THE HEIR

By the same author:

Summary Justice
Dieback

THE HEIR

S. J. Michaels

M

MACMILLAN

LONDON

First published 1994 by Macmillan London

a division of Pan Macmillan Publishers Limited
Cavaye Place London SW10 9PG
and Basingstoke

Associated companies throughout the world

ISBN 0-333-57761-2

Copyright © S. J. Michaels 1994

1 3 5 7 9 8 6 4 2

A CIP catalogue record for this book is available from
the British Library

Typeset by CentraCet Limited, Cambridge
Printed by Mackays of Chatham PLC, Chatham, Kent

As promised in life, this book is dedicated to
the memory of my dear father and mother.
It is also dedicated to those members of my
family who did not survive the Holocaust,
but whose spirit prompted this work.

Shall we only threaten and be angry for an hour?
When the storm is ended shall we find
How softly but how swiftly they have sidled back to power
By the favour and contrivance of their kind?

from 'Mesopotamia' by RUDYARD KIPLING

CONTENTS

INTRODUCTION

History records that Adolf Hitler and his wife, Eva Braun, committed suicide together in Berlin on 30 April 1945. However, it seems that the exact method of death remains somewhat questionable.

Therefore why did Stalin keep on insisting that Hitler was still alive, even months after seeing the evidence of the so-called suicide pact for himself?

Why, in 1972, after years of speculation as to Martin Bormann's fate and in light of an American journalist's revelation that he had located Bormann alive and living in South America, did the German authorities suddenly reveal, only days later, that they had just found the skeletal remains of Hitler's most faithful aide?

Why, during the Nuremberg trials and thenceforth, have the Allies been so concerned about keeping secret the Nazis' obvious preoccupation and involvement with devil worship and the occult?

How can anyone be sure of anything . . . ?

In the years preceding 1939, the Nazis established the Adolf Hitler Fund, or 'Adolf Hitler-Spende'. It was a fund solely administered by one man, Martin Bormann. Contributions were obligatory for all those who had 'benefited' from the Nazi regime and ostensibly the fund served to assist the Fürher's 'pet' projects. These projects included ex gratia payments made to many of the Nazi hierarchy, allowing them to indulge in their flamboyant lifestyles, but there was another underlying, more sinister motive behind the fund, a motive known only to Hitler and Martin Bormann.

By 19 October 1939, German High Command had formulated the detailed plans for the invasion of Holland and Belgium. The original battle plan had been called 'Operation Yellow' but, following its inception, the plans were to be changed, rechanged and even renamed in constant update until 10 May 1940, when crack German paratroopers spearheaded the attack into Holland. By the beginning of June that fateful year it was all over: the German Armed Forces were triumphant, but for some the German advance had taken on a more personal meaning.

Unknown to any of the German High Command, another devilish plan existed, a plan conceived before Hitler even came to power. Codenamed

1

'Operation Gold', its purpose was to plunder the financial centres of the captured territories. Apart from a small handful of top Nazis, only a select group of Himmler's SS 'Field Controllers' knew of 'Gold's' existence, but none had any idea of its full extent or evil purpose. Of the twelve SS officers summoned to the SS High Temple at Wewelsburg and initiated by Himmler in satanic ritual, all but one would die to preserve the secret, a secret so evil and frightening that in the aftermath of the war the British and American governments would stop at nothing to bury its very existence. The Third Reich would rise like a phoenix from the ashes, and nothing could be done to stop it.

But no one counted on a young Jewish woman called Elizabeth Goldmann, whose father had been murdered in Amsterdam by a ruthless SS officer called Rudolph Schiller and whose entire family – brothers, sisters, nephews and nieces – were to perish in the dreaded extermination camp at Buchenwald, on Schiller's personal order. In the years to come she would need every ounce of strength vested in her by her ancestors. Driven by a steel-hard determination to avenge her butchered family, Elizabeth Goldmann would take on the residue of the Third Reich, single-handedly and face to face.

PROLOGUE

It began on 10 May 1940, when German paratroopers penetrated the Dutch defences, securing the necessary bridgeheads for the advancing ground offensive. The bombing of Rotterdam broke the spirit of Dutch resistance and Holland capitulated five days later. The Blitzkrieg tactics had succeeded. By 26 May, the British Expeditionary Force would be squeezed on to the Dunkirk beaches. Western Europe belonged to Adolf Hitler, and already 'Operation Gold' was giving him the ability to secure him the rest . . .

AMSTERDAM
Thursday, 16 May 1940

PETER GOLDMANN stood by the open window of his second-floor office suite, overlooking the canal. He carefully drew back the net curtains, peering down towards the grey rows of soldiers as they marched three abreast across the canal bridge adjacent to his plush offices. For two days, vehicles and men had been pouring through the city, a city whose streets now echoed incessantly to the crunch of jackboots.

A black Mercedes-Benz saloon pulled up on the opposite side of the narrow canal, next to the colourful houseboats moored along the canal bank. A tall blond man in a navy pin-striped suit alighted from the vehicle and surveyed the German troops; from the look of things, it would be at least another twenty minutes before they cleared the bridge. The man would have gone unnoticed by Goldmann had it not been for an overzealous German military policeman who decided to check out the occupants of the Mercedes. The military policeman walked down the sharp incline from the bridge and directly up to the blond man. Goldmann watched as the German soldier hesitated momentarily before jumping to attention and saluting. The man began to address the soldier, who seconds later took to his heels and

3

ran back up the incline to report to his immediate superior at the bridge.

Peter Goldmann smiled to himself. It was amusing to see these pompous invaders being told what to do for a change. As he returned his attention to the Mercedes, his curiosity faded instantly: the blond-haired man was staring back at him, directly up at his second-floor window! Goldmann's heart began pounding in his ears as fear turned into panic. He moved away from the window, letting the net curtain fall back into place. Suddenly he felt quite dizzy, almost breathless. Had he been wrong? Had their eyes just met by chance? He peered through the curtains again. The man was no longer there; the Mercedes had driven up the cobbled incline next to the bridge. Peter Goldmann leaned back against the wall, adjusting his starched shirt collar as he breathed a deep sigh of relief.

The knock on the door alerted him instantly. Before he could say anything, the door was being opened. His panic had returned with a vengeance and for one frightful moment he expected to see a German uniform. His heart lifted upon seeing his secretary standing in the open doorway.

'Marie.' He squeezed the word from his dry throat upon seeing the woman's broad and happy features. The middle-aged secretary was carrying in his morning tray of coffee with the private post.

'Your coffee, Mr Goldmann.' The woman approached the desk. Then she noticed her employer's stressful state. 'Is everything all right?' Her face creased into a deep frown as she set the tray on the desk.

The elderly diamond merchant didn't answer. The echo of boots crunching over the cobblestone surface, intermingled with the sound of the motor-cycle escorts, revving up as they drove on to the sharp incline of the canal bridge, was almost overwhelming.

'Mr Goldmann?'

Suddenly he was aware of her words. He automatically turned and reached out to shut the window, and as he did so, his eyes were drawn unwillingly across the canal again. The black Mercedes had vanished. Goldmann pulled the window tightly shut before turning to face his secretary. No words were necessary. They both stood staring in horror at one another. The sixty-nine-year-old Jewish grandfather saw the woman's hands tremble as she set the silver tray down on his desk. He forced his tired features into a warm smile as he moved away from the window.

'That lot out there –' he shook his head – 'you must not take too much notice of them.' He widened his pale grey eyes. 'They'll probably just keep on going. Tomorrow another town, another city. Next week perhaps it will be another country. It will matter little to you or me, Marie. Their greyness will be lost in Amsterdam's flower market. You will see.'

'Mr Goldmann, I am afraid,' the woman said quietly.

'Marie, we are all afraid of something. It is only natural.' A reassuring smile again and a shrug. 'With me it's spiders, so what are a few Nazis?'

'Thank you, Mr Goldmann.' The woman began to cheer up.

Goldmann shook his head. 'It will be all right, Marie, you will see. I promise.'

For a moment the woman found herself almost believing the old man. She fought against the sudden urge to cry. 'I fear there's no morning paper again.'

'At times like this, who wants to read the news!' He gestured wildly.

'Mr Goldmann, may I be candid?' Marie continued.

'Marie, we've known each other a long time. If you can't be frank with an old man at a time like this . . .' His sentence ended on a habitual high note that seemed to turn anything he said into a whimsical question. Peter Goldmann smiled again, his warmth relaxed her.

'I cannot help but wonder why, with all your wealth and position . . . why you do not flee all of this and go to England, or even further?' It had always been Marie's inveterate opinion that no Jew would be safe under Nazi rule. Of course, they had all been hearing the stories for some time about persecution in Germany, but until now no one had accepted them or wanted to understand the risk.

Peter Goldmann returned to his desk, slowly easing his frail body into the leather chair. 'At my stage in life, why run, and indeed from what?'

'Mr Goldmann, everyone is talking. Forgive me for saying this, but the Germans are no friends of the Jews!' She moved closer.

'Germans! You mean Nazis, don't you?' he corrected her.

'Mr Goldmann! For the sake of your family then!' she pleaded.

'Marie – ' he raised a hand to halt further comment – 'as you say, we have all heard the stories of what the Nazis have done to their own people. Yes, they exercise more than just contempt towards my kind.' He leaned across the desk. 'But, you see, I remain a great optimist – unlike many in my synagogue, mind you.' He forced another smile. The woman stared back in bewilderment. 'The point I want to make is this,' continued Goldmann. 'Six of my seven children

5

live here in Amsterdam, not forgetting seventeen grandchildren. How on earth could I have arranged such an exodus? Do I look like Moses?' He raised his left eyebrow in that curious fashion she had grown to love and laugh at during her years of faithful service. But she no longer felt like laughing: all the signs pointed to perdition.

'No, Marie, without my family I am nothing. Two years ago I lost my wife to cancer. How on earth could I live with myself in exile, knowing that the rest of my family were left in the clutches of those "jackboots" out there?' Before the woman had an opportunity to answer, he cut her short. 'Now my coffee is getting rather cold.'

The words were not really meant as a rebuke, but at that moment Peter Goldmann was as close to nervous collapse as he could imagine. The woman excused herself and left the room. The diamond merchant sighed deeply as he removed the metal-rimmed spectacles from his jacket breast-pocket, adjusting them on to the bridge of his nose as he quickly scanned his morning mail. There was one letter that stood out from all the others, and amazingly it was from abroad. The overseas mail had become more than just erratic recently. The war had begun to affect Holland long before Hitler's troops crossed the border, but somehow this letter had found its way through. His tired eyes lit up. The handwriting was unmistakable; it was from his youngest daughter, in England.

Rachel Elizabeth Goldmann had gone to study in England in 1937, taking an English course at Girton College, Cambridge. Peter Goldmann could never understand why, of all his children, Elizabeth had taken to the academic life. She had been such a pretty, worldly little girl, full of the excitement and vigour of youth; hardly the ideal candidate for years of study in the dusty library of some foreign university. He missed her terribly but, although he had not seen her since her mother's funeral, took some comfort in the fact that, for the moment at least, his favourite daughter was safe and secure in England.

He hurriedly ripped the envelope open and scanned the contents. The letter had been written over six weeks previously. He checked the postmark; it had been posted in London at the beginning of April. He devoured the contents avidly, over and over again. It was full of the usual stuff, an update of events in her life, what she was doing, whom she had met, various questions about the family back in Holland. It seemed so normal, yet there was a strangeness in its tone, the hint of a job teaching somewhere but not the location; nor did she in any way clarify the position she had been offered, no hint of the establishment, nothing. He already knew that Elizabeth had been offered a temporary position at Cambridge University, but she made no further mention about this, and there was something else, something almost mysterious. After reading the three-page letter for the fourth time, he was still haunted by an uneasy feeling, which could well keep him distracted for the remainder of the morning.

He left his chair and crossed over to a large oak dresser, lifting a gold-framed portrait from amidst the array of family photographs laid out across the dresser. He studied the face: the beautiful deep-brown eyes and cheeky smile; the rolling auburn hair, cascading across her shoulders. It had been taken on Elizabeth's eighteenth birthday, in the halcyon days when God still favoured them all. Peter Goldmann returned to his desk, still clutching the photograph. Easing back into his chair again, he pondered on his favourite daughter. Of all his children, Elizabeth was the most outstanding – a remarkable mixture of beauty, charm and intelligence. Even as a child she was the only one of them who could twist him around her little finger. If he regretted anything, it was that none of his three sons was blessed with her independence of mind. Now he thanked the Great Jehovah for Elizabeth's waywardness; it had taken her away from home but thankfully out of the clutches of Hitler's thugs. He set the photograph to one side and placed the letter inside his jacket pocket.

Suddenly his attention was drawn to some sort of commotion emanating from the outer office. As he lifted the telephone to ring his secretary, the door burst open. Two men, dressed in black leather overcoats, stormed into the office.

'Replace the telephone!' snapped the taller man, speaking in Dutch.

The other one, a fat little man with beady eyes, snatched the receiver from him, ripping the wire from the wall socket as he moved next to the window. Goldmann was aghast.

'Who are you?' he demanded, knowing the answer in advance. He had seen their type over the last days, arriving and leaving the Police District Headquarters, now serving as temporary headquarters for the Gestapo.

The taller man shut the door and removed his right hand from the deep pocket of his coat. He was clutching a Luger pistol. There was no need to aim the gun at the elderly Jew; the point had already been made. Goldmann sat in silence, occasionally stealing a glance at the other Gestapo agent, who remained hovering beside the window, his face expressionless as he studied the display of family photographs on the dresser.

Goldmann tried to break the impasse. 'What have you done to

7

my secretary, please?' He addressed the one at the door. The man didn't respond. 'Who are you?' he persisted, turning his attention to the smaller man beside the window. The German sniffed and looked away. Suddenly something snapped inside Peter Goldmann; his anger boiled over instantly. 'I insist on knowing what is happening here!' he shouted, addressing the other man again as he began to rise out of his chair.

Suddenly a strong hand squeezed into Goldmann's left shoulder from behind. He winced as the fingertips penetrated deep into the soft tissue above his collarbone. The Gestapo agent was leaning over him now, his face barely an inch away, his sour breath overwhelming.

'Just sit there. A good little fucking *Jood* should know how to behave himself. Eh?'

Peter Goldmann cried aloud with the pain as the man squeezed even harder. Then, as the grip eased, he slumped back into his chair. Marie's words kept ringing in his ears. He could no longer blot out all the horrible stories he had heard about the camps in Germany now he was face to face with the actual reality of the Nazis!

At that moment the door opened again. Peter Goldmann's eyes widened. It was the blond man he had seen across the canal earlier! He was tall, with an air of confidence and a military bearing which could not be concealed by the navy pin-striped suit. His broad frame was accentuated by the camel overcoat he had draped across his shoulders. The man had the bluest, most piercing eyes Peter Goldmann had ever seen. His handsome features and dress set him apart from the other two scruffy weasels. He was from a different class altogether and much younger than they were, perhaps around twenty-five. The man was followed into the room by a uniformed German officer carrying two briefcases. Goldmann recognized the SS flashes on his lapels instantly. The officer remained just inside the doorway, whilst the blond man approached the diamond merchant.

The tall stranger threw off his overcoat, dropping it over the back of a nearby chair. Goldmann eyed him very carefully. The German wore his double-breasted suit like a uniform, immaculately creased and perfectly fitted. His blue silk tie was pinned into position a little under the knot by a gold tie-pin, bearing the crest of the German eagle and swastika.

'Herr Goldmann, I believe.' The tall man spoke in perfect English, with no hint of a German accent. Goldmann nodded in response. 'My name is SS Sturmbannführer Schiller of the Reichssicherheits-hauptamt. The officer behind me is SS Obersturmführer Kleist.' Schiller never took his eyes off Goldmann as he clicked his fingers.

8

Immediately both Gestapo agents left the room. Goldmann breathed a low sigh of relief; at least part of his problem had been temporarily removed, at least perhaps with this man he could reason.

'Herr Sturmbannführer – ' Goldmann was careful not to insult the German – 'what is going on, please?' He kept his voice level and respectful.

'Your English is better than I was led to expect.' Schiller grinned as he produced his identity papers, which included a part-profile photograph of himself in full SS dress uniform. He laid the documents out carefully on the desk in front of Goldmann.

'Please inspect my identification, Herr Goldmann, and then read this.' He set a further document down beside the identification papers.

Goldmann scanned the letter. It was typed in German, a language which he could readily understand, but the document was vague and ambiguous; it talked about the protection of valuable assets. In brief, it was an order naming SS Sturmbannführer Rudolph Schiller to seize all property, specifically 'precious stones, gold, silver and other items deemed relevant' for, as the letter droned on, 'safe-keeping'. Goldmann's eyes widened when he came to the final section: the authority came from no less a personage than Adolf Hitler himself. Immediately anger overcame his fear.

'Herr Sturmbannführer, could you explain what exactly you are here to protect me from?' Goldmann eased back in the chair, contemptuously shoving the papers away to the other side of the desk. It was his first mistake.

The young SS officer moved the papers back. His smile had evaporated. 'Looters, pillagers, thieves and suchlike.'

'Pillagers?' Goldmann raised an eyebrow. 'Herr Sturmbannführer, I thought only conquering armies pillaged.' He afforded himself a smile. It was another mistake.

'*Touché.*' Schiller grinned as he leaned across, raising his left arm. Goldmann was tossed out of his chair by the force of a back-handed slap across his left cheek. He landed heavily on the floor, jarring his ribs, the breath knocked out of him. Before he even realized, the German was crouched over him, grabbing him by his tie.

'You Jewish shit! Just what the hell do you think you are?' Goldmann focused on the icy-blue eyes. This man meant to give no mercy at all. 'I could have you gaoled for just looking Jewish!' Schiller snarled. Then he dropped his tone to a whisper, hissing out the next words. 'I could have you killed . . . right here . . . right now.'

Peter Goldmann held the side of his face and, for that matter, his tongue also; a bruised cheek was nothing in comparison to what these

9

animals could really do. Schiller pulled the elderly man up by his tie and forced him down into his chair again. It was then that Peter Goldmann caught sight of Kleist. From the look on the SS officer's face, it was clear that even he seemed fearful of his young SS superior.

'Now,' continued Schiller, releasing his grip on Goldmann's throat, 'I warn you not to give any invidious or false replies. I either get your complete co-operation or you will be arrested immediately. Is this understood?' Schiller spoke in an altogether quieter tone now, chilling to Peter Goldmann's ears; there was everything evil about this young man.

'Please, just tell me what you want,' he replied nervously, ready to agree to almost anything. He was no coward, but he could envisage his secretary and other staff enduring the same or perhaps worse treatment.

'We want access to your vaults. A complete inventory of all your diamond stock, both industrial and otherwise, including other precious stones and, of course, any gold, silver and currency you have on these premises or held elsewhere.' Schiller moved back, gesturing towards the exit. 'Shall we?'

Peter Goldmann picked himself up, using the edge of the desk for support. It was then that he saw Elizabeth's photograph, lying face up on the desk; the glass was cracked. As he stood, straightening his tie, he glanced down again at the photograph. The way the glass had broken distorted his daughter's eyes. She was no longer smiling. It was as if she was now crying.

After three hours in the basement vaults, the inventory was complete. During the entire operation Schiller had remained silently in the background, leaving Kleist to deal with the tiresome paperwork along with Goldmann and the chief factory manager. As Kleist and the manager stacked up the firm's ledgers for removal to Gestapo headquarters, Schiller's voice echoed across the basement vault.

'Tell me, Herr Goldmann, where is your private wealth kept?' Peter Goldmann swallowed hard. The bastards were going to clean him out and they were enjoying it.

'It is all in the anteroom over there, in a separate safe.' He gestured towards a red-painted steel door at the other end of the main vault room.

'Shall we?' Schiller gestured for the old man to lead the way.

'Is this absolutely necessary? You have my assurance that it has absolutely nothing to do with the business. You will see that from our books.' Peter Goldmann pleaded, but from the look on the German's face he knew he was wasting his breath.

'Open it,' insisted Schiller.

Peter Goldmann fumbled with his keys. Schiller watched impatiently as the heavy reinforced door finally swung open. The room was barely ten feet square, one side crammed with steel cabinets, whilst in the corner stood a tall, narrow black-enamelled safe, the door engraved with the words 'J. H. Goldmann and Company'. There was barely enough room for the two men to move. Peter Goldmann felt the German's breath on the nape of his neck as Schiller's attention focused on the old safe.

'Herr Sturmbannführer, may I be frank with you?' He began to perspire. 'I know only too well of the Nazi ·attitude towards my people; your own contempt is obvious.'

Schiller raised an eyebrow.

'I know that sooner or later my family will be arrested, just as others have been in Germany.'

'What you say is quite untrue. A typical distortion of the facts by world Jewry,' retorted Schiller angrily. 'In many cases the frustration of the good German people has resulted in anger and violence. Subsequently some prominent Jewish families have had to be temporarily taken into protective custody, but purely for their own convenience and continued well-being—'

'All right! All right!' Goldmann interrupted. He was becoming more unsure of what he was about to do by the second. 'Please listen! If I were to make a gift to your Führer of something, something unbelievable . . . could my family be granted a single favour?'

'What favour?' Schiller's voice quietened once again.

'Embarkation for America on the next available ship leaving Rotterdam,' blurted Goldmann. 'I will stay here in Amsterdam, if it is necessary, but my family . . . they are mainly children and women.'

Schiller paused and rubbed his chin. 'What you ask for is not entirely impossible, but you would have to agree to relinquish your family's control over this business and have it assigned to the German state.'

'Agreed.' Goldmann had accepted the loss of his business hours earlier.

'How many are in your family?' continued Schiller, with an air of congeniality.

'There are twenty-nine of us here in Amsterdam, including myself.' He watched for some positive sign from the Nazi.

'You Jews breed like rabbits,' Schiller chuckled. The diamond merchant ignored the insult and remained silent, his head bowed. 'Herr Goldmann,' continued the SS officer, 'that is twenty-nine favours, not one, as you first asked. I must stress to you that we are being propositioned all the time and by far more influential people than yourself.'

'I'm sure you are, I'm sure you are. I meant no offence, you understand!' Goldmann knew that he had only one chance.

'Just what is it that you consider so valuable as to suggest a personal gift to the Führer?' Schiller leaned back against one of the filing cabinets and removed a gold cigarette case from his pocket.

Peter Goldmann had run out of options. He braced himself. An aptitude for chess might have made him act more astutely, but it was too late for that now. This was not the time to be faint-hearted: his family was all that mattered; money was only a means towards an end and could be made again in the future. For one horrible moment he had a vision of a charred stump where his family tree should have been standing. He had no choice. He turned and knelt down facing the safe, silently reciting a prayer as he did so. On opening the old safe, he removed a shallow black metal case, setting it on the tiled floor at the German's feet. Withdrawing a small bunch of keys from his trouser pocket, he nervously fumbled for the correct key. 'This has been in my family for generations.'

'I hope for your sake that you don't have a gun inside.' Schiller grinned.

'Please! Herr Sturmbannführer, please! You do not know what this is doing to me.' There were tears in Goldmann's eyes as he unlocked the box. 'Do I have your word? Can my family go free?'

'You have my word that if what you have is good enough, you and your family can leave for America whenever you wish.' Schiller's blue eyes narrowed slightly.

'Thank you! Thank you!' Goldmann closed his wet eyes briefly as he slowly eased back the metal lid to reveal the box's interior. The contents were covered in a deep-red velvet cloth. Gently, almost reverentially, he pulled it aside to reveal the jewels.

The stones sparkled in the bright overhead electric lighting. Schiller gazed down at them. Never in his life had he seen anything quite like it. Three majestic, massive and identical red balas rubies were set geometrically into a gold mounting, almost surrounding a giant diagonally cut diamond centrepiece. The entire cluster was finished with the addition of four large pearls held in place by delicate gold clasps. It was beautiful beyond even Schiller's belief. After spending the last few hours looking at an incessant array of normal-sized diamonds by the trayful, he could see that this piece was indeed unique. Furthermore, judging by the gold work and craftsmanship, it was old, very old. Schiller knelt down and began to fondle the diamond centrepiece.

'Please!' exclaimed Goldmann. 'Be very careful. It is not used to being handled.'

'Where did you get it?' Schiller demanded.

'From history.' Goldmann stared down at the jewels. 'Are you not truly transfixed by its beauty?' Goldmann was almost in another world. Already his trepidation had disappeared. 'I know that I am each time I take it out of that box. Perhaps it is now time that the world sees it again.'

Peter Goldmann watched nervously as Schiller lifted the necklace from the box, raising it towards the light. He took his time, studying the piece, stone by stone, pausing to look again and again at the fine craftsmanship of the gold settings.

'It's called "The Three Brothers". We Dutch later called it "The Three Sisters".' Goldmann afforded himself a brief smile. 'I prefer to use the male gender myself.'

Schiller continued running his fingers gently over the balas rubies. He had never seen anything like this in his life.

'Queen Elizabeth I wore these jewels for the Ermine portrait in 1585, but I think you will find it was last recorded in a portrait of James I some years later.' Goldmann enjoyed the genealogy.

'Where on earth did you get it?' Schiller was mesmerized.

'One of my distant ancestors began as a jeweller in this very city, founding our family business.' There was pride in the old man's tone. 'It was purchased from agents sent by Charles I of England some time around 1650. It seems that before Charles went to the executioner, he was trying in vain to balance many of his royal debts by selling off part of the Crown Jewels of England . . .'

'So this is part of the British Crown Jewels?' Schiller interrupted.

'Was,' corrected Goldmann. 'The present British Crown Jewels have no relationship to "The Three Brothers". Frankly, some of them wouldn't be as valuable. The story has always been that this necklace was dismantled and sold off in bits and pieces after it came here to Amsterdam. My ancestor allowed the rumour to spread. It was a great deal safer to do so than to admit to its continued existence. In any case, I would imagine that it would have been too heavy a responsibility to carry. Can you imagine the dangers of trying to cut such perfectly matched rubies, let alone this exquisite centre diamond?'

'What is its value?' Schiller cut in impatiently.

'Priceless,' replied Goldmann firmly.

'But you must have some notion!' insisted Schiller, unable to hide his excitement.

'To give you some idea, Herr Sturmbannführer – ' Peter Goldmann took back the necklace, replacing it in the case – 'all the diamonds, gold and other stock you have just catalogued in the main vault are collectively worth far less. But due to the history of the necklace, any price I can think of could easily be doubled again.'

'My God!' Schiller's eyes gleamed as he began to rub his dry lips. 'Who else knows of its existence?'

'No one. It has been handed down from generation to generation in my family. Until a few moments ago, no one outside my closest family circle knew of its existence.'

'No written record anywhere?' Schiller couldn't believe his luck. He tried not to sound too sinister. 'I mean, you have no insurance on this piece?'

'None. It has been a family tradition to hold the jewels in reserve – emergency collateral which has never needed to be used, at least until now.'

It was the final wrong move on Peter Goldmann's chessboard. He had no more pieces to play and Schiller well knew the difference between logic and honour. The SS officer reached to close and pick up the box. 'I'll take the key, Herr Goldmann,' he said quietly.

'Then we have a deal as agreed?' Goldmann unclipped the silver-plated key from the chain ring and handed it over.

Schiller smiled as he carefully placed the key inside his jacket pocket. Goldmann breathed a deep sigh of relief. Then he turned to the safe, kneeling down to remove the remaining documents. The relief on his face was absolute until he heard the click from behind. He spun around, his eyes widening as he stared up into the muzzle of a Walther pistol only inches from his face.

'I'm afraid that things are just never that simple.' Schiller began to chuckle. Goldmann was speechless as he watched the German's finger tighten around the trigger. Schiller was still laughing as he pulled it.

The rising sickness in the old man's stomach was only momentary. The 9mm Kurz bullet slammed into his upper groin, exiting just above the left pelvis. Goldmann's frail body lurched backwards against the safe door. He was amazed to feel no pain and was trying to stop himself from falling over just as another bullet tore through his chest cavity. Blood spurted out through his shirt and jacket as he shuddered helplessly before toppling forward on to the floor.

14

Kleist and the factory manager rushed to the vault door. The SS officer stood mesmerized as Schiller emerged into the corridor. Reading the situation, the Dutchman tried to close the vault door in Schiller's path. Kleist began to draw his Luger as a third shot echoed around the basement vaults. The SS officer watched in astonishment as the Dutchman was flung backwards against the wall, his legs and arms flapping uncontrollably as he slid on to the floor. Kleist stared at the Dutchman's face. The eyes were already glazing over; a tiny trickling hole had appeared in the centre of the man's forehead. As he turned to ask Schiller what had happened, he saw the smoking pistol still pointing at the dead man.

'In God's name, Schiller! What have you done?' Kleist screamed as he fought to control his fraying nerves.

'The proper order of natural survival.' Schiller looked back coldly. 'God has nothing to do with it.'

'But Sturmbannführer, you can't just—'

'I have!' Schiller interrupted, waving his gun at the other German. 'Kleist, you really are a stupid little shit!'

The young SS officer stepped back in horror; for one awful second he thought he was next. He breathed a sigh of relief as Schiller returned his gun to his shoulder holster.

'If anyone asks,' Schiller said, walking over to him, 'you can say the Dutchman tried to take your gun.'

'I . . .' The man was uncertain of where this would lead. Killing was not in his brief.

'My dear Kleist, don't tell me you're worried about a silly old Jew and his servant?' Schiller laughed, and the coldness in his voice unsettled the SS officer. 'Who gives a damn about them?' Schiller eased Kleist's Luger pistol from his hand and went back to the manager's body, wiping his own fingerprints off the gun with a clean handkerchief.

'What are you doing?' asked Kleist nervously.

'I'm putting your gun into this creature's hand.' He turned sideways, looking up at the SS officer. 'After all, as you rightly say, I do need a reason for killing him, don't I?'

'I don't think this is a good idea,' Kleist stuttered.

Schiller smiled back at him. 'But, my dear Kleist, you don't need to think.' There was that eerie chuckle again. It was still ringing in Kleist's ears as the 9mm bullet cracked his sternum. Kleist stumbled backwards into one of the stone pillars. His head jerked as he looked down at the growing red patch on his chest. Slowly everything grew black. He slumped to the floor, his right leg caught under him awkwardly.

15

Schiller finished wiping the gun before forcing it between the Dutchman's dead fingers. It was just then that he heard it. At first he thought someone had followed them down into the vault, but then he realized.

'Damn you . . .' The voice seemed muffled. Schiller looked around, it was coming from the anteroom.

'Schiller!' The voice was louder now and much clearer.

The German moved next the open vault door, stepping over the Dutchman's body. He looked inside the anteroom. Peter Goldmann was lying where he had fallen, his head and shoulders propped up against the filing cabinets. Amazingly, the old man was still alive. On seeing his killer, his eyes narrowed. 'With all my heart and soul, I curse you!' He coughed, bringing up more blood into his mouth.

Schiller watched the frothy blood ooze from the side of the old man's gaping mouth. 'Don't worry, old man, you'll be seeing your precious family soon enough.'

Peter Goldmann felt his life ebbing away, but fought to stay conscious just a little longer. This evil dog had snatched his life from him and it was quite evident he also intended to kill his family.

'Schiller . . .' He was panting now, speaking in short and hurried bursts. He knew death would come at any moment: he could feel it entering his body; he was growing cold and dizzy. 'No matter where you go . . . I'll be there . . . Every time you turn the light out, I'm going to be . . .' Goldmann's voice died away. The coldness swept across his body like a giant wave. More blood bubbled up into his mouth and he began to choke. His eyes fell upon his daughter's letter, blood-soaked and protruding from his jacket pocket. The old man grasped the stained notepaper with his fingers. 'Rachel . . .' He gargled on the word. Peter Goldmann's soul was finally released. Schiller stooped over, ripping the letter from the Jew's hand. He examined the sender's name on the back of the envelope.

'Rachel Elizabeth Goldmann,' he said coldly.

HIGH NEWBURY GIRLS' PUBLIC SCHOOL, BERKSHIRE
The same moment . . .

ELIZABETH O'CASEY was just finishing for the day, collecting the books from the desks and tidying the empty classroom. The day had been long and tedious, and whilst not unlike any other school day, it was somehow different, for since rising that morning the feeling of gloom had never lifted; premonition had been hanging over her like a heavy dripping cloud, inexplicable and constant.

As she began to wipe clean the blackboard the pain struck. She felt it first in the pit of her stomach and then in her chest. She dropped the wooden-handled duster, leaning against the blackboard for support. Her heart was racing and she was suddenly perspiring. Another dart of pain again in her stomach, this time more severe than before and almost doubling her over. She tried to make it to a chair.

'No!' she screamed, stumbling and falling heavily against a chair, knocking it to one side. 'Please God . . . Let it not be so.'

Elizabeth fought hard to control her breathing. The baby was coming, but it wasn't time yet. She still had another eleven weeks to go; the baby wouldn't stand a chance. She tore open the high collar of her blouse, wiping the clammy sweat from her neck.

'God, please! Not my baby!' she cried out, too terrified to move in case of worsening the situation.

Elizabeth tried to focus on the wall clock at the rear of the classroom, but she couldn't see it. Everything was suddenly turning into blackness, deep and beckoning.

Six hours later

THE HEADMISTRESS tiptoed across the bedroom floor, peering down at Elizabeth, still fast asleep. The woman drew the bed-clothes up around Elizabeth's shoulders before retreating back to the door. She joined the school doctor in the living room. He was sitting at a drop-leaf table, bathed in the light of a standard lamp. The old doctor set aside the papers he had been studying. 'How is she?' he asked.

'Still asleep, poor lass,' she replied, her north Yorkshire accent quite evident.

'Aye.' He sighed, leafing through the Dutch passport for the second time.

'I feel terrible about us having gone through her personal belongings,' continued the headmistress.

'Don't give it a second thought, it had to be done,' insisted the doctor. 'The poor girl's family must be notified and she's hardly in a fit state to do it herself.'

'I suppose you are right,' she agreed reluctantly.

'She's pretty,' commented the doctor, pointing to Elizabeth's passport photograph. The headmistress nodded. 'What do you make of this?' He waved the Dutch passport in his hand. 'I thought you said her name was O'Casey.'

'O'Casey is her married name. She married an Irishman. I only met him the once, when she arrived here to take up her position four months ago.' She picked up a small framed photograph from a bookshelf and set it on the table in front of the doctor. 'That's him, he's called Eamon. I don't think they're very happy.'

'Why do you say that?' he inquired.

'Because she doesn't talk about him very much. He's away a lot, in America I think. But she speaks quite often about her family back in Holland; her father and she are very close. Her mother died just recently, if I remember correctly.'

'This passport's in the name of Rachel Elizabeth Goldmann.' He stared over the rim of his wire-framed spectacles. 'That's a Jewish name, isn't it?'

The headmistress nodded a second time. 'And her family are now all trapped in Amsterdam, under Nazi occupation. Can you imagine it?'

The elderly doctor frowned.

At first she was uncertain of where she was. Elizabeth's head pounded and she felt quite ill. Then she realized. She was staring up at the ceiling of her bedroom in the staff wing of the boarding school. The hushed tones of conversation alerted Elizabeth to another presence. The sounds were coming from the living room; at least two people, talking in muted tones. Stretching across to examine the clock on the bedside table, her shaking hand knocked the alarm clock on to the floor. It clattered noisily over the varnished floorboards. Almost

18

immediately the light came on. Then a friendly face appeared over her, blocking out the glare of the ceiling light.

'How do you feel, my dear?' The doctor looked at her concernedly, his voice warm and soothing. Elizabeth knew him quite well, he was in fact the local village doctor, paid a small retainer to look after the medical welfare of the children at the boarding school. She forced a smile.

'My baby?' she whispered, her voice dry and weak.

The doctor touched her shoulder, his face revealing the awful truth. Elizabeth shut her eyes as he replied, 'I am sorry, my dear, we did everything we could.'

'It can't be . . . it just can't be!' Elizabeth shook her head from side to side. 'No!' she howled.

Another face appeared beside her. 'Elizabeth?' The headmistress was clearly choked with emotion.

Elizabeth stared at her, shaking her head with disbelief. Then she broke down, weeping uncontrollably, choking on her sorrow.

'Easy, lass, easy.' As the older woman comforted her, she motioned the doctor to leave.

'I'll be outside if you need me,' he replied, heading for the door.

As the bedroom door shut, Elizabeth re-opened her eyes. 'What was my baby?' she whispered. There was no reply; the headmistress looked away when Elizabeth stared directly at her. 'Tell me!' she insisted, raising her voice.

'A boy,' replied the woman, squeezing Elizabeth's hand. 'I am so sorry, lass.'

'My son,' she said softly.

'Don't worry.' The headmistress patted her on the hand. 'There can always be another time.' She instantly regretted having uttered the words.

'No, there won't be another,' whispered Elizabeth.

'But the doctor says that you—'

'No!' Elizabeth shouted her down, squeezing the woman's wrist to the point of causing her pain. Elizabeth's heart sank further, for it was at that moment she realized that the feeling of foreboding she had experienced earlier was still within her. Whatever it signalled had not yet come to pass. The evil was still there, hovering close by, waiting. But for whom?

The headmistress recognized her inner torment. 'What is it, lass?' she asked anxiously. Elizabeth took a few moments to regain her composure.

'In Jewish kabbalistic teachings it is written that Lilith takes the lives of our infants and the unborn,' said Elizabeth, staring directly up at the white ceiling.

'I don't understand,' replied the woman, easing down on the bed beside her.

'Lilith is the consort of Samael.' Elizabeth swallowed deeply. 'Samael is the kabbalistic term for "The Angel of Death".' Elizabeth stared at her now. 'You don't understand, do you?'

'Understand what?' urged the headmistress.

'It might not yet be over,' whispered Elizabeth.

The headmistress fell silent. Nothing Elizabeth had said made any sense to her, yet her anguish was very evident. 'I'm calling back the doctor for you,' she insisted.

Elizabeth did not answer. She kept staring up at the ceiling, trying to understand her growing fear. Her father's face flashed before her again and again. Peter Goldmann was standing on the patio, smiling, just as always. She was five years old again, playing in the garden of their country house along with her older brothers and sisters. Then someone threw a ball to her and she jumped up, catching it between tiny fingers. Her father's voice rang in her ears, 'Elizabeth! Elizabeth!', but when she turned to throw him the ball he had vanished. She turned about, but now everyone had disappeared from the garden, she was alone, and afraid. Elizabeth tried calling out to her father, yet no sound issued from her. She turned around, again and again, but it was all in vain. Then she became dizzy, everything blurred, she was falling . . .

'Elizabeth!' A strange voice spoke to her. 'Can you hear me?'

Elizabeth tried to focus on the face before her, it was the doctor. 'What happened?'

'You fainted, my dear,' he replied.

'But I was speaking to . . .'

'It's all right,' he assured her. 'You need to rest a while. I'm going to give you something to help you get to sleep.'

'I've lost more than just my baby,' continued Elizabeth.

'In heaven's name, Doctor, what is she talking about?' asked the headmistress.

'I wish I knew.' Elizabeth felt the slight prick in her right arm. She glanced down at the stainless steel syringe pumping the sedative into her forearm. 'Whatever it is, it is not over . . . yet.' The tranquillizer began to have an almost immediate effect; within seconds she had begun to drift into a deep sleep.

20

'She'll sleep for at least five hours.' The doctor checked his patient's pulse. It was steady. 'We can leave her for a while.'

'Thank God,' sighed the headmistress, 'the poor lass needs all the rest she can get.'

AMSTERDAM
Later that night

SCHILLER brushed aside any possibility of a criminal investigation. Of course the civil Dutch police had their suspicions, but they, just as everyone else, were powerless to raise any objection or voice any doubt. Officially, an attempt had been made on the lives of two of the Reich's servants. Summary justice was more than an appropriate remedy. Now, in occupied Holland, the RSHA could do whatever they wanted. Above them there was no higher authority than the Führer himself.

Schiller smiled as he loosened his tie before easing back on to the massive four-poster bed. Now he was a wealthy man, rich beyond his wildest dreams. Memories of the poverty he had experienced in his youth had driven him to this goal. Schiller knew well what wealth really meant. It had nothing to do with glamour and comfort, it meant power and control; control over his own destiny. He had inwardly scorned those fools who surrounded his Führer; Goebbels and Goering with their expensive houses built and re-built, all paid for out of stolen money. He had nothing but contempt for the brazen power-crazy idiots, their homes littered with stolen art treasures. They could all play out their parts publicly, they were welcome to it, for he had the real power, something beyond their feeble imaginations, something that could never be taken away from him no matter what happened with the war. Of course he believed in Adolf Hitler. He also believed in his solemn oath when, during his SS initiation, his hand touching the consecrated flag, he had sworn 'obedience unto death'. He had believed in the concept of 'Operation Gold', when, along with the others of his hand-picked group, he had been sworn to further secrecy at Wewelsburg Castle. But above all else he believed in Rudolph Schiller. He had earned and deserved 'The Three Brothers'; the jewels were his investment for the future, no matter what the outcome.

21

He lay back on the bed, staring up at the ornate gilding of the ceiling decoration. From now on he would be accustomed to nothing less than this. The day's success in Amsterdam would be repeated in Rotterdam, The Hague, Brussels and Paris. In its initial stage 'Operation Gold' had already been proved to be a monumental success. He knew his signal to Berlin would elate the Führer as much as the phenomenal speed of the German advances against the French First Army Group and the British Expeditionary Force. He casually flicked open the metal box lying on the bed beside him and lifted out 'The Three Brothers', holding the jewels towards the light. The balas rubies glistened on his hand. What could they really be worth?

The knock at the door alerted him. Schiller quickly returned the jewels to the box, closing the lid just before the door opened. The young lieutenant appeared roused. Schiller raised himself off the bed.

'Herr Sturmbannführer. This has just arrived from Berlin.' There was an excitement in his voice as he handed the de-coded communications signal to Schiller.

Schiller unfolded the sheet of paper and read the short line message.

'*Kode Geheim* – For the urgent attention of SS Sturmbannführer R. Schiller, Reichssicherheitshauptamt, c/o SS Headquarters, Amsterdam – My deepest congratulations on the success of Phase One. You have my fullest support and confidence. Adolf Hitler.'

'Hirt, who else has seen this apart from you?' Schiller tried to hide his own excitement.

'Just the signals officer, *mein Herr.*'

'Very good.' Schiller refolded the paper and placed it in his trouser pocket. 'Anything else?'

'The information you asked for on the Goldmann family, Herr Sturmbannführer.' The man handed him a thin red folder. 'Everything is inside the file. Our initial information was correct, the entire family is listed as presently living here in Amsterdam.'

'All except one,' corrected Schiller as he ran down the list.

'*Mein Herr?*' Hirt was puzzled, as he had done his job meticulously. All twenty-eight members of the Goldmann family were listed in the file.

'Disregard what I just said,' Schiller dismissed the query, handing the file back to him. 'Have everyone listed in that file rounded up and processed for immediate transportation by rail to Westerbork Camp, pending transfer.'

'Westerbork, *mein Herr?*'

'Do you have a difficulty with that, Obersturmführer Hirt?'

22

'But the proclamation by the Reichskommissar . . .'

'To hell with the proclamation!' screamed Schiller. 'It does not protect Jews!' Schiller waved the folded signal at him. 'Need I remind you that I am personally engaged in the Führer's business?'

'*Nein*, Herr Sturmbannführer.' The violent outburst startled the younger officer.

Schiller took a step towards him, menacingly. 'Mark the transfer papers "Sonderbehandlung". Now do it. *Schnell!*'

'At once, Herr Sturmbannführer.' The young officer clicked his heels before scurrying outside.

Schiller picked up the jewel box and approached the desk at the far side of the bedroom. He removed the blood-stained envelope from the pocket of his jacket draped across the back of the chair and studied the blurred frank mark; it had gone through the sorting office in Reading. 'You will keep a little longer, Rachel Goldmann,' he whispered to himself. Then, using a penknife, he uncut the stitching along one side of the box's velvet lining, slipping the crumpled envelope inside and before tucking the velvet back into place. 'For future reference,' he murmured ominously. 'The world is a small place, too small for any Jewess to hide.'

Over the following four hours every member of Peter Goldmann's family, including in-laws, had been arrested. Westerbork would be only a staging point for their final destination. Before the end of the year those still living would perish in agony in Buchenwald.

HIGH NEWBURY SCHOOL, BERKSHIRE
Friday morning, 17 May 1940

ELIZABETH stirred to the sound of the birds chirping merrily just outside her window. She rubbed her eyes before focusing on the open window, the pale yellow curtains fluttering gently in the light breeze.

'Good morning.' The voice was cheerful. Elizabeth smiled upon seeing the headmistress entering the room. She was carrying a full breakfast tray, rather too precariously for Elizabeth's liking. 'How are you feeling, my dear?'

'I can't imagine a part of me that doesn't hurt, my head especially,' replied Elizabeth, drawing herself up against the headboard.

'You lost a great deal of blood, but rest will soon cure you. The doctor left some medicine, you can take it after you've eaten.' She set the tray down on the bed.

Elizabeth grimaced at the sight of the boiled egg and buttered toast. 'I'll just have some tea, if you don't mind.' She watched as the older woman poured from the pot, her hand trembling slightly. 'What about my classes?'

'Miss Prichard is looking after things until you get better. Don't you worry your head about it, just concentrate upon getting well again.' She smiled back.

'I'm sorry if I upset you last night.'

'Sorry?' The headmistress handed her the cup and saucer. 'There is nothing to be sorry for, lass.'

'Everything became . . . confused.' Elizabeth wiped her forehead, it was cold and damp.

'Forget it, my dear, these are confusing times we live in.' The headmistress shook her head.

'What did the morning news say?'

'It's not good, I'm afraid, but the word is that our boys are counter-attacking along with the French. The radio said that the RAF bombed industrial targets in the Ruhr valley last night.'

'Was there any mention of Holland?'

'None,' she replied flatly. 'Now drink your tea.' Elizabeth sipped the hot liquid gratefully. After a few moments the woman spoke again. 'My dear, there is something,' she said cautiously. 'The doctor and I were discussing it last night and we were wondering if there was anyone we could contact for you?'

'You mean Eamon?'

'He should know. He's in America, isn't he?'

Elizabeth set the cup and saucer aside before opening the top drawer of the bedside table, removing a notepad and pencil. Her stomach contracted with her sudden movement, forcing her to pause a moment before scribbling down the telephone number. 'Could you ring this number?' She handed over the notepad.

'Whitehall!' The headmistress couldn't hide her astonishment.

'Ask for a Mr McClean. Give him my name and tell him that I need to see him.'

'But, my dear, who is this, this Mr McClean?' The headmistress was perplexed.

'Just ask him to come.' Elizabeth stared back, her eyes pleading. 'Please.'

Sunday, 19 May 1940

ELIZABETH took a quiet stroll around the orchard in the walled garden next to the old school rectory. It was the first time she had ventured outside since losing the baby. Her own weakness shocked her and whilst the doctor had warned that it would be several weeks before she would be fully recovered, her fragility was nevertheless hard to take. She was forced to sit on one of the garden seats beside the garden path.

'Hello, Mrs O'Casey.' The man's Scots accent was unmistakable. Elizabeth turned to find Captain Tobias McClean standing next to the gateway at the orchard wall. She had only ever met him once before. It had been the week before her husband had left, almost four months ago. She remembered the occasion well; McClean had joined them for dinner at a London restaurant. Then, as now, he had been dressed in civilian clothes, and nothing about his bearing gave any hint of a military background. She had estimated him to be in his early thirties and had been struck by his friendly face and bright sparkling eyes. Given other circumstances, she recalled, McClean would undoubtedly have been, at minimum, an audacious flirt.

'Captain McClean.' She forced a smile. 'Thank you for coming.'

'I came as soon as I could.' He walked over and extended his hand to her before sitting down at the other end of the bench seat. 'I am sorry to hear about your trouble. I trust you are on the mend?'

'Some things can never be mended, Captain.'

'Indeed.' He sighed, removing a cigarette case and proffering it to her.

'No thank you, but don't let me stop you.'

She studied him as he removed the lighter from the pocket of his tweed jacket. This man was the only link she had to Eamon, her only possible avenue of contact. What he knew and what he would tell her could be as different as black and white, yet she had at least to try. She knew that McClean had disapproved of Eamon marrying her. He hadn't said as much, but she had seen it in his eyes. To him, and God knows who else in British Intelligence, Rachel Elizabeth Goldmann was a security risk, at minimum she was trouble for them. Of course she had played their game and answered their questions, mainly put to her through Eamon. She hadn't known anything about her husband working for MI5 until after their marriage in 1939. It was

25

humiliating to find that she was to be 'screened' by British Intelligence. After her initial anger at Eamon's deceit had abated, she had played McClean's stupid game and answered all the awkward questions. What did it matter to them who her great-grandfather was? Did they even know the difference between Sephardic and Ashkenazic Jews? Above all else, she had been surprised by Eamon's revelation, having taken him as an academic who simply romanced about the ideals of a united Ireland. That Eamon, the university lecturer, was a man of action at all, had been her greatest surprise, although she had always imagined that if his words were ever to materialize into any form of action, it would have been aligned to the IRA. Whilst Eamon O'Casey had all the physical attributes of some great Celtic warrior, he echoed nothing but peace and love; he was a poet, a linguist, a man of words.

'Have you seen my husband?'

'Mrs O'Casey,' McClean started slowly, carefully choosing his words. 'You understand of course that Eamon is not in England.'

'Yes.'

'Well, there's not much I can tell you, I'm afraid, other than to reassure you that he's safe and well.'

It was the standard reply she had heard a number of times from McClean's office since Eamon had gone away in January. It was no longer enough. 'I've just lost my baby!' she cried.

'Please, you must understand. I sympathize completely with your situation, but the nature of our business is such that I cannot tell you more.' McClean was finding it impossible to say much else. 'For Eamon's sake.'

Not without difficulty, Elizabeth stood up. 'I need him! I want him here!' she cried. McClean rose to his feet instantly, reaching out to touch her. Elizabeth pulled away. 'I have the right,' she insisted.

'It just isn't possible,' he said bluntly.

'Can you get a message to him then?'

'About the child?' McClean shook his head.

'Then what the hell are you doing here?' Elizabeth's anger suddenly abated. A tear trickled down her cheek. 'I just want him back. I need him, Captain McClean. He doesn't even know I was pregnant.'

'I'll see what we can do. But I can make no promises.' McClean tried his best to reassure her.

'Thank you.' Elizabeth stared back at him, wiping away a tear. 'There is something I need to ask you.'

'Name it.'

26

Elizabeth removed a folded sheet of paper from her skirt pocket and handed it across to him. 'As you know my family all live in Amsterdam. Captain McClean, I'm concerned for them. I know you already have all the information on file, but I took the liberty of writing it all down for you. I've included our house in the country. It may be that Papa has managed to get our family safely away from the city. The house would be large enough for them all to live there together.'

'When was the last time you contacted your family?'

'Not since last year.' She lied, praying that he wouldn't spot it. It had been one of the unwritten rules for Elizabeth, that after marriage to Eamon, she should always forward any foreign correspondence via MI5, for vetting and authorization.

McClean scanned the lengthy list of names and addresses, inwardly cursing his own generosity in allowing himself to be forced into a corner. 'I'll see what can be done. As you can imagine, things in Holland are somewhat sketchy at present.'

'I understand. Thank you.'

'How have you settled here at High Newbury?' he asked.

'Everyone has been very nice to me. I have my own apartment in the staff wing, it's very bijou, but it's comfortable.'

'No awkward questions from the other staff members about Eamon being away so much?'

'I've given the impression that Eamon is lecturing in America. It seems to have sufficed.'

'The headmistress, she rang me at Whitehall. She sounded more than curious.'

'She thinks we are cousins.' Elizabeth grinned. 'Twice removed.'

'I see.' He was slightly embarrassed; she had thought of everything. 'If there is any need for a change of residence or employment, you will let me know, won't you?'

'So that you can arrange another quiet job for me?' she replied sarcastically.

As McClean placed the list inside his pocket he removed a small brown envelope, setting it on the bench next to Elizabeth. 'That is for you.'

Elizabeth cautiously took the unsealed envelope and peered inside. It was packed with folded bank notes.

'It's legally yours. I know Eamon would want you to have it.' Elizabeth stared back blankly. McClean's embarrassment increased. 'You may want to take a short holiday, it's up to you.' McClean arose, taking the opportunity to retreat. 'We will do our best to find out all we can for you. If there is any further word on Eamon I will let you know.' He put out his hand to Elizabeth, but she ignored it, staring down at the money on her lap. 'Goodbye, Mrs O'Casey.' With that McClean turned and walked away, relieved to be getting away so quickly.

Elizabeth continued to stare down at the money. Was this what everything eventually came down to? The war had taken everything she loved away from her and yet it had only just begun.

PART ONE

The Seed

BERCHTESGADEN, AUSTRIA
Wednesday, 25 April 1945

THE STAFF car took him the final distance to the Berghof, the Führer's mountain retreat. The SS officer relaxed for the first time in days, enjoying the panoramic view of the thick mountain forest which enwrapped the craggy outcrops of the Austrian mountainside. The sunrise over the mountains was breathtaking; to SS Gruppenführer Rudolph Schiller it seemed the war was on another planet, the stark reality momentarily obliterated from his tired brain as he eased back into his seat and tried to snatch a little sleep, his first rest in over three days.

His thoughts were cast back to his earlier days. He had been born poor. His father, like so many others, had sacrificed his health in the trenches of the First World War. Plagued by ill-health and unemployment, his father had finally committed suicide, leaving Schiller and his mother to fend for themselves. They had lived hand to mouth for many years after that, dependent upon the charity of family members and friends. He had never forgotten the humiliation, the degradation, the menial tasks that his mother had to subject herself to, washing others' dirty linen, cleaning for them. He imagined she would have almost kissed their feet, if they'd asked.

Then, by chance, a distant uncle on his father's side died suddenly. He had made provision in his will for young Schiller to receive an education. So it was that young Rudolph finally made it to one of the Berlin *Gymnasien*. They had expected much from him and he hadn't failed them, but just as he was about to commence his tertiary education his mother had fallen ill with tuberculosis. What little remained of the money for his education was soon expended on medicines and doctors, but it was all to no avail. After four months she died.

With university unattainable, Schiller had wandered aimlessly from job to job, never staying in one town long enough to make any acquaintances. Then, by chance, whilst visiting Munich in 1933, he was introduced to Heinrich Himmler. The pair hit it off instantly, and shortly thereafter Schiller was quietly recruited into the Sicherheitsdienst, Himmler's personal secret civilian security organization. It was a power-base to build upon for Schiller, giving him, for the first time in his life, unrestricted opportunity. Himmler had looked after him well and Schiller's career had taken off in leaps and bounds following the successful completion of 'Operation Gold'. Of course he had betrayed his Führer by taking part of the booty, but he could justify that, even to himself. It was what he deserved. Apart from that one transgression, Schiller's loyalty to his Führer was beyond reproach.

Schiller's natural organizational skills had been put to good use. Himmler set him to work advising on the design and development of the death camps. He had taken his filthy job seriously, too seriously for some, even including Himmler. He had been frequently criticized for his overzealous acts; he was becoming too overt even for the weaselly Reichsführer. It was obvious to all at Reich Central Security that Schiller had a deep-seated hatred of the Jews. He had relished coming up with new and more 'efficient' forms of extermination for the 'low life', as he often referred to the camp inmates. When it became obvious that the camps were not going to complete the quotas set at the Wannsee conference, Schiller took his lead from Heydrich and instigated the formation of the Einsatzgruppen, specially selected SS mobile killer squads, with one objective: to speed up the extermination in the occupied countries, by whatever means at their disposal. As the death toll rose, Schiller's rewards had come swiftly, including personal gifts and decorations from a grateful Führer. He was now the youngest major general in the SS, but in reaching such exalted status he had marked himself as a major war criminal.

He had almost fallen asleep when the nudge on his arm alerted him. Schiller lifted the peak of his cap from over his eyes and glanced up at the SS major who had accompanied him on the drive up from the town. He focused his weary eyes on the other officer.

'We are almost there, Herr Gruppenführer.'

'What time is it?' grunted Schiller, shielding his eyes from the light.

'A little after five o'clock,' replied the major. 'Do you wish me to accompany you into the Berghof, *mein Herr*?'

'That will not be necessary. Return back down to Berchtesgaden and tell the airfield to stand by,' ordered Schiller.

'*Jawohl, mein Herr.*'

The six-cylinder Mercedes finally drew up at the bottom of a small flight of steps, leading to the main terrace of Hitler's mountain retreat. Schiller was greeted on the steps by a middle-aged woman, dressed in a grey service uniform. She quickly escorted him inside the main house. He had never been to the place before; it would have been a privilege to have been invited to Hitler's favourite country retreat, and on another occasion he would have lingered, taking his time to enjoy the experience, to admire the array of art treasures that festooned the apartments throughout the establishment. He was shown into the main lounge. A small Scottish terrier dog ran up to him and began to bark loudly.

'Be quiet.' The maid lifted the dog up. 'If you would make yourself comfortable, I will inform my mistress of your arrival, Herr Gruppenführer,' she said courteously.

Schiller removed his cap as he looked around. The room was massive, to one side stood a huge stone fireplace, above which hung a full-length portrait of Adolf Hitler. All the furnishings were covered in white dust-sheets and from the marks on the walls it was obvious that the remainder of the paintings had been recently removed.

'Depressing, isn't it?' The woman's quiet voice startled him.

Schiller turned to see Eva Braun, Hitler's mistress, standing in the doorway.

'Fräulein Braun,' he bowed slightly, 'It is good to see you again.' Eva Braun forced a smile as she moved over beside the empty hearth.

'I hear that Goering has some visitors,' she continued.

'News travels quickly,' he replied.

'Berlin sent a cable; it was hinted that our Reichsmarschall was in some sort of trouble and that I should avoid all contact with him.'

'And have you?' He studied the woman. There was a child-like quality about her. He could readily understand why Hitler cared for her so much, an uncomplicated oasis in the desert of the Führer's existence.

'He did try to telephone me. When that failed he sent a letter by messenger. I refused to accept it.' She ran her hands through her golden hair. 'What has he done exactly?'

'He sent a telegram, asking the Führer to relinquish the charge of the Reich to him.' Schiller frowned. 'It is being viewed by Berlin as treason.'

'The fool!' She looked away. 'I can have no sympathy for him.'

'As you said, he is being visited at present,' continued Schiller. 'The Führer has insisted on his full resignation from every public office.'

'No need to say any more.' She turned back to him again. 'And what happens to me?'

'I have orders to escort you to Berlin, at once.' The woman's elation was evident before she spoke.

'When do we leave?' She gripped the edge of the stone fireplace, trying to steady her shaking fingers.

'I have an aircraft waiting at the private airfield. We should go now, Fräulein.'

The woman began to laugh, almost hysterically. 'I hope your plane is big enough to take my luggage.'

'I am sure it is,' he insisted. 'But I must stress that we hurry, Fräulein. Templehof airfield may not stay open much longer, the Russians are closing in on Berlin by the hour.'

Without a word spoken, she was gone, and Schiller hadn't even finished his cigarette before she reappeared again. His eyes widened upon seeing the nurse who now accompanied the woman. The sultry-looking uniformed nurse was carrying a baby.

'We are ready,' Eva Braun said cheerfully, taking the baby into her own arms.

'Fräulein?' Schiller stepped forward.

'I should correct you on that score, Herr Gruppenführer. The Führer and I are already married.' She smiled back.

Schiller looked down at the tiny bundle nestling in the woman's arms. The baby's eyes were alert and bright. As he stared into the piercing grey-blue eyes, he didn't need to ask, there could be no doubt, for he had seen those same eyes before on so many previous occasions. Schiller wanted to say something, yet he was too choked up to speak.

'It's a boy,' she said proudly. 'He was born on 20 April, on his father's birthday! Can you imagine!' The pride in her eyes was evident, the trepidation of moments earlier had disappeared. 'He is called Pieter.'

'Pieter,' echoed Schiller, reaching up to touch the baby's hand.

'And today he shall at last be with his father!' she said gleefully.

Schiller found himself unable to keep his eyes off the child. He was angry at not having been told about him before, yet he could understand the imperative of total secrecy. Now he understood the full meaning of the escape plan. With the child as the Führer's future heir, 'Operation Herron' became a strategy, a manoeuvre rather than a retreat.

E AMON O'CASEY stared out from the window of his billet as the
strange convoy, led by two armoured cars, approached the outer
perimeter fence. He was curious, for no one had been allowed into
the main compound since the SS had sealed the place up, five days
previously. The armoured cars drew up on either side of the entrance,
allowing the remainder of the convoy to pass on into the compound.
A covered lorry, flanked by motorcycle escorts, swung through the
gateway. It was closely followed by a second lorry, open-backed and
crammed with Waffen SS. O'Casey raised an eyebrow: the barrier had
been lifted in anticipation – this new arrival had been expected.

As the covered lorry slowed to a halt outside the billet, the four
motorcycle-sidecar escorts pulled up short, forming a rough semi-
circle around the rear of the vehicle, their MG .24 sidecar-mounted
machine-guns trained directly on the tail-gate. Immediately the other
lorry disgorged the soldiers, the SS quickly forming two lines on either
side of the covered lorry, leading all the way up to the entrance of the
billet. An SS sergeant-major strode over to the covered lorry, pulling
the canvas back-flap aside and unbolting the rear-gate. As the tail-gate
swung down, the first of the sailors jumped out. The Irishman's
curiosity turned into puzzlement: from the look on their faces, the
German sailors were as bemused about their treatment as he was.

Then a staff car drew up alongside the sailors. A tall stern-faced
SS major alighted and approached the group, saluting one of them.
O'Casey recognized SS Sturmbannführer Karl Strassmann instantly.
He had not seen the thirty-year-old head of SS Security at Kiel for
several days and his sudden absence had mystified him. Strassmann
worked for Reich Central Security, the Reichssicherheitshauptamt, he
was Berlin's linkman at Kiel for the implementation of 'Operation
Herron'. O'Casey has disliked the arrogant officer from the moment
they had met; he was self-opinionated and clearly contemptuous of
him – that didn't worry him, but the German's inquisitiveness did.
The Irishman reinforced his resolve to get through the next days
safely. He had been walking a veritable tightrope for the last five years
and survived, and he certainly was not going to be undone now, in
the final days of the war, by some pompous Jerry bastard!

O'Casey stood next to the stove, pouring out some coffee from a battered enamel pot as the first of the sailors started filing inside the prefabricated billet. The Irishman ignored the submariners' curious stares as he waited for the last man to enter. The outer door finally closed behind the U-boat captain. O'Casey recognized the officer instantly by the white cloth covering on his cap.

'*Guten Tag*, Herr Kapitän.' O'Casey's German was perfect. For a moment the German took him to be a native countryman, until the Irishman continued in English. 'I'm told that your English is very good.' O'Casey approached the naval officer, offering him the steaming mug of black coffee. 'It's wet and it's hot.' He grinned.

The German took the coffee gratefully. 'Thank you,' he replied in English.

'The name's O'Casey; I'm what you might call the hired help around here.' He beamed broadly.

'Kapitänleutnant Petersen.' The naval officer gratefully sipped the hot sweet liquid. 'Real coffee, now I'm impressed.'

'Nothing but the best here, Captain, but I can't say as much about the accommodation.'

'Perhaps we can console ourselves with the fact that we won't be here too long,' replied Petersen, taking a further mouthful of coffee.

'I hear I'm to be sailing with you, or whatever it is you do on a U-boat,' continued O'Casey.

'You have me at a distinct disadvantage, Herr O'Casey.' The German was hesitant.

'Fear not, Captain, I'm not looking for information. Sure I'm just a simple Irishman wanting a lift home again. Help yerself to some more coffee, there's plenty in the pot.' O'Casey smiled and went back towards his own quarters. 'I'll be seeing you around,' he called out.

Petersen raised an eyebrow as he watched the burly red-haired Irishman disappear through an adjacent doorway. If he could be sure of one thing, O'Casey was anything but simple.

1.14 a.m., 27 April 1945

THE GUARD had just changed on the quayside and at the U-boat pens less than one hour earlier. He had studied their pattern carefully over the last three days. There would not be another change-over due for another two hours. O'Casey didn't much care for the conditions, the moon was too bright for one thing and the offshore wind guaranteed the harbour would be choppy, but he knew he couldn't delay any longer. The arrival of the U-boat crew signalled an imminent departure.

O'Casey had slipped out of the billet with relative ease, avoiding the SS guards by exiting through a broken roof-light above the latrine and crossing on to the flat concrete roof of the adjoining equipment store. From there it was easy: the building gave him covered access to within thirty yards of the sea-wall. He slipped down the rusty fire escape, careful to avoid the creaking metal steps that he had committed to memory. Pausing at the bottom of the open tread staircase, he listened carefully before crawling over to a pile of oil drums stacked three high and positioned half-way between the building and the sea-wall. It was the ideal hiding place: the oil drums were covered in a thick camouflage netting, draped loosely across and weighted down on two sides by concrete bricks. O'Casey checked his watch again. If his calculations were correct one of the German guards would be circling around the back of the building at any moment. He held his breath, counting down the seconds. A minute passed, then another, and another. The guard was late. He cursed inwardly.

The waiting was always the worst part – it gave him time to think. It was always the same and it never got any easier. Perhaps he was getting too old for it all, or was it simply fatigue? He sighed; the guard was now almost ten minutes overdue. He glanced over at the sea-wall, estimating the distance to be around twelve metres. O'Casey thought about taking a chance and not waiting any longer. He knew he could clear the distance and be over the low sea-wall inside four seconds, but the risks were great, any mistake in the timing and he was *kaputt*. Caught out in the open and in the bright moonlight, he wouldn't stand a chance.

He cleared the chill night air from his lungs and breathed in from the nose. He could smell the stench of seaweed left behind by the receding tide. Now that the tide was almost fully out there would be a drop on the other side of the wall of over thirty feet down to the rocks below. It was not an ideal situation, but a low tide suited his purpose. Suddenly he was alerted by a sound coming from his right. The studded heels of the soldier's boots gave him away well before he came into view. Seconds later, and ten full minutes behind schedule, the Waffen SS guard rounded the corner of the building. He paused, adjusting the leather chin strap of his helmet and scratching the stubble on his chin. The soldier leaned back against the wall of the store house, resting his foot against it. This was bad, for while O'Casey had made his plans hurriedly, he had at least taken comfort in knowing the guards' timing and procedure. He didn't recognize the guard, the man was obviously a replacement and from the look of him he wasn't very interested in doing his job. The precious minutes ticked by until the impasse was finally broken by the arrival of a second soldier.

'Rudi! *Komm!*' The second soldier clicked his fingers.

The first soldier grunted something indistinguishable and then proceeded to follow the other man around the corner of the building. O'Casey took his chance. He sprinted for the wall, his plimsolled feet hardly touching the surface except for his toes. Seconds later the black-clothed figure vaulted over the low stone sea-wall, dropping out of sight. O'Casey breathed a deep sigh of relief that his calculation had been accurate for he had landed on a small outcrop of concrete just seven feet below the wall, all that remained of the old pier which had been demolished years before to make way for the new U-boat pens. He clung to the stone wall, keeping within the shadows as he peered down into the darkness below. He couldn't see the rocks, but he could hear the occasional wave crashing just beneath him. If he had miscalculated he would almost certainly be lying amidst the rocks with, at minimum, a broken limb. Out in the harbour a small craft was patrolling the outer reaches, its searchlights sweeping out across the boom that stretched across the harbour entrance.

Then he started down, easing himself carefully into the unknown, feeling his way down the rough stone face. He was again fortunate, for as the wall dropped away it began to splay outward until it met the rocks. Suddenly he lost his footing, slipping on the seaweed. He was at the high tide mark, standing amidst the rubble of the old pier. As O'Casey eased himself down into the water, another wave crashed in, soaking him to the waist. Timing the next full wave, he let himself out with the tide, sliding between the rocks into the deeper water beyond. The water quickly saturated his black pullover and trousers, drawing him down as he cut out against the turning tide towards the U-boat pens. The three-hundred-yard swim was far more tiring than O'Casey had anticipated. The tide was stronger than he had expected, coming in at a steady pace and drawing him towards the jagged rocks beside the pens. It took every ounce of strength for him to keep on course towards the concrete mass. Minutes later he was there, treading water beside the massive steel sea-doors of the main pen.

The sea-doors were in fact steel-lined boxes, filled with concrete and several feet thick. They closed from either side across the mouth of each of the pens, suspended from heavy steel girders under the heavy twelve-foot thick concrete roof. O'Casey had studied his subject carefully: this was his only way in, as the other entrances into the restricted section were too heavily guarded for anyone to get past unnoticed, but if the place had one weakness it was the sea-doors. The pens were tidal, the sea-doors therefore were not hermetically sealed. The problem was that he didn't know for certain how far under the surface the steel doors extended. Continuing to tread water, O'Casey slipped on a pair of leather gloves to give himself some protection before taking a final deep breath and submerging into the cold, pitch black water. He groped his way down the barnacle-crusted sea-door, his lungs straining and ears hurting as he descended further.

O'Casey was about to give it up and resurface when his hand felt the underside of the door. He gripped on firmly to avoid himself rising again. Then, wedging his feet under the door he checked the distance to the sea-bed – there seemed just enough clearance for him to squeeze through. With every ounce of strength he could produce O'Casey pulled himself under the sea-door. With the coldness of the water he couldn't feel the barnacles slicing through his pullover and across his back. Suddenly he was in! He could sense the changing tone of the water. Light cascaded down to meet him as he began to rise again slowly. O'Casey tried to push towards the side of the basin before attempting to surface. His lungs felt as though they were at bursting point and his head pounded, but he knew that with the stillness of the water inside the pen any ripple would be detected instantly. He had somehow to reach the safety of the shadows.

Seconds later he came up, almost imperceptibly breaking the oily surface at the side of the fitting-out basin. He breathed deeply, almost coughing as he fought to regulate his breathing. He was next to a U-boat, but it was like nothing he had ever come across, longer than any other he had seen, and from the lack of rusting and the fresh paint work he could tell it had been recently launched. At the other side of the basin was an older Type-VIIC U-boat, its markings obliterated. Above he could hear the raised voices of the work crew hoisting provisions aboard the larger U-boat. Clearly, they were preparing for imminent departure. He began to move up the basin. Overhead, two gangways spanned the short distance from the quay-side down on to the U-boat's deck. Suddenly he froze. Just overhead two sailors struggled up the steeply angled gangway from the U-boat, the second man halting on the light metal gangway, his boots clearly visible through the light mesh. O'Casey's heart raced. Had the man seen something? Yes, the sailor was staring at the ripple in the oily surface created by the Irishman's movement.

'Come on, Erich,' urged the first sailor.

'I think there's something in the water!' the second sailor called out.

'Probably rats.' The other sailor grabbed him by the shoulder pulling him up the gangway. 'Come on, we have work to do.'

O'Casey couldn't believe his luck. He was just about to move again when the workshop doors began to roll back. Immediately a locomotive began shunting a wooden railway carriage into the pen. What intrigued the Irishman was the line of Waffen SS flanking the carriage on either side. The cattle truck was halted just several yards away from the quayside. Then the locomotive was uncoupled and reversed back outside. It had no sooner cleared the pen than the heavy door rolled back again across the railway tracks. It was then that O'Casey noticed SS Sturmbannführer Strassmann, the head of SS security at Kiel. The tall SS officer stood next to the railway carriage barking out orders to his men. O'Casey realized the workshop was being cleared of all unnecessary personnel. Once the area was cleared of all work-crews Strassmann went over and banged on the side of the carriage. The carriage doors opened and two further SS officers climbed out. For the next five minutes O'Casey watched, shivering in the cold water, as the heavy wooden boxes were unloaded one by one and taken aboard the large U-boat. From what he could make out each box was consecutively numbered and stamped with the German eagle and swastika. Now he knew that his source information had been correct.

'The gold,' whispered O'Casey. Suddenly he was aware of a new danger: he was shivering. He had to get out of there and fast before hypothermia set in.

He moved slowly back down to the bow of the large U-boat and judged the distance to the sea-doors. There could be no room for error; once out there in the open water of the pen he was totally vulnerable. He would have to make his exit first time. Filling his lungs again he drew himself under, using the serrated bow to draw himself under and gain depth. After submerging around six feet he shoved off from the cover of the U-boat hull, drawing steadily downwards as he propelled himself towards the sea-doors. O'Casey was in for a shock. The water level had risen considerably in the short time he had been inside. If he failed in his first attempt he would be forced to resurface inside the pen and in clear view of the soldiers.

His head pounded as he fought his way down into the blackness. His strength was being sapped by the current. The incoming tide had created considerable pressure under the sea-doors. Before O'Casey realized, he was almost breaking the surface again, but on the wrong

40

side! From somewhere deep inside O'Casey found new strength, the pain in his lungs and head vanished as he concentrated on getting out. As he kicked out, his heel broke the surface. Keeping his head he clawed his way down the riveted surface of the steel door, drawing himself further and further downward.

Suddenly, he was there! He grabbed firmly on to the underside of the door to stop his body being swung around by the current. His mouth opened as he exerted every last vestige of strength. He began to choke. For a few terrible moments everything hung in the balance. He was going up, but which way? O'Casey frantically struck out, trying to reach the surface before blacking out. He broke the surface, coughing and retching. He was outside! The waves lapping against his face and the blackness told him he had made it. As O'Casey's hearing returned he became aware of a high-pitched siren wailing from somewhere above. He cursed. So far God had indeed been merciful, but he wasn't making it easy. He had no time to rest – apart from the alarm he was freezing in the water. He had to strike out for the shore and very quickly.

Across the bay the searchlight alerted him to the approaching patrol boat. He struck out, sacrificing caution for speed as he headed straight back towards the old pier. The security lights on the sea-wall were still unlit. If he could just make it to the wall in time he stood a chance. Immediately the searchlights positioned on the concrete roof of the U-boat pens were switched on. Several arc lights splayed out into the rolling sea, searching for a target. O'Casey changed direction, heading straight for the rocky shoreline next to the pens and just managing to avoid one of the beams of light. Minutes later and close to exhaustion, O'Casey was washed up on to the rocks by the heavy swell. Gaining a foothold, he stumbled ashore, between the slimy rocks, recovering his breath a moment. Another searchlight suddenly illuminated the shoreline close by.

O'Casey picked himself up and ran, bounding across the open stretch of rocks until he reached the first section of the sea-wall. There was only the one way up and that was back the way he had come; climbing anywhere else would be too risky. He struggled alongside the sea-wall, through the foaming water, bracing himself against the incoming waves. He glanced out into the harbour: the patrol boat was closing in on the U-boat pens at full speed. Now he was in no doubt that he had been spotted. He covered his head as a large wave came crashing in over him. As it receded O'Casey waded through the waist-high water, groping his way alongside the slippery wall.

Progress was slow. Then, finally, he was there, standing under what remained of the old pier, the concrete projection just visible above him. He allowed the next full wave to sweep him up against the wall, and managed to grab hold of one of the rusty pier supports at the optimum moment. As the tide receded the Irishman was left dangling clear of the water. He climbed up until he had reached the concrete projection. Then, drawing himself up the last few inches he peeked over the sea-wall. Amazingly his way was clear, there wasn't a guard in sight. But where were they? Hadn't they been alerted by all the commotion at the pens? Shouldn't they have been at their stations? Maybe they were craftier than that, perhaps they knew after all, not just his whereabouts, but his identity! Was he about to walk right into a trap? He cursed. There was no time to wait.

O'Casey vaulted over the wall, landing lightly on the other side and keeping low. He ran for all he was worth, skipping past the pile of camouflaged oil drums, and heading directly for the rickety old fire escape. He had almost reached the stairway when something distracted him. Instinctively O'Casey ducked and side-stepped, barely missing the jabbing bayonet of the Mauser rifle. The soldier had burst out of the darkness like some vengeful Teutonic knight, charging head on into his avowed enemy. O'Casey moved fast, getting himself out into the open again. He needed space to manoeuvre. Whilst alerted by the alarm sirens, the young soldier had been caught unawares by the speed of his quarry. Levelling the rifle at O'Casey, the frightened soldier pulled the trigger, again and again, but nothing happened! The young German had been so eager to spring his attack that he had failed to release the safety catch. He was no longer thinking as a soldier – the sudden fear of coming face to face with death had taken hold of him.

O'Casey knew he had only seconds to dispose of the man, but he had to choose his moment well or he could still end up impaled on the end of a bayonet. As the young SS Oberschütze started to realize his stupidity and fiddle for the rifle's safety catch, O'Casey struck. Feigning a sideways movement, he went directly for the soldier, blocking the bayoneted rifle with his left forearm. The young Waffen SS soldier's eyes opened wide with fear as the black-clad giant closed on him. The cold blade sank into the soft tissue below the leather chin strap of his helmet. The soldier gasped and then began to shudder uncontrollably. O'Casey twisted the stiletto blade of the Sykes-Fairbairn knife and the man convulsed, dropping the Mauser rifle on to the concrete. With one hand clamped over the dying man's face, O'Casey yanked the knife clear. The soldier staggered backwards, looking on helplessly as his opponent sank the 6-inch stiletto blade into his chest. Death was almost instantaneous.

O'Casey stared into the eyes of the young man he held in his arms and cursed. It was all so needless, the bloody war was almost over after all. His conscience would have to deal with that later, but for now his instinct for survival advocated a more pragmatic approach. He stooped, drawing the stricken soldier over his shoulder and picking up the Mauser rifle in the same movement. O'Casey carried the body back to the sea-wall, tossing the soldier over at the optimum moment to coincide with the tide's retreat. The body hit the water right on cue, the sound of the waves obliterating the splash. O'Casey pitched the rifle out, well beyond the low tide mark. Already the white foaming water had begun to haul the body out beyond the rocks. Undoubtedly, the soldier would eventually be discovered, but with any luck the strong undercurrent would be adequate to deposit him somewhere over at the far side of the harbour complex.

Of course the guard's disappearance would fortify the original justification for a general alert, but without any body Strassmann would be running around like a headless chicken. With fresh rumours of wide-scale surrender and defeat rife within the Wehrmacht ranks, a soldier's disappearance could almost be expected. In any case O'Casey knew that with the strong tides it could be days before a body was found, and from what he had just witnessed in the U-boat pen, all he needed to get clear of the place was another twenty-four hours. With any luck at all he would be away by the time anyone realized.

Twenty minutes later . . .

H E HEARD the approach of heavy footsteps echoing around the corridor outside. O'Casey braced himself. Without any fore-warning the door burst open. SS Sturmbannführer Karl Strassmann walked inside, his face stern and accusing.

'Herr Sturmbannführer, how the devil are you?' O'Casey smiled up from the bath, a soggy-looking cigar between his teeth.

Strassman stared at the Irishman, his massive frame squashed up in the cast-iron bath, with one leg dangling over the side. 'You have been here all night?' he snapped.

'Now, doesn't it look like it,' insisted O'Casey, maintaining a steady grin.

Strassmann checked behind the door, examining the dry clothing draped across the back of a wooden chair. 'They are dry,' he commented to another SS officer standing next to him.

'Of course they're dry,' O'Casey quipped. 'I always take me clothes off before getting into the bath.'

'There has been a report of enemy saboteurs around the area of the U-boat pens. One of our men is missing,' he retorted.

'That's not so good now.' O'Casey pursed his lips.

'Stay in your quarters, Herr O'Casey. Do not attempt to leave for any reason.'

'Now, why ever would I be doing that?'

'My men have orders to shoot anyone found outside. Is that understood?' Strassmann glared at him.

'Naturally.' O'Casey smiled back. As the door was slammed shut the Irishman breathed a deep sigh of relief. He waited until the noise of their footsteps disappeared down the corridor before removing his left hand from the bath water and setting the dripping Mauser pistol on the soap shelf. If his time had finally come he wasn't about to go out all by himself.

HIGH NEWBURY GIRLS' PUBLIC SCHOOL, BERKSHIRE
Sunday, 29 April 1945

ELIZABETH was sitting alone in the staffroom, marking the third-form test papers. It had been a tedious afternoon, enlivened only by the atrocious weather, frequent thundershowers and a black and ugly sky. The knock at the door was more a relief than an interruption. Elizabeth looked up as one of the senior prefects peered round the door.

'Mrs O'Casey, you have a visitor.' The girl hesitated, lowering her voice. 'A Major McClean from the War Office.'

The mention of the War Office sent a shiver down Elizabeth's back. Since the war had started, she had only seen her husband three times, the last being well over a year ago. The war had changed everything: the man she had married no longer existed; they were virtual strangers now. During the last five years McClean had been

44

her only link with Eamon. She didn't trust the Scotsman, but then, she had little choice in the matter. 'Thank you, Sally. Please show the gentleman in.'

The girl smiled and disappeared again. Moments later the door reopened and the Scots army officer was shown in. He was wearing his uniform this time – perhaps it signified some sort of official business, she mused. The last time she'd met McClean, she had asked for two things, news about Eamon and once again news about her family back in Amsterdam. He'd failed to deliver on either score. So, what did he want this time? Perhaps he was going to be the bearer of bad news, not that she really cared any more, having lived without hope now these last dreadful years. As the door shut behind him, McClean removed his peaked cap. Elizabeth went forward and they shook hands.

'Is it news about Eamon?' Elizabeth asked nervously.

'He's fine. Please don't concern yourself, Mrs O'Casey, I'm not here to bring bad tidings.' McClean smiled.

'I don't understand?' Elizabeth returned to her desk beside the window.

McClean followed her across the room, setting his cap and swagger stick on the desk. 'Actually I was hoping *you* might have heard something.'

'Me!' Elizabeth was astounded. 'Major, I know very little about my husband's work, except that it is very dangerous and involves him being away on the Continent a great deal. He never discusses what he does and I don't ask questions. That is not the way I wanted it, but that is the way it is.' Elizabeth shook her head. 'Frankly, I find your comment rather obscure, bearing in mind that he works for you!' She was becoming angry now.

'Works with,' corrected McClean. 'I don't think Eamon has ever worked for anyone in his life. He's a free agent in more ways than one!'

'Your flippancy does not amuse me, Major,' Elizabeth rebuked him.

'Call me McClean, everyone else does.' He moved closer, ignoring the hostility. 'Are you sure you haven't heard from Eamon?' The smiling demeanour was gone now.

'You actually are serious, aren't you?' Elizabeth couldn't believe her ears. 'You think that I know where Eamon is!'

'Sometimes people with your husband's resourcefulness have their own private methods of contact.'

Elizabeth fell silent for a moment and turned towards the window.

It was raining outside, bleak and miserable – just the way she felt. 'Are you saying Eamon is missing? Is that it?'

'No, I'm not saying that.' McClean paused. The woman wasn't making this easy for him.

'Then what are you saying? What has happened?' Elizabeth turned on him.

McClean looked away.

'I have a right to know, Major,' Elizabeth confronted him.

'What I am about to tell you is strictly top secret. You cannot mention anything to anyone, and I must have your word on that.'

'What has happened?' Elizabeth said softly.

'Two days ago we received a radio signal from Eamon. He's on his way home.'

Elizabeth closed her eyes in relief. 'Thank God.'

'But we haven't heard from him since,' continued McClean.

She reopened her eyes, trying desperately to rationalize the situation. 'But there could be any number of reasons why he hasn't contacted you, couldn't there?'

'Mrs O'Casey, I'm not saying that he is in any trouble, but we are concerned that we didn't receive his scheduled broadcast. Look, I'm sorry for bothering you.' McClean picked up his cap and stick and moved towards the door. 'Knowing Eamon he'll probably turn up unannounced at some south-coast fishing port. On the other hand, you could hear from him first. If you do, you will let me know, won't you?' He paused, looking back at her.

Elizabeth shook her head, fighting back the tears. 'I've told you already. There is absolutely no way my husband could contact me. We have no mutual friends, no acquaintances. It has always been just ourselves and only ourselves.'

'Well – ' McClean removed a small white card from inside the lining of his cap and set it on a small Pembroke table next to the coatstand – 'There's my card, just in case.' He donned his cap, touching the peak with his swagger stick. 'Good afternoon, Mrs O'Casey.'

Elizabeth nodded. She couldn't bring herself to speak for fear that it might precipitate a flood of tears.

After he had left, she stood by the window, overlooking the forecourt and beyond towards the school playing fields and woodland. She saw McClean walking briskly through the heavy rain to an olive-green army staff car. The uniformed driver straightened himself and came round from the other side of the vehicle, opening the near door for his passenger. As McClean crouched to step inside, he glanced up at the leaded window, staring directly back at Elizabeth for a moment.

As the door closed the other passenger spoke up. 'Well?'

'I'm not sure.' McClean looked at the plain-clothes policeman sitting beside him. 'I want your boys to carry out a twenty-four-hour surveillance, effective immediately.'

The detective nodded. 'It'll mean drafting in some men from other areas. I'll need to see the Chief Constable about this.'

'Superintendent, the war has not ended yet.' McClean scowled. 'Where my department is concerned, you will do exactly as you are told. And immediately please.'

The policeman's face reddened.

Elizabeth moved back from the window and threw herself into the nearest chair as she finally burst into tears. McClean had brought it all back home to her, all the fear and trepidation, all the agony and the doubt. What did he know and what wasn't he telling her? She knew perhaps more than she should about Eamon's work. While Eamon had gone to great pains to understate and minimize the risks, she was too much a realist not to understand. Yet any protestations would be wasted. Eamon was a man of strict principle, driven by his burning desire to see a united Ireland. She couldn't comprehend how he justfied himself working for the British. She had asked him about it more than once, but the only answer she got was vague; he clearly didn't feel the need to explain his actions to anyone, even to the woman he purportedly loved.

Elizabeth's mind kept going back to the last time she had been with her husband. They had only had a short time together and it had been painful. She still blamed him for being absent when she had lost the baby. One part of her wanted to be loved by him, yet another held back in frustration and bitterness, forcing a deep wedge between them. Then, just before he left, Eamon had promised that this was the last time they would ever be apart again. She hadn't believed him, yet she had to believe in something to keep sane. What else was there for her?

Eamon had sounded somehow different that last time and now it troubled her greatly. For weeks afterwards she had felt an overwhelming feeling of foreboding, at one point almost having a hopeless expectation of the worst. Finally the feeling of dread had left her and she had become more settled, especially after the joyous news of the continued Allied victories all across Europe. The war was ending and so was her long wait. But was Eamon safe? Yet she knew he had to be still alive, something incomprehensible still told her that. Just as something had told her of her father's death even before Eamon had finally confirmed it, this same perception now told her that Eamon was coming back to her.

She dried her eyes and returned to the window. The sky was dark, and the rain was beginning to fall again. The distant rumble of thunder obliterated the noise of the rain beating against the window. Her head felt peculiarly light – perhaps it was the thunder in the air. She turned away and went across to the door, picking up McClean's card. She shivered as a chill ran through her body.

That evening Elizabeth went walking through the nearby woods as usual. Over the lonely months she had become a creature of habit. Every night she would head down the ash path, past the playing fields towards the local cricket pavilion. The meandering path led on into the woods and down to the riverside. It was her one and only daily opportunity to be totally alone and without interruption. It made her feel closer to Eamon somehow; at times she felt she could almost reach out and touch him, feeling his strong hands around her body, drawing her into him with all the emotion it evoked. But it was the loneliness that Elizabeth found the most difficult to suppress, especially since Eamon had brought her the dreadful news about her family back in Amsterdam. That moment still played vividly in her mind – a dashing of hope and an overwhelming despair. It had been in 1943, when Eamon had returned unexpectedly after an absence of almost two years. She had been in constant touch with McClean during that time and acutely aware of a change in the man's attitude over the latter months. There was something he wasn't telling her, and for a time she had suspected it was to do with her husband. Then Eamon had returned with the terrible news . . .

McClean had invited Elizabeth up to London, under the pretence of giving her some news about her husband. Elizabeth was to meet McClean as usual in the house close to Belgrave Square, an ordinary-looking, mid-terrace house, in a quiet residential area. She arrived early and was shown inside by the housekeeper, a young woman around her own age.

'Good afternoon, madam.' The housekeeper smiled as she shut the door behind Elizabeth. 'Please go on up to the drawing room on the first floor.'

'Thank you,' replied Elizabeth a little sheepishly. The place made her uncomfortable.

As she got to the top of the second flight of stairs, the drawing-room door opened. Elizabeth stopped in her tracks, for a moment not believing her eyes.

'Eamon? Eamon!' she cried, dashing up the remaining steps and throwing herself into his open arms.

'Elizabeth,' he whispered as he squeezed her body tightly against his own.

They kissed – she couldn't really remember for how long, but it had seemed like for ever, and she remembered her lips aching with the force of their passion. McClean had been with Eamon but had quickly excused himself, returning downstairs. They talked, mainly about how long he had to stay, and about how she had been coping after the miscarriage. For a while the recrimination and disappointment of the baby's loss was gone; the ecstasy of their reunion obliterated everything. But it was not long before Elizabeth realized her husband was hiding something. He was playing with words, and his embarrassment was becoming more acute by the minute.

'Eamon, what is it you have to tell me?' She took the bull by the horns, half imagining that he was about to leave her life that very next moment for good.

'Can I hide nothing from you?' he asked in a soothing tone, taking her hands in his.

'Are you leaving again, is that it?' She tried to prepare herself for the news.

'I wish it was that simple.' He paused. 'It's your father,' he replied slowly, averting his eyes a moment. 'Elizabeth, there's no easy way to say this . . .'

'Don't tell me – ' she raised her hand to his lips – 'don't say it.'

'Elizabeth,' he pleaded.

She stood erect, raising her chin defiantly. 'He's dead. I know he is. I've known since I lost the child.' O'Casey frowned, he wasn't quite sure what his wife was saying. 'When I was having the miscarriage, something told me that the baby was not my only loss.'

'Elizabeth.' He shook his head, wanting to draw her next to him, but she resisted. Her voice was shaky but resolute.

'How did he die?'

'The SS raided your father's offices and diamond factory. No one is quite sure of what happened. The police report was very brief.'

'What police report?' Elizabeth frowned.

'The Dutch police compiled a report on your father's . . . death.'

'You meant to say murder, didn't you?' She was angry now. 'Who did it?' she insisted, drawing away from him.

'An SS officer stated that your father had a gun. He allegedly shot a German official and then tried to escape arrest.'

'Arrest for what?' Elizabeth snapped. 'My father wouldn't have known how to hold a gun, never mind fire one! He was butchered!' She was close to breaking point.

'Elizabeth, that is not all.' O'Casey took her hands again. 'I can find no trace of your family in Amsterdam.'

'What do you mean?' She could sense the lie in his voice.

'Your family are no longer in Amsterdam. Two years ago the Germans rounded up the majority of Jewish families living in Amsterdam and moved them to concentration camps in Germany. It began in February 'forty-one. I can only presume they were amongst those taken. I'm sorry.'

'This SS officer, the one who murdered my father, does he have a name?'

O'Casey hesitated. 'All I know about him is that he was attached to Reich Central Security under a bastard called Heydrich, better known as the "Butcher of Moravia".'

'Heydrich,' Elizabeth repeated, staring blankly back at him.

'Heydrich was killed by Czech partisans last year, but I will find out more for you when I return. They can't have vanished.' O'Casey tried to sound positive.

'Return?' Elizabeth's face contorted. 'How can you return any-where! Haven't I lost enough! Must I go through the pain of losing you also?' Her voice almost dried up on the last words. Elizabeth shook her head in disbelief as O'Casey tried to reason with her.

'The war is not over yet.' O'Casey cursed the clumsiness of his own response.

She moved back from him and O'Casey went to grab hold of her.

'Don't touch me!' she screamed at the top of her voice. Elizabeth began sobbing just as McClean entered the room. O'Casey waved him back outside before consoling his wife. He took Elizabeth into his arms, nestling her head in his burly shoulder as she wept uncontrollably.

'Cry, my darling.' O'Casey ran his hand loosely through her thick auburn hair. He had almost forgotten how soft her hair felt . . .

Elizabeth closed her eyes. For a moment she could almost feel Eamon's arms around her. Then she shivered in the chilly southeasterly wind. Even though her husband had promised to investigate further the whereabouts of her family, Elizabeth had heard nothing more. All she knew for certain was that an unidentified SS officer had butchered her father. Even without knowing him, she could still curse him. She often found herself trying to imagine what he looked like and what she might do if she ever found him. It wasn't healthy, but she couldn't help herself.

She had cried many a night for her young nephews and nieces, a few of them only months old when the Nazis had taken them, now in some unthinkable hellhole, if still alive. Apart from them, Eamon was the only person that mattered to her now, he was the centre of her diminished universe. But Eamon O'Casey entered and left her life like some whirlwind, bringing such news as there was, bringing his loving tenderness, his strength, only to disappear again as suddenly as he had appeared. As predictable as his departure was, she could never face up to it. Like a condemned prisoner awaiting daybreak and the gallows, she would block out that dawning with every ounce of strength she could muster, yet it was inevitable that he would leave, like some cloud on the wind.

The wind was starting to pick up again and rain clouds were racing high above the darkening sky. She reached the fork in the path and checked her watch. It was already past eight o'clock and by the look of things there was going to be yet another rainstorm. Pulling her coat more securely across her narrow shoulders, Elizabeth circled back towards the cricket ground, walking faster now. What had McClean really been after? What did he mean by saying that Eamon was 'safe for the moment'?

A distant rumble of thunder echoed around the woods. The higher branches of the surrounding trees began to sway and pitch in the increasing wind. A minute later the rain began to fall, heavy and relentless. Elizabeth ran the last few yards to the top of the path and began the short dash for the pavilion. Another rumble, this time much louder; the storm was getting closer. Elizabeth reached the steps to the pavilion veranda just in time. Panting and out of breath, she removed her headscarf and shook her long auburn hair before throwing off the dripping coat and shaking it several times. Suddenly a man's voice cut through the noise of the rain dashing against the pavilion's tin roof.

'You made it back here just in time.' The voice was that of a stranger, yet there was something faintly recognizable about it.

Elizabeth couldn't hide her shock. She jumped back, almost too frightened to peer into the shadows of the veranda.

'Who's that?' She tried to sound as controlled as possible.

A figure emerged from the shadows – a man wearing a brown raincoat, tied at the waist by a knotted belt, his face partly concealed by the broad, flopping brim of a trilby hat. He raised his head, revealing a pleasant friendly face, but a face she did not recognize. 'Please, do not be alarmed,' he said candidly.

'You . . . startled me, coming out of the darkness like that.'

'Eamon said ya were beautiful. I can see he's a master of understatement.' The man smiled warmly.

'Eamon! You . . . you know my husband?' Elizabeth replied cautiously.

'I should do.' The man stepped forward, removing his hat and revealing a shiny bald pate with several straggly strands of wiry hair stretching across from one ear to the other. 'Eamon's my son.' He winked cheekily. 'That would make yerself my daughter-in-law.'

'Martin O'Casey!' Elizabeth gasped. Of course she had heard much about the man, but until now she had never met him and the only photograph Eamon had shown her of his father had been so faded by age it bore no resemblance to him. One part of her wanted to greet the man warmly while another part erred on the side of caution. She knew little of her father-in-law, the IRA chief, apart from his being on Scotland Yard's wanted list.

'I can see I've startled you.' He moved a little closer, hat in hand.

'But how do I know for certain?' Elizabeth replied slowly.

'That I'm himself, ya mean?' he interrupted, removing a crumpled-looking envelope from his coat pocket and handing it over. 'This will tell you everything. It's from Eamon.'

'Eamon!' Elizabeth took the letter hesitantly, examining the envelope. It was simply addressed with just her name, but more importantly it was in Eamon's hand. 'You have seen Eamon? He is safe?' She began to tear open the envelope.

'No, darlin', I haven't seen him, but I've a funny feelin' we'll both be seeing him soon enough.'

She scanned the one-paragraph letter. It read simply: 'Do exactly as told and we will be together in just a short time. This time for ever – Eamon.' Elizabeth shook her head in disbelief, before rushing into the man's arms and hugging him tightly.

'Now I know why Eamon's besotted with you. It's the smell of that beautiful hair of yers,' Martin O'Casey chuckled.

'What happens now?' asked Elizabeth pensively.

'Have you ever been to Ireland?'

She moved back, shaking her head. 'Eamon is there?'

'Not yet, but soon, very soon.' He grinned at her.

'When do you want me to go?' Elizabeth folded the letter up and put it in the sleeve of her cardigan.

'Would right now be soon enough?' He replaced his hat, adjusting the brim down across the right side of his face.

'That soon?' Elizabeth was stunned.

'This is not exactly a healthy place for the likes of me.' He took out a pipe and tobacco pouch from his coat pocket. 'I'm a very popular man, ya know. It's not just the Royal Ulster Constabulary who want me, ya know.' He winked again, that same cheeky glint that Eamon had.

'I had a visitor today,' Elizabeth said. 'Major McClean from the War Office.'

'Ah! Yer man.' Martin O'Casey nodded as if he already knew. Setting a foot on the guardrail of the veranda, he leaned back against one of the supports. 'Aye, Eamon's mentioned him a few times. He's MI5, British Counter-Intelligence.' He began to stuff his pipe with tobacco. 'Eamon does a wee bit of work for them from time to time.'

'I knew Eamon worked for the British, but I've never been quite sure just what he did for them.' Elizabeth moved a little closer.

'Aye,' he sighed, 'and it's best ya don't know either.' He stared back at her again. 'Tell me, what did yer man want?'

'He told me they had received a radio message from Eamon a couple of days ago, but since then nothing. He actually seemed to think that I might know where Eamon was . . .' Elizabeth listened to the echo of her voice as it died away under the noise of the pelting rain. 'He was expecting you to contact me!'

'Aye,' he replied drolly, replacing the pipe in his pocket as he stepped back from the guardrail again. 'He was anticipating my visit. Either a crafty piece of deduction or a serious bit of intelligence.'

'And you're a wanted man.' Elizabeth was aghast. 'Oh, my God!' She covered her mouth with both hands.

'Put your hands up and step out into the light!' The English voice cut the conversation short. It came from somewhere behind the Irishman. 'I am a police officer and I am armed.'

Elizabeth moved towards Martin O'Casey.

'Keep back from him!' snapped the voice.

'Do as he says,' Martin O'Casey replied calmly, raising both his hands. Elizabeth stood still, trembling with fright.

'Now, you,' the voice continued. 'Step forward again to the balustrade. And keep those hands in the air. No sudden moves.'

Martin O'Casey complied.

'Now, place both hands firmly on the balustrade and take one step back, spreading both legs.'

Martin O'Casey glanced across to Elizabeth and winked. Elizabeth didn't quite know what to make of it.

'Hurry up!' insisted the voice. Martin O'Casey moved back and stretched out at an angle towards the guardrail.

'Very good. Now stay as you are.'

The policeman appeared from around the side of the pavilion, clearing the three steps up on to the wooden veranda in one leap.

'Energetic,' muttered Martin O'Casey.

'Shut up!' snapped the young detective-constable, a look of satisfaction across his face as he trained his Webley revolver on the Irishman.

'Now, sonny, I think you might be a wee bit too quick for yer own good,' said Martin O'Casey.

'I said for you to shut it! Now on your knees,' he insisted, motioning with his gun for Elizabeth to step back. 'Looks like I struck gold. The Superintendent's going to be real chuffed when he sees you,' he went on cockily as Martin O'Casey knelt beside the guardrail.

'It looks to me as if you're about to make a complete ass of yerself,' replied Martin O'Casey, taking the opportunity to glance back at the young policeman, who was now standing directly in front of the pavilion doors. 'Liam!' he shouted.

Before the policeman could speak, both doors burst outward, one of them slamming into his shoulder and throwing him against a wooden bench seat. Elizabeth shrieked as a man's form materialized from the shadows of the open doorway and pounced on the young detective-constable. The third man was much smaller than the police-man but twice as broad and as fast as a cat. The policeman tried to put up a struggle but was forced on to the floor by a jab to the head. Immediately a size-nine boot stamped on to his right hand, pinning his fingers to the floor. The policeman screamed. Before he could let off a shot, the gun was wrenched from him. He lay prostrate on the wet floorboards of the open veranda, his assailant on top of him with a knee in his back. It didn't need anyone to tell the unfortunate policeman that any movement from him would result in a broken back. Martin O'Casey began to straighten himself up again as Liam handed him over the policeman's gun.

'Goodness, me old joints are getting a bit stiff.' Martin O'Casey pulled himself up with Elizabeth's aid. He looked down at the semi-conscious policeman. 'Young fella me lad, you could have caused

54

someone a serious injury waving this thing about.' He examined the gun. 'Well now, what have we here, a .38 Mark IV pocket model Webley revolver. A handy little piece, reliable, especially when the safety catch is released, which it wasn't.'

Liam Adams laughed as Martin O'Casey slipped the gun inside his raincoat. 'What shall we do with this 'un?' he asked.

'His car's around the other side of this building. Put him in the trunk and let him have a nice sleep,' replied O'Casey, moving over to Elizabeth, who was standing almost petrified.

She watched the dazed policeman being led away. 'Will he be all right? You aren't going to . . .' She couldn't bring herself to say the word.

'You mean kill him?' Martin O'Casey smiled as he guided her along the veranda. 'No, no, that wouldn't be good strategy at all. No, Liam there will give him a bop on the smacker and he'll sleep if off in the trunk of his car for the next few hours. By the time he finds the get-up and go to kick his way out of it, we'll be home and dry.'

Elizabeth tried to keep her mouth closed. Just what had she got herself into?

Shortly before midnight a blue sports car headed out of the grounds of the school. Instead of following the road through the grounds towards the main road, it sped off through a lane skirting around the woodlands, finally exiting on to the main road after three and a half miles of bumpy driving. Martin O'Casey's astuteness had placed Elizabeth and himself almost five miles away from the main entrance to the school grounds.

KIEL HARBOUR
Early morning, Tuesday, 1 May 1945

SS STURMBANNFÜHRER Strassmann stood pensively on the quayside alongside Kapitänleutnant Petersen and O'Casey. The Irishman was intrigued to see how nervous Strassmann had become within the last hour, checking his watch at regular intervals. The SS officer had spent most of the night in the communications room and the lack of sleep was telling on him. Strassmann began to pace up and down on the long quayside, snapping out needless orders to his men. O'Casey was impressed, since before dawn the entire area around the U-boat pens and warehouses had been swept clean by the SS, and not as much as a rat had gone undetected. At intervals of ten yards all along the quayside, Waffen SS guards stood at ease, their sub-machine-guns held at the ready.

'You know, Herr Kapitän, if I didn't know better, I'd say we were expecting royalty to arrive,' said O'Casey, cheekily.

Petersen said nothing in return. The Irishman had only just spoken when an SS Scharführer suddenly came running up to Strassmann and then started to point towards the southern horizon. Two black specks appeared out of the morning cloud.

'Look, there! To the south-east,' said Petersen, handing his binoculars across to O'Casey. The Irishman focused on the approaching aircraft as they slowly descended through the mist towards the docks. Then four further aircraft came into view, several hundred feet above the first pair, and clearly shadowing their descent. He identified the formation of grey-coloured Focke-Wulf Fw 190 fighter aircraft instantly.

'They have made good timing, considering the delay,' commented Petersen. O'Casey remained silent.

As the black-painted Fieseler Storchs swooped down over the warehouse roofs, their fighter escort banked out across the harbour. The two Storchs barely cleared the buildings as they dropped the final fifty feet to touch down together on the wide concrete quayside. Both reconnaissance aircraft came to a halt just yards from where they stood. O'Casey watched as the cockpit side door of the nearest aircraft snapped open and the tall blond-haired SS general emerged. He had met Schiller just once before, and it had been more than enough for him.

The SS major general had unsettled him during their brief meeting in Berlin. It was clear that Schiller hadn't trusted him, yet the success of 'Operation Herron' rested heavily on the active support of the IRA. Schiller had tried to pass off the operation as a tactical act of espionage, but O'Casey knew better: 'Herron' was an escape operation, pure and simple; a backdoor for the Nazi leadership in the event of capitulation. O'Casey had played his cards close to the chest, demanding a heavy price for the IRA's assistance. He had asked for two, but they had agreed on one million, in gold bullion, but it wasn't the gold that interested O'Casey, it was Schiller. To him, the SS general had another significance, far out-valuing anything else.

'Herr O'Casey, we meet again.' Schiller held out his hand to greet the Irishman.

'Herr Gruppenführer.' O'Casey shook hands, but his interest had already been drawn towards the nurse and baby being assisted from the aircraft by one of the other SS officers.

'And you are Kapitänleutnant Petersen?' Schiller turned his attention to the U-boat captain.

'*Mein Herr.*' Petersen saluted.

'Show me to your vessel,' grinned Schiller, turning back to Strassmann. 'See the others are shown down into the U-boat pens immediately.'

'*Jawohl, mein Herr!*'

'Come, gentlemen, we have much to discuss.' Schiller gestured for Petersen to lead the way.

As O'Casey followed up behind, he couldn't help but notice the stretcher being unloaded from the second aircraft. The patient's face was completely swathed in bandages and covered from neck to toe in a heavy army blanket. Then he noticed a tubby man, dressed in the brown uniform of the Nazi party. He was gesticulating wildly to one of the SS guards who was helping unload the stretcher. It was then he realized. O'Casey's heart skipped a beat. How could he have mistaken the man that had presented him to Adolf Hitler the previous year! He was looking at Martin Bormann, and if he was staring at Hitler's favourite mandarin, it didn't take much to guess who was lying on the stretcher.

'Herr O'Casey?' Schiller's voice cut through O'Casey's thoughts. The Irishman quickened his step, catching up with the two Germans. From the look on the SS general's face he could see that he had induced more than just his curiosity.

Petersen led the way down into the U-boat pens. O'Casey's eyes narrowed as he descended the steep concrete steps down into the basin. Since his brief foray much work had been undertaken. The two U-boats were now lashed together in the shallow dock over sixty feet beneath the reinforced concrete roof of the pens. Towards the far end a fragment of daylight protruded from between the heavy steel seadoors. The large pen was illuminated by overhead worklamps casting bright wells of light and contrasting deeper shadows. At 76.7 metres in length, the new Type-XXI U-boat was almost 10 metres longer than its companion, shining like a new coin by comparison to the rusty and weather-beaten hull of the smaller U-769. A work crew was busy loading torpedoes into the forward section of the smaller Type-VIIC U-boat whilst several other sailors were winching supplies on to the larger vessel. O'Casey cringed at the thought of living inside one of these 'tin cans'. He had been told that the journey to Ireland could take upwards of two weeks, but the thought of a single day seemed too much.

Schiller halted towards the bottom of the staircase, his eyes fixed on a navy diver who had just emerged from the water at the side of the larger U-boat. 'What is the frogman doing here?' he demanded.

'A security check, Herr Gruppenführer,' replied Petersen.

The SS general looked sternly at Petersen. 'Why should this be necessary?'

Petersen cleared his throat. He had been hoping to avoid this and leave the explaining to Strassmann. 'Several days ago, one of my men thought he saw someone in the water. Since then we have been sending down divers at regular intervals.'

'Why was Berlin not informed?'

'Nobody was found, *mein Herr*.'

'So?' quipped Schiller.

'Herr Gruppenführer, we are just being cautious. The incident would have been dismissed as the product of an overactive imagination except that one of the guards on the sea-wall went missing on the same night,' added O'Casey. Petersen's face reddened.

'What!' Schiller snarled.

'Herr Gruppenführer, every conceivable security measure has been taken, I assure you. We cannot be certain that the guard did not simply desert.'

'A German soldier! Desert?' shouted Schiller, his voice echoing around the concrete structure.

'Recently, there have been occasions, *mein Herr*,' Petersen replied quietly, so as to avoid being overheard by any of the work party. 'I am told that five men have already disappeared from the town garrison, within this last week.'

'Have SS Sturmbannführer Strassmann join me, immediately,' growled Schiller.

'*Jawohl, mein Herr*.' Petersen scowled at O'Casey before following after Schiller.

Wednesday, 2 May 1945

AT 1 A.M. PRECISELY the lights in the U-boat pen were finally extinguished. The sea-doors rolled slowly apart and the U-769 gently eased out into Kiel harbour. Forty minutes later the Type-XXI U-boat slipped berth and headed into the main navigation channel, exchanging the calm waters of Kiel harbour for the Baltic swell. The night was clear and a full moon shone down brightly on to the bows of Petersen's new command. He breathed a sigh of relief as his vessel passed over the anti-submarine nets which had been lowered just minutes before by Strassmann's shore party. Petersen relished these last moments, for he knew that shortly he would have to give the order to dive.

Below decks everyone tried to settle into their new abode. O'Casey had been given quarters in a cabin next to the nurse and baby. He'd seen nothing of the woman or her charge since they'd come on board, but he'd heard the baby crying, at times incessantly. His curiosity had grown by the way in which Schiller had reacted. Since the woman and baby had come on board, the SS general had placed their quarters strictly off limits to everyone except himself and Petersen. To O'Casey's certain knowledge Schiller had also spent some time in the cabin, clearly anxious about the child's welfare and such concern did not come naturally to the SS general. Something else was playing on the Irishman's mind. Since coming aboard, O'Casey hadn't seen Bormann or his 'patient'. That could only mean one thing, that they had gone in the other U-boat, but why?

The cabin door opened, without warning. O'Casey picked himself up off his bunk as Strassmann peered into his tiny cabin. 'Gruppen-führer Schiller wants you in the ward room.'

'Does he now?' he replied cheekily.

'Come.' Strassmann stepped aside, allowing O'Casey to lead the way towards the officer's ward room.

As he headed aft along the narrow passageway, O'Casey paused outside the door to the nurse's cabin. 'That youngster can make a hell of a racket, ya know.'

'Move,' snapped the SS officer.

On squeezing inside the narrow doorway of the officers' ward room, O'Casey froze. There on the table sat a brown suitcase, not unlike the one he'd planted in the roof-space of the billet before his departure. 'Top o' the mornin' to ya, General.' O'Casey smiled.

'I am curious,' Schiller said drolly, watching O'Casey ease himself on to the bench seat opposite him. 'Curious about what makes you tick.'

'Gold,' replied O'Casey without hesitation. 'Your people pay well, and of course I get one over on the British.'

'Surely there is more to it than just that, Herr O'Casey. The game perhaps? Playing one side off against the other?'

'Oh, there's that all right, General. In fact I was telling your Führer just that when he pinned a medal on me last year.'

'The Iron Cross.' Schiller leaned back against the wooden lining of the bulkhead. 'Of course, you were presented to the Führer in Berlin, were you not?'

'Sure, don't you know everything about me, General?' He grinned.

'Perhaps. I am curious however. I know what your friends in the IRA want from us, but what about you?'

'But I've got it already, General. I've a safe passage out of a tricky situation. If I'd been caught there back in Germany the British would have strung me up from the nearest tree.'

Schiller flung the case open, revealing the wireless transmitter set. He watched for a reaction from the Irishman, but got none. Finally, after a few agonizing moments O'Casey scratched his beard. 'Well now,' he sighed.

'It was found in the billet where you were staying,' Schiller said coldly.

'And you'd be wonderin' if it belongs to me?' O'Casey grinned a little.

Schiller slowly lit a cigarette before answering. 'Well, does it?'

'From first examination I'd say it's origin is British all right. Standard equipment issued by MI6,' replied O'Casey, in a factual voice.

Schiller blew the cigarette smoke straight into O'Casey's face. 'It has to be you.'

'General, you've got a security problem and you need to blame it on somebody, anybody. I'm the odd man out here so I'm good fer it. Stands to reason.' If O'Casey was concerned it never showed.

'Whoever owns this also probably breached security at the U-boat pen.' He drew on the cigarette again. 'No description; however, the swimmer had to be a man of incredible strength. The tide and currents were against him that night. To have entered and left the pen required a superhuman feat of strength.' Then he took O'Casey's hand in his, examining it. 'I am told that the swimmer would probably have injured himself on the barnacles attached to the sea-doors. Hands, back, that sort of thing.' O'Casey withdrew his hand as Schiller leaned back again.

O'Casey smiled, then he arose and turned around, raising his sweater to just under both armpits. There wasn't a mark on his back. As he turned back again the smile had vanished. He leaned across, shoving the wireless set aside with a sweep of his hand.

'General, you're playing a wee game with me. Whatever you're thinking about, just remember that without me you don't land in

Ireland and you don't get on to that aircraft my people have been looking after for you.'

'Do I really need you that much?' Schiller's hand moved on to the gun resting on his lap.

'Now listen to me very carefully, General. I can kill a man with me bare hands inside two seconds and if that hand of yours gets one inch closer to the gun on your lap, I'll be required to give a practical demonstration.'

Schiller drew on his cigarette again. 'It is interesting that you should say that. I forgot to tell you about that missing guard you mentioned earlier. He didn't desert, he was found washed up on the shore just a few hours before we left. They tell me he was knifed by an expert.'

'General, I don't need a knife.' O'Casey held out his massive hands. 'These do me nicely.' At that, Strassmann appeared at the cabin door, his pistol pointed directly at O'Casey's head. 'Look, General, just let me do my job of getting you and yours ashore and away safely an' you'll never see or hear of me again, for all I want is to get back to Ireland.'

'Just remember one thing, Herr O'Casey. If anything goes wrong when we land, you'll be the first to die. I can assure you.'

'Well now, to see Ireland and die, that'd be something in itself.' O'Casey winked.

'Get out,' growled Schiller.

'I'm glad we could see eye to eye on this, General. Good evening to ya.' O'Casey exited from the cabin, pushing past Strassmann. He walked casually through the U-boat until he came to the latrine. It was empty. Locking himself inside, he stared into the shaving mirror, wiping away the trickle of perspiration running down his left temple. 'You're a lucky bastard, Eamon m' boy.' He rubbed his left shoulder, it still hurt. He pulled off the navy sweater, turning to the side to get a clearer look in the tiny mirror. The deep lacerations across both his shoulders were still red and angry. 'Real lucky,' he added, wincing as his fingers ran across the ugly red gashes.

IRELAND
Sunday, 13 May 1945

ELIZABETH had never been to Ireland. Eamon had often talked about the 'twenty-six counties', but circumstances had somehow always prevented them from travelling there. His descriptions of the land had been graphic and full of nostalgia. She fell in love with the place instantly. Here, it seemed, the war had passed them by. Once away from the uneasy and nervous political atmosphere in Ulster, she was in another world altogether. After the years of uncertainty and worry she could already feel a great weight lifting from her mind. For now there seemed to be some respite from her constant anguish and uncertainty about her family. She satisfied her conscience with the promise of returning to Holland as soon as the war had finally ended.

Elizabeth's heart lightened with the prospect of a new life here as she watched the rolling drumlin countryside undergo a metamorphosis as they approached the border. The train clanked slowly to a halt at the customs post just south of Newry town. She stared across the carriage at Martin O'Casey, who winked at her reassuringly. Apart from the two of them, the carriage was unusually empty. It made a delightful change for Elizabeth after the constantly crowded trains in England. The guard rolled back the carriage door and stepped inside from the corridor, first examining Martin O'Casey's papers and punching his ticket. Elizabeth glanced up. Two armed policemen were standing in the corridor, peering down at her. She remembered what Martin O'Casey had told her: 'Relax and smile. It's the most disarming thing a woman can do.' So she did. The effect was instantaneous. One of the Ulster policemen touched the peak of his cap, the other smiled back at her.

She handed across her own ticket and the false identity papers that Martin O'Casey had furnished her with. Surprisingly, she felt no nervousness or fear. It was very much like some game she would have played as a child. Her mind flashed back to the halcyon days of childhood, the security and love that surrounded and protected her; it all seemed like yesterday, the nightmare of the last terrible years diminished by comparison.

'Miss?'

The voice awoke her from the daydream. She looked up to see the ticket inspector staring at her. For a heart-churning moment she thought the game was up, then she realized the man was just handing back her ticket and papers.

'Thank you,' she replied softly, returning the documents to her handbag.

The ticket inspector withdrew to the corridor outside, drawing the sliding door shut behind him again. Martin O'Casey waited until the two policemen had disappeared down the train before speaking.

'You had me worried for a moment there,' he said in a jovial tone.

'I'm sorry, I was on another planet.' She hunched her shoulders. 'Just memories.'

'Happy ones, by the look on your face,' he continued. Martin O'Casey knew very little about his daughter-in-law and he realized it would take time to come to know her properly, but he didn't need to be a psychic to see she needed to open up to someone. She reminded him of a well-shaken Guinness bottle, ready to pop at a moment's notice.

'I was just thinking of my family.'

'You haven't seen them in a long time, have you?' he inquired.

'Not since 1939 . . .' She hesitated as the train jolted forward and seemed to settle again. Then it began to move once more, slowly increasing speed as it pulled out of the border customs post.

'And you haven't been able to contact them at all?' Martin O'Casey sat forward, removing a pipe from his coat pocket.

'I tried writing. I sent a letter to my father just weeks before the invasion – I can't say if he even received it. I know he's dead . . . and Eamon told me there's no trace of all the others. Those bastards.' Her anger mounted.

'I hear the Red Cross is very good at tracing missing persons.'

'After Eamon told me, I approached the Red Cross, but I heard nothing. They told me that the displaced and missing run into millions. Can you imagine?' A tear formed in the side of her eye.

'What about your mother?' asked Martin O'Casey.

'Mother died just before the war started.' She stared out at the distant hills. 'Perhaps she was the lucky one. She avoided having to endure these years of living hell.'

Martin O'Casey patted her on the knee. 'Take comfort, child, it's over now.'

She stared back at him blankly. 'Is it?'

The journey through Ireland had been well planned. To avoid undue attention, they had first travelled across the Irish Sea to Belfast. Having taken the Dublin train south, they alighted in Dundalk, just south of the Ulster border, where they were met by another of

O'Casey's men and driven south-west, towards Mullingar. It was a change for the IRA commandant from following the black-market route between the British territory of Northern Ireland and the neutral territory of Eire, but he couldn't quite see this lady travelling inside a stinking cattletruck.

In Mullingar they transferred to another saloon car before heading southward towards Limerick on the west coast. They said little to each other during the tedious journey south. Elizabeth had pretty much kept herself to herself after sensing from Martin O'Casey that it was unwise to say too much in front of any of his men. O'Casey had travelled in the front, alongside one of his lieutenants, a droll man called Gerry, while Elizabeth had sat with Liam Adams in the back seat, dozing intermittently, jolted awake every so often by the poor road conditions.

Arriving in Limerick late that evening, they were taken directly to a boarding house near the town hall. The landlady had set the parlour table with sandwiches and a pot of steaming tea. Elizabeth watched with interest as Martin O'Casey beguiled the middle-aged landlady with his charm. It was easy to see where Eamon got his bravado from. Finally the lady excused herself and left for the kitchen, closing the glass-panelled door behind her. Martin O'Casey watched for a moment until the woman disappeared into the pantry. Then he spoke.

'Thank you for keeping from talking on the way down,' he said quietly. 'Our Gerry's all right, but he's a sorta nosy bugger.'

'I noticed.' Elizabeth poured out another cup of tea.

'It's his business ta be nosy, ye understand?' Martin O'Casey never waited for a reply. 'He can't help it. He's fairly distrustful of everyone. Most of the time that's to my advantage, but there's times like today when it can be a wee bit embarrassing.'

'He frightens me.' Elizabeth returned the teapot to the mat, replacing the knitted teacosy over it again.

'Aye,' Martin O'Casey nodded, 'but don't ya worry that pretty head of yers. Gerry does exactly what his Commandant says or I'll be fer setting Liam onta him.' He prodded himself in the chest with a teaspoon to emphasize the point. Then he produced a small flask from his coat pocket and added some to his tea.

'What Commandant?' For a moment Elizabeth imagined a German officer to be lurking somewhere in the background.

'That's me, ma darlin'.' Martin O'Casey grinned broadly, showing his missing upper teeth. 'Commandant Martin O'Casey of the Irish Republican Army, at yer service.'

'I didn't realize,' Elizabeth replied slowly.

'That I was in the IRA, ya mean?'

'Not that. Eamon was candid and seemingly rather proud about your exploits.' She glanced over. The woman had returned into the kitchen from the pantry. She lowered her voice, leaning across the table. 'I didn't realize that you were so highly placed in your organization.'

Martin O'Casey laughed. 'Here, take a drop of the critter in yer tea. It'll help ya sleep.'

'Critter?' She frowned.

'Poteen,' he replied, qualifying the statement for her. 'Home-brewed alcohol.' He poured a generous swig into her cup. Elizabeth was beginning to feel relaxed with this garrulous and amiable man. He waited until the woman returned again to the pantry before continuing. 'According to Eamon I'm number three on the wanted list over in England and in the north of Ireland. Mind you, it doesn't say a lot for the other two buggers in front of me. Eamon tells me they robbed a sweety shop!'

For a moment she thought he was serious. Then she realized and began to laugh. He was so different to her own father, yet she felt drawn to him in a similar way. She sipped some tea; the alcohol gave it a sting she wouldn't forget in a hurry. 'Tell me about Eamon.'

'Eamon! I'd prefer to tell ya all about meself!' He winked at her. 'But then ye wouldn't be interested in an old dog like me. Aye!' He shook his head, as if attempting to shake off the cobwebs. 'Eamon's a lad in a million. Intelligent, honest to the point of embarrassment and the kindest son a man could ever ask fer. Clearly, he doesn't take after the likes of his old father here!' He poked himself in the chest.

In between the funny stories and the frivolity, Elizabeth learned more and more about Eamon's background over the next hour. Her husband was indeed a dark horse; in some ways he was a total stranger. It was hard to understand. Here was Martin O'Casey on the run from both the British and Irish authorities and his son working for British Intelligence of all things! After listening to Martin O'Casey she wondered if she had really known anything about the man she had married. In ways it horrified her to discover the truth of so much that she had just taken for granted until now, yet in other ways she loved Eamon even more. She learned that his mother had died when he was only six years old. Eamon had gone to live with an elderly aunt until five years later, when she had also died. At that stage Martin's younger sister, Ellen, who had emigrated to America some years before, arrived back in Ireland for a visit. Childless herself, Ellen had offered to take Eamon back to the States with her. Martin

O'Casey, engrossed with his IRA activities, living a life almost constantly on the run, had accepted that it would be best for Eamon to return with his aunt to America, when, amazingly, the boy had stated his own case. Eamon had insisted, with an eloquence beyond his years, that he was going to remain in Ireland and stay by his father. Ellen had returned disappointed and a little embittered to America. She visualized a neglected child growing up under the influence of a hard-drinking rogue, with the clear prospect of washing glasses in some second-rate public house by the time he was fourteen. But Martin O'Casey had other ideas for his son.

Eamon was sent to a Dublin boarding school run by the Christian Brothers. He adapted quickly to the academic world, winning several scholarships. By the age of eighteen he had gained a place at Trinity College, Dublin, to read chemistry. He also discovered that he had a flair for languages and by the time he went to Oxford to read for his doctorate he could speak several European languages fluently, including German. Whilst Martin O'Casey believed fervently in his cause, he had dismissed the idea of Eamon following in his footsteps. He had a vision of his son becoming one of Ireland's leaders, rather than another warrior. It was a dream wasted. Instead, Eamon confronted him, demanding to join the IRA.

It was easily accomplished. Eamon had already come to the notice of the IRA's hierarchy while he was attending Trinity. Very soon afterwards he was recruited, but under very special circumstances and with one very special reason in mind: the infiltration of British Intelligence. As Europe shuddered under the shouting and stomping jackboots, Eamon was a perfectly placed candidate for MI5. His academic career took him to various universities and institutions throughout Germany, Austria and even as far east as Ruthenia. Then overnight Eamon became one of the most important agents the British had on their payroll when, in 1937, whilst living in Berlin, he was approached by German Intelligence.

The Germans had viewed Eamon as a passionate United Irishman, the perfect candidate to assist them in subverting the British presence in Ireland. Furthermore, while failing to identify Eamon's link with MI5, Abwehr had uncovered a profile on Martin O'Casey, by then wanted by the British for 'capital crimes against the state'. Playing the game even better than the IRA hierarchy could ever have envisaged, Eamon started to weave his web of intrigue, playing off the British against the Germans. As war loomed closer he could see just where it was taking him and, for that matter, Ireland.

Astutely or by chance, he had rightly determined which way

Ireland would tip in the event of all-out war. Following Hitler's failure to seize the opportunity to invade either England or Ireland, Eamon was left in a vacuum. He couldn't go forward or go back; he was forced to play off MI5 against Abwehr in the hope that he, and therefore the IRA, could salvage something from the mess. The war tipped and swayed; Eamon played his hand extremely carefully. Whilst the British knew of his involvement with German Intelligence, they didn't know just how important he really was.

Finally, after the landlady passed through the parlour, excusing herself as she went off to bed, Martin O'Casey came to the heart of the matter.

'Eamon's on his way to Ireland right now. He could be here anytime.' He lit his pipe.

'How do you know?' Elizabeth asked.

'He got word through by radio.' Martin O'Casey smiled and squeezed Elizabeth's hand reassuringly.

'You were in contact with Eamon?' she asked incredulously.

Martin O'Casey shook his head. 'No, but our people received a Morse-code signal. It confirmed his imminent arrival.' His eyes lit up. 'Tomorrow I'm for taking you a short drive down the coast. A little sightseeing you might say, along the Ring of Kerry.'

Monday, 14 May 1945

THE COLD, shimmering sea had at last fallen calm following five days of continuous storm conditions. The fog that had plagued the south-west shoreline all day and well into the evening had finally drifted out to sea, allowing the moon to illuminate the swelling surface.

Elizabeth stepped down off the rugged stone path leading from the cliff top to the shingle, careful to avoid slipping in the damp kelp washed up over the previous week. She joined the lone figure standing at the water's edge, scanning the horizon through a pair of small binoculars. On hearing the woman's approach over the loose shingle, Martin O'Casey lowered the field glasses and spat into the frothing water at his feet.

'Nothing. Not a damned bloody thing!' The frustrations of the last days were beginning to tell on the old man. Eamon was already well overdue.

'He will come, I know it,' Elizabeth said softly but determinedly.

The old man turned, gazing down into her deep-brown eyes. 'You say that with such conviction.'

'He'll come. You will see.' She smiled up at him. His rugged features softened.

Elizabeth O'Casey took up the vigil, staring out over the waves. Watching the heaving rollers just past the three-mile reef reminded her of the past hectic and depressing years, filled with ups and down, hopes dashed like helpless waves against unrelenting rocks. Pushed and shunted in one direction without a choice, it was as if her life had been plotted out somewhere, in some majestic map amidst the stars. She stared up at the star configuration and wished just one more time.

'Holy Mary, Mother of God! It's here!' Martin O'Casey cried. 'Look! Look!' He pointed out to sea. The bow and conning tower of a U-boat was breaking the surface just inside the three-mile reef. Elizabeth didn't need the confirmation of her own eyes, she knew already in her own heart. She continued staring up at the sparkling stars and beyond; whatever would happen was already foretold.

Several shadowy figures rushed out from the cover of the cliffs and joined their leader just as the second U-boat surfaced, further out to sea, beyond the Reef. The IRA men began to jump and cheer, waving their Lee Enfield rifles in the air and congratulating one another on the fruitful outcome of their long vigil. Another IRA volunteer, carrying a back-pack radio, knelt down beside Martin O'Casey and began transmitting in Morse code on the short-wave radio.

The excitement went unnoticed by Elizabeth. She quietly moved away, captured in her own thoughts of the past, trying to understand her situation. Where had it all started? Perhaps it had been that fateful day in spring, all those years ago, when she had met Eamon, or perhaps it went back further to her own Jewish roots . . .

Eamon O'Casey had captivated her from the first moment she'd set eyes on him. It was one of those inexplicable things, more suited to the pages of some romantic novel than to real life, as she saw it. She had always thought of herself as a pragmatist, not readily affected by emotion and certainly not headstrong, no matter what her father had always insisted.

They had met while she was in her final year of a postgraduate course at Cambridge University. Elizabeth had travelled down to Oxford for the day in support of the varsity Rugby team. They'd lost, but the social evening that followed had made up for everything. O'Casey had been teaching at St Hugh's College. From the first moment they had hit if off: she had been mesmerized by him; never in her life had she ever met anyone like him. Inside weeks they were married – secretly of course, partly so as not to upset the university authorities, but more importantly because Elizabeth wanted some time with her new husband before broaching the subject to her own family. Elizabeth was fully aware that the marriage would never have her father's blessing: no Gentile had ever married into the Goldmann family and Peter Goldmann was a stickler for tradition. The death of her mother the previous year had left Elizabeth without the voice of moderation. She was alone with her decision and the consequences. She decided it to be wiser to keep the marriage secret, at least for some months, until she could determine how best to approach her father, but with the onset of the war she never had.

THE TYPE-XXI U-BOAT
Less than two miles off the Irish coast

O'CASEY was invited up on to the bridge for the first time since leaving Kiel. He breathed in the cool night air as he squeezed out of the deck hatch. After almost two weeks cooped up in the smelly confines of the U-boat, to him breathing in the fresh air was like nectar to a bee. 'Permission to come aloft, Captain?' O'Casey asked cheekily.

'Granted,' Petersen replied in English, but without turning round. He was too busy scanning the landmass of the Dingle peninsula through a pair of heavy binoculars. It was a bright moon, not the most favourable conditions for closing undetected on any coastline, the weather was surprisingly mild and the wind strength had dropped away to a negligible level. The U-boat slowed slightly, cutting through the swell at a steady six knots.

'Where's the other U-boat?' asked O'Casey, scanning the northern horizon.

'U-769 remains further out to sea,' replied Petersen, pointing to the outline of the Conning tower a mile beyond the reef.

'What about its passengers?'

'There are no passengers aboard U-769,' he said flatly.

'Well now, Captain, I've a slight problem with that. In fact I've got two, one's wearing a brown suit and the other's on a stretcher.'

'Herr O'Casey,' Petersen rounded on him, 'you ask too many questions for your own good.'

'I'm just curious by nature,' grinned the Irishman.

'Save your curiosity,' retorted the captain.

'Beautiful, isn't it?' O'Casey changed the subject, gazing over at the rugged shoreline and breathing in the fresh sea air.

'But is it safe?' Captain Petersen glanced at him.

'It's as safe as you want it to be, Captain,' O'Casey replied drily, drawing a suspicious stare from the other sailors standing on the bridge watch with their captain. 'But then you'd be referring to them rocks over there,' O'Casey said, pointing towards the Blasket Islands, projecting out into the sea from the end of the long peninsula. 'Cut you to pieces, they would. Many a vessel has foundered there.'

'Herr Kapitän!' shouted one of the watch party. 'Message from the radio room. We have shore contact! Code confirmation.'

'Confirm contact and prepare landing party as arranged,' replied Petersen, turning his attention once more to the Irishman. 'Tell me, Herr O'Casey, what makes you do what you do?'

'Ah! That's the million-dollar question, Captain, but now that the war's ending I'm going home. All that's behind me now.' O'Casey leaned back on the bridge support with both elbows, turning his back on the sea breeze. 'Tell me this, Captain, just when will you be going home?' O'Casey jibed. The captain was stumped. The cocky Irishman had touched a sore point, something that had weighed heavily on his mind for some days now. Petersen returned to scanning the shoreline with his binoculars again, for he had no answer.

It took another twenty minutes for the U-boat to move into position. Eamon O'Casey waited on the swaying forward deck as three of the sailors inflated a rubber dinghy, using a compressed-air line brought up from the forward section. He was too interested in gazing upon his homeland to notice the SS colonel and the Luftwaffe pilot officer climbing out of the conning-tower hatch.

'Soon you will be home, Herr O'Casey.'

The Irishman turned to see the two German officers walking unsteadily towards him. Both were dressed in civilian clothes: navy donkey jackets and poloneck sweaters. Strassmann, the SS colonel, was a cool customer. O'Casey had had little contact with the man since leaving the port of Kiel almost two weeks previously. Unlike the steely-eyed young general, the older Strassmann had been a true soldier once, having blooded himself in the mountains of Crete and on the Russian front. For that reason alone, O'Casey found himself having a certain respect for the man. The SS colonel carried a

Schmeisser sub-machine-gun strapped around his bull neck, whilst the young Luftwaffe lieutenant wore a pistol belt over his jacket.

'Expecting trouble, Herr Sturmbannführer?' O'Casey grinned.

'That depends on you, does it not?' replied Strassmann grimly.

For once O'Casey said nothing. He was already busy getting a final fix on the torch signal from the beach.

They paddled ashore in silence, three of them in the tiny rubber dinghy. Strassmann took up the front, whilst the Luftwaffe officer and O'Casey paddled side by side. As they pulled away, the SS colonel glanced over his shoulder at the U-boat, overwhelmed by a strange feeling. The U-boat had seemed to him to have many similarities with the womb, offering security and comfort, a brief haven from the realities of war. Whilst he could never relax in the artificial atmosphere, it surprised him to realize that he was now suddenly missing it, heading off into the unknown and on the word of an unscrupulous Irishman. Suddenly he was aware that O'Casey had been watching him. It was an unsettling feeling: what was the Irishman really up to, was he as genuine as he seemed?

The tiny rubber dinghy made the shore, rolling in on top of a giant breaker. The wave disintegrated upon hitting the steep incline of the shingle beach. Strassmann jumped clear of the dinghy, closely followed by O'Casey and then the pilot. All three men waded through the frothing water, steadying the dinghy and tugging it further up on to the beach with the help of the next incoming wave.

'Lead the way, Irishman,' insisted Strassmann.

O'Casey smiled back as a solitary figure emerged from the darkness, walking slowly down the beach towards them. O'Casey turned just in time to see Strassmann levelling his Schmeisser sub-machine-gun at the approaching figure.

'Put that bloody thing aside,' O'Casey snapped.

'I don't take chances,' retorted Strassmann angrily.

O'Casey rounded the dinghy like a raging bull, standing directly in front of the SS colonel, his face less than an inch from the German's nose.

'Listen, and listen good. Either you play by my rules or I'll kick yer arse right back out to sea!'

Before Strassmann had time to think, O'Casey shoved the sub-machine-gun back against his chest, making the German almost fall backwards into the tide. O'Casey grinned at him before moving off to meet the figure, now standing only yards away at the top of the steep incline where the fine sand met the shingle and seaweed. Strassmann was tempted to blast half a dozen holes in O'Casey's back and damn the consequences, but as he touched the Schmeisser his heart skipped a beat – the gun's magazine had vanished!

Eamon O'Casey could tell the stranger's saunter a mile off. He rushed forward to greet his old father. Martin O'Casey's eyes lit up on seeing his son for the first time in over a year. 'Now, you're what I call a sight for sore eyes,' he said drolly.

O'Casey shook his head and threw both arms around his father, hugging him tightly. 'It's good to be back, Da,' he replied.

'And what about yer man down there?' Martin O'Casey stared over at Strassmann.

'Pay no attention to him, sure he's nothing.' O'Casey grinned. 'Excess baggage until the rest of them come ashore.'

'Are they going to pay up as agreed?' whispered Martin O'Casey.

O'Casey nodded. 'They'll pay all right and perhaps a wee bit extra. But there's a problem.'

'Something we can't handle?'

'It's something I can handle,' replied O'Casey. 'It's personal.'

'Eamon.' Martin O'Casey frowned. 'Dublin's depending on this. We can't afford a balls-up.'

Eamon O'Casey grinned back at his father, a mischievous glint in his eyes. Martin O'Casey roared with laughter; he was his father's son all right. They were joined by Strassmann and the young pilot.

Martin O'Casey looked into Strassmann's angry face. The German was hardly in control of himself.

'Aren't ya going to introduce me?' He prodded his son in the arm reproachfully.

'SS Sturmbannführer Strassmann, meet me father, Commandant Martin O'Casey of the Irish Republican Army.' He gestured with his hand towards the older man. 'Oh, aye, and before I forget, you dropped this.' O'Casey removed the missing gun magazine from inside his jacket and handed it across to Strassmann. The German was dumbstruck. The pilot tried hard not to laugh.

Strassmann snatched back his property as he addressed Martin O'Casey. 'My pleasure, Herr Commandant.'

'Well now, isn't that nice,' Martin O'Casey replied nervously.

'And this is Oberstleutnant Lenard of the Luftwaffe,' continued Strassman.

'Pleased to meet you.' Martin O'Casey shook the young pilot's hand, before raising his fingers to his lips and whistling. Moments later three other men appeared from amidst the sand dunes and headed straight for the dinghy, immediately carrying it back up the shore. A fourth man, wearing a Sam Browne belt and sporting a .45

72

Colt revolver over a grubby-looking raincoat, came running over to Martin O'Casey's side.

'Pat here will show your pilot to the aircraft,' continued Martin O'Casey.

Strassmann nodded for Lenard to go with the man before returning down the incline towards the water's edge. Removing a torch from inside his jacket, he began signalling to the U-boat.

'I suppose that will mean more company,' commented Martin O'Casey.

'Imminently,' replied his son.

Martin O'Casey took his son by the arm and guided him up the remainder of the steep shingle incline. 'By the way, there's someone here to see you.'

O'Casey's eyes followed his father's over towards the sand dunes. There, illuminated in the moonlight, her auburn hair fluttering in the wind, stood Elizabeth. O'Casey's mouth fell open. Immediately he rushed up the beach, his feet slipping on the shingle and loose sand. Elizabeth ran forward, throwing the raincoat off her narrow shoulders. She tried to cry out his name, but her mouth was suddenly too dry. Throwing herself at him, Elizabeth was swept off her feet and twirled around by O'Casey as their mouths finally touched. Suddenly the past, all the doubt, the self-recrimination, the suffering and fear they had endured these long years abated. Now, for the moment, all was set right again, now they were finally reunited.

'Who is she?' asked Strassmann, returning to Martin O'Casey's side again.

'Me daughter-in-law, an' a fine lass she is too.' Martin O'Casey smiled.

'Is it far to the aircraft?' continued Strassmann.

'Not far. It's up at the farm, about a quarter of a mile inland. We can take the cliff path, it's more direct.' Martin O'Casey led Strassmann and Lenard up the beach past his son and Elizabeth. The couple hardly noticed as they continued embracing.

'C'mon, you two, everyone's staring.' Martin O'Casey chuckled.

O'Casey eased Elizabeth gently down again. 'We'll stay here for the moment,' he replied, without taking his eyes off her. Martin O'Casey shrugged his shoulders and continued on up the cliff path, followed by the two Germans.

Elizabeth and O'Casey stood staring at each other.

'So it isn't a dream, you are real?' she said softly.

'As real as you're ever going to get.' O'Casey beamed. 'And this time there will be no more goodbyes.'

'No more goodbyes?' she whispered, her eyes filled with tears. 'I like the sound of that, if it's true.'

'It's true.' He kissed her again.

Several more IRA men ran down the beach past them, attracting O'Casey's attention. The Type-XXI U-boat had moved closer inshore and in the moonlight he could see various figures gathering on the vessel's forward deck. Half a mile down-shore a small fishing boat had already left the safety of the cove and was on its way out to meet with the U-boat. It wouldn't be long before the rest of the Germans arrived.

'What are they doing?' asked Elizabeth.

'Coming ashore,' grunted O'Casey. Elizabeth stared into her husband's eyes. She could recognize his concern.

The track to the farmhouse began on the other side of the thirty-foot-high sand dunes, amidst the rocks, where the thick grass began to force itself up through the coarse sand. The steep path wound up to the top of the two-hundred-foot limestone cliffs. Meadowlands Farm lay in the moonlight, a small cluster of low, whitewashed buildings and a ramshackle old barn set within a sixty-acre meadow.

'Well, there it is!' smiled Martin O'Casey, out of breath after the steep cliff climb and the quick pace that he had set ahead of Strassmann. The German did not answer. He was looking back towards O'Casey and the woman. 'Don't you worry about those two lovebirds. They'll catch up with us in their own good time,' chuckled Martin O'Casey.

'I hope for your sake this place is as desolate as your son says,' replied Strassmann.

Martin O'Casey laughed again, as he opened the low wicket gate in front of the farmhouse. 'Sure only the seagulls and the odd guillemot would be seein' anything. An' the last aircraft that flew over here belonged to them Wright brothers! Well now, how about some Irish hospitality?'

Strassmann checked his wristwatch. 'I would like to see the aircraft first.'

'Right ya are,' answered Martin O'Casey, leading the way around the side of the farmhouse.

He took Strassmann to the largest of all the farm buildings, a dilapidated wooden barn on the other side of the lime-washed stone farmhouse. The old barn had been converted some years earlier into a giant hay-storage shelter, open on one side, along which bales of last year's hay had been stacked three deep to within inches of the sagging roof. Strassmann followed Martin O'Casey through a side door into the darkened interior. Standing in the middle of the barn was a Douglas C-47 Skytrain, covered in camouflage netting from nose to tail. Lenard was already checking over the aircraft.

The Douglas C-47, otherwise known as the Dakota, was an aircraft in common use by the Allies. Powered by two Pratt and Whitney 1,200hp engines, it was the main troop and supply transport used by both the British and Americans. Normally the C-47 had a range of only 1,600 miles, but this aircraft, seized from the RAF during Rommel's sweep through North Africa during 1942, had been altered by Kämpfgeschwader 200, the Luftwaffe's covert operations unit, headquartered at Flensburg in northern Germany. Disposable fuel tanks had been fitted under each wing by the engineers at Flensburg to double the aircraft's range. The aircraft was in fact a 'ringer', perfect in every detail to an existing aircraft based at a US supply depot and airbase in West Sussex. Now painted US Army olive green, the aircraft carried a yellow identification 'B' marking and serial number on the tail section, and on the fuselage 'K4' markings, matching it to a US Supply Squadron. If detected on the outgoing flight, it would be properly identified by its squadron insignia; by the time the discrepancy was discovered, if at all, it would be too late.

Lenard emerged from the aircraft to meet Strassmann. 'She's OK. Apart from one of the batteries needing recharging, she's ready for take-off. I can have her ready inside the hour.' He motioned towards a stack of oil drums at the far end of the barn. 'All the fuel we need is over there.'

'Good,' replied Strassmann, sounding relieved. He turned back to the Irishman. 'And now for some of your famous Irish hospitality. *Ja?*'

'Right ya are,' said Martin O'Casey.

The entrance door into the farmhouse was low and in two sections; the top half of the door was already open. O'Casey could see Strassmann staring curiously inside.

'Don't worry, Colonel. Contrary to what you Germans think, not all of us Irish keep our pigs in the parlour!' O'Casey grinned as he opened the door latch and ushered Strassmann inside, ahead of him.

The cottage had appeared smaller from the outside, and was indeed deceptive, the low-ceilinged parlour having been extended out towards the rear. The floor was covered in undulating red-stone slabs. In the centre a large round table rested on a tattered Wilton rug, whilst at the far end of the room a steaming pitch-black pot hung from a chain directly over a crackling log fire in a large open fireplace. Beside the blackened fireplace, a heap of sawdust had been piled up against the wall, next to a basket of firewood.

The furniture was spartan – a few wooden chairs scattered around the room and a sideboard, squeezed into a corner to one side of the fireplace, apparently to block off a disused doorway. In contrast, a very new-looking upright piano sat next a window. The only light in the room came from a single oil lamp suspended from a beam directly over the table. Suddenly the kitchen door opened and an old man carrying a kettle shuffled in and over to the fireplace. To Strassmann's amazement, he began pouring the kettle of water over the sawdust. Strassmann's smirk almost developed into laughter.

Eamon O'Casey was standing just outside the kitchen door, in hushed conversation with two other IRA men, when Elizabeth came into the kitchen from the rear of the farmhouse. From the looks on all their faces, she knew she had real cause to be frightened. Eamon O'Casey had not seen his young wife for so long, he could hardly remember the way her eyes changed colour in the different light, but one thing he had not forgotten was her look of fear when they had parted that last time. He quietly excused himself and led her outside into a small, low-walled yard at the rear of the farmhouse, and then on towards the cliff path.

'Talk to me.' He smiled, hugging her gently at his side as they continued walking. Elizabeth pulled away. 'What is it, woman?'

'You!' she said in a raised voice. 'It's you, Eamon, and your father and the complete mess you're all mixed up in! Just when is this all going to end?'

'Elizabeth.' His pleading tone was ignored. Elizabeth looked away. 'After tonight I'm finished. We both can walk away from it all for ever, believe me.' His deep melodic voice could usually soothe her, but not this time. Perhaps it was all those missing years, all those promises not fulfilled. She had taken enough and something was very different now, inexplicably different.

'I can't go on any more, Eamon.' She looked at him, tears filling her deep-brown eyes.

'I know.' He sighed, running his hand through her long auburn hair.

'That's all you can say to me? I don't believe it!' Elizabeth raised her voice. 'You walk out of my life, all for God and Country. I only get to see you briefly and without notice for two maybe three days at a time. Then your father summons me to a "family reunion"!'

'Elizabeth, please!'

'And what do I find when I get here?' continued Elizabeth undaunted, turning to confront him as they reached the top of the path. 'I have to stomach a handful of murderous Nazi thugs!' She stepped closer now. 'Eamon, what do you take me for? Am I not a person in my own right? Do you so easily forget what happened to our unborn child?'

'Will you ever forgive me for that?' he snapped.

'Where the hell were you? Where were you when I was lying flat on my back in a strange bed, going through the hell of labour pains and contractions for the child I had already lost?' Elizabeth could contain herself no longer. She began pounding him on the chest with both fists, pounding against the agony of her own heart. The Irishman stood there, accepting each blow without question or objection. When she had finally worn herself out, Elizabeth fell against his chest, sobbing uncontrollably.

'It doesn't make it any easier, does it?' He stroked her head soothingly, sniffing in the scent of her hair. She shook her head.

Waiting until his wife had regained her self-control, O'Casey walked her away from the farmhouse towards the cliffs and along the cliff-side path to the headland. They paused, staring out towards the far side of the bay. The bright moon was reflected in the rippling surface of Dingle Bay, warming the sea's grey tones. Ten miles north, across on the other side of the inlet, the dark profile of the landfall played games with the dark clouds blowing in from the west. For a moment Elizabeth thought she could identify the outline of the mountains beyond, then almost imperceptibly the slow-moving cloud obliterated and transformed the images before her very eyes.

'Life's like that,' she said softly. 'You think you can see it all before you, understanding and knowing what it is, then suddenly it's all changed. Nothing like what you imagined it was.'

'But now we're together.' He buried his face in her hair.

'It's so peaceful here,' whispered Elizabeth, 'almost like another planet. It's hard to imagine man's inhumanity under this very same sky.'

Eamon O'Casey was slow to answer. None of the words that filled his head could suffice to express the love he felt for this woman, the peace that he had at last found after the years apart. Then his mind came down to earth with a thud as he thought over what he must yet do.

She looked up, recognizing his inner dilemma. 'What is going to happen?'

'Hopefully nothing, at least nothing for you to worry about. But I don't need to remind you that dealing with these Nazis is akin to inviting a cobra to tea.'

Elizabeth stared out into the bay below. 'So the IRA is to double-cross the Third Reich,' she said slowly. His silence confirmed her words.

'God please be with us.' Elizabeth closed her eyes in prayer.

Minutes later the curragh, a long, open fishing boat favoured for the conditions off the western coast, touched the shimmering shoreline and the black-uniformed SS officers disgorged on to the beach, like a plague of black rats.

Elizabeth stood at the open door of the farmhouse as the men approached. As the small group entered through the farmhouse gate, a chill rose up her spine and she moved back from the doorway.

'We can wait inside the farmhouse until we get confirmation from the pilot.' Martin O'Casey opened the latchgate.

The tall blond officer in the uniform of an SS major-general eyed the Irishman with suspicion. 'The less time we spend on your soil, the better it will be,' he grunted.

'Herr Gruppenführer, I can assure you that I want you out of here just as much as you do. But if we all stay together, then there's less possibility of one of your men there gettin' trigger-happy.' He waved towards the door. 'Please.'

The SS general begrudgingly went inside, but his eyes lit up upon seeing the tall and slender woman standing in the kitchen doorway, her image silhouetted by the brighter light streaming in from behind her. As she stepped forward, the light from the kitchen penetrated Elizabeth's light cotton dress, exposing the outline of her shapely legs, much to the German's obvious pleasure. He watched intently as she came closer. The way she moved reminded him of the models he had seen on the Paris catwalk in 1942; she had style and class, something totally alien to these surroundings. He raised his eyes slowly up her body, staring into her oval face. He smiled. She was indeed very beautiful, her brown eyes inviting, despite the coldness of her stare.

'Herr Gruppenführer, may I have the pleasure of presenting my daughter-in-law, Elizabeth.' Martin O'Casey was obviously proud of the fact. 'Elizabeth, this is SS Gruppenführer Schiller.'

The German's smile was hungry. 'Madam, it is indeed a pleasure.' He stepped forward and went to take Elizabeth's right hand to kiss it. She drew back from him and for a long moment Rudolph Schiller and Elizabeth O'Casey stared into each other's eyes.

'Frankly I am surprised.' Schiller shrugged. 'O'Casey never mentioned having such an alluring creature for a wife. I should have expected him to be shouting such a thing from the rooftops.'

'As you know, my husband is something of a dark horse,' Elizabeth said sarcastically, staring over at the strange sight of the German army nurse emerging from the darkness into the light of the doorway behind. She was carrying a baby!

'Touché.' Schiller nodded, a slight grin filling his face.

Elizabeth continued staring at the nurse and an SS guard standing next to her. The soldier was holding a sub-machine-gun in readiness.

'The gun alarms you, yes?' asked Schiller. Elizabeth nodded. 'A necessity of war, I fear.'

'But the war is over, General.' Elizabeth's voice was quiet but steady, no hint of the fear she felt rising from the pit of her stomach. She stole another glance across to the nurse and baby again.

'But others may not view it the same way.' Schiller looked at O'Casey as he came in from the kitchen, behind Elizabeth. The Irishman pursed his lips, undoubtedly about to make some retort, when there was the sound of hurried footsteps on the gravel path just outside the entrance. Strassmann rushed in. The SS colonel went directly over to Schiller, whispering to him. Schiller turned to Martin O'Casey as Strassmann went outside again. 'My adjutant tells me that the gold has arrived ashore. Your men are inspecting it right now.'

'Right ya are.' Martin O'Casey turned to his lieutenant, Pat McManus. The man had been after his position for some time now, but after tonight Martin O'Casey would be bidding to take over the IRA's entire army council in Dublin, and there would be little else to stop him. 'Pat, see the pilot and get some help from the boys to get the plane out of that barn and into the field.'

McManus picked up his Lee Enfield rifle and left. It was clear to Schiller that the Irishman had nothing but contempt for his leader.

'Well then – ' Martin O'Casey rubbed his hands together – 'since we've a few minutes to spare, how's about some food and drink?'

'Thank you,' replied Schiller.

Elizabeth leaned against the kitchen sink, staring up at her own reflection in the uncurtained window. The thought of these Nazis in such close proximity was enough to disturb the dead. Why had God brought them together like this? She thought about her family. What had really become of them all? Elizabeth's mind conjured up old family images. She was playing in the garden of their country house again, just six years old, skipping in the afternoon sunshine with her brothers and sisters. Then her father appeared at the french windows to the rear of the house. He was walking towards them, arms extended, as he rushed down the steps from the veranda, beckoning for them to run to him. She ran towards him, only realizing his look of terror as she got closer. He was screaming something, yelling at her now. The images in the glass suddenly changed. She was looking at herself again and just over her right shoulder stood the devil himself. Schiller!

Elizabeth jumped. 'I startled you,' said Schiller in a low voice, his icy stare penetrating and unsettling her.

She flushed. 'Is there something I can get you?'

'You are not Irish?' he said inquiringly.

Elizabeth grasped the side of the worktop to steady herself. 'I'm Dutch.'

'Are you?' He was playing with her.

'Why yes,' she insisted. Schiller watched closely; the woman was quite petrified.

'From?' continued the German.

'Amsterdam,' replied Elizabeth.

'That is very interesting. I have been in Amsterdam myself. A most beautiful city.' He nodded agreeably. 'Tell me, just when did you meet your husband?'

'In 1939. Eamon was lecturing at Oxford University, I was studying at Cambridge at the time.' She tried in vain to hide her nervousness.

'Not at the same university?'

'No. We met socially.' Elizabeth turned away from him. The German's overbearing attitude was intolerable. Part of her wanted to strike out at him with something, whilst the other part simply wanted to run as far away as possible. She looked into the window again. He was smiling, but not in any friendly way.

'So what were you studying?' pursued Schiller.

Elizabeth looked down at a bread knife just inches away on a cutting board. 'Languages,' she replied, reaching over until her fingertips touched the handle of the knife. All she had to do was take hold of it. She struggled internally.

'What are ya trying to do, General, steal me daughter-in-law?' Martin O'Casey appeared at the doorway and came over to Elizabeth, touching her on the shoulder. 'Well, woman, do you enjoy burning the bread?'

She looked at the frying pan, where smoke was gently rising from the bread. The Irishman laughed heartily as Elizabeth began to rescue what she could.

'Your adjutant is calling for you, General. I think everything is just about finalized,' continued Martin O'Casey.

'Good,' snapped Schiller. 'Frau O'Casey, it has been a pleasure.' It was about all she could do to stare back at his image in the steamy window. The German smirked as he squeezed past Martin O'Casey. Once he had gone, the Irishman's smile turned into a serious frown.

'What did you tell him?' he asked quietly.

'Nothing much. He just took me by surprise, that's all. He knows I'm Dutch. He frightens me.'

The Irishman nodded.

'What is going to happen?' she asked, lowering her voice.

'Leave well alone.'

'It was like an interrogation.' Tears began to trickle down her face. 'I . . . I didn't know what to do.'

'The cheeky bastard!' replied Martin O'Casey. Elizabeth buried her head in his chest. He looked across at the frying pan – the bread was now going to burn on both sides.

Outside the weather was starting to deteriorate. A heavy fog was blowing in from the sea, shrouding the nearby fields and reducing visibility. Lenard approached the German officers, a worried look on his young face.

'*Mein Herr.*' He addressed himself to Schiller. 'If we don't get off immediately, we won't be going anywhere.'

'Start up the engines. We are ready now,' insisted Schiller. 'Get the flare gun! *Schnell!*' he shouted over to one of the other soldiers.

The Pratt and Whitney aircraft engines roared into life as Lenard made the final preparations for take-off, easing the aircraft out into the open meadow and in line with a series of flaming beacons, tar barrels burning brightly down one side of the makeshift runway area as a guide. Lenard had already paced out the grass runway; he could make a safe take-off blindfolded.

The SS general walked just ahead of the group, clutching his briefcase to his chest. He was followed closely by Nurse Toller, carrying the baby. As instructed, Greta Toller's tall SS bodyguard kept beside her at all times, keeping a watchful eye on his charge. Strassmann and the other SS officers followed, accompanied by a small detachment of Waffen SS grenadiers. Eamon O'Casey joined

Schiller, walking along beside him. He stared down at the briefcase handcuffed to Schiller's left wrist. 'You don't intend to lose that in a hurry,' he shouted over the noise of the aircraft.

The German stared back suspiciously.

'No offence intended,' shouted O'Casey, raising both hands jokingly, at the same time keeping a careful eye on his distance from the low stone wall to his left. He couldn't leave it much longer.

At the same instant Strassmann spotted the movement in the small copse adjacent to the barn. He was unsure at first, as the fog was thickening. Then he saw it again – someone moving inside the tree-line. His eyes narrowed: there were at least three or four figures, all carrying rifles. He looked across to the barn again. Five of O'Casey's men had filed into the back of the tumble-down building and taken up position behind some of the discarded bales of hay. They were walking into potential crossfire.

Just as Strassmann was about to shout out a warning, the sky above the cliffs lit up. Even in the fog the red flare was plain to see.

'Something has happened on the beach,' growled Schiller.

'It's a trap! They're going to take us on!' shouted Strassmann.

As Schiller turned towards the SS colonel, O'Casey shoved him aside and started running for a nearby hay cart. Strassmann rounded on the Irishman and opened up with his Schmeisser sub-machine-gun. The 9mm bullets tore into the cart, splintering the wood, as O'Casey disappeared over the four-foot dry stone wall just beyond.

'*Verdammt!*' cried Strassmann, running to his master's aid.

'Get to the aircraft! *Schnell! Schnell!*' shouted Schiller, getting to his feet.

'Get the child to the aircraft!' Strassmann waved the nurse and her bodyguard forward.

SS Sturmmann Müller guided his charge and the baby towards the waiting plane. The remaining Waffen SS men and several of the officers rushed forward, forming a defensive line. Then all hell broke loose.

As the nurse and her SS escort ran towards the Dakota, the IRA men in the barn opened fire, cutting down one of the soldiers instantly. Nurse Greta Toller screamed as the young soldier fell at her feet, his chest splattered in blood and tissue. Müller grabbed the nurse and steered her over to the cover of the hay cart. A grenade suddenly exploded just feet away from the other soldiers, engulfing two of the men momentarily in a white cloud of dust and flame. The nearer man took the full blast in his stomach and groin, and was killed outright, while his comrade fell on to both knees, blinded by the flash. Raising his hands up to his face, he started to scream, just as a .303 bullet passed between his fingers, exploding his cranium and tossing him around like a spinning top. He crashed into the earth beside his smouldering comrade, dead before he hit the ground.

'The child!' cried Schiller as Strassmann crawled over beside him, keeping his head below the zinging gunfire.

'He and the nurse are all right,' Strassmann assured him.

'Can we make it to the aircraft?' yelled Schiller, catching his breath as he unholstered his Walther pistol.

'It's our only chance!' snapped Strassmann. 'They've got at least a dozen men and a heavy machine-gun across that field on the other side.' Strassmann pointed across to the small copse, now almost obscured by the swirling fog. 'If we keep away from the centre of the field and stay close to the wall, we can get close enough to the aircraft to make a dash for it.'

'The child must be protected at all times!' insisted Schiller. 'Schnell! We have no time to waste.'

The Germans started running towards the transport aircraft, Schiller and two of his men ahead of the rest. They were just yards away from the aircraft's tail section when a massive explosion rocked the entire area and Schiller felt himself enveloped in a blinding white flash and flung into the air like a rag doll. He landed on his back, the momentum somersaulting him backwards until he lay sprawled face-down on the grass.

Strassmann was following with the nurse and child when he was stopped in his tracks by the force of the massive explosion. He dived to the ground, drawing the nurse and the baby down next to him. Unseen by anyone, several of the IRA men had moved up from the other side of the aircraft and had hurled a bag of Mills grenades under the starboard wing. Flicking a live grenade on top of the bag, one of the Irishmen had ignited the fuel tank under the wing, sending a sheet of flame through the aircraft and exploding some munitions in the rear fuselage section. The resulting explosion effectively broke the aircraft in two, sending most of it up in a sheet of flame, claiming four lives – an IRA volunteer, Lenard and two of the men accompanying Schiller.

'Follow me and stick close!' ordered Strassmann, picking the man nearest to him. 'The rest of you give covering fire!' He clicked a fresh magazine on to the Schmeisser as he ran forward towards Schiller, closely followed by the other soldier. The German line opened up as both men began twisting and weaving their way out into the drifting fog. The IRA volunteers returned fire with all they had, aiming their bolt action .303 rifles towards the running Germans. Strassmann was fortunate: the fog was working to his advantage, giving the IRA a very limited target. Skidding to his knees beside Schiller, he lifted the unconscious general up and over his left shoulder, careful at the same time to keep a firm grip on the trigger of his sub-machine-gun. Then he realized that Schiller's briefcase had been ripped from him in the explosion. He quickly found it, lying some yards away, the leather flap still smouldering. 'Get the briefcase!' he shouted to the other soldier.

'Jawohl, mein Herr.' The young SS grenadier had no sooner answered than two IRA men appeared out of the fog, running low and directly at them. From the look on the Irishmen's faces, they were just as alarmed at seeing the Germans as they were.

'Look out! To the right!' warned Strassmann. The soldier dropped the briefcase just as one of the IRA men opened up, the bullet skimming past his right ear. Strassmann replied with automatic fire. The Schmeisser jumped in his hand as he fired a prolonged burst. Both IRA men were cut down instantly by the 9mm bullets, but by now the gunfire had attracted the attention of others. Bullets were starting to chop up the turf at Strassmann's feet. 'Grab the briefcase and cover my back!' Strassmann started heading back again. As the grenadier again picked up the briefcase, two high-velocity rounds smacked into the small of his back, throwing him on to the damp grass face-first. Strassmann didn't look back, he kept on going as fast as his legs could carry him. Reaching the low stone wall, he cleared it in a single movement, landing heavily on the other side as he absorbed the effects of the impact on Schiller. Passing the SS general over to one of the other men, Strassmann quickly forgot all about the briefcase as he began regrouping his remaining party. He had no other choice but to fall back to the farmhouse. His priority now was to protect the child and try to hold out until reinforcements could be sent ashore, but he also knew there was little chance of any such operation succeeding until dawn. By then they would be wiped out.

As they reached the farmhouse Strassmann paused, crouching against a stone wall for support before gently easing Schiller on to the grass verge at the side of the dusty limestone track. The SS general was breathing heavily and just starting to regain consciousness. Strassmann checked Schiller's injuries for himself. The left side of his tunic was saturated in blood; his left forearm had been badly lacerated by shrapnel. The entire left side of his face and neck had been badly burnt and his left eye was bleeding profusely. Schiller opened his right eye and tried to speak.

'We . . . must get back to the shore,' he grunted.

Strassmann concurred. Even in delirium, Schiller's thinking was accurate. It was the only way now. 'In good time, *mein Herr*,' Strassmann assured him as he applied a field dressing to Schiller's arm. 'Help is on the way.'

'The child . . .' Schiller was almost overcome by pain.

'He's safe, *mein Herr*,' insisted Strassmann, staring over at the nurse, the baby screaming in her arms. Nurse Toller was crouched behind the stone wall, shaking with terror as she tried her best to calm the child. Schiller stared at his torn arm. There was a small section of chain attached to the handcuff around his bloody wrist. 'The case!' he cried. 'Where is the briefcase?' He fought to stand up, but was easily dissuaded by his adjutant.

'The briefcase is gone. There is nothing that can be done about it for now,' he insisted.

'Karl! You must get it back. It is crucial I have it!' Schiller tried to force himself up again, but then collapsed. Strassmann checked his pulse, it was still strong. Propping his sub-machine-gun on top of the wall, Strassmann stared out into the fog. The shooting had ceased for the moment, but nevertheless the briefcase would have to wait. He had other priorities more pressing.

The explosion and shooting had been heard aboard the Type-XXI U-boat. Quickly the Nazi back-up plan rolled into action. Out of sight, on the lee side of the U-boat, three rubber dinghies, each containing four men, had already been launched into the choppy sea following the flare. Equipped with outboard petrol engines, they started racing towards the shore. Petersen stood on the U-boat's bridge in frustration, listening to the gunfire and explosions; without the right co-ordinates he couldn't even use his deck guns.

On the beach the Germans had already started loading the gold crates back on to the curragh. The beach party had managed to beat off the initial attack by the Irishmen, but not without incurring their own casualties. From the eight-man party, now only five remained active, with another badly wounded. The sailors waited, just as they had been instructed.

Back at the farmhouse it wasn't long before the fighting recommenced. By now the Germans were well and truly pinned down at the house by the machine-gun and small-arms fire from the tree-line at the edge of the meadow. Strassmann cursed his position, for all he had remaining was a handful of men, but he quickly began to reorganize what was left. He was down to three able-bodied men and several wounded, including the tall SS corporal assigned to look after the nurse and child. Strassmann was no stranger to combat and knew their position was untenable. Their survival depended on two things: quick relief or exit and the IRA continuing to make mistakes.

'Is the radio still working?' He turned to the young lieutenant next to him.

'*Jawohl, mein Herr*,' panted the officer, having just run on all fours along the length of the stone wall to avoid the now almost continuous sniper fire.

'Contact the U-boat and give me the handset,' Strassmann snapped, looking at the nurse still cowering behind the stone wall. 'Müller!' he called over to the nurse's bodyguard. As the tall SS corporal scampered over, Strassmann noticed he was holding his arm stiffly. There was a heavy patch of blood around his left shoulder and blood was dripping from between the fingers of his hand. 'Is it bad?' he asked.

'I'm all right, *mein Herr*.' Müller gritted his teeth.

'Get the nurse and child inside the farmhouse and stay with them. We are going to have to hold these bastards off until help arrives.' He had no sooner finished than the radio crackled into life. Strassmann took the handset instantly.

Müller kicked open the door and sprayed the kitchen with his sub-machine-gun before going inside. He appeared at the door seconds later, ushered the nurse in and then slammed the door shut again. Nurse Toller was almost hysterical. The baby was now scream- ing and she couldn't control him any more. '*Mein Gott!* What will happen to us!' she cried.

'Shut up!' growled Müller, peering into the darkness of the parlour. 'I'm checking the rest of the house. Stay here and don't leave!' The battle outside reached a new crescendo as both sides opened up simultaneously. Somewhere near by several grenades exploded, shattering one of the kitchen windows and showering the nurse with glass.

'Don't leave me!' she cried, grabbing Müller's leg. He pulled away.

'Control yourself!' he insisted, unholstering his Luger pistol and handing it to the nurse. 'Here, take it! The safety catch is off and there's one up the spout.' He pointed towards the back door. 'If anyone comes through that door, pull the trigger.' At that a stray bullet splintered the back door and smacked into the wall above their heads. The nurse wasted no time squeezing into a corner, beside an old oak dresser. 'Take it,' insisted Müller, forcing the gun into her hand. She took it hesitantly, her hand shaking so much that she almost dropped it. 'Just remember who you are protecting! I will be back for you both in a moment.' Müller looked down at the baby, touching his tiny head before vanishing into the blackness of the parlour. The nurse was almost rigid with fear, unable to move a muscle. Suddenly more stray bullets smashed through another window beside her, ripping the fluttering curtains and showering her again. The baby screamed. Automatically she crouched to shield him from the falling debris. The shooting continued; someone had now directed a machine-gun on the farmhouse. The bullets blasted an uneven pattern across the rough plaster wall of the kitchen. The SS nurse prayed for the first time in her life.

Müller cleared the parlour, satisfying himself that he was alone. Then he checked the main door. He was surprised to find that it had already been locked and bolted from the inside, just the same as the back door had been. If both doors had been barred from the inside, it could only mean one thing – someone else had to be inside the house! Müller turned, half expecting to find the 'someone' behind him, but all he saw were the flickering embers of the log fire. There was a break in the shooting outside. Müller could hear his own breathing. He wiped the sweat from his brow. The pain in his shoulder was getting worse. He pulled out a handkerchief from his pocket, tucking it inside his tunic over the wound.

Then he heard it! A creaking sound from upstairs. Someone was directly above him in one of the bedrooms. From being inside the house earlier he knew where the staircase was, but he didn't need it. Steadying the Schmeisser in his good arm, he wedged it against his chest and squeezed the trigger. The entire 32-round magazine emptied into the beamed and plaster ceiling, spraying it from side to side in several waves. He closed his eyes against the falling dust as the 9mm parabellum bullets tore into the rough plaster between the timber beams.

Above him, Elizabeth froze in terror as the bullets erupted through the floor and all around her. Luckily she was standing directly over one of the main beam supports. She closed her eyes, expecting death at any second, but it never came. Then the shooting stopped. Elizabeth opened her eyes. She had expected and almost wanted death and was confused to find herself still breathing. Suddenly she was alerted by the sound of someone kicking open a door and running up the wooden staircase. They were coming to get her!

She moved blindly towards the door, brushing past the bed and almost stumbling in the darkness. The noise grew louder. Someone was at the top of the staircase now and rushing towards her door. She stood to one side, bracing herself against a washstand. The door flew open, smacking against the low-pitched ceiling. Müller rushed inside, spraying the room with his sub-machine-gun. Instinctively Elizabeth struck out at the shadow, sinking the twelve-inch bread knife into the pit of Müller's neck at a downward angle, just above the breastbone. The German swung around in horror, trying to see his attacker, before crashing forward into her, pinning her to the floor by the weight of his body. She could smell him, the sweat of his body mingling with the foulness of his dying breath. Elizabeth screamed, beating him with her hands until she realized that the German was finally dead. She struggled free, crawling out from under the heavy body.

Outside, Martin O'Casey's men were closing in on the remaining Germans, while his son headed down towards the beach to try and stem any advance. The Irishmen knew they had to be quick, for undoubtedly help would be soon arriving from the U-boat. As the IRA volunteers advanced across the field under the cover of the drifting fog, disaster struck. The burning aircraft lay in two sections directly behind them, its back broken and one of the wings completely gone, but the fire hadn't yet done its worst. The flames, rekindled in the light breeze, were fanned towards the last remaining long-range-fuel tank under the port wing. The aircraft exploded in a mountainous orange and yellow flame, illuminating the advancing Irishmen like targets on a shooting range.

'Fire! Give them everything you have!' cried Strassmann.

'Get back!' shouted Martin O'Casey, realizing the situation too late.

The Germans opened up. Inside those few seconds sixteen of Martin O'Casey's men lay dead or dying in the field. He himself was one of the few fortunate ones, having flung himself behind a haystack just as the shooting started. After almost a minute the shooting finally halted. The silence gave way to the moaning sounds of the injured. Across the field someone started screaming in Gaelic, garbled and incoherent. Another shot rang out. The screaming stopped.

*

Elizabeth crept down the stairs, carrying the dead German's Schmeisser. All she could see in the darkness around her were images of her lost family. She didn't care any more about living; all she wanted was revenge. As she reached the parlour she heard the baby crying. She stood listening. Then she heard a woman sobbing and pleading in German for the baby to hush. Elizabeth gripped the gun firmly. They were German and she had just killed a German. Listening to the screaming baby, she felt sick to the pit of her stomach.

The SS nurse was shaking the baby in her arms, begging him to stop crying. Nurse Toller was getting hysterical. She had heard the shooting both in the parlour and from upstairs. It had been some minutes ago and Müller had still not returned. It could only mean one thing. She trained the Luger towards the kitchen doorway, trying to steady her aim.

'Come over here. I can help you.' Elizabeth spoke in German.

The nurse was devastated by the sound of the female voice speaking to her in perfect German. The voice was coming from the direction of the open doorway leading to the parlour. Nurse Toller tried to strain her ear to hear above the almost incessant gunfire outside.

'Please. You have nothing to fear from me. Come inside the parlour. It will be much safer for the child.' The voice sounded concerned, but the German nurse was petrified. 'Where is Müller?' she said nervously.

The reply came slowly. 'Müller is dead.'

The nurse almost dropped the gun with fright. Her mind raced. Whilst she knew she was safe in the kitchen corner, she could not imagine just how the fight was progressing outside. Already she had heard a number of men run past the window and the battle seemed to be raging on well into the distance. Would she be left behind? Perhaps they had already forgotten about her? Perhaps Strassmann was already dead?

'The soldier tried to kill me. I had no choice,' continued Elizabeth, still speaking in German. 'Please hurry. I do not know what is happening outside, but you . . . and your baby, will be safe here at the other side of the house, away from the fighting.'

The baby, still screaming, had by now started thrashing around in the nurse's arms. 'Who are you?' she cried.

'A friend. Do not worry. Unlike your friend Müller, I do not make war on children and women.'

The SS nurse listened intently. She was certain she could detect sincerity in the woman's voice, but could she trust her?

'All right. I'm coming.' Against her better judgement, she slowly got up into a crouching position and began to move across the floor, being extremely careful to support the child in her arms. She comforted herself in the knowledge that she still had the pistol in her hand and if necessary she would use it. She tried to flex her wrist and keep the gun trained on the doorway. Several more shots rang out from somewhere close by; the nurse hurried. Just as she reached the centre of the room there was another shot, the bullet ricocheting around the kitchen. Nurse Toller didn't hear the sound. Her eyes ignited in a blinding flash. She slumped on to the cold stone floor, unable to hear her own cries as the blood pumped forth from the gaping hole in the side of her head.

Elizabeth was still crouched behind the dining table and chairs in the parlour when she heard the woman's scream. Casting all caution aside, she left the sub-machine-gun on the floor and crawled into the kitchen, where she stumbled against something. Groping with both hands, she discovered she was beside the now silent nurse. The woman appeared dead. Elizabeth drew back on finding her hands warm and sticky with blood. Then she heard the baby's muffled cries and realized that the woman had fallen on top of her charge. Elizabeth quickly pulled the nurse on to her side. She was still clutching the baby in her left arm. The child coughed a little and started crying again. Elizabeth lifted the baby from the woman's arms. To her amazement, the crying stopped instantly. Elizabeth was then startled to see some movement in the nurse's body. The very action of taking the child from her seemed to jar the nurse back into consciousness again. Her eyes flickered open and she stared up at Elizabeth, just able to make out the baby in her arms. Elizabeth was about to speak when she noticed the gun in the woman's hand. For a terrible moment she was convinced the SS nurse was going to use it, but it slipped away from her fingers, clattering noisily on to the stone floor beside her.

'Is he . . .' Nurse Toller's voice drained away.

'He's fine,' insisted Elizabeth.

She moved closer as the woman tried to speak again.

'He's stopped crying . . .' She coughed up a little blood and grabbed Elizabeth by the wrist. 'Listen . . . I have little time . . .' She coughed again, bringing up some frothing blood, which started trickling down her cheek. 'You are a woman. You understand these things . . . Look after him.' Her eyes bulged as she fought to utter her next words. 'He is the heir!' she cried. The grip on Elizabeth's arm suddenly relaxed. The air rasped out unevenly from the nurse's throat, ending with a gurgle as her lungs finally gave out.

Elizabeth's face mirrored her confusion, then another stray bullet

90

smashed into the wall above her head. Fuelled by a mixture of fear and rising panic, Elizabeth fled back inside the parlour, taking the now-screaming baby with her. She took refuge behind a couch as she tried to settle him down again. As she sat there trapped, listening to the sound of gunfire and exploding grenades outside, she thought about what the nurse had said. It made no sense at all. She stared down at the baby boy. Just who was he?

Suddenly the kitchen door was booted open. Elizabeth jerked, almost making the baby start to cry again. She heard footsteps on broken glass; someone was inside the kitchen. Then a voice in German cried out.

'Herr Sturmbannführer! The nurse is dead!' The voice appeared to be echoing in the opposite direction; it was being directed back outside.

There was a muffled reply. Then a clunking noise.

'*Handgranate!*' the voice cried out just before a massive explosion ripped apart the kitchen, sending a cloud of dust into the parlour. Elizabeth was thrown on to her side by the force of the blast, her ears searing with pain. Unsure if the baby was still making a noise, she covered his mouth with her hand as he thrashed about inside his thick blanket. As she lay waiting, she only then realized that she couldn't hear a thing and her right ear was agonizingly painful. Then following a popping sensation in her left ear, Elizabeth found she could hear again. The shooting outside had now changed direction. The battle had moved away from the farmhouse. She removed her hand from over the baby's mouth. He screamed aloud, in one way relieving her and in another terrifying her of the possibility of discovery.

Slowly, she got up from behind the couch, rocking the baby in her arms, but it had no effect. The front of the rose-patterned couch was speckled with metal shrapnel from the fragmentation grenade. It was then she realized just how close they had both come to dying. Creeping forward to peer into the devastated kitchen, she saw the nurse's body, covered in debris and partly concealed by the body of a German soldier. The man was lying spread-eagled on his back, his blackened body peppered with shrapnel. Elizabeth turned away, her stomach churning. She knew she had to find out what was happening outside and escape this place. After some further minutes had elapsed, she took the baby upstairs and placed him in her own bed, lining him on either side with pillows so he wouldn't fall out. Back in the kitchen, she stepped on the Luger pistol, instinctively picked it up and went to the door. She could still hear shooting but it seemed to be coming some way off, from the direction of the cliffs.

Racing round the far side of the house, she slipped on the wet grass. As she tried to stand up, Elizabeth halted in her tracks: through the swirling fog she could just make out the profiles of some men running across the field, beyond which the aircraft was still burning brightly. All around her the wooden-framed farm outbuildings were also ablaze, set on fire by Strassmann and his men to cover their escape. Across the limestone track winding down towards the cliff, several figures could be seen running slowly as if in the final stages of some marathon race. One man, just ahead of the group, stumbled and fell forward. It was only then that Elizabeth realized that the man was carrying someone across his shoulder.

She wanted to run after them and kill them all, every last one, yet something held her back. She turned away and flopped against the bullet-riddled wall. As she stared across towards the burning outbuildings, a young German sailor came running around the corner of the farmhouse. She could see by his panicked face, illuminated by the fires, that he had been left behind in the turmoil. He halted, training his Mauser rifle menacingly at her. They were only feet apart; she could almost smell his fear. He seemed so young. Her first reaction had been to shoot him, but his youthfulness distracted her. Before Elizabeth realized, she began speaking to him in German.

'I mean you no harm,' she insisted, careful not to raise the pistol in her right hand.

The boy's face lightened. He had been clearly disoriented by the sudden violent events. 'I must get back to the U-boat!' he panted.

Elizabeth turned towards the cliff path and pointed.

'They have gone that way.' She looked at him. He was trembling. 'Go! Go quickly! *Schnell! Schnell!*'

As the young sailor went to run, another figure hobbled into view from the other side of the house. It was one of Martin O'Casey's men. The Irishman raised his Lee Enfield rifle and trained it on the sailor only ten yards away; he could not fail to miss the youngster. Elizabeth amazed herself at the speed of her own mind. Eamon had told her about the way the mind works faster in a highly dangerous situation, and now she knew exactly what he meant. She looked at both men, seeing clearly in the subtle movements of their bodies that they were prepared to kill each other.

'No!' she yelled at the top of her voice at the IRA man and then automatically jumped the short distance to get between them, turning towards the young German. '*Nein!*' She gestured for him to lower his rifle. The sailor wavered, but stood his ground, petrified.

'Get out of the bloody way!' demanded the Irishman, still training his rifle on the boy.

'You'll have to shoot through me,' retorted Elizabeth, before slowly pacing towards him.

The Irishman tried to sidestep her. Elizabeth had betted and was now praying that the young German would stand his ground and not try to shoot.

'Damn you, Mrs O'Casey, get the hell out of it!' The Irishman pointed the rifle at her head.

'Let him go. He's only a child. He'll do you no harm.' She was now only a couple of yards from the Irishman; she could see his eyes from behind the gun sights. He had to have a heart! She prayed with every ounce of strength that she could muster, too afraid to close her eyes. It was yet another thing she had learned from her husband during their brief periods together. 'Always stare a man in the eyes, never take your eyes off his for a second,' Eamon had said. She hadn't really understood, until now.

'Please,' she pleaded as she drew up in front of him. Suddenly it was all over. The Irishman capitulated, realizing his edge over the youngster had dissipated. He lowered his .303 rifle.

'Tell the fucker to get outta here before I changes me mind,' he snapped.

Elizabeth smiled and turned towards the young sailor. 'Go! *Schnell!*' The sailor hesitated. 'Go now!' she insisted.

His movements were jerky and slow, then suddenly, like a fox released from a snare, he bolted across the grass and over a low stone wall towards the track. The IRA man stood shaking his head in disbelief.

'I must be fuckin' mad,' he grunted.

'Not mad,' replied Elizabeth with a smile. 'You're compassionate.'

Elizabeth turned and walked back towards the door of the farmhouse. She had almost reached the kitchen when the shot rang out. She turned, expecting to see the IRA man with a smoking rifle in his hands, but instead she found him slumped against the gable wall. She ran to him, but she could see it was no use. The wall behind him was splattered in blood and brain tissue. He had been shot through the forehead. She looked back towards the young sailor. He was standing on the far side of the wall, with his rifle pointed at her. Elizabeth didn't hesitate. She dived face-first on to the earth just a split second before a second bullet smashed into the wall above her head. Her thigh took the full brunt of the fall as she fell on to the

Irishman's rifle, yet she felt no pain. Another shot rang out, followed quickly by yet another. Plaster and limestone showered over her as she lay flat against the damp earth, trembling.

As the firing stopped, she looked up towards the low wall, expecting the sailor to return and finish off what he had started. Anger rose inside her. Suddenly she realized she was still clutching the 9mm Luger in her right hand. She looked at it incredulously. She had absolutely no idea of how to fire the gun, yet she still got to her knees and rushed forward to the stone wall, pointing the muzzle of the gun out into the swirling fog. There was no more hesitation or compassion left in her. The young sailor was running again and had almost disappeared from view down the path towards the beach. Elizabeth trained the gun in his general direction with both hands and pulled the trigger. The gun kicked in her hands, again and again, until she had exhausted the magazine. Straining her eyes, she couldn't see if she'd hit him or not. He had disappeared.

'Bastard!' she screamed, throwing the empty pistol after him. In the distance she could hear the sound of small-arms fire intermingled with the heavier thudding sound of the U-boat's deck gun. A whistling sound preceded an explosion from the direction of the shore. Two more IRA men raced past her, one shouting something to her in Gaelic. Elizabeth ignored him and climbed over the stone wall, running through the fog, towards the cliffs. She was mesmerized by the horror of what had just happened. Unthinking, she walked on, following the limestone path until finally she arrived at the small copse close to the top of the cliff path. Below, somewhere on the beach, sporadic shooting had recommenced. Elizabeth was oblivious of the noise created by her feet crunching on the loose chippings.

'Over here! And keep down.' A strongly accented Belfast voice echoed from somewhere over on her left. She turned, startled. One of the men who had run past her minutes earlier appeared from the tree-line.

'Why the hell didn't you stay at the farmhouse like you were told?' said the Ulsterman, guiding her back to the trees.

'I didn't understand. I don't know Gaelic,' she replied in a whisper.

'You stay with us. It ain't safe down there.' He pointed towards the beach. Somewhere below a grenade exploded, followed by rapid fire. 'What's left of them bastardin' Jerries is tryin' to get back to their submarine,' continued the man looking down.

'Have you seen my husband?' she asked.

'Eamon?' The man turned to her. 'Last seen, he and the Comman-dant were headin' down there.' He pointed at the cliff path. Everything was blotted out by the heavy fog. 'We'll end up killing our own if this weather keeps up!' The man then communicated in Gaelic to his partner. Before he realized it, Elizabeth had flashed past him, disappearing down the narrow cliff path.

'Come back!' shouted the Ulsterman, but she was gone.

All along the beach and amidst the sand dunes pockets of German sailors were fighting their unsteady way towards the water's edge. The weather conditions had provoked a state of confusion; already the German sailors had claimed one of their own mistakenly.

The curragh carrying the gold had by now returned to the U-boat. Now the Germans had formed themselves into a small bridge-head around the remaining beached craft, awaiting the arrival of their comrades, trapped further inland.

Kapitänleutnant Petersen had already ordered the U-boat's diesel engines to be restarted again, giving the returning sailors a sound by which to guide themselves back safely through the swirling fog.

'Can you see anything, Herr Kapitän?' asked one of the young sailors standing next to the captain on the open bridge.

The captain turned on the youngster, letting his frustration explode in a most unusual outburst of anger. 'Can you?' he growled before turning to the bridge control panel and passing a message to the control room below. 'Chief? I want this vessel moving at a moment's notice. Prepare to head for open waters on my orders!'

Jawohl, Herr Kapitän.' A voice echoed back, through the pipe. The captain looked back towards the shoreline. He dared not take the U-boat any closer to the shore for fear of running aground. He felt totally helpless. He had risked firing one salvo from the deck gun, following radio direction from the shore, but the shell had fallen hopelessly short, almost killing his own shore party. His guns were useless and he could not afford to send any more of his men ashore. He was about to turn towards the control panel again when the young sailor he had just reprimanded stuttered out a warning.

'Herr Kapitän! Boarders off starboard bow!' The sailor trained his machine-gun sights on target. He was about to open fire when Petersen placed his hand over the gun barrel, pushing it aside.

'That's our men out there!' he snapped.

They watched as the curragh's narrow bow cut through the water, bringing the fishing boat alongside the foredeck. A work party ran forward, throwing the bobbing fishing boat a line. Captain Petersen felt ill as he watched the wounded and dead being brought aboard.

95

He stopped counting after the fourth body. The captain turned to a young second lieutenant standing beside him. 'Take charge of the vessel. I'm going ashore,' he snapped.

Strassmann and two remaining sailors were now trapped in the sand dunes, some hundred yards away from the beachhead position. The SS major examined Schiller. He was still breathing, but his pulse had weakened. Strassmann checked the bleeding and realized that it had intensified. He quickly ripped off the leather strap from his Schmeisser, applying it as a tourniquet just above Schiller's shattered left forearm.

Two red flares were launched skyward almost simultaneously. Strassmann cursed under his breath. It was the emergency signal they had agreed on earlier; the beach party was planning to pull out. They had to get through to the boats and fast. Schiller started to regain consciousness again, his face taut with pain. Strassmann covered his mouth to muffle his groans.

'*Mein Herr!* Someone is coming!' One of the young sailors frantically pointed towards the far side of the sand dunes.

Strassmann motioned for the sailor to come over beside him. 'Stay with him. And make no sound.' He scrambled up the side of the dune and on to a grassy knoll some fifteen feet above. He made out a crouched figure moving down past their position towards the beach. Just as the man passed round the side of the sand dune, Strassmann struck, leaping from his perch with a short bayonet clenched in his left hand. He landed uncomfortably on the man's shoulders, falling badly to one side. Under normal circumstances the mistake would have given the other man an edge, but instead the man lay face down in the sand. Winded, the SS major leapt back on top of his victim, grabbing the man by the back of the hair and bringing the razor-sharp bayonet down to slice his throat.

'*Nein!*' groaned the man. At the very last second Strassmann pulled back on the bayonet. It was one of the young sailors from the U-boat. The youth was about to speak again and Strassmann quietened him.

'Shut up!' he panted in the young sailor's ear as he tried to regain his breath again. 'I could have killed you. Where the hell is your helmet?'

'I lost it . . . I had to jump over a wall at the farmhouse. I shot one of the Irishmen. Then the woman started shooting at me . . .'

Strassmann was disgusted. He let go of the sailor's hair, thudding his head back into the sand. 'Excellent! You run away from a female.'

Schiller started groaning again. At the same moment Strassmann identified other noises somewhere to his right. He quickly motioned for the sailor next to the SS general to quieten him. They could all hear the Irish voices now. Then the sound diminished as the IRA men started moving away from them. Strassmann crept over to the sailor. 'Stay with him and keep him quiet.' He crawled off on his belly, supporting the Schmeisser on both forearms as he moved forward from the cover of the dunes, heading towards the sound of breakers crashing on shingle below. Seconds later he felt damp sand with his fingers. If they could make it to the water, they could follow the shoreline to the boats. He waited a moment, listening. The immediate area seemed safe. Crawling back, he heard Schiller shouting at the top of his voice. Strassmann got to his feet and sprinted the final distance to the dunes. He found the sailors trying in vain to quieten down the SS general.

'What's going on?' growled Strassmann, shoving the sailors aside and raising his hand to Schiller's mouth. 'I told you to keep him quiet.'

'But we couldn't . . .' blurted one of the young sailors.

'Karl! Is that you!' Schiller pulled Strassmann's hand away from his face.

'*Jawohl, mein Herr.*' Strassmann waved the sailors back as he leaned over his master. 'You must keep your voice down,' he whispered, but the SS general didn't seem to understand.

'My briefcase! The child!' Schiller was consumed by panic.

'It's no use. The child and nurse are dead, a grenade caught them.'

'*Nein!*' yelled Schiller.

'The briefcase was blown to pieces when you were caught in the explosion,' whispered Strassmann, hoping it was true. 'It probably saved your life and took most of the shrapnel.'

'But everything was in it!' Schiller grabbed his adjutant by the arm, almost fainting again. 'The jewels, Karl!'

Perplexed by the remark, Strassmann took the opportunity to lift him over his left shoulder again. 'Move out. This way,' he ordered, waving for the others to follow him towards the shore. Then, like some ghost, Eamon O'Casey appeared out of the mist in front of them, barely twenty feet away. He was brandishing a captured German sub-machine-gun.

'Just where would you lads be thinkin' of going now?' O'Casey spoke first in his native language.

Strassmann stared back in horror. The barrel of O'Casey's sub-machine-gun was pointed directly into his belly. For days on end he had studied the Irishman in the confines of the U-boat. He was a professional. There would be no room for mistakes and, with the added disadvantage of Schiller's weight over his shoulder, he was definitely no match for the Irishman. O'Casey had them all in view as he moved forward up the slight incline from the shore. The two sailors looked on despondently as the big Irishman moved closer.

'Now, let's be dropping those guns, like good lads.' O'Casey returned to speaking in German. They slowly complied. 'That's good of you.' O'Casey grinned again, motioning with his gun for Strassmann to step away from his discarded Schmeisser. 'Now! *Schnell!*' O'Casey's aggressiveness startled the SS major into compliance. 'Major?' continued O'Casey, reverting to English. 'Now, you look like an intelligent man to me. So what do you say to me letting you and your pals there go free?'

'I can arrange to have the gold brought to you, if that's what you want,' Strassmann said hurriedly. 'I feel sure that we can come to some arrangement.'

'Not the gold,' snapped O'Casey, nodding towards Schiller. 'It's him I'm fer wantin'. You and yer pals there can piss off as far as I'm concerned.'

'He's almost dead, for God's sake!' Strassmann played for time. He could feel Schiller's right hand moving steadily around his leather belt towards the open flapped holster at his right hip.

'Major, I don't think you're understanding what I'm sayin',' snapped O'Casey.

'But why?' demanded Strassmann. Schiller's hand reached the gun just as O'Casey's attention was drawn to something in one of the sailor's eyes. Following a well-honed instinct, O'Casey threw himself aside, rolling over on the soft sand. Spinning around, he aimed the sub-machine-gun from a crouched position. Another sailor was just five yards from him, his rifle aimed directly at the Irishman.

'Fire!' screamed Strassmann, just as O'Casey's sub-machine-gun obliterated the echo of his voice. The sailor fell forward. O'Casey fired another short burst, hitting him in the chest and spinning him to one side. O'Casey turned like lightning, rolling backwards over the sand. The first sailor had by now retrieved his Mauser rifle and fired at the Irishman. He missed. The Schmeisser spat again, four bullets ripped into the young German's stomach. The youngster doubled over with the force of the bullets, punched backwards almost a yard before falling face-down on to the ground. O'Casey lay still, awaiting the next move. There was none.

'That's better, girls!' he chuckled coldly. 'Now let's be having no more of your nonsense. This is no way to treat an Irishman and on Irish soil too!' O'Casey rolled over again, drawing his knees into his body and springing back on to his feet. For a man of such giant size and weight, O'Casey could move like a ballet dancer.

'You still haven't told me why you want him,' shouted Strassmann.

'That's between him and me!' growled O'Casey. 'Now, I've already had to kill two more of your boys, Major. Don't push me!'

'I must insist upon the Geneva Convention being adhered to. This is neutral territory after all,' replied Strassmann.

'Geneva Convention? Don't make me laugh! Set him down and get the hell out of here while I'm still in a generous frame of mind.'

Strassmann turned to the left as if to ease the injured man down on to the ground. O'Casey hadn't seen the SS major's gun being slipped from its holster. Two shots rang out in rapid succession. Eamon O'Casey's head jerked, his body convulsed for a moment. He staggered for a second before slowly straightening up again. His white sweater had two spreading dark patches around the area of his chest. Any normal man would have been tossed helplessly on to the ground. The Irishman chuckled. The pain had yet to hit him, and although he was well aware he'd been shot, shock had blocked out any pain.

O'Casey swung the Schmeisser unsteadily in his right hand, snatching at the trigger as he saw Schiller, the smoking Walther P38 pistol still in his hand. O'Casey emptied the magazine, his shots going completely wild as Schiller fired again and again, hitting the Irishman continuously in the chest and stomach. The SS general grinned at his handiwork; the Irishman was dying. Then, unbelievably, O'Casey started forward. He no longer thought of survival, just revenge. Strassmann watched incredulously as O'Casey kept on coming. Schiller fired once more, hitting O'Casey in the left thigh. This time he went down, thudding on to both knees. O'Casey steadied himself with the empty Schmeisser as he struggled to get up again.

The Germans watched, mesmerized, as the Irishman staggered to his feet again, almost doubling over as he took another step forward. He was only a few paces from the SS officers when he tossed the empty Schmeisser aside and pulled out a long curved fish knife from a leather sheath at his side. Schiller went to shoot again, but his gun was also empty, the slide was projected backwards, showing the empty magazine. A smirk appeared on O'Casey's dying lips as he closed the last few feet. In combat Strassmann had witnessed many acts of courage and bravery. He knew the extent to which the human body could persevere, or at least he thought he did until now. He moved backwards, but stumbled, dropping Schiller heavily and landing partly on top of him. The SS general groaned loudly as his adjutant jumped back to his feet, ready to defend himself against the gleaming knife. Another shot echoed round the dunes and O'Casey again dropped to his knees.

Behind him stood the remaining sailor, his face emanating a satisfied pleasure at finishing off the Irishman with a single shot from his Mauser rifle. O'Casey shuddered; his eyes could not hide his utter surprise. With all his remaining strength, he strained to get back on to his feet, but it was useless. His limbs had gone numb and he could no longer feel the handle of the knife in his right hand. His head slumped forward, a shock of red curly hair falling about his eyes. The sailor strutted forward, a new sense of purpose in his manner. Shooting O'Casey had given him an almost sensual feeling of dominance and power. O'Casey leaned forward, supporting his dying body with his left hand outstretched on to the blood-soaked sand beneath him.

'You're hardly worth the price of another bullet, Irish scum!' The young sailor kicked away O'Casey's arm and he fell on to his side, groaning. As the sailor stepped over the Irishman O'Casey swung around, using his bodyweight as a pivot. His almost useless right arm was flung upwards by the momentum of his body. The sharp blade sliced into the sailor's boot, cutting through the leather like melted butter. The youngster yelped like a scolded puppy. O'Casey flopped on to his back, the very last vestige of life seeping from his veins and arteries.

'Bastard!' cried the sailor, firing his rifle into the Irishman's face. The gun recoiled against his shoulder as he snapped back the bolt action and fired again. It took Strassmann to stop him in the end, grabbing him by the wrist.

'Enough!' he ordered.

Elizabeth was relieved to meet up with Martin O'Casey at the bottom of the path. She had been crouching half-way down the cliff path since the shooting restarted. The IRA commandant was overjoyed at seeing her, yet angry she had strayed so far into the mêlée.

'The saints preserve us! Just what the hell are you doing here?'

'I must find Eamon,' she insisted.

'Look, no one has seen him for some time. I've been down on

this blasted beach for ages meself, but in this pea soup, I could have danced with the Devil himself and not known who he was.'

She forced a smile.

'That's better.' He grinned before turning to one of the three men with him. 'The boys here will take you back up the cliff. I'll be seeing you later, and so will Eamon.'

Elizabeth turned to walk off as another of O'Casey's men ran out of the mist from the direction of the shore and spoke to O'Casey in hurried Gaelic. Elizabeth turned again in reaction to the man's obvious panic. O'Casey's face answered her worst fears.

'It's Eamon! Isn't it?' Her voice quivered in the cold night air, O'Casey senior closed his eyes and then beckoned the man to show him the way. As she moved to follow him, the men tried in vain to hold her back, but they were not fast enough. Elizabeth ran on through the fog, desperately trying to keep up with the two men. It did not take long for them to stumble on the scene. The first sight to meet her was the body of a German sailor, lying face-up in the sand. It took her a moment to realize that he had been the one she had saved at the farmhouse. Her attention was drawn to where Martin O'Casey and the other IRA man had stooped over one of two more bodies lying some yards away from the sand dune. Elizabeth began walking forward, a tight knot gripping her stomach as she tried to blot out the dawning horror. There, no more than ten paces away, lay Eamon, cradled in his father's arms. She rushed forward, but O'Casey's man barred her path.

'Let me past! Let me go, damn you!' she yelled.

'Let her be,' whispered O'Casey senior. The man stood aside and allowed her to pass.

She threw herself down beside Eamon. The bullets had almost obliterated his face beyond recognition. His nose had been smashed. A gaping hole now replaced his right eye. The cranium had erupted and his head was now a misshapen mess. A trickle of yellow mucus intermingled with a pool of bright red blood, oozing from between his shattered teeth.

Elizabeth turned away and began to retch until there seemed to be nothing left inside her. When she finally regained her composure and turned around, Eamon's upper half was covered by Martin O'Casey's coat. The other IRA man was already reciting the rosary as he was joined by several more of his comrades, one nursing a bleeding shoulder.

She looked over towards Martin O'Casey. He was sitting several yards away on a low rock, his head cupped forward in his hands.

Elizabeth touched Eamon's hand. It was already cold. She stood still for a moment before going over to Martin. Beyond the intermittent crashing of the waves, they could hear the submarine's diesel engines roaring and then gradually fading away.

'Hear that?' he said absently. 'They're going now.' He looked up, his eyes red and wet. 'They've taken everything and now they're gone.' The despair in his tone was pitiful.

'Let them go. They can do no more,' she replied, staring out into the fog. 'Some day they will have to answer before God!' The pain in her chest made her feel as though her heart was cracking apart.

'Elizabeth, listen to me very carefully.' Martin O'Casey spoke softly, touching her hand. 'You must leave here at once and try and forget what you have seen and what has happened.'

She shook her head. He stood up, leading her away from Eamon's body and out of earshot of his men.

'You must,' he insisted. 'There is much you do not understand and I have no time to enlighten you. Life is a fragile thing, and God knows you've learned that lesson tonight, but you have now got to put it all behind you. You must live. It's what he would have wished, you know that.'

'But how?' she whispered.

'I have an idea, but first we must get you back to the farmhouse.' He guided her towards the cliff path again. She tried to resist and go back to Eamon, but he stopped her. 'Let the dead be. It's for you now. Don't look back.'

'But it seems I've been looking back all my life,' she replied despondently. Martin O'Casey watched Elizabeth struggle for words. 'I . . . I don't know anyone. Everyone is dead.' She looked at him blankly. Martin O'Casey was concerned. She was not handling the loss naturally; it was as though there was a blockage inside her.

'Come, let me get you to the farmhouse first,' he insisted.

'First? And then what?' She frowned.

'We bury the dead,' he replied softly.

She looked back towards the sand dunes. 'What about Eamon? Where is he to be buried?' She could hardly bear to ask.

'We called him Finn MacCool, did you know that?' He forced a smile. 'It's the name of a legendary Irish giant who's supposed to lie in an unmarked grave somewhere. That was the way we buried our warriors in the past.'

'And now also,' she replied softly, looking back at Eamon's body still being prayed over by one of O'Casey's lieutenants.

'It must be. And no one must know where.' The words hurt, but he had to be brave enough for both of them, 'Otherwise, too many questions would be asked.'

Back at the farmhouse they were met by another of Martin O'Casey's men, who took the IRA leader aside and spoke to him in hushed tones. Elizabeth stood watching the burning embers of the outbuildings and the smouldering wreck of the aircraft. She wanted to die. Martin O'Casey came back to her side again.

'I hear they left something behind.' He nodded towards the farmhouse.

'The baby!' exclaimed Elizabeth, suddenly consumed by a fear for the child's safety. Martin O'Casey recognized her concern.

'It's all right. The wee nipper's not harmed, but he's balling his head off right now,' he assured her, guiding her towards the house.

Inside, the parlour was as she had left it. The fire now had gone out, its steady glow replaced by the rising sun's rays angling through the window. As she crossed the stone floor, she could hear the baby crying in the bedroom above. She became aware that Martin O'Casey was staring at her.

'Before you ask, I can't,' she insisted.

'If he stays here, he's as good as dead.'

'I can't, I tell you!' she cried, covering her ears with both hands as she tried to blot out the baby's cries.

Martin O'Casey went over to her, removing her hands. He smiled at her, comfortingly. 'Well, at least be fixing me something to feed him with.'

'There's a bag somewhere.' She looked around her, her head jerking nervously. Then she spotted it, the nurse's canvas shoulderbag, lying just inside the doorway to the kitchen. As she reluctantly lifted it up, she couldn't avoid looking over at the nurse's body, now lying beside that of the SS soldier. Two flies were crawling over her face, one playing with her open lips.

Elizabeth felt ill. She rushed outside, leaning over the garden wall as she retched again. On the other side of the wall, a string of men were still hurriedly passing slopping water-buckets to the barn. They were fighting a losing battle, for already the old timber rafters had crumbled down into the burning interior. Not understanding why, Elizabeth found herself racing out into the open field until suddenly she was aware of standing amidst the strewn wreckage of the aircraft. She walked on a little farther, towards the smouldering aircraft, taking her time, trying desperately to decide what she was going to do. But suicide was not the answer she sought.

She stopped as her foot hit something. Elizabeth looked down. Her toe had collided with a small battered black-metal box. She turned it over with the toe of her shoe. It was charred all along one side and badly misshapen and dented. She almost kicked it aside until she noticed the charred remnants of a briefcase lying beside it, a broken handcuff still attached to the twisted leather handle. Elizabeth flipped the briefcase over with her foot. Suddenly she felt ill again. She was staring down at the silver-embossed German eagle and swastika. She booted the case away, sending it into the air and scattering its charred paper contents over the scorched grass.

She was just about to do the same with the metal box when suddenly something within urged her to pick it up. As she did so, the lid fell open and the red-velvet-wrapped bundle dropped the short distance to the ground. She studied the box; its velvet-lined interior was empty. She stooped to pick up the bundle at her feet, unwrapping it warily. Elizabeth was completely dumbfounded by the sight of 'The Three Brothers', its rubies, diamonds and pearls glistening in the morning light. She stood, mesmerized, as the wind began to whip up the strewn papers and blow them directly into the burning aircraft wreckage. As she knelt, unknowingly staring at her father's jewels, the pages of Adolf Hitler's will and testament went up in flames. Suddenly she was aware of a coldness about her. She quickly covered up the jewelled setting again and returned it to the battered box. As she walked back to the farmhouse, there was renewed purpose in her step. Something had changed. She wouldn't understand for some time to come, but a metamorphosis had occurred.

Stepping inside the farmhouse, she realized that the baby had stopped crying. Her fear returning, she rushed to the staircase, almost stumbling as she skipped up to the bedroom. She stopped at the door, half expecting to see the SS man she had stabbed still lying on the floor. Much to her surprise and relief, all that remained were some bloodstains on a mat and scuffmarks where someone had dragged the body from the room. She looked over towards the bed, a little taken aback with the evidence of her eyes. Martin O'Casey was sitting there, feeding the child from a bottle. He smiled upon seeing her.

'I got it from the nurse's bag. The water was still warm in the kettle above the fire.'

'It should be boiled,' she said, wiping away a tear and smudging her face in the process.

'I imagine it was at one time,' he replied whimsically.

The baby struggled and coughed a little. Then he brought up some of the milk on to Martin O'Casey's shirt. 'Damn,' he grumbled. 'I wonder who he is?'

'He's German, that's enough for me,' Elizabeth sneered.

'He can't be more than a few weeks old by the look of it,' he mused. 'Funny that Eamon didn't mention him . . .' He stopped talking, the pain of uttering his lost son's name too much to bear.

'Let me take him.' Elizabeth surprised herself with the suggestion, setting the charred metal box on the dressing table as Martin O'Casey gratefully handed over the baby.

'In case you're wonderin', I took the soldier's body outside with the others.' Elizabeth did not reply. He ran his fingers over the battered box. 'What have we here then, a souvenir?'

'Open it and see for yourself,' she replied, wiping the child's mouth with a clean handkerchief, before resuming its feeding.

He flicked open the burst lid and drew back the velvet cloth, revealing 'The Three Brothers'. 'Holy Mary!' he cried. 'What's this?'

'I found them. Close to the aircraft. They seemed to have fallen from a briefcase one of the Germans was carrying.'

'They'll have belonged to that bastard Schiller then.' He took the jewels over to the low window, to get a clearer view of them. 'He was the only one carrying a briefcase.' He nodded approvingly as he studied the jewels. 'These are old, antique.'

'Throw them away,' she insisted.

'What!' He looked astounded.

'Don't soil your hands on anything those Nazis had.'

'And where do you think they got them from, eh?' He nodded. 'Go on now, ask yerself that one.' There was silence. 'Well, I'll tell you then, shall I? They bloody looted the stuff. Stole it themselves. Just the way they've stolen Eamon's life away from us.' There was pain in his voice and he turned away, concealing his anguish from the woman. He sniffed back the tears as he changed the subject. 'Now, what was it you were sayin' about a briefcase? Any papers in it? Money, bonds, that sort of thing?'

'I think so. They blew away when I kicked it.'

'Ya kicked it?' He turned to her, laughing. 'Ya kicked it?' he repeated.

'Yes,' she replied slowly. 'I think the papers blew into the fire.'

'The fire, ya say! You realize you probably burned the only existing access papers to some bloody Swiss bank accounts!' Martin

O'Casey began to roar with laughter. He couldn't explain why, but it felt good.

Elizabeth spent the next few hours alone, nursing the child back to sleep and packing her things together. She tried not to think of the baby in personal terms. He was German after all, probably Schiller's own son by the look of it, yet every time she thought of the nurse's last words, she knew she was wrong. After she got the baby settled back to sleep, she finished packing her small leather suitcase before slipping outside for some fresh air. The fog had lifted and the sun was splitting the trees again. Over by the barn stood Martin O'Casey's main lieutenant, Pat McManus. The man stared back at her blandly. As she walked down to the garden gate, she could feel his eyes burning into the back of her head.

Without hesitating, she headed down the path a slight way towards the cliffs again. The wind had picked up, bringing a chill with it. She shivered, drawing up the shawl across both shoulders as she took in the same view she had shared only hours earlier with the man she had loved. The fragrance of the plants and the smell of the grass covered in a blanket of morning dew filled her mind with a sensuality she had almost forgotten. She closed her eyes once again, reflecting back to moments of ecstasy, filling her heart with expectations of pleasure and excitement. Suddenly she felt quite sick. Eamon was gone for ever, along with that part of her life.

'There you are.'

Elizabeth was startled by the voice. She turned hesitantly to see Martin O'Casey coming up to her.

'It's over,' continued O'Casey. 'He's been put to rest with our other dead.'

'May I see where?' She shivered.

It had been against his better judgement to allow her to know, yet she had the right. No one could deny her that. 'Of course you can.' He gently guided her back down the steep path and on to the beach and past the sand dunes, walking slowly towards a small risen area, set back against the cliff face. Helping her up on to the grass bank, Martin O'Casey indicated a section close to the cliff face. The grass sods had been replaced carefully so that they would grow back and re-form quickly.

'We'll put some rocks on top just to make sure. It'll look like a rockfall from the cliff above. No one will ever know.'

She knelt down, running her fingers into the broken sandy soil. 'How many are here with Eamon?'

Martin O'Casey paused. She could hear the tremor in his voice as he continued. 'Seven of my men, including Eamon.'

Elizabeth looked up on hearing the fishing boat's engine. A small trawler was just coming around the head into the bay.

'Don't worry. They're on our side. I had most of the German bodies weighted down and dumped out at sea. A cable-length from shore, as those Protestant Freemasons say, and a wee bit more for good measure.'

Elizabeth started to pray just as five of O'Casey's men strolled down the path, past them, guns slung loosely across their shoulders. Martin O'Casey went over to the leading man and spoke to him briefly. The men went over to the bottom of the cliff face and began collecting the smaller rocks.

'It's time,' Martin O'Casey said, gently touching her shoulder. Elizabeth paused for a final moment before standing up.

By the time they returned to the farmhouse the car had arrived. Elizabeth went inside the house, whilst Martin O'Casey spoke to the driver. After a couple of minutes he followed her inside, finding her standing in the parlour.

'Got everything together, have you?' He walked forward and set the battered metal box on the table next to her baggage.

'I think so,' she replied nervously. 'But I'm not taking that.'

'Then I'll take it.' He placed his hands on her shoulders and smiled. 'You're the bravest colleen in the world.'

'And the loneliest.'

He pretended to ignore the remark and went over to the armchair, where Elizabeth had set the sleeping child. 'He's still asleep,' he said softly.

'You must understand that under no circumstances will I be keeping the child,' she said adamantly.

'As you wish.' He went back to her, kissing her on the forehead.

'I mean it, Martin. I couldn't handle that.'

'Don't worry. Everything will be taken care of, I promise.' He lifted her baggage from the table. 'Now let's be getting you away from here while you still can.'

'I don't understand.' She halted him.

'I told you earlier that there was things you didn't understand.

107

You're not one of us and to some losing Eamon won't mean too much. It doesn't give you immunity.' He could see she was about to explode and raised his hands in protest. 'You're a security risk. Didn't I take you from under the noses of British Intelligence and slip you out of England?'

'You would harm me? The IRA?' She frowned.

'Not me, but there are those that might.' He sensed something in her face and turned about. Pat McManus, his IRA lieutenant, was standing at the open doorway. From his smug look he'd heard everything. Martin O'Casey glanced down at the captured machine-gun slung over his right shoulder. McManus's fingers were ominously close to the trigger. 'Yes, Pat, what is it?' he said coldly.

'The boys were wonderin' what to do with the weapons we collected,' McManus said drily, staring curiously at the metal box on the table.

'Is that a fact, now,' snapped Martin O'Casey, boldly thrusting both hands on his hips. 'And what would you be doing with them, Pat?'

'I'd load them in the lorry and take 'em to Mullan's public house in Castlemaine,' McManus said reluctantly.

'There you are now,' nodded Martin O'Casey. 'Didn't it only take a genius like meself to be dragging that out of you?'

McManus hovered for a moment, then stormed outside, slamming shut the half-door and shaking the doorframe.

Martin O'Casey turned back to Elizabeth. 'Now that one's worth a watching,' he said. 'I'm not saying it's fer sure, but I'd feel a lot safer if I got you outa here. I've some friends in Cork. I'll tell you about it when we get there.'

The black Morris saloon was waiting just outside the farmhouse, with Liam Adams behind the steering wheel. Martin O'Casey didn't waste a moment in loading the baggage and ushering Elizabeth and the baby outside. As Elizabeth eased herself into the rear seat she looked out to her right. Pat McManus was standing at the gable of the farmhouse, watching. For the second time in as many hours her stomach churned. Martin O'Casey casually walked from the house and climbed in beside Liam Adams.

'All right, Liam. Take her easy, no rushing, mind.' She watched him open the glove compartment and remove the revolver. He glanced back at her. 'A little insurance,' he added reassuringly.

The car moved off past McManus, who was then joined by several others. The Irishmen watched in silence as their commandant drove off. McManus couldn't help but smile as the car disappeared from sight over the slight hump in the road.

'We should have stopped them,' growled one of the men standing beside him.

'He'll keep,' McManus said ominously.

'Auld Marty's just signed his own death warrant,' added the other man.

'An' he knows it too,' replied McManus. 'He knows all right.'

CORK
Later the same day

THEY ARRIVED in Cork that afternoon. Elizabeth found no comfort in the sights around her. The place appeared cold and grey. She was close to exhaustion, both physical and mental. Fortunately, the child slept for most of the journey, giving Elizabeth the opportunity at least to rest a little.

The house was on the northern side of the town, in a tree-lined avenue next to some open parkland. The car drew up outside the large Victorian terraced house. A round-faced and heavily built woman in her late thirties answered the door. Clearly she had been expecting them, for she went straight down the steps to the pavement and opened the rear door of the car. Her face lit up on seeing the sleeping baby in Elizabeth's arms.

'Here, let me take the wee lamb for you.' Smiling, she extended her arms towards Elizabeth.

'Thank you,' replied Elizabeth. 'It's been a long journey.'

'And undoubtedly a bumpy one,' remarked the woman, taking care not to disturb the sleeping baby. 'By the way, my name's Mary.'

'Elizabeth O'Casey.'

'And what do we call you then?' The woman cuddled the baby as she stood on the pavement.

Elizabeth didn't know what to say.

'Never mind that now, just get them inside,' snapped Martin O'Casey, taking the baggage from the boot.

The woman ascended the steps back into the house, carrying the baby. Elizabeth looked up at the mid-terrace house, uncertain of whether or not to follow.

'Come on, there's sure to be tea in the pot,' smiled Martin O'Casey.

Elizabeth stood for a few moments, paralysed by trepidation and sadness. As she forced herself to go up the steps, Martin O'Casey leaned into the car and lifted a small brown leather case from the back seat. 'I'll be staying here tonight. When you get clear of here, dump the car where it won't be found,' he said, flicking open the glove compartment and slipping the Walther pistol inside his coat. He grinned at his long-standing bodyguard and driver.

'I'll be waiting at the boarding house,' replied Liam Adams.

Martin O'Casey nodded back. 'I'm not a hundred per cent sure about this place. McManus and the boys may know about it. They just might put two and two together. See if we can get the use of the old cottage over in Churchtown. They don't know about that place.' Liam Adams nodded back as he was handed a thick envelope. 'Four hundred quid. Pick up another car – fast but nothing flashy, mind.'

'Right, boss,' replied Adams.

As he was about to close the door, Martin O'Casey added another instruction. 'When you're at the boarding house, slip down to the docks and check up on the sailing schedule for America.'

After settling the baby down in the parlour room, the smiling lady prepared a light meal for her weary visitors. Over tea in the kitchen, the woman and Martin O'Casey conducted a limited and stilted conversation. Elizabeth was unsure whether her presence was inhibiting them or there was another meaning behind their reserve. The woman had introduced herself as Mary O'Dwyer, a schoolteacher by profession, married without children to a doctor at the local hospital. Both she and her husband, Sean, were staunch Republican activists and had been involved with the IRA for many years, but they were also personal friends of Martin O'Casey and the old IRA leader appeared to be banking on their friendship coming before organizational loyalty. From Mary O'Dwyer's tone, it was also evident that she was already aware of what had occurred at Dingle Bay.

When the baby started to get restless in the next room, Elizabeth excused herself, glad to be away from the stifling atmosphere pervading the conversation in the kitchen. Through the open door she inadvertently listened to the others' hushed tones. Several times she was certain she could hear Eamon's name being mentioned; at one stage Mary O'Dwyer was reduced to crying. Elizabeth sat nursing the baby on her lap. She was devoid of feeling. She no longer possessed the energy to cry; nothing mattered any more. Several times Martin O'Casey peered inside the parlour, to where Elizabeth sat expressionless on the *chaise-longue*. Her demeanour frightened him. She was withdrawing into herself more and more every minute.

'I don't like the way she's behaving,' he whispered to Mary O'Dwyer.

'She's been through hell, from what you've been saying,' replied the woman. 'When did she start becoming so unresponsive?'

'On the way here.' He stubbed out the cigarette on the saucer of his empty teacup.

'She looks as if she could do with a rest, poor child. I'll show her up to a bedroom.'

Martin O'Casey took his turn at looking after the child while Mary O'Dwyer showed Elizabeth up to the second floor. When she returned downstairs half an hour later, the grave look on her face alerted him instantly.

'What is it?' He stood up.

'Sean will confirm it of course, when he returns from the hospital. I've telephoned him.' She closed the kitchen door. 'Martin, I'd say she's having some sort of breakdown.'

'What do you mean, breakdown?'

'She didn't respond to anything I said. I undressed her and put her to bed. She never said a single thing to me. She just lies there, staring up at the ceiling. It's not a good sign.' Mary O'Dwyer shook her head. 'I think you'd better be telling me what happened before Sean gets here.'

Sean O'Dwyer arrived within fifteen minutes from the cottage hospital. He followed his wife straight up to Elizabeth's room. Mary O'Dwyer returned downstairs several minutes later, taking the baby and its carrycot back upstairs with her. Martin O'Casey went into the front drawing room. From memory he knew where the whisky was kept. Cursing O'Dwyer's preference for foreign brews, he removed the bottle from the walnut sideboard, taking one of the crystal glasses from beside the empty decanter and filled it almost to the brim. He was on his second glass when Sean O'Dwyer came into the room. He was a small, weak-looking man in his late fifties, almost twenty years his wife's senior. His jet-black hair was clearly dyed, with its neat waves cemented by the copious application of hair cream. The little doctor had a stern look about him as he peered over the rim of his gold spectacles. There was no welcome for his old friend. Instead he went over to the bay window and examined the street outside from behind the lace curtains. It was starting to get dark.

'I'm sorry about Eamon.' O'Dwyer kept his eyes on the street. 'He was a fine man and a good son.'

While he could hear the words, the platitude meant nothing to Martin O'Casey. 'Get to the point, Sean,' he sighed.

'Just what have you brought down upon this house?' O'Dwyer said angrily, twirling around to confront his uninvited guest.

'Now, that's a fine way to say hello to an old comrade.' Martin O'Casey took a further sip from the glass.

'The word's out on you, Martin,' O'Dwyer cautioned.

'I'll straighten it all out with Dublin tomorrow.' Martin O'Casey waved his half-empty glass dismissively.

'Tomorrow might be too late!' O'Dwyer raised his voice angrily.

'How is she?' Martin O'Casey changed the subject.

'She needs rest. A great deal of rest,' replied O'Dwyer. 'And she should be in hospital.'

'Out of the question.'

The door opened and Mary O'Dwyer popped her head inside. 'Shall I make us all some tea?' she asked cautiously.

'Martin won't be staying that long,' snapped her husband, glowering over the rim of his spectacles. Without a word, she was gone again, quietly closing the door behind her. 'I hear you didn't get the gold either,' continued O'Dwyer.

'News travels fast.' Martin O'Casey eyed his old friend with suspicion.

'Pat McManus rang me at the hospital,' replied O'Dwyer. 'He wanted me to tell him if you got in touch.'

'And have you?' Martin O'Casey's eyes narrowed.

'Don't be ridiculous. You are my friend, God help me.' He was clearly affronted.

'I'm sorry, Sean. I didn't mean it the way it sounded.'

'Why the hell did you leave Dingle Bay the way you did? McManus says you ran out on him and the boys.'

'I had to get the girl and the child out of there,' he insisted.

O'Dwyer shook his head. 'Maybe it's you I should be examining instead.'

'I'm not crazy, just tired.' Martin O'Casey rubbed his eyes.

'You look exhausted.' O'Dwyer's anger abated; he could see his old friend was close to collapse.

Martin O'Casey nodded. 'If you can put me up tonight I'd appreciate it.

'No sooner said,' O'Dwyer capitulated with reluctance. 'How the hell did it happen?'

'Eamon said he had a score to settle with one of the Germans he brought ashore. A bastard called Schiller, an SS general no less.' He took another drink to numb his anguish.

'So you're telling me that Eamon started all this?' O'Dwyer turned on him again.

'I'm saying nothing – ' Martin O'Casey eased back in the armchair, staring up at the ceiling through bleary eyes – 'except that Eamon set up the operation. Without him we wouldn't have had anything.'

'Martin, I don't want to sound too cynical, but we *don't* have anything. You lost the gold and Dublin was counting on it.' O'Dwyer moved over in front of him again. 'I may tell you, Martin, that the army council is damned angry at what happened. I rang Dublin after McManus had been on to me. Naturally very little was said over the telephone, but sufficient for me to understand that heads will roll on this one.'

'Sean, I couldn't give a shit.' He sighed.

'Listen to me. If Eamon was acting on his own and out of order, they can't place the blame on you. But you've got to tell them that. You have to convince Dublin. It's clear to me that McManus is using this disaster to his own advantage. With you out of the way, he has a clear run for the summit. And his sort don't moralize.'

'Indiscriminate bombing? Women and children as legitimate targets? You don't have to remind me, Sean. These youngsters don't see it the way we do.' He gulped down the remaining Scotch, wiping his lips with his hand.

'That's why you've got to explain it to Dublin yourself.'

'I knew Eamon was going to try something.'

'I didn't hear that,' he rebuked him.

'Eamon had his reasons.' Martin O'Casey stared back at him. 'But he didn't tell me why. He didn't have to. If Eamon had to do something, it was not without purpose.'

'Has this anything to do with the girl?' persisted O'Dwyer.

'What are you driving at?' Martin O'Casey was becoming annoyed now.

'I've examined her, remember. The baby isn't hers.'

'The baby would have died if it had stayed at Dingle Bay. It made sense that me daughter-in-law took the child with her. There's nothin' more to it than that!'

'But why did Elizabeth have to be there in the first place? You took a terrible risk getting her out of England like that.'

'Eamon wanted her to be there when he arrived. It was something that we had agreed on months ago. At the time he didn't know for certain if he'd even get himself out of Germany alive. But he wanted his wife to be there if he did. Sure he even had me arrange entry papers for them to get into the United States.'

'And that's another thing,' retorted O'Dwyer. 'What gave Eamon the right to decide to flit to America? He pledged himself under the tricolour to take orders just the same as you and me.'

'Hell's gates!' Martin O'Casey was on his feet. 'My son is dead! He gave his life to this organization. He gave more than any of those shuck warblers in Dublin!'

'Take it easy, Martin. I'm on your side.' O'Dwyer went over to the large sideboard and poured him another whisky. Martin O'Casey downed it in a single gulp.

'What about the girl? She looks awful sick to me,' he continued, extending his glass for yet another refill.

'She is suffering from a psychosis. Nothing organic. Obviously caused by the shock of what she's gone through.'

'What can be done?' he asked.

'She needs immediate treatment, admission to a hospital,' said O'Dwyer.

'Impossible! You know what we're involved in here. We can't afford to admit anyone to a hospital. It would be the first place they'd check.'

'Martin, I don't think you realize the potential seriousness of the girl's condition. She can't be moved from pillar to post. There's every possibility that when she comes round, she'll be suffering from traumatic neurosis, reliving over and over again the terrible experience she has locked up inside herself. She needs medical attention and, above all else, rest. I'll concede to keeping her here, but I can't give you any guarantees about how long recovery will take, or for that matter even if there will be a full recovery. Realistically I'd be a lot happier with her in hospital.'

'No.' Martin O'Casey was resolute.

'Very well.' He shrugged his shoulders. 'Mary can look after her and the child here at the house and I'll be near at hand if she needs me.'

'I'll be staying near by meself in case you've need of me.'

'Where?' asked the doctor.

'Better you don't know. But I'll keep in touch.'

'If that's the way you want it.' O'Dwyer returned to the bay window. Everything was quiet outside.

'How long could it take her to get fit enough to travel?' Martin O'Casey asked guardedly.

'How long's a bit of rope? Look, Martin, she could be ready to go in a few weeks. But it might be more.'

'Christ!' Martin O'Casey was exasperated.

O'Dwyer turned away from the window, his face grim. 'But even so, she'll undoubtedly need further treatment and a great deal of rest. She's clearly been through hell.'

'We've all been through hell.' Martin O'Casey was unequivocal.

THE TYPE-XXI U-BOAT
24 May 1945

THE SCREAMING was driving Strassmann out of his head. He had listened to the constant rambling and cries for the last four hours. Schiller's condition had deteriorated. A fever was now ravaging his body and despite all the medical treatment Petersen could muster, the arm wound was beginning to fester and swell. The left hand was swollen to twice its size and had turned almost black. Strassmann burst into the cabin banging the plywood door against the bottom of the bunk. Schiller lay in semi-consciousness, his head swathed in bandages, covering one side of his face. Petersen and his first officer, Erich Kordt, looked up in mutual alarm as Strassmann glowered at them both.

'Can anyone do something for this brave son of the Reich?' he yelled.

'We have done everything, Herr Sturmbannführer,' Kordt stood erect. 'The burns are bad enough, but we can do nothing more with the shrapnel wounds to his arm.'

'Let me see!' insisted Strassmann, pulling back the blanket. The open wounds had been disinfected and loosely bandaged with wads of padding to stem the flow of blood, but it hadn't been enough. The discoloration in the hand was plain enough to see. Schiller started moving his head from side to side.

'Something must be done, otherwise he will die,' insisted Petersen.

'But what?' Strassmann shook his head.

'The arm will have to come off,' said Petersen firmly.

'Amputation! Here? In this stinking tin can!' Strassmann was appalled at the very idea.

'It is the only solution,' urged Kordt. 'Otherwise the poison will

115

spread throughout his system. You can see for yourself that his temperature is running close to fever point.'

'But how? What facilities do you have here?' Strassmann remained unconvinced.

'It can be done. I am only repeating what young Mohr said earlier, Herr Sturmbannführer,' interrupted Petersen.

'And just who the hell is Mohr?' demanded Strassmann.

'Our hydrophone and radio operator.'

'So what does he know?' The SS major replaced the blanket.

'Mohr was a medical student, before joining the Kriegsmarine. His father is an eminent surgeon,' replied the captain.

Strassmann thought for a moment. There was little option. 'Get him in here. Then see me in the ward room.'

Less than five minutes later Mohr was shown into the ward room by Petersen. The SS officer studied the youngster; he looked no more than sixteen. 'Well, Herr Doktor, what is your prognosis?' Strassmann asked sarcastically.

'Herr Sturmbannführer, the arm will have to come off,' replied the young sailor. 'The infection from the shrapnel wound is spreading rapidly and the blood supply to the hand has been restricted for too long. The hand is useless, *mein Herr*.'

'But can you do it?' The SS officer narrowed his eyes.

Mohr looked up at Petersen before venturing to answer. 'I think so. I have never done anything like this before, but my father is chief surgeon at a Hamburg hospital. I have seen similar operations before.'

'If you go ahead, what chance of survival does Gruppenführer Schiller have?' Petersen interjected.

'There are two dangers, Herr Kapitän. First is the continued infection to the rest of his arm and ultimately to the chest; it may already be too late to amputate. The second danger is the shock of such an operation. The trauma could kill him,' Mohr answered nervously.

'What surgical equipment do you have on board?' Strassmann addressed the captain.

'All our morphine is gone. We do have disinfectants and ointments and some mild drugs which could hopefully reduce the infection. The operation would be without anaesthesia.'

'Monstrous!'

'What do you think my predecessors did in cases of such injury?' Petersen looked at Mohr. 'It was the captain's duty or that of the first mate to carry out amputations. I am fortunate in having young Mohr on board.' He smiled at the youngster.

'You were a medical student; for how long did you train?' asked the SS officer.

'A year, *mein Herr*.'

Strassmann shook his head. 'What equipment do you have?'

'We have some scalpels in the medical kit. I have already been down to the galley, I can sterilize one of the cook's hacksaws and some of his butcher's knives,' replied Mohr.

'Do it. *Schnell!*'

Mohr moved his patient next to the galley, clearing out some space in the crew's living quarters. He needed a constant supply of boiling water, but most of all, several of the larger butchery knives would have to be heated over the gas flame until red hot. The only safe way to end the operation was to cauterize the stump, sealing the blood vessels and reducing the prospect of further infection. He had watched his father perform similar operations. Now he was regretful at not having paid more attention, but one thing he was certain of, the cutting and severing of the limb had to be completed as fast as was humanly possible, with the wound cauterized instantly.

Schiller, meantime, had stirred slightly from his feverish ramblings after being moved on to the makeshift operating table consisting of two tables pushed together in the middle of the crew quarters. He was also asking some awkward questions about his condition. Petersen was by now in the control room steadying the vessel at periscope depth while Kordt stayed with Mohr, helping to prepare for the operation. Strassmann had insisted on being present, asking Mohr if it would be possible to link himself up to Schiller for a blood transfusion, knowing himself to be of the same 'O' positive blood group. His offer had been flatly rejected as being too impractical, they didn't have the equipment to rig up a transfusion. Instead he remained at Schiller's side, plying him with schnapps.

'What is happening?' asked Schiller, barely able to muster a whisper.

'Herr Gruppenführer.' Strassmann looked over at Mohr standing at the galley door. He was busy giving instructions to the cook regarding the heating of the knives. 'You are very ill.'

'Karl?' Schiller raised his head off the table. 'The child? Where is he?'

'Killed, *mein Herr*, along with his nurse.'

'*Nein!*' Schiller shook his head. 'It cannot be. It cannot.'

'I saw the evidence myself at the farmhouse.'

'*Nein!*'

'*Mein Herr*, you must think of the present, not the past.'

117

'What about the other U-boat?' Schiller frowned.

'We were in radio contact with U-769 yesterday. They are on course and everything is normal. We estimate their arrival will be within five days of our own.'

'Do the crew yet know about our destination?'

'Only Kapitänleutnant Petersen and his first officer know the details.'

'That is good.' Schiller raised his head off the table, just enough to catch a glimpse of the cook heating several knives over a gas light. 'Karl, how bad are my injuries?' Strassmann didn't reply. 'Tell me!'

'The arm has to come off,' said Strassmann grimly. 'At the elbow.'

Schiller took another sip of the schnapps, coughing as the burning liquid entered his throat. 'And my face, what of my eye?'

'We will not know for certain until you have been seen by an optometrist.'

'Where . . . are we?' he asked.

'Well into the Atlantic, *mein Herr*. Almost out of range of enemy reconnaissance aircraft.'

'Are we surfaced?'

'We are about to, just before . . .' Strassmann paused, looking down at the floor.

'Before you cut off my arm, Karl,' Schiller finished the sentence for him.

'There is no anaesthetic, *mein Herr*.'

'Then I shall experience something of those operations our SS doctors were performing in Auschwitz.' Schiller chuckled coldly. 'If the Jewish scum can tolerate it, so can I.' His body went into spasm as a wave of pain hit him.

In the control room, Petersen studied the weather conditions. A heavy sea fog was blowing up from the south-east. He directed the vessel straight into it, finally giving the order to surface and cut engines. He was first up on to the bridge. The fog was dense, with any luck they could sail past an enemy vessel at one hundred yards and still remain undetected. For the next few minutes he listened to the sound of the pumps extracting the remaining sea water from the ballast tanks. The sea was like plate glass, with barely a ripple, visibility so poor that he could barely see the stern of his own U-boat.

'You could lose yourself in this,' whispered Kordt.

'Just what the doctor ordered,' said Petersen wryly.

Below deck, fresh air vented through the U-boat's interior, much to the relief of the entire crew. In the cramped crew quarters Mohr made his final preparations. Schiller looked up at the young sailor, his shirt sleeves rolled up high over both elbows, his hands and arms discoloured by the brown iodine. Mohr removed the covering sheet; his patient had already been stripped naked except for his bandages. Schiller's left arm, still swathed in the heavy green and brown field dressings, was now extended over one side of the table, hanging ungainly, blackened fingers pointing towards the deck.

Strassmann looked across to the young sailor. Mohr nodded, everything was now ready. Without a word spoken he began cutting away the bandages, dropping them into the metal bucket on the floor.

'This will be interesting, if nothing else, eh, Karl?' said Schiller jokingly. Strassmann couldn't reply.

Mohr shook his head. The smell rising from the rancid flesh made him nauseous. He continued working as fast as he could. Schiller gritted his teeth, every part of his body seemed to ache. The burned tissue on the left side of his face and neck felt as if it was bubbling underneath the dressing. Strassmann pinched his nostrils, blocking out the stench as Mohr began covering the upper arm in iodine, extending up to Schiller's armpit. Then he gave the nod to Strassmann and the cook. The two men began tightening the leather belts around the patient, securing his legs, torso and uninjured arm. Schiller groaned as the straps tightened.

'Herr Gruppenführer, can you hear me?' asked Mohr. 'This will take only a few seconds, no more than a minute and it will be over.' He went to set a piece of leather between Schiller's teeth. 'Bite on this.'

'Nein! *Schnell! Schnell!*' insisted Schiller, swallowing deeply as Mohr fixed yet another leather belt loosely around the upper part of his left arm before tightening a further strap around the wrist, securing the arm to the table leg underneath. Strassmann came to his side, taking his cue from the young sailor. He quickly ran a metal cleaning rod under the loose belt and started twisting it around, tightening the belt into a tourniquet. The leather began to twist like a corkscrew, cutting deeply into the flesh. Schiller flexed his swollen hand for the last time and let out an almighty yell.

'Aaaah!' he cried, then screaming aloud, 'The future belongs to us!'

His voice echoed around the U-boat as Mohr began. He quickly ringed the skin just an inch below the elbow joint with one of the scalpels, cutting in as neatly and deeply as he could in one go.

'*Nein!*' Schiller screamed anew, gripping on to the side of the table with his other hand. His body rose up from the metal tables, arching into the leather securing straps. The cook threw the full weight of his body across him to keep him down on the table. Full of nerves, Mohr dropped the scalpel.

'*Dummkopf!*' rebuked Strassmann. 'Hurry, damn you!'

Mohr quickly snatched up another scalpel from the tray beside him. The arm was now bleeding profusely despite the tourniquet.

'Apply it tighter, he's losing too much blood!' urged Mohr, trying to retrace his previous cut. 'Get ready,' he said to the cook. The man rushed off into the galley, leaving Strassmann to control the patient. The SS major twisted the belt with all his might, bending the cleaning rod in the process. Schiller ground his teeth together, pulling further at his bonds.

'I can't hold him down!' cried Strassmann. At that moment Kordt arrived and immediately gave assistance by throwing his weight across Schiller's torso.

Mohr then cut the skin in a single stroke, running upwards from the main cut, revealing a clean opening directly down on to the joint of the bone. 'Now!' he called out. On his instruction Strassmann grabbed hold of the injured arm by the wrist, pulling with all his might, flexing the arm to full extension.

'Aaargh!' cried Schiller, the very veins on his head seeming ready to burst.

'The knife!' shouted Mohr.

The cook came out of the galley with a glowing red-hot butcher's knife held by a pair of vice grips.

Mohr quickly grabbed the hacksaw from the instrument tray beside him and gripping the arm just below the joint he set the blade into the frayed tissue. Schiller's head shook uncontrollably as the saw began its journey back and forth into the bone and remaining tissue. He could feel the reverberation of the instrument throughout his entire body. Blood spurted into Mohr's face as the main artery severed. Then another scream, this time more sickening and deafening than anything before.

On the bridge Petersen gritted his teeth, clasping the bridge rail with all his strength as the sickening cry echoed from below.

'Poor bastard,' he whispered to himself.

Schiller's final cry ended as the glowing blade cauterized the wound. The smell of burning flesh and smoke filled the U-boat's interior within seconds.

'Another hot iron!' demanded Mohr. The cook rushed back to the galley to fetch a bayonet that he had also heated up over the gas light. 'Be quick!' urged Mohr, slightly burning his own hand in the process. Holding the flat side of the blade against the area of the main artery, he made sure that the seal was perfect. With his patient now unconscious, Mohr quickly got to work on stitching up the remainder of the wound with catgut fishing line while Strassmann concentrated on keeping the tourniquet tight. After another couple of minutes it was all over. Mohr wiped away the blood from around the wound, examining his handiwork.

'Release the tourniquet, and slowly,' he insisted.

Strassmann gently removed the rifle cleaning rod and unbuckled the belt. The charred stump began oozing very slightly. To Mohr's relief, his job had been a success, the cauterization held. Strassmann breathed a deep sigh of relief. Mohr quickly covered the charred stump in white antiseptic powder, bandaging it tightly, using several thick sterile wads to soak up the excess blood before applying a heavy dressing. By the time he'd finished, Schiller's entire upper arm was bandaged and secured around his neck and chest. Mohr stood back, wiping the sweat from his eyes.

Whilst his patient was still unconscious he took the opportunity to check Schiller's facial injuries. The skin on the entire left side of his face had wrinkled and burst into a series of oozing sores, but more importantly the eyelid had been partly burnt away, making it impossible for the eye to shut fully. On flashing a pencil torch into the cornea he shook his head.

'What is it?' asked Strassmann.

'The eye is gone,' he said solemnly.

'But will he live?'

'The next twenty-four hours will tell.' Mohr shrugged. 'If he makes it that long and we've caught the infection in time, who knows.'

Wednesday, 6 June 1945

MARTIN O'CASEY was forced to remain in Cork for over three weeks, waiting for some improvement in Elizabeth's health. He had remained in hiding, along with Liam Adams, staying away from the O'Dwyer household as much as possible, moving from the dockland boarding house to a rented cottage on the eastern outskirts at Churchtown. Twice he had attempted to mediate with his principals in Dublin, but circumstances and Pat McManus were weighted against him. He was a dead man or just as good as.

Elizabeth lay in bed all this time. She understood where she was, yet her muscles seemed powerless to act; her mind seemed to be locked away from reality. They helped to feed her in relays. She didn't verbally object, yet there was no comfort for her in taking sustenance. They usually gave up after trying unsuccessfully to spoon the food into her. All she wanted was to die. If her body gave up on her, it would all be over, but she knew she couldn't help speed up the process by any personal action; nature would have to take its course. Sean O'Dwyer wasn't a psychiatrist, but as a student he had had extensive experience with patients in states similar to Elizabeth's. The problem was, how long would her withdrawal last? Apart from the vitamin injections, he began treating Elizabeth with a series of drugs, helping her to relax in the hope that it would give her body the opportunity to stage a recovery.

Martin O'Casey had stayed well away from the house, but he couldn't leave it any longer. It was late that evening. He walked briskly down the rain-swept street, drawing up his coat collar against the wind. As he approached the door, the curtain moved in the bay window of one of the houses further down the avenue. He was met in the hallway by Mary O'Dwyer. She looked excited and didn't take any notice of the briefcase he carried under his arm.

'Martin, thank God. We've some good news about the girl. She came round yesterday. Sean's very confident.'

'Where is she?'

'Upstairs. Sean's with her now.'

As she spoke, Sean O'Dwyer called down, 'Mary, bring me up my other medical bag. It's beside the coatstand.'

She picked up the bag and hurried upstairs.

Martin O'Casey flung off his wet raincoat and hat and followed her, surprising even himself at the speed with which he climbed the stairs to the second floor. Elizabeth was lying back in the bed, her head and shoulders supported by pillows. She smiled upon recognizing him, the first voluntary action he'd witnessed her make in nineteen days.

'Thank God for miracles.' Martin O'Casey rushed to her side.

'*Shalom aleikhem*,' she whispered.

'Whatever that means – ' he squeezed her hand – 'at least you're back with us again.'

'I feel quite fine, really,' she replied.

'Fit enough to travel?' he asked.

'No, not yet,' interjected O'Dwyer.

Elizabeth shook her head. 'I'll be fine, Doctor. From what you told me earlier, I've taken up enough of your time.'

'What nonsense,' he rebuked her gently.

'I must go,' she insisted, turning back to Martin O'Casey, 'but where?'

'America.'

Elizabeth's eyes widened.

'I'll leave you two to talk.' Sean O'Dwyer left the room.

'Why America?' she asked.

'I'll explain that to you in the morning.' He frowned. 'Tell me the truth, just how fit are you?'

'The doctor and his wife have been helping me around the room and down to the bathroom on the first floor. I can manage, really.'

'But could you handle a baby?' he asked hesitantly.

'Martin, you know what I said about the child.' She shook her head and he could see that the very mention of the baby was upsetting her again. 'I wouldn't even see the baby this afternoon when they had me out of bed.'

'Elizabeth.' He took her by both hands. 'I know you've been through much more than anyone could imagine. All I'm asking is that you take him with you and when you get to America you can arrange for his adoption.'

'No!' She shook her head and started crying.

'Hush now.' He stroked her head, drawing her against his chest. He held her, he couldn't say for how long. Finally she quietened and closed her eyes. Martin O'Casey eased her back down on to the pillows, tucking the bedclothes around her before tiptoeing from the room.

After he'd gone, Elizabeth sat up again and moved slowly over to the window. She was weak and cold. From downstairs she heard the grandfather clock strike the half-hour. She peered out. It was raining. The flickering gaslights on the pavement patched the darkness with tiny wells of yellow light. She watched the rain stomping incessantly into the puddles at the kerbside gutters. Suddenly the wind changed direction and rattled the window, blowing the rain directly on to the windowpane and obliterating her view. She moved back and sat on the edge of the bed. Elizabeth was depressed and frightened, but her uncertainty was beginning to lift. A new perspective was forming. She was now coming to terms with her obligation to pick up the pieces again. She thought about the baby. He was so small and frail. How could she have ever thought of him in the same light as those

Nazi butchers? She picked up the dressing gown from the bottom of the bed.

Martin O'Casey had joined the O'Dwyers in the front drawing room. He'd immediately sensed anger in the atmosphere, but played around it until he could contain himself no longer.

'Anybody would think I wasn't welcome here,' he said grinning.

'Martin, we have to talk,' Sean O'Dwyer spoke up. 'There's things that need saying.'

Martin O'Casey flopped himself down in one of the armchairs, opening his jacket. 'Well, I'm listening.' He ran his hand through his dishevelled strands of white hair.

'I had a visit today,' continued Sean O'Dwyer. 'Pat McManus called to see me at the cottage hospital with some of his chums. He started quizzing me about you and he said a few things.'

'Like what for instance?' inquired O'Casey.

'Like, for example, where that baby came from.' O'Dwyer pointed towards the rear parlour, where his wife had left the baby sleeping in his Moses basket. 'Why didn't you tell us about him?'

'Would it have made any difference if I'd told you?' replied O'Casey.

'McManus claims the child in there belongs to some German general. He says they came off a U-boat. Is he right?' he persisted.

'He might be.' O'Casey shrugged his shoulders. 'Then again, he mightn't.'

'McManus also says that you took something that rightfully belongs to the organization. He claims you recovered some jewels from the Germans.'

'That boyo's got some imagination.' Martin O'Casey cocked his head cheekily to one side.

'Stop playing games, Martin! We've put up with enough. We've both taken terrible risks these last weeks. Look at what this is doing to Mary!' He pointed towards his wife, now crying as she stood beside the fireplace.

'All right, I'll get them both out of here.' Martin O'Casey stood up. The little doctor went for him, trying to grab the old man by the collar. Mary O'Dwyer screamed. As O'Dwyer reached forward, steel hands clamped around his wrists, forcing his hands down and bringing him within inches of O'Casey's face. 'Now you listen to me. Don't think I don't understand what you've done. I owe you both and I'll pay you for it. But don't ever think about layin' a finger on me again.' The fire in his eyes alarmed the doctor. He tried to draw

124

back, but he was still being held firm. The fire went out of O'Casey's eyes as he looked over O'Dwyer's shoulder and saw Elizabeth standing at the door. She was holding the baby in her arms. Martin O'Casey let go of his friend and went to Elizabeth's side.

'Can you manage all right?' he asked.

'Yes.' Her lips twitched into a faint smile. 'But he's put on weight since I last saw him.' She looked down, drawing back the crocheted shawl. The baby gurgled, his blue eyes gazing back at her. O'Casey guided her over to the sofa and sat down beside her. The O'Dwyers watched in silence as she nursed the baby on her knee. 'I heard most of what you were saying,' Elizabeth said quietly, looking up at Sean O'Dwyer. 'It was hard to avoid.'

'I'm sorry,' he replied.

'But you're right, of course. We cannot stay here.'

'There's a ship leaving in two days. New York-bound out of Southampton,' commented Martin O'Casey.

'Can we get the baby aboard?' asked Elizabeth.

Martin O'Casey cleared his throat. 'I fear I have a confession to make. I've already registered the baby in yours and Eamon's names. I took the liberty of calling him after your father.'

'Peter,' she said softly, drawing back the edge of the blanket from around the child's face and gently touching his forehead.

'The good doctor here signed the registration papers himself.' Martin O'Casey looked up at his old friend.

Sean O'Dwyer placed an arm around his wife. 'We'll leave you both to talk. We'll be in the kitchen if you want us.'

Martin O'Casey smiled back at him. 'I'm sorry, Sean, things got a little hot there.'

'Forget it,' replied O'Dwyer, closing the door.

'I hope you don't mind – about the registration, I mean,' said O'Casey.

'Peter O'Casey sounds fine to me.' Elizabeth smiled as she nursed the baby on her lap.

The next two days passed slowly. Martin O'Casey kept coming and going at all times of the day and night. Elizabeth could sense trouble from the atmosphere in the house. Mary O'Dwyer kept herself mainly downstairs at the rear of the house, whilst her husband and Martin O'Casey conducted a series of meetings in the front room. At the end of the second day Elizabeth ventured from her bedroom and went

125

downstairs, finding Mary O'Dwyer ironing some clothes in the kitchen. The woman looked up on realizing that Elizabeth was standing at the doorway, then continued with her chores.

'Am I disturbing you?' asked Elizabeth.

'Now why would you be saying a thing like that?' Mary O'Dwyer kept on working.

'You haven't spoken to me since I arrived here.'

'Perhaps it's best we don't,' she said sternly.

'Is it that you don't like me?' continued Elizabeth.

The woman shook her head. 'That's got nothing to do with it.'

'Then what is it?' Elizabeth stepped forward.

'You bring bad fortune to this house.'

'What on earth are you talking about?' demanded Elizabeth.

'Ask O'Casey. He will tell you.' The woman slammed down the iron and brushed past Elizabeth.

Elizabeth sat up the entire second night. She couldn't sleep a wink. Over in the corner of the bedroom, the baby stirred in his wicker Moses basket. She slipped over and peered down at him. As usual, he was asleep on his stomach, his tiny hands flexing out and in as if he was trying to grab hold of something. She reached down, touching a little hand with her finger. He grasped it instantly, squeezing tightly. No matter where he had come from, he was still one of God's children. He was also part of her obligation now, at least until she got him safely to America. Gently, she tucked him in again, drawing the blanket up around his neck. A sudden noise startled her, the car tyres screeched as a car skidded to a halt directly outside the house. Elizabeth crept over to the window. A dark-blue saloon had drawn up directly opposite. Two figures emerged from the back of the car, which then sped off. The two men walked quickly across the street and into the house.

Sean O'Dwyer and Martin O'Casey were standing in the vestibule, removing their wet overcoats and hats when Elizabeth appeared at the bottom of the stairs carrying the baby. Sean O'Dwyer took one look at the Dutch beauty and excused himself. Martin O'Casey removed his wide-brimmed hat, shaking the water from it.

'What is it?' Elizabeth had recognized the look of concern on the men's faces.

'You two go into the front room,' suggested O'Dwyer. 'Mary should have left a fire on.' He went forward, opening the drawing-room door for them. Elizabeth went in ahead of O'Casey.

The room was warm. The fire was now dying but had done its job well, keeping the room at a pleasant temperature. Outside she could hear the rain pelting incessantly against the windows, now shaking and vibrating in the strong wind. Martin O'Casey went over and peeked through a chink in the curtains before switching on the standard lamp in the corner.

'Don't worry yer little head about the storm. It's to blow over by the morning.' He smiled at her. 'It won't affect yer sailing.'

'That's not what is concerning me.' She shook the baby gently in her arms.

'Then what is?' he asked coyly.

She looked directly into his face. 'What is going on?'

'I don't know what you mean.' He moved over beside the fireplace, rubbing his hands together as if trying to generate heat in them. 'I've been busy. Nothing that concerns you, child.'

'You are lying,' she said softly, embarrassed at saying it.

'Now, why would I do a thing like that?' he retorted.

'Martin, for God's sake! You can keep making questions out of my questions all night if you wish, but it isn't going to change anything. I want to know what's happening. I have a right!' She rebuked him. 'Even Mrs O'Dwyer made a comment to me earlier tonight.'

'Did she now! And what was she saying?' He thrust his hands on to his hips defiantly.

'She told me I had brought bad luck to this house.'

'If anyone did that, it was meself,' he said candidly.

'Is someone after us?' She moved closer to him.

'Aye.' He sighed. 'I told you at the farmhouse that things wouldn't go too well after what happened. And I was right.' He looked directly at her.

'Pat McManus?'

'That piece of cow dung! Excusing the description.' Martin O'Casey grunted. 'He's part of it all right, but it's Dublin. The army council held a court last week and it was just as well that I didn't turn up for it, because they found me guilty.' He sniffed.

'Guilty of what?' Elizabeth frowned.

'I'll not bore yer pretty little head with the technicalities of it, but in simple terms I suppose you might say I'm taking the blame for the botched-up military operation and the death of our men.' He forced a smile. 'But in real terms I'm the boyo who lost a million in gold. That's what it comes down to.' He nodded. 'That's what it always comes down to.'

'And Eamon's death means nothing to these people? They don't consider the loss of your son as punishment enough?' Elizabeth fought to hold back her tears as she sat down on the couch.

Martin O'Casey sat down beside her and ran his hand through her soft hair. 'No, child. You see, they know about the jewels. I kept them.'

'You still have them?' She was astounded.

'They're down in the cellar of this house, under a loose stone in the corner. I hid them there the day we arrived here. I thought they might come in useful for your future.'

'No.' She shook her head, rejecting the idea. 'I don't want them. I want nothing that belonged to those animals.'

'All right, if that's the way you want it.'

'Can't you give them back?'

'Too late.' He sighed, touching the baby's tiny hand.

'So what happens now?'

'Now I'm playing cat and mouse. I don't think they know about this place – the O'Dwyers are loyal to me. They think I'm staying down in a boarding house near the harbour. First thing in the morning we get you and the wee one to Cobh and then aboard the ship. It anchors just offshore to take on more passengers. Then I'll get outa here, probably over the border into Ulster. We'll be OK.'

'Come with us,' she pleaded.

Martin O'Casey shook his head. 'I'm sixty-seven years old, child. Too old to run and too proud to think about it.'

'I can't leave you!' she cried. The baby began to stir.

He removed a crumpled, grubby envelope from his jacket pocket and set the bulky packet beside her. 'This is for you. I've been carrying it around for days now.'

'What is it?' she asked.

'An Irish passport in the name of Elizabeth O'Casey and I took the liberty of including the child on it.'

'Very presumptuous of you.'

'Don't worry, the passport's real enough and you'll find I included a birth certificate for the child. There's also over two thousand dollars in fifty-dollar bills, and before you ask, they're not forgeries either.' He grinned. 'Now, I'm cabling my sister Ellen. She lives in New York. She'll be awaiting your arrival. Just in case, her address and details are on a letter inside that envelope. Make sure she gets it.'

'You've thought of everything,' she said.

'Not quite.' He stood up again. 'The papers for your entry to the

128

States were originally in Eamon's name. He had planned on taking you there himself.'

'I see,' she said solemnly.

'The papers will permit you entry to the United States for up to six months. It should give you enough time to try and make your stay a permanent one. Ellen will help you all she can.'

'I just don't know,' she said despondently.

'Well, there's plenty of other places to see. Just don't be too quick on hurrying back to Ireland.' As he removed a further envelope from his coat, Elizabeth couldn't avoid noticing the butt of the pistol protruding from the pocket. He flicked over the coat, concealing the weapon again. 'This is your ticket. You're travelling second class on the SS *Olympic Star*. A deck cabin with a sea view. You should be fairly comfortable.' He handed her the envelope. 'All meals included.' He chuckled.

'This was for you, wasn't it?' She took the manila envelope.

'It's perfectly legal. Tickets are transferable, provided notification is given to the shipping line in advance. They'll be told first thing in the morning.'

'That isn't what I asked.' Elizabeth tried to control her anger as she opened the envelope and examined the contents. 'If you stay here, what happens to you?'

'My child, I broke a cardinal rule of my organization. It makes no difference whether I stay or go. In the end it'll be the same.'

'They're going to kill you!' She couldn't believe her own ears. 'And there's two tickets here. You can still come with me,' she said, removing the tickets from the envelope. Martin O'Casey took one of them from her. Without hesitation, he threw it on the coal fire. It went up in flames almost immediately. 'Why?' She was stunned.

'You can't run for ever.'

She had no answer.

Elizabeth was ready and waiting the next morning when Liam Adams drew up in a navy Vauxhall saloon right on time. While Martin O'Casey took her baggage outside, she stopped in the hallway to thank the O'Dwyers.

'I owe you both so much. I hardly know where to start.'

Mary O'Dwyer was the first to speak. 'Start by getting to the docks on time.' She forced a smile.

'Thank you.'

129

'Take care of the wee one.' Mary O'Dwyer surprised Elizabeth by kissing both her and the baby.

'You can send us a postcard,' added Doctor O'Dwyer.

'Come on.' Martin O'Casey appeared at the door again, clearly a little out of breath.

'Goodbye,' she said finally, following him out to the car.

'You can see them to the car. I'm in my shirt sleeves,' Sean O'Dwyer urged his wife as he shivered in the chilly morning air blowing up the hallway.

'Then you can get the kettle on.' Mary O'Dwyer smiled at him, before following Elizabeth outside. She held Peter while Elizabeth got into the back of the car. 'I'm going to miss him, you know.' Then she kissed him.

'So you mean we're not bad luck after all?' Elizabeth smiled as she took the baby into her arms.

'No, bad fortune,' replied the woman, blowing a kiss to her as she closed the door.

After watching the car leave the street, Mary O'Dwyer went back inside and shut the door. Entering the kitchen, she froze rigid. Her husband was lying spread-eagled on the tiled floor, a man standing over him, brandishing a sawn-off shotgun. A second man was sitting at the kitchen table with a stupid grin on his face.

'So this is the missus.' The man at the table prodded Sean O'Dwyer with his toe. The doctor grunted.

'Who are you?' she demanded.

'I'm the man who yer husband here has been giving the run-around,' replied Pat McManus. 'Show her what I mean, Jamsie.'

The man with the shotgun took a step back and fired both barrels into Sean O'Dwyer. The doctor's body lifted off the floor and slumped down again. Mary O'Dwyer screamed at the sight of her husband's torn body. She turned away, burying her face against the door. McManus stood up and went over to the shaken woman, grabbing her roughly by the chin and forcing her to look at her husband.

'No! Please!' she cried.

'Now look at 'im!' Mary O'Dwyer's head was forced down to within several feet of her husband's body. 'I don't make war on women,' continued McManus. Mary O'Dwyer stared down at her husband. Sean O'Dwyer's back was a mass of pulsating red, the open wound extending from the peppered shotmarks in the back of his neck down as far as his buttocks. His shirt had been blown away, along with most of the skin and tissue of his back, revealing several sections of white lumbar vertebrae. McManus snatched her by the hair, forcing her face into his. 'But you might just become the exception to the rule, if you don't tell me what I want to know.'

They arrived at Cobh Island a little after 8.30 a.m. The SS *Olympic Star* had already anchored in the deep water just offshore. A procession of smaller craft surrounded the 15,000-ton ocean liner. The combination of the war ending and the arrival of the first scheduled liner in some time had resulted in a party atmosphere. Martin O'Casey emerged from the ticket office after a few minutes and joined Elizabeth on the crowded quayside.

'There you are.' He handed her back the ticket. 'All in your name. I checked there's no problem with the baby. They have facilities on the ship.' A ship's horn sounded off in the distance. Elizabeth looked over towards the liner. The ferry was coming alongside the quay to take the final passengers out to the waiting ship. 'It's strange, you know.' He stared down at the baby. 'You lose your only son one minute and yet if you held on to this wee one here, he'd almost be a grandson to me.'

She knew exactly what the old man was getting at. Elizabeth went over and kissed him on the cheek. She watched the tears rolling down his wrinkled face. 'I can't make a promise like that,' she said firmly, 'but I will write to you.' She took the child into her arms and let one of the porters carry the Moses basket and her baggage over to the steps.

'I never was one for letter-writing.' He smiled. 'There's just one more thing. I left a little something inside your case. If not for you, then keep it for the child.' As he stroked the baby's head, Peter made a cooing noise. 'And as for you, young fella me lad, you take care of this fine lady.' He bent forward and kissed the baby's forehead. The child touched the stubble on his chin and started to laugh.

'Madam?' Elizabeth looked aside. It was the porter again. 'Ready to board now, please.'

'Thank you.' She turned to Martin O'Casey. The old IRA chief was wiping his eyes with his hand. 'Here, take this.' She handed him her own handkerchief. He took it gratefully.

'Well, this is it.' He tried his best to sound happy.

'I'll pray for you,' she answered, stretching up and kissing him on the cheek. '*Lechaim uleshalom.*'

'Now, that sounded nice.' He raised an eyebrow.

'It means "To life and peace". My father used to say it quite often when dealing in business back in Amsterdam.'

131

'Amsterdam! Now doesn't that sound a fine place to be! Maybe I'll be going there for a while.'

'Madam, please,' interrupted the young porter, eager to get her aboard the ferry.

'I'm coming now,' she assured him.

'God bless you both.' Martin O'Casey stroked the baby's head one last time. He watched her walk away. She stopped and looked back at him before disappearing down the stone steps to the gangway. As she did so, Pat McManus appeared from out of the shadows of the customs shed behind O'Casey . . .

THE SS *OLYMPIC STAR*, WHITE STAR LINE – 400 MILES EAST OF NEWFOUNDLAND
Wednesday, 13 June 1945

THE TWO men walked on to the promenade deck from the second-class saloon. The taller of the pair paused to light another cigarette, cupping the match in both hands as he struck it against the box. His attention was immediately drawn towards the side rail, to a lone figure standing just under the canopy of the flying bridge.

He had seen the woman with the young child in her arms just twice since they had boarded at Ireland. She intrigued him. Perhaps it was his reporter's natural instinct, but somehow or other, she stood out from the rest of the women aboard the liner. He turned to his associate as he flicked the match over the side of the ship.

'Charlie, I'll see you in the bar around seven.'

'Sure you will.' The glint in the other man's eye annoyed him.

'Wipe yer mind clean, Charlie, the lady's got a baby in her arms. That means there's a guy somewhere, see?'

'Well, if it ain't stopped Ed Morrisey until now, I guess it never will.'

'Get outa here.' Morrisey took a playful swipe at his colleague. The man headed off, chuckling to himself.

Elizabeth was totally unaware of the stranger's presence until he spoke. 'We seem to be making good time.' The man's casualness and American accent caught Elizabeth off balance. She averted her eyes from the rolling sea, somewhat relieved at being distracted from such painful visions of Ireland. The man seemed to sense the sorrow in her eyes as she forced the glimmer of a smile.

132

'I'm sorry? What were you saying?' Elizabeth adjusted the shawl across over the child's head, against the chilly sea breeze.

'I said that the crossing is going well. We're making good time.' Morrisey smiled as he watched the woman's long auburn hair ruffled in the gathering wind. A sudden gust almost blew her beret overboard. As she tried to straighten it, Morrisey stepped in and held the baby for a moment. 'Allow me.'

'Why, thank you.' Elizabeth quickly recovered the baby.

'The name's Ed Morrisey.' He touched the brim of his hat, taking the opportunity to pull it down more firmly over his forehead.

'Mrs O'Casey,' Elizabeth replied guardedly.

Morrisey looked down at the baby, stirring in her arms. 'She's real cute.'

'She's a he, Mr Morrisey.' Elizabeth raised an eyebrow. A slight grin began to form on her lips. 'His name is Peter.'

'I'm sorry, mam, kids were never a real strong point with me.'

'You have children of your own?' Elizabeth could not avoid speaking to the man, and while she did she decided she may as well go on the offensive. It had taken over three days alone in her cabin for her to decide she was not going to waste the remainder of her life in anonymity. If someone wanted her, if someone was hunting for her, they could come and get her, but she was not going to run.

'Nope, never had the time for it.' He sounded pleased with himself for having admitted it.

Elizabeth eyed the plump, greying man with the rosy cheeks and round gold spectacles. Under his flapping overcoat he was wearing a three-piece green tweed suit, sporting a dark bow tie and a yellow silk handkerchief that flopped out from his breast pocket and matched nothing else he wore.

'You've been away during the war?' she continued, already eyeing the door next to the saloon, her retreat down below deck.

'For the duration, I'm a newspaper man. Got caught up in London way back in 'thirty-nine. My paper made me an offer I just couldn't refuse. They told me to stay in England and get paid or come home and get fired.' He grinned. 'And I've been in Europe ever since. But now I'm going home.' He puffed on the cigarette, careful not to allow any of the smoke near the child.

'Well, it was a pleasure to meet you, Mr Morrisey. Thank you for letting me save my beret in time.' Elizabeth went to go back indoors.

'Say, that accent of yours, it doesn't go with the Irish name.' Morrisey tried to prolong the conversation a little longer.

'No, I'm Dutch. My husband is Irish.' She didn't know why she

133

had lied. It came so naturally it shocked her a little. She took another step towards the door.

'Your husband isn't travelling Stateside with you, mam?'

'No, he'll be joining me there later.' It was much harder the second time, and she could see from his eyes that he sensed her deceit.

'Mam, if I had a pretty wife like you, an' a cute youngster like that, I'd make sure I was with 'em, yes, mam.'

'Yes.' Elizabeth stood erect, her chin thrust forward, her nostrils pinched more against the memory than the increasing chill wind.

'But there's a lot of people in the same position as yourself. Families split up for years on end.' It was Morrisey's turn to be embarrassed now. He felt he had somehow offended the woman, his curiosity had backfired.

'Good day, Mr Morrisey.' Elizabeth politely nodded before heading inside. Morrisey rushed forward, holding back the door for her. 'Thank you,' she smiled faintly.

'My pleasure, I assure you.' Morrisey touched the rim of his hat as Elizabeth passed by. 'Nice talking to you, mam. Perhaps we'll see each other again before we dock,' Morrisey called after her, but she never looked back.

At the same moment Morrisey's companion reappeared from out of the saloon, catching a glimpse of Elizabeth as she headed down the passageway. 'Now that's what I call class,' grunted the smaller man, approvingly.

'Yep, but there's something else.' Morrisey shook his head, tossing his unfinished cigarette over the guardrail. 'Remember when I told you about entering those camps in Germany, an' the look on those miserable faces?'

'A thousand times Ed, a thousand times,' the other man sighed. Was he going to have to hear the same old story all over again? 'It was misery everywhere,' he added, hoping to cut short Morrisey's propensity to ramble.

'Sure there was misery there, but there was also a pride. It was still there, deep inside each of those poor wretches. They were proud, every last one of 'em.' Morrisey removed his hat and scratched his forehead. 'Charlie, I'm tellin' ya, that dame has that same pride.' He stared after Elizabeth and wondered.

Elizabeth went straight back to her cabin, hoping that the steward had finished his daily rounds. As she turned the corner she saw the two men standing outside her door. She recognized the captain and bursar instantly. Then the steward appeared at the cabin door and pointed towards her. Elizabeth tried not to panic. What did it mean?

Had someone discovered the diamonds? Had someone realized who she was? She clutched the baby even more tightly.

'Mrs O'Casey?' The captain stepped forward, his grim face told her it was serious.

'What is it? What's wrong?' she insisted.

'Perhaps we could discuss it inside your cabin.'

Elizabeth went ahead of the two officers, settling Peter into his cot.

'Perhaps you should sit down, Mrs O'Casey,' continued the captain.

'I'm perfectly all right standing, thank you,' she said firmly. 'What is wrong?'

'Mrs O'Casey, do you know a man called Martin O'Casey?'

'He is my father-in-law. Why?' She frowned.

'Mrs O'Casey, you should prepare yourself for some bad news.' The captain guided her gently over to one side. 'I regret to inform you that Martin O'Casey is dead.'

'Dead!' She looked back in astonishment.

'I'm truly sorry, madam. His body was discovered at the docks shortly after we sailed from Ireland. He had been shot. The police found a receipt for your tickets on the body. That was how they were able to trace you to this ship.'

'Trace me? Am I a suspect?' She was horrified at the very thought.

'Heaven forbid, good lady. I have it on authority that your father-in-law died after we set sail. I fear he was murdered, along with another man. The Irish police would like a word with you, if you would consent.'

She shook her head. 'I can't go back, I have to reach America.'

'I'll see what I can do, but you must understand that under the circumstances they could insist upon your return. You would be what they term a material witness.'

'I see,' she said absently.

'We'll leave you for now. If there is anything you want, the steward will be just outside. I could arrange for someone to look after the baby, if you so desired?'

'Thank you, but I will be fine,' she whispered.

'As you wish.' The captain and bursar then withdrew. As the door closed, Elizabeth threw herself on to the bed and wept.

NEW YORK HARBOUR
Friday, 15 June 1945

ELIZABETH had taken Peter up on deck in the hope of catching a glimpse of the Statue of Liberty. She had been disappointed by the thick morning fog which had reduced visibility to merely a few hundred yards. Below her, she could see the pilot's boat drawing away from the steps which had been lowered from the lower cargo deck.

'Mrs O'Casey?' Elizabeth looked around to find the captain standing next to her.

'Captain.' She smiled nervously.

'I have only a moment, I've a ship to dock, but I thought you should see this.' He handed her a telegram. 'The harbour pilot's boat brought it on board for my attention. It seems that the Irish authorities no longer require your presence.' Elizabeth scanned the message. 'The Irish police have apparently apprehended Mr O'Casey's killer, a man by the name of McManus.'

'McManus,' she repeated.

'Do you know him?'

'Why, no.' She blushed. 'Who is he?'

'I have no idea.' The captain touched the peak of his cap. 'Well, I mustn't keep the pilot waiting. You will excuse me, Mrs O'Casey.'

'Thank you.' She smiled again.

'My pleasure. If I shouldn't see you before disembarkation, may I wish you a pleasant stay in the United States.'

'Goodbye, Captain.' Elizabeth looked down at Peter, nestled in her arms. God was indeed looking down on both of them.

The quayside loomed into view, its profile diminished by the morning fog. The liner was being eased into berth by three tugboats, two at the bow and one positioned aft. A horn sounded up on the top deck, a five-second blast, followed by two shorter ones. Already people could been seen gathering on the quayside, waving and shouting at the passengers as they crowded at the guardrails on the lower and upper decks. The atmosphere of gaiety and laughter amongst the passengers seemed total; everyone was frantically trying to catch sight of someone they knew ashore. Of course with the morning fog it was virtually impossible, but that did nothing to dampen their determination.

The deck was now becoming quite crowded as the other passengers filed out from the dining room, following the final breakfast sitting. Elizabeth suddenly found herself being squeezed against the guardrail. She pushed back frantically, so as to protect the baby in her arms, but the crowd surged against her. Peter began to cry and Elizabeth started to panic, when suddenly someone came to her rescue, blocking the shoving mass with his body.

'Hey, watch the lady and kid!' shouted Morrisey. 'Give 'em some room there, Mac.' He pushed one of the male passengers back before guiding Elizabeth safely away from the thronging crowd.

'Thank you, once again, Mr Morrisey,' replied Elizabeth.

'Maybe you'd be better outa this!' he shouted above the noise. 'It's a lot safer over on the promenade section.'

'I'll take your advice.' Elizabeth was in no mood to debate the matter.

Once they had reached the quiet of the promenade deck, Elizabeth started to relax again. Peter suddenly started cooing. Elizabeth looked down at him, his little head covered in the blue bonnet she had knitted for him since coming aboard. She had surprised herself, for the last time she could remember knitting was just prior to her sixteenth birthday. Filled with ambition, she had started to knit her father a cardigan, but time and patience had beaten her and he'd ended up with a woollen scarf instead. 'Thank you for getting me away from all that.' She breathed deeply, then a grateful smile filled her face as she cuddled the child.

'Are you OK?' asked Morrisey.

'I think I was probably about to expire back there.' She could laugh about it now.

'Or get shoved overboard,' he quipped.

'Quite,' she agreed wholeheartedly. 'I am for ever in your debt, Mr Morrisey.'

'If you don't mind me saying, I heard about your father-in-law. I'm very sorry.'

'Don't tell me, you sniff a story?'

'I'm too close to home to even think about it.' He lit a cigarette.

'How did you know?'

'The steward on "C" deck has a big mouth. He was telling everybody about the visit you had from the captain and bursar. He says you've to go back to Ireland.'

'Let me update you, Mr Morrisey.' Elizabeth handed him the telegram.

'That's a relief for you,' he said, perusing the message.

The ship's horn blasted again. The baby shook in her arms, stirred by the sudden noise.

'Your family's in New York?' he continued.

Elizabeth rocked the baby gently. She didn't want this conversation, but she was finding it unavoidable. 'An aunt, by marriage.'

'I see.' He pouted, surprised at her readiness to impart the information.

Morrisey removed a business card from his pocket. 'Listen, if there's anything I can ever do for you, look me up. Here's my card, I'm with the *Boston Tribune*. For the moment.'

'Thank you,' she replied shyly.

'Attention! Attention!' The broadcast system crackled into life and a voice started echoing around the ship. 'Would all remaining passengers on "C" deck please make your way to the main banqueting room for the return of passports and visas. I repeat, this is the last call for . . .'

'I really must go.' She propped the baby against her shoulder and shook hands with the reporter. 'Goodbye.'

'Goodbye, Mrs O'Casey, and good luck.' Morrisey grinned, showing off his yellowed teeth.

As he stood watching her walk away, Morrisey realized he was still holding the telegram in his left hand. For a second he was tempted to follow her, but instead he folded the blue paper into his pocket.

Elizabeth descended the gangway to the quay, following the line of passengers towards the customs shed. One of the stewards walked alongside, carrying her baggage, consisting of one medium-sized case and a small travelling bag. In comparison to some of the other passengers, with their trunks and a multitude of baggage, she felt quite inadequate. The queue halted and Elizabeth looked around the massive clearing shed. It was completely crowded, with the first-class passengers already standing in line.

She pondered over the woman she was to meet. She really knew very little about Ellen O'Casey, other than she had come to the United States during the 1920s, married and divorced within two years and now lived alone in New York, working in some factory. She really had no idea how the woman would react to the child – had she even received Martin's message? The queue started moving again. Elizabeth followed the young steward through the rows of waist-high barriers; clearly he was used to procedure, short-cutting the main queue and taking her aside to one of the vacant customs desks. She waited while the steward spoke to the customs official. She watched the other passengers going through the customs point. The officials appeared more interested in identification than what was in their luggage.

'C'mon, lady.' Elizabeth looked over, upon hearing the gruff voice. She was being addressed by the taller of the two customs officers standing at the other side of a long bench-type table.

'I am sorry?' She stepped forward to the table.

'Anything to declare, mam?' The tall customs man spoke without looking at her. He appeared to be busy, checking something off a list on his clipboard.

'No.' Elizabeth tried to sound calm.

'Papers?' The customs man held out his right hand, sticking his pencil behind his ear, looking at her for the first time. His face lightened up when he caught sight of the baby.

As she handed over the documents a scuffle broke out at the customs point next to her. Elizabeth turned to see a stocky middle-aged man being wrestled to the ground by two other customs men. The man put up a fight, booting one of the customs men in the face, before being finally overpowered when a third officer punched him on the nose. The man crashed into a wooden bench. Before he could do anything, he was handcuffed and roughly hauled off between two officers towards the customs office at the far side of the clearing shed.

'What was that all about?' Elizabeth gasped.

'We get 'em all the time. Criminals, Nazis, fascists, all trying to sneak in on false or stolen papers,' the man grunted. 'Now, you don't look like a Nazi, do you?' The customs man grinned across at Peter, gently squeezing his tiny hand. He was just about to let Elizabeth through when his supervisor approached, whispering in his ear. As the supervisor moved on down the line, the official leaned over and spoke to Elizabeth. 'I'm real sorry, mam. I've just been told to check all baggage from now on.'

'Why, of course,' she replied willingly.

He quickly checked through her suitcase, with the speed of an expert. 'I'll take the small one now.' He passed the suitcase aside for the steward to re-seal and quickly went straight to the bottom of the travelling bag. His fingers felt the metal box almost immediately. 'What's in the box, mam?'

'The baby's bottles,' she replied without hesitation.

'I'll have to see inside.' He removed the box, examining its battered appearance. 'This has been through the wars, all right,' he quipped.

'I suppose it has,' she said nervously.

He glimpsed inside before closing the lid again. 'Everything's in order, mam. Sorry for the search,' he apologized, helping to re-pack the bag.

Elizabeth watched with relief as the second officer stamped her papers, before returning them.

'Enjoy your stay in the United States, mam,' said the second customs man.

'I will, thank you,' she said gratefully.

'Just follow the white line on out the far side of the building. I'll get you a porter, the steward has to stay this side of the line.' The customs official clicked his fingers, beckoning one of the porters over.

As she walked on through the giant shed, Elizabeth's fingers gently groped around Peter's nappy. 'The Three Brothers' were safe and well, and probably a lot warmer than they had been in previous centuries. She followed the porter outside, along a wide pathway, marked out by another two rows of navy grey barriers, towards the gateway. The eight-foot-high spiked iron railings separated the docks from the public street. Outside, a handful of New York cops were trying to keep back a veritable swelling sea of people, all jostling for a better view of the new arrivals. Two further policemen stood behind the gates, glad they were on the inside. As Elizabeth neared, she could see some of the people were holding up pieces of paper and card with various names written on them, but most chose to yell and shout over the noise of the others in vain attempts at attracting the attention of their loved ones and friends.

'Coming out!' yelled the porter. There was another sudden surge. The police tried shoving everyone back as the gate opened, barely enough for Elizabeth and Peter to get through, following the porter.

'Get back, will ya!' shouted a tough-looking police sergeant, using his night stick as a ram to force home his message. 'Go ahead, lady,' he shouted to her. Peter was already crying, clearly upset by the noise and bustle. Elizabeth wasted no time in thanking the man, she passed on through, grateful when she caught sight again of the Negro porter, standing on the sidewalk with her luggage.

'Want a cab, mam?' He smiled warmly.

'I was hoping to meet someone here.' Elizabeth looked around, in vain, for she had absolutely no idea what Ellen even looked like.

'Elizabeth O'Casey?' The woman's Irish accent was crystal clear.

Elizabeth turned about to find herself confronting a small plump woman, in her fifties, her grey hair pinned up under a small green hat. The woman was dressed in a brown tweed suit, hardly fitting into any fashion trend, but worn smartly, like a uniform. As she stared into the woman's eyes she could see the family resemblance. 'You are Elizabeth, aren't you?' The woman's voice was shaky, she sounded nervous. It was then that Elizabeth realized she hadn't even answered yet.

'Yes,' she replied, sounding inadequate.

'I'm Ellen.' She leaned forward and kissed her. 'Thank God, you're here safely. I was getting worried, I've been standing for almost two hours. Here was me beginning to think that you weren't on the passenger list after all.' She kissed her again before looking down at the baby. 'And this here must be my great-nephew! Isn't he cute, would ya look at him! Isn't he so big!' she said excitedly.

'His name is Peter,' she answered.

'An' a fine name it is, too.' Ellen was beaming, clearly ecstatic at their meeting. Then she gestured for the porter to take the baggage over to the waiting cab rank. 'May I?' She held out her arms and took Peter from her. He stopped crying immediately. 'Now isn't that a good sign, or isn't it?' She laughed. 'We're going directly to my place, it's not that far from here.'

Elizabeth sat in the back of the cab, oblivious of Ellen's continuous monologue directed solely at Peter. She was glad that Ellen had become so engrossed in the baby, for she knew that she had to pick the right moment to tell her the terrible news and she doubted her ability to lie successfully. She had deliberately avoided any discussion about the O'Casey clan back in Ireland.

As the journey continued Elizabeth quickly let herself be immersed in the sights and sounds of the city. She had read and heard so much about New York that she thought herself prepared for the experience, but the sheer size of the buildings astonished her. The journey to the apartment took much longer than Elizabeth could ever have imagined. She had never seen so much traffic in her life. Watching the people on the sidewalk, shoppers, workers: they seemed all the same to her, always in a rush. If she was certain of one thing it was her utter determination to conquer this city. There was no room for second best, no room for the defeated. This town didn't accept strangers unless they were completely successful, and the best. At that precise moment Elizabeth knew, above everything else, that she was not going to be like the rest of them out there on the sidewalk, watching their backs, wondering how to pay the next bill and hiding from the postman. She deserved to be above all that, and she knew she could be, for with God as her judge, she had it in her and she knew that with the jewels the dream could become reality.

141

The apartment was in the east side of Brooklyn, situated next to a subway viaduct. Even on a sunny afternoon it was a dull and drab place. The street was narrow and overshadowed by the iron structure. It appeared to Elizabeth that whatever the time of day, the sunlight would find it almost impossible to grace the street, squeezed between the railway structure and a row of four-storey brick-faced apartment houses. As the cab drove up the street, Elizabeth looked across through the broken wire fencing, between the steel stanchions, towards the open area beyond. For a moment she thought it was a park, not much, but something. At least it would be somewhere to take Peter. Then she saw the clouds of dust and the machines; the mechanical diggers and heavy lorries. The area was a large building site; they were just clearing away the remnants to build again, no doubt a little higher, she reckoned. Elizabeth looked at the children playing in the shadows beneath the railway line, they were dirty and shabbily dressed. The reality collided with her dreams of moments earlier. Was this Peter's destiny? Was this hers? She tried to counter the welling doubt and kept a stiff upper lip. She was no failure. She could rise above this, and somehow she would!

'Nearly there now,' consoled Ellen, reading the expression on Elizabeth's face to mean tiredness. Peter had by now fallen asleep. Ellen gazed down at him. 'He must take after your side of the family, he looks nothing like Eamon, does he?' She smiled again.

Before Elizabeth could reply the cab drew up to a halt outside a blue painted door.

Ellen was first out, carrying the baby. By the time Elizabeth had joined her on the sidewalk, Ellen was already immersed in conversation with a woman in a maroon coat with a fur collar. Elizabeth caught the woman's snappy nasal tone; it was new to her ears.

'Ya kept that kinda quiet, didn't ya?' The woman chuckled at her own words.

'Sally, I'm twenty years past the sell-by date,' retorted Ellen. 'This here's my nephew, Petey.'

'His name's Peter,' corrected Elizabeth.

'Sorry, pet.' Ellen smiled. 'Elizabeth, I'd like ya ta meet Sally Lomax. She lives just opposite me, on the second floor.'

'Pleased to meet you,' Elizabeth replied softly.

'Me too.' The woman bent over Peter, pulling at his feet. 'Isn't it cute.'

'He is not an *it*!' replied Elizabeth matter-of-factly. The woman was speechless.

'I think we'd better go inside, don't you?' interrupted Ellen, averting a potential conflict.

Inside, Elizabeth was more than shocked by the size of the apartment. She had been used to living in small rooms, especially over the last five years. While the place was by no means Buckingham Palace, the rooms were bright and very spacious. An old sewing machine sat on a metal stand next to a tall window, which reached up to the ceiling of the living room. The carpeting was of a poor quality and badly worn in several places, but the furniture seemed fairly new, modern, the sort she had seen advertised in the glossy American magazines which had been all the rage in London before the outbreak of war. In the centre of the room sat a long four-seater sofa covered in uncut Moka with matching armchairs sitting at right angles and forming a square in front of a small gas fire and wooden surround. After settling Peter down for a nap she returned to the living room.

'Make yourself at home.' Ellen's voice filtered out from the kitchen. 'I'll just be a minute with the coffee. You do like coffee, don't ya?'

'Coffee's fine,' replied Elizabeth.

'What about Peter, is he still asleep?'

'He's in the bedroom, fast asleep.' Elizabeth went over to the kitchen door and watched Ellen preparing the food on the worktop beside the gas cooker.

'What about that brother of mine? Not to mention my wayward nephew! Say, I sure as hell hope Eamon makes a better father than he's been a son to Martin.'

Here it was. Elizabeth had been dreading the moment. She had gone over what to say time after time, but the more she thought about it, the worse it had all come out, yet here she was, standing at the door of the kitchen and the question had been asked. She looked into Ellen's eyes. How much did this woman really care about her brother? The woman had no one to support her, no husband to comfort her, nothing. This could kill her. She walked reticently into the kitchen. Elizabeth's silence had already alerted Ellen.

'What is it?' She stopped cutting the sandwiches.

'Ellen . . .' Elizabeth found herself unable to tell the woman.

'Martin's dead, isn't he?' she said bluntly, her chin raised defiantly, ready to take the news like a punch on the jaw.

Elizabeth simply nodded. It took her a few moments, but Ellen began to cry. Elizabeth guided her inside to the living room, helping her into one of the armchairs. After some minutes Ellen's grief turned

143

to anger, the only thing left to her. 'Why didn't you tell me before?' she demanded.

'Ellen, I had reasons, believe me,' Elizabeth tried to assure her.

Ellen stood up, heading back into the kitchen again. Elizabeth followed, reaching out and trying to console her further.

'No! Don't you touch me!' she screamed, turning to face her. 'You damn well knew, you could have told me before!' she repeated.

'I thought it best if . . .'

'*You* thought it best!' she screamed. 'Martin was the only family I had left, and now a stranger comes into my home and tells me he's dead!' Suddenly Peter's cries could be heard from the bedroom beyond.

'You must understand,' insisted Elizabeth, trying to ignore the baby's cries for the moment.

'To hell with you!' cried Ellen, wiping away the tears from her cheek with her apron. 'So what's Eamon doing? Why isn't he here to tell me himself? Eh? Well?'

'Eamon's dead too.' Elizabeth's heart ached at the thought.

'You . . .' Ellen was completely stunned. Her bitterness melted as she saw Elizabeth's face begin to fall away in an avalanche of despair. Then Peter's screams cut into their conversation.

'I had better see to him,' said Elizabeth. Ellen stood alone in the kitchen, unable to offer her guest any comfort for the moment.

Neither woman slept that night. As the conversation wore on, Elizabeth confided as much as she could in the woman. Ellen was not unsympathetic, although it was clear that she found certain aspects of the related events quite unbelievable. Elizabeth did most of the talking, her dry throat eased by several Jack Daniels.

'You don't spare anything in your measures of whiskey, do you?' Elizabeth's head was light, a combination of tiredness, relief and the alcohol.

'After what you've told me, I'd say you need it. Here, have another.' Ellen leaned over to the coffee table and snatched the open bottle nearly spilling the contents over the floor. 'Oops!' she hiccuped. 'Here, honey, have another slug.' She began pouring into Elizabeth's empty glass, sliding down on to the floor as she replenished her own glass. Some of the whiskey spilled over her tweed skirt. She seemed either not to notice, or not to care as she leaned across, setting the bottle back on the glass-topped coffee table. Elizabeth sipped at the neat whiskey, her face contorting as the alcohol entered her throat.

'You know, honey,' continued Ellen, waving her glass around, 'you and me, we're the only family we've got.' She hiccuped again before taking another swig. 'I was married once, ya know. It lasted just seven months, an' he left me.' She slammed her glass on to the table, almost smashing it. 'Ah! What the hell anyway. He didn't care about me, did he?' She shook her head, agreeing with herself.

'You miss him, even now after all this time?' asked Elizabeth.

'Miss him? Never! I hate the son of a bitch! Hate . . . him.' Ellen nodded this time. Then another hiccup, followed by a long deep breath. 'You know, Liz, you don't mind me calling you that, do you, hun?' She looked up, focusing her eyes on the younger woman. ''Course ya don't.' But before Elizabeth could answer she pointed accusingly at her. 'Yes you do! I can see it in your eyes!' Ellen saluted her by raising her glass. 'You're quite right, hun, I'll call you E-liz-a-beth.' Ellen forced her mouth into a contortionist's nightmare as she tried to pronounce the name correctly. 'You know, I'm fifty-three years old and I've never had a baby.' Then she began sniggering like a schoolgirl. 'An' I'm hardly likely to, now, am I?'

The two women stared at each other before bursting into laughter, neither understood precisely why, but the bond was there. They had already forged a common understanding.

'Can you imagine . . . me!' Ellen prodded herself to emphasize the point. 'Me having a baby?' Then she roared aloud, making a hooting sound. 'Immaculate . . . that's what it'd be. The immaculate perception!'

'Conception!' laughed Elizabeth.

'What the hell,' replied Ellen waving her hand in the air, 'I'd say that son of yours will be enough handling for the two of us.'

'The two of us?'

'You're living here now.'

'I can't stay here indefinitely,' replied Elizabeth, overwhelmed by the offer.

'Why ever not?' Ellen was beginning to sound offended. 'What-ever's wrong with "Sunset Boulevard" anyway?' They laughed again. 'Look, you're not imposing, you two can stay here for as long as ya want to.' She prodded her on the knee. 'An' I ain't taking no for an answer, you hear?'

'You are very kind,' blurted Elizabeth.

'Hell, no, we're kin, ain't we?'

'Kin,' Elizabeth nodded.

'Now, tomorrow we're going job hunting. Auntie here is taking her little niece down to the Labor Exchange.'

'The Labor Exchange?' Elizabeth frowned.

'The place that tells ya where to get a job, honey.'

'But what about Peter? Even if I get a job, who would look after him?'

Ellen smiled back, winking. 'You leave that all to Auntie here.'

After several more drinks the conversation drifted back, as always, to Ireland and the recent events. Ellen still could not take it all in, especially Elizabeth's account about the Germans.

'Tell me once again about this bastard, what you call him . . . Schiller, is it?'

Elizabeth paused, her memory of the SS general painful at best. 'He's an SS general.' She shook her head. 'There was something about him. He was pure evil. I can't explain it, but when he walked into that farmhouse, it was as if I had been waiting for him.'

'Waiting for him! God, I need another drink!' Ellen steadied herself as she reached for the bottle again. 'An' you honestly think the bastard's still alive?'

'I can't explain why, but I know he is.' Elizabeth stared directly at her. 'I just feel it, his evil seems to penetrate my very soul.'

'Holy Mary, you poor child.' Ellen forgot the bottle and took Elizabeth's hand. 'It sounds to me as if you've just imagined you encountered the devil.'

'I didn't imagine anything. I think I have,' whispered Elizabeth. 'I did.'

'Gold help you.' Ellen held her in her arms.

'I swear, if God spares me and gives me the opportunity, I'll put him in hell, where he belongs.' Elizabeth tried to fight back the tears in vain.

It was five hours later and the sound of the constant snoring from the next bedroom had kept Elizabeth awake for the last hour. Elizabeth struggled out of bed, careful not to disturb the baby. She crept into the living room and partially drew back the patterned curtains. The sunrise was already beginning to illuminate the grey sky above the city. A train was slowly clattering its way along the track opposite, on the far side of the street. Elizabeth watched it disappear up the incline of the viaduct, the red tail-lights disappearing into the morning mist. In the street below a solitary cop strolled along the sidewalk, rattling his long night stick against the railings.

Ellen, she recalled, had described the miserable place as 'Sunset Boulevard': nothing could have been further from reality. Elizabeth sighed, this city was now home and she had to adjust, not only for herself but because of Peter. Ellen was right, she had to put everything behind her and start again. She gritted her teeth. Somehow she would do it: failure was not in her vocabulary, determination had been instilled in her from birth. She closed her eyes. Even as she looked towards the future the past still crept back like an on-coming fog, dark and forbidding. Even now, in the quiet stillness of the morning, she could hear the gunfire and exploding grenades, momentarily she was back again in Ireland amidst the battle and confusion. Through the cloud of battle there emerged a figure moving steadily towards her, a black-clad man with a sneering face. Rudolph Schiller was walking directly towards her! Elizabeth clutched the curtains, almost ripping them down as she forced the vision from her mind. But four thousand miles south the terror lived on . . .

THE BRONX, NEW YORK
Wednesday, 11 July 1945

WEDNESDAY morning at the Labor Exchange was a rather crowded affair. Arrangements had been made for the woman in the apartment below to look after the baby for a few hours while Elizabeth went back to the local Labor Exchange, several blocks away. She had been trying for some weeks to get a job, but without any success. Elizabeth had been warned to expect to complete a few forms, but nothing had prepared her for what lay in store. The place was a virtual sea of bureaucracy. After queueing for several hours and having completed yet another fresh wad of forms, she was finally interviewed by a less than interested female official. After quickly scanning the various forms, the middle-aged woman tossed them back across the desk.

'Sorry, I can't help you.' The woman shoved Elizabeth's papers back across the counter, at the same time looking over her shoulder to the next in line, at the head of the long queue. 'Next!' she called out.

'Excuse me? I've been standing, waiting since nine this morning. I don't understand . . .' Elizabeth was close to tears as Ellen came to her aid.

'My name's Ellen O'Casey. This young lady is my niece by marriage. She's just recently arrived from Ireland and she's got a little baby. She needs work.' Ellen O'Casey pleaded as best she knew how, trying to cap her own hot Irish temper as she forced a smile.

The female behind the counter looked back with obvious

147

annoyance at the intrusion. 'See, she's an alien, OK!' She stressed the point, a little aggravated at having to do so.

'Clearly it is not OK!' growled Ellen, letting her anger burst forth.

Elizabeth tried to calm the situation. 'So how do I rectify the matter?' she asked.

'Look, she's no work permit and without that you can't apply for work. Period.' The woman official continued referring her answers to Ellen.

'Please have the courtesy to address me,' insisted Elizabeth. The official glanced over at her, a little stunned at the outburst. Ellen touched her arm. Elizabeth took the message and tried to tone down her manner. 'But what about my credentials? I have been teaching for these last five years. Please, see them for yourself.' Elizabeth tried to hand back her papers again.

'It's no use,' the woman drawled. 'You might be a qualified teacher in England, or wherever you've been, but not according to the regulatory controls of the State of New York.' She smirked.

'And what about another state?' asked Ellen hopefully as Elizabeth quietly drew back her papers.

'My guess is they'll say just the same thing. Nothing I can do about it,' the woman said disparagingly.

'But there must be *something* I can do?' said Elizabeth.

'Look, go see the Department of Education.' The woman shrugged. 'Perhaps they'll help. But don't bank on it,' she added sarcastically, ticking her list and calling out over Elizabeth's shoulder for a second time, 'Next!'

'Thank . . . you.' Elizabeth was almost brushed aside by the next eager job-hunter. As she walked away, she overheard the official speaking to one of her colleagues in the next booth.

'Irish immigrants. Slumming it over here. Just who the hell do they think they are?'

Elizabeth turned around, a fire igniting in her heart. Ellen tried to halt her but was shoved aside. The official caught Elizabeth's glare and blushed slightly. Elizabeth walked back to her and tore up her application papers, letting them flutter down on to the counter. 'Some day I will own most of this city,' she snapped. The woman stared back in amazement. 'Some day I will have people such as you coming to me for employment, but I will at least treat them with dignity.' The controlled anger in Elizabeth's voice dumbfounded the official; she was unused to anyone speaking to her in anything but submissive tones. A general hush fell over the entire Labor Exchange. Every head

148

in the public area turned towards Elizabeth as she walked confidently towards the exit. Ellen caught up with her on the steps outside.

'I could swear to hearing a pin drop in there,' smiled Ellen, as Elizabeth fought back against a terrible urge to cry. 'But what did you do it for?'

'Why not?' Elizabeth breathed in deeply. 'It wasn't going to make any difference, was it?' She sighed. Ellen shook her head. 'Well, Ellen, what now?'

'Now, we walk.' Ellen took her by the arm and guided her down the block.

Nothing was said by either woman for several minutes, then Ellen broke the ice.

'Apart from marrying the first bozzo who comes by, the only other alternative you have for work is to play the relief game.'

'The what!' Elizabeth stopped in her tracks, fuming at what she saw as a scurrilous insinuation. 'I'm no prostitute!'

'You, a streetwalker?' said Ellen in a loud voice. Then she began to laugh. Several nearby pedestrians turned their heads towards Elizabeth on overhearing Ellen's comment. She could almost feel their eyes burning into the back of her head as they inspected her from head to toe. 'I'm sorry, Elizabeth. I meant for you to work part-time relief in one of the restaurants or hotels here in the city. Very little's asked and the pay's not too bad, provided you're prepared to work the hours. It ain't easy, but what the hell is!' She took Elizabeth's arm again and guided her off towards Harlem River.

Elizabeth thought about it. She would need time to obtain the qualifications necessary even to teach in this country and whilst she had the jewels, she was uncertain of just how to dispose of them quietly and profitably. There was also the child to consider. How could she look after him properly? She was confused, but undeterred.

'Look at it this way, Elizabeth, I've got this day job in the factory, so I arrive home around five o'clock. That gives you time to get out to work on the evening shift and I stay home and look after little Petey.'

'Peter,' insisted Elizabeth.

Ellen smiled and squeezed her arm a little tighter. 'Awh, what the heck, I'll only call him Petey when you're out at night.'

'Like hell you will!' Elizabeth raised her voice over the noise of the constant street traffic and the shrill of the cop's whistle as he stood at the island junction, directing the traffic ahead.

'You're catching on,' replied Ellen, still laughing.

'But where do I start looking?'

'Start here in the Bronx. And if that's no good, check out Queens. But now we go home for some lunch.'

That afternoon Elizabeth scoured the Bronx area. She was about to give up hope of finding anything in the neighbourhood when she happened on Larry's Diner, close to Madison Avenue Bridge. The ad was crudely taped into the side window, directly under the menu, such as it was. It said simply, 'HELP WANTED. 6 TILL LATE'. Elizabeth peered inside the diner. It was poky, a long narrow place, stretching back as far as she could see. She went inside, the hinges of the glass door squeaking as it was fully opened. A long bar counter stretched down one side of the diner, and down the other was a series of wooden booths, with fitted tables and benches. Between the plate-glass window and front edge of the counter someone had crammed no less than five tables and an assortment of chairs. Whoever owned the place was ready for a voluminous trade but, apart from herself and a solitary customer at the far end of the counter, it was empty.

'What'll it be?'

Elizabeth was a little startled by the voice. The man's head appeared over the counter.

'I . . . I'm sorry. I didn't realize anyone was there.'

'So, what'll it be?' repeated the little man in the chef's hat.

'I was looking for Larry.' From the screwed-up look on the man's face, she realized there was need for elaboration. 'The ad in the window. It says there's a job vacancy.'

'Might be.' He gave her the once-over. 'An' who are you?'

'Elizabeth O'Casey.' She chose to keep to her married name, although it was altogether uncertain what minority would get better treatment in this town: in general, both the Jews and the Irish seemed to be viewed as low caste.

'Irish, eh?'

'My husband,' she answered hurriedly.

'Uh huh,' replied the little man. 'Any experience?'

'You mean cooking? Serving?'

'I mean, lady, have ya ever worked in a diner before, see?'

'Why, no. Not exactly.'

He frowned. 'Work permit?' She didn't answer. He turned his back on her and continued working at the large range, flipping pancakes. Elizabeth was unsure whether or not the interview was terminated, or in fact if she had actually been speaking to Larry

150

himself. She cleared her throat, but the little chef seemed to take no notice. She repeated herself.

'Are you Larry?' she asked politely.

He peered at her from over his shoulder.

The solitary customer at the far end of the counter started to guffaw. Elizabeth stared down at the man. He was shaking his head.

'Lady, you have the privilege to be addressing none other than Elmer Byrd, otherwise known as "Larry", and on occasions by other names too, none of which bears repeating.' The man's voice was deeply accented. Elizabeth imagined him to be Italian. He saluted her with his coffee cup. She nodded back to him before returning her attention to Larry. The little proprietor had stopped flipping pancakes and eyed her up very carefully.

'OK, lady, so you want a job. An' you ain't got a work permit an' you says you ain't got no experience working tables an' I don't know a damn thing about you!' He leaned over the counter, lowering his tone a little. 'Now, why should I take a chance on letting you work around here?'

Elizabeth felt like walking out, but already that day she had been called into over twenty premises. For someone without the proper papers, work in New York was at a premium and she needed a job, any job, and quick. She gritted her teeth. 'Mr Byrd – ' she could see that the form of address disturbed him – 'from the advert in your window you need someone to work nights, and from the salary that you'll probably be offering I honestly don't see too many takers. As for my experience, I've dined in some of the very best establishments throughout Europe, so please don't tell me what I do or do not know.' She paused, slamming her handbag on to the counter. He jumped back a little. 'Now, I am honest and I'm prepared to work my fingers to the bone for you. In other words, Mr Byrd, I'm prepared to give you a chance, and I think it logical that you should at least reciprocate.'

'Reciprawhat!' Elmer Byrd gulped. He was totally unused to 'broads' speaking to him like this; nor was he at all used to confrontational situations where someone repeatedly used a surname that he'd prefer to forget. He was speechless, and going redder by the second.

'Aw, Elmer!' The man sitting at the end of the counter spoke up again. 'Give the lady a chance, will ya? You're disturbing my apple pie an' coffee.' The man's deep voice resonated around the empty diner.

'OK! OK! You're hired,' Elmer snapped. Elizabeth smiled. 'But only for a trial period, see!'

'Thank you,' replied Elizabeth courteously.

'Don't ever thank me, lady. The dough's bad an' so's the hours. Six till four, six days a week, Sundays off.' He pointed his finger accusingly at her. 'An' another thing, see, no time for a break. You take that when you can an' when I says!' Elmer Byrd didn't like being pushed into anything, and he was still hoping to put her off the job.

'I understand, thank you.' Elizabeth continued smiling, and she was glad she had, for when Elmer Byrd stepped out from behind the counter she almost burst out laughing, just managing to make do with broadening her smile. He was no more than five feet tall. Clearly the other side of the counter was somehow raised. To his amazement, Elizabeth shook hands with him. It was clear that he was quite unused to such behaviour.

'You start tomorrow night. Be here five-thirty sharp.' He continued.

'I can't,' Elizabeth replied.

'You can't?' Byrd perked his head to one side in disbelief.

'I've a baby to put to bed and you did say six until four if I recall.'

'Lady's got a point there, Elmer!' The man with the Italian accent shouted up from the far end of the counter again.

'OK! OK! Dames!' snarled Byrd, smacking his dishcloth on to the bar counter. 'Six it is!' he yelled. 'Write down your address on this.' He tossed over a small notepad and pencil.

'Thank you.' Elizabeth scribbled down Ellen's address, then she started to walk down to the man at the end of the counter.

'Lady,' whispered Elmer Byrd, 'take it from one who knows and stay away from that guy.'

Elizabeth ignored the warning and approached the man. He was casually dressed, in a brown leather jacket and a brown floppy-brimmed hat which he wore at an unusually jaunty angle. He seemed to be in his fifties, his black hair now turning white at the temples, but he was also clearly very muscular and fit for his age, his ruddy complexion indicating an outdoor life. He stood up to greet her, removing his hat and offering her a seat. He was much taller than she had anticipated, well over six feet.

'You look as if you could do with a cup of Elmer's coffee.' He smiled.

'I think perhaps under the circumstances I shouldn't.' Elizabeth glanced back. The little proprietor was keeping a careful watch on her from the side of his eye. 'I just wanted to thank you. I was clearly getting nowhere until you interjected.'

'Never mind Elmer there, his heart's really in the right place.' The

152

man then shouted up the bar, 'Hey, Elmer, two more coffees down here!'

'Thank you, but no, honestly.' Elizabeth waved her hand in protest. 'It's been a very long day for me and I have to get home to my child.'

'Child?' The man seemed almost disappointed. Then he appeared to realize the embarrassment he was causing. 'The name's Joe Costello.' They shook hands loosely.

'Elizabeth O'Casey,' she replied.

'Irish?' he continued, clearly eager to avoid her leaving his company. 'You don't sound Irish.'

'No . . . I'm Dutch. My husband . . . was Irish.' She still found she could not come to terms with the reality. 'He died.'

'I'm sorry.' Now he was embarrassed.

She simply nodded. It was easier that way, it didn't hurt so much. Elizabeth forced herself to keep up a brave face. 'I must go. Thank you, Mr Costello.'

'At least I know where to find you.' Costello glanced across to Elmer Byrd. He was pretending to clean the soda fountain as he listened in on their conversation.

'Good-night,' Elizabeth replied, turning towards the doorway.

Joe Costello watched her leave. She stopped at the doorway, examining the heavy black clouds. There was something about her that excited him; she was different from the other dames. He watched her drawing a yellow scarf over her head before venturing out from the shelter of the doorway. As she disappeared from his view, Joe Costello sat down again to finish off his coffee, catching the look on Elmer Byrd's face. He motioned for the little man to come over. Elmer Byrd knew better than to refuse.

'Let me see that address,' demanded Costello.

'Hey, Mr Costello, she's a bit young for you, ain't she?' chuckled the little proprietor, trying to make a joke of it. Costello clicked his fingers and the notepad was handed over instantly.

'Aw, gee, Mr Costello, I need part-time staff in this joint. Give me a break,' pleaded Byrd.

'She's got class,' replied Costello coldly. 'Something this joint ain't.'

The little proprietor knew not to push this customer too far. The man was renowned for his short temper and viciousness. Elmer Byrd had learned it was better to swing with the punches than to argue. 'Sure, Mr Costello, anything you say,' he replied humbly. Suddenly he was grabbed by the front of his apron and hauled tightly up against the counter by the man.

'In future, keep yer comments to yerself, see, "Byrd-brain",' Costello said gruffly. Before Elmer Byrd could answer, a cup of coffee was poured over the counter.

He stood shaking, while the man slowly got up and left the diner. As the front door banged shut, he breathed a deep sigh of relief.

Elizabeth was beginning to find her own way around the Bronx district. Shortly after Ellen left for work the next day, Elizabeth hurriedly prepared the child, setting him into the small pram that Ellen had procured for her from the pawnshop on the next block. His dark hair was in contrast to his pale complexion. The baby stared back at her with steel-blue eyes. It was unsettling. She shook off the feeling as she hurried out.

She had an idea of where she was going, she'd seen the place only the day before yesterday, but finding it herself was another thing. She had to ask directions twice before finally locating the right street. The building was in poor shape, squeezed between a laundry and a delicatessen. She watched from across the busy street. It looked as if it was locked up and deserted.

Some young boys ran up the sidewalk, one of them drinking from a Coke bottle. As they neared the building, some of the other youngsters started egging on the one holding the Coke bottle. After a moment of hesitation, while his pals moved cautiously on past the delicatessen, the boy finally plucked up the courage. He ran forward and chucked the empty bottle towards the door of the building next to the delicatessen. The Coke bottle shattered on impact, then the boys started running, yelling and whooping at the tops of their voices.

She was starting to convince herself that the place was derelict when the heavy front door suddenly opened. An old man appeared in the doorway and began shaking his head on seeing the broken glass at his feet. Elizabeth crossed the road with care, waiting for nearly a full minute in the central reserve until she got a break in the heavy traffic. By the time she had crossed to the other side, the old man had brushed the broken glass away with his foot and was closing the door again.

'Excuse me!' she shouted above the noise of a heavy truck as it rolled by. The old man seemed not to hear her. 'Hello!' she tried again, this time gaining his attention just as he had almost shut the door.

He looked at Elizabeth for a few seconds. He seemed to be trying to form some impression of her before opening the door any wider. The old man pulled open the grubby painted door further and moved forward. He wasn't tall, a little over five feet, his hunched shoulders visible even under the heavy black overcoat and broad grey woollen scarf he had draped from his neck. He wore a black woollen hat, pulled down around his ears, and displayed several days' stubble on his chin. His eyes narrowed behind the thick lenses of his spectacles as he took a closer look at her.

'How can I help you?' Elizabeth detected the strains of some East European language in his accent.

'Is the synagogue not open?' she asked pensively.

'Why? Who are you, young lady?' He wasn't hostile, just cautious.

'I am Jewish. My name is Elizabeth O'Casey.'

He looked at her suspiciously. 'O'Casey? Is that not Irish?'

'My late husband was Irish. My family name is Goldmann. I'm Dutch.' She looked down at the baby, stirring in the pram. 'This is my son.' She looked up again. The old man was in front of her, staring down at the baby, his grey face lighting up on seeing the gurgling child. 'I was wanting to see a rabbi.'

'Come inside.'

Elizabeth manoeuvred the pram up the single step from the sidewalk. The entrance hall was dank and drab. All the windows had been boarded up. She waited while the old man closed and bolted the door. He shuffled inside, shutting the frosted-glass vestibule door. 'Can't be too careful, vandals . . . kids. It's always the kids.' He shook his head and beckoned her to follow him towards the back of the building.

She followed until she was standing in the middle of a small synagogue. It was a long room with high fanlights and an extraordinarily high ceiling, broken up by a series of roof lights along one side. The grey clouds above added to the gloom within. The walls were discoloured and running with damp, and the plasterwork boasted in part. The smell of decay was everywhere.

'It's seen better days.' The old man's voice echoed around the empty room. He led her down towards the back of the synagogue and into a small anteroom, which appeared to be the caretaker's quarters. It was windowless, the only natural light coming in through a cracked and dirty skylight. Elizabeth looked around as the man switched on the light. The room had a narrow cot in one corner and a gas stove in the other. A battered roll-top desk sat next to the cot. The old man pulled over a chair from beside the desk and gestured

155

for her to sit down. 'I'm afraid it's not much, but it is all I have.' As she went to sit, he waved his hands jerkily in the air. 'Just be careful,' he continued in a shaky voice. 'Don't lean too far back or the back legs might collapse.'

'Do you think it's wise for me to sit at all?' She smiled back, drawing the pram beside her.

The old man began to chuckle. He crossed over to the stove and, after shaking the kettle to see if he had enough water in it, began to light one of the gas rings.

'Is the rabbi around?' Elizabeth continued.

The old man turned around slowly. 'You are looking at him.' He hunched his shoulders. 'For what it may be worth, I am Rabbi Jacob Bronowski.'

'I'm sorry, I thought you . . .'

'I know, you thought I was the janitor.' He shrugged his shoulders again. 'So, I'm the janitor as well, but do I get paid for it?'

'Forgive me for asking, Rabbi, but from your accent and your name, are you Polish?' inquired Elizabeth.

The old man nodded. 'I came here just after the Great War. It was in 1919. In some ways it seems just like yesterday, but in others . . .' His voice died away as he stared up at the ceiling, raising both hands.

'I understand. I feel myself that I have aged twice over these last weeks.' Elizabeth sniffed back the welling tears. Then she was silent for a moment. 'Is the synagogue closed down?'

'Not the synagogue, just the people.' He moved across beside the small stove. 'This synagogue is similar in many ways to its flock, worn out and old. All our young people have moved away from the area. There are few of us left.'

'And now you have two more.' She looked down at the baby, rocking the pram gently.

'There is a much more attractive synagogue across the river, you know.'

'I like it here.' She forced a smile. The old rabbi shook his head.

'Tell me about yourself, my dear. You say you are from Holland?' He eyed Elizabeth suspiciously.

'Amsterdam, my family . . . they lived there for generations.'

'Until the Nazis came?' the old man asked.

Elizabeth nodded, head bowed. 'They were taken away by the Nazis.'

'I am sorry, my dear. Tell me, have you any knowledge of their whereabouts?'

156

'They are all dead . . .'

'Words cannot suffice,' he said, clasping his hands together.

'Nor can deeds.' Elizabeth looked him sternly in the face. The old man was impressed by her courage.

'What can I do for you?' he asked softly.

Elizabeth turned away. 'I don't really know.' She suddenly felt cold, her hands shaking. She crossed her arms, grasping both shoulders tightly.

'Perhaps you just need to remember what you are, my child.' The old man's voice echoed around the room.

'And what am I?' She sighed.

'You know the answer as well as I do.' He paused, smiling. 'You are a Jew, and you must remember that, for the rest of the world won't let you forget it.'

She turned on him, her eyes filled with tears. 'And this is going to see me through the remainder of my miserable existence?'

'It is only miserable if you so choose it!' He was angry now. It startled Elizabeth a little. He stepped forward, like a boxer moving in to jab his opponent. 'You have your life to live. God has spared you for something other than just existing.' He grasped her firmly by both arms. 'You owe it to him.'

'But I have nothing.'

'You have everything!' insisted the rabbi. 'Most of all, remember just what you are. If you fail to do so, it is your forebears you are denying, not just yourself.' He stood back, letting the words register. 'Come with me.' He took the kettle off the gas ring and opened the door again. She followed him back inside the synagogue, leaving the pram behind. 'Listen very carefully to what I am about to say,' he cautioned as they approached the ark. She waited as the rabbi removed something. As he hobbled back to her, she realized he was carrying a small, tattered book. 'This was my grandfather's. A copy of the Bible. It was his wish that my father follow in his footsteps and become a rabbi, but my father died before he could fulfil my grandfather's wishes, so I fulfilled that wish instead. That is the way it is. In your case, your entire family perished, you lost everything, but now it is up to you to make amends. Plant a new sapling to grow in place of your old family tree. Living up to the expectation of one's forebears is a challenge in itself. It gives you the edge to survive, something we Jews must inherit.' His voice dropped away. For several moments they stood in silence, facing each other.

The rabbi shook his head. 'You have a son. Bring him to the chair of Elijah.'

How could she, yet how could she not? 'But you do not understand,' she said slowly, bursting into tears.

The old man took her gently into his arms and guided her over to one of the bench seats. It took a few moments for Elizabeth to regain control of herself.

'I have to tell someone,' she blurted out. 'I can't go on with this.'

'Then tell me.' He squeezed her hand.

'It's so very hard for me to explain,' she said cautiously.

'Try, my dear,' said the old man.

'I suppose it all started back in April . . .' Elizabeth related the entire events of the last few months, leaving nothing out. It was a relief to unburden herself to another. The old man listened sympathetically, halting her several times to verify specific points. She could see from his face that he was having difficulty in fully believing her story, yet somehow, she had to convince him. After almost one hour she finally drew to a close. Elizabeth felt completely drained of all emotion. '. . . So now you see.' She sighed deeply.

The old rabbi looked up at the *ner tamid*, the 'eternal light' hanging just above the ark. The light flickered and then grew strong again, as if a gust of wind had just blown across the synagogue. Then he stared into Elizabeth's eyes; the pain was there to see, raw and bleeding. 'My child, what can I say?'

'You don't believe me, do you?' she replied defensively.

'On the contrary.' Rabbi Bronowski gazed down at the threadbare Bible on his lap. Then he nodded to himself, as if agreeing to some inner question of conscience. 'Here, take this.' He handed the book to her.

'I can't,' protested Elizabeth.

'It was mine and now it is yours,' he said slowly.

'No.'

'No matter what you think and whether or not you like the idea, God has given you a son. Look to him for your future. Pass on to him what your father would have wished. Take it, for I have no son.'

Reluctantly, Elizabeth accepted the Bible, nestling it against her chest.

'Will you call on me tomorrow?' asked the old rabbi. 'Just to let me see how the child is,' he added.

'I would like that,' she replied courteously.

'God bless you both, Elizabeth Goldmann,' he said, using her family name.

It was only when she reached the sidewalk outside the synagogue that Elizabeth realized the manner of his address. Had he used her

158

maiden name by mistake? She stopped and turned back. The old man was standing in the doorway, smiling down at her. It was then that she realized: there had been no mistake on his part. She smiled back and walked off towards the taxistand at the end of the block. The rabbi stood, watching Elizabeth, a look of satisfaction on his wizened face.

PART TWO

The Serpent Sleeps

LONDON
Friday, 13 May 1960

MCCLEAN had been summoned to Whitehall for a consultation with Sir Arthur Hanning, the acting head of MI6. He had been avoiding the thought of the ordeal for the last two days, ever since the news had broken, but now it was time to face up to the reality. He had known weeks before about the Israeli Intelligence Service plans to scoop one of the top Nazis from Argentina and he had done absolutely nothing about it. Now the news had broken officially, and it was a much bigger fish than even he could have imagined. Mossad had apprehended and brought back to Israel one 'Ricardo Klement', better known to the world as SS Obersturmbannführer Adolf Eichmann.

Now the bubble had burst and British Intelligence were wanting to know all about it, amongst other things. McClean knew this would be the catalyst to get him out of the Secret Intelligence Service South American operations for good. They had wanted that for so long; he couldn't remember when his work had pleased any of them. Up until now there hadn't been reason enough to clip his wings – he had always managed to stay one step ahead of the Whitehall mandarins – but no longer. Now they had their excuse, apart from which he *was* superstitious and it *was* Friday the 13th after all! McClean climbed the steps of the Old Admiralty Building, feeling quite uncomfortable in the navy pin-striped suit; a sports jacket and flannels would have been more in keeping with him, but a meeting with *the* boss required that little extra, even if one was about to be carpeted.

As McClean walked into Sir Arthur Hanning's outer office, he found his own section head, an ex-lieutenant-colonel from one of the Guards regiments, sitting in the corner. The man ignored him and kept reading from his copy of *The Times*. McClean knew for sure now that his apprehension was justified: he was for the chopping block.

'Major McClean?' asked the secretary knowingly. 'You're to go right in.'

He was shown into the first-floor office, a large, bright room. Sir Arthur Hanning stood next to the window, staring out across Horse Guards Parade. There was no welcome, no handshake; the man didn't even have the courtesy to turn around and face him.

'Sit down,' he said coldly. McClean looked at the hard-backed

163

chair which had been set in the centre of the floor, opposite the large knee-hole desk. McClean sat down, trying his best not to fidget. The acting head of the Secret Intelligence Service finally turned about, staring angrily at him. 'Heard the news from Tel Aviv, I suppose?'

'Sir.' McClean looked straight ahead.

'You were in Israel ten years ago at a conference, were you not?'

'Yes, sir.'

'And ever since then you've been keeping a watchful eye on developments there.'

'Yes, sir.' McClean sat up more rigidly.

'And you had no idea that Mossad would try this kidnapping?'

'No, sir.' God forgive me, thought McClean.

'McClean, you are supposed to be our expert in these matters, aren't you?'

McClean looked at the floor, he didn't have an answer for that one.

Hanning glanced down at the file before him as he spoke. 'I've been doing a bit of checking on you and what I've seen I do not like. This Nazi business, for example, just what in damnation is going on?'

'It's all in my last report, sir,' replied McClean.

'I have that, but it seems somewhat contradictory and quite ambiguous in parts.' Hanning flicked aggressively through the top pages of the file.

'Sir?' McClean frowned, for he knew the statement was quite untrue.

'Who authorized you to continue the investigation into this alleged Neo-Nazi "Spider" organization that you reported on two years ago?' Hanning's eyes narrowed.

McClean cleared his throat. 'I took it upon myself, sir. It does exist, I assure you.'

'Evidence! McClean, you haven't got any. You deliberately mis-used your position in South America to carry out an unofficial investigation into the unsubstantiated existence of some neo-Nazi organization, and as a direct result your normal work has suffered, has it not?' He snapped the file closed.

'I wouldn't agree with that, sir.'

'Your section head does.'

'He's entitled to his opinion, sir.'

'Entitled? He's damn well right, McClean! And I have that evidence here!' He lifted the buff-coloured file, flinging it to the side of the desk. 'There's enough in there to rewrite the service's disciplin-ary code.'

164

'I'm sure there is.' McClean couldn't help but permit himself a smile.

'This amuses you?' Hanning jabbed a finger towards the file. 'What you were doing could well have embarrassed HMG. The present situation in the Middle East and in the Soviet Union is alarming, to say the least. Even the Americans have lodged a complaint with us about your meddling in their South American affairs. Their man in Buenos Aires, Agent Clancy, has made specific mention of you compromising CIA operations there. You seem to take it all as some sort of irrelevant joke!'

McClean cursed under his breath. Ever since Clancy had arrived in Argentina, he had made life impossible for both McClean and the Israelis. Of course, the man had always explained his attitude as complying with US foreign policy, but the seed of doubt had been sown in McClean's mind. Some things about the man no longer added up. The more McClean dug, the more he discovered. The man had declined a promotion to take the South American job and, knowing Clancy from old, that didn't add up at all. Also, Clancy had some dubious German connections in both Paraguay and Argentina. There had to be something else in it for him and it was clear to McClean just what that was. Clancy liked the high life, and it had to be paid for; in simple terms, he was on someone else's payroll.

'McClean, you are totally incompetent!' shouted Hanning, breaking into his thoughts.

Something finally snapped inside the Scotsman. 'If anyone's incompetent around here, it's you and people like you!'

'How dare you! That's quite enough!' Hanning was stunned by the sudden outburst. Normally by this time in a 'carpeting', he had his subject grovelling.

'No, it isn't!' McClean was out of his chair. He strode forward, leaning over the desk. Hanning stepped back. 'There's something going on in Paraguay and Argentina that we should know about. This "Spider" organization could lead us somewhere. It's run on the same lines as "the Odessa" organization. I just need a little more time!' But he knew it was useless; he had gone too far. Hanning exploded.

'Your closeness with these Israelis has caused much embarrassment. You are through, McClean. Finished! History!'

'And you're a stupid bastard!' snapped McClean. 'You got your bloody knighthood on the backs of people like me, but when the shit gets stirred up a little, you're the first to dive for cover!'

'Dismissed.' Hanning pressed the buzzer on his desk.

McClean headed for the door. 'I was sacked from the moment you sent for me.'

The door opened and Hanning's secretary rushed in. McClean stared back, pointing a finger at the man. 'Hanning, you just pray to God that I'm wrong. Because if I'm right, you're going to have to fight the Second World War all over again!' Then he stormed out, past the frightened female secretary.

McClean's section head was now standing in the outer office, a smug look of satisfaction on the passed-over colonel's face.

'Happy, are we?' asked McClean. The man's smugness was too much for him. Suddenly the colonel was staring at a clenched fist. The blow caught him on the left eye. He fell back into the filing cabinets and slumped to the floor. 'And that, Colonel, is for doing nothing. Just wait until you actually do something!' McClean straightened his jacket and walked out, slamming the door against the wall.

To his surprise, and for the first time in ages, McClean actually felt good about something. He headed straight out of the building, loosening his necktie as he passed the guards at the main entrance. There he was, standing on a London pavement, with no job, just under £100 in his bank account and the rent on his flat due by the end of the week. He looked in his pocket: four one-pound notes, a ten-shilling note and three sixpences. McClean headed for the West End where he knew he could call in a favour and get a start on getting drunk, free of charge.

A few hours later McClean emerged from the basement Soho club and looked again at the remaining change in his pockets.

'Just about enough to get drunk on in Florrie May's,' he sighed, walking off, oblivious of the man tailing him from the other side of the street.

Florrie May's was actually called the Empire Arms, a small corner pub in Pentonville, close to where McClean had his accommodation. Florrie May was the elderly cockney proprietress. She ran the place like an army mess, according to the strictest of rules – *her* rules, for ever since her husband had died, she had had to take on the burden of the business herself or go under. A lot of punters had chanced their luck with Florrie, much to their regret. She was only four foot eight, but she had a voice on her that would have matched any sergeant-major on a drill square, and a catalogue of swear words that would have widened the eyes of any ship's captain. The place was already beginning to fill up with regulars. McClean squeezed up to the bar.

'Hello, Mr McClean, don't you look the smart one in your new suit.' Florrie smiled across the counter at him. 'The usual?'

'Make it a double, Florrie.'

'Something troubling you?' She moved a little closer.

'You could say that,' replied McClean, sifting through the change in his hand.

The evening wore on, as did McClean's money. Florrie sensed his predicament and sent a barman over to his corner table with several large drinks on the house. McClean was in no mood to argue, and gratefully accepted the offer. He mused over the day's events for the umpteenth time. McClean just could not believe the stupidity of his masters. They were burying their heads in the sand whilst the neo-Nazi cancer started to emanate from South America. He was sure that the 'Nemesis' organization already had controlling interests in West Germany and Italy, and they were not going to be satisfied with financial growth: if they had wanted just wealth, they could have sat back on their behinds in their South American hideouts and enjoyed the high life. Something was happening and for a purpose, but why? Why? He downed the remainder of his glass.

'Want another one?'

He looked up. A woman in a beige coat and matching beret smiled down at him.

'Anna?' McClean couldn't believe his eyes. 'Anna Poetach!' He went to stand up, but she eased him back into his seat, sitting opposite him at the small, round table.

'It must be five years!' he continued.

'It's been seven.' She smiled back. He held her gloved hand tightly.

'I didn't know you were in London. How long are you here for?'

'Until tomorrow, then I fly back to Tel Aviv,' she said quietly.

His face dropped. 'That soon.' Then professionalism took over. 'How did you find me here?'

'Easily.' She leaned across and whispered, 'Too easily for your own good, McClean.'

He looked around the crowded pub. It was full of all the usual regulars, except for two men standing by the door into the snug. They had their backs turned, facing the bar, but the one nearest was watching McClean's every movement in the large mirror above the counter.

'They're all right. They're with me.'

'Why? Protection?' He drew back from her.

'Something like that.' She smiled again. 'Simon has been having you monitored for some time now.'

'Simon?' He looked at her curiously. She was referring to the codename for the chief of the Israeli Intelligence Service. 'But you mean "watched", don't you?'

'Call it whatever you like. Look, can we go somewhere?' She touched his arm.

Florrie came over, clearly curious about who was talking to her favourite customer. 'Another drink for you, Mr McClean? And of course your friend here. What will it be, my dear?'

'I'm fine, thank you,' replied Anna.

'Florrie, this is Anna. She's an old friend.' McClean felt forced into the introduction. It was the only way he was going to get rid of the inquisitive old lady.

'Nice to meet you, love.' Florrie shook hands with Anna. 'Sure I can't get you one on the house?'

'No, thank you,' replied Anna.

'Nice to meet you anyway.' Florrie turned to leave, giving McClean her wink of approval.

'She likes you,' remarked McClean.

'And that's important?' Anna raised her eyebrows, in that way he'd almost forgotten.

'In here it is. Just look at Florrie the wrong way and you'll be out on your ear.'

Suddenly there was a commotion at the bar. Florrie was shouting at one of the two men who had been shadowing McClean.

'Come on, let's get out of here.' McClean stood up and escorted the female Israeli Intelligence Officer outside. Behind him Florrie could be heard cursing and yelling. She had mistakenly taken the two men for homosexuals and they were getting a mouthful of abuse, much to the roars of laughter and encouragement of her regulars.

'I missed you, McClean,' said Anna, taking his arm as they walked along Pentonville Road.

'Now that is saying something, coming from you.' He smiled.

'You're drunk!' she protested.

'Not that drunk, thank you,' he insisted. 'By the way, thanks indirectly to your kidnapping of Eichmann I lost my job.'

She didn't appear surprised by the news. 'I wouldn't have called it a kidnapping, more an arrest,' she said quickly.

'That's not what the papers are saying.' He glanced around. The two men had now exited from Florrie's and were walking behind at a distance. 'Tell me. Have your two boys there got a mobile back-up?'

'No, I don't think they were expecting you to drive tonight.' She laughed as he straightened his crooked tie.

Suddenly McClean hailed a passing taxi, shoving Anna into it before she could say a word. The two Mossad agents were left standing on the pavement as McClean waved goodbye to them. 'The Embankment,' he instructed the driver, before taking Anna into his arms and embracing her. She didn't argue.

They strolled along the Embankment for the next hour. McClean listened at first, updating himself on what Anna had been doing with her life since they had last met. She told him what she could. It was clear to McClean from the outset that she was after something; sooner or later she'd come to the real point of the visit. In the meantime, he played with her, trying to determine what really made this beautiful woman tick. They were crossing Waterloo Bridge when she arrived at her reason for being there.

'We've been tailing you for weeks now, off and on. Not all the time, that would have been too obvious,' she said candidly – too candidly for his liking.

'May I ask why?'

'For your safety as much as our own information.'

'What are you talking about?' He stopped, leaning over the wall and staring into the rippling water.

'You're on to something, McClean.'

'You mean "Nemesis", don't you?' He looked at her. She was standing next to him, watching a barge heading downstream towards Blackfriars.

'Yes.' She couldn't deny it.

'Well, I'm off the case now. Maybe you didn't hear me earlier when I told you.' He turned around, his elbows resting on the wall. 'I was sacked this morning.'

'I knew something had happened the moment our people reported back about your afternoon drinking session around the clubs and pubs in the West End.'

'So I've actually told you something that you didn't quite already know!' He sounded pleased with himself.

'Not exactly. We got confirmation about your storming out of Sir Arthur Hanning's office and punching Colonel Seymour just minutes after the surveillance report.' She smiled back at him.

He let out a deep sigh. 'And now what?' He pulled out a packet of Embassy cigarettes from his pocket, but it was empty. He crumpled it up and threw it into the river.

'Tell me about it, the time you first found out about "Nemesis",' she urged him. Then she moved over beside the stone wall, peering over into the Thames. 'You never did quite tell me all about how you got interested in it.'

169

'I suppose it all started in 1945. I was summoned to Winston Churchill's Cabinet War Rooms . . .'

THE BRITISH CABINET WAR
ROOMS, LONDON
11 p.m., Wednesday, 25 April 1945

THE JOINT CHIEFS of staff were all seated around the blanket-covered tables, which had been formed into a rough open rectangle. The gathering was like any other of the numerous meetings held in the underground rooms beneath the government offices in Great George Street since the beginning of the war. The chiefs of the three services gathered with eight ministers from the war cabinet, along with several permanent secretaries to the various ministries.

Tea was served whilst they awaited the arrival of the Prime Minister, Winston Churchill. For a change, the general attitude was joyous, intermingled with a feeling of relief now that the cold, dark days of war had receded and an end was in sight. In the cramped confines of the cabinet room, no one gave much notice to the arrival of the Prime Minister's private secretary and a tall, rugged-looking army major. The chatter continued until Churchill's arrival, when the entire gathering rose as he entered the room. As usual, he appeared in a hurry, the smoke from his puffing cigar trailing behind him. It was the first time McClean had seen Churchill in person. He was slightly taken aback by the Prime Minister's diminutive stature; he had never quite imagined him to be that small.

'Old Winston's looking more and more like a steam engine each time I see him,' muttered one of the ministers to another. McClean tried to keep his face straight.

'Thank you, gentlemen. Please be seated, if you can all find the room to squeeze in,' Churchill said loudly, moving around to take his seat directly in front of a large wall-map of the world. His private secretary began to open the red cabinet dispatch box in the middle of the table and removed a bundle of files when Churchill motioned him to halt. Churchill took his time, staring around the room. 'Gentlemen, I have called you all here today on a matter most grave indeed.' A general hush fell over the room; the euphoric feeling of seconds before had vanished. 'I have just come from a meeting of the Joint Intelligence Committee, where I was addressed on a matter most urgent and of great consequence.' Churchill looked across towards McClean in the far corner. 'May I introduce to you the newcomer to our little gathering. He is Major McClean of MI6. I think it appropriate that he should tell you of what we know.' Then he nodded to McClean.

McClean arose. He had not expected that day to come face to face with his Prime Minister and now he, the renegade soldier, was about to address a war cabinet meeting. He nervously cleared his throat and began speaking in his strong Highland accent. 'Prime Minister, gentlemen, we have reliable information that Adolf Hitler and a top-level party of Nazis are going to slip out of Berlin imminently.'

There was a general murmur. The Prime Minister banged the table with the palm of his hand and silence quickly reigned once more. He nodded again for McClean to continue.

'Earlier today, at 10 a.m., German local time, over three hundred Lancaster bombers began a bombing raid on Hitler's home at Berchtesgaden, near Salzburg. This was done following our initial report that he was there with his friends, preparing to make their final plans of escape. Since then, we have received further information that the only person of any significance to have been there at the time was the woman called Eva Braun. Most of you will know her as Hitler's mistress.' Several of the ministers nodded their heads in agreement. 'Braun left the Berghof along with an unidentified SS general, returning to Berlin literally only minutes before the mountainside around the Berghof was flattened. This, along with a further wireless report we received from Berlin, would strongly indicate that Adolf Hitler is still in that city, but only just. We believe he is planning to move from Berlin before the Russian stranglehold on the city tightens any further. An unrelated intelligence report from Kiel indicates that two U-boats are being prepared for an ocean voyage. There might just be a connection.' McClean paused.

'Why do you say that?' asked one of the ministers.

'The area where the U-boats are being kept is under the control of the SS,' replied McClean.

'That is very interesting, thank you,' replied the minister.

'Do we know how and when Hitler will make his move?' inquired one of the senior naval officers present.

McClean cleared his throat. 'No, sir, not as yet, but we may have a lead shortly. We have liaison officers with the Red Army forces around Berlin. Of course we are able to intercept all German wireless traffic through our monitoring stations and this may just give us the confirmation we need.'

'Gentlemen!' interrupted Churchill, nodding to McClean to sit down. 'Judging by what I was told at my earlier meeting, the Red Army hopes to take total control of Berlin within the next forty-eight hours. That does not give Hitler much leeway to get out. Marshal Stalin has assured me that by the twenty-eighth no airports will be left open for the Nazis to escape from, and until then his fighter aircraft remain constantly in the air, operating from just south of the city. Their orders are to intercept and destroy any air traffic entering or leaving Berlin.' Churchill paused, drawing on his cigar once more. 'You all know what a personal blow it has been for me to see that coveted prize going to Stalin, but I am swayed in consideration of expedience to bow to Russia's advantageous position and let them take Berlin without delay. There is an overriding factor in all of this.' Churchill stopped for a moment, eyeing the gathering from over his spectacles. 'As well you know, the war in Europe will not be completely over until that animal Adolf Hitler is brought to God's justice. I am prepared, therefore, to concede to Marshal Stalin this bloody first bite at Berlin, given his personal assurance that he will see to Hitler's capture, alive or dead.'

The telephone rang in a far corner. Churchill's private secretary left the conference table and answered briefly, quickly returning to the Prime Minister's side and handing him a scribbled note. Churchill glanced at the message, then nodded affirmatively.

'Gentlemen, you will have to excuse me. President Truman has just telephoned on the transatlantic line.' The Prime Minister then whispered to his private secretary before rising from his chair. McClean watched Churchill leave. There was a heavy tiredness about him that even the imminent arrival of peace could not seem to alleviate. As the Prime Minister left, the ministers began talking amongst themselves once again. In many ways it reminded McClean of being back at school, with the pupils in uproar once the master left the classroom.

'Major, would you come with me, please.'

McClean looked up. The Prime Minister's private secretary was standing behind him. He had imagined that, with his briefing now over, he was being invited to leave, but to his utter surprise he was shown down a claustrophobic corridor and into a small bedroom, fitted out with a utility desk and chair.

'The Prime Minister will be with you presently, although I must caution you that he is prone to spend quite some time on the transatlantic connection,' the private secretary said stuffily.

'Well, I suppose for President Truman it's a change from playing the piano.' McClean smiled.

'I'm sorry?' The private secretary thought he'd missed the point.

'The last photograph I saw of Harry Truman showed him playing a piano with Lauren Bacall on top of it,' McClean replied rather cheekily, trying his best to keep a straight face. 'Now that is a tasty lady.'

The red-faced private secretary hastily excused himself and disappeared.

After more than forty minutes McClean was starting to think he had been forgotten. Then the door opened and Churchill walked in. The army major was on his feet instantly.

'I apologize for keeping you waiting here, but I need your advice.' Churchill closed the door behind him.

'Sir,' McClean replied humbly.

'Major, how reliable do you rate our Russian allies?'

McClean stared back at the Prime Minister for several seconds before answering. 'If we are talking about the dissemination of intelligence information, I'm not sure, sir.'

'So we cannot be sure of exactly what is happening in Berlin?' Churchill raised an eyebrow.

'No, sir. We lost contact with our only Berlin source just over two weeks ago. At that time the source thought there was a definite commitment by Hitler towards escaping from Berlin. We outlined the information to your office last week.'

'I read the report.' Churchill shook his head despondently. 'This business you mentioned in Kiel. From what you said earlier, you seem to think there could be a connection.'

'It makes sense, sir.' McClean didn't like going out on a limb, but he had a gut feeling about this one. 'It could be quite possible for a light aircraft to still get out of Berlin, even if the airport has been seized. Kiel would be well within flying range.'

'We cannot allow these criminals to escape.' Churchill puffed away at his cigar for several moments. McClean watched the Prime Minister's cheeks shake as he enforced his words. 'Report any development to me personally. No matter how obscure it may seem, I want to be kept informed.'

173

CIC OPERATIONS ROOM, WESTERN
APPROACHES, LIVERPOOL
Tuesday, 15 May 1945

MCCLEAN was using Derby House in Liverpool as his *ad hoc* base of operation in attempting to locate the escaping Nazis. Information was flowing in at a colossal rate now. Germany had already surrendered and elements of British and American Intelligence were scouring Berlin for any trace of Hitler and his associates. Of course German radio had been broadcasting news of the Führer's death days in advance of the surrender, but McClean was taking nothing for granted: even if Hitler was dead, many of his senior co-conspirators were still unaccounted for in the confusion of Germany's capitulation.

Derby House had been used from the very beginning of the war to track the campaign in the Atlantic, helping to keep the sea lanes open and let vital supplies arrive safely in Britain. It had not been an easy task, especially in the first two years after the commencement of hostilities, but finally everyone in Derby House had begun to relax, at least until McClean's arrival. Shortly after midnight, McClean received the message from MI5, based at the British Representative's Office in Dublin. They had been contacted by G2, the Irish Army's Intelligence Service. An incident had occurred close to Castlemaine on the south-western coastline of Ireland. The report indicated that a gun battle had taken place between elements of the IRA and apparently German forces. Apart from the mention of the C-47 aircraft, McClean's eyes were drawn by the fact that several of the dead washed up on the shoreline were German sailors and, from the detail of their dress, the MI5 official had ventured to suggest that they had come off a U-boat!

'Looks like you may have come up trumps, McClean!' The admiral handed back the deciphered radio message.

'It certainly does, sir,' mused McClean.

'So what are we after, Major? The PM says we have to give you every assistance on this one.'

'We're after at least one but probably two U-boats.'

'Destination?'

'South America.' McClean stared at the giant map of the North Atlantic. It stretched out across almost the entire width of the wall, rising from the skirting to the ceiling. The ocean was depicted in dark blue and the tiny orange and white markers pinned sporadically across it depicted the last known positions of Allied shipping. Somewhere out there were two U-boats and there was every possibility that Adolf Hitler was in one of them! At that, another naval officer came into the room. The admiral introduced McClean immediately.

'Major, may I introduce you to Captain Thorburn. He's our main submarine expert, attached to Naval Intelligence. I had him come up from London to assist you.'

'Major.' Thorburn nodded courteously.

'Well, it looks as if you and I are going to share a few sleepless nights, Captain.' McClean grinned as they shook hands.

McClean and Thorburn worked all day and into the night preparing their plan of action. By the end of the day they had a small staff already busy sifting through the relevant intelligence files.

'Well, we'll just have to wait and see what the next couple of days bring,' said Thorburn. McClean went back to studying a file under the desktop light.

'There is one other thing, Captain. I am told that you are an expert on U-boat statistics.'

'What would you like to know?' Thorburn replied casually.

'How many of the damned things are still around?'

'That, old chap, is the million-dollar question, I'm afraid. Even if every U-boat complied with the ceasefire agreement and headed for port, it could still take several weeks for us to be sure of the numbers.' Thorburn set aside the file he was reading. 'Why do you ask?'

Before McClean could reply a young Wren officer interrupted them. She handed Thorburn a sealed envelope. 'This has just arrived from Dublin, sir.'

'I think you should open it, old chap.' Thorburn handed it over to McClean.

The Scotsman hurriedly tore open the white envelope and scrutinized the contents.

'Well?' prompted Thorburn.

'We're in business,' snapped McClean.

OXFORDSHIRE
The following day

WINSTON CHURCHILL was standing on top of wooden scaffold-ing, four feet off the ground, busily repointing the brick course of the garden wall with a trowel. It was something which, although he enjoyed, he had not done in some time and his stiff back and sore shoulder amply bore out the fact.

'Winston! Someone to see you!' Clementine Churchill stood on the steps of the rear patio just outside the tall french windows. Churchill looked over, adjusting his white panama hat against the glare of the afternoon sun. McClean was standing next to his wife. He watched the officer salute her, before walking briskly towards him, the gravel crunching under his feet. Churchill remained up on the scaffolding, taking the moment to relight his cigar.

'Sir, I apologize for the intrusion, but I must see you.' McClean saluted the British Prime Minister.

'Your phone message said something about a U-boat.' He set the trowel aside, placing it in a bucket of murky water. 'Help me down.' He started easing himself on to a small stepladder set beside the scaffolding. McClean assisted and then followed the Prime Minister over to a nearby garden seat.

'Sir, there have been some serious developments,' continued McClean.

'So soon?' Churchill sat down.

'Sir, do you recall I submitted a report to you mentioning one of our agents in Germany. An Irishman called Eamon O'Casey?'

'You received a wireless signal from him at Kiel, if I recall, about two U-boats being prepared for sea.' The Prime Minister removed his panama hat and rubbed the sweat from his face with a handkerchief. 'Go on.'

'Early this morning, we received a message from the Irish authorities about a massacre at Dingle Bay, on the west coastline. It would appear that a gun battle had taken place between elements of the IRA and German forces. So far they have accounted for almost thirty bodies, nine of which were dressed in German naval uniform, and overalls the like of which are worn by the U-boat arm of the Kriegsmarine. The other dead are reportedly all Irish; several have

176

already been identified as having IRA connections. One of the dead has been confirmed as Eamon O'Casey the agent I mentioned.'

Churchill frowned. 'How long ago did you say all this happened?'

'The bodies were discovered yesterday, after someone reported gunfire and explosions in the vicinity of Castlemaine.'

McClean removed several photographs from his briefcase and handed them across. They showed the burnt-out remains of the C-47 aircraft. 'I received these within the last hour, sir. The wreckage of a Dakota aircraft with American military markings was found just a quarter of a mile inland from the beach. Our man in Dublin managed to steal a look and take these photographs. It seems that the aircraft had been fitted with long-range tanks.' He pointed to a corner of the photograph. 'It confirms our previous suspicion that they were intending to fly on to South America.'

'Well, at least they won't make the journey in any style, or quickly for that matter.' Churchill eased his sore back into the wooden-slatted garden seat. 'I think you had better pass this one over to our navy. A U-boat can't have travelled too far inside a day.'

'Coastal Command are already scouring the area and will extend the search as necessary.'

'Good! Well then, all we do is wait.' Churchill clapped his hands and stood up. The meeting was over.

'Sir, I'm returning to Derby House tonight. Could I have permission to approach Washington? Their people could help in this.'

Churchill looked up, nodding once. 'Agreed, but I want no flares fired. Keep it quiet, Major. No undue panic.'

'Sir.' McClean saluted as Churchill shuffled back towards the scaffolding again . . .

McClean coughed as he moved back from the wall and started walking slowly down the Embankment again. Anna took his arm, squeezing it gently.

'What happened then?' she urged.

'After my meetings with Churchill, I was assigned to special duties, ostensibly to locate the two U-boats. At first it seemed like something of an impossibility, for out there, stretched almost across the entire seven seas, was a multitude of enemy U-boats. But nevertheless, following that second meeting with Churchill, a full-scale hunt was mounted throughout the North Atlantic.'

'I remember. They reached Argentina, didn't they?'

'Purportedly yes, but I had my doubts.' McClean stopped again. 'What do you mean?'

'Some time later, long after Admiral Dönitz had ordered all the U-boat Wolf-Packs to surrender, two U-boats reached South America. During our investigation we had accounted for the whereabouts of 377 U-boats; officially only two still remained at large. U-977 had taken just over a hundred days to reach the shores of Argentina, sailing into Buenos Aires just ahead of U-530.'

'And they carried no passengers?'

'Of course not.' He looked directly into her eyes. 'And everyone fell for it, hook, line and sinker.'

'I don't understand?'

'They were decoys.' McClean went back over to the wall again.

'Just how can you be so sure?' She caught up with him.

'One of the two missing U-boats was a Type-XXI, one of the new electro boats. Both vessels that sailed into Buenos Aires were older versions.'

'Go on,' she urged.

'During the following months I tried to convince my superiors that they were wrong, but of course all the time the evidence was building up to indicate the exact opposite. It was decided that there had been no grand escape plan. Hitler's remains had of course been located and identified in Berlin, and Bormann had been witnessed as dead. From my information I knew of just one man who could possibly know and confirm the existence of the escape plan and possibly "Nemesis": Admiral Dönitz. I finally got permission to see him in Nuremberg city gaol. It was 15 October 1946 – the night the executions started, a night I'll never forget . . .'

NUREMBERG CITY GAOL
Tuesday, 15 October 1946

McCLEAN arrived a little after 7 p.m. The rain was being driven steadily against the side of the army staff car. McClean sat alone in the back of the vehicle as it waited in queue, behind an American army jeep, just outside the main gates of the prison.

'What's up, Corporal?' McClean eased forward in his seat, trying to focus ahead through the lazy windscreen wipers and the glare of the bright lights beyond.

'Another Yank checkpoint, sir,' replied the Welsh RCT driver.

A US military policeman, his uniform covered in a soaking poncho but clearly distinguishable by his white helmet, approached from the right. The driver rolled down his window. 'What's up, pal?' he said jovially.

The stern-faced policeman avoided any conversation. 'ID,' he demanded, flashing his torch into the interior of the staff car, temporarily dazzling McClean. 'Sorry, sir.' He removed the torch and checked the British driver's identification card. McClean then stretched forward and handed over his own, along with his authority from the Allied General Commander for the Nuremberg district. 'I'm Major McClean, on the authority of General Millwell. You should be expecting me.'

From the policeman's quick response, it was obvious he had been. 'Yes, sir.' He saluted. 'We've been expecting you, all right. But I'm afraid you're going to have to walk the rest of the way from here. No vehicles allowed past this point until further notice.'

McClean climbed out of the car and stared at the towering walls of the old prison. Drawing up his raincoat collar against the driving rain, he followed the military policeman through the checkpoint. Passing under a red-and-white painted barrier, McClean pushed his way through at least two dozen newspapermen as they stood impatiently, getting soaked outside the nine-foot-high wire fence. Then he waited whilst the military policeman spoke with one of his buddies on the other side of the fenceline.

'There ya have it, boys!' an American voice boomed out from just behind McClean. He turned around, a fat-faced reporter with tight-fitting wire-framed glasses and a small pencil moustache was pointing straight at him. The man was clearly angry about something. 'Our guys win the war for 'em and they still get in ahead of us.' Several of the gathered reporters began to laugh, but from the look on the speaker's face the comment was not intended to be humorous.

Suddenly the military policeman stepped in front of the reporters. 'Major McClean?'

McClean turned again. His escort had finally got the fence gate unlocked and was waving for him to follow. He walked the final yards to the tall double gates at the prison's main entrance.

'Why are the press here?' asked McClean.

'Don't rightly know, sir,' replied the policeman, knocking on the picket gate. 'All I know is the army press office told them to be here.'

The picket gate opened and McClean was shown inside, having to produce his identification yet another time. The policeman then led him through into a courtyard towards a door marked 'Military Administration Office'. An American army major was standing beside a desk at the far side of the office. As McClean walked in, he rounded his desk to meet him.

'Thank you, Sergeant, that will be all.' He dismissed the policeman.

'Sir.' The MP saluted smartly and exited.

'I'm Major Dooley. You must be McClean.' He smiled and extended his hand to the British officer.

'Major,' replied McClean.

They shook hands and McClean produced his authority. The American examined it carefully before sitting back on the edge of his desk.

'Take a seat, Major.' Dooley gestured to a chair set next to the fireplace built into the corner of the small office.

'Thank you, but I'm in a hurry,' replied McClean.

The American pouted as he scanned the order. 'Colonel Arnold is in charge of security around here. He's preoccupied right now, but I know he'd like to see you first.'

'I understand,' replied McClean.

'You're Intelligence, right?' The American handed back the order.

'Yes.'

'The general's office said something about you wanting to speak to one of them damned Nazis.'

'I want to interview Admiral Dönitz.'

'You'll need to be quick then.' The American lit a cigarette, inhaling deeply.

'Why?' McClean moved back inside the fire again.

The American handed him a sheet of paper listing eleven names, the first being that of Hermann Goering. 'That's the death list you're looking at.' Dooley glanced at his wristwatch. 'Very shortly the shutters will come down all over this gaol and it'll stay that way until it's over. You don't get your meeting over in time, Major, and you're here for the duration of the executions.'

'I'll try and be quick,' McClean assured him. Even in victory and after what he had seen and learned about Nazi atrocities, McClean still couldn't bring himself to join in the American's clear delight. He'd seen enough killing to last him a hundred lifetimes. Suddenly another officer came into the office. Dooley stood to attention as the man took off his cap, shaking the water from it. The officer couldn't help but notice the list in McClean's hand.

180

'Is that the execution list?' he said gruffly.

'Colonel Arnold, this is Major McClean from British Intelligence,' said Dooley, obviously embarrassed at being caught waving the sheet of paper around. He took the list from the Scotsman and handed it to the colonel.

McClean brought both feet together, briefly nodding his respect to the colonel. It seemed to mellow the white-haired officer.

'So you're Major McClean, pleased to meet you.' He shook hands with the Scotsman. 'AGC said to facilitate you as much as we can under the present conditions. Just who the hell is it that you want to see, Major?'

'Dönitz, sir.'

'You picked a hell of a time, Major, a hell of a time. I see Dooley here has been filling you in.' The colonel looked at his subordinate and then at the execution list.

'I'm sorry, Colonel, but it's imperative I see Admiral Dönitz tonight. I'm due back in London again tomorrow.'

'Admiral?' He frowned. 'You mean the prisoner, don't you? Major, we don't allow prisoners to have rank. These people are all tried and convicted war criminals,' he said sternly. McClean kept quiet. 'OK, Major, Dooley here will show you to the cell.'

McClean was taken by Dooley through a maze of corridors leading to the main prison cell block. After two further security checks he was shown down yet another corridor to a steel-barred gateway. McClean waited while Dooley spoke to a tall MP sergeant at the gate. He looked through the steel bars, down the long corridor. It was brightly lit by comparison with the rest of the prison; he could see right down to the bottom of the cell block. Military police personnel stood directly outside the cell doors along the entire length of the corridor, each man with his face up against a small open inspection panel. Both officers walked inside, McClean having to stoop a little because of the low headroom at the entrance. Once they had taken a few steps, the steel gate was banged shut behind them. The noise reverberated around the entire cell block.

'At least none of the bastards are going to sleep,' commented Dooley.

'What's this for?' asked McClean, waving towards the line of military police standing at the cell doors.

'Special arrangements, by order from the top brass. The condemned prisoners have to be watched twenty-four hours a day. Just in case they try and cheat the hangman.' Dooley moved closer to

McClean and whispered; 'One word of warning, Major. None of these Nazis know about the executions yet; the sentences are to be read out to them at midnight. Until then it's under wraps.'

McClean nodded back.

As they continued on down the corridor, McClean couldn't help but glance at the chalked nameplates beside each of the cell doors. It read like something from the Nazi *Who's Who*. First there was Goering, next Ribbentrop, and after that came Field Marshal Keitel and then Alfred Rosenberg, Hitler's philosopher and co-conspirator in the Final Solution. As the list ran on, McClean found it hard to take in the fact that here they were, the men who had been the cause of so much death and destruction, all under one roof, all about to die.

'It's just the condemned ones up here,' continued Dooley. 'The rest of the bastards are way down the back some.'

'When is it to be?' whispered McClean.

Dooley waited until they'd cleared the corridor before replying. 'As soon after midnight as possible. The death warrants are to be read out to each of the condemned in his cell. It's supposed to save time for them up on the gallows. Can you believe that, after all that they've done!' The American was clearly disgusted at the condemned being given any consideration at all.

McClean followed him up a short flight of stone steps and into an adjoining cell block. They passed through another gateway into a similar-looking corridor, but without the same level of security. Four guards stood at intervals down the corridor, their mood relaxed. The prisoner McClean wanted to see was in the second cell to the right. Dooley flicked open the spyhole, peering inside first before beckoning one of the men over.

'Open this up, soldier,' he ordered.

A baby-faced military policeman checked through the spyhole before opening the door. Dooley went in ahead of McClean and spoke to the prisoner in fluent German.

'Good evening, Admiral.'

McClean found it curious that despite the colonel's opinion of the prisoners, Dooley still accorded respect to the fifty-five-year-old German. Hitler's supreme naval commander from 1943, and successor during the final days of the Third Reich, had been lying back on his bunk. He slowly stood up as McClean entered the tiny cell.

'This is Major McClean from British Intelligence,' continued Dooley.

Admiral Dönitz nodded courteously. He had the appearance of a weary man, his fine grey hair dishevelled and his pale face unshaven.

His studded shirt was collarless and his trousers without belt or braces. McClean was aware that the tall admiral had escaped the death penalty that conviction on all charges would have brought, but had been given ten years on two other counts. It seemed to McClean that the proud ex-naval commander would have preferred a quick end to enduring the humiliation of defeat and incarceration.

Dooley turned to the British officer. 'Officially no one's supposed to be alone with this prisoner, but I guess in your case it's OK. I'll be outside if you need me. I take it you can speak the lingo?' McClean nodded and Dooley left, slamming the cell door shut again.

'Herr Major, you understand that I cannot even now discuss certain military issues.' The admiral declared his position as he sat down again.

'I am not here to talk about military matters,' replied McClean.

Dönitz raised an eyebrow, clearly doubtful of his comment.

'Accepted,' he agreed.

The conversation was slow and exacting. Although the discussion was courteous, McClean was getting nowhere with Dönitz. He denied any knowledge of an escape plan and kept repeating the information he had offered during earlier interrogation: as far as he was concerned, all U-boats had been accounted for.

Suddenly, just after midnight, all hell seemed to break loose. Voices echoed around the corridor outside, then there was yelling, followed by the noise of hobnailed boots. It sounded to McClean as if a full platoon was running up the corridor. The cell door swung open.

'Sir, you'd better come outa there pronto. We've gotta initiate "shake down".'

The baby-faced military policeman prepared to usher him outside. McClean noticed that he had drawn his baton and was clearly flushed and nervous about something.

'What's the matter?' asked McClean.

The soldier ignored him, keeping his eyes firmly fixed on the admiral. Almost immediately a burly master-sergeant appeared at the doorway. 'You'd be best to step outside, sir,' he said firmly.

McClean complied, and instantly two further military policemen rushed into the cell past him, one of the soldiers closing the door in McClean's face.

'Sergeant, what is going on?' demanded McClean.

'"Shake down", sir. All cells and prisoners have to be searched,' snapped the sergeant.

'But why now?'

183

The sergeant drew McClean to one side as several soldiers and a doctor, all dressed in white coats, ran past in the direction of the condemned cells.

'Goering's taken poison,' replied the sergeant.

'Is he dead?' asked McClean. His question was answered for him when Dooley appeared around the corner, coming from the condemned cell block. The blank expression on his face said it all.

'One down and ten to go,' he said drily, raising the open palms of both hands and indicating only ten prisoners now for execution. 'Sergeant, I want a full body and cell search of every prisoner in these blocks!'

'Already in hand, sir,' snapped the sergeant.

'Carry on.' Dooley took McClean down the corridor, towards the empty cells. By now soldiers were pouring into the corridors by the dozen. A gate was unlocked and McClean stepped through.

'What happened?' he asked.

'Cyanide poisoning,' groaned Dooley, shaking his head. 'There'll be hell to pay for this.'

'But how did he get it?' asked McClean.

'That, Major, is the million-dollar question,' answered Dooley.

'So what happens now?' McClean halted just beyond the gateway.

'The colonel says we go ahead with the executions as planned and in the meantime every goddamn prisoner and cell in this joint is going to get hauled inside out.' He pulled out a packet of cigarettes, flicking one into the side of his mouth, but not lighting it. 'You finished with Dönitz?'

'I've a couple more questions I'd like to pursue. If I could?'

'I don't know.' Dooley shook his head.

'Two minutes, that's all,' pleaded McClean.

Dooley removed the cigarette from his mouth, crumpling it in his hand. 'Shit! You'd better make it damned quick, 'cause when the top brass hit this place no one's getting to see anyone.'

'Thanks.'

McClean was shown back to the cell. The soldiers had just finished searching both the admiral and his cramped accommodation. McClean noted that the mattress had been removed from the bed, as had the pillows. Dönitz was sitting on a chair in the corner. By now another military policeman was standing just inside the open door, watching the admiral.

'He stays,' insisted Dooley, before leaving again.

184

'Goering . . . is dead?' asked Dönitz, a look of amazement on his face.

The MP stepped forward. 'I don't know that you should answer that, Major.'

'It's my responsibility, Corporal.' McClean turned to the prisoner, continuing in German. 'Yes, apparently he took poison.'

Dönitz shook his head in disbelief.

'I have just a few more questions for you, Admiral, and I haven't much time. I'd appreciate your frankness.'

'If I can help and it is not against the Geneva Convention or against my conscience, I will answer you.'

'Have you ever met SS Gruppenführer Rudolph Schiller?'

'Schiller?' The admiral thought for a moment. 'Briefly, just a few times. He was one of Himmler's aides. The last time was in early 'forty-five, I think.'

'Can you tell me anything about him?'

'Nothing. I had no direct dealings with him. When I met him the last time, he was in the company of Reichsleiter Bormann.'

'Schiller and Bormann, they were friends?' McClean persisted.

'*Nein*, nothing like that.' He shook his head. 'Bormann was not a friendly type, in the true sense of the word. He is an opportunist. He would sell his own mother if he had too.'

'Now, that is interesting.' McClean paused, moving a little closer to the German. 'You said "is" when you referred to Bormann. Everyone else around here seems to think he died in the Berlin rubble.'

'Major, if you believe that then you are not the man I take you for,' answered Dönitz.

'Why do you say that?' McClean asked.

'Bormann was always a survivor, first and foremost,' Dönitz replied solemnly.

The door opened and Dooley peered inside. 'Time's up!' he insisted.

McClean put his cap back on and saluted the naval officer. The guard's face echoed his disgust.

'Thank you.' Dönitz stood up.

McClean saved his most important question for last, giving the impression he already knew the answer. 'Just one more thing, Admiral. What was your involvement with "Nemesis"?'

'"Nemesis"?' The admiral raised an eyebrow. 'Why do you ask this, Major?'

'McClean?' Dooley interrupted again. 'The colonel's heading this way.'

'Admiral?' urged McClean.

'All I know is that "Nemesis" was the codename for a diplomatic mission Schiller and Bormann were working on along with Reichsminister von Ribbentrop.'

McClean thought for a moment. 'Did you know what the diplomatic mission was about?'

'*Nein*, except that it involved a sea journey. I was simply asked to provide certain logistical support.'

'What support?'

'Two U-boats.'

'And did you?'

'*Nein*. In the end, circumstances overran events. With the enemy advancing through our lines, I was never approached again.'

'Sir? I must insist.' The guard touched him on the shoulder.

As he stepped into the doorway, McClean fired another question at the admiral. 'When and where was this final meeting?'

'Why, it was in the Führer Bunker, some time in March, I think.' Dönitz began to smirk. 'They were all discussing business together, talking in hushed tones. Of course, there was nothing unusual in that, Bormann always operated that way.'

'Thank you, Admiral. You have been a great help.' McClean stepped outside. The relieved MP slammed the door shut again just as Colonel Arnold reached them.

'There you are, McClean,' he snapped.

'I'm sorry to hear about your trouble,' replied McClean.

The colonel grunted, he clearly didn't want to comment. 'You'll have to leave by the other exit, Major, and I'd appreciate your leaving right now. Dooley, you come with me.'

'Sir.' Dooley led McClean aside. 'Wait in my office. I'll get there as soon as I can.'

McClean grabbed him by the arm as he went to move away. 'Dooley, I need to see Ribbentrop.'

'Are you crazy?' Dooley hissed. 'It's out of the question. Ribbentrop's scheduled for execution, he's top of the list now that Goering's dead.'

'There must be some way I can get to see him!'

'Major Dooley!' the colonel called out from the end of the corridor.

'I'll have to go.' Dooley rushed off after his superior officer.

McClean was shown down another corridor away from the

186

condemned cells. He was taken out through a door leading into a small rectangular yard. It had stopped raining, but water was still dripping down from a wire mesh suspended about twenty feet above his head and covering the entire open courtyard. He followed his escort across to another door, which was duly unlocked from the inside. Going the roundabout way, it took him almost ten minutes to arrive back at the Administration Office. The courtyard clock struck once as he went up the steps into Dooley's office. A young second lieutenant was using the telephone at Dooley's desk.

'Where are the executions taking place?' asked McClean.

The young officer looked a little startled at first. 'Wait a minute, will you?' he spoke into the telephone, then, dropping it to his side, 'They're hanging them in the old gymnasium, sir. It's in the inner courtyard.'

'Show me!' insisted McClean. The young officer hesitated and McClean ripped the telephone from his hand. 'This is an emergency.' The young lieutenant looked back, wide-eyed.

They raced out across the courtyard and into the facing building, next to the block where the condemned prisoners had been incarcerated. The small tunnel brought them to the inner courtyard, which contained a small building at its centre. The brick building was in fact the gaol's gymnasium, now the final destination for the ten war criminals. The building was ringed with MPs, all brandishing submachine-guns in the port position. McClean had to negotiate yet another security check before getting to the door of the old gymnasium. Suddenly his path was barred by a sombre-looking MP captain.

'No one's permitted entry,' he said flatly.

'My name's Major McClean. I've got to speak with Major Dooley. He should be with Colonel Arnold.'

'Sorry, sir, I have orders. No one's to get in or out. Colonel Arnold's own words.' Then the captain addressed the young second lieutenant. 'Take the major back to the Administration Office, Lieutenant.'

'Yes, sir,' snapped the young lieutenant.

McClean was almost ready to explode when a familiar face appeared at the doorway, behind the captain. 'Dooley! Thank God!' exclaimed McClean.

'McClean, you'll never learn.' The American shook his head. 'It's all right, Captain, this man's an official observer.'

The captain moved aside and let him pass through.

'Dooley, I need to see Ribbentrop. It's vital I see him,' pleaded McClean.

187

'Come with me.' Dooley showed him through into a wide hallway which ended at a set of double doors. A military policeman was posted at either side, both men equipped with a sidearm and baton. 'I suppose getting you in here isn't going to make much difference to me after Goering's suicide,' commented Dooley.

'What happened exactly?' asked McClean.

'A cyanide capsule. How the hell he ever got it, I guess we'll never know for sure. The provost marshal's investigating right this minute.' Dooley pushed up the peak of his cap and scratched his forehead. 'Come on, I'll take you through.' He nodded to one of the sentries, who unlocked the door.

They were now standing inside the gymnasium itself. McClean shielded his eyes from the bright lights. Facing him were three black-painted scaffolds. Each consisted of a simple cross-beam which spanned between two eight-inch-thick posts, a hemp rope suspended from a metal ring on the centre of each cross-beam. The lower section of the scaffold platform had been covered with a heavy curtain. A lone American army sergeant was standing on the middle eight-foot-high scaffold with his arms folded. In front of him hung a noose, coiled once and tied up with light string. Dooley guided the British officer to one side, where they joined a small gathering of reporters and representatives from each of the Allied forces. They were all standing behind a roped cordon, stretching across the back of the gymnasium.

'Well, well. We meet again,' a voice said.

McClean looked to his left. It was the same fat-faced reporter he'd seen at the checkpoint outside the prison.

'No hard feelings about what I said outside, Major, but we were getting kinda wet waiting for the main feature to start.' The reporter grinned.

McClean ignored the man. He had more important things on his mind. 'Where is Ribbentrop?' he demanded. Just as he'd finished speaking, a door at the top-right side of the gymnasium opened. A man was led into the room, accompanied by Colonel Arnold. He stood erect, wearing only a collarless white shirt and black trousers.

'There's your man, McClean,' whispered Dooley. 'Foreign Minister Joachim von Ribbentrop.'

McClean's heart sank, but from the look of contempt on the condemned man's face he knew he would have had no chance of getting him to talk. Two soldiers held the German, whilst a third unlocked his handcuffs and began to tie his hands behind his back. Once they'd finished, Hitler's ex-Foreign Minister was led up the thirteen steps to the gallows. He stood, looking down at the mixed gathering as the hangman and his assistants tied Ribbentrop's legs together with leather straps.

'May God save Germany!' Ribbentrop shouted out in a clear voice to the gathering of reporters and witnesses standing down at the far end of the gymnasium. Then he mumbled something to one of the soldiers. The soldier nodded and Ribbentrop continued. 'My last wish . . . is that Germany realize its entity and that an understanding be reached between East and West.' Then the rope went down around his neck, the hangman careful to make the final adjustment to the knot, before resting it on Ribbentrop's right shoulder. The rope had been looped to take up the slack and then tied with a light cord which was designed to break under the weight of the falling man. McClean watched as the black hood was finally placed over Ribbentrop's head.

Silence pervaded the gathering. Suddenly there was a loud creaking and cracking sound as the trapdoor was sprung. The prisoner fell, disappearing from sight behind the covered lower section of the scaffold. The rope went taut. McClean swallowed deeply as he watched the slowly gyrating rope.

'Want to go?' asked Dooley. McClean couldn't speak; he nodded and started for the door.

'What's up, "Limey", no stomach for it?' The fat-faced reporter was standing casually popping some more chewing gum into his mouth. He was grinning like some Cheshire cat.

'What's your name?' asked McClean, regaining his earlier composure.

'Ed Morrisey, *Chicago Tribune*,' he replied. 'Why?'

'Oh, nothing,' smiled McClean. 'I just wondered if your father knew it?'

'My father?' The reporter stood open-mouthed as he watched the two army officers leave.

'. . . and that was the end of my investigations into "Nemesis". It all ended when Ribbentrop fell through that trapdoor.' McClean sighed again.

'McClean, can I give you a bit of old-fashioned advice?' Anna leaned against him.

'What?' He appeared a little perplexed.

'McClean, you know just as well as we do that "Nemesis" is hot stuff. It's what controls the "Odessa" and "Spider" organizations. If these Nazis, and they are still Nazis, knew how much you know,

189

you'd be as good as dead.' He started to laugh. 'Being off the job is not going to afford you any protection and you know it.' She was slightly angry now.

'Well, there's not much I can do about it, is there?' he said sarcastically.

'We want you to work for us.'

He looked directly at her. 'Seriously?'

'Very.' Anna paused for a moment, lending effect to her words. 'It's been on the cards for some time to make an approach to you, today just brought it to a head.'

'And what terms and conditions do you offer?' The glint in his eye told her what she wanted to know.

'Money, rank, flexibility – none of that is a problem, if that's what you want. But it stops short of me getting into your bed.' She tantalizingly pursed her lips.

'I get a chance to follow through on "Nemesis"?' He stuck to business.

'I imagine that's why Simon wants you.'

'But you don't?' He pulled her close to him.

'You haven't accepted yet.' She held her lips back from him.

'Accepted.' Then he kissed her. There was no objection as she melted into his arms. At least it was a start, he thought, and Tel Aviv was not until the next morning.

ISRAEL
Tuesday, 11 April 1961

THE TRIAL had begun in a specially prepared courtroom in Jerusalem. The progress of the prosecution was made painfully slow by the mass of evidence necessary to support the case. McClean had taken a special interest from the first moment. Not only had Eichmann's arrest been the catalyst of his departure from England, but the man knew things that might clarify "Nemesis". McClean watched from the public gallery as a thin, balding, middle-aged man entered the courtroom and went directly into the dock, which was surrounded by a bullet-resistant glass case. There was a murmur from the gallery as the insignificant-looking man sat down between two guards. McClean listened intently as the court opened and the man rose, putting on his earphones. He fiddled nervously with them, then he looked up at the gallery. For a few moments McClean and Eichmann were staring at each other, then the ex-SS officer gave a slight grin.

Eichmann was made to stand and answer all fifteen charges. He listened impassively as they were read out, acknowledging where necessary and saying little through his interpreter. Twelve of the charges carried an automatic death penalty, yet it seemed from the accused's attitude that he had little concern for the proceedings. As the final charge was being read aloud, Eichmann returned his attention to the gallery. McClean had gone.

The trial plodded on for weeks, amidst an air of unprecedented publicity, the like of which McClean hadn't seen since the Nuremberg trials of 1946. By 20 June, Adolf Eichmann started to give his own evidence. He created some commotion in the court by refusing to swear on the Bible before commencing to speak.

McClean slipped into the public gallery just in time to hear the defendant speak. As he sat down on a vacant seat, he couldn't help but notice the attention he was getting from a heavily built man with a ruddy complexion sitting just two seats away from him. He ignored the man's interest and continued watching the proceedings until the man changed seats with another spectator and moved up beside him.

'You don't recognize me, do you?' the man whispered to him.

McClean stared back at him. It was only when the man donned his gold-rimmed spectacles that McClean had the recollection of having met him some time in the past.

'Nuremberg city gaol, 1946?' the man continued.

It was then that McClean realized he was sitting beside the newspaper man whom he had met briefly on the night of the executions. He knew he couldn't avoid him, but he couldn't afford to start a conversation there and then. He motioned for the man to follow him outside. As they stood to leave, Eichmann glanced up from inside his glass box. McClean averted his eyes as he led the way outside.

'Ed Morrisey.' The American shook hands with him. 'And don't tell me, it's McClean, isn't it?' He smiled.

'How did you know that?' McClean felt stupid.

'I'm a newspaper man, Mr McClean.' Morrisey felt pleased with himself. 'So, are you still with the British army. Last time you were a major, weren't you?'

'I'm not in the army any more,' replied McClean.

'Ah.' Morrisey was clearly unsatisfied with the comment. 'So what are you now? Official observer for Her Majesty's Government?'

'Just an observer.' McClean smiled as best he could under the circumstances. 'Are you here in Jerusalem for long?'

'As long as it takes.' Morrisey rolled his eyes towards the courtroom door. 'I did some talking to get my editor to agree to my coming over here. I don't intend to rush back.' He handed McClean a business card. 'My card – the hotel number's scribbled on the back. Give me a shout if you're free some time.'

'I'll do that, thank you.' McClean put the card inside his pocket and headed out of the building.

An hour later, McClean was in Simon's office. The Mossad chief's platitudes were beginning to wear a little thin, but McClean had too much respect for the man to let it show.

'My favourite Scotsman! Come in, McClean, and sit down.' Simon, his shaved head glistening under the strong electric light, rose from his desk and pulled up a chair for McClean. 'How are things in Jerusalem?'

'Slow.' McClean eased down into the chair, hot and sticky after his car journey from the court.

'The law must take its course, even when it's someone such as Eichmann,' Simon said solemnly.

'You said you wanted to see me?'

'Yes. Look at this. It's a report from one of our people in West Germany.' He handed him a file.

McClean scanned through it. The report was a detailed financial analysis, with a number of names, all German. However, it was the concluding section that got McClean's attention. It mentioned the word 'Nemesis'.

'When did you get this?' asked McClean.

'Interesting reading, isn't it?' Simon ran his hand across his billiard-ball head. 'Our man picked up the mention of "Nemesis" just the once. It was in a Berlin night-club – two German businessmen were a little more than intoxicated. I delayed showing you the file until I ran a few checks of my own. This is what we found.' He handed McClean a further report. It cross-referenced most of the names mentioned in the first, giving a brief war-time history of each man. Every one of them had been a high-ranking Nazi party member.

'Incredible!' McClean was totally overwhelmed.

'I want to put something to you, hypothetically of course.' Simon

192

started walking around the room again, his usual form. 'Supposing we had it all wrong. Whilst our information indicates that these ex-Nazis are assisting certain Arab states in creating "the bomb", could it be that we are placing our bets on the wrong horse?'

'What horse?' McClean always hated it when Simon started off in riddles.

'What if this "Nemesis" that we've been hearing about for the last fifteen years has got nothing to do with an improved armoury for the Arabs? What if it's to do with finance?' He leaned over the desk, facing McClean. 'Money begets power.'

'It would make sense. The Reichsbank gold reserves that disappeared for example. They've never been found,' commented McClean.

'Exactly.' Simon started walking again. 'Think of it, McClean. Over two billion dollars' worth of gold, notwithstanding the art treasures and diamonds that we know are still missing.' He turned on McClean. 'The true figure could be five or six times that, and increasing all the time, every minute of every day, growing stronger and stronger. You control an economy, you control the country.'

'On the basis of what we know already, do you surmise that the control for "Nemesis" is coming from South America?'

'For the moment it is the safest way for them to operate. It has to be.' Simon's eyes narrowed. 'It's too early yet for the big cats to come back out of the jungle.'

'And the foundation of this organization?' asked McClean.

'You said it yourself. The "Odessa" and "Spider" organizations only help ex-SS and top Nazi officials. It is they who form the nucleus of this new organization. Even if they don't know its aims or objectives, it offers them a safe haven in return for their continued services.' He went back to his desk and removed a sheet of paper from the drawer. 'This is a verbal statement that our people obtained in Germany last year. At the time it meant very little, uncorroborated and unsubstantiated.' He handed it to McClean. 'It was obtained from a German woman who was secretary to Martin Bormann for some time at the beginning of the war. We had contacted her in the hope of getting some further trace on Bormann; instead our people got a lot of boastful, clap-trap nonsense. The conversation was recorded from the next room. In it she described a document she had typed for Bormann, a document supporting a plan proposed by an SS officer called Schiller. The plan was to conquer Europe, not by force but by financial constraints to bring the other countries to their knees. Hitler liked the idea, but for one reason or another Germany ended up invading.'

McClean scanned the typed extract from the conversation. It said little that he didn't already know. The *Adolf Hitler-Spende*, Hitler's private finance fund controlled by Bormann, for example, but the woman also mentioned an SS operation entitled 'Operation Gold'.

'What is this about "Operation Gold"?' asked McClean.

'We're not sure, but it seems that special SS units were sent in along with the spearhead battalions of the German army when they invaded in 1939 and 1940. The object was to asset-strip the financial institutions of whatever they could get their hands on.'

'What do you want me to do? Go back to South America?' McClean handed over the transcript.

Simon smiled. 'I already have someone working on that. The best chance we have of finding out more about this is right here in Israel.'

'You mean Eichmann?' McClean shook his head, scoffing at the idea. 'When you located him Eichmann was working for a water company of all things. It's hardly the centre of a financial empire.'

'But he worked for Rudolph Schiller. He should know whether Schiller's alive or not. He's bound to,' insisted Simon.

'So you want me to talk with him?'

'McClean, if he talks to anyone it will be someone such as you. You're not one of us – he'll know that. It might make a difference.'

'Can I offer him a deal?' asked McClean.

Simon shook his head. 'No deals.'

McClean stood up to leave. 'Get me everything you have on Eichmann, what he did before as well as during the war.'

'Very well.'

'And while you're at it, run a check on this man.' McClean tossed Morrisey's business card on to Simon's desk. 'I met him at the trial today.'

The intelligence chief picked up the card and stared at it a moment. 'Interesting. Yes, I've heard of this man. He syndicates work around all the main American newspapers. He used to work for a Chicago newspaper.'

McClean shook his head. Was there anything Simon didn't know about, he wondered.

'Are you worried about this Morrisey?' continued Simon.

'Not worried, just curious. He met me at the Nuremberg prison on the night of the executions and he remembered me. It could be just a coincidence.'

Simon smiled. 'Caution? McClean, some of our ways are actually rubbing off on you already.' As McClean reached the door, the

Mossad chief shouted after him, 'By the way, Eichmann was a salesman before the war, so be wary of some fast talking.'

JERUSALEM
Friday, 15 December 1961

T HE TRIAL ended on 14 August, but the verdict was not given until four months later. Adolf Eichmann was then brought back into the same courtroom to face judgement. McClean had deliberately avoided going back to the court since his brush with Morrisey. He waited until Eichmann was standing in the dock before slipping into the courtroom gallery. The American reporter was sitting with his colleagues in the front row, intently watching the proceedings below. Adolf Eichmann stood ramrod straight and immobile as a statue, looking into the judge's eyes and showing no emotion whatsoever as the judge completed his summary and read out the sentence.

'This court sentences the accused to death . . .' There was a pause before the judge continued. Throughout the courtroom the silence was absolute. '. . . For crimes against the Jewish people, crimes against humanity and war crimes.' Eichmann didn't even blink. The entire proceedings had lasted fifteen minutes in total and the German had never flinched once. Eichmann then turned on his heel and left the dock.

McClean slipped outside again. He had reached the steps of the courthouse and was starting to push his way through the crowd when Morrisey caught up with him.

'Hey, McClean! Hold up there!'

McClean winced at the sound of his name being shouted aloud. There was nothing else to do. He would have to speak to the American.

'Mr Morrisey.' He tried his best to smile.

'Hey, old buddy, it's Al, not Mister. Say, I've been looking all over for you since the last time we met,' Morrisey said excitedly.

'I've been busy,' replied McClean.

'How about a drink to mark the occasion?'

McClean agreed with some reservation. They headed away from the crowds, finishing up at Morrisey's hotel. Of course, McClean had known exactly where the American was staying, not just from the telephone number on the back of his card but from the report Simon had shown him. As far as Mossad were concerned, Morrisey was clean. He had been commissioned by one of the main US weekly magazines to cover the events in Jerusalem.

As they sat down over some drinks at the bar, Morrisey tried to develop the conversation. 'Tell me, McClean, just what exactly do you do here? I take it you're working for the Israelis?'

'I'm working for a British oil company. Survey and exploration work.' A cover story had been a standard prerequisite for the job. 'We're surveying just off the coast, not far from here.'

'So that's why I haven't seen you lately.' It seemed to satisfy the American.

'But I thought I'd make a point of getting to the court for the judgement.' McClean sipped his whisky.

'You were lucky to get in without a pass.' Morrisey watched carefully for his reaction.

'Not really. Some of the government boys here owed me a favour.' The barman served up another round. McClean was glad of the interruption. After the barman finished, he was first to speak up. 'So, is this you finished and ready for home?'

'I've got to file my final story later today. I suppose they're not going to let me into Ramle to see Eichmann before he hangs.' Morrisey shot the gin and tonic into the back of his throat.

'I would doubt it.'

'A pity, that.' Morrisey grinned. 'I suppose your friends wouldn't pull a few strings for me too?'

'I'm not that well connected,' replied McClean.

'Aren't you?' Morrisey leaned over, careful not to let anyone else overhear him. 'They told me at Nuremberg that you were in Intelligence, right?'

'That was the war; this is now.'

'I suppose a guy like you wouldn't still be doing the same job under the cover of some oil company?' Morrisey nudged him with his elbow.

'I left the British army a long time ago,' insisted McClean.

'Say no more.' Morrisey gave him that knowing wink.

McClean decided to change the subject. 'So what do you do now? I mean after filing your story.'

'Back to the States – another scoop, another place. Anything for a few bucks! What I'd like to do, of course, is write an exposé on these neo-Nazis and what they're about, but then I'd be tramping on too many toes.' Morrisey picked up a fresh drink.

'I suppose it depends on whose toes they are.' McClean checked his watch and tried to look surprised by the time. 'Look, I was expected somewhere half an hour ago. I'd better get out of here.' He waved over the barman again, handing him some shekel notes. 'Give this gentleman a drink on me.'

'That's very kind of you.' Morrisey stood up and shook his hand. 'Hate to write anything on an empty stomach.' He laughed again.

McClean excused himself and headed out of the hotel. The American watched him leave. Even he had to admit to himself that there were some things more interesting than a drink.

RAMLE GAOL
Wednesday, 30 May 1962

FIVE MONTHS had lapsed since the death sentence had been passed. McClean had been able to interview Eichmann in gaol on four different occasions, but time was running out now. It seemed that there was little chance of clemency: the condemned man was due to hang in less than twenty-four hours. McClean had built up a rapport with the prisoner, but little else. Eichmann was saying nothing that could incriminate or damage his friends and old comrades. Today McClean planned one final bid to get the information he so desperately needed.

As on previous occasions, McClean was shown into the exercise yard at Ramle gaol. It was a small area, set aside exclusively for one prisoner. McClean waited for a few minutes until the rattling noise from the door at the far side of the compound alerted him. Eichmann was shown in – a frail-looking figure, dressed in a threadbare V-neck pullover, prison uniform trousers and carpet slippers. At a signal, the prison guard then left.

'Herr McClean, how nice to see you again,' commented Eichmann, speaking, as always, in his native tongue.

'Good afternoon,' replied McClean, producing a packet of cigarettes from his pocket and offering them to him.

'Unless that contains some self-determining phial, I have no use for it,' commented Eichmann.

'Just tobacco,' replied McClean, returning the packet to his jacket pocket.

As Eichmann walked out into the centre of the yard, the sun

caught his forehead. He shielded his eyes from the glare. 'Well, do you have an answer for me?' he asked without any apparent emotion.

'Nothing to your benefit. The Israeli authorities are in no mood to listen to plea-bargaining, I'm afraid.'

'Then our meeting is at an end.' Eichmann squinted. 'A wasted journey for you.'

'You could still talk to me anyway,' commented McClean.

Eichmann shook his head. 'You miss the point, Herr McClean. I did what I had to for the Führer, I simply obeyed the laws of my country. I have no guilt, I make no apology – not to you or to anyone else. So why should I help you, tell me?'

'Your friends have done nothing to help you, have they?'

'They helped me for fifteen years, before I was kidnapped.'

McClean ignored the last remark. 'You told me earlier that the "Odessa" helped get you to Argentina. What can you tell me about the organization?'

'Herr McClean, this is a waste of time and I have little time left.' Eichmann shook his head.

'You know what they are up to, don't you?' persisted McClean.

'Perhaps you'll all find out, soon enough,' he said menacingly. 'This meeting is terminated.' Eichmann started to head back to his cell.

'They've left you here to die!' McClean was furious. He was losing the last chance he had to get what he wanted from this man. 'What do you know about "Nemesis"?' he shouted, but Eichmann kept on walking. 'It's run by your pals, isn't it?'

Eichmann waited whilst the guard on the other side began unlocking the door for him. He turned slowly, looking directly into McClean's eyes as the door opened. McClean's heart sank. He had lost him. Eichmann's face broke into a smile, giving McClean momentary hope, but then the German spoke.

'Goodbye, Herr McClean.' Eichmann turned on his heels.

'Is there nothing I can get you?' McClean surprised himself by asking such a question.

Eichmann stopped just inside the doorway and looked back at him. 'A bottle of wine would be nice, preferably red and French.'

'I'll see what I can do,' replied McClean as the door closed between them. McClean stood alone in the small exercise yard. It was over. There would be nothing more forthcoming from Eichmann.

The next day, on Thursday, 31 May 1962, after a visit in the death cell from the Reverend William Hull, a British nonconformist minister, Adolf Eichmann went to the gallows at Ramle, unrepentant and refusing all religious consolation. In his cell, he left behind him a half-finished bottle of red wine.

One hour later

THE TELEPHONE rang on the reading table next to him. The tall, grey-haired man set down his brandy glass and book, casually picking up the telephone.

'*Ja?*' he snapped.

'Our friend passed on.' The voice at the other end sounded a little excited.

Karl Strassmann said nothing for a moment. 'When?'

'Around midnight their time, about an hour ago.'

'So, that is the end of that,' said Strassmann.

'So it seems,' replied the caller.

'Did he talk to anyone?' asked Strassmann, stirring the brandy with the end of his cigar.

'Negative. He told his visitor absolutely nothing.' The caller chuckled.

'This visitor is the same one that you reported on before?'

'That's affirmative. His previous visit was two weeks ago.'

There was silence for more than several seconds before Strassmann spoke again. 'A personal interest. How curious.'

'Shall I check him out further?'

'But of course,' replied Strassmann.

The line went dead just as Ed Morrisey was going to speak again. 'Of course,' he repeated to himself, staring at his bloated image in the hotel-room mirror.

PART THREE

The Serpent Stirs

1963

B USINESS *could not have been better for the Elizabeth Goldmann Collection. The jewellery retail company had expanded well beyond even Elizabeth's greatest expectations, opening up further outlets in Rome, Paris and Cape Town. Until now Elizabeth's contract for diamonds had been entirely with Israel, but now she was having to negotiate with other suppliers in South Africa. She had hoped that she would have been able to spend more of her time at home, but each year things just seemed to become more hectic. She was America's success story.*

The years since her arrival in New York seemed to have been struck off the calendar in the time it took to dash the pen across the page. She had worked, planned, conceived, prostituted herself in a loveless marriage with that Mafia bastard Joe Costello. He and his construction company had been the bottom rung in her ladder, but she had not shed a tear at his murder. She had been glad, glad for Peter's sake. That Costello had beaten up on her was one thing, but when he had lifted his stinking hands to her four-year-old son! She had sworn then that she would kill him for that, but others had done it instead. Maybe, as the psychiatrists had suggested, Costello and his violence had been implanted into Peter's subconscious, disturbing him, making him withdraw from her – the one who loved him. It probably accounted also for that terrible incident in 1956, at the military academy, when he had knifed Senator Knight's son. They said Peter had meant to kill him, but she knew that couldn't be true. Maybe she had tried too hard to make the boy love her. Peter had grown steadily further and further away from her as the years passed. There had been more schools and more disappointments, with his academic record starting to resemble a patient's temperature chart, changing with his constant moods of depression. Vacations were usually spent at the house in Long Island, with Peter passing most of his time sailing, or for that matter doing anything that would keep him out of his mother's way. They were strangers now.

She had used the jewels one by one to build up her empire, and in 1960 had married a businessman called Oliver Hoover, yet another rung on that glittering ladder of success. Peter hadn't got on with his stepfather, but as time marched on he had accepted him, in a limited fashion. If anyone could communicate with Peter, it was Jacob Bronowski. The elderly rabbi had become Peter's guardian during most of his vacation time, replacing Elizabeth whilst she was away more and more on her various business trips abroad. She hadn't realized it herself, but her business trips were fast becoming an excuse for Elizabeth: the pain of handling a stubborn, questioning and constantly moody son was too much for her to cope with.

On advice, she had started ploughing some of the profits from her jewellery business back into the construction company inherited from Costello. She had been aware for some months now that whilst the construction company was expanding, its overheads had increased dramatically; the outlay at times seemed greater than the eventual profit. Hoover had talked her into agreeing to the purchase of an office block on 42nd Street. One of the city's investors had lost badly on both the New York and London commodities markets and needed a fast cash-raiser. Hoover had made a convincing argument and she had to agree that the asking price was well below its real market value. A Manhattan address would not only enhance both the construction company and her own image, but the leasing of the other office space would pay for any outstanding loans. Elizabeth had her own views on what should be done, but this was her new husband's ball game.

Her third marriage had been love initially, but as time progressed it became clear to Elizabeth that all was not as it should be with Oliver Hoover. Recently Peter's melancholia seemed to have rubbed off on him also. She knew of his flirtatious behaviour before they had been married, but she had been blind to it ever since. On returning unexpectedly from Paris late one night, she decided to stay in their New York apartment rather than drive all the way to Long Island. She had discovered them in bed: her husband and a young actress, locked together in the act of sex. To compound the situation, the woman was even known to her, having been a frequent visitor to parties at their Long Island home. In the days that followed, Elizabeth came to realize that just about everyone in New York society had known about the affair, everyone but her. She had tried to hold on to her marriage, but by the time the society columnists had finished she had only one course of action left.

HIGHFIELD BOYS' BOARDING SCHOOL, BRIDGEPORT, CONNECTICUT
February 1963

T HE YEARS had been good to her in other ways. Elizabeth still maintained her exquisite figure and, with her auburn hair cut in a smart, shorter style, she looked at least fifteen years younger than she was. However, the pace of her lifestyle troubled her. Peter was supposed to have been the priority in her life, but he'd taken a back seat. She had promised herself that somehow things would work out differently, somehow she would take that rest and hand the reins of the business over to her husband completely, but each year it had been just the same – pressure after pressure, excuses following excuses.

It had all come to a head just before his entry to Yale. All the way up to Bridgeport she'd tried in her mind to reconcile herself to the gap between them. It had widened so much that she could no longer even be sure of speaking with the seventeen-year-old properly; he was becoming more and more defensive with her. She had arrived at the school and been shown into the principal's office. The principal had greeted her warmly. They hadn't met before because she had left all the arrangements to Oliver.

'Welcome, Mrs Goldmann. A great pleasure to meet you at last.' The principal shook hands with her, before showing her to a seat. Dr Hogan was thick-set and in his late fifties, with a congenial manner.

'Thank you for seeing me at such short notice,' she replied.

'Don't mention it.' He sat down opposite her. 'Now, you're here to see Peter? A fine young man, just fine. He's settled down well here. Work is no problem to him.'

'So I've been told.' She leaned forward slightly. 'Dr Hogan, may I be blunt? My son and I, we haven't exactly had a close relationship over the years. I'm aware that he is academically bright, but how is he really? Inside?'

'Well, Peter is a quiet type. He keeps himself very much to himself. At first I thought it had something to do with his military-academy background – some of those schools can be awfully tough.' He shook his head. 'But as time went on, it became apparent to us all here at Highfield that he is very much a loner. It's partly to do with his high intellect, you understand.' He shook his head again. 'You may not be aware, but despite his age, Peter could have passed his university entrance exams a year ago. He could have attained a place at any of our leading universities, but he displays a certain immaturity.'

'Immaturity?' Of course she'd heard the comment before, but never put so directly.

'It's something undoubtedly that Peter will grow away from. We just felt that entering any university at his age would have a detrimental effect on his development. Look, I can understand his frustration at being kept in a class with those who are just not as quick as he is, and I'm sorry that it brought you all the way here, but there is very little more that we can do about it.'

'Are you telling me that Peter is some kind of teenage genius?' Elizabeth frowned.

'Well, Peter's intelligence quotient is extremely high. I won't bore you with the details, but it's the highest I've ever experienced in my entire career. Don't get me wrong, Mrs Goldmann, I assess genius not just on IQ, but on how someone applies himself to achieve his aims. To put it bluntly, in Peter's case there can be a certain lack of direction at times.'

'What do you mean?' she insisted.

'Peter prefers to do what he wants rather than what is expected of him, although I must say he does what he does very well.' The principal chuckled.

'He refuses to work?' she asked.

'Hmm, not exactly. He's top of his year.' He rubbed his chin.

'Could you give me an example?'

'Certainly. For instance, when your husband was visiting here last fall, he suggested that Peter should prepare himself for a profession in the financial world, but Peter was just not interested. In the exams before Thanksgiving, instead of achieving his usual top mark, Peter flunked his math examination.'

'I recall reading the report card.' Elizabeth was annoyed with herself for not having paid more attention to her son's achievements. 'Dr Hogan, I can only apologize if the meeting with his stepfather upset Peter emotionally. I can assure you that it will not happen again.'

The principal sat forward. 'Mrs Goldmann, I fear you are missing the point. You see, I'm convinced that Peter deliberately failed the examination, just to reaffirm the message to his stepfather that he wouldn't be studying business management.'

'My goodness.' Elizabeth was amazed. 'Tell me, Dr Hogan, just what is my son interested in?' Elizabeth was embarrassed at having to ask a stranger to explain about her son.

'History, specifically military history. He's actually written several treatises on the subject. I have them here if you'd care to see them.' He produced several bound volumes of papers from a side table, already bundled in red ribbon and clearly prepared for her. From the look on his face, he was clearly very proud of Peter's achievement.

'This is all news to me, Dr Hogan.' She undid the ribbon and flicked through the top papers. The first and second documents were on Napoleon's and Hitler's Russian defeats. Peter had compared and analysed in detail the two campaigns, drawing close similarities between them.

'Our head of history has forwarded some of Peter's work to colleagues at Harvard. They are extremely impressed, I may tell you,' the principal continued, clearly proud of his prize student.

Elizabeth barely heard him. She was too interested in studying the last of the documents, entitled 'The German Defeat, 1942–5: A Comparative Analysis'.

'Peter seems preoccupied with the Second World War. I would hardly have classed it as history in the proper sense.'

'It's all part of modern history. We encourage our students here to take a close look at how their worlds have been moulded and formed, especially in a recent context.' He smiled, adding, 'In Peter's case, it is perhaps a little more exciting for him.'

'Whatever do you mean, Doctor?' She handed back the papers again.

The principal frowned. 'Why, your son speaks fluent German of course. He's been able to sift through material that our other students wouldn't even understand. Our head of history had some archive material sent down from Harvard and Yale for him to peruse. Peter can be quite insatiable when he wants to be.'

'I knew he was interested in foreign languages, but I didn't know he spoke German.' She felt sick inside. All the fears and doubts she had suppressed about Peter suddenly came bubbling back up to the surface again.

'Mrs Goldmann? Are you all right?' The principal rose from his high-backed library chair.

'I want . . . to see my son. Now!' she insisted.

They met in the school library – a large room, approximately sixty feet square. It was in the old part of the building; a plaque over the doorway read '1640', just twenty years after the Pilgrim Fathers had landed on Plymouth Rock. The library smelt of age – the fustiness of old books and ancient timbers. The walls above the crammed book-shelves were unevenly plastered, segmented into panels by rugged pitch-black timber supports which stretched up to meet a vaulted ceiling. It was bright outside, the sunlight cascading between the swaying branches of the trees and through the opaque leaded stained-glass windows, bathing the well of the library in a rainbow of colour.

The place had been empty of both students and staff. Peter came in from the top door, staring down at his mother sitting at the far end of the main reading table. She stood up and he walked slowly down the side of the long oak table, his face illuminated more fully as he entered the well of light towards the centre of the room. Finally he appeared before her, his blue eyes as piercing as ever, his dark hair shining in the light. He looked pale, but his eyes were full of vitality.

'Hello, Mother.' He smiled warmly. It took her by surprise.

'Peter.' Her fear abated and she kissed him on the cheek, as she always did.

'How nice to see you again,' he continued, now just the hint of sarcasm in his tone.

'You've grown,' she replied, trying not to make the words sound stupid.

'A little.' His eyes narrowed slightly. 'Now, to what do I owe this pleasure?' Then he flicked back his dark hair, setting it into place with his left hand – a habit that she'd grown to detest.

'Peter, please. We need to talk,' she pleaded, trying desperately to avoid their usual confrontation. 'Look, can't we at least sit?'

Peter then sat down and began tapping his fingers on the table.

'Must you?' She glowered at him. He stopped instantly.

'I saw the newspapers,' he continued. She was expecting him to say 'I told you so' and then make some smart comment about his stepfather, but instead he surprised her. 'I presume that both you and my stepfather are going to become somewhat richer.' He referred to a recent merger that Oliver Hoover had negotiated, adding more muscle to the Costello Construction Corporation, which now ranked within the top three construction giants in the United States.

'It will be yours some day,' she said emphatically.

'How nice.' There was a smugness in his tone.

'Peter, I'm here for a reason. I've decided to leave Long Island. I'm moving down to the summer house in Key West. It should be ready in a about a month.'

'And Oliver?' he asked coldly.

Elizabeth ignored the comment. 'Peter, I want you to come and live with me in Florida. I know you will be going to university in the fall. Dr Hogan has high hopes of you going to Harvard, but we would at least have the summer together.'

'If I'm going anywhere it will be to Yale.'

'Yale?' She was surprised, but not disappointed. 'Well, at least we can have a chance to get to know each other again before you go.'

'Did you ever really know me?' he asked casually, too casually to sound healthy.

'Please, Peter, this is difficult enough for me. I'm having to apologize and I don't find that very easy to do, even with you.'

'Apologize?' He eased back in his chair.

'I should have been paying much more attention to you than I have been. I'm sorry. I let work come before us and that should never have happened.'

'I should imagine that with all the countries you've been staying in you could apologize in any number of languages.'

She hesitated, unsure of whether or not to proceed. 'I believe you have something of a gift for foreign languages yourself.'

'Is that a crime?' he asked sarcastically.

'Peter!'

'There are perhaps a lot of things you don't know about me, Mother, dear.'

'That is what I want to rectify,' insisted Elizabeth.

'And do you think you can?' His coldness unsettled her. The penetrating blue eyes cut through her façade with ease.

'Let me try, please.' She averted her eyes.

'I read the recent article about you in *Time* magazine. It referred to one of your hobbies as gardening, but you never mentioned me. Not even once.' A chill ran off the last words.

'I will not have my private family life dissected in public!' she said angrily.

'Strange. The gossip columns are full of it!'

She had expected him to say it, but his smugness brought her closer to boiling point. 'Peter, you've become totally distant.' Elizabeth frowned. 'Is there no way we can come to understand one another again?'

'Too much water has passed under the bridge for anything meaningful to happen between us,' he replied.

'There was a time once when you made me promise never to leave you.' She thought back to that awful day when she found Peter locked in his room, following one of the many beatings by Costello.

'I remember.' He shook his head. 'But you put business first and once too often.'

'Don't you see? I had to! Where do you think we would have been without me striving for something better for us? Well?'

'Together?' He stared at her accusingly.

'Together at the bottom of the pile.' She modified his statement. 'And you, Peter, were never destined for the bottom of anything.'

There was an awful silence for a moment. 'Then what am I destined for?'

'To take over the family business.' She hesitated. 'Provided, of course, that is what you want.'

'Family? But you never speak of my father.' He raised his voice a little. It was controlled, but the aggression was very obvious. 'Never in all this time have you ever mentioned his name.'

Elizabeth bit her lip. She always dreaded discussing the subject and each time it was becoming harder to satisfy his curiosity. 'Look, you know he died a long time ago. It was just after you were born. What was there to tell you? There seemed little point in any discussion.' She looked away. This was not what she had come for.

'Mother! Do you know how ridiculous that sounds?' He pounded the table with his fist. 'How many times have I heard that? Three? Four? Well, I'll tell you, shall I? You've evaded the subject and denied me the truth on seventeen different occasions, since I was five years old. That's one for every year of my life so far! You know, Mother, you make St Peter look like an amateur by comparison.'

'Peter, please! We have each other. Isn't that enough?'

'If we had each other, yes!' He nodded his head. 'But we haven't!' Then he leaned forward. 'For you, Mother, dear, it's your work, your growing empire. And me? All I have are growing pains!' She looked away. 'Pains I've had to suffer alone, crying myself to sleep in some stinking school dormitory, burying my head between the pillows so as not to alert the other boys!' He jumped to his feet, his chair crashing noisily to the stone floor. Peter lowered his voice as he continued, 'Oh, yes, you've really been there when I needed you.' He moved away from her.

'I never . . .' Elizabeth stood, choked with emotion.

'Never what?' He turned on her instantly. 'Realized? Cared?' He flicked his hair back out of his eyes again. 'It really doesn't matter, does it? It's all the same.' There was no response. 'Isn't it?' he persisted.

'Stop this! Stop it!' she cried, covering her ears.

'Why don't you go back to your husband. He needs you more

than I do, according to the graphic account his girlfriend gave to the newspaper.'

'Stop!' she commanded.

Peter shook his head. 'But I don't need you and I don't want anything from you.' He wasn't shouting any more. There was a firmness in his voice, a commanding tone with much more authority than she could ignore.

'I love you!' she cried.

'It's too late!' he shouted, his voice echoing around the empty library. 'What I needed from you was a long time ago. Neither of us can go back. It's lost, Mother, gone for ever.'

'I did it all for you,' she pleaded.

'You did it for yourself.' He breathed in deeply. 'Oh, yes, I benefited. I had the proper schools, but I still didn't have you. Your love was either so overbearing that it smothered me or too far away for me to feel it.' He flicked the hair from across his eyes. 'To you love was down the other end of a telephone line or contained in some brief note stuck inside a food parcel, courtesy of the US Mail.'

'It was not like that!' Elizabeth shook her head defiantly.

'You were never there to know what it was like.' He pointed a finger accusingly. 'Never!'

Elizabeth stared into his ice-cold eyes. There was no emotion, no sign of reconciliation. She rushed from the library.

She was not to see her son again for almost six months. Things between them wouldn't get any better . . .

PART FOUR

The Awakening

ELIZABETH *immersed herself in the business. It became her whole life and her decision paid dividends as the corporation flourished. Whilst declining separation officially, her marriage to Hoover was purely for show. Now they lived almost totally separate lives, their frequent appearances without each other explained away as 'due to the exigencies and pressures of business'. Although Elizabeth could see that her husband at times lowered his guard enough to display his regrets at what had happened, she was determined never to be betrayed by him again. He could keep his actress friend, and his quiet and discreet weekends aboard his yacht at Cape Cod, just so long as they remained exactly that: 'discreet'.*

Her contact with Peter was infrequent by now, especially since he had started at Yale. She relied upon 'Uncle' Jacob Bronowski to act as her immediate go-between and ensure that the young man wanted for absolutely nothing. The old rabbi relished his role, gaining Peter's confidence in almost every respect. As a retirement present, Elizabeth had purchased an apartment for the old man in Manhattan. She had wanted to get him something more substantial, a retirement cottage in the country perhaps, but the old man loved the city. He relished its atmosphere and even its more seedy aspects, maintaining that he would get withdrawal symptoms if he couldn't wake up in the morning and listen to the traffic noise! The purchase had a two-fold purpose: apart from being a thank-you gift it gave Peter a place to come and stay during his vacations from Yale, when he frequently declined to travel to Long Island or Key West. If she couldn't have him with her, at least she knew that he was safe.

LONG ISLAND, NEW YORK
Tuesday, 1 June 1965

ELIZABETH had just arrived back at the Mansion House from another buying trip to Israel, selecting diamonds for the Elizabeth Goldmann Collection. She was sorting through some mail with her secretary, Katie, when Oliver Hoover rushed in. She had little contact now with her husband and they had an 'understanding' that when she was in residence at Long Island, he would stay at the apartment in New York. Her initial reaction was to order him out, but from the look on his face she could see that something was terribly wrong.

'Oliver?' she said pensively.

'I . . . I need to see you, Elizabeth. It's important.' He was pleading to stay.

'We'll finish the correspondence later, Katie.' She dismissed her secretary.

'I just heard over the radio,' he blurted. 'Wendell's dead – a massive coronary.'

Elizabeth was stunned upon hearing the news about her closest rival. For the last seven years she and Charles Wendell had been locked in a bitter conflict. Wendell's corporation had suffered heavily in the marketplace as a result of the Costello Construction Corporation's rapid growth, but he had fought back ferociously, using every trick in the book. There had been severe casualties on both sides, including Oliver Hoover having to leave his father's old company because of his association with Elizabeth. Part of her had grown to hate the sound of Wendell's name, yet deep inside she had a quiet respect for the man; he had been a fighter, just like her.

'When?' she asked.

'I rang Tom Pakenham at the stock exchange. Apparently it happened on the floor of the exchange. He was talking one second and then just keeled over. There was nothing anyone could do.' He flopped down into one of the chairs.

'My God, that's terrible.' Elizabeth rose from her chair and went over to the window.

'I suppose the country club will be a little quieter at the weekends now without Wendell's constant wheeling and dealing.'

'I suppose that your old company will now be up for grabs.' She stared out towards the Chrysler Building, its ornate spire pointing up into the clear blue morning sky.

'Not a bit of it,' answered Hoover without hesitation. 'As Pakenham said, they move fast in this game. The company already has a new president, decreed by long-standing agreement.' He paused before giving her the really bad news. 'Elizabeth, Tony Mortimer's the new president of Caldwell and Hoover.'

Elizabeth looked back at him. The despair in Hoover's face was nothing to what she felt in her heart. Tony Mortimer was Wendell's nephew and probable successor to the Wendell empire. He was also one of Elizabeth's most bitter opponents. Whilst Wendell had fought against her with all the business acumen he could muster, including

216

some underhand actions that she could never forgive, Mortimer was something else entirely – he was evil. For as long as she'd known him, Tony Mortimer had tried his best to destroy her. His actions ranged from trying to discredit her personally to the deliberate sabotage of her business. Of course, nothing could ever be proved, nothing could be linked directly back to Mortimer, but when a certain type of trouble occurred, she knew where it came from.

'How?' Elizabeth gritted her teeth.

'Apparently his late father, old Senator Thadeus Mortimer, had bought a substantial share in the business when his son took over the London side of the operation. It was part of the codicil agreement that his son would succeed in the event of Wendell's retirement or death.'

'The world is full of rats.' She felt sick.

'They don't come much bigger.'

'I can think of one,' she said firmly.

Oliver Hoover fell silent, a little unsure of just whom she might be referring to.

Over the next few days Elizabeth watched the parade and spectacle of the numerous tributes to the dead financier. Tony Mortimer appeared on television, paying his own personal and undoubtedly hollow, respects to 'the great man', as he had been titled by one of the leading newspapers. Even the White House paid its own special tribute and the upper house joined the House of Representatives in a minute's silence. It was during that time that Elizabeth saw another death notice listed in the *New York Times*. Her blood ran cold as she peered again at the name. The notice had been inserted on behalf of a Felix Kessler, representative of the Kessler and van Riel Merchant Bank in Amsterdam. The man's name was German yet the bank's Amsterdam address was that of her late father's diamond business!

The week following Wendell's funeral Elizabeth made a few inquiries of her own. From her list of possibilities, one name kept consistently reappearing: Sam Conrad. She rang the Pittsburgh district code and got through immediately.

'Conrad.' The man's voice was gruff.

'Mr Conrad, my name is Elizabeth Goldmann. I have a job for you,' she said without any hesitancy.

'Mam? I'm sorry, but do I know you?' The gruffness diminished slightly.

'No, but you will,' she said bluntly.

'I'm sorry. I'm kinda busy right now.'

Elizabeth sat forward in her chair. 'Mr Conrad, I have a cheque made out in your name to the tune of ten thousand dollars. It's your retainer if you accept my proposal.' She waited a moment, letting him chew over the sweetener. 'If you are interested, I suggest you go along to your local American Express office, where you will find an envelope in your name, containing my home address in Long Island, a plane ticket and reservation to New York.'

'Lady, is this a joke? Are you serious?'

'Mr Conrad, my offer is valid until midnight tonight. If you're interested be at my house by then. Good morning.' Then she hung up.

Sam Conrad arrived at the house a little after ten that evening. He was shown into the library by Rosetta, Elizabeth's Puerto Rican housemaid and cook.

'Mr Conrad.' Elizabeth got up from the sofa and went forward to greet the private detective. He was much as she'd imagined him to be – tall, but fat, with a boxer's face.

'Mrs Goldmann.' He shook her hand. 'Forgive me, but don't I recognize you from some place? A magazine maybe?'

'Probably. The *New York Times* did a profile on me last month.' She showed him to a chair next to the cocktail cabinet. 'Would you care for a drink, Mr Conrad?'

'No, thanks, not when I'm working.'

'So I take it you've accepted the job?' She went across to the desk, removing a large envelope from the top drawer.

'That depends on what it is, Mrs Goldmann,' he said cautiously.

Elizabeth handed over the envelope. 'Nothing illegal, if that is what worries you. You will find it all in there, including your retainer.'

He peeked inside the envelope. 'What is it?'

'I want you to go to Amsterdam and wherever else is necessary. I want to find out what happened to my family, Mr Conrad.'

'Your family?' He raised an eyebrow.

'They disappeared at the start of the war, just after the Nazis invaded Holland in 1940.'

Conrad whistled. 'Is this not a matter for the Red Cross?'

'If you want the retainer, take the job, Mr Conrad,' Elizabeth said abruptly. 'They say you are the best private investigator in this country. Now prove it to me.'

Conrad slipped the envelope inside his coat.

PARK LANE HOTEL, LONDON
Wednesday, 16 June 1965

THE NEXT week dragged for Elizabeth. She had come so far, yet still she could not break away from the spectre of the past. Could Conrad help ease the heavy burden or would his revelations make matters worse? As previously arranged, Elizabeth went ahead with her London business trip, bringing along Fred Rickman, the company lawyer and one of her junior partners, to handle private legal matters for her. She had 'inherited' Rickman along with the construction company following Joe Costello's death. Initially she was dubious about his methods and intentions, but after time he had become one of her most trusted confidants. Likewise, the little lawyer worshipped the ground upon which Elizabeth walked. She had been like a breath of fresh air to him after having to contend with Costello's underhand wheeling and dealing.

Elizabeth booked a suite at the Park Lane Hotel, on Piccadilly, on the recommendation of her husband, after he had told her about being billeted there for a short time during the war. Elizabeth was enthralled by the 1920s ambience of the place. It reminded her of some of the places she used to visit with her father and mother when on holiday in Paris.

On the third day she received word from Conrad. He was in Frankfurt and on his way to see her. She counted away the minutes and hours until the private investigator arrived. Fred Rickman disappeared as Conrad was shown into the suite. From the lounge window, Elizabeth looked out over the trees in Green Park, towards the bandstand beyond, where a military band was striking out a section from one of Mendelssohn's overtures. It had been her father's favourite.

She thought back over her previous attempts to find out what had really happened to her family in Amsterdam back in 1940. Using what little information she had, several times she had travelled to the city, but on each occasion she came up with absolutely nothing. Her

219

search for any clue as to her family's fate had been fruitless, but now there was hope. The van Riel family had been merchant bankers in Amsterdam for some time and although her father had never had any dealings with the bank, he had often spoken about his friend, Paul van Riel. On her last visit, her father's old premises had been lying vacant, partly gutted by a fire some years before. Elizabeth had been tempted to do something about it and lay claim to her family's remaining estate, but something held her back. Perhaps it had been too painful to contemplate, perhaps she had been too frightened of releasing all her pent-up emotions. Instead she had walked away from it, content with the present and trying desperately to forget her terrible past.

'Mrs Goldmann?' Sam Conrad's voice interrupted her thoughts.

'Mr Conrad.' Elizabeth turned around.

'I came straight from the airport.' Conrad lumbered across the room, carrying his extra weight with seeming difficulty. 'My report.' He proffered a grey envelope to Elizabeth.

'I was expecting you to have taken far longer,' commented Elizabeth, tearing open the envelope.

'I wrote it out on the plane here. Sorry it wasn't typed, but I knew you'd be in a hurry to see it. I'm afraid it isn't good news. It's very much as you suspected yourself,' he warned.

Elizabeth's eyes widened as she picked up the papers. The file contained a brief statement from one of her father's retired employees. The old man had witnessed three bodies being carried out of her father's Amsterdam factory on 16 May 1940.

'The date, is he certain?' She looked up from the papers briefly.

'Yes, mam,' nodded Conrad, 'the old man was sure. He had just retired from your father's business after thirty-five years with the firm. Your father had presented him with a gold pocket-watch and chain only the week before, so he remembers the day well. The German army were marching into the city. He says he witnessed the Gestapo raid your father's offices and factory. Everyone who worked there was hauled away to the local police headquarters for questioning.' Conrad halted a moment. 'Everyone except two people.'

'Go on,' she urged.

'The old man was standing on a street corner near by. He saw an open-backed army lorry taking the workers away from the rear of the premises. The reason he was interested was that his son-in-law wasn't on board. He was your father's manager, Jan Huygen,' Conrad stuttered.

'Yes, I remember him. My father respected and trusted him.'

'The old man saw the bodies being carried out of the rear of the building and put into the back of an army lorry.' Conrad's throat was dry; he referred to his notebook before continuing. 'First Huygen was carried out, then a German officer and then finally your father. The bodies were partly wrapped in blankets but the faces were uncovered.'

Elizabeth turned away, staring back outside again. 'What about this officer?'

'The old man doesn't know exactly, but this was the same guy who went inside originally along with the SS officer in charge.' He fumbled through his notes. 'Yeah, here it is, his name was Schiller.'

'What did you say?' Elizabeth felt her heart jump. Her hands began to shake.

'An SS major called Rudolph Schiller. You'll find his photograph somewhere in those papers you've got.'

Elizabeth fumbled through the papers until she found the document she wanted. It was a photostat of an SS personnel record that Conrad had procured from the War Crimes Commission. She stared into the grainy photograph. It was there, in the eyes. How could she forget those horrible moments when she stood facing him in the kitchen of that Irish farmhouse in 1945?

'Look, mam, that's not all. Following your instructions, I visited Buchenwald concentration camp. Where I found this.' He removed another photostat from his inside pocket and set it on the desk beside her. 'It refers to a batch of prisoners brought to the camp by rail from Amsterdam. It mentions the prisoners by number only. There were twenty-six in all, two having died during the journey.'

'What?' she said absently, still staring down at the blurred photograph.

'Mrs Goldmann, the numbers refer back to a holding camp at Westerbork. I checked – the records from Westerbork still exist. The numbers all refer to the Goldmann family, your family.' Conrad held up the paper. 'This document also lists them as being of no useful purpose and instructs the camp officials to instigate special treatment. They died in Buchenwald, there can be no doubt, Mrs Goldmann. I'm real sorry. "Sonderbehandlung" meant just one thing, extermination.'

Elizabeth picked up the photostat copy. 'It was . . . what I'd expected,' she replied hesitantly. She felt sick to the very pit of her stomach.

'I did a follow-up check on this Schiller character. He ended up a general in the SS. It seems he disappeared in Berlin some time around the closing days of the war. He's listed as officially missing, presumed dead.' Elizabeth started shaking, uncontrollably. The papers she had been holding slipped from her hands and fell on to the floor. 'Say, are you all right, Mrs Goldmann?' The detective hastily put away his notebook. 'Mam?'

'Leave me, please.' Elizabeth waved him away as he stepped forward. 'Get out!' she cried.

The door opened and Fred Rickman rushed in. Reading the situation immediately, he ushered Conrad outside to the hallway, shutting the door as he glanced back at his boss. She was weeping.

'What happened?' demanded Rickman.

'Look, buddy, I'm real sorry, she wanted to know and I told her,' said Conrad.

'But it still doesn't make it any the easier, does it?' quipped Rickman.

Thursday, 17 June 1965

IT WAS well into the early hours of the following morning and Elizabeth was still awake. She was sitting next to the window, staring out across Green Park and beyond, towards the dark outline of Buckingham Palace, just visible through the trees. She was unsure of just how long she had been sitting there; time seemed irrelevant, yet unrelenting. She stared across at Conrad's report, still lying on the carpet. A shiver ran across her shoulders. She rubbed her arms with both hands. She found it hard to believe that fate could have been so horribly cruel as to bring her so close to Schiller after what he had done. Why had God allowed it to happen?

Schiller had been seriously injured during the clash in Ireland. Could he really have survived? For until now she'd really given the matter little thought.

Conrad's report had been very concise. There was no doubt now, her entire family were dead and all on the word of one man, Rudolph Schiller. But why? It could not have been because they were Jews. The first Jewish transportations from Amsterdam didn't commence until February 1941, she already knew that. Yet her entire family had received this 'special treatment' nine months earlier.

She thought back to Ireland once again. Unknowingly they had faced one another for a short time. She had served him tea. She had spoken to him. And through him she had also lost the man she loved, yet also gained the son she otherwise could never have had – a sick

222

irony. Schiller had been suspicious of her from the start and she of him, playing on words, like cat and mouse. To listen to him, it had sounded as if Germany had won the war; his confidence had been overflowing. He had come ashore with his bodyguards, strutting around the old farmhouse with a briefcase handcuffed to his left wrist. She thought about the jewels. They had been his and she had used them to start up her own business empire. It made her feel sick and cheap inside. Her business was founded on the sale of the jewels she had found in that battered tin box lying beside that shredded briefcase.

'The Great Jehovah works in ways often unclear to mortal man.' Elizabeth had often heard her father speak those words. Now she understood how cruel the statement really was. There in 1945 she had faced the man responsible for her father's death and the subsequent annihilation of her entire family. Why did she have to survive and yet have her husband taken as a consequence of know-ing the same man? God had cursed her and yet blessed her with a child she loved above all else. God also had given her the opportunity to amass a great fortune. Her mind froze for a second time that evening.

Elizabeth was to stay on in London for the next couple of days, rarely leaving the hotel suite. She had tried contacting her husband by telephone, without any success, but not without surprise. His secretary informed her that he had left New York on a business trip to LA, but Elizabeth knew better. Just so long as Oliver Hoover kept his indiscretions private she didn't much care what he did any more. She no longer believed in love and certainly not in romance, and any such pretence in her life could only cloud the real issues.

She replaced the telephone receiver. In a strange way she was relieved to have been unable to speak with him, for she had to face this thing alone and rationalize matters for herself. She lifted the receiver again and telephoned the suite on the floor below. It rang for almost half a minute before being answered.

'Hello?' Fred Rickman sounded as if he'd been asleep.

'Did I wake you?'

'Wake me? No, not really,' Rickman lied, so as not to offend his boss.

'I need you to go on ahead to Ireland as discussed.'

'Elizabeth, are you sure about this?'

'How long will it take?' she continued.

'A few days. I've already been in contact with a firm of solicitors in Dublin.'

'Very well then. See me at breakfast before you leave. Good night.'

'Good night,' replied Rickman, aware that she'd already hung up on him. He didn't quite understand his boss's motives but he knew better than to argue with her.

BONN
Friday, 18 June 1965

THE WAITER walked across the floor of the fashionable restaurant carrying a telephone. He approached the man dining alone at the corner table. 'Herr Kruse?'

'Ja?' Karl Strassmann looked up from his dinner. The waiter stood before him, holding a silver-plated telephone in his hand.

'A call for you, *mein Herr,*' replied the waiter, plugging the telephone into a nearby wall socket, setting it on the table before withdrawing several paces and then waiting.

Strassmann slowly removed his napkin, setting it beside his unfinished fish dish. He lifted the telephone receiver, dismissing the waiter with a wave. 'Roland Kruse,' he said.

'Herr Kruse, this is Hilmar. I've just had confirmation about that matter I discussed with you yesterday. The American works for a construction company called the Costello Corporation. That's all we know so far.'

'Where is he now?' asked Strassmann.

'He took a flight to London. I'm told he had a meeting there before boarding a plane for New York.'

'Very well. Contact our friends in New York and see what can be done. Just remember, nothing too direct.' Strassmann hung up and quietly continued with his dinner.

NEW YORK
Ten hours later

ED MORRISEY had just got back into his office following an extended liquid lunch when the intercom on his desk buzzed. 'Morrisey,' he answered, yanking off his jacket and adjusting his braces.

'Ed, a call for ya, long distance. Take it on line two.' The voice switched off again before the newspaper man could reply. He lifted the red telephone at the side of his crowded desk and punched the second button.

'Morrisey here.' He sat down.

'This is Wolf.' The words made him rise out of his chair again.

'I told you never to call me here!' He glanced around the large and bustling office. No one had noticed his anxiety.

'Shut up and listen. There's a package on its way to you. You will get it this afternoon.' There was no reply. 'Did you hear me?'

'I heard,' replied Morrisey grudgingly.

'This is urgent. We want action immediately. We will be in touch.' The line went dead and Morrisey was left staring down at the telephone in his hand. He had no sooner set the receiver down than the office messenger arrived at the foot of his desk, handing him a large buff-coloured envelope.

'This one's for you, Mr Morrisey.' The youngster dropped the envelope on his desk and continued on his mail round.

'Hey, sonny!' Morrisey shouted back to him as he examined the envelope. 'Where'd you get this?'

'The mail room, sir, where else?' The messenger continued on his rounds.

Morrisey opened the envelope. The first thing that hit him was a copy of the yearly accounts and shareholders report for Goldmann the Costello Construction Corporation. The first page was folded back and one of the directors' photographs was ringed in red ink. The newsman's eyes lit up as he stared down at Elizabeth Goldmann's face.

DUBLIN
Saturday, 19 June 1965

ELIZABETH flew into Dublin International Airport on the first scheduled morning flight from London. Rickman was there to greet her. Since the corporation had been formed, she had started to use the lawyer more and more. It had been over seven years now since Fred Rickman had practised law on his own. The corporation work had become increasingly demanding and, when Elizabeth offered him a high salary on top of his percentage share from the construction business, he jumped at the chance to work for the Elizabeth Goldmann Collection. She had picked well, for Rickman was a loyal servant and faithful to the letter. He waved to her as she strode smartly across the Tarmac from the Boeing airliner.

Elegant in a lemon suit and white silk blouse, she looked well, much more the woman he knew than the shaken wreck he'd left back in London just two days before. A tall, well-dressed man in his late twenties strolled alongside, bending to every movement of her lips. Rickman felt down. For a long time he had harboured a desire for Elizabeth himself, but he had to make do with being close to her on their numerous business engagements instead. In many ways it satisfied his need for her – she needed him, she confided in him, he was her confidant – but it still upset him to see the way she continually flirted with other men. They were attracted to her like some sort of magnet, and she relished being the centre of attention.

Rickman thought back to what his old grandfather had once said to him: 'What profit a man if he gains a woman and then walks into a crowded ballroom knowing that every other man in the damned place had probably balled her first!' The old soldier had been quite right. Not until now did Rickman understand fully the meaning of his wisdom.

Elizabeth, for all her business genius and ability, was anything but discreet. She was a natural flirt and whilst he knew it went no further, the problem was that no one else did. Even Oliver Hoover had harboured suspicions over the years, which in its own way contributed to their separate existences and his adulterous behaviour. She should have been getting invitations to all the major social events back in New York, and if it had been up to the menfolk she probably

226

would have, but Elizabeth's reputation through the ladies' circles had grown steadily and totally out of proportion. But then that was the nature of things. Yes, Elizabeth Goldmann didn't make life any easier for herself.

Elizabeth returned Rickman's wave as she passed under the viewing gallery towards customs. He threw away his cigarette and headed down to the arrivals suite just in time to see Elizabeth's six-foot escort kissing her on the hand. By the time he squeezed through the crowd and reached the barrier, Elizabeth had bade the man farewell and was handing her luggage tag to one of the porters. A few minutes later she cleared the customs desk and met him in the arrivals area.

'Darling! How are you?' As always, she kissed Rickman on the cheek. He looked at her, a glint in his eye.

'Who was the boyfriend?' He smiled.

'Someone I met on the aircraft. We were seated together.'

'Looks like you created a real impression,' he replied.

'You know me by now, Fred, I can't resist the attention.' She smiled back.

'At least you're looking better than you were two days ago,' he added.

'Time heals.' She pouted. 'Or is it that time allows you to think how to get even?'

The words puzzled him a little. He changed the subject. 'Did you have a good trip?'

'A bit bumpy just after we left the English coast, but the company was entertaining.' She smiled at him. 'Fred, darling, you're not jealous, I hope.'

He flushed slightly as she took his arm.

The journey back to Dublin was like a journey back in time for Elizabeth. Rickman was struck by her unusual silence. The bubble seemed to have burst again, her earlier exuberance vanished. She was too intent on looking out of the window and staring at the changing countryside as the green fields gave way to more and more concrete.

'Penny for them?' he asked.

'What?' She turned around, a little startled at the intrusion.

'I said, a penny for your thoughts.'

'There's definitely something in what they say about the forty shades of green,' she said absently, shaking her head as if stirring herself awake. 'Excuse me, I'm just tired, that's all.' She forced a smile before returning her attention outside. Rickman watched her cross her legs. She was patting her knee continuously with all four fingers – a nervous sign he had long since recognized to respect. He would ask no questions until later.

CONNAUGHT HOTEL, DUBLIN
the same day

RICKMAN finally got his opportunity over morning coffee in Elizabeth's hotel suite. Elizabeth emerged from the bathroom, her blouse unbuttoned and her hair swept down across her shoulders. She flopped on to the long velvet-covered sofa. 'The coffee smells good,' she said, pouring out some for herself.

Rickman set his cup and saucer aside a moment. 'So what's the matter?' he asked.

'Whatever do you mean?' She finished pouring and sat down facing him on one of the settees.

'Something's been bothering you since London. What is it?' he persisted.

'Fred, you're imagining things. Just a little tiredness, that's all.' She dismissed his concern but could see that he wasn't convinced. 'What about Meadowlands Farm?' she asked.

Reluctantly, he let himself get drawn on to the new topic. 'I did what you asked.'

'I never doubted it for a moment.' She sipped the steaming black liquid. 'Any problems?'

'No. I had a bit of trouble with the name, though, but finally the blasted bureaucrats at the companies' register conceded. It's registered just as you asked, in the name of "Oisin Enterprises". I've hired a Dublin-based solicitor called O'Neill to take care of things for us. He seems a discreet enough individual and comes highly recommended.' He leaned a little closer to her. 'Elizabeth, do you still want me to go ahead with this deal? I mean, OK, in money terms it doesn't cost much, but what are we going to do with a piece of farmland on the Kerry coast?'

She answered with a question. 'That's why we set up the company, isn't it?'

'OK, OK, it's your money, Elizabeth,' he said reluctantly.

'Did you find out about the other matter?'

'Mrs O'Dwyer is still living at the same address in Cork. She even

228

works in the same national school. Her husband was killed all right, just as you heard.'

'She doesn't suspect?'

'You mean that you're here in Dublin? No, she doesn't even know I've been checking up on her.'

'It's time I made amends with her. I still keep blaming myself for her husband's death.'

'You crazy? You can't blame yourself for what some half-crazed Irish terrorists did nearly twenty years ago,' he argued.

'But I do,' she said emphatically. 'I'll see her later tomorrow, perhaps just before I leave for New York.'

'Is there anything else you need?' he asked.

'I don't think so.' She took another sip of coffee.

'There's a pile of papers waiting your signature. I left them on the briefcase on the table over there.'

'I'll go through them after. Will you join me for dinner tonight, at say eight?'

'Sure, but will I not be a sort of letdown from the guy you met this morning?' He smiled, she frowned. He took the hint. 'If you'll excuse me, I've got some calls to make back home.' Then he stood up.

'Ever the efficient one.' She smiled back. 'By the way, can you try and locate Oliver for me?'

'Sure thing.'

It had just turned seven o'clock that evening and Elizabeth was putting on her stockings when the telephone rang. She paused in front of the full-length mirror to examine the seams of her nylons. They were fine, but she had to frown at her sagging buttocks – not a good sign. 'You need more exercise,' she groaned aloud, before answering the telephone.

'Elizabeth?' It was Fred Rickman, there was panic in his voice.

'Fred, what is it?'

'Elizabeth, you've got to get back Stateside right away. I've just been talking to Oliver. The reason why you couldn't get him is because he left LA. He's been in Washington, trying to avoid a crisis. The Monopolies and Mergers Commission and the IRS are after us.' He paused, catching his breath. 'Elizabeth, a Senate Committee has been appointed to investigate the construction corporation.'

'Don't say any more. Come up and see me straight away.'

Elizabeth had dressed by the time Fred Rickman arrived at her hotel suite. He padded the room like some caged animal as he related all the events to her.

'But why?' she asked finally.

'Some newspaper printed an article about us. It's alleged that we got some contracts by paying bribes and furthermore that the IRS has pinpointed serious irregularities in our accounts. If that wasn't enough, there's even some sort of allegation about us laundering Mafia money!'

'Well, are we?' Elizabeth asked bluntly.

'Of course not!' he said firmly. 'Look, we've been stitched up. I don't know just how serious the matter is, but what we're talking about here is the credibility of our stock. The corporation is into some heavy borrowing over the new real-estate deals recently. It's our confidence that's at stake here.'

'Our interests are very exposed,' she agreed.

'There's just one more thing. If this blows up the way I see it, our corporation finances could be frozen by the IRS, pending the outcome of the Senate Committee's findings!'

'Then we have to act quickly,' snapped Elizabeth. 'Tell me, how long could all this take?'

'How long's a piece of spaghetti? It could take months, even years. And the longer it is, the worse it'll be for our business confidence. Look, Elizabeth, I've seen these government guys in action at close quarters. They have the power to seize whatever they want, right down to personal property, everything!'

'That's monstrous!' Elizabeth sat down beside the dressing table. 'When's the next flight to New York?'

'There's one just after midnight.'

'Get me a seat on it,' she said firmly.

'What about me?'

'You wind up the deal here and get back as fast as you can. Now, while I'm packing try and get through to Oliver. I must speak with him!' She headed back to the bedroom.

Elizabeth started to pack. She thought about everything. Whether she wanted him or not, Oliver was now a necessity in her life. She had just finished packing when Fred Rickman knocked at the door, his face pale and sweating.

'Can I come in?' The worried look on his face said it all. She walked forward to meet him. 'I couldn't get Oliver, but I spoke to the office.'

'Well?' she asked impatiently.

'They've really got the knives out back home.'

'Speak logically,' she reprimanded him, moving to pick up her baggage from the ottoman.

'Hugo Knight is heading up the Senate Committee.'

'Now, that *is* bad.' Elizabeth stopped in her tracks. Senator Hugo Knight was a long-standing adversary in business and politically. He had also borne a personal grudge against her ever since Peter had attacked his son at boarding school. The fact that his son was a chip off the old block, a natural bully who had pushed Peter beyond all reasonable limits, didn't seem to enter into it. The senator had pushed to have Peter charged, even alleging attempted murder, but Elizabeth knew his type well – where words were not sufficient to pacify, money was.

'Elizabeth, New York says that apparently Lou Adams has been taken into special protective custody by the FBI. He's obviously the one who's been stirring up the shit!'

She couldn't believe her ears. Adams had been one of the other partners she had inherited when taking over the failing business following Joe Costello's death. Certainly the accountant had no love for her, but she had turned around a sinking company and made him a very rich man. To everyone's surprise, Adams had insisted on staying within the corporation, declining to be bought out on several occasions. It didn't make any sense. The man stood to lose everything if the corporation now went under.

'The corporation has made him rich!' She shook her head.

'Rich or not, he's spilling the beans,' replied Rickman.

'But what can he tell them? I got him to remain on the board just after Joe died. I helped him, even after the mistakes he had made, letting Joe borrow so heavily and at interest rates even the King of Siam couldn't afford! What can he say that could damage the corporation? He got a substantial sum for his percentage and, considering all the trouble he was, he was damned lucky to get a bean!' She noticed something in his eyes. 'We are clean, aren't we?'

'Elizabeth, he knows about me.' Rickman sat down. Suddenly it had smashed him in the face. Now he knew what it was all about.

'I . . . I did some underhand dealing for Joe in the early days, a little tax evasion. Sure, Lou was a part of it – he was the damned accountant – but I helped cover it up.'

'Fred, that was before it became my corporation.' She tried to reassure him.

'Yes, but there's more.'

'More?' She was exhausted.

'Elizabeth, they found out about me . . .' he said shamefacedly. 'I was in bed with another . . .'

'A man?' She finished the statement for him. Rickman nodded in agreement, putting his head into cupped hands as he sat down on a stool next to the dressing table.

'Are you saying that you are homosexual?' she asked.

'No. Not the way you think,' he said emphatically. 'It was a long time ago, in Richmond. I was just a kid of nineteen, a law student. He was much older. I can't really say what happened, it just kinda did . . . there never was a time before . . . or since.'

'Well, it will undoubtedly add some colour to the proceedings, but I don't think it's a hanging matter.'

'The point is the man I knew . . . he was murdered . . .' His voice fell away. After a moment Rickman recovered his composure enough to continue. 'The police suspected me of homicide. I didn't do it, of course, but that didn't stop them charging me. I was held in gaol for over seven weeks before they found the killer.' He shuddered at the memory. 'Have you any idea what it was like in that county gaol?' He looked at her, his eyes revealing his torment.

'I can imagine,' she said, kneeling down in front of him and taking him by both hands.

'Oh God! Elizabeth!' He sniffed, averting her eyes and staring up at the ceiling.

'We'll get through this. I know we will,' she said, trying to reassure him.

'They convicted me on a minor charge of indecency. I was forced to plead guilty to avoid the glare of a full trial. I got off with a small fine.' He looked into her eyes. 'Elizabeth, I never disclosed the conviction to the New York Bar Association. I couldn't practise if I had.'

'The Mafia and a homosexual – all the press needs for a field day.' Elizabeth got up again and went over to the window, staring down at the grey Dublin roofs. She could just picture the headlines tomorrow and shivered at the very thought.

'I'm so ashamed. I'll resign, of course,' he stuttered. That was the last thing she needed.

'Fred, don't tell me that! At the moment I need solidarity, not apologies. Save that for whoever calls you to the Senate Committee hearing!' Elizabeth immediately regretted having said it. 'Look, forget about yourself. This is about me, not you. Senator Knight vowed to get me some day. He's been waiting in the wings for this opportunity for a very long time and this is his chance to hit me where it matters. It's a perfect opportunity for him to undermine our corporation, and, like every set-up job, it'll have its flaws, if we can only find them.'

'I am sorry, Elizabeth. I would do absolutely nothing to hurt you, honestly!' The look of utter despair on his face melted her anger. She regretted having been so cutting. She went over to his side. 'They won't hurt you through me,' he said firmly.

'I know that.' She rested her hand on his shoulder. 'We'll face this thing together. But in the meantime, I want you to stay here in Ireland. You're better out of it.'

'As you wish,' he replied slowly. If Elizabeth had seen the look on his face, she would have had second thoughts.

JFK AIRPORT, NEW YORK
Sunday, 20 June 1965

THE INTERNATIONAL arrivals area was bustling with newsmen and reporters and four separate television crews. Over the last twenty-four hours Elizabeth Goldmann had become something of a national celebrity. The gossip columnists' coverage of Oliver Hoover's exploits had whetted media appetites. One of the more sleazy New York dailies had even ventured to run a story claiming that the Mafia godfather Hector Giovanni had been one of her old boyfriends and now everyone was speculating on her sexual appetite: even Hollywood stars were being mooted as her lovers. Newsrooms were scoured for their most glamorous photographs of Elizabeth. The airport security officials met her aboard the aircraft to offer a quiet exit, but true to form Elizabeth chose to face the music head-on. She was met just inside the VIP lounge by Oliver Hoover. The area had already been cleared of reporters.

'No matter what you think of me, Elizabeth, I'm standing right beside you until we see this through,' he said resolutely.

'Thank God,' she whispered, grasping his arm and, to his surprise, kissing him briefly.

'Elizabeth, we've got to talk. Right now, before we leave this lounge!' he said excitedly.

'Oliver, please calm down and don't sound so alarmist,' she cautioned him. 'Now, tell me what's been going on.'

'It's Hugo Knight,' replied Hoover, 'the bastard's made a media feast out of a bar snack. The word is he's called in old favours. They're out to get you, Elizabeth, from all sides.'

'It's nice to know it's personal, as always.'

'The airport director has just told me there's a lobby out there packed full of newsmen,' he continued.

'Well, I suppose I may give them what they want.' She forced a smile. 'Oliver, darling, would you care to hang in there, on the arm of a slut?'

'Elizabeth, there's no need for this,' said Hoover remorsefully. 'It's me who should feel ashamed, not you.'

'If I've thought about anything during the last twelve hours, it's us.' She squeezed his hand. 'Oliver, if we can get through this, do you think there's still a chance for us?'

'Elizabeth,' he said softly, kissing her full on the lips.

As they walked arm in arm towards the exit, he continued to speak. 'I should have seen all this coming.'

'Whatever do you mean?' she asked.

'Some time ago, I picked up on a rumour circulating on Wall Street about Adams. He'd been seen in the company of Tony Mortimer on several occasions.' He shook his head. 'And I was so damned busy I didn't do anything about it.'

'This is no time for self-pity, Oliver, darling.' She squeezed his arm again. 'I just hope that we can keep Peter out of all this.'

'I was talking to him earlier on the telephone. He's taking it all in his stride. You have nothing to worry about.'

'Some chance!' She raised an eyebrow. 'Come on, *Daniel*, the lions await!' She tried to sound jolly as she guided him towards the swing doors.

Immediately they were both blinded by the flashing lights. The questioning was fast and furious, lights popping all around them. Elizabeth could hardly get one answer out before another three or four were simultaneously fired at her. She and Hoover eased through the crowd with the aid of airport security guards. They ignored the more obvious and insulting questions, trying to keep an air of dignity. Just as they reached the elevator, Ed Morrisey confronted them. Elizabeth vaguely recalled the fat reporter with the gold-framed spectacles. She smiled at him, just as he spoke.

'How do you feel about Fred Rickman?' he asked candidly.

Elizabeth was unsure just where the question was leading, but she took it in her stride. 'Mr Rickman is a hard-working board member of our corporation and also one of its closest advisers.'

'You ain't heard yet, have you?' There was a wide grin of satisfaction on the newspaperman's fat face.

'Heard what?' asked Elizabeth.

'He topped himself, just hours ago in Dublin.'

'You're lying!' Elizabeth's blood ran cold. All around the cameras clicked and flashbulbs ignited anew as Elizabeth's eyes flashed to Hoover and back again to Morrisey.

'We know nothing about this,' retorted Hoover angrily, shielding his eyes from the glare as he tried to guide Elizabeth into the elevator.

Elizabeth stayed her ground, rounding on Morrisey. 'You must be mistaken. I've just left Mr Rickman in Dublin!' she insisted.

'Well, it must have been a hell of a farewell, for he hanged himself just a few hours later. It's all on the transatlantic wire.' Morrisey waved a crumpled piece of yellow paper in her face. Elizabeth snatched it from him. 'See for yerself,' continued the reporter. 'He topped himself in the bathroom, or maybe it wuz in your bathroom.'

Elizabeth smacked him hard across the face, knocking his spectacles to the floor. Hoover gripped her tightly by both arms and shoved on through the remaining reporters to the safety of the elevator.

'Keep them back until we get clear of the building!' he growled to the security guards.

The elevator doors closed. Elizabeth buried her head into the corner. 'Tell me this is just a bad dream,' she pleaded.

'Honey, I wish it was,' replied Hoover as he scanned the Reuters telegram for himself.

Morrisey didn't join his colleagues in the rush for the staircase. He wiped away the blood trickling from the edge of his fat lips with a handkerchief, then turned to the photographer standing next to him. 'Did you catch all that?' The man grinned back; they had got their scoop. 'See it gets on to the front page of the next edition, will ya? The city editor's expectin' it. I'll ring in the story from here.' The man was gone in an instant, rushing back to beat the deadline. Morrisey stood scratching his bald head. Something puzzled him about the Goldmann woman. He had seen her before, he was sure of that, but where?

LONG ISLAND, NEW YORK
Sunday, 20 June 1965

THEY WENT straight back to the house. Elizabeth had insisted upon buying the mansion after marrying Hoover, with the intention of giving Peter a stable base and, more than that, making them into a family. Things hadn't quite worked out that way, for Peter had grown more and more distant as the years progressed, and Elizabeth found herself staying in the house only on the occasional night. The limousine swept up the driveway, coasting to a halt outside the front portico.

Elizabeth went to her bedroom while Hoover joined a group of accountants and lawyers in the library to discuss damage control. Once she was alone again, she looked at the crumpled yellow telegram in her hand, still finding it hard to believe the paper-strip message. Why had he done it? He was one of the nicest people she'd known – gentle, understanding, trustworthy and, above all, her friend. Over the years she'd grown to depend on his advice on many matters, and he had always been there when she needed him.

On reflection she found it strange that for some reason she'd never questioned his being without constant female company before. He had always been such a fastidious and busy little man that she just took it for granted that he was married to his work, nothing more. At the many dinner and business engagements they had been forced to attend, he had always turned up alone, and she had never thought anything of it. She looked back at their last moments together. Had she pushed him over the brink? Perhaps if she'd been a little more sympathetic with him instead of venting her anger, this would not have happened. She tore up the paper, scattering the pieces across the floor. Why was it that everything she loved deserted her?

The telephone rang and she picked it up, half expecting to hear her husband's voice asking her to come downstairs. Instead, much to her delight, she heard the familiar Polish accent of Rabbi Jacob Bronowski.

'*Shalom*,' he said softly.

'Jacob, it's wonderful to hear your voice again.' She sniffed back the urge to cry.

'Take it from an old man, Elizabeth, don't let the bastards grind you down,' he said firmly. She laughed. 'I mean it, my child. You can turn this thing around if you really want to.'

'How do I do that?' she asked.

'Pray, my child. Trust in God for your deliverance. Remember what I told you once about being Jewish and what it means?'

'Of course I remember.'

'Do not lose sight of that, my child, and in the meantime keep your powder dry and your musket loaded.'

'Will I see you?' She wanted nothing more at that very moment.

'Peter called me and asked me to go up to Yale to see him. I feel I should do that first.'

'How is he?' She felt embarrassed asking someone else about Peter, but between Peter and the old rabbi a rapport existed that few could understand – to one here was the father he never knew, an unchanging influence in a difficult development, and to the other, Peter was the grandson he had always wanted.

'He's fine, just fine,' the rabbi assured her.

'Give him my love, even if he doesn't want to hear it.'

'He wants to hear it, deep down, where it counts.' He stopped for a second, then added, 'At heart, he is a good boy, Elizabeth. Just give him a little more time.'

'I may not have a little more time to wait. In fact, after this he may not even want to see me again.' The tears were unavoidable now, and she hung up, unable to continue the conversation. After a while, she went over to the portrait of herself that Hoover had commissioned the year of their marriage. She looked at the younger woman – the bright sparkle in her eyes, the determination and resilience. Did she still have it? She unclasped the side catch and the oil painting swung out, revealing the wall safe. Elizabeth quickly went through the numbered sequence, lifting out the battered black metal box. She hadn't set eyes on it for some time now, since its transfer from the safety deposit box shortly after her marriage to Hoover.

She carefully carried it across to the dressing table and opened it, unfolding the faded red velvet and staring down at what remained of 'The Three Brothers'. At one time Schiller's murdering hands had stroked and caressed these stones. Were they his? Had he stolen them from one of his victims? The anger surged through her body. She began to tremble, not with fear and trepidation, but with total hatred. She lifted the jewel box and its contents and hurled them across the room with all her might, crying out at the same moment. The tin box smacked violently against the wall, splitting the lid off.

'God!' she screamed at the top of her voice, the veins standing out on her neck. 'Why me? Why let me live through this? Why? Why?' Elizabeth flung herself on to the bed and wept uncontrollably. Nothing seemed important any more. Even the thought of Peter couldn't give her any solace. She was hard – life had caused her to be so. It was endemic to her, something she imagined every Jewish boy and girl took for granted. She could tolerate her entire family being wiped out. Millions had similarly suffered during the Holocaust and she was no different, except in one respect: she now knew her family's killer. The collapse of the business seemed nothing by comparison. It was something personal now; not just another crazed or sick mind acting under the auspices of an SS uniform and open mandate from his Führer, but something deliberately personal. But why? And what if the bastard was still alive? She had even echoed her fears years ago to Simon Wiesenthal. Had the famous Nazi-hunter in fact acted on her information? Had he even believed her?

The telephone started to ring. She ignored it. Finally she eased herself forward and picked up the receiver.

'Elizabeth?' It was Hoover. 'Could you come down here?'

'Can't you handle it alone? she asked nervously.

'Are you OK?' Hoover's question went unanswered. Just at that moment she saw it, the yellowed and stained envelope lying next to the wardrobe. It had fallen out of the smashed jewel box. Setting the receiver back, she went over and picked it up. She was unsure of the brown stains at first, but not of the writing or the addresses both on the front and back. It was in her own hand! Her very own letter, the last one she'd sent to her father just before the invasion of Holland. She hastily opened the envelope and confirmed the contents. There was no doubt about it. All this time she had always wondered if he'd ever received it and now she knew. Now she knew much more.

Her legs buckled and she fell on to her knees, staring at the battered tin box and running her fingers along the red-velvet lining of the broken lid. It seemed almost impossible that she hadn't noticed the rip before. The letter had been hidden in the lining all this time. For all these years she had carried her father's letter unknowingly. For all these years she had used the jewels, believing them to be Schiller's, stolen from whom didn't seem to matter. Had she ever imagined in her wildest dreams that they could have been hers legally? Her father's only remaining possession that she could identify.

She looked again at the envelope in her hands. The stains were dried blood, probably her father's blood! She was numb with anguish, too stunned to cry further. The hatred that she now felt for Schiller blotted out all other reason and understanding. She stared blankly at the letter. It was as if her next thought would be too much to bear, too hard to face. Slowly raising it to her lips, she kissed the blood-stained letter. God had given her another sign, but what did it mean?

Downstairs, Hoover emerged from the meeting two hours later, looking as exhausted as he felt. She met him in the main lounge, where he was pouring himself a large brandy.

'Would you like one?' he asked.

'No, thank you.' She sat down beside the fire, stretching out her hands towards it. 'What happened?' she continued.

'What happened to you?' he replied. 'I telephoned and you just hung up.'

'I . . . was tired,' she said softly.

He walked over beside her, partly blocking the fire with his body. 'The IRS claim that our tax returns for the last five years are incorrect. They've slapped a lien amounting to thirty million dollars on us.' He gulped down his brandy, spilling some on to the carpet as he gesticulated wildly. His flushed appearance confirmed that he had been drinking for some time.

'That is preposterous,' she said bluntly.

'Look, someone's fingered our business. Lou Adams is telling Senator Hugo Knight and his cronies exactly what they want to hear. Now, you and I both know there's nothing to it, but if the IRS insist on following the letter of the law they can even seize our personal bank accounts. Think of that! They can crucify us.'

'What have you instructed?' she asked.

'I've a team of lawyers and accountants working on it right now, but with Fred Rickman having killed himself, it's looking pretty bad.'

'We can beat it,' insisted Elizabeth.

'Oh, yeah, but time will kill us. We'll have to lay off work on all our major projects. It'll ruin us.'

'Get a court injunction to stop them,' she suggested.

'Elizabeth, you don't take out injunctions against the IRS,' Hoover said sarcastically.

'Then perhaps it's time someone did,' she said resolutely.

'There's something more.' He downed the remaining brandy before continuing. 'The Senate Inquiry is investigating allegations that the corporation is controlled by the Mafia.'

'On what grounds?'

'Lou Adams claims that the Giovanni family handed us a million to get the Washington Manhattan Bank off our backs. That lying bastard turning state's evidence is one thing, but can you believe the gall of the guy? It's one specific too many. Our lawyers will make mincemeat out of it, that's for certain.'

'He's not lying, Oliver. I was loaned that money by Hector Giovanni,' she answered coolly. 'But before you say anything, it was a legitimate loan, which I repaid with interest two years later. It was all strictly above board.'

'Jesus! I can't believe how stupid you've been!' He tossed the glass into the fire, the remaining brandy erupting in blue flames as the glass cracked. 'Why?'

'Because I had to. There was no other choice. Our financiers were going to foreclose. In fact, they were in the process of doing just that. It was worth it just to see their faces when I handed them the money and told them to count it.'

'We're finished!' he yelled.

'Why? Is Hector Giovanni finished? Is he under Senate investigation? Don't you see, Oliver, they haven't a leg to stand on. I had a legal contract drawn up with Hector. He had collateral. The contract was completed and he got his money back. There was nothing underhand, nothing concealed.'

'I'll never forgive you for this, Elizabeth!' he retorted.

She stood up. 'The problem with you, Oliver, is that you've no backbone. In fact I'm surprised that you can even stand up at all.'

NEW JERSEY
Friday, 25 June 1965

THE NEXT week dragged along, with a flurry of excitement and speculation in the press as the corporation pre-empted the IRS and filed a petition to the New York State Court to protect the ongoing operation of the business whilst the investigation was pending. Ten days after the news had broken, Fred Rickman's remains were returned to the United States. He had no family, apart from an elderly aunt in Wisconsin, so Elizabeth took it upon herself to organize matters. She knew that Rickman had been born a Roman Catholic and had lived as a child near the sea – he had often spoken about its beauty to her and others. The quiet funeral took place in New Jersey, at a small church graveyard overlooking the sea. It was

240

attended by just a handful of close friends, excluding Lou Adams. The publicity had frightened most people away, for fear of being associated with the stricken corporation.

As they were leaving the church grounds, Elizabeth was approached by Don Giovanni's only son, Nico. She hadn't seen the young Italian for some time. Nico Giovanni had put on a little weight around the neck, but still looked as fit as ever.

'Nico.' She was surprised.

'Mrs Goldmann,' he replied respectfully. 'May I offer my family's condolences on Mr Rickman's untimely passing.'

'Thank you.' She forced a smile, removing her black veil as she spoke.

'My father was wanting to speak with you.' He gestured towards a long black limousine parked to the other side of a small grassy knoll.

'Do you think that would be wise at present?'

'Mrs Goldmann, whatever might have happened to your business, both you and my father acted properly. You should fear nothing.'

'Yet why is it that I fear everything?' She looked back at him.

'Please,' he insisted.

'Elizabeth?' Hoover started walking towards her.

She waved him back. 'It's all right, Oliver. I will see you later, back at the house.'

Hoover and the others watched as she went up the path towards the limousine. The driver alighted and opened the door for her. Hector Giovanni welcomed her. He looked frail and tired.

'Mrs Goldmann, please do me the honour of sitting with an old man for just a moment.' He smiled warmly.

Elizabeth got in without a word. No sooner had she sat down than the car started moving.

'I am truly sorry about Mr Rickman. I knew very little about him, but what I saw I liked,' continued Don Giovanni.

'What do you want?' She looked at him.

'You allowed me to help you once. Let me do it again,' he said bluntly.

'But why should you help me?' she asked. He stared ahead through the smoked-glass panel at his son sitting beside the driver. 'I see,' she added.

'Debts are debts, Mrs Goldmann.' He smiled as he handed her an envelope.

'What is this?'

'Everything you need to know about the IRS investigation. The Senate Committee, bahh!' He waved his hand. 'That is nothing and will remain nothing. It is just unfortunate that you picked up a few enemies along the way.'

'And the IRS?' She looked down at the white envelope on her knees.

'Now that is another matter. There is no easy way to tell you this, but your husband has been a very foolish man. For some years now he has been dabbling on the stock exchange and has made several massive losses. He covered himself by playing around with the construction company's books and selling off some of its shares.'

'What!' Elizabeth was alarmed, especially about the shares.

'It is all in there,' he said softly. 'I am so sorry, but you should know.'

She opened the envelope and scanned through the pages. It was the fifth page that drew her attention. It was a debenture, a fixed-interest security issued by the corporation in return for a bank loan. Hoover had used the New York office block and house at Long Island to pay off his debts. She looked at the name of the receiver: it was Tony Mortimer, the new owner of the Washington and Manhattan Industrial Banking Corporation. She was too numb to speak.

'I know that you have been having discussions on how to raise the money demanded by the IRS,' continued Hector Giovanni. 'I would earnestly suggest that you forget about such a move. To take money from your own holdings and thriving company and put it into a sinking wreck would be disastrous.'

'You know, I was almost talked into negotiating a settlement with the IRS.' She was nearly overcome with emotion as she continued. 'How did you know all this?'

'Your husband even approached me for a loan last year. Of course I declined upon finding out that you had not been consulted. But afterwards I ran my own check. I fear it was worse than even I had suspected.'

'I should thank you, but such news . . .' She shook her head.

'My advice to you is simple. Let the construction company go into liquidation. There will be sufficient to pay off any demands from the IRS. The loans have been secured. Of course, it means that you will forfeit the house and office block, but your own business will not be affected.'

'Just like that, give it all up!' She stared back angrily.

'It is the only way. Otherwise you will get drawn into this mess, and even if you salvage something out of it, the construction business will never be the same again. Believe me, I know about these things,' he assured her.

'And Senator Knight?'

'All hot air. Remember, it's really not you he's after. It's me. Of course, I heard your son and his had a run in at a boys' academy one time, so he would enjoy getting you on the stand, but I think you would be a fair match for the bombastic senator, if it comes to that.' He grinned.

'What do you mean by saying "if it comes to that"?'

Hector Giovanni tapped his nose with his finger. 'One must always keep something up one's sleeve.'

'And I have nothing.' She sounded devastated.

'You have this.' He removed a small silken handkerchief from his pocket and handed it to her. As she unwrapped it, her eyes widened. It was the balas ruby she had sold to 'Fixy' Fox, the shady New York jeweller she had approached soon after her arrival in the country.

'Where? How?' She looked at him open-mouthed.

'Do you not recognize my driver?' He tapped the glass partition with his silver-tipped cane and 'Big George' Francetti glanced back. The face didn't register with her at first. Hector Giovanni continued, 'He came into Fixy's shop just as you were leaving.' Then she remembered, the man with the mole on his forehead.

'But how did you realize?'

'You forget you gave me the rest of the jewellery as security when I lent you the money.' He patted her hand. 'And now it is time that you should have it back again, where it belongs.'

'But why?'

'My dear, did no one ever tell you never to look a gift-horse in the mouth?' He laughed.

LONG ISLAND, NEW YORK
Friday, 25 June 1965

ELIZABETH arrived back at the Long Island mansion in the late afternoon. From the number of cars along the gravel driveway and in the main forecourt, it looked as if a convention was taking place. As she alighted from the cab, she heard the jazz music coming from the direction of the house. Rosetta, Elizabeth's housemaid, met her at the front door, a look of bewilderment on her face.

'Mam, I sure don't know what the master's doing,' the Puerto Rican maid rolled her eyes as she spoke.

'How long has this been going on?' asked Elizabeth.

'Since they got here! And now Rosetta's kitchen is empty.'

'We'll soon see about this,' she said angrily, handing her coat and bag to the maid as she went inside.

Hoover was giving a supper for some of those who had attended the funeral, but clearly it had got out of hand. From the moment she walked into the lounge, she could tell that the fool was drunk. On seeing her, he waved across the crowded floor.

'Honey, come and join us!' When she didn't move, he walked over to her, rather unsteadily, attempting to kiss her on the cheek, but she moved back from him. 'What did that old bastard Giovanni want?' he said, rather too loudly for comfort. Near by, heads turned towards them.

'Come out to the hall,' she insisted, trying to guide him outside.

'What's wrong? Can't a buddy have some fun?' he said loudly.

'I think we should talk.' She looked around the crowded room. There were far more faces here at the party than had turned up at the graveyard. It looked as if her husband had invited half the local golf club! 'In private,' she added firmly.

'Come and meet everyone first,' he insisted.

'I'll be in the library, when you're ready.' She turned on her heels and strode out.

It was another ten minutes before he joined her. Elizabeth was already packing some of her private papers into two briefcases. The stupid grin left his face when he realized what was happening.

'What are you doing?' he demanded, shutting the door.

'I'm leaving,' she said flatly.

'After what you said to me at the airport?' he hiccuped.

'You know, Oliver, when you're drunk you really are pathetic.' She slammed the case shut. 'I'm leaving you and I'm leaving this house, for good.'

'You're bluffing.' He staggered across the floor, swaying at the opposite side of the desk from her.

'Go back to your party, Oliver. It'll be the last you'll be having in this house.' She glared back at him.

'You're angry because I'm drunk, is that it?' Another hiccup.

'No,' she snapped, slamming the copy of the debenture down in front of him. 'I know all about your stupidity on the stock market, all about the secret loans. Why you never came to me in the first place or sooner I'll never know, but now it's too late, for both of us.' She closed the second briefcase and started for the door.

'Elizabeth, can't we talk about this?' he pleaded, steadying himself against the desk.

She stopped at the door. 'Oliver, you've made some very stupid mistakes in your life. For that I can forgive you. But not to have confided in me? Your dishonesty? That's different.' Tucking one of the cases under her arm, she opened the door. 'I've already instructed Rosetta to pack my luggage and forward it to the Plaza Hotel in New York. I'll be staying there until the house in Key West is ready. You can have the New York apartment. You'll need a place to stay while this house is auctioned. My lawyer will be in touch with you, you can rest assured of that.'

'You've got it all worked out, haven't you?'

'Someone has to. Goodbye, Oliver.' Then she walked out.

'Elizabeth, for God's sake!' He tossed aside his glass, holding out both arms to her. His charm no longer worked. She was gone.

PLAZA HOTEL, NEW YORK
Saturday, 26 June 1965

CONRAD had been shocked to get the early morning call. Having followed the last days' events and publicity closely, he hadn't expected his client to be in much of a state to see anyone, let alone him again. He arrived at the hotel shortly after 9.30 a.m. and was shown in by Rosetta. Elizabeth stood in the main lounge of the top-floor suite, dressed in a blue silk blouse and matching skirt, with a thick gold necklace worn outside the unbuttoned collar of her blouse. Conrad was, as usual, overawed by the woman's style and good looks. He was surprised to find that, unlike at their previous meetings, she was not alone this time. A small, swarthy young man, dressed immaculately in a dark Italian suit, was standing next to her.

'Thank you for coming, Mr Conrad.' Elizabeth shook his hand warmly. 'Please accept my apologies for my abruptness when we last met, but as you can understand it was something of a great shock to me.'

'Forget it, Mrs Goldmann. I can understand perfectly.' He glanced over her shoulder at the other man.

'Mr Conrad, this is Nico Giovanni. He works for me.'

Conrad went to shake the other man's hand, but got no reaction.

245

'By any chance, you're not one of the New York Giovannis, are you?' he asked cautiously, studying the muscular-looking stranger. Conrad got a simple nod from the younger man. From the cold stare on Nico Giovanni's face, it was all he was going to get.

'Mr Conrad,' continued Elizabeth. 'I want you to work with Nico here. I want you to tell him everything you know about the case and from here on take your orders directly from him.'

'Mam? I don't understand?' Conrad stepped back. 'All you wanted was for me to try and track down your family and determine what became of your father's property and wealth.' He shook his head. 'There's nothing more that I can do. It's all in the summary of my report.'

'I've studied your report, Mr Conrad.' Elizabeth went over to a sofa and sat down. 'What I want from you now is entirely different.'

'How different?' replied Conrad.

'I want to find Rudolph Schiller.'

'But, Mrs Goldmann, from what I could ascertain the guy's supposed to be dead. No one's seen him since 1945.' Conrad was adamant.

'Money is no object.' Elizabeth nodded to Nico. He handed Conrad a small but thick envelope. The detective took it with some hesitation.

'That is a bank book, Mr Conrad,' Elizabeth spoke up. 'The account has been opened in your name. There is no ceiling on the amount you can draw. All I ask is that a careful record be kept of your expenses. While I intend to pay well for your services, I don't expect to get ripped off,' she said sternly. 'No entertainment in the red-light districts, the way you did on your last trip to Amsterdam.'

'Mam! I can assure you—' Conrad was cut sort.

'If Schiller's alive, just find him,' Elizabeth interrupted.

'And if I do?' Conrad was more than embarrassed that Elizabeth had found out about his 'leisure activities' in Amsterdam when carrying out his European investigation for her.

'Nico here will kill him.' Elizabeth nodded towards Nico.

Conrad's mouth dropped. 'I don't know about this . . .' he stammered.

'You said yourself Schiller's dead.' Elizabeth shrugged. 'You can't kill a dead man, can you?' she added cheekily.

Before he knew it, the other man was guiding him reluctantly out of the suite. While they waited for the elevator, the detective tried to start up a conversation.

'You don't say much, do you, pal?' Conrad said nervously.

246

'Just do as the lady says and we'll get along fine,' Nico replied in a low voice. Conrad sensed the veiled threat instantly.

'Say, pal, that dame's just joking, isn't she?' He chuckled. 'We can always play her along . . .' Suddenly Nico squeezed Conrad's right shoulder, forcing him into the elevator. 'Hey, pal! Take it easy, will ya!' Conrad winced at the sharp pain invading his right shoulder. Then the elevator arrived and the doors parted. Nico shoved Conrad in, punching the lobby button. He held the doors open while he spoke.

'Listen to me good, see? Now you draw some money from that bank account you just inherited. Enough for a long trip. I'll stop by at your hotel and pick you up around two.' Then he released the doors and stepped back into the lobby. 'Be ready.' He pointed at him threateningly just as the doors started closing.

'Ready for what?' Conrad shouted.

'South America,' replied Nico, just before the doors closed.

Conrad massaged his shoulder as the elevator took him downstairs. He looked at the bank book and shook his head. He hadn't been very cautious about not drawing too much attention to himself when he'd been in Europe; it had been a terrible mistake. He swallowed deeply. Annoying some hot-headed neo-Nazis seemed a piece of cake by comparison to aggravating his new partner.

UNIVERSITY OF YALE
Sunday, 27 June 1965

THE NEXT day, Elizabeth finally travelled up to Yale to visit Peter. Rabbi Bronowski had reported back to her, stating that the boy was in fine health. Then she had telephoned him herself. The conversation had been strained as usual. Peter had mentioned that he was preparing for some summer school and didn't want to be disturbed. Although she had capitulated on the telephone, she knew that she had to see him personally and the sooner the better.

Elizabeth had driven up by the scenic route, taking in the beautiful Connecticut countryside. Alone in the back of the chauffeur-driven limousine, she had time to think. She had been trying to determine what to say to him since her telephone call the day previously, and still she'd come no closer to a decision. How could she avoid the usual slanging match, the usual verbal confrontation? She thought back to his childhood. Just where had they gone wrong? He had been such a difficult child to understand. Even from an early age he had been consumed by heavy, deep moods that would last for days on end. He was stubborn and ultimately a loner. She had tried to integrate him with other children, but it was to no avail.

Then Joe Costello's violence consumed them both. At first it was a gentle scolding and, although she had tried to keep the boy apart from her husband, she had to concede that there were occasions when Peter needed a firm and guiding hand. No one could understand the relationship she'd had with Costello, for theirs was a marriage of convenience. In her case she needed to stay in America and marrying a citizen was a certain way of doing it. In Costello's case he had tolerated the indignity of a pre-nuptial agreement to a sexless marriage and separate bedrooms, in the belief that in time she would grow to accept him. But he was wrong, terribly wrong.

To the outside world, it was a perfect marriage. Elizabeth carried out her marital duties religiously in all but one way. As time marched on, Costello's frustration began to boil over. Perhaps that had been the fuel that had driven Costello on to exact his revenge on the boy more and more. Peter's punishments no longer fitted the crime. For the slightest misdemeanour he was beaten with his stepfather's belt, until the skin was almost lifting off his legs and buttocks. Elizabeth blamed herself for allowing the situation to get out of control, and by the time she finally took Ellen's advice to do something about it, it was too late. She recalled that evening vividly. Costello had been out drinking with his friends, as usual. When he had finally returned with two of his buddies, she had ordered the two drunkards from the apartment.

After they left she had started on Costello. His construction business was in severe difficulty and he was in trouble. That day, while tidying up his bedroom, she had uncovered documents pertaining to his business. Contrary to what Costello had been telling her, he had been borrowing heavily and was well behind with bank and other repayments. Joe Costello exploded in a fury. Elizabeth had expected harsh words, but not physical retribution. Peter had watched through a crack in the hall doorway as his stepfather started into Elizabeth with his fists. After the first punches she hadn't felt much more. Costello had dragged her unconscious into the nearest bedroom and finally consummated his 'marriage', but he hadn't stopped there.

Elizabeth shut her eyes as she thought back to that October night. What had Peter seen, while she lay unconscious on that bed, being raped and sodomized over and over again? What had gone through his mind as he watched his stepfather taking a knife to her breasts and groin? She had finally come around some hours later. Hardly able to walk, she had crawled from the bedroom on her hands and knees, leaving behind a trail of blood. It had taken her some minutes to locate Peter, locked inside a broom cupboard. She had found him huddled up in a ball, his face swollen and bleeding. She could vividly remember the look on his face as he saw the blood trickling down the inside of her legs. Painfully, she had tried to cover up her shame with the dressing gown, before taking him into her arms. That had been the last time Peter had allowed her to hug him, to hold him. After that, things were different between them.

Costello had met his end the following morning, after being confronted by some of his Mafia friends. Instead of reasoning with them over his outstanding loan, he took them on – and lost. Of course, the NYPD had tried to make a case against Elizabeth, suggesting a motive of retribution for the attacks on her and Peter, but their investigation ran up against a brick wall.

Elizabeth found herself hospitalized for nearly six weeks. Whilst her mind was irrevocably scarred, the plastic surgeons had done a remarkable job. Her body gradually healed, but some things could never be undone. She could never have any children of her own. With Rabbi Bronowski's assistance, Elizabeth maintained a positive attitude and fixed her eyes firmly on the future. During her recuperation, Elizabeth had taken Ellen's advice and gone away with Peter for a brief holiday to Cape Cod, but it made no difference to their relationship. Something was stopping Peter from displaying any emotion whatsoever.

Over the following years she had taken him to various psychiatrists, but none could offer any real advice, for without Peter's participation there could be no change. As the years swept past, she virtually gave up any real hope of ever regaining her son's confidence. After that her business interests drew Elizabeth steadily away from home. Even after her marriage to Oliver Hoover, she still maintained a hectic travel schedule, much of which was out of the United States altogether.

With Peter at boarding school, Elizabeth drew more and more on the contact maintained between her friend Jacob Bronowski and the boy. She allowed Peter to visit the elderly rabbi frequently and as much as possible saw to it that the old man came to visit at Long Island when Peter was home on holidays. Although the old man and the boy were close, even Bronowski could see there was a distinct reticence on Peter's part to communicate with him fully. It was as if the boy was always holding back his innermost thoughts, as if there was an inner person lurking behind the façade. It would be a source of constant agony for her over the years to come.

The car circumnavigated the Yale campus area and minutes later pulled up at the apartment block where Peter lived. Elizabeth had arranged the timing of her visit to suit her son, but going by previous experience that wouldn't be any guarantee he'd be there. She walked slowly up the two flights to the first floor of the old building and pressed the buzzer on the door of number 1B. Peter opened the door, his pale blue eyes gleaming as he stared back at his mother. She hadn't seen him in over two months. His hair was much longer and, from his lean appearance, he didn't appear to have been eating.

'Hello, Peter,' she said with some apprehension.

'Mother.' He opened the door wider, allowing her to enter.

The apartment was a poky affair. A small bed-settee lay in one corner of the room, close to a gas fire, with a rusty coin meter beside it. The place smelt damp. She tried to refrain from saying anything that might upset him as she looked around. There were two other doors, one open and leading into a small kitchen area. Elizabeth presumed the other, closed door led to the bathroom, for what it would be worth.

'Have a seat.' He directed her towards the only chair in the room, a rocker set beside the fireplace. 'Don't worry. The bugs won't bite.'

'How have you been keeping?' she asked.

'So, so.' He sighed. Elizabeth ignored the attitude.

'Peter, I'm here for a reason. I must tell you that Oliver and I have unofficially separated. I'm moving down to the summer house in Key West permanently.'

'I see.' If he was annoyed, it didn't show.

'Don't make this any harder for me than it already is. Please,' she pleaded.

'Well, what do you expect me to say, Mother?' The way he belaboured the last word worried her.

'Rabbi Bronowski says that you're doing very well here at Yale.' As usual, she was always the first to change the subject.

'So, so,' he replied.

'Peter, must it always be like this?' She sat forward in the rocking chair.

'You drew the lines, Mother, dear. Not me,' he snapped.

'I?' Even Elizabeth was surprised at how quickly the meeting had deteriorated. 'Everything was done for you, Peter. Everything!'

'Ah, that's my mother, as defensive as always.'

'When we first came to this country, I slaved night and day just to keep us here. If the emigration authorities had had their way, we'd have been on the next boat back to Ireland.'

'So you married the first bastard that came along.' Elizabeth stood up. 'What, going so soon?'

'I had hoped to have a proper discussion with you, but obviously I've failed miserably.' She headed for the door.

'What! No kiss?' As always he had to have the last word, and as always she would let him. Elizabeth flung the door open and ran down the stairs.

Elizabeth said nothing other than directing the driver to return back to New York. She held back her tears as she glanced up at the first-floor window. Peter was standing in the middle of the bay window, staring directly down at her. She averted her eyes. The journey seemed the longest Elizabeth could remember. Every facet of the past seemed to hurtle back at her again, everything was upturned in her tortured mind. As the car neared the outskirts of New York, the driver turned on the radio. The news broadcast was announcing the collapse of the Costello Construction Corporation. Elizabeth leaned forward and spoke to the driver.

'Turn up the volume, James,' she commanded, listening to the words of the broadcast.

'. . . and it has just been confirmed that the Costello Construction Corporation stock has dropped over fifty points on the stock exchange. So what does it mean for the construction industry? With me in the studio is Ed Morrisey, the man who broke the news of the company's alleged evasion of taxes and collusion with a well-known New York Mafia family. Ed, what do you make of all this?'

Elizabeth recognized Ed Morrisey's deep drawl as he started speaking. 'Well, Johnny, it looks like the end of the Costello Construction Corporation. The IRS has already frozen the company's assets and the personal assets of the leading company directors. It was bound to happen, it was just a matter of time. A serious blow to thousands of Americans living all across this country.'

'And the allegations of Mafia involvement?' prompted the broadcaster.

'It wouldn't be proper for me to comment on that, Johnny, especially with Senator Knight's committee looking into these allegations, but my guess is that there's no smoke without fire.'

'Thank you, Ed Morrisey. I now go back to our man in Washington . . .'

'Turn it off, please. I've heard enough,' insisted Elizabeth. The driver complied.

PLAZA HOTEL, NEW YORK
Monday, 28 June 1965

ELIZABETH emerged from the elevator directly opposite her hotel suite to find two soberly dressed men standing outside the doorway of the suite. Arnie Ellis, the corporation's main architect and one of its junior directors, stood beside them.

'Rachel Elizabeth Goldmann?' The taller of the pair walked forward to meet her.

'Yes,' she replied cautiously.

'This is for you. A subpoena to attend a Senate Committee on alleged corruption.' He thrust the paper into her hand. 'And this also,' he added, slapping a further document on top of it. 'It's a court order, freezing all your personal assets.'

Elizabeth stood in bewilderment as the two men pushed past her into the elevator. She had half expected it to happen, but her involvement with the construction corporation had been purely in name only for the last decade. Clearly reason didn't enter into it. Her name was associated with the company and there was no escaping it.

Arnie Ellis approached her. She hadn't seen him since Fred Rickman's funeral. 'They got me too. I was on my way over here to tell you, but those two were already waiting.'

'I think we could do with a drink, don't you?' She tried to keep up appearances.

'Elizabeth, I took the liberty of hiring Christopher Topping. He's the best there is. He's going to call over here and give us the low-down on this thing.' He followed her inside the suite.

She looked back at him. 'Arnie, the low-down is that we're in trouble. I don't need your lawyer to tell me that.'

An hour later Ellis's lawyer arrived hot foot from the courthouse. He had a grim look about him as Ellis introduced him to Elizabeth. 'Chris Topping, this is Mrs Goldmann, one of the corporation's directors.'

'Mrs Goldmann, I've heard much about you.' Topping sounded almost English, with just a hint of his Boston background evident.

'And likewise, Mr Topping.' She shook his hand.

'What's the news from the courts?' asked Ellis.

'As expected.' Topping sat down on one of the armchairs, facing them both. 'Everything is frozen until the outcome of the IRS matter.'

'I was told that there was enough equity in the corporation's assets to get us out of this,' said Elizabeth.

'That's true, but there's these allegations against your husband. The government is looking for blood. They will want a conviction.'

'What happens to my husband is his concern, Mr Topping. My own lawyers advised me that my concern is in keeping my own business out of this.'

'That's true. The Elizabeth Goldmann Collection can't be touched unless they can prove some sort of collusion between it and Costello Construction. But I'm afraid that your personal assets will remain affected by this until such time as the situation is resolved.'

'Fortunately, everything I have is in my company's name, including my house in Key West.'

'That's good,' he concluded. 'Now, with your consent I will get together with your own lawyers and we'll thrash out a line of common defence on this.'

'Agreed. But what about this subpoena I've received to attend this Senate hearing in Washington?'

'I'll find out what you're up against on that. Will you be in town for long?' he asked.

'I was going down to Key West for a few days. The reporters and the fuss in this city are starting to get to me.'

'I understand. The hearing isn't for another three weeks. It will give me time to get things together. Of course, if you wish I can accompany you to Washington.'

'Thank you.'

He stood up to leave. 'Just one other thing. Arnie told me that you and Hector Giovanni are old friends. I think it would be best if you didn't see or speak to him before the hearing.'

'Guilty by association,' replied Elizabeth coldly.

WASHINGTON, DC
Monday, 19 July 1965

ELIZABETH arrived for the Senate Committee hearing as directed. As she walked into the room, she saw a familiar face she hadn't seen for some years. Jake Bartholomew was standing talking with another man towards the front of the room. She hadn't seen him since after Costello's death. The New York detective had been the only one in his department to believe Elizabeth when she was protesting her innocence over Costello's death. Whilst he had accepted her innocence in that matter, he had almost persecuted her over her association with Don Giovanni and his family. The line had been drawn between them long ago. Bartholomew recognized her instantly and excused himself, strolling confidently across to her.

'Mrs Goldmann, nice you could make it.' He grinned at her.

'Captain Bartholomew, this is my lawyer, Mr Topping.' Elizabeth introduced the lawyer, trying to keep control of her temper.

'Mr Topping.' Bartholomew and the lawyer didn't shake hands. 'From what I hear, you're the best there is.'

'I'll take that as a compliment, Captain,' replied Topping drily.

As they took their seats, Hector Giovanni came into the courtroom, accompanied by 'Big George' Francetti and his own lawyer. As he took up his seat close to Elizabeth, he looked over, bowing courteously to her. She couldn't help but notice his frailty. He had looked ill before, but now he looked deathly.

'Mr Giovanni appears quite sick,' Topping whispered.

'I can't say I blame him,' replied Elizabeth, just as Hugo Knight and five other US Senators emerged from a side door, taking up their respective positions around a long curved bench at the front of the room. Instantly the numerous cameras at the back of the courtroom started whirring into action and the bright camera lights were switched on. Elizabeth found the proceedings more than just unsettling. She looked over again at Hector Giovanni; the proceedings were also having a profound impact on the old man. His usual confidence seemed to have diminished.

Hugo Knight started the ball rolling, glancing down once or twice at her during his thirty-minute introduction. Finally he came to the first witness of the afternoon. Captain Bartholomew took the stand giving testimony as to his background and knowledge of the

New York Giovanni 'family'. Hector Giovanni watched impassively as the detective told what he knew to the committee. As time went on, it became clear that it wasn't so much what Bartholomew knew as what he was insinuating. The innuendo was sticking like mud; they were paving the way for the old man's downfall. Finally that afternoon, Hector Giovanni was helped to the front by his 'minder'. He waved Francetti away as he took the oath. Then the relentless questioning began. Elizabeth cringed as the old man took battering after battering from the silver-tongued senator from Virginia. Hugo Knight kept up the pressure during an hour of incessant interrogation, hardly giving Giovanni time to answer.

'I put it to you, Mr Giovanni, that you gave this money to Mrs Costello, as she was then, as payment for your family's connection with the construction company,' insisted Senator Knight.

'That is not correct.' Hector Giovanni's voice was becoming tired and broken. 'This was a proper loan between two friends.'

'Friends? But we heard earlier from Captain Bartholomew of the New York Police Department that you maintained the first time you met Mrs Goldmann, or Costello as she was then, she was in a hospital.' He then shouted. 'Where she was recovering from being raped and brutalized by her husband, a man you had killed!'

'That is a lie!' The old man rose to his feet. 'Joe Costello was a close friend of mine. Our two families go back all the way to the old country! I can tell you this, Senator, that so long . . .'

'Ah! So you admit there is a connection between you and the Costello Construction Corporation after all, a long-standing one within the Mafia, or is it called Cosa Nostra?' Hugo Knight's voice drowned out the old man completely.

'I . . .' Hector Giovanni hesitated, swaying unsteadily on his feet for a moment. Francetti was at his side immediately, but the old man waved him away. 'You twist things, Senator. I may have done many things in my life, but this lady is innocent of having any connection with them.' He pointed a finger back towards Elizabeth as he continued. 'For Elizabeth Goldmann is indeed a lady, in the truest sense of the word.' He forced a smile from his broken features as he looked over at her. Elizabeth smiled back. Then Hector Giovanni returned his attention to the committee, addressing himself directly to Hugo Knight. As he was about to speak, Hector Giovanni suddenly clutched his chest, his face contorted in pain. Francetti tried to assist him. 'I'm all right,' he insisted, looking Senator Knight directly in the eye as he continued. 'Yes, Senator, Elizabeth Goldmann has class and breeding – something that a person such as yourself would perhaps have difficulty comprehending.' The Senator's face turned bright red, then some of the spectators and press began to laugh.

As he was about to continue addressing the committee, Hector Giovanni's mouth dropped open. Before Francetti realized, his boss had collapsed across the table in front of him, his head to one side. One of the stenographers screamed as several of the court officers rushed forward to assist him. Elizabeth watched in horror as life was extinguished in the old man. His eyes rolled up into his head as they eased him on to the floor. Moments later one of the court officers stood up. He shook his head as he looked directly at Senator Knight.

ARGENTINA
Monday, 19 July 1965

NICO GIOVANNI had to admit to being impressed with Conrad's performance. The overweight detective was good at his job. They were into their second week looking for answers in Argentina when Conrad got to hear about a certain country club well out of the way somewhere. What it was all about he couldn't be too sure, but there was one sure-fire way to find out.

The car bumped along the dusty road. They had been out all day and without any success, apart from watching some cattle moving across the plain. Now they were heading back to town. Nico Giovanni checked his mirror again. Apart from the constant jolting his arms and wrists were taking, the other thing that was decidedly annoying him was the company that had been keeping pace with them for the last hour and a half. He glanced across at his partner. Conrad was still stretched back in the front passenger seat, dozing, his hat tilted forward, covering his eyes.

Nico nudged him. 'We've got company.'

'So I noticed,' said Conrad drolly.

'They've been tailin' us now close on two hours,' said Nico, peering through the brown dust as they rounded the narrow road cut into the side of the steep gorge. The black Cadillac was still there, maintaining its hold-back position.

'What do ya suggest?'

'According to the map, there's a split in the road just up ahead. I think we should take the upper cut and see what happens,' said Nico.

256

'You're driving, pal,' sighed Conrad, easing himself upright in the seat again.

Three miles later they hit the junction. A road branched off to the left, leading up through the forest, whilst the main road looped down towards the plain. Just as they were on the junction, Nico booted the car and steered left, increasing speed. The tailing car followed. Nico judged his moment well. The height differential between the two roads was now over fifty feet and increasing rapidly, but a short distance ahead the shrubland on the hillside had been burned away, leaving just the dusty hillside between themselves and the lower road. He slowed down, letting the black Cadillac catch up. Nico's well-honed instinct saved the moment, for as he peered into his side mirror he just caught the sun's reflection off the gun barrel protruding from the passenger side of the ensuing vehicle.

'Hold on to yer hat!' he snapped.

Before Conrad could answer, he was thrown against the door as the car veered off the road and into the air. The car bounced on to the hillside, its bonnet bursting open as it took off again, tilting sideways. Nico kept his head, judging the next landing just right. The car slammed into the hillside again, this time skidding the remaining twenty odd feet on to the lower road, before coming to rest amidst a massive cloud of dust. Conrad was just about to thank God when the first bullets ripped into the side of the vehicle just behind them.

'Automatic fire!' shouted Nico, slamming the car into gear and racing off down the main highway. Another burst of gunfire ripped through the roof of the car, narrowly missing both men. It was only after they reached the next town on their way back to the city that they breathed a final sigh of relief.

They stopped beside a water fountain in the town square and Conrad got out of the car to inspect the damage. The vehicle had been raked with several bursts of machine-gun fire. He climbed back in again.

'Those bastards weren't messing, were they?' He wiped the sweat from his brow.

'Well, if they were, they sure as hell won't be the next time!' growled Nico.

Two hours later they arrived back at their hotel in the city of La Plata. Nico was dusty and hot and definitely ready for a cold beer or two. He and Conrad had been reluctant partners now for the past few weeks, without a hint of success, except for stirring up a hornets' nest.

All they were doing was making a nuisance of themselves and they knew it. They could have easily been killed on the road earlier but someone had just wanted to frighten them off for the moment. The longer they stayed about the place, the worse it was going to get.

Both of them had agreed to call it a day. It was just a question of who was going to break the news to their 'client'. Conrad went into the hotel ahead of Nico. After getting rid of the car, Nico headed up to the first-floor suite. As he entered the room he took one look at Conrad and knew something was wrong.

'What is it?' he demanded.

'It's your father, Nico. It's not good.' Conrad handed him the telegram.

Nico Giovanni read the terse message: FATHER DEAD. NATURAL CAUSES. WASHINGTON DC THIS DATE. REMAINS TO NY TONIGHT. COME QUICK. G. FRANCETTI.

'I'm real sorry, Nico.' He patted him on the shoulder. 'I'll make the travel arrangements.'

Nico was unable to reply.

KEY WEST, FLORIDA KEYS
Tuesday, 17 August 1965

ELIZABETH settled into her new permanent home. The place had been built originally as a summer retreat for her family, but now it was all she had. She had hoped that Peter would join her at the white-painted house nestling between the palm trees, overlooking the clear blue waters of the Gulf of Mexico, but during the university vacations he chose instead to go and stay with his 'Uncle' Jacob in New York. She could readily understand why. The old rabbi had a way with him that she envied.

She looked out over the sea. The sun was going down, casting a cold shadow across the water. For a moment she was back again, standing on the Kerry clifftop, looking out and waiting for the U-boat's return. She shivered, looking for the tall, thin periscope out in the shimmering sea. She breathed a sigh of relief on recognizing the mast of a small fishing boat, making its way back home after a day's work. She had been too overcome with the events of the last weeks to think about Conrad's failed attempts to find any trace of Schiller.

Perhaps the fat detective had been right after all, perhaps she was really only chasing ghosts. She prayed he was right.

Hector Giovanni's death had ended the Senate Committee's investigation. The manner of his passing had caused a minor political storm and, in the face of adverse public opinion, Senator Knight had been forced to roll down the shutters. The IRS had since accepted a negotiated settlement from Oliver Hoover's lawyers and were also no longer pressing charges, but the down-shot was that the construction business was finished, carved up between Tony Mortimer, the IRS and several of the other main creditors. Hoover had tried reaching her on umpteen occasions, but she had flatly refused to have any contact with him, even to the point of returning his mail unopened.

PART FIVE

The Coming

THE PAMPAS REGION, ARGENTINA
Friday, 3 September 1965

THE PRIVATE twin-engined Lockheed jet aircraft flew in from the north-west, just a thousand feet above the mountain range as it began its descent towards the airstrip. Otto Matz sat uncomfortably in the rear of the fourteen-seater aircraft. For once he was not enjoying himself. If greed could drive any man to the brink of insanity, it was Otto Matz. He had been an eager participant in the formation of the ultra-secret organization from the very outset but 'Nemesis' had not lived up to his fullest expectations.

His father had been a German engineer who had emigrated to Paraguay just after the First World War. Shortly thereafter, he had met and married a wealthy Paraguayan lady and consequently inherited the Los Milanos ranch, a massive, sprawling property along with mining interests, some of which stretched into Brazil. Born in 1920, Matz had been raised initially on the family plantation in Paraguay, with tutors flown in especially from the United States, but as time marched on it became apparent to his father that the young man would have to complete his education in the Fatherland. So it was that in 1937 young Otto was sent to Berlin, to study in one of the top gymnasiums, ostensibly with the intention of gaining a place at one of the main universities, but then war broke out and young Matz was ordered home.

It was with much reluctance that he returned, reaching Rio de Janeiro on a tramp steamer, outbound from Hamburg. He was furious about his father's decision to order him back to Paraguay. His contempt for his parents grew into hatred. To the young idealist, Germany was now his home, where he belonged, supporting his Führer. Over the next years he fermented, driven by a constant anger at being excluded from what he saw as 'the greatest battle of all'. Then his spirits lifted when, during 1944, he received a visitor. The stranger identified himself to Matz as SS Sturmbannführer Karl Strassmann and, to him, Strassmann was the epitome of everything he dreamed of being – a tall Teutonic knight.

Matz had relished the secret discussions he had with Strassmann. He was needed at last, but there was one minor obstacle to his involvement. It came as no surprise to Matz when, a short time after, both his parents were killed when their light aircraft crashed in the jungle, just north of Asunción. They had been killed outright, the crash blamed on a simple navigation error. Otto Matz was the immediate successor to an estate valued in the millions, but, more importantly, his lands and resources could now be put to a better use.

Because of his privileged background, Matz had become the organization's main man in both North and South America during the post-war years. His antecedents could pass the closest scrutiny. He could travel the world without arousing suspicion. Because of his unique position, he could see the potent and awesome power of 'Nemesis', but even he had no idea of its real purpose. The group's strength lay in its control as much as its anonymity. Beneath it stood the 'Odessa' and 'Spider' organizations, working independently and without full knowledge of 'Nemesis'. Only those at the very top of the two illegal organizations knew the name 'Nemesis', but even they knew little else. They had long ago sworn their undying support for 'Nemesis'; they would follow their instructions to the letter, no matter what the consequences. 'Nemesis' had remained dormant for the first couple of years, but then it slowly began to move. In time its tentacles had reached back across the ocean and into the very heart of Europe.

Matz enjoyed his position, mainly jetting around both continents on his private aircraft. Life had been good since the pact with his German friends two decades before, but now something was wrong, very wrong. He looked across the narrow walkway of the private jet towards the other passenger and shivered. He didn't like being too close to the man; he frightened him. The aircraft banked sharply to the starboard side and Matz got his first glimpse of the country club, a cluster of whitewashed buildings set amidst a wide plain. He had known about the place since its purchase and construction back in 1946, but until now he had avoided going to it. The less these men knew about him the better, but now he had been commanded to attend. He looked over again at the other passenger and shivered. Rudolph Schiller was staring back at him!

The country club had been set up in the pampas area of Argentina, inaccessible and totally exclusive. There all the meetings were held between the representatives of 'Odessa' and the 'Spider'. This was where the executive orders originated and the decisions were made. In essence, the two Nazi organizations were there as a buffer for 'Nemesis'. Through them the neo-Nazis could get footholds in various Latin governments. Twice a year special meetings were held at the country club, with the 'Odessa' organization represented by Heinrich Keller and 'Spider' by Josef Gross. As always, the meetings were chaired by a little-known individual called Mark Renan. The country club was run in essence by 'Odessa', used primarily as a final staging point for the escaped comrades.

More from convenience than by coincidence, an Argentinian army base was located just fifteen miles away to the south-east. The Argentinian army used the base as a remote training facility for their special forces and various specialist marine units, but it also served as a necessary back-up to the small in-house security unit at the club. The club's security unit was locally recruited, made up of hand-picked ex-military and police personnel, under the supervision of Colonel Ortega, an ex-police commander with a successful track record in counter-insurgency. Ortega liked the job. It was perhaps a trifle boring, but the money was something he could have only dreamed about. The Germans were prepared to pay well to get the best.

Miguel Ortega was a single man in his late fifties and was well suited for the appointment. The job required him to live permanently on the country-club estate. It was a twenty-four-hour commitment and, whilst Ortega had his aides, he was the man in the saddle, and he had no intention of falling off. He had been in charge of security for over seven years, during which time he had seen the 'guests' come and go from every part of the globe, from Italy, from South Africa, even from Australia. He was a shrewd man – he had to be in his business. Asking questions got a man unwelcome attention and asking too many got a man killed. During his time he had seen many things. The blond-haired leaving as auburn, the hooked noses straightened, the rounded faces squared off, the eyebrows raised, the chins altered. The club's in-house medical team performed all the surgical transfor-mations with polish, using every medical advantage known to man.

The more he saw, the more he was sure he would never be leaving the place. He knew too much for his own good. That was why, three years before, Miguel Ortega had come to a decision. It was not an easy one to take – disclosure in the early stages would have meant certain and probably protracted death – but now he was glad and sure he had made the right choice. For he did not care for the man calling himself Mark Renan. He was a cold customer and one of the chilliest Ortega had ever met. Ortega went to the private airfield to await the arrival. Normally, Renan only came to the country club twice a year, but this time a special and urgent meeting had been called less than a month after the last one. Something had happened, something serious, judging from the expressions of the other two gentlemen who had arrived earlier.

He heard it first, before catching sight of it. The twin-engined jet aircraft came down out of the low cloud surrounding the mountains to the west, its silver wings reflecting the afternoon sun. The private plane swooped low and came in for a direct landing, its undercarriage popping out as the changing shriek of the engine noise alerted the ground staff on the runway apron. Ortega got out of the white stretched limousine and straightened his tunic as the jet streamed past, its nose pointed upwards and flaps fully extended as the main wheels bit the dusty Tarmac.

Inside minutes the aircraft was taxiing back up the runway and on to the apron. Immediately it stopped, Ortega's men surrounded it in a wide arc, facing outward, automatic weapons at the ready. It was the drill; nothing less than absolute vigilance was acceptable. As the side hatch was unlocked, several of the ground staff rushed forward to pull out the steps from just under the open hatchway. Rudolph Schiller alighted through the narrow hatchway, his left arm fixed in front of his chest, his hand gloved as always. He was carrying an attaché case handcuffed to his right wrist. Ortega went forward and saluted him.

'Welcome, Señor Renan. How delighted I am to see you again so soon.'

Schiller did not reply, but limped past and climbed into the back of the limousine. Ortega watched as a second person alighted. He hadn't seen the small, tubby man with the swarthy complexion before. The man smiled at him nervously before following Schiller into the limousine. Ortega shrugged his shoulders and quickly followed, getting into the front of the car. The driver pulled off instantly, pursued by two jeeps, each carrying four of Ortega's best men.

'I trust you had a pleasant flight, Señor?' inquired Ortega, turning back towards the man with the eye patch and facial scarring. Schiller studied him for a moment. The security chief had several beads of sweat about to trickle down the side of his hooked nose. He also had a devious manner which Schiller had noted from the very first moment they had met – suitable for the job, but under a tight rein.

'Are the others here?' Schiller ignored the question, looking across towards a group of aircraft parked next to the hangar and maintenance buildings.

'Sí, señor.' Ortega removed his cap, flicking the last remaining strands of his greasy hair across a barren scalp. 'Five hours ago. They flew in from Montevideo, in one of the club's aircraft.'

'How many guests have you at present?' Schiller kept staring out of his side window.

'We have thirty-seven. Two are due to leave at the beginning of next week.' Ortega adjusted his tie, a habitual nervous reaction. This man made him uneasy, very uneasy.

'Whilst I am here, no one is permitted to leave or enter the country club, is that understood?' snapped Schiller.

'Sí, señor,' Ortega hastily responded.

The remainder of the five-minute car ride passed in silence. Ortega found himself unable to keep his eyes away from the brown attaché case on Schiller's knees. Why chain a case to your wrist when you're surrounded by the very best security that money can buy? He tried to curb his curiosity as the limousine began the slight incline towards the summer house. As normal the meetings were held away from the normal clubhouse activities, the venue being the summer house down by the old swimming pool.

Over the years the country club had been extended and developed to facilitate the increased numbers of old comrades who had finally made it safely to South America. The main clubhouse was akin to a small five-star hotel, with over fifty private suites, bars, restaurants and leisure facilities. Every form of relaxation had been catered for, including a cinema and even an eighteen-hole golfcourse within walking distance of the main complex. The medical station was now developed into a small hospital, capable of taking up to twenty patients at any one time, with three operating theatres, an X-ray department and a research and laboratory section capable of diagnosing and treating just about any tropical disease known to man. The hospital even had its own isolation section, with specialist burns and intensive-care units. It had been the intention initially to have any surgical work done in private clinics in Buenos Aires and Rio de Janeiro, but things had begun to hot up and it had long since become unsafe for the brotherhood to use them. The country club was as near as anyone could get to total comfort combined with total security, yet Ortega had been careful to keep the security low profile and enhance the relaxed atmosphere of a tropical paradise.

The limousine drew up at the old summer house, an area now used exclusively by visiting VIPs. Schiller went inside, followed closely by Otto Matz, leaving Ortega at the limousine. Inside the summer house awaited Heinrich Keller and Josef Gross. Both men stood as Schiller limped into the large sun room. Keller had removed his jacket and tie and was clearly sweating in the heat, whilst Gross was dressed more casually in a cream open-neck shirt with a pink cravat. He had a tall glass in one hand and was about to pour himself another vodka and orange juice from the small corner bar.

'Renan, old chap.' Keller smiled at the newcomer nervously. They adhered strictly to protocol, never referring to Schiller by his real name, even privately. It was the unwritten rule; any transgression was fatal. 'How the devil are you?'

Schiller nodded as he unlocked the handcuff and set the attaché case on a large circular table in the centre of the room. He then began fiddling with the combination lock. 'Gentlemen, you have not been called here for the benefit of your health or relaxation. Please refrain from any indulgence until the meeting is terminated.'

Keller set his glass aside and went over to stand beside Gross as Schiller removed a green file from the briefcase, beckoning both men to sit down. 'Gentlemen, this is Herr Matz,' he continued. Both nodded curtly to the small, swarthy stranger. They all sat down around the table and Schiller began.

'Gentlemen, we have a breach in our security.'

'Ridiculous!' scoffed Keller. 'I can vouch for every Kamerad!'

'I am sure you can, General, but our problem doesn't lie there,' replied Schiller coldly.

'Then where?' urged Gross.

'That is for you to decide.' Schiller handed over the file to Gross. 'Both of you please study that and then give me your conclusions.'

The two men studied the document for several minutes. Then Gross spoke out. 'Mossad knows about the country club!' His eyes widened.

'Correct. But more importantly it knows about the existence of "Nemesis",' replied Schiller, looking over at Matz. The little Paraguayan flushed. Did the ex-SS general suspect him, of all people?

'How did the Israelis find out?' inquired Keller. 'Eichmann?'

'No, we're certain that our late comrade gave nothing away before his execution. Although I can tell you that SS Obersturmbannführer Eichmann was interrogated at some length about such matters, he never talked. He died a soldier's death.'

'At the end of a Jewish rope.' Keller shook his head in disgust.

'You miss the point, gentlemen. The Israelis already knew of "Nemesis"'s existence before Eichmann was captured. The question is how much they know.' Schiller looked again at Otto Matz. 'I have asked Herr Matz here to explain to both of you something of our North American operations.' Matz's eyes widened. He was unsure of the wisdom of such a disclosure.

The other two Germans listened in silence as Matz explained how monies had been invested through certain sectors of industry both in Canada and in the United States. They were clearly impressed, if not a little confused. Finally, Schiller came to the point of the meeting.

'Gentlemen, we are going to set a trap for our enemy. It has been decided that the "Odessa" organization will draw some of the Israeli agents into Argentina. We are going to teach them to keep to their own backyards.'

'This will only bring unwanted attention,' commented Keller.

'It is an order!' snarled Schiller.

'*Mein Herr.*' Keller sat upright.

An hour later both Schiller and Matz were boarding the aircraft. Ortega watched as the jet roared down the runway, throwing up a small dustcloud behind it before lifting into the heat haze. Matz had said little following the meeting. He wanted to choose his moment well. Now was as good a time as any.

'Schiller, why was I at the meeting?' he inquired.

'To draw the lice out of the woodwork,' Schiller replied without hesitation.

'You mean Keller or Gross could be the cause of the leak?'

Schiller looked back at him. 'No one is above suspicion, my dear Matz. Not even you.' Matz began to sweat and flush again. 'But don't worry. I'm sure our problem will shortly be resolved.'

Matz remained numb for the remainder of the flight. He could hardly think straight. Then finally, just before they landed at the ranch, Schiller spoke again. 'Come on, Matz, cheer up. We're almost home again.'

'I find nothing cheerful in having my loyalty questioned,' said Matz indignantly.

Schiller started to laugh. 'I'm sorry, Otto, it is easy to tease you. My amusement was at your expense.'

'So I am not under suspicion?' asked Matz excitedly.

'Of course not,' replied Schiller bluntly. 'But if news of any of our North American operations gets back to the Israelis, then I will know two gentlemen to approach, eh?' He barred his yellow teeth as he grinned.

'We've been so careful with everything, it hardly seems possible.' Matz scratched his balding head.

'Which reminds me,' continued Schiller, 'I want you to check the location of the remains of the U-boat crew we dispatched in 'forty-five.'

'Why?'

'I want all avenues rechecked. Make sure that no one escaped, or for that matter that no one has discovered the bodies.'

'But I personally saw to it myself!' insisted Matz.

'I want it double-checked,' insisted Schiller.

THE PARANÁ REGION, BRAZIL
Thursday, 9 September 1965

MATZ WENT to Brazil the following week, using one of the turbo-prop aircraft to land at the disused mines at San Diablo. Even from the air the place unsettled him, the memory of what he had to do all those years ago still came back to haunt him. As the aircraft circled the valley, preparing for the final approach, he thought about the dramatic events during 1945. After the rendezvous with the U-boats on a deserted stretch of the Brazilian coast, they had travelled inland by aircraft supplied by his company.

The German sailors had thought they were landing in Paraguay, but instead they had arrived here at San Diablo. Before the day was over, they had all been killed, machine-gunned by the SS as they ate a meal under the canopy of one of the prefabricated buildings. With their U-boat safely scuttled in a deep trench off the Brazilian coast, all that remained was to dispose of the bodies. Using Indian labour, Matz had had the bodies dumped into the deepest mine shaft. As the final body had been tossed into the abyss, Strassmann's men had killed the Indian workers who had witnessed the events – nothing was left to chance. Until now Matz had been certain that the dastardly deed had remained a secret, but the seed of doubt had been sown and it was eating away at his confidence.

As arranged, the survey team of engineers from São Paulo was waiting for his arrival. The men, mainly Bolivian and French engineers contracted from Santa Cruz, had been brought out to the mines by helicopter, under the guise of reopening the tin mine. They knew little about the job, only that it paid four times better than anything they'd worked on before. From knowledge, Matz was already aware that the shaft in which the bodies had been thrown was now filled almost entirely with water. The only way to check properly was to pump it out, or, better still, divert the water into one of the other connecting shafts further down the valley.

After landing, Matz was taken by jeep to the small cluster of tents erected beside the old mine works. He had had an eerie feeling about the place ever since arriving: the memory of all those sailors' faces still haunted him to this day. He had been able to ignore the guilt pangs until now, but even though the jungle had encroached on to most of the mine works, it couldn't cover up what had occurred. He was

270

shown into a large ex-Red Cross tent, covering over seventy square metres. It clearly served as the hub of the operation and housed four drawing boards and a large map chest. Matz was eager to hear the proposals. The team leaders had been on site for the last three days and knew exactly what he wanted. All he wished for now was a quick and hasty departure from the place. The two leading surveyors on the team awaited him patiently inside the main tent.

'Ah, Señor Matz, how good it is to see you again.' The main surveyor, a Bolivian called Rosati, smiled.

'Just spare me the pleasantries, Señor Rosati, and give me your report,' snapped Matz, slumping back in a folding chair next to the main planning table.

The surveyor blushed and cleared his throat as he looked across at his other colleague. Then he turned to a map pinned on a large display board, standing next to the table. With a pointer in his hand, he began to elaborate his conclusions.

'We have examined the west side of your mining seams – that was where we believed it most likely we would find an answer to your problem – but, alas, the shaft in question is now under so much water I doubt if we can ever clear it.'

'How much water?' retorted Matz, getting increasingly more anxious by the moment.

The engineer pointed to the map on the table. 'This western section was mined at a considerable distance deeper than the area where we now are standing. As you know, the mines were last used over forty years ago. Since then, subterranean water has been seeping into and rising in the western shafts, in some places to a depth of several hundred feet.'

'Pump it out then,' continued Matz, unabashed.

'No estoy de acuerdo, señor. It is just not possible,' the other surveyor spoke up. 'We have tried several times to see what effect our emergency pumping equipment had on the water level. On each occasion the effect was negligible.'

'What are you saying?' Matz ground his pearly white teeth as he sat forward.

'Water is entering from the high lands here to the north-west.' Rosati circled an area on the map in red ink. 'What started as seepage has now developed into subterranean pools. We cannot recommend the expenditure required to pump the shaft out. Even if we succeeded, I imagine that the old shafts would be totally unsafe to work again.'

'So, that is it.' Matz flopped back again in the chair. Schiller would just have to accept that it was impossible.

271

'Not necessarily.' The senior surveyor looked across again at his junior. 'We are in agreement that the eastern seams indicate that where we are now standing is the most probable location for a successful mining operation.'

'But I told you that this section is no use.' Matz was on his feet instantly. 'There is only one shaft that remains a probable success.' He recognized something on the engineer's face. What was it? 'You didn't go into it, I hope?'

'No, señor, we followed your instructions to the letter,' replied Rosati. 'But our survey results would disagree with your opinion, señor.'

'And what the Indians had to say about it would have convinced us anyway,' interjected his assistant.

'What Indians?' Matz screwed his face up.

'The local tribe around these parts tells some tale about ghosts. They claim that the shaft in question is haunted. They wouldn't go down there even if it was safe,' continued the other man.

'Señor – ' Rosati was clearly annoyed at his colleague's interruption. 'We can still have a successful mine here. But you must listen to our recommendations.'

'I've listened to enough. The survey is complete. Pack up,' insisted Matz.

'Think on it, señor. It could be very profitable. Here are some initial figures that we have prepared. Study them at your convenience and reconsider.' He handed Matz a rolled copy of the plans.

'Very well, I'll take them with me, but I want all work on this mine stopped immediately. Gentlemen, thank you and good day.' Matz lifted his panama hat and strode from the tent, just pausing a moment at the entrance flap. 'If we do have ghosts, I want no one going down the mine shaft and stirring up these local Indians.' He tried to make light of the situation.

'As you wish, señor.' Rosati nodded in agreement.

Matz walked swiftly from the tent, ignoring the gathering of local Indians all curious to get a glimpse of the white man who had stepped out of the flying machine. He did not see the look on the face of the insignificant little Indian woman standing next to his car. The Indians stepped aside as Matz approached and some of the children were shooed away by the Brazilian driver. The Indian woman didn't move so readily. She stood in his path, staring at Matz with dark eyes. He raised an eyebrow at her arrogance and brushed past, climbing into the open jeep.

'To the airfield, señor?' asked the driver.

Matz nodded. 'From what I remember of them, these Indians still stink as badly as they used to,' he said drily, getting a laugh from the driver as he walked round to the other side of the jeep.

It was then that she knew for certain. The white man's appearance had changed from all those years ago. He had lost most of his hair and had broadened out around the stomach. He walked now with a hunch and no longer had the facial hair, but it was him. His voice could not deceive her. The Indian woman wove her way through the gathering, careful to keep the small sack in front of her so that it shouldn't be knocked from her hand.

The driver had by now climbed into the seat beside his passenger and was ordering all the Indian children away from the front of the vehicle. Just as the diesel engine roared into life, the little Indian woman appeared at Matz's side. She said something in her local dialect. Matz looked at her, a little unsure if the wizened Indian was speaking directly to him or to the driver. He stretched across, just about to roll the window up in her face, when it happened. The woman tossed the sack in through the opening. It was already open and fell inside top-first. Even before the sack landed, its contents had fallen on to Matz's lap. He looked down in horror as the green viper snake curled around his thigh, hissing loudly. He tried to scream, but the shock was almost too much for him. The driver dived from the vehicle, rolling over in the dirt and calling out to Matz.

'Jump, señor! Jump!' he screamed. Stupidly, Matz tried to brush the snake aside and jump clear, but as soon as he made the sudden move it struck, biting him on the neck.

Matz gave out a sickening scream as he writhed in panic. The deadly venom shot through his system. His neck felt as if it had been prodded by a thousand white pokers simultaneously. The snake held on, emptying its venom sacs. The driver drew his revolver, watching Matz sprawled back across the seat, his face puffed and contorted, the agony of his death fixed for ever. As the snake slithered away on to the floor of the vehicle, the driver fired, cutting it in half. Immediately the Indians started running back. Several of the women and children screamed. Everyone gathered round the little Indian woman. She just stood there staring at Matz, a contented look on her wizened and haggard face.

LOS MILANOS RANCH, PARAGUAY
The next day

BACK AT Matz's ranch, Schiller had taken the news calmly. He simply ordered the woman to be brought back to Paraguay. The Indian woman had been kept in the cellars of the main house since she arrived. She had driven her captors almost crazy at the beginning with her constant chanting and muttering. No one was quite sure what she meant and no one was taking any chances even going near her. Rumours of her involvement in witchcraft and even sorcery already abounded throughout the ranch. Schiller ordered her interrogation by one of his men, a blond-haired sadist called Roth. The ex-SS captain wasted no time in extracting what he needed from the woman.

'Well, Roth, have you ascertained what happened?' Schiller hobbled down the uneven steps into the basement with some difficulty. He stared over at the Indian woman, now hanging by her wrists from a metal bar, her feet dangling several inches off the floor. She was completely naked and now semi-conscious from the beating and electric shock treatment had already received.

'The Indian threw a poisonous snake at him, *mein Herr*. It bit him and Matz was dead inside seconds,' said the blond-haired man.

'Why?' snapped Schiller, limping over to the woman and lifting her chin up. She was almost unconscious. She looked a great deal older than her thirty-five years – a natural development of the ageing process amongst the South American Indians.

'Her name's Yarima. She also has the baptismal name of Maria. It was given to her by a priest from a Catholic mission, located close to the mine.' Roth moved up beside his master. 'She says she was the wife of one of the Indian workers killed along with the white men at the mine shaft in 1945.'

Schiller turned abruptly. 'You mean she is a witness?' he growled.

'Apparently so.'

'How untidy,' commented Schiller. 'Find out everything. I want to know what she's said, who she's said it to and everything you can about this priest and mission.' Schiller turned and limped back towards the stairs. 'And quickly!' he barked.

'*Jawohl, mein Herr*,' Roth replied obediently, turning back again to the semi-conscious woman. 'Get me the cattle prod,' he ordered one of his men.

Just over an hour later Roth found Schiller sitting on the sun terrace, overlooking the swimming pool. The SS general was dividing his time between flicking through a five-day-old copy of *The Times* and watching several young topless women tossing a ball to each other at the poolside. He looked up at his aide.

'She died a few minutes ago,' said Roth.

'You must be losing your touch,' replied Schiller.

'She mentioned telling a Father Andrés and a Dr William Thomas. They run a Roman Catholic mission in Paraná.'

'A French priest and Welsh doctor in the middle of darkest South America, how intriguing.' Schiller folded the paper with one hand, tossing it on to the table in front of him.

'Apparently the doctor is an American.' Roth wiped the blood off the knuckles of his right hand with a handkerchief.

'And she spoke of this to no one else?'

'*Nein.*' As Roth answered, the beach ball landed at his feet. Schiller picked it up as the young blonde ran up the steps to recover her ball, her full breasts bouncing.

'*Bitte?*' She smiled, extending her hands to him. Schiller blew her a kiss as he handed back the ball. '*Dankeschön, mein Herr.*' She then turned and ran off back to rejoin her two friends, now jumping into the swimming pool.

'Roth, find the mission,' said Schiller bluntly.

THE CATHOLIC MISSION, PARANÁ, BRAZIL
Sunday, 12 September 1965

THE THREE Bell helicopters flew down, through the tropical rainstorm, landing in the middle of the leper colony and Catholic mission early that morning. The sound of the heavy rainfall drowned out the noise of the aircraft. No one knew what was happening until after they had landed, and by then it was too late. The Indians and mission staff were herded through the rain at gunpoint and rounded up together in the small chapel. The last to be taken there were the priest and the new mission doctor, a young Brazilian from Campos.

The old priest looked over at his flock, huddled together at the other side of the chapel at gunpoint. It angered him. '*Pour l'amour du ciel!* I demand to know what is going on!' he insisted, refusing to be frightened by the men with the Armalite rifles.

Roth was waiting for him just inside the porchway of the wooden chapel. 'Are you Father Paul Andrés?' he demanded.

The priest stared at the blond-haired man for a moment. 'I am Father Andrés,' he replied defiantly. 'And you are committing sacrilege, so I should at least know your name!'

Roth looked over at the young man in the white coat with the stethoscope around his neck. He couldn't be the other one they were looking for. 'Where is Dr William Thomas?' The elderly priest looked bewildered. 'Where is he?' insisted Roth, pointing the rifle at him.

'If you had taken the trouble to come in here correctly, you would have passed him on the road,' replied the priest.

'Do not mince words with me, Frenchman!' insisted Roth, prodding his chest with the muzzle of the M16 rifle.

'He is in the graveyard over there.' Father Andrés pointed towards the low-lying stone wall at the perimeter boundary of the Catholic mission. 'Dr Thomas died here ten years ago,' added the priest. Roth was silent. He stared out at the tiny graveyard beyond the rain-swept compound. 'What is this all about?' demanded the priest.

'Against the altar!' shouted Roth, firing a short automatic burst above the heads of the frightened Indians. His men began to move them up to the front of the chapel, where they huddled like frightened children against the altar rail. The young doctor stood next to Father Andrés, a human barrier between the evil visitors and the terrified Indians. Several of the Indians, expecting the worst, fell to their knees before the cross and started praying aloud. Father Andrés began to pray as one of the Germans recocked his rifle. An instant later, the four gunmen opened fire in unison, emptying the 30-round magazines of their 5.56mm Armalite rifles into the group.

The firing continued for over a minute, the gunsmoke rising up through the rafters towards the tin roof as each of the gunmen changed magazines and resumed firing. It amazed the Germans that none of the twenty-three Christians had tried to run. As the shooting ended, Roth walked forward, firing the occasional shot into anyone that still moved. He found the priest lying sprawled at the foot of the rough wooden cross, a small alabaster statue of Mary clutched in one hand. Before leaving, Roth raised the M16 at the statue's head and put a bullet through it, showering the dead priest in plaster dust.

Anna Poetach found Simon in conference with several army officers and a cabinet minister. She waited outside the glass-walled room for over an hour before the meeting broke up. The others traipsed out, leaving the chief of Israeli Foreign Counter-Intelligence alone. Anna spoke to one of the aides standing next to the door before entering. Simon was beside a map of the Middle East, studying the clearly defined Israeli defence lines, and barely noticed her until she was right beside him.

'Anna! You are back with us. How was Washington?' asked Simon, kissing her on the cheek.

'You know that from my report.' She raised an eyebrow.

'We are living in dangerous times, young lady. Look at this.' He pointed to the map. 'Our enemies are poised all around us.'

'Will it ever be any different?' she asked, staring down at the report on the September massacre at the Catholic mission in Paraná. It had been codenamed 'Bloody Sunday', the title scrawled across its blue cover in Hebrew.

'What has this to do with us?' she added.

'Our people in Brazil think that the neo-Nazis are responsible.'

'But why?'

'That's what you are going to find out, but first, this.' He handed her another report. 'It's an update on this "country club" in Argentina. As you know, we've been getting good-quality information out of it for some time now. It's time we paid it a closer look.'

'Who's Colonel Ortega?' she asked, scanning through the report.

'A rather disenchanted Argentinian army officer and a very brave man. He's been feeding us the information on this "club". A good contact, but we think it's time he was extracted for his own safety. Get him to Israel for de-briefing. Apparently he has photographs of many of the Nazis passing through the place, before and after their plastic surgery.' Simon was excited. It often didn't show, but this was the biggest break that Mossad was going to get in South America.

'Herr Wiesenthal will be dancing cartwheels if we pull this off.' She smiled.

'And I shall join him.'

'When do I leave?' She handed him back the reports.

'After full briefing, in about a week. You'll be going in via Peru, a tourist on holiday. Now, you will have strong back-up on this one.' He held her by both arms. 'Anna, be careful, I fear you might need it.'

'I will be all right.' She leaned forward, kissing him on the forehead.

AZUL TOWN, THE PAMPAS REGION OF ARGENTINA
Thursday, 21 October 1965

ANNA POETACH arrived back at her hotel just after 9 p.m. She felt tired and more than a little disillusioned after her wild-goose chase. Colonel Ortega had seemingly vanished. She had already decided on a hot bath and an early night. As her legs were tired, she took the elevator to the second floor. It was air-conditioned, with a sweet fragrance in the air, all in stark contrast to the sweat and smells she had had to tolerate all that day. The elevator jolted to a halt and the doors folded back. She went to walk out into the corridor. Then her stomach flipped over. Two middle-aged men stood before her, blocking her path. The one on the left she had seen before in the hotel lobby, but the other man she didn't recognize – not that she was too interested in faces when trying to work out what to do about the gun in the first man's hand.

'*Zurücktreten!*' said the other man.

There was nothing else for it: she moved back inside the elevator. Her shoulderbag contained a small .22 semi-automatic Mauser pistol, but she needed several moments to get at it. These two bastards were going to have to make a mistake. Anna moved backwards until she touched the cold metal of the elevator wall, her mind working overtime. They stepped inside, the one with the gun first. It was a Walther by the look of it, with no silencer, and these people couldn't afford any attention, even if they did seemingly run the country. It was an oversight that could help her. Just as the other man entered the elevator and began to reach for the control panel, she struck.

Swinging her shoulderbag, Anna deflected the first man's gun, before kicking him between the legs. Both men had been taken unawares. What they'd been sent to get and what they'd found were two different things. The second man swung round to grab for her throat, but he was overweight and clumsy. The little schoolteacher from Mannheim, meanwhile, had turned into a minor tornado. She wove expertly, using the man's momentum against him. She got behind him and slammed the knuckles of her index and middle fingers into his kidneys. The man gave a sickening groan that sounded close to a dying man's last exhalation, not that Anna was waiting to see the result. She grabbed him by the back of the hair and tossed him on top of his partner. Punching the ascent button on the wall control panel she skipped across the two prostrate forms just before the automatic elevator doors closed. The corridor was empty. She thanked God as the elevator began to whine. Anna watched as the arrow on the circular brass display began to move clockwise – her two 'escorts' were on the way to the twelfth floor.

She pulled out the Mauser pistol, slipping the safety catch. Then she raced up the corridor, ignoring her bedroom and heading for the nearest fire escape exit. She halted at the fire door, panting through excitement rather than any unfitness. No matter how you prepared for the real thing, it could never be the same. She closed her eyes a second and thought about Simon. He would expect her to be logical in a situation such as this. 'Always have a plan "B",' he would say. 'Think ahead and always have another way out, and remember they're going to be thinking just the same way as you are.' And Simon was right. If these buffoons had back-up, it could easily be on the other side of this fire door, or anywhere down to the ground floor.

She gritted her teeth. She was on her own. If they were waiting for her, they'd be on to her partner, Hilmar. She tossed away the shoulderbag. All she needed was the gun now and absolutely nothing to hold her up. Slipping off her high-heeled shoes, she put a shoulder to the fire door. It bounced back noisily against the wall. She quickly panned the darkened interior of the stairwell with the gun in both hands, crouching low. It was clear. Anna raced down the four flights of steps towards the bottom exit.

She was just reaching the landing at the top of the final flight when a door burst open somewhere above her. Hurried shouting followed. It was her two 'escorts'. Just as she reached the exit door, a shot rang out, ricocheting off the metal balustrade, then a further three shots. They clearly weren't worried now about drawing attention to themselves. This could only mean complicity with the local police or that they felt themselves above the law and beyond reproach. The shots went wide, the nearest powdering the concrete three yards to her right.

Anna raced forward, snapping down the door's horizontal opening bar. She was now at the rear of the hotel, close to the main carpark. She raced barefoot across the concrete and then through the flowerbeds and lawn that screened the rear service area from the public car-park. She hesitated, taking cover in a cluster of palm trees at the edge of the car-park. She looked across. Hilmar was still sitting in the car. What the hell was he doing! Hadn't he heard the shots?

She raced over, weaving low through the rows of parked cars. The place was empty except for some revellers arriving at the main entrance to the hotel in a taxi.

She halted at the row next to the car. Hilmar still hadn't moved. Anna checked around. The vicinity was apparently clear. Moving very carefully, she went along the row of cars until directly in front of her own. She peered up, looking through the small gap between the parked vehicles. Hilmar was looking straight at her, his eyes open and fixed, the surprise of death on his face. From the bright lights surrounding the hotel entrance, she could see the dark blood-stains down the front of his white shirt. He had been garrotted, his throat cut across to a depth of almost two inches by the thin wire still protruding from his neck.

Anna looked across at the hotel entrance. The taxi was still there, engine running. She didn't want to leave Hilmar – it hardly seemed proper – yet they would have immobilized his car or, even worse, one of them could still be inside, waiting. She fought back her urge to cry and raced the final yards through the last row of cars towards the entrance. The taxi driver was more than startled to find the dishevelled young woman jumping into the back of his cab.

'Drive!' she panted in English.

'What!' The local taxi driver turned around in puzzlement. It was then that he had the cold muzzle of the pistol thrust at his neck.

'Drive! Now!' she insisted.

'OK! OK!' he cried out, using up most of the English he knew. He wasn't going to argue the point. Putting the old car into gear, he headed round the car-park towards the main road. He was driving too slowly for Anna's comfort. As the taxi rounded the sweeping drive, a figure jumped out from the bushes, yanking open the front passenger door and diving into the front of the car. It was the German with the gun! He grabbed hold of the steering wheel for support and the car swerved violently. At the same time the German raised the gun in his free hand. Anna didn't hesitate: she fired instinctively at his head. The German slumped onto the seat. The loud crack at his right ear deafened the driver. He panicked and the vehicle bounced up on to the kerb, almost coming to a halt. Anna stretched across, pulling up sharply on the steering wheel, and the taxi jerked back on course again.

'Faster!' she insisted. The driver looked in the mirror, his eyes filled with a mixture of fear and shock. '*Schnell! Schnell!*' she shouted. Somehow he seemed to understand the German words more readily, stamping on the accelerator.

The car raced on towards the gates of the hotel grounds. To Anna's horror a strong hand reached up from the front passenger seat and grasped her right wrist. Terrified, Anna looked down. Amazingly, despite the deep graze an inch above the right eye, the middle-aged German was still conscious, with a grip like a vice. She couldn't get the gun pointed down at him as he began to force himself up from the seat, his eyes burning with rage and pain. She looked over, the front passenger door was still ajar, with the German's left foot trapped in it. As the man raised himself more fully out of the seat, grabbing hold of his own gun, she struck. Using the flattened palm of her left hand she punched up, under his flabby chin, forcing his head back so violently that the sinews in the nape of his neck crunched. Before he could yell he fell back into the door, forcing it open more widely. Both legs were now outside the car, his well-polished black shoes being torn up against the rough surface of the road. He still held on to her wrist but dropped his gun, grabbing hold of the seat instead. Anna struggled against him, lashing his face and head time and time again, but the man was possessed of supernatural strength. As the taxi approached the pillared gateway Anna stretched across and yanked the steering wheel to the right. The car swung against the open wrought-iron gate, catching the door and the German's legs. The man let out a scream as the door was forced closed on his lower torso and upper legs. Then his right leg caught under the gate and dragged him against the stone pillar. He was finally wrenched from the car. Anna gave a sign of relief. She was living on nervous energy, most of it borrowed and running out.

'*Beeilung!*' she shouted at the petrified driver. He gave a series of jerky nods and swung the taxi left into a wide, tree-lined avenue. Anna made him take her out of the city in a southerly direction. Simon had earmarked a small aviation company she could use in case of emergency. After leaving the city limits, they drove straight into what seemed like dense jungle. The road surface became rougher and extremely narrow, shrouded in thick vegetation. Memorizing a map was one thing; interpreting it on the road and by moonlight was another. They had just passed across the small bridge when, twenty minutes late, they ran into the road-block. Two police cars were angled across the road, their blue and red emergency lights flashing continuously. A truck of what appeared to be militia or army personnel was parked at the side of the road, just behind the police cars. The driver glanced back at Anna.

'*Policía!*' the driver stuttered.

'Act natural. If they ask you, we're going to Tandil.' She moved over behind him and stuck the gun in his ribs, keeping her arm down low and against the door. 'Say one word and I'll shoot.' He nodded. He could understand English after all!

They were waved down by a policeman holding a flashlight. He immediately noticed the damage to the front passenger door and the deep scores along the paintwork. Anna gulped. This could be difficult. He looked inside the taxi, flashing the light at Anna, who smiled at him as pleasantly as she could under the circumstances. He ignored her and turned his attention to the driver.

'*Carnet de conducir, por favor.*' The policeman held out his hand and the taxi driver passed across his driving documents.

'*De donde vienen?*' continued the policeman.

Anna strained to understand him. He was asking where they had just come from.

'Azul,' replied the driver.

'*A donde?*'

Anna dug the gun muzzle into the driver's rib-cage. The man flinched slightly but it went unnoticed. The policeman was busy studying his driving and identity documents.

'Tandil,' replied the driver.

The policeman then turned his attention to Anna. She rolled down the window slightly, using her right hand.

'*Documentos de identidad, por favor.*' He studied her carefully.

'*Siento . . . no hablo español.*' She struggled with the pronunciation.

'English?' The policeman frowned.

'No, German, but I can speak English.' She kept smiling up at him.

'And I . . . a little.' He nodded. 'Señora, you have papers?'

'No, they are back at my hotel. I was in a hurry, you see.'

'Why?' The policeman was not going to be put off easily. She couldn't decide whether it was professional curiosity or her unbuttoned dress front.

'I have an appointment . . . with a man.' She pretended to feign embarrassment.

'Your name, please?' He actually smiled. She felt she was getting somewhere.

'Anna Kupfer. I am here on holiday. I just arrived from Peru.' He nodded, handing the papers back to the driver. The taxi was suddenly lit up in the headlights of another vehicle. Anna tried not to glance

282

around as it slowed to a halt a short distance behind them. The policeman was about to let them through when he was called to one side by his superior.

Anna tried not to tremble. There was clearly a flurry of movement from behind, shadows moving back and forth in front of the car headlights. What was happening? She attempted to hide her fear as the policeman returned again beside the driver's door.

The very next moment a sub-machine-gun was jabbed through the open window next to her and the muzzle put to the side of her head. From the corner of her eye she could see it was another uniformed policeman. Before she could do anything a third policeman appeared at the other side of the taxi, pointing a revolver at her head.

'Get out,' commanded the first policeman, careful to keep out of the way of his colleague's gun sights as he opened the door. She carefully set the Mauser on the floor, kicking it under the driver's seat, thinking she still might just be able to talk her way out if the taxi driver kept his mouth shut. As she stepped barefoot out of the taxi, the first policeman grabbed her roughly and thrust her on to the car bonnet, face-down. The policeman with the sub-machine-gun covered her while the other began a body search. She smelt his foul breath as he leaned across her, his sweaty hands groping down around her buttocks. She braced herself as a hand slid up between her legs, raising her skirt to the obvious excitement of the other policeman. The policeman's fingers lingered, playing with her. Anna's anger grew. Suddenly she twisted sideways, slamming her elbow up into the man's face. The policeman screamed. His colleague raised his sub-machine-gun at her as Anna tried desperately to protest.

'You can't treat me like this!' she shouted, trying to control her temper. The policeman seemed to understand what she was saying. For a moment, she thought she was gaining his sympathy, but then one of the other policemen located the gun under the driver's seat. Anna cringed, visualizing the next ten years in a Buenos Aires prison. The one she'd hit came back at her, pistol drawn. Whilst she felt she could have taken him on, she knew she wouldn't win the battle. The incensed policeman pistol-whipped her across the side of the face. Anna slammed back against the car bonnet, momentarily stunned. The policeman cocked his revolver, jabbing the muzzle up under her chin.

Anna lay sprawled out across the warm bonnet, waiting for him to squeeze the trigger.

'Jetzt habe ich dich.'

Anna's eyes flashed sideways on hearing the words. The fat

German she had evaded in the hotel was standing at the other side of the taxi.

The third member of the Israeli team was still in Azul. He was to act as the communications channel and back-up to the first two. He sat impatiently beside the telephone at the rented house on the outskirts of town. He hadn't heard from either Hilmar or Anna in over twelve hours. He checked his wristwatch again. It was already past 3 a.m. A noise alerted him. Outside, somewhere in the street below, a dog was barking.

Picking up his handgun from the table, he switched off the overhead light and crossed to the window. The first-floor window of the old town house overlooked a narrow, cobbled street. Apart from the faint light emitted by a lamp at the far corner, the street was in complete darkness. The barking ceased as quickly as it had started. The young Israeli readjusted the roller blind and went back to the table. After another cigarette he decided he would give them one hour and then he would have to go to the Hotel Astoria and check up on Anna.

Anna had been tied to the kitchen chair for several hours, with two Nazis watching over her constantly. Her face ached and her wrists and ankles were by now badly swollen from the tight bonds. She could hardly flex her fingers and her feet were already numb. They had taken her from the police road-block to a house in the middle of an old orange plantation on the outskirts of the town. Surprisingly, they hadn't questioned her. They had gone to considerable trouble to catch her, yet now she was left tied up in a darkened kitchen, waiting, but for what? Little did she know that she was about to get an answer she could never have imagined in her wildest nightmare.

A door was opened and then closed somewhere off on the far side of the disused mansion house. Approaching footsteps echoed over the marble floors. Another door creaked open. The steps grew louder now and changed in tone: someone was walking down the parquet-floored hall towards the kitchen. The swing door creaked open and a man was silhouetted in the bright light streaming in from the hallway. He was squat and of medium height, the long coat draped over his shoulders hiding the outline of his body but not the flabbiness of his neck. He walked across until he was standing just six feet away from Anna. She could see him clearly now, his face illuminated in the light of the overhead oil lamp.

284

She didn't recognize him immediately. The job the country club's plastic surgeons had done on him was magnificent – even the eyelids had been altered. His closest family would have been fooled. Then he ran his left hand across his chest, as if trying to alleviate some imaginary heartburn, and it was then she knew – the way he held his fingers, the little finger splayed out from the rest. She had seen the very same mannerism over and over again while studying the grainy photographs in the old intelligence files. She was looking at Martin Bormann!

'I believe you have been looking for me?' He spoke in barely accented English.

'Really?' She tried to hide her realization.

'Mossad. Israeli Intelligence! This is the face of intelligence?' He pointed to her mockingly. The others began to chuckle. 'Is this the best they can do?' He began to laugh.

'I don't know what you mean. I am German. My name is –' Bormann lunged forward and struck her hard in the face. Anna reeled back, almost capsizing the wooden chair. It was immediately steadied by one of Bormann's henchmen.

'Your name is shit! Jewish shit!' he screamed.

Someone grabbed Anna by the hair and pulled her head forward to face the monster again. She tried to speak, but her lips were already beginning to swell and one of her teeth had been almost knocked out.

'You –' he jabbed a finger at her – 'are going to deliver a message from me to Tel Aviv.' Anna pushed her chin out, her eyes daring him to take another swing at her. Instead Bormann stepped back. 'A message of medieval proportion and significance to you Jews,' he sneered. 'Strip her,' he commanded.

The other member of the team returned to the town house just before dawn, even more perplexed than before. There had been no sign of Hilmar or Anna at the hotel and neither had answered their bedroom telephones. Their car was no longer in the hotel car-park. If nothing happened soon he would have to make a report. He went back upstairs without turning on the downstairs lights. In the darkness he missed the figure in the doorway leading from the lounge towards the dining room. He switched on the upstairs light and threw his coat across the bed. Just as he went to sit down the telephone began to ring.

'At last!' He gave a sigh of relief, setting his gun and shoulder-holster next to the brimming ashtray. He lifted the receiver to his ear. 'Yes?'

There was an eerie silence from the other end of the line. He thought he could hear someone breathing, then a voice spoke.

'Look downstairs.' The man's voice was cold.

'Who is this?' demanded the agent. 'Who . . .'

The line went dead before he could finish. The young Israeli threw the receiver down and snatched the 9mm Mauser from the shoulder-holster. His cover had been blown! Cautiously he descended the stairs and slowly worked his way through the house. After clearing the hall and kitchen, he went to the front lounge, switching on the light from the panel in the main hall. The door was ajar – he was certain he had left it closed before going out.

He took a deep breath and kicked it fully open, moving into the doorway on one knee, his gun held in both hands, ready to fire. He almost did. The very presence of the figure in the facing doorway was enough, but something held him back at the very last moment when he took up second pressure on the trigger. He stared down the gun sights towards Anna at the far end of the room. Afterwards, when relating the story to his people, he couldn't say for sure just how long he had knelt there staring at her, transfixed with horror and shock.

Anna had been nailed by each hand to the top corners of the architrave. She had been drawn and quartered, her chest opened from just below the breastbone to the groin and then cut horizontally at the waist. Her intestines and organs had been laid open and partly pulled from her, but one organ was missing. Her womb, the most sacred part of any Jewish woman, had been cut out and removed. Anna's defiled body had been left as a most hideous and gruesome warning to her Jewish masters, a warning that could not be ignored.

TEL AVIV
Sunday, 24 October 1965

MCCLEAN arrived back from Frankfurt, having changed over to a scheduled El Al flight in Rome. A car picked him up at the airport and took him straight to the office. The head of Mossad was waiting for him, his normally beaming face filled with sadness.

'*Shalom*. Come in and sit down.'

McClean sank into one of the leather armchairs. He was tired after the long trip from Frankfurt. Simon turned and stared at the various maps pinned to the wall just behind his desk.

'What's wrong, Simon?' asked McClean.

'Bad news is never easy to break.' Then he looked directly at the Scotsman. 'Anna's dead.'

McClean fought hard for breath. He sat forward with his head in his hands. The risk of death was something they had all lived with for a long time now, but somehow he had always believed Anna and he were immune; someday, he always believed, they would quit and rejoin the rest of the world as normal people.

He cleared his throat. 'When?'

'It was in Argentina,' replied Simon, 'three days ago.'

McClean raised his head, his grief overcome by a surging anger. 'What the hell was she doing there?'

'A recovery mission.'

'For what? Nazis?' McClean stood up, a little unsteady on his feet. Simon kept silent. 'She was after those Nazis! It was this "Nemesis" thing, wasn't it?'

'You know our rules. I cannot tell you any more.'

'Stuff your bloody rules! I want to know what happened. I have a right!' McClean was screaming now.

Simon shook his head. 'You are personally involved in this thing. Leave it to me.'

'Leave it! You got Anna killed!' He pointed a finger accusingly at him. 'I was working on "Nemesis". It was the reason I agreed to join this bloody outfit in the first place. You sent me off to Germany on a wild-goose chase and all the time you'd planned to send Anna in, hadn't you!'

'McClean . . .'

'How did she die?' he interrupted.

'Her body has just arrived back in Israel. I can't tell yet . . .'

'Fuck you!' McClean stormed out of the office. He couldn't bear it any longer.

McClean couldn't recall the last time he'd gone on a binge. Then he remembered the night Anna had met him in Florrie's pub in London. She had looked so stunning – sensual yet seemingly untouched by the hardness of life – and now she was gone, gone for ever. He tried washing the sickness from his stomach with copious amounts of whisky, attempting to drown his memories of those fleeting hours together. The next morning he woke in his bedroom with a very sore head and a peculiar buzzing sound in his ears. He sat up slowly. He was still fully dressed except for his shoes and necktie, and had obviously fallen asleep across the bed. He was just about to lie back

287

down when the door buzzer went off again. He was tempted to ignore it, but then it sounded a third time and now it was continuous.

He struggled to the door, forcing one eye open to peek through the spyhole, then pulled the door back a fraction.

'What . . . do you want?' He forced the words through a dry mouth.

'May I come in?' asked Simon as he pushed past, followed by another of his men. 'I think you've met Saul before.'

McClean supported himself against the wall as the two men went on into the lounge. By the time he followed them in, Simon was sitting on the sofa next to the window, whilst Saul was standing, flicking through a magazine he'd picked up off the coffee table.

'What do you want?' McClean squinted and tried to shield his eyes from the bright sunlight.

'I want you back,' said Simon resolutely.

'Why the hell should I?' snapped McClean.

'Because you want to get them just as much as I do.'

'But yesterday you said . . .'

'That was yesterday.' The head of Israeli Foreign Counter-Intelligence stood up. 'Get showered and changed. Saul will stay here to make you some black coffee.' Then he headed for the door. 'I'll see you at the "Half-way Hotel". Saul will drive you.'

McClean watched him leave with some disbelief. Saul set the magazine aside. 'I'll fix you breakfast, shall I?' McClean didn't answer. He was already headed for the bathroom. After a long, cold shower he emerged fully clothed to join Saul at the kitchen table. The Israeli poured him some coffee in silence.

'Tell me why he's changed his mind.' McClean was curious.

Saul shrugged his shoulders, but McClean could see the question embarrassed him.

'Tell me!' he growled, shoving the coffee mug aside.

'He saw Anna's body last night.'

McClean's eyes narrowed. There were a thousand things he wanted to know about what had happened, but with the trauma of the news his mind had been numbed. Suddenly McClean lurched forward, grabbing Saul by both lapels of his jacket with crossed hands. He pulled the Israeli agent almost across the table, uncrossing his hands and tightening the collar against Saul's neck. Even though Saul was expertly trained in unarmed combat, he was absolutely helpless now, held tightly against the table as he was.

'Tell me, God damn it!' He watched the man's eyes bulging as he increased the pressure on his windpipe. 'Tell me!' he insisted, releasing him a little.

'She was . . . carved up.' McClean could see it was upsetting for the man to go on any further.

'Where is she?' He tightened his grip again and Saul gasped.

'At an army base here in the city. The military hospital there has an emergency mortuary.'

'Get your coat and hat,' snapped McClean, releasing the man from his grip.

An hour later, Saul and McClean were standing in the mortuary. A female army orderly checked a clipboard that hung on the wall next to the door.

'Number five,' she said without emotion, before going across to a row of stainless-steel lockers and opening one of the refrigerated compartments. Then she rolled out a metal tray containing a black plastic body-bag. McClean went to her side. The orderly unzipped the first part to reveal Anna's face. The skin was already turning black, the bruising to her mouth and face barely visible with the discoloration. Her eyes were closed. She seemed almost peaceful lying there.

'Unzip the rest,' insisted McClean. The orderly looked over at Saul. The Mossad agent nodded before turning away.

McClean and Saul arrived at the 'Half-way Hotel' by mid-afternoon. It had been a dusty drive all the way down the bumpy roads to El Kubab. The 'hotel' was west from the town, well away from any kibbutz or village. It amazed McClean how the Israelis had managed to keep the place a secret. The underground complex was the size of an American football stadium. The amount of excavation alone must have raised a few eyebrows somewhere, yet miraculously they had achieved the impossible. From the distance the 'hotel' looked like any other small army training camp. Indeed, to the curious observer it functioned as exactly that, except the 'recruits' were in fact seasoned Israeli soldiers on constant guard.

Simon joined McClean down on the second floor at the main conference room. He was accompanied by a short, bald-headed man with a black patch over his left eye. The man was unknown to McClean yet his uniform shirt displayed the shoulder insignia of an Israeli army general.

'Nice to have you back,' said Simon.

'I saw her,' McClean answered as Saul left the room.

'I know,' replied Simon in a matter-of-fact way. 'Without my approval you wouldn't have been able to.'

'Always one step ahead.' McClean nodded.

'One has to be in this job.' Simon sighed. 'McClean, I'd like to introduce you to a good friend of mine, this is General Moshe Dayan.'

'General.' McClean nodded to the man and the general smiled back.

'McClean, what I am about to tell you is never to be repeated outside this room,' continued Simon.

'Go on.' McClean drew a cigarette from his pocket and lit it.

'Anna's death, as you will be aware, is a secret that we must all live with. It cannot be made public. The Israeli cabinet was informed yesterday of her death and whilst it is our policy to avenge such things, there are other considerations that override any such action.'

'Like what?' McClean was becoming annoyed again. This sounded very much like a fob-off.

'Israel is heading for war.' Simon let his words sink in. 'Take it from an old man, it's an inevitability in any case, but it will happen much sooner than anyone imagines.'

'Why?' asked McClean, looking across to the general. The soldier said nothing.

'To secure the State of Israel,' replied Simon.

'The Egyptians?' asked McClean.

'And Jordan and Syria,' replied Simon.

'What's this got to do with Anna's death?'

'I can't prove it, but from recent field reports I've seen I believe this "Nemesis" organization is backing the Arabs.'

'Explain.' McClean drew deeply on his cigarette.

'The one thing the Arabs need now more than anything is money. With that they can buy their way into Israel with tanks, rockets and aircraft. Yes, the Soviets are supplying them, but they need paying, and the money, we believe, is coming from these neo-Nazis.'

'Stop the money and you stop a war,' replied McClean. He watched the general move over to one side and take a seat. He was clearly there as an observer.

'We hope so, McClean, but at the least it will make a war winnable.'

When the general left an hour later, Simon and McClean mulled over everything they knew about 'Nemesis'. Finally they emerged into the ebbing sunshine, strolling together around the compound.

'It doesn't perhaps look like much to you,' said Simon, 'but this land means everything to me – not just because I'm Jewish, but because I can breathe freely.'

'I can understand that,' sympathized McClean.

'Can you really? You only entered Germany when the war was finally over. I grew up there as a boy under repression, and that was before the Nazis had their day. Do you know what it is like to be bullied and ridiculed every day of your life? No, of course you don't.' Simon dug his hands deeply into his jacket pockets. 'When the Nazis came to power, I was forty years old. I had a family – a wife and four beautiful children.'

'And are they . . .' McClean hadn't the heart to continue. Anna had told him before of Simon's hermit-like existence. She always said that if he ever stopped working, it would be like turning off a machine.

'They all died in the camps.' Simon stopped and sniffed in the early evening air as he stared over the hills towards the setting sun; in a few minutes it would be dusk. 'The Holocaust took them all.' McClean was about to say something, but then Simon continued. 'All except my eldest daughter. You saw her in the mortuary in Tel Aviv yesterday.'

McClean was speechless. He watched the old man walk away before shutting his eyes, trying to blank out the memory of the last two days, but all he could visualize was Anna lying in the plastic bag; all he could think about was the horrible torment she must have endured before dying. As he re-opened his eyes the sun went down behind the hills, a blackness descended about him and entered into his very heart.

NEW YORK
Tuesday, 2 November 1965

ELIZABETH was in New York to finalize the severance of her involvement with the Costello Corporation. It had taken a long time, but finally the saga of the failing construction corporation was drawing to a close. To keep Hoover out of prison, she had used several millions of her own capital from the jewellery business to pay off the outstanding debts. Despite everything, she still cared for him

291

in some way. Perhaps it was fear of being alone again that had stopped her ending their relationship completely.

Elizabeth arrived in the lawyer's office a little later than expected. Christopher Topping chaired the meeting between the ten lawyers representing all the creditors and interested parties to the formal winding-up of the Costello Construction Corporation. Oliver Hoover sat with his own lawyers across the table from her. She looked into his eyes. The pain and humiliation he was suffering were obvious. He had been truly brought down. His word would no longer count for anything in the financial institutions of New York.

The meeting dragged on for over an hour. With the final settlements out of the way, each of the lawyers filed out of the room, leaving Elizabeth and Hoover alone. She had thought very carefully of what to say to him, but his demeanour indicated he was close to a breakdown.

'How have you been?' he asked in a broken voice.

'Fine, considering. And you?'

'OK, I guess. This has sort of taken the wind out of my sails.'

'I can imagine,' she replied.

'They let me move into the gate house at Long Island, until things were settled here.' He nodded his head several times.

'And now what?'

'I'm a bankrupt.' He breathed in deeply. 'I don't know.'

'Come home with me to Key West,' she said softly.

Hoover looked at her for a moment. He couldn't believe that he was being given a second chance. 'I don't want charity. I've had enough of that already.'

'I'm not offering charity. I'm offering myself,' she said firmly.

He reached across, taking her hand in his. 'I can't . . . I don't deserve it.'

'I know you don't.' She smiled at him for the first time. He burst into tears.

YALE UNIVERSITY, CONNECTICUT
Monday, 8 November 1965

WHEN PETER had decided on history and economics, Elizabeth was surprised. She had noticed his constant interest in animals and wildlife at one stage and half imagined he would decide on veterinary surgery or perhaps biology. There was even the faintest of hopes that he might choose medicine, although Elizabeth knew the idea to be a fait accompli – Peter was less interested in people than insects or birds.

For the first months at Yale, Peter had kept himself to himself, settling into his rooming house on the edge of the university campus. The History and Economics lectures were boring. He found he knew more about most of the subject matter than the lecturers did, but at last he was free to do what he wanted. With a private income from his mother, he was his own master and answerable to no one.

Declining the constant invitations to join his mother in Key West, he had either visited Rabbi Bronowski in New York or stayed on in his rooms on the university campus. It also gave him an opportunity to catch up on a history lecture series being run by one of the senior professors. It was a privilege to be offered the chance to participate in Professor Snyder's history sessions. Students and academics had been known to travel from all over the country, and even further afield, just to hear the great man deliberate. This week's theme was 'World Politics and Strategy, 1944–5'. Peter had jumped at the chance to hear someone else expound theories on his favourite subject.

He crossed the square between the science block and the lecture theatres. A girl was sitting at the side of the steps to the main lecture hall with two young men. He had spotted her the day before. She was beautiful: fair-haired and a little older than him – in her mid-twenties, he reckoned. She had something the other girls on the campus lacked; it was called style. As he walked up the steps, he was conscious of her watching him.

'Hi there!' She looked up at Peter.

He looked at her, taken aback as she smiled. 'Hello.' He stopped for a moment.

'What's your name?' she asked cheekily, leaning back on both elbows against the wall.

Peter hesitated. It had to be some sort of a joke. No one had ever taken any interest in him before. 'Peter O'Casey.'

'Irish?'

'Not really.' He shrugged.

'I'm Catherine.' She cocked her head to one side, blotting out the morning sunlight shining from directly behind her. Then she stood up, ignoring one of the two boys as he continued trying to chat her up. She held out her hand. 'Hello, Peter.'

He shook her hand cautiously, expecting the joke to hatch any second, but it didn't. This wasn't real. What did he have to offer anyone? All he was good for was passing exams.

'You're here for the Snyder lecture?' he asked, studying her UCLA sweatshirt.

'I should be. It's too cold to sit out here,' she replied.

'Yeah.' He looked down, slightly embarrassed.

'So you're what they call a real Yale freak.'

'It beats getting drafted,' he retorted.

Before she could answer, two of the other male students came down the steps from the main entrance.

'Hey, Catherine, want to go with us for a malt maybe?' the nearer of the two burly nineteen-year-old students butted in.

'You guys go on. I'll catch you up later.' She smiled back disarmingly.

'Sure, whatever you say, Catherine. Catch you later.' He turned after giving Peter a hard stare and moved off with his pal.

'Excuse me, I'll be late for class.' Peter fumbled with his pile of textbooks. Several dropped on to the steps. The other students guffawed loudly.

'Wise up!' she shouted back. To Peter's amazement, she picked up one of the books for him. 'Are you usually this clumsy?' She smiled again, but it wasn't meant to make fun of him – she seemed genuine.

'I think it must run in the family.' He smiled nervously.

'I see.' She nodded her head gently. She really was pretty and she had character, a combination he had never witnessed before, except in his mother. He wiped the thought from his mind instantly.

'I'd better go now,' he insisted.

'Or you'll be late for class, right?' she said mockingly.

'Right first time.' It was his turn to smile. The ice was already cracking.

'I'll walk with you.'

'OK.' He turned and she walked beside him up the steps. He

noticed that she carried her books in a leather shoulderbag which hung at an uncomfortable angle from her left shoulder.

'Can I carry that for you?' he asked, surprising even himself.

'Sure, why not.' She handed over the bag. He saw that the top book was on sociology. 'I'm doing a post-grad course in sociology,' she continued.

'Sounds interesting.'

'Actually, it's full of crap. I only joined the course last week. I missed the start of the semester due to illness.'

'That's a lot of catching up to do. I hope it was nothing serious you were down with.'

'Down with . . . Oh!' She hesitated. Peter put it down to embarrassment. 'No, I was looking after my sick mother. The university was very understanding about it all.' She smiled at him.

'I see.' He accepted the reason without question. She glanced at him from the side of her eye as he stopped outside the lecture theatre. 'This is where I get off. I'm already late, I'm afraid.' He paused, looking through the glass panel in one of the double doors. The lecture was just about to begin. Professor Snyder's assistant was already cleaning the blackboard at the rear of the dais.

'Hey! I'll join you.'

'What!' Before he knew it, she was shoving him through the swing doors.

'I've a free period anyhow, and the library's usually packed at this time of day, so what the heck! Who's going to notice one more face?' She smiled at him again as they took their seats in the back row. Peter shrugged. How could he refuse?

The lecture was examining the effect of the various Allied war conferences, with special reference to the Yalta Conference between Churchill, Roosevelt and Stalin. Catherine shifted uncomfortably in her seat as the lecture rolled on. It seemed to Peter that she was quite uninterested in it. Professor Michael Snyder was one of the faculty's oldest fossils. He was well known for his repetitive nature and for rambling on about the most obscure of issues, but he knew his subject better than any other man. The lecture was delivered at dynamic pace, with many of the students unable to keep up with their notes. The professor's assistant produced a constant slide display of supporting material. Somehow or other, the professor managed to get side-stepped into commenting on a cartoonist's impression of the Yalta Conference.

'. . . take cartoonist satire, for example,' he continued. 'The

English used it to great political advantage in the nineteenth century. Things that could not be said for fear of the civil tort of libel could now be entered into via the use of the artist's sketchpad. Many believed cartoons to be a side issue, an irrelevance, something that attracted the illiterate towards the publication. But during the 1930s and 1940s, of course, the cartoonist did much to awaken world opinion to Adolf Hitler, and even with Hitler's power and control over the news media, the cartoonist did his job well . . .'

'What an old bore,' Catherine whispered in Peter's ear.

'Shush!' he replied anxiously. The lecture droned on, the professor summing up with a resumé of the Potsdam Conference and the various war crimes conferences, but as usual his propensity to get waylaid led the lecture off on a tangent, discussing journalistic responsibility and abuse, and how politics could be remoulded by the antics of national newspapers.

Catherine watched as Peter followed the subject matter with an intensity she had thought couldn't exist. He seemed mesmerized by the lecture. For the next thirty minutes she studied him, trying to decide what was going on behind those piercing blue eyes of his.

'. . . then we come to the final question of whether to believe everything that is written. For example, did Hitler really kill over six million Jews, did . . .' Professor Snyder continued.

'I've had enough. This old shit must be the biggest pain I've ever heard,' she finally whispered again.

'He's also the head of my faculty,' replied Peter. 'Don't rock the boat, *please!*' He groaned.

'Any questions.' Professor Snyder began to pack up his notes. He was used to silence after his lessons, no one wanting to prolong them.

'Yes, I have one!' shouted Catherine. Heads turned from all over the packed lecture theatre. Peter tried to ease over to the other arm of his chair. Perhaps there was a crack in the raised floor that he could get through.

'Yes, Miss . . .'

'Beaumont, Professor, Catherine Beaumont. My question is simple enough. You mentioned briefly that the press in Nazi Germany kept silent over Hitler, yet dozens of leading journalists either went missing or fled Germany in the years when Hitler was coming to power. The way you make it sound, the press could have printed what they wished and all with Uncle Adolf's blessing! Now, you question the reporting of the Holocaust, you stand there and question Hitler's participation. The fact is that over four million, perhaps as

296

many as six million, and not just Jews but Gentiles too, died in Hitler's death camps, under his control.'

'But, Miss Beaumont, you miss my point. No documentary evidence exists to show that Hitler even knew about the death camps.'

'No official records exist to show that Socrates was queer, yet we all know it as a fact!' The lecture hall resounded to the sound of laughter.

'*Touché*, young woman.' The professor bowed to her, just as the bell rang for the end of the session.

Catherine joined Peter for a walk in the park afterwards. For the first time in as long as he could remember, Peter was actually enjoying himself. 'You gave that old bastard in there hell.' Peter was proud to walk by her side. Not only was she pretty but she was intelligent too.

'Yes, maybe, but did you see him writing down my name? By tomorrow he'll know I'm not one of his students.'

'So tonight we have a final feast! The condemned ate a hearty meal and all that!' insisted Peter.

'You realize that you've just invited me out tonight?' She smiled.

'I'm surprising myself.' He laughed.

And the laughter didn't stop. They spent the evening in a little Italian place close to where Peter roomed. The food was slow in coming but the company made up for everything. Peter had never met anyone quite like Catherine before. Certainly in many ways she reminded him of Elizabeth, except for one major detail: she seemed interested in him for himself. It was the first night of many. Peter found himself wanting to see her at every opportunity – at lunch-time, then for study periods, just sitting next to her in the library.

It was several weeks before Catherine invited him back to the small single-room apartment she had rented temporarily, just a few miles from the university campus. It was a cold and wet night, and appropriately they'd just seen the movie *Judgment at Nuremberg*, starring Maximilian Schell. Then they snatched some burgers and french fries at a nearby café. It was after eleven and by now Catherine knew that her landlady, a creature of habit, would be fast asleep. The old lady lived alone in the basement apartment with her cat. She did things like clockwork – always took the milk in at the same time each day, always went for her morning stroll at the same time, meals at the same time and finally to bed at the same time. Catherine also knew that the old woman removed her hearing aid when she went to bed, so even if Peter smashed down the front door she wouldn't hear it.

'Come on up. I've got a bottle of Chablis. It won't be chilled, but you can't have everything.'

'Catherine, I don't know.' He hesitated.

'Bullshit, O'Casey! Come on. I'm not going to bite!' She raced out of the Sunbeam Alpine sports car and stood at the top of the steps. 'Last chance!'

He jumped out of the car, tossing the keys into his jacket pocket and following her inside. Her room was on the second floor, to the front of the building. He watched from the window as the rain began to fall again: outside his car was open and getting drenched, but suddenly it didn't seem to matter any more. She disappeared off to get the wine, leaving him to look around the place. The room was small but cosy. She had posters up everywhere – some she'd obtained from a circus, others from the local movie house. The one advertising *Casablanca* took pride of place, just above the mantelpiece of the small fireplace.

'Sorry, no glasses. Will these do?' He turned to see her with the wine in one hand and two mugs in the other.

'I think so,' he said agreeably, taking the wine bottle.

'You surprised me tonight,' she continued, sitting down cross-legged in front of the fire. 'I didn't know you could speak German. Did you learn that from your mother?'

'I taught myself actually.' He stared back suspiciously.

'You never talk about her much, do you?' she asked just as he pulled out the cork and began pouring the wine.

'There's nothing to talk about. She lives in Florida now – that is, when she's not jetting around the globe.'

'And your father's dead?' she prodded him.

'As far as I can tell.' He shook his head. 'She doesn't exactly talk about him very much. In fact, she doesn't talk about him at all.'

'That hurts?' She sipped some wine.

'What is this? An interrogation?' He leaned forward and kissed her. She set her mug aside and took him into her arms. Slowly he eased on to the rug beside her, their bodies locked together.

Peter woke up the next morning with the warm sun beating down on to his face. He sat up in bed and shielded his eyes to the sunlight streaming in through the uncurtained window. Catherine lay on the bed beside him. She was still asleep, curled up snugly under the blankets. The night had been like a dream for Peter. It had been everything he could ever have wanted – wonderful, exciting . . . Words failed him for the first time in his life. She stirred, reaching over and drawing him down again.

'Don't go just yet,' she whispered into his ear.

'I think I can hear your landlady downstairs.' He was certain he could. She sat up in the bed, the blanket falling to her waist. Peter stared at her nakedness. He still found it hard to believe that he'd made love to such a beautiful woman.

'Love me.' She nibbled his ear.

'That's the problem,' he replied with a seriousness. 'I think I do.'

Catherine opened her eyes and stared at him for a moment. He really meant what he was saying.

Later that morning, after successfully sneaking him out of the house, Catherine headed down towards the main post office and used one of the pay phones as usual, placing the call direct to the Manhattan number. She checked around just to make sure she hadn't been followed before dialling the last three digits.

'Hello? Ed Morrisey.' The man's voice was gruff as always.

'Ed? It's me.'

'Catherine! Hey, how's it going at Yale? Scored any good points for the team yet?'

'Ed, this isn't working. I think you should pull me off this assignment.'

Morrisey sat forward, leaning on his desk with both elbows. 'What the hell do you mean, young lady? Do ya know the trouble I went to, getting you on to the features team?'

'Ed, the magazine wouldn't print the story. In essence, there isn't one. Peter's just a nice kid, learning to be himself.'

'Hey, you ain't gone soft on this one, have ya?' he snapped.

'Please Ed, take it from me. There is no story,' she persisted.

'What about the mother? Has he opened up on her yet?'

'Not really. I don't think he cares for her very much. They don't even see each other. He's supposed to be spending his vacation with her down at the Florida Keys, but he won't go.'

'Make him.'

'Ed, don't make me do this, please,' she begged him.

Morrisey ripped off his gold-rimmed spectacles and rubbed his face. He wasn't being put off that easily. 'Stick with it, kid. Ring me next week.'

'But, Ed, I don't . . .' She stopped speaking, he'd already rung off.

US NAVAL ACADEMY, ANNAPOLIS, MARYLAND
Saturday, 4 December 1965

THE REUNION of the officers and men of the Second World War destroyer USS *Cheyenne* was held as usual at the Naval Academy at Annapolis. For some time now it had been customary to meet on a tri-yearly basis, to assist those with heavy business commitments or perhaps living far away. The organization of the reunion was arranged by Lieutenant-Commander Abe Charles (Retired). As always, he tried to obtain one or two guest speakers, just to break up the evening a little, but he was fast running out of people to ask. Those who had had authority over the *Cheyenne* during the war years were dropping like flies due to ill-health or just plain old age.

Oliver Hoover was more than usually reluctant to attend this time, his commitment to rebuilding his marriage being total, but Elizabeth had insisted that he take the break and see his old buddies at the reunion dinner. Reluctantly he had accepted. Elizabeth needed him more than ever now. It was a nice feeling and something he wanted to savour, but this reunion was going to tie him up for nearly twenty-four hours when he took in his travelling time. As always, he contacted Jimmy Drexel at his restaurant, arranging to meet up at the reunion. They arrived together. Rank didn't matter to Hoover any more – both he and Drexel had been long-established friends before the war had even started – but for just one evening every three years they would revert to officer and subordinate. It was the way things were and nothing could change it.

The old USS *Cheyenne* had long since gone to the scrapyard at Norfolk. Whilst only a reserve officer, Abe Charles had stayed on as captain until the de-commissioning date, when he had brought the ship into harbour for the last time in 1952. By then, most of the conscripts had already returned to civilian life, including Hoover of course. Abe Charles felt that a bond had developed between himself and his crew, something that went beyond the normal run of things. It was because of this that he fought determinedly to maintain contact with the other crew members.

Hoover reckoned that his ex-captain must have made it his life's work to organize the reunions – the effort involved was unbelievable.

The old gymnasium at the academy had been decorated in some splendour. The walls and ceiling were festooned with red, white and blue streamers and balloons, and each of the tables had been laid out fit for a king. It looked to Hoover more like a political convention than a reunion. They had all expected something special to be arranged, but Abe Charles had gone overboard.

'Jumping Jehosaphat!' exclaimed Jimmy Drexel, casting an eye hurriedly around the place.

'Impressive,' replied Hoover. 'Just who have we coming? All it said on my invitation was a guest speaker.'

'Must be the President!' sighed Drexel.

Their questions were answered when Abe Charles came in, accompanied by the well-known Second World War veteran Admiral Radcliffe, now seventy-four years of age and in failing health. The admiral was an enigma in military matters. A White House adviser and ex-chief of the Pentagon, he had retired to write his memoirs, but instead had been called back to the White House several times to act as the President's personal envoy. He had a unique knowledge that transcended politics, with successive Presidents clamouring to gain Radcliffe's expertise.

The party got under way just a little after 7 p.m., with cocktails being served at one side of the gymnasium. Already all the ex-officers had split into a small group on their own, reminiscences filling the air. Hoover didn't much care for the 'them and us' situation, but it was a fact of life he was forced to accept, something to be tolerated for just one evening in every thousand or so. He watched the admiral. The old man now walked with the aid of a stick, following a fractured pelvis the previous year. Amazingly, Radcliffe still kept his stiff military bearing and there was an air of authority about him.

By comparison, Abe Charles looked like a passed-over bank clerk, his rounded shoulders and protruding stomach adding more years to his appearance. He would have been better off sticking to his vegetable patch in San Francisco, thought Hoover. He cast an eye around the rest of the gathering. Time was indeed catching up with them all – the swollen girths, the bald and greying heads, the double chins. Was he as bad as the rest of them? Of course, he had to be, but his ego hadn't let him face up to it until perhaps now. It seemed to hit him all at once, making him feel utterly miserable.

As always, the dinner menu never altered: a salad followed by soup and then fish. It didn't take much to guess that the main course would be steak Diane – this had been the tradition since after the first reunion back in 1947, when something went haywire in the kitchens and the entire reunion abandoned their dinner midstream. It amazed Hoover that anyone still took the trouble to print out the menu. Apart from any invited guests at the top table, everyone knew exactly what they were getting. He stared along the top table to the admiral, sitting three away beside another guest of honour, the rear-admiral in charge of the Naval Academy, Admiral Holden. Abe Charles was in his element in his role as great American warrior, his tuxedo resplendent with a row of miniature medals. From what Hoover could see, Admiral Holden was trying his best to put up with the situation, picking at his food and nodding politely at the conversation.

The after-dinner speeches were pretty much as usual – rambling with a pretence to humour, the sort of thing Hoover had come to expect. Abe Charles started off the speeches as usual, thanking everyone for their attendance, making reference to their dwindling numbers and announcing the demise or indisposition of those not in attendance. His speech would be the longest by far – it always was – and, as usual, it was a revamp of speeches he'd made in previous years.

Admiral Radcliffe was next to speak. Hoover watched as the old man eased himself up from the table with difficulty, leaving his stick on the floor next to him and using the table edge for support.

'Admiral Holden, Captain Charles, officers and men of the USS *Cheyenne*,' he said in a weak voice.

There was total silence in the hall. The navy waiters and orderlies clearing up the dishes stood quietly at the back of the gymnasium. Even in retirement the admiral still commanded a respect that Abe Charles would have given his right arm to share.

'I was very pleased to get Captain Charles's invitation to be here tonight, but I didn't know that I should really accept.' There was a general murmur around the hall. 'You see, I . . . I had a speech all made out but now it just doesn't seem proper any more.' The admiral's voice was becoming shaky and unsteady. It was now dawning on Hoover that the old man had suffered a slight stroke at some time. 'The last time I saw you all was on a certain dash down the South American coast during 1945. The war in Europe had ended but there we were, in the South Atlantic, chasing after a U-boat. Well, none of you knew exactly why and that was correct . . . the way it should have been.' He paused for a moment. 'I lived my life like that, doing things the correct way . . . the proper way and . . . and sometimes, when you look back with hindsight, it doesn't after all seem proper or indeed correct. And we never did get that damned Kraut U-boat!' Everyone laughed, perhaps realizing the strain the old man was under. He waved for them to cease. 'But . . . but nobody could feel too bad. We did things by the book, played by the rules, and that, that is what it's all about . . . I . . . I . . .' Hoover watched the old admiral look all around him, a lost expression on his face. It was as if he'd suddenly awakened to find himself standing there in front of a room full of strangers. 'Rules . . . that's what it's all about . . .' continued the Admiral, sounding like a stuck record.

Hoover was first on his feet, moving over just behind the admiral. 'Sir, sit down, take the weight off your feet,' Hoover urged.

'Hoover, get back to your seat. I'll take care of this!' retorted Captain Charles, indignant that Hoover was presuming on his guest speaker.

'Shut up, you arsehole!' snorted the admiral. Charles was mortified, pretending to ignore the remark and covering the microphone a second too late. The entire gathering on the floor began to chuckle. The admiral's words had gone a long way to sum up their own feelings about their ex-captain.

'Get me outa here, son.' Radcliffe turned to Hoover, pleading through painful, red-rimmed eyes. Hoover lifted the old man's stick and helped him away from the top table and out of the nearest exit. They followed the corridor and then exited through a door on to the lawn.

'There's a seat over by that tree,' said the admiral. 'You can see clear across the bay from over there.' He waved his stick towards a tall maple standing alone in the middle of the sweeping lawn, just before it began to bank and slope downwards towards the shoreline. Hoover helped him across and got him rested on the bench seat built around the bottom of the giant two-hundred-year-old tree.

'Used to come up here when I was a student instructor at the academy,' sighed the admiral. 'Proposed to my first wife right here.' A smile cleared the wrinkles from his face momentarily. Then he looked at Hoover. 'You're Hoover, the ship's exec, aren't you?'

'You have a clear memory, sir.' Hoover smiled.

'I've a bad memory, son, parts of it obliterated for ever.' He breathed in the fresh evening air. 'You ever wonder just how much the brain can retain? I do,' he continued, answering his own question. 'Then we wonder sometimes why the train runs off the tracks. Maybe it's all too much. I sure as hell don't know any more. For someone always so sure of himself in his career, it's sure as hell a bit unsettling now. Got a cigar?' He breathed deeply again.

'Cigarettes, I'm afraid.' Hoover removed his gold case and opened it for the old man. The admiral took one, puffing deeply and then coughing.

'They don't allow me to smoke any more, say it constricts the blood vessels or something.' He puffed again. 'I had a stroke, you know.'

'I thought so,' replied Hoover, sitting down beside him.

'Does it show that much?'

'My mother had a stroke just before she died. It was something about the way you spoke back there.' Hoover tried to lighten the situation, a little embarrassed by the comment.

'Some speech, eh!' He pulled out several folded sheets of paper from his jacket pocket. 'I was going to read this, then that buzzard Holden in there says I can't! Still under a security blanket! Huh!' The old man was filled with indignation. He threw the folded papers on to the seat beside him. 'Then I decided to say something short and funny, but the funny thing was that I couldn't remember what I was going to say. Hoover, I'm falling apart.'

Oliver Hoover didn't reply. He was too busy scanning the admiral's discarded notes. They were all about the *Cheyenne*'s hunt for the Type-XXI U-boat, perhaps in more detail than the old man should have contemplated revealing publicly, especially the aspect of military action inside Argentina's territorial waters, which would give more than just a few headaches to the US State Department. Then he got to the final piece and his eyes widened. The U-boat had been located, and what was written about its passengers was almost unbelievable

'Adolf Hitler was believed to be on board the U-boat!' Hoover gasped.

'Close your mouth, son . . . This place is damned famous for those beach flies. They come inland just about this time each evening.' The admiral chuckled.

'Admiral, may I ask you about what you've written here?'

'Sure, son, be my guest.' The admiral was enjoying his cigarette.

'You say here that Intelligence believed Hitler was on board the Type-XXI U-boat.'

'That's what they said all right.'

'But it was never confirmed?' continued Hoover.

'Nope. The U-boat escaped, as you know.'

'But you also say here that the sub was located.'

'An oceanographic survey ship from the US Navy was charting down in the South Atlantic during 1962 when they located something peculiar on their sonar. From what they found, they knew it was a piece of an old wreck of some sort, but the question was, what wreck? There was nothing listed as having been lost in the vicinity and they discounted its being a very old wreck because of the clear definition of their signal. It was in deep water, in a trench just off the Brazilian coast. But the survey ship did carry some new experimental remote-control submersibles that they were testing out at the time.'

'They found the U-boat!' Hoover rested his head back against the tree. All these years it had puzzled him. It was also one of the main talking points each time the *Cheyenne*'s crew met.

'They found the crushed hull of one of the electro U-boats we'd heard so much about at the time . . . You know, if the Krauts had gotten more of them into the water in time, it could have made all the difference to the war . . . Britain might have capitulated. Its supply lines across the Atlantic would have been severed irrevocably. Those Kraut scientists . . . led by that guy Walter, they were light-years ahead of any of us. Put into service in adequate numbers, just three or four years earlier than they were, those Type-XXIs would've given the Krauts complete control of the seas. Think about it – the British fleet and ours would have been annihilated.'

It seemed to Hoover that the old man had got his second wind. He was off on a tangent now and enjoying it, but Hoover was desperate to discover what had happened.

'What state was the sub in?' he urged.

'They took some shots . . . using one of those underwater cameras . . . The hull was fairly crushed. From what they could tell, it appeared the vessel had been scuttled.'

'Scuttled!' Hoover sat forward.

'Apparently they'd placed charges in the sides of the hull and again at the pressure doors.'

'So then the crew must have escaped,' prompted Hoover.

The admiral nodded his agreement. 'Damned crafty, those Krauts . . . You know that they'd disguised the vessel to appear as one of ours.'

'I don't follow.' Hoover was on the edge of his seat.

'The salinity at that depth is enough to reduce the corrosive powers of salt water. The submersible was able to get pictures of the markings still on the side of the conning tower. The Krauts had painted the Stars and Stripes on both sides!' Admiral Radcliffe coughed, tossing away the remains of his cigarette. 'The cheek of those bastards . . . using our national emblem to cover their escape.'

'Clever,' commented Hoover. 'So what happened to the crew and whoever else was on board?' His mind was racing now. 'What's

305

Admiral Holden so worried about that he asked you to curtail your speech tonight?'

'He didn't ask me, son . . . he ordered me.' The admiral looked over at Hoover. 'Joe Holden didn't turn up here tonight by accident, Hoover. He was sent here to make sure that an old fool didn't go overboard.'

'I don't understand, sir?'

'Don't you?' The admiral coughed again. 'Well, I'll tell you.' He stared straight at Hoover now. 'A few years ago I decided to write my memoirs. That was how I found out about the Type-XXI having been located. I put out an ad in one of the naval journals, asking for anyone with material that might assist my project to contact me. In the main I was searching for photographs and that sort of thing.' Another cough. 'Well, that was how a young naval lieutenant-commander called Burnett arrived on my doorstep in Boston. He'd read about my planned book in the article I'd written in the journal. He knew one of my last wartime experiences was chasing U-boats in the South Atlantic. He was on board the navy survey vessel that located the wreck. He brought along some shots he'd developed himself before the negatives were seized by Naval Intelligence.'

'Intelligence? Why should they have been interested after all that time?' Hoover was really intrigued.

'Can't say. Burnett told me that after they'd reported finding the U-boat, a Naval Intelligence officer was waiting for them at the dockyard at Maryland when they arrived home. The entire crew were given a very lengthy and pointed lecture on national security.'

'Burnett gave you these photographs?' Hoover folded the unused speech prepared by the admiral and shoved it inside his jacket pocket.

'Just as well he did too.' The admiral coughed again. 'He was killed two days later in an auto accident.'

'My God!' Hoover started to feel quite uneasy.

'That's how the Pentagon found out about me seeing the young-ster. I attended his funeral in North Carolina . . . Felt I had to, was the least I could do for him.'

'Someone approached you?'

'Not immediately . . . about six months later I was approached by the CIA. I'd just forwarded the first draft of my memoirs to the publisher in New York. The CIA had already obtained a copy of what I'd submitted, even photostats of Burnett's photographs of the U-boat.'

'And what happened next?' urged Hoover.

'The CIA demanded that I hand over the photographs.'

306

'And did you, sir?' Hoover turned around. He could hear voices coming closer from the direction of the building.

'As I said in my speech, son, I lived my life the proper way. The navy was in no doubt that I would hand them over and I never disappointed them.'

Hoover looked over again. He could hear two men's voices more distinctly now. He stood up, glancing around the side of the tree.

'There you are, Hoover!' It was Abe Charles, accompanied by Admiral Holden. 'I've been looking everywhere for you. Is Admiral Radcliffe still with you?'

'Yes, sir,' replied Hoover. The two men walked round the tree.

'There you are, Admiral. We've been quite worried about you.' Charles tried to sound charming.

'Shut up, Charles!' grunted the old man. 'The only thing you're interested in is making an impression.' He stood up, aided by Hoover. 'Thank you, son.' He smiled at him. 'I've enjoyed our little . . . smoke.'

'Me too, Admiral.' Hoover smiled back.

'C'mon, Jack, I've arranged for a car to take you home,' interjected Admiral Holden.

'I'm sure you have, Joe.' Then he winked at Hoover, before allowing Abe Charles to guide him back towards the main complex. 'You think of everything.' Hoover went to follow the old man, but was halted by Admiral Holden.

'A moment of your time, please.' Admiral Holden raised a hand to Hoover's chest. Once the old admiral and Charles were out of earshot, he continued. 'You shouldn't take anything Admiral Radcliffe says too seriously. As you can see, he's quite a sick man. Shouldn't even be here this evening.'

'I can see that, Admiral,' replied Hoover curtly.

'Sit down, Mr Hoover. I want a word with you,' invited Holden. Hoover obliged him.

'You were in the stock market, I believe.'

'The past tense is quite correct, Admiral. I was made bankrupt following the collapse of Costello Construction Corporation.'

'Yes. I was sorry to hear about that. Of course, your wife is Elizabeth Goldmann. She has a business stretching across this entire globe, I believe.' The admiral's concern sounded unconvincing. 'Your wife is quite a celebrity.'

'Admiral, what do you want?' Hoover turned on him.

'Admiral Radcliffe is a very sick man. I just wanted to thank you personally for what you did for him back there.'

'It was nothing,' replied Hoover cautiously.

'You were out here for a while,' continued Holden. 'I'd like to think that if Admiral Radcliffe in any way compromised himself, you wouldn't use that for any personal advantage.'

'What does that mean?' Hoover glared at the man.

'You're a businessman at heart, Mr Hoover. Businesses rely on trust and goodwill,' the admiral replied sharply.

'Was that some sort of threat, Admiral?'

'Just stick to your own business, Mr Hoover, that is all.' Holden rose. 'Good night,' he said curtly, before walking back inside. Hoover ignored him, watching the ships out in the bay.

Hoover said nothing to Jimmy Drexel on the way back to New York about what Radcliffe had said. He didn't dispute anything the old man had told him. Undoubtedly Radcliffe had physical problems and perhaps memory lapses, but the old man had been certain about his facts relating to the U-boat. In his day, Admiral Radcliffe had been at the hub of events, one of the main driving forces of his country's navy, a man with considerable power and prestige. Now he was a fearful old man, his mind full of Machiavellian plots and subterfuge. Was it his imagination, some direct result of his illness, or were they real?

What intrigued Hoover more than anything was the way in which the US authorities insisted upon keeping the discovery of the U-boat a secret. What was to be lost by making public such a revelation? Then there was the intelligence report that Hitler was supposed to have been aboard the submarine. Why did someone as far up as the White House want to keep silent on that? Was someone being paid, or even forced, to avoid a hunt for escaped war criminals? He had to discuss it with someone, but who? After all these years of helping to build the brave new world, as it had been so described by various politicians over the last two decades, Oliver Hoover was suddenly thrust into confusion. The only person he could talk to was his wife.

KEY WEST, FLORIDA KEYS
The following evening

'I'M TELLING you, Elizabeth, it's a fact. The U-boat made it to South America. They scuttled it before going ashore.' He spoke with conviction.

Elizabeth had listened intently to Hoover's story for the last forty minutes. She walked quietly out on to the veranda and breathed in the cool sea air with mounting excitement. Now she had something to go on. Something tangible for Conrad to follow.

ASUNCIÓN, PARAGUAY
Monday, 6 December 1965

'WE HAVE to talk, *mein Herr*.' Roth approached his master. Schiller was sitting by himself in the Turkish bath, a towel drawn loosely across his stomach. He looked up, unamused by the interruption.

'This had better be important, Roth.' Schiller never liked being disturbed at anything he did.

'Herr Renan, yesterday two Americans arrived in Asunción. They checked into the La Palma Hotel. One is called Conrad, a private detective of sorts. The other man appears much more interesting. His name is Nico Giovanni and he has strong Mafia connections. His family runs New York City. They are the same two who were in Argentina, snooping around and asking questions about the country club.'

'And how does this concern me?' asked Schiller, adjusting the black patch over his left eyesocket.

'They're looking for a certain Rudolph Schiller.'

'I see,' Schiller replied, calm as always. 'Who sent them? The Israelis?'

'*Nein*, a woman called Elizabeth Goldmann. An American businesswoman.'

'And from the sound of it a Jewess,' snapped Schiller. 'No doubt the World Jewish Congress has a part to play in all of this, eh?'

Roth shrugged. 'There is something else you should know, *mein Herr*. This Conrad is the same person that Herr Kruse reported on from Bonn. He was snooping around, trying to find out about you.'

'Why was I not told of this before?' Schiller frowned.

'The matter was attended to, *mein Herr*. It was arranged by our American contacts to give the lady something to worry about on her own doorstep. It cost her dearly. She lost a great deal of money when the Cartello Corporation collapsed.'

'But clearly not enough,' insisted Schiller. 'Goldmann, that name sounds familiar. Find out what you can about her.'

'I already have, *mein Herr*.' Roth handed his master a copy of *Time* magazine. Elizabeth's face was on the front cover, advertising a ten-page feature on her inside. Schiller's right eye narrowed. 'I know this bitch!' He flicked open the magazine. It contained a short resumé of Elizabeth's family background.

Roth watched as Schiller stood up, his face bulging with anger. 'I want this woman thoroughly researched. Everything there is to know about her business background and present business. In the meantime, have the local police pick up these two Americans and get them deported. *Schnell!*'

Schiller tossed the magazine on to the floor as Roth left. The paper slowly began to wrinkle with the heat and moisture. He watched as Elizabeth's face began to distort and Peter Goldmann's face began to emerge in its place. Schiller stomped on the magazine.

LOS ANGELES
Dawn, Tuesday, 18 January 1966

A BUSINESS crisis soon put paid to Elizabeth's intrigue, following Conrad and Nico's deportation from Paraguay on what were described as 'visa irregularities'. A small but significant company in the Goldmann chain was in serious difficulties. The company produced garments for the Elizabeth Goldmann Collection, repeating the better-selling lines that Elizabeth had procured from the Paris and London fashion markets. A senior manager at the Los Angeles company had somehow managed to embezzle over $2.6 million and the company was about to go bust. Up to now only the company directors and management knew of the affair, but if news got out it could affect the share price of the entire United States business operation. It could also have a knock-on effect that would be harder to stop than a runaway train.

Elizabeth asked Hoover to intercede. She knew it was about time he got back into the swing of things again and this was a perfect opportunity for him to regain some of his old confidence. What was needed was damage-control of immense proportions.

Hoover flew straight to California, taking along Sam Conrad at Elizabeth's suggestion. They were met at the airport by the company president, Bill Andrews. The sixty-one-year-old Californian was close to a state of panic. Once the introductions were over, Hoover and Conrad transferred to the waiting limousine. Andrews climbed in beside them, winding up the security window and cutting them off from his chauffeur in front. As the car started to roll, Hoover opened the conversation.

'Give it to me straight, Bill, no bullshit,' Hoover said in a low voice. He'd met the man just twice before, when Elizabeth was taking over the company, and had been impressed with his frankness and direct approach. Now, he was depending on them.

'His name's van Riesen. He was the finance director. You met him last year.'

'Van Riesen? He's German, isn't he?'

'Yes, he came here in 1951. Married a local girl.' Bill Andrews could hardly think straight.

'If I recall correctly, the local girl was your sister, Bill.' Hoover looked across accusingly.

'Oh, God! This is devastating.' He wiped the sweat from his glistening brow.

'Did she know anything about this?'

'I swear, Oliver, she knew nothing, not a damn thing! This will kill her. She's been left, abandoned, with two kids and a king-size mortgage.'

'No collusion? No outside assistance or involvement?' continued Hoover.

'None so far. It looks to us as if the bastard operated on his own.'

'OK. Elizabeth's sent Mr Conrad here to ascertain a few things about all of this. I want you to give him your fullest co-operation, is that understood?' insisted Hoover.

'Totally,' snapped Andrews, clearly frightened.

'OK. I want all your senior management and accounts staff in the company offices within the next hour,' continued Hoover.

'Now?' Andrews glanced at his watch. It had just turned 5.20 a.m.

'Have you got a problem with that?' Hoover fired the man one of his boardroom glares. 'Because if you have . . .'

'No. I'll get them. I'll get them,' he stammered.

Ten minutes later, the limousine wheeled to the left on to the main highway towards town.

'Where the hell are we going?' quizzed Hoover.

'I . . . thought you'd want to go to the hotel first, to freshen up or maybe rest,' replied Andrews, realizing the inadequacy of his own words.

'I rest when this thing is in the bag, and that goes for you too, Bill,' retorted Hoover, flicking on the intercom panel to the driver. 'Driver? Take us to the factory, and step on it!' Then he flicked it off again, looking across at Conrad. The private investigator shook his head as the startled driver complied immediately, wheeling the stretched limousine around 180 degrees across the highway.

Whilst Hoover handled things at the factory, Sam Conrad headed for van Riesen's house, just five miles south down the highway. Mrs van Riesen had been pre-warned of his arrival. She showed the investigator into her home with some reservation.

'Have you found my Herman?' the woman asked nervously.

'Not yet, mam, but we will.' Conrad looked at the woman who was accompanying her. 'Who are you, mam?' he said bluntly, as always.

'I'm Bill Andrews's wife. Anne is my sister-in-law.' The woman was defensive. He looked back at Mrs van Riesen again.

'You reckon your husband's in Mexico, right?'

'He left a note.' She went over to the table, picked up the handwritten note and offered it to him. Conrad removed a handkerchief from his pocket, careful not to add his own prints to the document. 'Who else has touched this?'

'Just me and Jennifer here.' She looked across at Bill Andrews's wife.

'OK. I'd like to see your husband's study.' He wrapped the note inside the handkerchief for the moment after scanning it.

'It's back here, through the family room. I'll show you.' She led the way through the house.

10.06 a.m.

AT THE FACTORY Hoover had just completed his grilling of all the senior management. He looked across towards Bill Andrews, sitting hunched up in the corner of the office as he took the telephone call. The company president looked as if he was undergoing the first stages of a coronary thrombosis. 'Bill?'

'Hold on a second,' he said into the receiver before handing it over to Hoover. 'It's Conrad. He's found something. Something real bad.'

'Hello, Sam.' Hoover looked pensive as he listened.

'I'm in this jerk's study. He hasn't exactly tried to hide his exit route. I'm holding a booking reservation in my hand. A one-way to Mexico City.'

'When did the flight leave?' asked Hoover.

'Last night. He'd have landed and been long gone by now. My guess is he probably hitched another flight from Mexico City. He wouldn't hang around there.'

'Thanks, Sam. I have all the staff at the factory. I'll keep them here until you arrive.' He set the telephone aside as he eyed up Andrews. 'Bill, don't let family loyalties get in the way here.'

'I won't.' Andrews gritted his teeth. 'What about the cops? Do you want me to call them in?'

'No way,' retorted Hoover.

'I needn't tell you that this is a federal offence. The Feds can come in pretty useful sometimes.'

'Bill, you miss the point entirely. If news of this leaks out, it could damage us seriously. We can't take a body blow like that, especially in the wake of the Costello Construction Corporation.'

'I understand,' replied Andrews despondently.

'No you damned well don't! I want this kept quiet, deathly quiet,' rejoined Hoover adamantly. 'I'm remaining here at the factory. I intend to inspect every ledger and file that this man has worked on since he started here. I want your preliminary report and recommendation on my desk today.'

The dejected company president headed out of the office to organize matters. Oliver Hoover fought off tiredness as he studied the first reports from the accountants he'd had flown down from San Francisco. Herman van Riesen had been more than crafty; he

313

was starting to emerge as one of the most cunning and calculated embezzlers Hoover had ever come across. He had left such confusion in his wake that it was going to be one gigantic task to prove a thing against him. There was a knock on the door and Sam Conrad walked in alone.

'Did you see Andrews on your way in?' Hoover opened the conversation.

'He's gone to his office. If you ask me, the man ain't well, Mr Hoover. It ain't just tiredness. There's something else.'

'Perhaps it's guilt,' replied Hoover, sitting back in his chair. 'Give it to me from the top, Sam, the very worst.'

'Well, he didn't go to Mexico like Andrews said and I told you earlier.' Conrad sat down facing him. 'He laid out a fake trail. I had it checked out. This guy headed for Rio, bought a seat on the plane to Mexico all right, but he never boarded. But when you check the passenger list at LA, at first inspection it looks like he was on the plane. Now that's crafty.'

'You've done well,' remarked Hoover. 'And now?'

'Now we go after him. It shouldn't be that hard. But it's the money that gets me,' continued Conrad.

'What do you know about the money?' Hoover sat forward instantly.

'He burned his trash before leaving, but he didn't do a thorough job. That sorta surprised me. Struck me as a meticulous son of a bitch.' Conrad was enjoying his moment. He popped another piece of gum into his mouth and began to chew.

'Get to the point and I'll throw in a pack of chewing gum with your ten per cent,' urged Hoover.

The detective pulled out a clear plastic bag from his coat pocket. It contained the charred remains of a bank document – part of a ledger, it seemed. 'Got that in the bottom of a fire at the vegetable patch in van Riesen's garden. Musta thought he'd burnt it all, then covered it over with grass cuttings.'

'It's in German.' Hoover's eyes widened.

'I found this too.' Conrad produced another bag, containing part of a bank book cover. The words were embossed and, although badly disfigured by the fire, were still legible: COMMERCIAL BANK OF SWITZERLAND.

'This, Mr Conrad, is my department, I think. I shall let you attend to Rio alone.'

'On my way. I have a connection leaving LA in just over two hours,' replied Conrad. They shook hands. 'I just hope that my reception in Rio's better than the one I had in Paraguay.' He chuckled.

'Paraguay?' Hoover was puzzled.

It was only then that Conrad realized the man had no idea about his wife's hunt for Schiller. 'It's a long story,' he said, skipping over the subject.

'When Elizabeth said that you were the best, she was clearly right.' Hoover smiled.

'You haven't said what you want me to do with this guy when I get him,' commented Conrad.

'Get him first,' insisted Hoover, 'quickly and quietly.'

Once Conrad left, Hoover lifted the telephone and spoke to the switchboard operator. 'This is Mr Hoover. Get me patched through to my wife in Florida. You should have the number on your classified management index.'

An hour later Oliver Hoover walked into Bill Andrews's office. The company president was slumped across his desk, exhausted.

'Oliver . . . I didn't hear you come in.' Andrews went to stand up.

'Stay where you are, Bill. I only came in to say goodbye,' replied Hoover, now quite overwhelmed with tiredness himself. Then he thought of the company's financial director, sunning himself on the Praia de Copacabana and the adrenalin of anger started to flow again.

'I'll be out of here today,' replied Andrews solemnly.

'Get out now, Bill, and get some rest. You'll be needing it.'

'Needing it?' Bill Andrews's face became contorted.

'You don't think you're escaping that easily from the stricken ship, do you?' Hoover leaned across the desk. 'You're remaining here at the helm until this mess is cleared up. Then we decide what we're doing, not before.'

'Thank you,' groaned Andrews. 'You don't know what this means to me, to keep my head up like this and not be chucked out on my butt.'

'Like you deserve to be, you mean?' commented Hoover. Bill Andrews nodded his head. 'Just get back in here by late afternoon. In the meantime, I've put the accountants into van Riesen's office and department. They'll be reporting direct to you. I'm leaving for New York straight away. I want you to ring me tonight and give me an update on what they've discovered.'

315

'OK,' replied Andrews. 'And thanks.'

'By the time this thing is all over, old buddy, you mightn't be in the mood to thank anyone.' Hoover lifted the brass letter-opener from the desk and set it down, point facing him. Then he strode out, leaving the office door open. Bill Andrews stared down at the letter-opener. He knew exactly what the old naval custom meant: a finding of guilt had been passed on him.

NEW YORK
Tuesday, 18 January 1966

THE PRIVATE jet got into the airport five hours later. It had been raining steadily all day and the air was damp with the expectancy of another downpour. Oliver Hoover transferred to his waiting car in silence. Normally he enjoyed chatting to the company's New York chauffeur about the latest ball game, but not on this occasion. He eased back in the plush rear seat of the Lincoln and closed his eyes. He had planned on a hot shower and a bite to eat once he reached the hotel but Elizabeth was already waiting for him. She'd arrived just an hour earlier. She met him in the hallway of the hotel's penthouse suite.

'Oliver!' She hugged him warmly, kissing him on the lips. 'You look terrible. Come into the lounge and get warmed.'

'I'd prefer to have a shower first.'

'Business first!' she insisted, guiding him across to one of the matching sofas. He flopped into it and she sat down next to him. He relayed the events at the factory and outlined the action taken. Then he showed her what Conrad had found. It became apparent that Elizabeth was just as tired as he was, for she had been busy herself, checking with various contacts in the financial institutions and houses in New York and Washington, trying to unravel some of the mess created by van Riesen.

'What do you know about this van Riesen anyway?' she asked.

'He's Bill Andrews's brother-in-law.'

'How dreadful for poor Bill.' She sipped her wine slowly.

'Dreadful! The blasted fool promoted his in-law to a position of infinite power and control with the company and let him off the leash. He deserves to answer for this thing personally.'

'And will he?' asked Elizabeth.

'That depends upon what Sam Conrad comes up with. He's sure he's traced this guy to Rio de Janeiro.'

'How nice for him. Spending the company's money, I presume?'

'No, van Riesen transferred it all through a Swiss bank in Zurich.' He took another gulp of his wine as he showed her the scrap of letterheading that Conrad had located. 'It was all done in advance, last week. He didn't take anything with him as far as I know. He didn't need to.'

'He must have had accomplices,' she said with some certainty. 'So what happens now?'

'We have our people going through the accounts department at the company offices. With any luck we can get this mess sorted out quietly and without any fuss. If Conrad locates this asshole, we can force him to return the money hopefully.'

'Hopefully.' She poured him some more wine. 'Now I would like you to take me to bed, Mr Hoover. You still have some work to do before you can sleep.' She kissed him on the cheek.

'Yes, mam,' he quipped.

Wednesday, 19 January 1966

ELIZABETH was awakened by being shaken on the arm. She stirred and looked up to find her husband staring at her. Elizabeth could sense something ominous as soon as she focused on his face. 'Good morning, darling, sleep well?' she asked.

'I've bad news, Elizabeth,' he said sternly.

'How bad is bad?' She sat up, covering her breasts with the silk sheet. 'Was it a phone call from Bill Andrews?'

'Nope.' He exhaled deeply. 'It was the other one from Rio.'

'Conrad can't locate him?'

'Conrad's dead,' Hoover said coldly.

'What!' she cried in anguish as she drew her dressing gown around her shoulders and got out of bed. 'What happened? He only went there yesterday, didn't he?'

'He managed to fall out of his hotel window or balcony or something. The caller was very abrupt. He rang Bill Andrews at the LA plant.'

'But what else did the police say? They must know something?' she replied angrily.

Hoover stared up at her. 'You don't understand, Elizabeth. It wasn't the police who telephoned. It was Conrad's killer!'

Elizabeth closed her eyes for a moment, trying to let the words sink in. 'Was it this van Riesen character?'

'Nope, Bill says he didn't know the man, but he sounded German too.'

'My God. That poor man, he did so much for us!' She blinked back the tears. 'So this accomplice, I suppose he told Bill to stay away and stop any further investigation.'

'No.' Hoover's eyes were fixed on the far wall. Elizabeth looked at him. She could see the anguish and concern on his face. 'The caller said that the Californian company was just the start.'

'The start of what?' She was angry now.

'You tell me.' Hoover sighed. 'You tell me.' He buried his face in his hands and tried to blot out the image of Sam Conrad and how he must have looked after being thrown from the twelfth floor of his hotel.

BUENOS AIRES
Thursday, 3 February 1966

THE WHITE Mercedes-Benz limousine drove steadily through the noonday traffic in the outskirts of Rio de Janeiro. It was heading for Copacabana, on the southern side of the city, where it was to be met on the jetty of the private yacht club. The traffic slowed, almost to a halt. Schiller sat uncomfortably in the darkened rear interior of the stretched limousine. He glanced from the silver-plated clock mounted just above the cocktail cabinet panel and back to the gold and diamond Rolex watch on his wrist.

In fifteen minutes the car travelled just over two hundred yards, the traffic moving in fits and starts. Finally all three lanes sat motionless in the one-way street, with the heat rising from the car bonnets and exhaust fumes of the several old diesel lorries just in front clouding the stifling atmosphere. Schiller turned up the air-conditioning control in the rear of the car, but it was already running close to maximum. He looked again at his watch and then tapped the smoked-glass partition with his gold-topped walking stick. The window whirred down automatically.

'Mark! What the hell is going on in front?' He spoke in clipped English.

The driver rolled down his window and peered out to the side, looking past the dirty rear wing of the car in front. 'There appears to be some sort of accident at the junction ahead, sir.'

'Can't you get around it?' he snarled.

The driver stared across at the busy pavement, cluttered with traders' brightly coloured stalls. It was market day and the traffic round Rio was double its normal level. 'No, sir.'

Schiller smacked the release button on the panel in front with the base of his stick and the partition window whirred up again. The driver gulped against the dryness in his mouth. For a few moments he had had the pleasure of full air-conditioning blowing at him from the rear compartment; now he was stifling again in the heat. The traffic began to move and he breathed a sigh of relief. He could smell food cooking at the pavement-side restaurant. People were sitting under shady trees, gorging themselves on chilli and barbecued beef. A waiter was carrying out a large tray of cold beers. The driver fought off the urge to grab a glass as he passed by.

They were getting close to the junction now and by peering out he could see what was holding them up. A fruit lorry had collided with a van and had spilled most of its load. A small army of people were helping to lift up the melons, oranges and grapefruit lying across the road, whilst the two drivers and a local policeman stood arguing beside the steaming and mangled front section of the lorry, now firmly wrapped around the van's tail section. From what he could see, most of the women and children helping to lift the fruit were helping themselves, then disappearing back into the crowds with baskets filled to the brim. The Mercedes halted again, as another policeman tried to direct the traffic across the junction from the left. The cane smacked against the glass partition once more. Nervously, the chauffeur lowered the panel by an automatic switch.

'We are late! Tell that policeman over there to move this traffic out of our way!'

'Sir, it would be best if . . .'

'Do it! *Schnell! Schnell!*' Schiller snapped up the partition again and stared out of the side window once more. He hated the sticky heat, his old injuries aggravating his temper. The leather patch he wore permanently over his left eye was a constant source of irritation. He still suffered pain in the empty socket and the black patch he wore always made the skin around it sweat. But he had learned to live with the loss of his left forearm and now wore a plastic and metal replacement, permanently covered by a black leather glove. He stretched out his left leg. The knee now cracked every time he bent it and, although the pain had long ago stopped, numbness persisted, giving him a terribly exaggerated gait and necessitating a walking stick.

Schiller looked across at the corner newsagent's. The paper stand outside was filled with the various South American dailies and periodicals; the magazine stand stood next to it. It was all the usual rubbish that sold – the glossy French and American magazines. He glanced at the last row. It was that woman's face again! This time there was something other than just her bright, defiant eyes glittering out from the photograph – something he'd only dreamed about seeing again. He threw open the car door and climbed out as fast as his body would allow. The chauffeur was already walking back after speaking to the policeman directing the traffic.

'Sir!' he called out.

Schiller ignored him as he hobbled over to the news-stand, snatching one of the magazines. He turned back, quickly flipping through the pages with his fingers. An irate shop assistant raced out on to the pavement, shouting for him to halt, but Schiller was too engrossed in what he had found to listen to the rambling woman. She ran up to his right elbow, pulling at him and shouting.

'Money! Pay money!'

He shoved her away immediately and glared down at her. The little woman stopped in her tracks. The look on Schiller's face horrified her. The chauffeur read the situation instantly and quickly thrust a fifty-dollar bill into her grubby hand. The woman hesitated and then looked at the money, nodding her approval humbly as the chauffeur followed his master back to the Mercedes, which had now attracted five dirty street urchins to peer inside the open rear door. He shooed them off just before Schiller hit one a smack across the head with his stick. The SS general glared at his chauffeur and bodyguard. 'Get me to the marina!'

'Jawohl, mein Herr.' He held the bullet-proof door open while his master climbed inside. Schiller was instantly engrossed again in the magazine. He stared down at the photograph of Elizabeth. She had deliberately got herself on to the front cover of another magazine, and all for his benefit, for around her neck she wore 'The Three Brothers'! The red balas rubies glistened in the photographer's studio light. He read steadily for the remainder of the ten-minute journey. The bitch was issuing a personal challenge to him!

The yachting marina, covering over ten acres of shoreline, was a very fashionable area, privately owned by the 'Nemesis' group. The floating jetties served as mooring for three hundred yachts and small craft, whilst the inner, more private quayside was for VIPs. The Mercedes raced along the causeway, having been waved through the outer security cordon, and finally stopped at the end of the pier. The two-hundred-and-fifty-foot-long private yacht was berthed at the very end. The *Lady Christina* had three decks. The lower one was for the crew's accommodation, stores, kitchens, engine rooms and the like. The main deck consisted of luxury accommodation for twenty people: eight private double suites and a further four single suites. The upper deck was made up of the private saloon, stateroom, games room, a small swimming pool, a dining room and the smoking room. Without waiting for his aide to open the door, Schiller alighted from the car with the air of a much younger man. Moving past the two guards standing at the bottom of the wooden gangway, he hobbled up on to the main deck to meet Roth.

'Herr Renan!' Roth clicked his heels. 'It is good to see you again.' He glanced down at the crumpled magazine tucked under Schiller's arm.

'Where is he, Roth?'

'In the billiards room, *mein Herr*.'

'Show me! I keep getting lost on this blasted vessel!'

Roth went ahead of Schiller, showing him to the main staircase – a grand, wide affair, carpeted in deep, red pile. The two men walked up on to the upper deck, where two young women were at the pool, one swimming about whilst the other dangled her long legs over the side. Her bikini hardly covered the essential parts; she was dark, swarthy and, whilst well developed, looked no more than sixteen. The girl in swimming was a blonde. She smiled up at Schiller as they walked past and said something in Spanish. Schiller ignored the remark and limped on towards the billiards room.

'How long have they been on board?' he asked Roth.

'Since Venezuela, sir.'

'His doing, I presume?' he said angrily.

'*Jawohl, mein Herr*.'

Schiller stopped just outside the white-painted louvred doors at the entrance to the games room. 'Dangerous. I don't like it.'

'I tried telling him, but you know what he's like, *mein Herr*.'

Schiller glared at the blond man. 'Get rid of them! Get them off this ship immediately.'

'But, sir—'

'No argument, Roth, just do it. And I don't care how you do it – make it clean and simple, no bodies, nothing. Understand?' Roth looked around. The dark-haired girl waved casually over to him. 'What are you waiting for, Roth? Don't tell me you've been fucking them too?'

Roth looked back, a mixture of anger and embarrassment filling his mind. 'As you order, *mein Herr*.' He clicked his heels again and went off towards the pool, calling out to both young girls.

Schiller opened the double doors. Bormann was stretched out across the full-size blue-baize table, about to take a shot into the corner pocket. Karl Strassmann was standing to one side, leaning on his billiard cue. He nodded to Schiller. He hadn't seen much of his old master since his arrival in South America a couple of days before.

'Schiller! My dear chap!' Bormann turned his head towards Schiller, smiling. 'I never realized you were aboard. Come in and join us.' Bormann placed the shot, easily getting the ball into the pocket. 'Ha! I wish every hole was entered that easily!'

Strassmann grinned. Schiller slammed the doors shut, gaining both men's attention instantly.

'Karl, get out,' ordered Schiller.

Bormann stood back from the table, setting his cue in one of the empty wall brackets. 'Really, Schiller, there is no need for him to leave. He is one of us. You ought to have seen the way he handled the Swiss deal – magnificent!'

'*Schnell!*' shouted Schiller, smacking the edge of the table with his stick. Strassmann knew better than to stay. He threw his cue down on to the table, scattering the remaining billiard balls. It was his only defiant gesture. He was no match for Schiller. He walked past him, within inches of his face, keeping his head partly bowed as he left, slamming the door closed once he reached the safety of the other side. He cursed quietly under his breath as he walked past the pool. The girls had gone already; both had followed Roth below deck.

'Look, old chap, you must change your attitude towards our younger friend there. That is an order.'

'Shut up!' insisted Schiller.

'How dare you!'

'Don't you know that half the world and their pet dogs are out there searching for you? Yet here you are, gallivanting about on this floating gin palace, picking up youngsters at every port of call and attracting attention to yourself.'

'You are in no position to speak to me like that, Schiller! Just remember your place!'

322

Schiller grinned and threw the magazine down on to the table just in front of the ex-Reichsleiter.

'What's this? Taken to reading glossy magazines?'

'Look at the front cover!'

Bormann picked it up. The woman's face meant nothing to him. 'Attractive, nice jewels. I wouldn't shove her out of bed! But I don't know her. Should I?'

'I met her when I landed in Ireland with the child. She was the wife of one of our Abwehr agents, a man called O'Casey. Remember?'

'Ah, yes. Now I recall.' Bormann nodded. 'So what?'

'Look at the jewels. Don't you recognize them? They belonged to me!' hissed Schiller. 'She's now one of the wealthiest women in the United States, with business interests in almost every Western European country. Read the article. You might see why.'

Bormann leafed through the magazine carefully, but he had still not mastered reading in English very well. He looked at the photographs. There was one of a young man carrying what seemed to be a pile of schoolbooks. He was dressed casually, not much taller than five feet eight, standing beside an old Ferrari sports car. The date at the bottom of the photograph said April 1963.

'Bormann, ask yourself how a woman of no means in 1945 becomes so wealthy. The article mentions some scandal relating to her involvement with the Mafia, but she needed capital of her own and my guess is that she used the jewels. This Jewess has grown fat on my property!' Schiller stepped forward. 'Bormann, the month of June is not very far off and our sacred bond was given to the Führer. The Reich will rise from the ashes, more powerful this time, stronger, more vengeful than ever before! Have you forgotten the magnitude of our mission?' Schiller trembled at the very thought. 'June 6th, this year, 1966, with all the sacred signs of the millennium!'

Bormann began to laugh, much to Schiller's disgust.

'What is so funny?' he growled.

'It's just the thought of a woman getting one over on you, Schiller, dear boy. It really is quite rare, don't you think?'

'She's made her blasted fortune from our money! That which belongs to the future of the Reich!'

But Bormann wasn't listening. He had leafed back again to the previous page, with the young man's photograph. 'Schiller, look at this photograph of her son. What age do you think he is?' Bormann passed back the magazine and set it on the table next to him.

'How the hell should I know! What difference does it make?'

'Eighteen, nineteen perhaps?' mused Bormann. There was a tremor in his voice. 'This photograph was taken just three years ago. Look at the boy's face. Look at it! It could be a snapshot of him as he was in his younger days. I know, Schiller. I was at his side day and night from the beginning. I knew his every mannerism, his every action. At a glance I could sense what he wanted. He didn't need to say.'

'What on earth are you rambling on about?' demanded Schiller.

'Look at the photograph, will you. I may not be able to read English very well, but I can read a photograph. Look at his eyes, his stance, his build. He is almost his father's double!' He was shaking now. 'Don't you understand, Schiller?' He jabbed the magazine with a chubby finger. 'He is the Führer's son! He must have been saved! The bitch must have taken him and raised him as her own.' Bormann laughed excitedly.

Schiller looked again at the photograph, confusion turning into a glow of excitement, burning in his heart as he recalled those first moments when he had seen the child . . .

BERLIN
8 p.m., Wednesday, 25th April 1945

BERLIN *was a doomed city. It was only a matter of time before its final capitulation. Stalin had wasted no time in forcing his troops onward towards the main prize of the war. On 1 April 1945 all the senior commanders of the Soviet forces had been summoned to Stalin's office. Convinced of treachery by the other Allies, Stalin was in no mood for waiting at any agreed demarcation line. Berlin had to be taken before some deal was done with the enemy. Stalin asked only one question of his commanders: who was going to get to Berlin first? From then on, the war had become a race between each of the Soviet army commanders, Zhukov commanding the 1st Byelorussian Front and Koniev commanding the 1st Ukrainian Front.*

Marshal Zhukov had the distinct advantage of having already secured a bridgehead over the River Oder and, after getting the order from Stalin, he did not hesitate. His mechanized forces surged across the last natural line of defence in his break-neck race for Berlin. Marshal Koniev's army group was to the south of Zhukov's, effectively splitting the German forces as he swung elements of his 1st Ukrainian army north-west.

The 1st Ukrainian Front had by far the hardest task. Both distance and the enemy's gut determination were against them reaching Berlin first. In the face of opposition, Koniev's armoured and mechanized divisions burst through Juterbog, whilst other elements pushed west towards the River Elbe. Koniev's tanks swept through Potsdam and on to the southern outskirts of the main German defence line around Berlin itself, having ignored several major pockets of resistance in favour of reaching the main objective first. But it was not enough.

After many setbacks and in the face of a multitude of hardships endured by both Soviet commanders, Stalin declared Zhukov the winner of the race. The Red Army had beaten the Americans and British to Berlin. Now the city was completely surrounded by over half a million Soviet troops. The time had almost come.

Schiller had safely arrived in the city that morning with the two women and the baby. He never even got a chance to say goodbye to Eva Hitler before she was whisked away from Templehof airfield by two of the Führer's adjutants. Since then he had spent his time down in the cellars of Prinz-Albrecht-Strasse, headquarters of Reich Central Security, destroying all traces of 'Operation Gold' and 'Operation Herron'. It had also given him the opportunity he needed to clear out his own personal safe of any specific incriminating evidence. More importantly than anything else, now that his departure from the beleaguered city was imminent, he was finally able to retrieve the old box containing 'The Three Brothers'. No matter what else happened, the jewels were his ticket to freedom.

The staff car sped up the street and into Voss Strasse. Rudolph Schiller stared out at what remained of the new Reich Chancellery building. Aerial bombing and constant Russian artillery barrages had taken their toll, the building was little more than a shell. The car slowed now as it circumnavigated piles of rubble which had been swept to either side of the wide street, giving it the semblance of a narrow snake-like track, merely three metres wide in places. All around them fires were still burning amidst the heaps of rubble, some billowing thick black smoke across their path.

Was this what they had striven for all these long and bitter years,

325

their dreams finally done to death in the ruins of Berlin? They deserved more; he deserved more. These last fifteen years he had faithfully served and sacrificed himself for the Fatherland, and for what? His beloved Führer had been misguidedly directed into questionable treaties and alliances. The High Command had consistently miscalculated the enemy. Even the Jewish annihilation had been suspended, and instead the camps and Einsatzgruppen were now busily involved in acts of concealment. Schiller sneered at the very idea of it. How did these idiots think they could hide the disappearance of over six million? He stared around at the collapsed buildings and burnt-out shells, peering through windowless openings into the smoke-filled sky beyond, but he did not feel despondent. Out of these ashes there would rise a phoenix that the world would soon recognize and fear. Germany's enemies would pay dearly for this victory.

Schiller stared ahead as the car slowed almost to a halt. Out of the smoke emerged a disheartened-looking group of Volkssturmmänner, the Home Guard, shuffling towards the vehicle. The motley group consisted of old men and young boys in civilian clothes, each one wearing his distinctive red armband bearing the inscription 'Deutsche Volkssturm Wehrmacht'. Most of them were carrying ancient Austrian Mannlicher rifles, while a lucky few had managed to get hold of more up-to-date weaponry. Schiller noticed that the group's straggler was a boy, only twelve or thirteen years old. He was carrying a Panzerfaust-60 anti-tank projectile over his shoulder with obvious difficulty.

'Is this what we have been reduced to?' he asked the SS driver, himself a Berliner, attached to Colonel Kempka's motor pool at Hitler's headquarters.

'It gets worse, *mein Herr*, believe me,' sighed the driver.

As with most of his peers, lethargy had set in. Just days before he would not have dared answer a superior officer in such glib fashion, but he no longer cared about protocol.

Schiller rubbed his tired eyes and refocused on the road ahead. They were approaching Wilhelmstrasse. Less than ten metres away he could make out the semblance of a barricade, constructed out of burnt-out vehicles and broken paving stones. A Tiger tank sat on each side of the wide street, both surrounded by sandbags, topped with rows of barbed wire. The turret of the nearer Tiger whined into motion as the barrel of the 88mm gun trained on the staff car. Schiller watched the unsettled driver fidget nervously in his seat before they were approached by an officer dressed in the tight-fitting black battledress uniform of the SS tank battalion.

'Sit still,' commanded Schiller.

'I would respectfully remind the SS Gruppenführer that only yesterday someone from our pool was killed by a nervous tank crewman . . . in circumstances not dissimilar to this . . . his vehicle was blown to pieces,' stuttered the driver.

Schiller climbed out of the vehicle with a briefcase in his hand.

'*Heil*, Hitler.' The SS captain saluted smartly upon seeing his uniform and rank. Schiller returned the salute, silently handing across his papers. The officer inspected them quickly.

'Thank you, Herr Gruppenführer.' He returned the identity papers. 'I presume you are heading for the bunker?'

'*Ja*,' replied Schiller.

'From here on no vehicles are permitted. You will have to walk, *mein Herr*. All side roads have been sealed, on the Führer's express orders.'

'Hauptsturmführer, I do not intend to take the scenic route, nor do I want a tourist guide, but before a further artillery barrage commences I would like to find the blasted entrance!'

'If you follow me, *mein Herr*,' the officer humbly replied.

Schiller followed the man across the rubble-strewn grounds of the chancellery. It took five minutes to negotiate their way to the emergency entrance to the underground bunker complex, located in the chancellery kitchens. In the distance they could hear the thunder of the Russian artillery. The Red Army was making way for its final offensive on the Reichstag. Schiller looked over his shoulder. The flashes of gunfire were growing brighter, illuminating the rain-heavy clouds.

From the chancellery kitchens, they passed down into the main bunker complex, situated some twenty feet below ground level. The tank officer excused himself, returning back above ground, leaving Schiller in the Führer's adjutant's office. The large underground office was bustling with men and women, some dressed in uniform and others in civilian clothes. They were all crating piles of papers and boxes of files into the centre of the room, ready for removal to the busy incinerators. Hitler's headquarters were being stripped of the very last vestige of evidence that could link the Nazis with their many crimes against humanity.

'Papers, please.' The colonel from Hitler's bodyguard regiment, the Leibstandarte SS Adolf Hitler, rose from his desk beside the main entrance to the deeper Führerbunker complex.

'I am in a hurry,' snapped Schiller.

The young colonel examined the photograph on Schiller's papers, returning them instantly, clearly nervous of provoking any further reaction. 'Everything is in order, Herr Gruppenführer. You may proceed.' He motioned for one of the SS guards standing next to the doorway to approach. 'Show SS Gruppenführer Schiller down to the lower bunker.'

The orderly led the way down a flight of concrete steps into the lower reaches. The maze of corridors and staircases wound down towards the inner sanctum, known to Hitler's staff as the Führerbunker. It was designed to withstand the very worst bombardment any enemy could throw at it, but it had never been envisaged as the Führer's headquarters and was lacking in both space and comfort. Hitler's staff were squeezed together into a tiny area deep below the chancellery gardens, accessible only by a long underground corridor from the adjutant's quarters in part of the old Reich Chancellery.

They eventually came to a steel security door at the end of a long corridor. Schiller examined the doorway: two metres wide by three metres high, it was capable of being hermetically sealed against gas attack. On all sides the door was fitted with steel clamps, now in the open position but capable of closure in seconds. Two SS guards covered the entrance, each man shouldering a Schmeisser submachine-gun. The orderly spoke to the nearest of the guards, who stared at Schiller curiously before nodding to his partner. The soldier slowly pulled back the massive door. Schiller's eyes narrowed – the steel plate was over 200mm thick.

The corridor continued beyond, its brown plaster walls bathed in a dull yellowish light emanating from high wall-mounted lamps, fed by conduit running down from the arched ceiling. As the door clunked shut behind them, the first thing that struck Schiller was the artificial atmosphere.

'The air seems stale.' Schiller found the damp atmosphere almost overpowering.

'One gets used to it, *mein Herr*. Especially, if you stay down here for a while.' The orderly gestured for Schiller to follow him. 'The air ducts don't work very well – an engineering problem, so I'm told. The further down you go, the worse it becomes.'

'The further down! Just how deep are we?' asked Schiller, keeping pace with the man.

'Already we are some eight metres beneath the grounds of the old Reich Chancellery building,' replied the orderly. 'But if you think this is deep, *mein Herr*, the Führer's quarters are over seventeen metres beneath ground level.'

Schiller covered his nose against a noxious smell as they passed a corridor to their left. The orderly noticed the SS general's discomfort. 'A pipe blockage in the main sewer, *mein Herr*. It happens sometimes.'

Schiller nodded as they came finally to another doorway, leading to a concrete staircase. Unhappy to be descending further into this hellhole, he was nevertheless somewhat relieved to have escaped the stench above. Clearly the orderly was accustomed to such nauseous smells. Schiller wondered if he would be down here long enough to build up the same immunity. Once past another set of double solid-steel doors, they entered a maze of narrow corridors, the vaulted ceiling just inches above Schiller's head. Then they came to another staircase, leading to the lower reaches of Hitler's bomb-proof quarters.

Finally he was shown into a long, narrow conference room just outside Hitler's office suite. The orderly approached the duty officer – a small, weary-looking colonel, bearing the yellow lapel insignia of a cavalry regiment. Schiller looked round the room. It was simple enough – whitewashed concrete walls, with a long oak table at the centre of the narrow room. The brown carpet was wrinkled and dirty, clearly damp in patches. One door stood out from the rest, padded in brown leather and embossed with a silver German eagle. Schiller's eyes narrowed. He was looking at the entrance to the Führer's office suite.

'SS Gruppenführer Schiller?' The colonel limped over to him. 'I am Oberst Horstmann, adjutant to the Führer.'

Schiller handed over his orders.

'Reichsleiter Bormann is waiting for you,' replied the colonel, just as the burly shape of Hitler's private secretary emerged from a doorway at the far end of the room.

'Schiller! My dear chap,' Bormann greeted him.

'*Heil*, Hitler.' He saluted.

'*Heil*, Hitler,' responded Bormann, his salute more a dismissive wave than anything else. He strode towards him. 'My dear chap, we were beginning to get a little concerned about you.' They shook hands, Bormann staring up at the tall, blond SS general. 'Come and tell me everything.' He guided Schiller towards a side office, turning to Horstmann as he opened the door. 'The moment the chief is free, tell him SS Gruppenführer Schiller is here.' Bormann had referred to Hitler using the slang word common amongst the headquarters staff.

'*Jawohl, mein Herr*,' snapped Horstmann.

Closing the door behind him, Bormann continued. 'The chief is busy for the moment. Horstmann will let us know when he's available. It will give us a chance to talk.' He grinned, showing two rows of yellowed teeth. 'Be seated, Schiller. Make yourself comfortable.'

Bormann went over to a small wall safe and began fiddling with the tumbler lock. Opening the safe, he removed a bottle of brandy and two small glasses, setting them on the table before the SS general. 'I'm sure you could do with some refreshment after your hazardous journey.'

'That would be very welcome,' replied Schiller, taking a seat beside a metal-topped mapping table. As Bormann poured, Schiller removed his cap. He couldn't avoid staring at the large wall map of Europe directly in front of him. It had been overdrawn, obliterated almost completely in places, with red and black pen markings. Partly overlapping it was a Berlin street map, showing the city defence system and communication lines. Schiller was wondering how much of the city was still in German hands when Bormann's voice broke his concentration.

'Tell me about your trip.' Bormann handed him a brandy.

'We got here, but only just.' Schiller downed the brandy in one gulp. 'The aircraft was badly shot up as we left Berchtesgaden.'

'They levelled the Berghof,' Bormann replied solemnly.

'So I heard.' Schiller sighed. 'And what of Berlin? On our way into Tempelhof it looked as if the city was completely surrounded.'

'It is, dear fellow. By the way, my heartiest congratulations at getting the woman and child safely here.'

'Where are they?' asked Schiller.

'In the Führer's quarters on the other side of the conference room. I had them quietly brought down from the chancellery gardens. The Führer wanted no fuss or excitement.' Bormann sat down on the edge of the table next to him. 'Now, to business. How are things in Kiel?'

'Everything is ready as planned. Two U-boats are waiting in a restricted section of the U-boat pens. When do we leave?' asked Schiller, impatient to be away.

'Soon,' Bormann grinned again, 'but first I have to arrange another wedding for the chief!'

Schiller stared back contemptuously at the Reich Leader. This did not go unnoticed. He detested the sight of Hitler's favourite mandarin: the man had been a manipulator from the first moment he had set eyes on him in 1933. Now, over the last few months of the war, Bormann appeared to have gained total control over the dying embers of the Third Reich.

They had just finished coffee when the telephone tinkled faintly. Bormann snatched up the receiver and, after listening briefly, replaced it without reply. 'He will see us now.'

Schiller stood, removing his leather overcoat and straightening his crumpled uniform as best he could. Lifting his briefcase, he followed Bormann out into the main conference room towards the Führer's leather-panelled door. He drew Bormann aside just before they entered. 'Tell me honestly before we go in, just how is he?'

'Moody would be an understatement,' Bormann whispered. 'I wouldn't do anything to upset him, if you know what I mean.'

Schiller did not need any reminder. He had already witnessed Hitler's wrath following the July bomb plot the previous year. Bormann knocked on the door, pausing before entering, just ahead of the SS general.

'*Mein* Führer,' Bormann spoke up, 'SS Gruppenführer Schiller is here, as directed.'

Schiller's mouth dropped open. The man he had come to worship no longer existed. A stooped body slowly arose from behind the oak desk. The black patches around Hitler's eyes were accentuated by the terrible pallor of his skin. His face and stomach were bloated from constant overuse of the drugs administered by his personal physicians. Hitler's hands trembled as he stood unsteadily behind the desk. Almost instinctively he thrust both hands into the deep pockets of his grey tunic, seemingly to avoid the further attention of his visitors. Schiller came to attention and saluted smartly.

'*Mein* Führer, it is good to see you so . . . well.' Bormann flashed a glare across towards Schiller. Adolf Hitler's features changed, almost imperceptibly. He forced his face into a faint smile.

'SS Gruppenführer Schiller, thank God you made it through the Russian lines, to bring me the woman I love and the child I had never seen. This is indeed a debt I can never repay.'

'It was a privilege, *mein* Führer,' insisted Schiller.

'Reichsleiter Bormann informs me that everything is in readiness for the commencement of Operation Herron.'

'*Jawohl, mein* Führer.'

Hitler gestured for both men to be seated. They sat facing him on a narrow sofa.

'What time do I have?' Hitler asked bluntly.

'In my opinion, we must leave Berlin at the earliest possible moment. Yet if it is too soon, the secrecy of the entire plan could well be jeopardized,' Schiller said without reservation.

Hitler nodded his agreement.

'I think the optimum moment for action will be around the 30th,' Bormann interjected, much to Schiller's displeasure. 'I have been assured that the city defence force can hold out until the beginning of May. After that nothing can be guaranteed.'

Hitler shook his head. 'It is over, finished.' Removing his hands from his grey tunic pockets, he banged the desk with both fists. 'The people have failed me!' he cried.

'But Germany is resilient!' Bormann interrupted with a raised voice. 'We can rebuild!'

Hitler shook his head. 'Perhaps Reichsminister Goebbels is correct. I should end it all here, where it began.' He grasped his left arm to stop it shaking.

'We need a figurehead, *mein* Führer,' retorted Bormann.

Hitler waved him to be silent. 'Leave me now,' he mumbled.

Schiller and Bormann both stood as Hitler turned his back on them and shuffled off into the adjoining room.

Once outside the leather-padded door and out of earshot of the SS bodyguards, Schiller turned on Bormann.

'Just how long has he been like this?' he demanded.

Bormann shook his head. 'Since early February.'

'What if he decides to stay?'

'I will take care of everything,' replied Bormann.

10 p.m., Saturday, 28 April 1945

SCHILLER had mainly kept to his quarters since his arrival at the bunker, apart from the time he had had to spend in the communications room or in consultation with Bormann and Hitler. His cramped bedroom was situated close to the SS guards' quarters, well out of the way of the round-the-clock activity down in the Führerbunker. He was frustrated by the waiting. Whilst the timing of the operation was all important, everything had been in place for days now. All he needed was the go-ahead from Bormann and they could all be out of this subterranean hell within twenty-four hours.

He lay on the camp bed, stripped down to his shirt and trousers, the constant droning of the overhead extractor eating away at his tolerance as he stared up at the yellowed, flaking ceiling. He kept mulling over their situation; as each day passed their chances of successfully escaping from Berlin diminished markedly. The knock at the door came as a welcome relief to him. Schiller sat up, running both hands through his short-cropped hair before unlocking the door. He had half expected a messenger from Bormann, but instead he found himself looking into the attractive, but pitiful face of Eva Hitler.

'Frau Hitler,' he said with some astonishment.

'May I come in?' she asked cautiously.

'But of course,' Schiller opened the door more fully, allowing the woman to pass inside. The scent of her French perfume was a pleasant distraction from the dank conditions of his quarters. He hadn't seen the woman since she had been whisked away from Templehof airfield. She was wearing a blue silk dress, with a lace shawl covering her bare arms. The female he had met at the Berghof had since vanished. Before him stood a tired, pasty-faced woman with drawn features. She had been completely overshadowed by an aura of tiredness. Clearly, Eva Hitler had not been sleeping.

'I must apologize for having disturbed you at such a late hour,' she continued. 'May I sit down, Herr Gruppenführer?'

'Of course.' He quickly pulled over a chair for her.

'Thank you.' She eased herself into the chair, seemingly in some sort of pain.

'Are you unwell?'

She shook her head as she continued. 'Pieter has not exactly been easy to handle these last few days, even with Nurse Toller's assistance.'

'Is he sick?'

'*Nein*, just difficult,' she replied blankly.

'I am sorry, he is such a fine boy.'

'You mean that, don't you?' She looked into his eyes.

'Of course,' he assured her.

'At Berchtesgaden you struck me as a loyal officer. My husband speaks very highly of you. I am relying on that judgement still holding,' Eva Hitler's nervousness was obvious.

'I am at your command, Frau Hitler,' he replied instantly.

'I often wondered if I would ever get myself used to that title.' She shook her head several times. 'But now I won't even have time to find out.' She bit back the urge to cry. 'As you are probably aware, my husband has decided to end his life here in Berlin.'

'Reichsleiter Bormann informed me earlier today,' he said solemnly.

'I am going to join him,' she said bluntly.

Schiller couldn't hide his bewilderment. 'But what about Pieter?'

'I have no option, I cannot explain. But I first need your guarantee that Pieter will leave this place safely.' Eva Hitler almost choked on her words.

'I . . . You have my word. On my most solemn oath,' he said instantly.

'Do you have any idea where my husband is right now?' Before Schiller could answer she continued, a tear running down her cheek. 'I'll tell you, shall I?' There was a tenor of accusation in her voice. 'He's ascertaining from Professor Haase the most appropriate method for us to . . .' She burst into tears, weeping uncontrollably. It took a few minutes for Eva Hitler to regain her self-control. Finally she regained enough composure to continue. 'That lout, Bormann, he cannot be trusted,' she said angrily. 'He hates me almost as much as I loathe him. I know for certain that he has been trying to convince my husband that there is no place in this world for Pieter once we die.'

'Frau Hitler, I find that hard to believe.' He poured doubt on her comment.

She shook her head again. 'Herr Schiller, I accept fully that it is my place to die at my husband's side, but an eight-day-old-baby? I didn't bear him for this! He can place no threat to anyone on this earth.' She looked pleadingly at him. 'If at all possible Pieter must be taken away from this place and given a chance for life. Only you can do it.'

'You think Bormann would really harm Pieter?'

'Don't you see how vulnerable my son is? No one knows of Pieter's existence, apart from a small handful of people. I have been living in seclusion these last months at the Berghof. My pregnancy wasn't even showing before I went there. Apart from Bormann and yourself, no one knows that Pieter is still down here. He remains out of sight with Nurse Toller, in our private quarters.'

'I promise you that Pieter will remain safe,' Schiller reassured her.

Eva Hitler stood up and kissed him on the cheek. 'I can at least have peace of mind now.'

'I will not fail you,' he insisted.

BERLIN
Sunday morning, 29 April 1945

To SCHILLER'S frustration, he had to wait around for four more days before getting the opportunity to initiate his escape plan. He found Bormann a little after 10 a.m. in the map room of the

Führerbunker. He was clearly suffering from a hangover, bleary-eyed and sweating profusely.

'I had a visitor last night.' Schiller opened the conversation.

'Who?' replied Bormann, loosening his collar and tie.

'Frau Hitler.'

'What did she want?' Bormann frowned.

'She is under the impression that the child leaves with us.'

'Impossible!' Bormann sprang out of his chair. 'What did you tell her?'

'I agreed. What else could I do?' Schiller smirked.

'Good. Let her think just that. It will console her during her final hours.' Bormann nodded.

'I think it actually makes sense,' commented Schiller.

'Rubbish! Preposterous! Are you mad? We don't want a trail leading right to us,' insisted Bormann.

'The child should go also,' pressed Schiller.

Bormann was in no mood for a confrontation. 'We shall see.' He was dismissive.

'Are the papers ready?' continued Schiller.

Bormann turned to a large safe and fumbled with the combination lock. Turning the side handle, the safe door swung back. He stooped down and produced two identical black leather briefcases, both embossed with a silver German eagle. As the briefcases were set before him on the table, Schiller noticed that they both had a set of handcuffs snapped around the handles.

'The Führer's last will and testament and a copy of his authority is included in each of these cases.' Bormann's beady eyes lit up. 'Just think of it, Schiller. You and I will become the guardians of the future!'

Schiller's icy-blue eyes narrowed.

It was shortly after 3 p.m. that afternoon when Adolf Hitler emerged from his quarters to bid farewell to the small group now standing in line along the narrow conference room. Bormann stood next to Joseph Goebbels, with Generals Krebs and Burgdorf at the end of the line. He glanced over at Schiller standing in the background. The look on the Reich Leader's face made Schiller's stomach churn. Bormann emanated a smugness that distinguished him from the rest of the gathering. Hitler slowly shuffled down the line, shaking hands with each person in turn, stopping briefly to speak to one or two. Eva

Hitler stood nervously at her husband's side as he stopped again. It was then that her eyes met Schiller's, standing at the back of the gathering. From the look on her face he could see that she had been crying. Then, without warning, she broke from her husband's side and went over to him.

'Gruppenführer Schiller, I must not forget to thank you.' Her voice sounded shaky.

'My pleasure, Frau Hitler.'

'You will take care of him, won't you?' she whispered, her eyes pleading. 'This is for him.' She squeezed something into his hand before moving back to rejoin her husband. Schiller opened out his fingers: a solid gold signet ring lay in the palm of his hand. He looked up. She was already back beside her husband as he addressed his valet, Heinz Linge.

'Serve the one who comes after me,' insisted Hitler.

Schiller could see the look of puzzlement on the valet's face as his master turned away from him for the final time. Moments later, the farewells over, the Hitlers went back inside their private quarters to die. Hitler stood aside, gesturing for his wife to go before him, finally closing the door on the gathering outside. As they started to break up into smaller groups, Schiller examined the ring more closely. It was stamped with the swastika and eagle; just inside, along the inner rim, he could make out the imprint of the words 'Heute Deutschland! Morgen die Welt! – Adolf Hitler 1938' and a name, barely visible due to wear. Then he realized – the ring had belonged to Adolf Hitler! Schiller followed Bormann down to the map room, where the Reich Leader was met by Dr Ludwig Stumpfegger, the last remaining physician officially on Hitler's staff and still present in the bunker. Bormann and Stumpfegger sat down at the map table and became immediately locked in hushed conversation. Schiller went over to the map wall to wait. He checked his wristwatch. It had just turned 3.12 p.m. Bormann and Stumpfegger continued talking in subdued tones until some minutes later a noise from outside interrupted them. Anticipating it to be over, Bormann left the table and ventured outside to the conference room. Magda Goebbels was being led away, crying, from Hitler's quarters. Bormann drew one of the junior officers aside.

'Is it over?' Bormann asked pensively.

The grenadier captain shook his head. '*Nein, mein Herr*, just an interruption. Frau Goebbels forced her way into the Führer's quarters, hysterically pleading for him to flee to Berchtesgaden.'

'Foolish woman!' growled Bormann. 'Make sure there are no

more interruptions and have Linge report direct to me the moment it happens.'

'*Jawohl, mein Herr.*' The army captain came smartly to attention before positioning himself next to the entrance to Hitler's office.

Bormann returned to the room again, a scowl across his reddened features. He went directly over to Stumpfegger to resume their conversation. After some minutes, they stopped talking and Bormann went over to a side cabinet, pouring himself yet another drink. Stumpfegger remained at the table, fidgeting and scuffling his feet as he kept checking his watch over and over again.

Schiller moved across, beside Bormann. 'What happened?' he asked.

'Magda Goebbels, hysterical bitch!' grunted Bormann. 'She got past the guards somehow and interrupted the Führer.' He swallowed some of the brandy. 'Everything is all right now, thanks solely to my intervention. Don't panic, old chap, we should know any second.' He lifted the glass to his lips again. Before he could drink, a strong hand clenched his wrist, squeezing it to the point of pain. Bormann glared at the SS general, but his words stuck in his throat as he realized Schiller's pique.

'I just hope for your sake your assumption is correct,' Schiller said menacingly.

He let go of Bormann's wrist, causing some of the brandy to spill over the Reich Leader's trousers. Bormann struggled to control his temper as he watched the SS general move across beside the main map wall. Schiller examined the electric clock. It was almost 3.38 p.m. He cursed inwardly. They had all expected to hear something by now. What did the delay mean? Stumpfegger looked over at the SS general and suddenly something inside him snapped. 'Why the hell doesn't something happen! Linge was to check after fifteen minutes!' he shouted.

'Perhaps Linge is too frightened,' suggested Bormann, regaining some of his earlier composure.

'Frightened! Bah! Indecisive, if you ask me. Just like the rest!' Stumpfegger snarled. At that very moment the door was flung open and Heinz Linge rushed into the room.

'Herr Reichsleiter, come quickly! The Führer! He's dead! Cyanide – the smell is terrible.'

Just for a moment all that could be heard in the terrible silence was the constant droning of the overhead extractor fans. Bormann and Schiller stared across the room at each other.

'Stumpfegger, come with me!' insisted Bormann, never taking his eyes off the SS general for a moment. 'And you also, Schiller.'

They all immediately followed Linge outside. In the conference room they were met by the Reichsminister for Propaganda, the diminutive Dr Joseph Goebbels, Major Otto Guensche, one of Hitler's adjutants, and Artur Axmann, Head of the Hitler Youth Organization. Several other senior officers from the general staff stood aside in muted discussion. Bormann wasted not a moment in taking the initiative.

'Right, Linge, lead us through.' He turned towards Goebbels. 'Herr Reichsminister, would you please accompany me.'

Goebbels nodded his agreement as Bormann scanned the sullen faces of the others present, beckoning Guensche and Axmann to follow. Linge unlocked the outer door and Bormann went in just ahead of Goebbels, whilst the others trailed behind. Schiller stood in the vestibule doorway, blocking any further access. The smell hit him first – the bitter almond stench of cyanide. He looked over Guensche's shoulder to the scene inside. Bormann was stooped over a long sofa with a handkerchief held to his mouth and nose. As he stepped back, Schiller saw the two bodies lying on the blue sofa. Adolf Hitler was sprawled out on one side and his newly wed bride lay curled up against the sofa cushions at the other end, looking at first glance as if she were just asleep.

On a small table next to Hitler lay a Walther pistol and a couple of blue phials containing cyanide. A vase had been knocked off the table, splattering the floor and sofa with water, the red and white carnations scattered across the blue velvet sofa and over Hitler's legs. It was instantly evident that both were dead. Hitler's right temple and mouth were oozing blood, whilst Eva Hitler's contorted face registered her choice of cyanide poisoning. Still covering his nose against the stench, Bormann signalled for Stumpfegger to examine the bodies and pronounce death. Hitler's physician carried out his last official act, his eyes watery as a result of the cyanide. Stumpfegger went over to Hitler first, resting on one knee beside him. He checked his wrist for a pulse. There was none. Then he checked Hitler's eyes. They had already begun to glaze over. Shaking his head, he moved over to Eva Hitler, but there was no need for him to examine her. Her contorted face and bulging eyes told the story. The discoloration of her lips confirmed her use of the cyanide poison.

'They are dead,' he said reverently, standing up and going back beside Bormann again. Had Stumpfegger done his job properly, he would have discovered the bruising and marks on Eva Hitler's wrists. She had been held down while the poison was administered.

The group stood there, seemingly transfixed by the sight before them. Bormann glanced across at Goebbels, standing uneasily on his club foot. He was clearly too upset to act for himself. It was apparent to Bormann that he had to take charge of the situation. He hadn't wanted to be seen to do so, but the indecisiveness of the others left him with little choice. Nothing could be left to chance.

He stepped forward. 'Gentlemen, if you would all leave the room, I can arrange for the transfer of the remains up to the chancellery garden.'

Goebbels nodded his agreement. Just as Bormann had anticipated, none of them was keen to stay in the acrid atmosphere any longer than necessary. Apart from Stumpfegger, they all solemnly filed out. Bormann nodded to Schiller, still standing in the vestibule. The SS general relocked the outer door. Bormann moved around the bodies and went to the adjoining bedroom door, knocking once. The door opened immediately. A white-coated doctor stood in the doorway, his forehead perspiring. 'Well, Ruchmann?' Bormann asked pensively. The SS doctor stepped aside to allow Bormann a clear view inside. A man sat in profile on a leather armchair at the far end of the bedroom, his body covered in an army blanket, his head completely swathed in bandages, except for two eye slits and a small open section around the bottom of the nose. Bormann went over to him, peering into the narrow eye slits. The grey-blue eyes were open, yet somehow lifeless – no flicker of movement, no sign of response.

'Is this to be expected?' Bormann was concerned.

'Quite normal.' Dr Ruchmann replied. 'In a catatonic state, this lack of response is quite normal.'

'How long will it last?' continued Bormann.

'As long as necessary,' Ruchmann replied resolutely, replacing the empty syringe into his medical bag.

All eyes were fixed on the first body being carried from the room. The rug in which it was wrapped was barely enough to cover Hitler's head and torso. The leading SS guard supported the body just under the shoulders whilst two more tried their best to support the legs while moving slowly to the staircase. The gathered senior Wehrmacht and SS officers of Hitler's general staff watched mesmerized as a second body was carried from the room. This time no attempt was made to cover up Eva Hitler's body. Bormann carried her remains to the bottom of the emergency staircase, where others took over for the difficult climb to the surface exit.

Bormann then waved Schiller over. 'Come with me,' he insisted, glancing back at the small gathering. Three guards from the SS Leibstandarte Adolf Hitler, Hitler's personal bodyguard detachment, stood shoulder to shoulder across the corridor, blocking the path of anyone attempting to follow. Schiller followed Bormann up the winding staircase to the chancellery garden, where Goebbels and the others were already waiting.

By the time Bormann and Schiller got to the garden, Hitler's body was already being removed from the rug and eased into a shallow pit, supervised by the tiny figure of Joseph Goebbels. Schiller stayed at the bunker entrance, more intent upon listening for incoming shells. To the north, artillery bursts were intermixed with the sound of heavy and light machine-gun fire. Then Schiller's attention was drawn to several palls of smoke rising from somewhere just beyond the Tiergarten. The fighting had encroached into the heart of Berlin, much closer and sooner than any of them had anticipated.

Eva Hitler's remains were hurriedly placed next to her husband's, almost floating on a bed of petrol. Immediately two SS guards began emptying the remaining jerrycans over the two corpses. Goebbels withdrew to the bunker entrance just as a Russian artillery burst rained down too close to the chancellery garden for comfort. As the two guards retreated, Bormann stepped forward, igniting his cigarette lighter before tossing it into the open grave.

Suddenly the air was filled with yellow and blue flames as the petrol exploded skyward, creating a black mushroom-shaped cloud and momentarily blotting out the sun. Bormann was first to draw himself to attention and raise his right arm in the Nazi salute. Slowly he was followed by the others as they all stood peering towards the burning pit. Goebbels and the rest remained as Bormann headed back inside the bunker again, followed closely by Schiller. They hurriedly descended the concrete staircase.

'What do you think?' asked Bormann.

'I think we should get the hell out of here.'

'On that issue we both agree.' Bormann grinned.

Schiller stopped on the second landing. 'What about Goebbels?'

'He's made his own arrangements. His wife and family are in the upper bunker complex. He plans to move them down to the lower section tonight. He says he is going to dictate his will, following which he will kill himself and his entire family.'

Schiller raised an eyebrow. 'So he suspects nothing?'

'My dear fellow – ' Bormann patted him on the arm – 'we can't afford to take unnecessary passengers!'

Schiller and Bormann went directly to the map room again and Bormann immediately began to pack some of his personal papers from the wall safe. 'Think of it, Schiller, freedom and sunshine!' He chuckled. 'Send the signal to Flensburg. Get the aircraft here.' Schiller quietly locked the door, before approaching the Reichsleiter.

'Where is the child?' he asked in a low voice.

'What does the brat matter?' Bormann was furious. He turned towards Schiller, scowling. 'Follow orders. Don't be an ass!'

'I want the child to come with us,' replied Schiller resolutely. 'Now, either you tell me or I take the journey alone.'

'For God's sake, why?' insisted Bormann, his tubby face getting red with anger.

'I made a promise to his mother,' replied Schiller coldly.

'Don't be ridiculous! It was never agreed!' Bormann snarled, turning back to the wall safe again. Suddenly a large hand grabbed him on the right shoulder, spinning him around until he smacked hard against the wall. Before Bormann could do anything, a Walther pistol dug into the soft tissue under his chin. He looked into Schiller's cold eyes. Fear replaced his anger. The SS general drew back the gun hammer, the metallic click sent a shiver through Bormann's entire body. He braced himself for the very worst.

'The child,' hissed Schiller.

'All right!' Bormann blurted out, trying to catch his breath. 'I had the child drugged. He's perfectly safe and well. Asleep in the dressing room just off the Braun woman's bedroom. The nurse is still with him.'

'Show me!' Schiller demanded.

Bormann led the way across to Hitler's quarters, unlocking the outer door and moving through the anterooms into Eva Hitler's bedroom. The same nurse that Schiller had escorted from Berchtesgaden was sitting with the baby boy, nursing him in her arms.

The nurse stood on seeing Bormann. Schiller shoved the fat Reich Leader aside. 'Is the child all right?' he asked.

'Perfectly,' replied the astonished nurse, looking back at Bormann, who was cowering against the wall.

The waiting was the worst part. Because of a delay in summoning the aircraft from Flensburg, the escape plan had to be postponed a further twenty-four hours. Schiller waited impatiently in the damp, acrid atmosphere of the bunker. He spent hour after hour in the solitude of his room, happily passing the time by studying 'The Three Brothers'. He had worked through five years of hell for the Reich: he had given them everything, he'd done everything – all their dirty work, all the unrepeatable assignments. He had fouled himself in every thinkable way. He held the jewels up towards the light. They made up for everything. The balas rubies and massive pearls glistened and sparkled in the stark electric light. He was wealthy beyond his wildest dreams. With the jewels he could be his own man, do what *he* wanted for a change, and most of all he would no longer be subservient to idiots such as Bormann.

THE BUNKER
2.56 a.m., Tuesday, 1 May 1945

THEIR DEPARTURE from the Führerbunker had been well timed. Those remaining in the bunker were either asleep or too drunk to notice. Bormann led the way, a briefcase handcuffed to his left wrist and wielding a Schmeisser sub-machine-gun in his right hand. They moved up into the main bunker complex and towards the little-used section leading to the Propaganda Ministry. The area was deserted. Nurse Toller and child followed directly behind Bormann, carrying Pieter, now asleep again due to a small dose of sleeping medicine administered an hour earlier by Dr Ruchmann. Next came 'the patient', covered in a grey army blanket and lying on a stretcher carried by Stumpfegger and Ruchmann. Schiller followed several paces behind, carrying an identical but heavier briefcase to Bormann's. He looked down at it, chained to his left wrist, and smiled. He had it all now: Hitler's authority to carry on the struggle from foreign shores and, of course, 'The Three Brothers'.

Once through the empty staff area, they almost broke into a run down the long connecting corridor until they reached the double steel doors. Bormann was already sweating profusely and clearly out of breath. The SS general pushed past the stretcher and went up to him.

'What is it?' Schiller was impatient.

'I need to unlock the doors,' replied Bormann.

'So, unlock them!' urged Schiller.

'Do you see the red light above?' said Bormann angrily.

342

'What are you driving at?' Schiller stared over at the baby nestled in the SS nurse's arms. He was still asleep.

'At 3 a.m. precisely, one of my men will turn off the central alarm. That light will automatically change to yellow. Then we have precisely thirty seconds to get through before the alarm is switched back on again. That way we can get out without causing a complete security scare.'

'I say we go on anyway. By the time the guards get themselves into some kind of order, we will be long gone!'

'I'm not risking a complete security alert.' Bormann's eyes narrowed. 'Remember, I am the one who is in charge.'

Unconvinced, Schiller returned to the back again, staying close to the child.

Precisely on schedule, the light changed colour. 'We go now!' insisted Bormann, slinging the Schmeisser over his right shoulder and fumbling with a small bunch of keys, almost dropping them, much to Schiller's disdain. The SS general rushed forward, snatching the keys from the nervous Reich Leader and unlocking the door for him. After some nerve-racking moments, they were through. The heavy double doors firmly swung back into place and locked with just seconds to spare. Almost immediately the alarm light turned to red again.

'That was close,' panted Bormann.

'Too close,' glowered Schiller. 'Where now?' He was trying to adjust his eyes to the very dull lighting of the next passageway. The wall lights began to flicker and then to fade completely.

Bormann produced a battery torch from his satchel. 'Don't worry about the lights. It always happens during heavy bombardment. This section is powered from the auxiliary electrical source under the Propaganda Ministry. Come on, keep everyone close behind me.'

They forged ahead, going downhill again. The gradient increased, until suddenly Bormann's feet were in water. He stopped, scanning ahead with the torch. Schiller came up beside him again and studied the problem. In the torchlight it was impossible to determine just how deep the water was.

'What is this?' demanded Schiller.

'I don't know. It was all clear yesterday,' said Bormann shakily. 'There must have been a burst in the water mains due to the shelling.'

'Is there another way?'

Bormann shook his head.

'How much further downhill do we travel?'

'Not far. Just to a service entrance. It's somewhere on the right-hand side.' Bormann's vagueness angered the SS general.

'But is it over or under the surface?' barked Schiller, snatching Bormann's torch and wading into the water.

They kept going, slowing down completely as the water level began to reach waist height. Ruchmann and the lanky Stumpfegger lifted the canvas stretcher on to their shoulders, while Bormann assisted the SS nurse with the child. Finally Schiller called out to them.

'We have reached it!' he shouted.

Bormann was first to his side. He looked at the steel door, rusty rivets running diagonally across it. '*Ja*, this is the door.'

Schiller drew back the top bolt and shoved against it, but the door failed to budge.

'There is a second bolt near the bottom,' said Bormann.

Schiller holstered the gun and stretched down into the murky water. After some anxious moments, he located the second locking bolt. He gave it a violent tug and then another. Suddenly the door burst open, the force of the water knocking him back against the wall. As the water level settled again, they passed on through into the service corridor and up a series of concrete steps leading into a rubble-strewn cellar in the ruins of one of the annexes belonging to the Propaganda Ministry. Schiller threw back the cellar door and breathed in the fresh night air, peering up through the partly collapsed floor to the star-lit sky above. They were out! He had no sooner turned back to help the nurse up the last steps when several figures emerged from the darkness at the far end of the cellar.

'Leviathan,' the voice shouted out clearly.

'Vesuvius,' answered Schiller.

Three soldiers in camouflage drill uniform came into view, illuminated partly by the burning Berlin skyline and the moonlight. Two of them halted as the central figure continued towards him, moving in a leopard crouch. The man knelt down beside Schiller, resting his MP-40 sub-machine-gun across his knees. He pushed back his camouflage-covered helmet, revealing a young face smeared in cam cream.

'SS Hauptsturmführer Heidler at your service, *mein Herr*.'

'What about the aircraft?' Schiller asked pensively.

'They landed just over an hour ago. Everything is ready.'

'Excellent.' Schiller was relieved. 'How far to the aircraft?'

'Not far. We should make it in under thirty minutes, *mein Herr*,' replied the SS captain.

'Lead on,' said Schiller resolutely.

The Russian 79th Rifle Corps had begun their final push to overthrow the Reichstag. The fiercest of the fighting was now only a couple of blocks to the north at the Moltke Bridge, over the River Spree, where the 1st Byelorussian Front had blasted through, seizing the bridge and Himmler's old quarters at the Ministry of Internal Affairs. Now the fighting had become so fluvial that no one could be certain who exactly controlled which sector. Heidler's men went ahead first, clearing the way and drawing any possible enemy fire in advance of the main party. Another twelve SS grenadiers flanked the escape group with a further four soldiers bringing up the rear.

Bormann had carefully planned the escape route, constantly updating and revising the route to the very last second. It worked. In under twenty-five minutes they had arrived at the underground car-park close to the Brandenburg Gate, without a single hitch. The remainder of Heidler's party had already secured the car-park and temporary landing strip in advance of the radio signal being sent to Flensburg, summoning the aircraft. The location had been chosen very carefully, mainly because of the protection it offered against the constant Russian bombardment, but also because of its access to the temporary airstrip running to the Brandenburg Gate. The pilots from Kampfgeschwader 200, the clandestine operations unit of the Luftwaffe, waited impatiently in the darkness of the underground car-park.

The senior pilot, Oberstleutnant Max Lenard, checked his wrist-watch again. His passengers were already over an hour late. He looked up towards the entrance and saw their shadows first – a number of figures illuminated by the constant overhead flashes of the Russian artillery as they ran down the incline from the street outside, their footsteps echoing as they disappeared into the darkness. 'Gustav!' Lenard called over to his colleague. 'I think they're here.' A voice then echoed across the empty car-park.

'Leviathan!' shouted Heidler.

'Vesuvius!' responded Lenard, pointing a flashlight in the direction of the voice.

Bormann led the way across the car-park.

'*Mein Herr.*' Lenard and his companion came to attention upon recognizing the Reich Leader's sweating features. 'Oberstleutnant Lenard and Leutnant Weber from Kampfgeschwader 200. At your service, Herr Reichsleiter.'

'Let's get the hell out of here,' insisted Bormann gruffly.

'Sir.' Lenard directed the flashlight across the car-park, checking the other members of the little group. He paused upon seeing the covered stretcher, but when he came to Schiller his mouth dropped open. The SS general had a baby in his arms. 'Herr Gruppenführer!'

'Close your mouth, Herr Oberst. You are not seeing things,' replied Schiller.

'Jawohl, mein Herr,' the young pilot replied snappily.

'Are the aircraft ready?' interjected Bormann, eager to depart the place.

Lenard turned the flashlight behind him, revealing the two Fieseler Storch Fi 156 aircraft, both experimental versions that the Germans had kept under wraps since the French Morane-Saulnier plant had ceased development. 'Warm-up should take around five minutes,' commented Lenard, staring over at the stretcher party. 'The stretcher could be taken on board and secured while we carry out the instrument checks.'

'Get on with it,' ordered Bormann.

Lenard boarded his aircraft in preparation, while Bormann signalled for Ruchmann and Stumpfegger to bring forward the stretcher and follow him across to the second aircraft. On closer examination, Bormann was dismayed by the flimsiness of the unarmed little aircraft. He had serious doubts about their ability to get them out of Berlin, but appearances were deceptive. The aircraft had been specially adapted and prepared for their night-time role in clandestine operations. Painted completely matt black, they were almost impossible to distinguish once airborne. Each capable of carrying a pilot and up to two passengers, the tiny aircraft, with their wing spans of just over 14 metres and an overall length of 9.9 metres, had an incredible capacity for short take-offs and landings, perfect for their covert role. Each aircraft was powered by a 240 hp Argus engine, adapted and silenced for the special operations role, reducing overall noise emission by more than sixty per cent.

Lenard jumped into the cockpit seat of the first aircraft and switched on the power system. The engine ignited, revving in pitch to the point of shaking the very wing tips of the aircraft. Almost immediately the second aircraft followed suit, sending exhaust smoke over the remaining spectators. Finally, Lenard gave the thumbs-up; they were ready for take-off. The baby began to stir in Schiller's arms as he went forward, careful to avoid the propeller, and round to the side hatch, situated under the left wing.

To allow for the stretcher, one of the seats had been removed from the second aircraft. The stretcher had already been taken aboard and eased down inside the fuselage, where 'the patient' had been strapped in securely. Dr Ruchmann made a final check with his stethoscope and administered another injection before the journey. Exiting from the aircraft, he joined Bormann and Stumpfegger, who were standing back at the aircraft's tail section.

'Everything is in order. The patient is fine,' he shouted over the aircraft engine noise. 'He will not need any further medication for twelve hours.' He handed Bormann his black medical bag. 'Everything that you need is in there. Are you clear on the instructions?'

'Of course,' shouted Bormann, impatient to be off.

'Good fortune, Herr Reichsleiter.' Ruchmann shook Bormann's hand. He was followed by Stumpfegger.

'Until we meet again, *mein Herr*.' The lanky Stumpfegger had to stoop for Bormann to hear him properly.

'Until then!' shouted Bormann.

Both Ruchmann and Stumpfegger stood back as Bormann went across to the first aircraft to speak with Schiller. The SS general emerged from the aircraft just as Bormann came up to the door.

'Ready?' Bormann shouted as they shook hands. 'One of us must make it out, Schiller!' The SS general nodded.

Schiller finally closed the aircraft door and began to buckle on his safety harness. The engine changed pitch and they began to move forward at greater speed, bouncing over the uneven concrete. Reaching the incline to the road, Lenard gave it more throttle. The aircraft negotiated the steep incline with relative ease, rolling up on to the rubble-strewn street outside and swinging right towards the emergency airstrip, less than ten metres behind the other aircraft.

The airstrip was only a few metres beyond them when the ground in front erupted. The Russian artillery had begun a further bombardment in their final push on the Reichstag. Lenard pulled hard on the controls, stomping on the pedal with his left foot as he tried to avoid a massive crater in the road. Schiller imagined that the other aircraft had received a direct hit. Suddenly their own was enveloped in a cloud of brown dust, totally reducing visibility for several moments. Lenard pressed on instinctively, then without warning they were clear again and bouncing over the broad kerbstones on to the makeshift airstrip. He stared over Lenard's left shoulder. Bormann's aircraft was moving to the edge of the airstrip.

In the first aircraft, Bormann could see the unmistakable form of the battle-scarred Brandenburg Gate looming ahead. Smashed and gouged by artillery and mortar fire, it was somehow still standing. The pilot scanned the runway before him for fallen debris. Two more shells blasted into a tall building on their right, demolishing the top floors in a sheet of yellow flame. He turned towards Bormann and raised a finger skyward. As Bormann looked back at his patient, the aircraft lurched forward without warning, quickly building up speed. Bormann closed his eyes.

In the second aircraft Schiller checked that the nurse was holding the baby securely. She smiled nervously back at him, understanding his concern.

'Here we go!' shouted Lenard.

Suddenly the aircraft shot forward, its tail weaving from side to side as it accelerated along the street. From somewhere on the right a sniper opened up, the bullet smashing through a side window between the pilot and Schiller. Ahead Lenard could see the Brandenburg Gate looming closer and closer, bathed in the intermittent flashes of the artillery barrage. A tremendous force slammed into Schiller's face and chest as the aircraft lifted into the air. It shot skyward at an incredible angle, skimming over the Brandenburg Gate with just inches to spare. Schiller glanced out of the side window. Already the smouldering ruins of Berlin were hundreds of feet below them.

Bang! The aircraft lurched and then began to shudder violently. Lenard rolled thirty degrees sideways. Bang! Bang! Again the tiny aircraft was thrown sideways, like some troublesome moth.

The air around them lit up as the Red Army's anti-aircraft batteries on the western bank of the River Spree tried desperately to reach their target. Dozens of searchlights scoured the sky. Lenard pitched the aircraft into an immediate dive and it started spiralling down. For a few nerve-racking moments, Schiller honestly believed that they had been hit. As the ground rose up to meet them, though, the little aircraft suddenly pitched sideways and upwards, levelling off just feet above the Berlin roof-tops.

Ruchmann and Stumpfegger had watched the aircraft take off from the safety of the entrance to the disused car-park. Their jobs now done, they approached SS Haupsturmführer Heidler to be escorted out of the battle zone towards the American lines, as arranged. Heidler was standing in the middle of the car-park, talking to one of his men, as the two doctors approached. They were less than five paces from him when he turned, his sub-machine-gun pointing directly at them.

'What is this!' cried Ruchmann.

'Sorry, Herr Doktor. Orders,' said Heidler.

'Lower that weapon this instant! I hold the rank of SS Obersturm-bannführer. I outrank you,' cried Ruchmann defiantly, but Heidler cocked the Schmeisser. *'Nein!'* shouted Ruchmann, shielding his face with raised arms.

A clatter of gunfire temporarily blotted out the sound of the artillery bombardment beyond. Ruchmann took the bullets in his chest and was killed almost instantly. He was lifted off his feet and hurled backwards, landing spread-eagled on the ground. Stumpfegger tried to run and caught the Schmeisser's full force in his back. Seven 9mm parabellum bullets tore an uneven pattern across the surgeon's back, shattering his spine and ripping through the kidneys into his liver. The impact spun Stumpfegger sideways. He slumped on to the concrete, his back covered in oozing patches. Stumpfegger stared up at the SS officer as he approached him, the look of bewilderment fixed on his face as he tried to speak. As Heidler raised his weapon to fire again, the SS doctor convulsed, then he expired.

Heidler's men worked silently. Both bodies were immediately carried back to an armoured personnel carrier waiting in the shadows of the underground car-park. The steel doors clanged shut and the engine roared into life. Slowly the massive APC shunted forward, bumping over the fallen debris towards the upper exit. Five minutes later it trundled to a halt just south of Stettinnen railroad station. The transfer was completed in under a minute, then the carrier drew away, heading west towards the Tiergarten.

Two bodies lay on the railway line: Ludwig Stumpfegger was face upwards, whilst Ruchmann was sprawled face-down beside him, dressed in Martin Bormann's uniform. In his tunic pocket, Ruchmann now carried papers which, not immediately but in time, would identify him as one Martin Bormann, and if anyone ever took the trouble to check the medical and dental records, they would find the corpse a perfect match. Witnesses would later testify at the Nuremberg war crimes trials that they saw Martin Bormann's corpse lying next to that of SS Doktor Ludwig Stumpfegger on the railway line. Their evidence went largely unchallenged.

PART SIX

'Nemesis'

NEW YORK
Wednesday, 16 February 1966

OLD HABITS die hard. Hoover couldn't resist the temptation to visit the Templeton Hotel in South Queens once again. Now that Elizabeth had returned to Florida he had some free time on his hands and against all his better judgement, he would make the most of it. He had just left a meeting with the bankers. He was tired, but not too tired to pass up an opportunity. Hailing a cab, he ordered the driver to take him to the south of the city, dropping him off close to the hotel. He slipped in the side door, going up the fire exit to the second floor as usual. He knocked on the door as always, three short raps, followed by two longer ones. The door opened after a few seconds. The new girl was a brunette, small and vivacious. He'd only spoken to her on the telephone. From what he saw, she was even better than she'd sounded over the line.

'You must be Bob.' She smiled at him. It was the name he always used; it was safer that way.

'I only have an hour,' he replied.

'Well, then – ' she pulled off his overcoat – 'let's get started.'

The prostitute was wearing a black see-through négligé. Hoover's smile broadened as she started unzipping his trousers. He didn't waste a moment, pushing her on to the bed and quietly easing himself on top. He had barely pulled his shorts off when the door burst open and the camera flash-bulbs began exploding.

'Say! What is this!' He tried to cover himself up by pulling a sheet across his body. The two photographers continued taking photographs. The brunette hauled him towards her, wrapping her legs around his torso. More bulbs exploded.

'Get off me, will ya!' he snarled, trying desperately to elbow the woman away. She bit his shoulder and Hoover cried out in pain.

When he looked up, the two photographers were leaving the room. He shoved against the woman again. This time she released him. As Hoover started to pull on his shorts and pants, the prostitute jumped off the bed and fled the room, just as she'd been told to do. Her job was over now.

'Damned whore!' he shouted, jumping to his feet and nursing his shoulder. The teethmarks were bleeding. 'Bitch!' he growled to himself, picking up his shirt and tie from the bottom of the bed.

It was only then that he realized he was not alone. A blond-haired man was standing at the door, staring down at him.

'Get out of here! This is private!' insisted Hoover.

Roth stepped inside and closed the door.

'Listen! Did you hear what I said just now?' continued Hoover.

'Just get dressed, Mr Hoover.' The man spoke with a heavy German accent.

'Say, who the hell are you?' demanded Hoover.

Roth sat down facing the American. Hoover went for him instantly. Before he had taken three steps forward, the gun was pointing at his belly.

'Jesus!' exclaimed Hoover in a shaky voice.

'You are going to listen to me, Mr Hoover.' Roth gestured for him to move backwards. 'You work for me now, unless of course you want some sleazy magazine to get hold of those photographs.'

'What is it you're after?' Hoover sat down on the bed.

'Your wife,' replied Roth. Hoover's eyes widened.

NEW YORK
Tuesday, 8 March 1966

ELIZABETH had arrived in the city to sort out some legal matters. Whilst she was there a message came through from Nico Giovanni. He wanted to see her urgently. They met over dinner at the Stork Club in Manhattan.

'He's not acting natural.' Nico was adamant.

'You're imagining it,' retorted Elizabeth.

'Judge for yourself.' Nico handed her some papers. 'He's been transferring around some of your company funds. Inside the last month over twenty million has gone into one of the Zurich accounts.'

'Oliver's just making some necessary adjustments for me. That's all.' Elizabeth shook her head as she flicked through the papers. She had no idea what Hoover was up to, but how could she admit that to Nico or anyone else. 'I gave him power of attorney to act on my behalf in certain matters. That's all.'

'And what about the Bogotá trips? Three times inside the last five weeks,' he persisted.

'That's OK. I know about them. He went at my request.' Elizabeth set the papers aside and looked up.

'Your request! I didn't know . . .' Nico was stunned.

'Nico, you are a dear friend – ' she reached over, squeezing his hand – 'but you don't know everything around here.' Elizabeth raised an eyebrow. 'Now, is there anything else?'

'That's it,' he replied softly.

'OK, thank you.' She smiled again. 'Now can we eat? I'm famished.'

As they commenced the meal, Elizabeth's smile faded. It was all news to her, painful news.

Whilst she was in the city, she went to see Rabbi Bronowski. There were matters more pressing than her idiotic husband. The old rabbi greeted her like a long-lost daughter. He had retired to the small apartment, which Elizabeth had bought for him some years before. It was a happy place, cluttered with old photographs and memorabilia of his early life in Poland and first days in the new country. Over tea he brushed aside the small talk and got to the point of her visit.

'I know why you are here, my child.'

'You do?' She smiled at him.

'You want to know if I've seen Peter recently.' He lifted a copy of the magazine from the table and waved it at her. 'Letting the boy's photograph appear in a magazine! What are you trying to do to him?'

'I wasn't aware that they'd publish his photograph. When the magazine photographers came down to Key West, one of them noticed his photograph on top of the grand piano. They copied it without me knowing anything about it.'

'He's very angry, you know.' Rabbi Bronowski waved his finger accusingly at her. 'Peter likes his anonymity, especially with the young lady he's courting.'

'What young lady?' Elizabeth was upset. She had no idea that he had a girlfriend.

'A nice young woman, called Catherine.' His eyes lit up. 'And Jewish too.'

'And you kept this from his mother?'

'Elizabeth, he's a young man now, about to make his own way in the world. Perhaps if you didn't expect so much from him, you would receive something instead.'

'I've given up hope of ever getting Peter back.' She looked totally dejected.

'Something else is bothering you. What is it?' he asked.

'I don't want to talk about it,' she insisted.

'When did talking ever hurt?' he rebuked her. 'Is it Oliver again?'

She nodded, and spent the next couple of hours talking about the embezzlement and Hoover's behaviour over the Zurich monies. She didn't come up with any new answers, but it didn't hurt to talk.

KEY WEST, FLORIDA KEYS
Wednesday, 9 March 1966

HOOVER was already back at the house by the time she arrived herself. She joined him on the beach for a swim, then they went back to the house to get changed for dinner.

'Oliver?' she called out from the bedroom, on hearing the shower stop.

'Yeah?' he replied.

'I was talking to Switzerland today.'

'Oh, yeah!'

'They said you had been transferring large amounts of our money from the French and English banks.' She looked into the dressing-table mirror and began fixing her hair. Suddenly Hoover's image appeared behind her. He had one towel wrapped around his waist and was drying his hair vigorously with another.

'That's right,' he replied casually.

She studied him. Was he hiding something? 'Why didn't you tell me?'

'Tell you?' He sat on the edge of the bed, still rubbing his head. 'I didn't think it necessary. We talked about the possibility of a merger with the Italians over the fashion chain just last month. I wanted to get us into a good bargaining position, that's all.'

'We discussed the merger, but not the accounts.'

He stopped drying his tousled hair and looked directly at her. 'Sorry, honey. It didn't seem like a big deal. The money is safe where it is.' He shrugged his shoulders.

'But why did you do it?' she persevered.

He stood up and headed back into the adjoining bathroom. 'All right, I'll tell you,' he shouted back, 'but you'll have to promise to keep this a close secret.'

'Oliver!' She was becoming angry. They couldn't afford any more mistakes after the last disasters.

He popped his head round the doorway. 'Sorry!' he said, raising both hands in surrender. 'The Italians are in problemville. One of

356

their main investors has sold off close on forty per cent of their shares. They've taken a dive on the market that they're not going to recover from.'

'What's that got to do with you transferring our company's European funds?'

'Everything! The Italian company is a very hot acquisition, even with its financial crisis. It's going to be up for grabs within the next seventy-two hours at a knock-down price. We can get it, provided they don't know exactly who we are!' He raised a finger to halt any interruption. 'That's why I wanted our negotiators to have something to play with over in Rome. Waving around a fat Zurich account under another name will just about pull the deal off. Saving the Elizabeth Goldmann Corporation a cool twenty million, minimum.'

'I . . . had no idea.' She was taken totally unawares.

Hoover winked before returning to the bathroom.

Elizabeth turned her attention again to the mirror. 'Well, my smart husband, you'd better hurry or we'll miss the first half of the concert!'

Oliver Hoover didn't respond. He was standing with his back propped against the cold tiled wall, gasping for breath. He'd just pulled off the biggest bluff of his life. He exhaled, wiping the perspiration from his forehead.

NEW YORK
Friday, 11 March 1966

ROTH ARRIVED in New York several days later on a scheduled flight from Kingston, Jamaica. The journey and method were a tried and tested procedure used many times in the past. No one in their tight little circle travelled directly to South America. There was always a stop-over at an acceptable mid-way point. Customs world-wide paid less attention to a traveller from one of the more respected locations, especially when they were known to have travelled from the same place in the past.

Roth had used the Australian passport on over a dozen occasions during the last five years. His heavy Germanic accent was never questioned. Like other countries, Australia had taken in thousands of refugees following the war; he was only one of many. His passport was in the name of Paul Rozzenberg and described him as a businessman. If anyone inquired, an import/export company had been established in Sydney, Australia, in 1952 in his name, specializing in the clothing trade. The name was deliberately Jewish-sounding. If anyone quizzed him on his background, he had a cover story which could fool the Documentation Centre at Geneva. He had been given the identity of a Jewish prisoner from Dachau concentration camp. The real Rosenberg had vanished in the years following the war, only to re-emerge in Australia in 1949 with Roth's face.

The forged documents had been readily accepted by the Australian authorities. They were desperate for immigrant workers, especially tradesmen such as Rozzenberg the master tailor, who had kept himself alive in Dachau by tailoring uniforms for the SS oficers and guards. But not only did this Rozzenberg have experience; he also had money, Swiss francs, supposedly stashed away before the war began. That too had been 'fixed' by the 'Spider' organization. Roth had spent the next two years establishing his identity and business structure, as ordered by his superiors. It was a legitimate foothold in yet another country and all part of the greater plan.

Even approaching middle age, Roth kept himself at the peak of fitness. He hadn't liked many of the jobs Schiller allocated to him – they were petty and boring. He was a trained assassin and had expected to be used as one. Instead, he had been used to wet-nurse a bunch of old cronies in South America, has-beens who were afraid of their own shadows half the time. Yet the ex-SS major felt a compulsion to obey Schiller right to the very end. As Schiller had told him on several occasions, 'The war is not ended until we are all dead! The fight must and will go on.'

This trip was different however. They wanted him to reconnoitre the ground in New York. They wanted all the information he could get on Elizabeth Goldmann. He was to start with a reporter called Ed Morrisey, quite an unscrupulous man by all accounts. The 'Odessa' had supplied his name to Schiller's contact in the United States. He would be met on arrival at New York's airport and everything would be taken care of. He would gather all his information and make his report in one week, when the *Lady Christina* was due to arrive in the Dutch West Indies.

WALL STREET
4.02 p.m., Monday, 14 March 1966

PAUL BECKER sat in his president's suite studying the report from the New Jersey foundry when the telephone burred into life. He looked up from his papers. It was his private line. He picked up the receiver, half expecting his wife.

'Yes?' he asked in his usual quiet manner.

'Herr Becker?' The voice was distant and sounded as if the caller was shouting down a long tunnel. The manner of address also startled Becker. His father had taken the family away from Germany in the 1920s. Whilst Becker had been born in Germany, he had left as a young boy of seven. He had never been referred to as 'Herr Becker' in his life.

'This is Paul Becker. To whom am I speaking, please?'

'Herrenklub,' the caller responded.

Becker gasped. He had not heard the codeword since 1940, when Nazi agents had blackmailed him into helping them establish a network on the eastern seaboard of the United States. Instantly his mind went into overdrive. Was this the FBI trying to trick him? A ruse by a McCarthy-style administration? After all, they had had their day in the courts with the alleged Communists. Why not Nazis?

'Who is this?'

'608 Fifth Avenue, by 49th Street. The Goelet Building. Can you remember that, Herr Becker?'

'Look! Who is this?'

'Third floor, office suite 3G. Be there at nine o'clock this evening. Use the rear entrance. You'll find the fire escape staircase open.'

'I won't do this,' insisted Becker, slamming down the receiver.

Just over an hour later the private telephone rang again. He was going to ignore it, but it kept on ringing. Finally he picked up the receiver and listened.

'The Goelet Building, third floor, suite 3G, nine o'clock,' the man's voice repeated impassively.

'Look, I told you before, I'm not interested in meeting anybody. I don't know who you are or what you want. Now, if this persists, I'm calling the police,' he said defiantly.

'We thought about that.' There was a chilly silence before the caller continued. 'Ring home.' Then the line went dead.

Paul Becker slammed the receiver down and jumped out of his chair. He opened the cocktail cabinet and poured out a shaky measure of gin, splashing a little on to the wooden service counter. He bypassed the tonic water and fired it back straight. Why him? What did it mean? He cursed himself for not having answered the caller more positively. They had his private number, known only to members of his closest family and the directors of the property corporation. Suddenly it hit him. He slammed the empty glass down and returned to his desk, ringing home first to check on his family.

To his relief everything was all right. His wife had just returned from the school along with the youngest of his three children. The older children were already home and safely watching television. After setting down the telephone, he thought again about what the German had said. Then he called his elderly father, living out at Long Island. The telephone rang for over a minute before being answered.

'Hello?' The woman's voice was strange to him. She also sounded nervous.

'This is Paul Becker, who is this?' he demanded. Becker could hear an exchange of voices, then a man came on to the line.

'Mr Becker! Thank God!' Becker identified the voice of his father's gardener.

'Lloyd, what's going on over there?'

'I'm real sorry, Mr Becker, but your father has met with . . . an accident. He's been taken to the County General.'

'What! What's wrong with him?' insisted Becker.

'He's all right, Mr Becker. Look, the police are here with me, they want a word with you.'

'What?' Becker was now regretting having telephoned. He could have made more sense out of a blithering idiot.

'Mr Becker? This is Officer Higgins. It appears there's been a burglary here at your father's home.'

'Is my father hurt?' It was a stupid question of course.

'It looks like some sort of break-in or robbery, but we can't say yet what's missing.' The policeman appeared to ignore his question.

'Look, Officer, shove the house! What happened to my father? He's eighty-two years old, damn it!' yelled Becker.

The journey to the County General Hospital was the longest that Paul Becker could remember. He admonished his chauffeur five times during the car journey, demanding that the man put his foot down, jump lights and, for that matter, ignore pedestrians crossing the road. The driver was ready to quit his job by the time the black limousine pulled up outside the skyscraper hospital building. Becker rushed through the casualty department like a whirlwind, eventually pulling a staff nurse from her station to take him to his father. The old man was lying in the cubicle nearest the emergency operating rooms. A young doctor was in attendance, checking his blood pressure. On seeing Becker, he moved him back, drawing the curtain across the cubicle.

'We haven't operated yet. But his condition is not serious. He is stable and the bleeding has stopped. We'll be taking him down to the theatre in about five minutes.'

'What the hell are you talking about?' growled the businessman.

'Your father's lost the little finger of his left hand,' answered the doctor solemnly. Becker almost pushed him aside as he went into the cubicle. 'He's sedated, so please take it easy!' the doctor called after him.

'Papa? Papa, can you hear me?' Becker leaned over the bed. The old man opened his eyes. Becker could see the beads of perspiration running down from his forehead. His left hand was supported in a sling and raised up on a small frame above the bed. Becker stared at the tubes now inserted into the eighty-two-year-old's right arm, feeding him a fresh supply of plasma and sedative.

'Paul,' he whispered, his throat dry.

'Yes, Papa.'

'Paul . . . are we alone?'

Becker looked around. The nurse and doctor had left. He drew over the cubicle curtain. 'Yes,' he finally answered.

'They . . . they cut off my finger with a cigar clipper!' The old man shook with fear. Then he began to cry, sobbing almost out of control.

'Who were they?' demanded Becker.

The old man's eyes widened and danced as he lifted his head partly up off the pillow to clarify they were still alone.

'Who was it? You know, don't you, Papa?' he persisted.

'The brotherhood,' whispered the old man.

'Nazis?' replied Becker, trying to look startled.

The old man grabbed him by the arm, tugging at his sleeve. 'You know! Don't lie to me!'

'Papa, I don't know what you mean! You're suffering from shock and are in pain. You need to rest.' The old man flopped back on to the bed and ripped out the plasma drip from his arm.

'What the hell are you doing? Nurse! Nurse!' Becker called out.

The old man turned to him just as the staff nurse rushed back in. He no longer cared who heard. 'Paul, they cut off my finger to make

361

sure you'd keep your appointment . . . perhaps if I die you won't need to!' The nurse tried to calm the old man as she pulling out the taped needle still sticking out of his forearm. It was now pumping blood over the white sheets.

The doctor returned and took Becker by the arm. 'I think it would be best if you left now.'

Paul Becker didn't need any prompting. He pushed past, heading for the nearest exit. At that moment he had no idea where he was going, but he knew exactly where he had to be at nine o'clock that evening.

THE GOELET BUILDING
9 p.m., that evening

OFFICE SUITE 3G was at the end of the marble-walled corridor. Paul Becker stopped at the opaque-glass-panelled door. There was darkness on the other side. Ever since his childhood back in the Ruhr valley, he'd been terrified of the dark, but now at fifty-one years of age it had a further hidden fear for him. He gritted his teeth and turned the handle. The door opened quietly.

'Anyone here?' Silence. 'Hello?' Still silence. He checked his watch, turning slightly to catch its face in the light from the hallway. Then he felt the entire world crash on to his shoulder and neck. Becker crumpled under the force of the blow. He slumped on to the linoleum floor, totally helpless. It felt as if his entire left side was paralysed. A door shut behind him. Suddenly strong hands were dragging him across the floor, lifting him up on to a swivel chair. Becker's head was light. The room felt as if it was circling around him. If it hadn't been for the armrests, he was certain he would have toppled off. A light was switched on at the table next to him. The anglepoise was bent directly into his face, merely a foot away.

'Are you alone?' a voice asked in German.

Becker was disorientated. He didn't understand the words at first. It had been so long since he had spoken his native tongue, especially with the anti-German feeling around in the years following the war.

'Are you alone?' This time there was an underlying threat in the man's tone.

'*Ja*,' Becker grunted. His head was pounding now and his collarbone was excruciating. Suddenly someone pulled him into a more upright position in the chair, forcing his face towards the lamp.

'Your services are still required, Herr Becker,' continued Roth.

'Look, whoever you are, I don't know what you mean,' he pleaded in English.

'You still serve the Reich until we say otherwise,' insisted Roth, still speaking in German.

'Why was my father hurt?' Becker could hardly speak for the pain.

'To teach you obedience,' he replied coldly.

'What do you want from me?' Becker began to slump down in the chair. A hand grabbed his hair from behind and pulled him sharply up again. He yelled out.

'Tell me everything you know about Elizabeth Goldmann,' the man said, reverting to English. It was only then that Becker identified him as the voice on the telephone. 'Your company handles all the Goldmann acquisitions, does it not?'

Becker's eyes widened. Then he began to talk and talk.

It had just turned 5.10 a.m. when the street-cleaners found the man's body lying on the sidewalk on 49th Street. The police began by searching the seventh floor of the Goelet Building. The open corridor window indicated the place from where the suicide victim had jumped, and the fingerprints of the dead man would be found on both the window latch and the frame. The note found on his body confirmed the matter. A broken collar-bone amongst the victim's other multiple injuries would never be questioned by the busy coroner's office. Paul Becker's family would even be denied his insurance money.

NEW JERSEY
Tuesday, 15 March 1966

ED MORRISEY was very much as Roth had suspected he would be: fat, rude and with a smell of whisky and stale tobacco from his clothing. Their meeting was in the Sands Inn. Roth's helpers had made sure that Morrisey was brought there secretly. The reporter believed that he was going to be given a scoop relating to Elizabeth

Goldmann's involvement with illegal drugs. He was shown into the chalet at the far side of the mountain-road motel. It was a quiet location – in fact, although it appeared to be busy, with lights blazing and music drifting through the night air from three of the other chalets, the place was totally empty.

Morrisey had been driven to the complex by an attractive young woman. She had said little to him at the start of the drive – just enough small talk to keep him relaxed and comfortable. As they pulled into the forecourt area, Morrisey could hear the loud jazz music booming forth from the main motel building. It sounded as if a party was in progress. He was starting to believe he was in heaven, for his female companion had even let him stroke her leg on several occasions and had taunted him sexually for the last half-hour of the long drive up to the motel. They stopped outside chalet number 23.

'Hey, honey, why don't we go up there for some fun before my meeting.' He climbed out of the Ford sedan and looked over at the main motel building they had just passed. 'Listen to that beat. Now that's my kinda music, sweetheart!' He looked across at the woman. She smiled and gestured for him to follow her into the chalet. The lights were out and it seemed empty.

'We've got another hour to waste before the man arrives, and the place all to ourselves,' she said, tempting him.

'Now that's my kinda gal.' He clapped his hands against the chill night air and followed her around the car, over to the sheltered porch and into the unlocked chalet. 'They're kinda trusting up here, ain't they? You wouldn't get away with doing that in New York City!'

She smiled as she walked in ahead of him, switching on the light. The place was warm and cosy, with orange walls and curtains and a pale-green carpet. There were two single beds next to the far wall and a television next to the dressing table and built-in wardrobe. Morrisey closed the door and took off his raincoat.

'Well, one thing's for sure. We ain't goin' ta need both them beds.'

'You're the boss,' she said tantalizingly. He watched as she removed her suede car coat. Her tight yellow sweater outlined her large breasts. Then she sat on the bed and silently began to undress, firstly unzipping her knee-length boots.

Morrisey moved over beside her and started fondling her breasts from behind. 'I'm going to give it to you doggy fashion first. Ever had it that way, hun?' he whispered in her ear.

'Later,' she said softly. 'I want to shower first. Don't you?' There was more than a suggestion in her voice.

'Yeah,' Morrisey licked his lips. 'In the shower first, standing up.' He stood back from her and started pulling off his clothes. The girl quickly stripped down to her bra and pants and then disappeared into the bathroom.

'Hey, where are ya going? Wait for me!' he called after her, half out of his trousers as he hopped towards the bathroom door.

'I'm just running the water!' she called out.

'With your clothes still on?'

'So I'm shy!'

As Morrisey removed his trousers and socks, a bra was tossed out through the open door, followed quickly by a pair of flimsy pants. Morrisey then locked the chalet door. He could hear the girl singing and splashing around in the bathroom. As he picked his jacket up off the floor, he remembered the flask in the inside pocket. He needed a drink right now. He downed the whiskey in three gulps before removing his shorts. Morrisey walked naked into the steam-filled bathroom. As he entered, he received a sharp punch to the kidneys.

'Arrragh!' Morrisey fell in agony on to his knees and before he could react another blow landed on the side of his neck, rendering him unconscious. The reporter went down like a sack of potatoes on to the tiled floor.

Roth emerged from behind the door and drew back the shower curtain, revealing his naked accomplice. The young woman looked down at the fat reporter sprawled across the damp floor. After turning off the hot tap, she left the bathroom, making no attempt to cover herself whatsoever. Then, picking up her fallen underwear from the bedroom floor, she closed the door. When Morrisey came round, he was hanging from some overhead pipes, his toes barely touching the damp tiled floor of the wide shower. Roth was standing before him, putting on a pair of rubber kitchen gloves. Morrisey nearly passed out again and Roth put the smelling salts to his nose for a third time.

'Ach! Stop!' His neck ached and his arms felt as if they'd been pulled from their sockets. 'What'd ya want? Do I know ya?'

'No,' said Roth, picking up the bowie knife from the vanity unit. 'Elizabeth Goldmann and her corporation. I want to know everything.'

'What?' Morrisey was confused. He focused on the blond-haired man standing before him. 'Look, pal, you don't need to beat me and tie me up to find out that! I've been with you guys from the very start. You keep me in booze money. You do work for Kruse, don't you?' Roth nodded. 'You speak to Kruse. He'll confirm who I am,'

Morrisey said confidently. 'Now stop arsing about an' let me go, will ya?'

'We can do this the hard way,' said Roth, slicing the skin just above Morrisey's left nipple. The American squealed, more from shock than pain. He couldn't believe the man had done it.

'Stop! For Christ's sake! Please!' he blubbered. All semblance of confidence had deserted the fat reporter.

The German immediately opened the door and the young woman re-entered. She was carrying a portable tape-recorder which she connected up to the shaver socket, angling the microphone towards Morrisey.

'This is crazy,' maintained Morrisey.

'Talk!' insisted Roth.

Morrisey answered every question Roth asked and everything was recorded. The German was leaving nothing to chance. Morrisey was able to tell him practically everything about Elizabeth – her business, her house in Key West and even the story he'd got from the old jeweller and 'fence' nicknamed 'Fixy' Fox.

'Now, tell me about the boy.'

'What boy?'

'Peter Goldmann,' retorted Roth.

'Naw, ya got it wrong there. He's called O'Casey. His old man died at the end of the war. She brought him over here from Ireland.' Roth's eyes widened. This was exactly what he had been wanting to hear. 'Go on,' he insisted.

'The boy's a kinda weirdo. I even got a piece off Senator Hugo Knight about how the boy stabbed his son with a bayonet when they were both at some military academy in Virginia.'

'The boy, he is at Yale University now, isn't he?'

'Yeah, but I don't know where he is at the moment. I tried to contact his girlfriend just yesterday, but her landlady says she hasn't seen her for several days. Then I spoke to one of the teaching staff an', according to him, the boy left the campus nearly a week ago.'

'What are you to this girlfriend? Who is she?' demanded Roth.

'Catherine Beaumont. She's one of my features staff. I had her placed at Yale to try an' fall in with the jerk in the hope of busting a scoop on the mother.'

'So, you don't know where he is now?'

'Your guess is as good as mine, pal. Say, do ya want to hear something real interesting?'

'What?' retorted the German.

366

'How about letting me down first, eh?'

'Don't play games with me.' Roth slugged him in the stomach, just enough to knock the wind out of him.

'Arrgh!' cried Morrisey. The sight of the man drawing back his fist again made him answer. 'I saw her and the boy before, it was in 1945.'

'You are wasting my time.' Roth scoffed at the idea.

'I'm serious! I couldn't remember at first, but when I interviewed the dame last year, I was sure I'd seen her somewhere before. It was the name that shook me. She wasn't called Goldmann then, it was O'Casey.'

'And this was in 1945?'

'On a ship, heading for the States. She and the baby came from Ireland.' Then, suddenly it became clear to him. 'Say, that baby, he'd be around twenty-one now. So it's gotta be that weirdo, right?' Roth nodded. 'Now, how's about untying me an' letting me outa here? I won't say a word, honest. You know you can trust me.'

'And I believe you, honest.' Roth moved closer. Morrisey grinned. 'You did a series of articles recently on gang killings in New York.'

'So what?' The grin evaporated.

'I read that you said one of the gangs had the habit of killing by cutting its victim's heart out while the unfortunate was still alive.'

'Sure, some Puerto Rican freaks did it, but . . .' The reality started to dawn on Morrisey. 'Hey, hold up a minute! No! Please!' he shrieked.

'I am sorry, Herr Morrisey, but you can understand that it must look genuine. It will be as painless as I can make it, I promise.'

'No!' cried Morrisey. A sickening scream filled the air.

Five minutes later Roth re-emerged from the shower room, carrying the portable tape recorder.

'You can tidy up now. You know what to do?'

The young woman nodded as she looked into the bathroom. Ed Morrisey was still dangling from the pipes, his chest cavity gutted.

VIENNA
Wednesday, 16 March 1966

ELIZABETH hadn't wanted to delay her visit, but the mopping-up operation after the embezzlement was considerable and had taken much longer than anticipated. It was imperative to keep a lid on the incident. Public confidence in the entire corporation was at risk.

Instead of going to the Documentation Centre in Linz, Elizabeth invited Simon Wiesenthal to her hotel, on the banks of the River Danube. The tenacious Nazi hunter did not accept her first invitation. He wanted to check out the validity of her call. It was only after her second telephone call to his office that arrangements were made. Elizabeth hadn't seen the man since New York in 1946. She had not revealed her identity to him as she related the incident in Ireland after Wiesenthal's public appeal for information about Nazis on the run. Would he remember after all these years? Would he even trust anything that she said now?

As agreed, she waited in the hotel's main restaurant for the 7.30 p.m. appointment, but Wiesenthal never showed. By 8.45 p.m. she had run out of patience and was feeling quite angry with herself for having placed herself in such a situation. The business needed her and she had cancelled her meeting in Paris to come to Austria to meet someone who hadn't even bothered to accord her the politeness of turning up. Finally she returned to her suite on the first floor.

Upon opening the door, Elizabeth was confronted by three men, two of whom she had never seen before. Her heart skipped a beat before she realized she was looking at Simon Wiesenthal, seated in an armchair at the far end of the lounge.

'Herr Wiesenthal! What is the meaning of this?' she demanded, deliberately leaving the door open.

'I must apologize, Mrs Goldmann, but a man in my position has to be extremely careful. Please come in and close the door,' replied Wiesenthal.

Elizabeth was rather hesitant; his two young companions looked quite menacing. Then her mind was made up for her when a fourth man appeared behind her, blocking the doorway.

'Please, Mrs Goldmann.' Wiesenthal stood up, waving the other two into the bedroom.

Elizabeth obliged, closing the door in the fourth man's face quite deliberately. 'I demand to know what is going on.'

'A man in my profession has to be very careful, Mrs Goldmann. Have you any idea just how many attempts have been made upon my life since I started up the Documentation Centre?' He shrugged his shoulders. 'There have been so many I've just about given up counting.' He smiled and crossed the room until he was standing directly in front of her. 'It could have been a trap, you see. I do apologize.'

'How did you get in here?' she asked.

'I have many friends, Mrs Goldmann. Believe me, it is safer both for you and for me to meet here in private.' He smiled. 'May we sit together?'

'Be my guest!' she snapped, going directly to one of the chairs over by the fireside.

Simon Wiesenthal moved across and sat down opposite her. 'I always wondered about you, following our last meeting, Mrs Goldmann, and for some strange reason I also expected to meet you again some day.'

'And what do you know about me, Herr Wiesenthal?'

'I know that you are probably the most powerful business woman in the United States. You were the head of the Costello Construction Corporation and of course the Elizabeth Goldmann Corporation, an organization which seems to have its hand in nearly every country in the civilized world.'

'I don't see too many signs of civilization, Herr Wiesenthal,' she replied bluntly.

'I know.' He nodded in agreement.

'Let me ask you one thing. Do you trust me?' she said bluntly.

'I would not have taken the trouble to be here otherwise.'

'Then I shall continue the story that I started to tell you in 1946 . . .'

Elizabeth spoke for the next fifteen mintues, occasionally interrupted by Simon Wiesenthal in order to clarify certain points. Finally she drew to the end.

'. . . so now you have it. This Schiller, I feel certain, is alive and probably living in Paraguay.'

Wiesenthal nodded in agreement. Elizabeth watched him. He was staring into the flames of the coal fire. She was starting to wonder if she had indeed come to the right man – he seemed almost to be in a daydream of some sort. Then he came to life again. He looked across at her, beaming from ear to ear. 'I do apologize, but this all brings back vivid memories for me. You have no idea the effort I have put in to making these men accountable.'

'I can imagine,' replied Elizabeth. 'Tell me, Herr Wiesenthal, do you think that Hitler could have been aboard that U-boat? Do you believe that he could still be alive?'

'I discount nothing.' He looked back at her, squeezing her hand reassuringly. 'Nor should you, my dear lady. This knowledge, if true, could place you in very serious danger.'

'Thank you for your concern.' She smiled back.

'Just don't go opening any business deals in South America. If you go down there, you may not come back,' he replied. 'South America has become a haven for the majority of the escaped war criminals I have on file. The place is teeming with them, with both governments and officials corrupted and controlled by their organization.' He could see that he was startling her. 'Yes, they are anything but finished, these men, and I use that term guardedly. They are still scheming, still planning. Yes, Germany might have been defeated, but these evil men will never accept it.'

'I didn't realize it was so serious, so organized.'

'Not many do. Governments, yes, but the general public are oblivious of it.'

Elizabeth kept thinking about van Riesen and Sam Conrad.

'Mrs Goldmann, something else is on your mind. What is it?'

'You're very astute, Herr Wiesenthal.' The awful truth was suddenly dawning on her. 'Yes, you are correct, there is something else. My corporation might be in trouble from these evil men that you describe.'

Elizabeth went on over the next hour to describe what had happened at the Los Angeles company and how Sam Conrad had mysteriously 'fallen' to his death when he went down to Rio in pursuit. Simon Wiesenthal listened carefully. The more he heard, the more he was convinced of one thing. Finally he stood up. 'Mrs Goldmann, supposing that these people who embezzled from your company are in fact neo-Nazis, does anything strike you as peculiar about all of this?'

'I don't follow,' she replied.

'You, Mrs Goldmann, you are the focus of all this.'

'They want me?' Elizabeth frowned.

'You said the man on the telephone to your husband said something about it being just the beginning, correct?'

'Yes.'

370

'The beginning of what, Mrs Goldmann, that is what intrigues me. Fate in many ways has allowed you to follow your own destiny. You were there in Ireland when these dogs landed. It turns out that your present husband, Oliver Hoover, was first officer on board the very ship chasing the same submarine in the South Atlantic. You have gathered considerable and important information against these thugs. Does it not strike you, Mrs Goldmann, that God has been instrumental in taking you along this path?'

'And allowed them to infiltrate and attempt to destroy my business?' Elizabeth countered. 'That's preposterous!'

'Perhaps.' He rubbed his face. 'You must let me digest what you have told me. In the meantime, I caution you to take great care. Check your own personal security arrangements and wait. I shall be in touch with you as soon as I can.'

'You mentioned that these men are known to various governments. How does that explain the United States' attitude towards keeping the discovery of this U-boat a secret?'

'That I can't tell you,' replied Wiesenthal, putting on his hat. 'Mrs Goldmann, I can't make you any promises, but I will look into this.' He shook her hand. 'Leave Vienna tomorrow and take the first available flight back to the United States. This place may no longer be safe for you.'

She looked at him, unable to hide her puzzlement.

'I will have someone call for you in the morning and see you safely to the airport.'

They said goodbye to each other and he left with his 'minders'. Once back at the Documentation Centre, Simon Wiesenthal telephoned Tel Aviv. While waiting for the call to be put through, he spoke to the man sitting opposite him in the dimly lit and cramped little office, packed to the ceiling with pile upon pile of files.

'She has something and they want it,' he said after placing a hand across the receiver.

McClean nodded back at him. 'They're certainly after something.'

YALE UNIVERSITY, CONNECTICUT
Wednesday, 23 March 1966

THE CAR pulled up outside the apartment block. It was seven in the morning and raining in torrents. The man limped from the car, his highly polished shoes splashing in the puddles of rainwater now gathering at the roadside – the drainage channels had already overflowed, unable to cope with the freak weather conditions. His steel heel-tips clipped loudly against the tiled surface as he walked up the corridor to the first-floor address. The door bell rang only once at apartment 1B. Peter shook himself awake. No, he had imagined it. His head fell back on the pillow again. He looked across at Catherine, sound asleep just inches way from him, her blond short-cropped hair dishevelled, her body fragrant – it was paradise. Then the bell rang again, this time twice. Peter focused on his bedside clock. The alarm had been set for 7.30; it was only just coming up to 7.04. Reluctantly, he slipped out of the warm sheets and pulled on his shorts and corduroy trousers. Meanwhile Catherine arose and headed for the bathroom. He was still trying to get himself fully awake by the time he got to the door. He opened it partially, the security chain still in place – even so close to the university it paid to be careful.

'Hello, Peter.' It was Jacob Bronowski.

'Uncle Jacob, what are you doing here?' He was astonished.

'Where have you been for these last days, my boy? We've all been looking for you.' Peter opened the door wider for him to enter. 'You'd better come inside, Uncle Jacob.'

Bronowski entered, removing his wet hat and going into the lounge. 'You look tired.' He observed the dishevelled double bed unfolded across the floor of the cramped little room.

'What do you want, Uncle?' Peter yawned. He held no personal animosity towards the man – he loved him. But being one of his mother's closest advisers was enough to cause distrust in his mind.

'You. Your mother rang and she wants you to come down with me and spend a few days at the Keys.'

'Whatever for?' Peter asked.

'She must tell you that herself, my boy.'

At that moment Catherine appeared at the door of the bathroom, a short nightgown barely wrapped around her slender form. The old rabbi was speechless. Of course, Peter had told him about the girl and his feelings for her, but whilst the old man had looked forward to meeting her one day, he had never contemplated an introduction under such circumstances as these.

'Uncle Jacob, this is my wife.' Peter went over and placed his arm around Catherine.

Jacob Bronowski recovered his composure only after several moments. 'Wife, you say?' He watched as the young couple looked into each other's eyes. It was indeed love. 'My heartiest congratulations to you both.' He stepped forward, kissing Catherine and then Peter on both cheeks. 'Now I understand why no one could find you both these last few days.' He laughed.

'Of course, it was just a civil ceremony. We were hoping that you would officiate properly,' said Catherine.

'It would be my honour, my child,' smiled Rabbi Bronowski before turning his attention back to Peter. 'But now we must leave, for there is much urgency in getting you to Florida. Your mother wants you there today.'

'Is she sick?' asked Peter.

'No.'

'Then why all the rush?' he insisted.

'Peter, I've just got orders to see you safely to the house.'

'Peter, perhaps we should go. It's time I met with your mother,' urged Catherine.

'I've booked the airline tickets.' He shrugged. 'One more is no problem.'

'Uncle Jacob, what do you mean by safely? Am I in danger, then?'

'Peter, I cannot explain. You must simply trust,' pleaded the old man.

'For you, Uncle Jacob, I would travel the world.' Peter smiled. 'So Florida isn't that far.'

They all laughed.

KEY WEST, FLORIDA KEYS
7.15 p.m., Wednesday, 23 March 1966

ROCKY POINT was a sprawling whitewashed house, nestling amidst luscious gardens and palm trees on a rocky promontory of approximately twelve acres surrounded on three sides by the gin-clear waters of the Gulf. The Mexican-style sixteen-bedroomed house was serviced by a private driveway sweeping down off the main highway. Apart from a secluded stretch of golden sand on the south side, the property boasted its own tennis court, solarium and gymnasium, and for the more adventurous guests with a yearning for watersports, a speed boat was moored alongside the private jetty on the west shoreline.

None of the leisure activities interested Peter. He was there for a reason. They arrived in the early evening and were greeted first by Rosetta, Elizabeth's long-serving Puerto Rican maid and housekeeper. Rosetta hugged and kissed Peter warmly, just as she always had. Then, much to her astonishment, she was introduced to a new family member. They congregated in the library, and Peter was in the process of showing Catherine the collection of first-edition eighteenth-century books when the door opened. Elizabeth strode into the room, closely followed by her husband.

'Hello, Mother.' For once Peter did his best to sound pleasant.

'Peter, I shall make this as simple and as painless as possible!' Elizabeth was angry. 'What is she doing here?'

Peter swallowed his pride. 'Mother, this is Catherine. She and I were married five days ago.'

Elizabeth was stopped in her tracks. She looked across at Jacob Bronowski, who nodded in confirmation to her. 'You are hardly soul mates!' Elizabeth stood against the reading table at the centre of the oval-shaped library. She had intended to try to repair her relationship with her son, but now she had to reveal this young woman for what she was.

'Is there any need to be rude, Mother?'

'You are aware that this woman is an employee of a certain newspaper and ferreted her way into Yale just to get the inside story on you!'

Peter smiled. 'I know all that.'

'Then why all this?'

'We love each other.' He put his arm round her.

'Don't be nauseating,' she mocked him, waving away her husband when he tried to silence her. 'And what about you, young lady? Are you going to tell me that a young woman of your obvious beauty and charm is really interested in my son?'

'That is an insult to both of us, Mrs Goldmann! I won't stand for that!' retorted Catherine.

'Come on.' Peter started to guide Catherine outside.

'Walk out of this house, Peter, and you walk out on everything!' Elizabeth said determinedly.

Peter and Catherine ignored her. Outside, on the veranda, Catherine turned to him. 'Peter, go back in there. Make your peace with her.'

'Never! Catherine, I know I'm not much of a catch, but you wanted me and now you've got me, and it's probably for the worse.'

She smiled back at him. 'Let's walk back to the road. I saw a bus-stop just a quarter of a mile back on the highway. We can get a lift somewhere.'

He kissed her in full view of the others inside. Hoover moved beside his wife, urging her to retract. 'What the hell's gotten into you? Go after him. Tell the boy you're sorry. Welcome that young woman into our family while you've still got a chance!'

She looked back at him, the tears forming in her deep-brown eyes. 'I have my pride,' she said in a low voice.

'And very soon that's all you'll have,' he snapped, turning to the old man. 'Rabbi, maybe you can talk some sense into her, for I've just about given up!' Oliver Hoover walked out, trying to catch up with the young couple as they headed off along the path.

Everyone at Rocky Point was too busy to notice the 350-foot luxury yacht steaming between the islands, a little over two miles offshore from them. Roth watched the house through the binoculars. Everything was coming along nicely, very nicely indeed.

MIAMI
Later that night

HOOVER drove the young couple into Miami, dropping them off at a motel. Peter brooded for the remainder of the night and the next day. This was a side of him that Catherine hadn't seen before and it frightened her. They ate lunch in their room in silence. Finally she decided to break the ice.

'Do you ever think of your father?'

'Sometimes. Why?' He watched the flames lapping the logs on the fire.

'Who was he?' she asked.

'My mother never talks about him. She told me reluctantly when I was younger that he was an Irishman, an academic. He lectured at Oxford University before the war.'

'And what about during the war, what did he do then?'

'You know, I don't really know.' He laughed. 'He must have done something. I was born in Ireland, after all.' She joined in the laughter.

'In Dublin?'

'No, it was in Cork. I suppose that makes me an Irish citizen by rights.'

'What's it like, I mean Ireland?'

'You know, I've never been back there.' He took another deep swig of wine.

'Peter, I could be wrong but I think your mother is hiding something. From what you've told me, she keeps deliberately playing down your father. It's quite unnatural for a mother to do that unless . . .'

'Unless what?'

She hesitated, trying to frame her words so as not to offend him. 'Unless there's something about him that she doesn't want anyone to find out about.'

'So, in the interests of investigative journalism, you want me to go and find out for myself, eh?' he asked.

'No, not you alone.' She smiled at him. 'Never alone again.' Then she kissed him gently on the lips. Peter set the drink aside as they fell back on to the cushions strewn across the floor. Catherine started unzipping her slacks as she kissed the nape of his neck.

'So let's do it,' he groaned.

IRELAND
Friday, 25 March 1966

PETER WAS glad finally to land at Dublin International Airport. The flight had been long and cramped, and he hadn't slept much, unlike his fellow traveller, who had slept at one stage for a full six hours uninterrupted. As agreed, they booked into a hotel and then went on to Cork the next day. They found the Register of Births, Deaths and Marriages in a large building, close to the city centre.

Using Peter's date of birth, it was easy to obtain a full copy of the birth certificate. The document was in Irish with the English in brackets underneath. It gave his place of birth, the address of the house and the names of two witnesses to his birth. The birth had been registered not by Elizabeth, but a doctor called O'Dwyer. There was nothing unusual in that, but it seemed curious that his mother had never mentioned the fact to him before. Apart from that, there was little else to go on for Elizabeth had always been economic with any information about Ireland. Peter then requested the clerk to check the records for the death of his father, Eamon O'Casey, but without a date of birth or date of death it was going to prove impossible. The only lead they had was Dr and Mrs O'Dwyer.

The street had not changed much over the years. Apart from the odd paving stone that had been replaced and new electric street lighting, it was pretty much as it had been two decades before; only the style of the curtains and some of the paintwork on the terrace houses looked new. As they left the taxi, Peter was frightened for the first time in his life. He couldn't explain why – perhaps it was fear of the unknown, of what he might find out.

The door bell chimed loudly and a woman opened the door. She appeared to be around sixty years of age, with a total lack of make-up, and grey hair tied back in a bun. The high-necked frilly blouse she wore over the plain tweed skirt and grey stockings, not to mention the sensible shoes, gave Catherine the impression the woman had somehow been caught up in a fashion time-warp. Or maybe fashion had yet to catch up with the quiet suburbs of Cork.

'Mrs O'Dwyer?' said Peter nervously.

'Yes. How can I help you?' Her eyes skipped between Peter and Catherine.

'Mrs O'Dwyer, I really don't know how to say this but I'm Peter O'Casey. You probably last knew me as a baby. I was apparently born in this house.'

Mary O'Dwyer clutched the door for support. Her legs felt suddenly weak and she couldn't hide her anxiety from the two young people on her steps.

'Mrs O'Dwyer, may we come in and speak to you for a moment?' asked Catherine, stepping up to the woman.

There was some hesitation, briefly, then she opened the door in silence. Peter was reticent but was pushed forward by Catherine. They were shown into the front room. Both sat on a *chaise-longue*, recently upholstered and moved in from the other living room.

'So, you say that you are Elizabeth's boy.' Mary O'Dwyer stood beside the fireplace as she studied Peter. 'How do you think I can help you? How is your mother anyhow?' She sat down heavily on one of the corner armchairs. From its worn appearance it was clearly her favourite seat, with a view out across the street.

'My mother is fine, thank you. She sends her regards.'

'Does she now.' It was the first lie. She knew Elizabeth would never have said that. The woman had not been in touch with her once since 1945.

'I'm trying to trace my roots and I was wondering if you could perhaps help me?' he continued.

'If I can.' She sat forward slightly. Catherine watched her carefully. The woman was frightened of something.

Catherine squeezed Peter's hand as he continued. 'Did you know my father?'

'No.' His first disappointment.

'But according to my birth certificate I was born in this house.'

'That is what it says.' There was a callousness in her tone.

'But that isn't true, is it?' Catherine's journalistic tendency to seek out what lay behind the words suddenly manifested itself.

'I didn't catch your name, my dear.' Mary O'Dwyer frowned.

'It's Catherine O'Casey. Peter and I were just recently married.'

'I see. My congratulations,' she replied, with the hint of a smile on her face.

'I was born in this house, wasn't I?' persisted Peter.

'That's what it says on the birth certificate,' she repeated.

Catherine sensed something was quite wrong as Peter continued. 'But why wasn't I born in hospital?'

'Home births were the norm quite often in those days.' She changed the subject. 'Would you both like some tea?'

'Thank you, that would be very nice,' agreed Catherine.

Mary O'Dwyer arose slowly. She wasn't going to be drawn, of that they were certain. After an interlude of some ten minutes she wheeled a small trolley back into the room. As she handed out the tea and scones, Mary O'Dwyer did a little digging of her own.

'I haven't heard from your mother in years, you know.'

'Were you two very close?' asked Peter.

'Not particularly. Distance changes a lot of things.'

'It says on my birth certificate that a Dr Sean O'Dwyer was present. Is that correct?'

'Yes, that's what it would say all right.'

'Does he still practise at the same address?'

'Dr O'Dwyer, my husband, is dead.' She said the words without expression. 'Some scones? They were freshly baked this morning.'

Peter stared at her. 'When did Dr O'Dwyer die?'

'The very day your mother and you sailed for America.'

Peter and Catherine looked at each other in disbelief.

'I'm . . . I'm sorry,' said Catherine, unsure of what to say.

'So am I, but then, you can't turn the clock back, can you?' Mary O'Dwyer forced a smile, then looked at Peter with curiosity. 'Isn't it strange that I can remember yer wee blue eyes, piercing as they were when you were just a nipper. And I'd swear they've got bluer as you've got older.' She almost smiled again.

'Mrs O'Dwyer,' continued Peter, 'did you ever know my father, Eamon O'Casey?'

'I just met him the once. My husband knew him quite well of course. He taught at Oxford University, if I recollect properly. Something to do with science, I believe. I think that's how they met, your mother was at Cambridge at the time.'

'She went to Cambridge?' he replied, clearly surprised.

'You didn't know?'

'She never speaks of her past. I know only that he, my father, was a teacher of some sort. Is there anyone who could tell me about him?' Peter persisted.

'No, I doubt that now.' She seemed definite.

'Well, what sort of a man was he?' asked Catherine.

'He was quiet, gentle for his stature and size.'

'You mean he was tall?' queried Peter.

'You don't even know what he looked like?' She frowned.

'My mother never discusses him. I reckon it must hurt her.'

The woman set aside her cup and saucer and went over to a small bureau. 'I think I actually have a photograph of Eamon with my husband.' She found what she was looking for relatively quickly – a small, pocket-size photo album, full of faded old black-and-white photographs. 'Yes, here it is. I fear it's not very good. It was probably taken with our old Brownie box camera.' She removed the photograph from its setting, examining the pencilled handwriting on the reverse side. 'It was taken on holiday in Galway, August 1936.' She handed it across, looking over his shoulder as Peter eagerly examined it.

The photograph was of three men on a beach. The smaller of the three was Sean O'Dwyer. He stood in the middle of the group, holding a fishing rod and the fish he'd caught. 'Is that my father?' Peter pointed to the tallest of the group.

'That's Eamon on the right,' she confirmed. Peter stared at the burly, curly-haired Irishman. He was wearing a pair of dark swimming trunks. His muscular physique reminded Peter of one of those Charles

379

Atlas adverts – the 'after' shot. Peter looked at the third man. His father bore a striking resemblance to him. 'You've noticed the similarity, haven't you?' asked Mary O'Dwyer.

'Yes.' Peter nodded. He realized he was looking at his grandfather.

'Martin O'Casey was a very close friend of my husband,' she added.

'My grandfather,' echoed Peter.

Catherine examined the photograph for herself. 'Peter, you look nothing like your father.' She could see that he was thinking along similar lines.

'Eamon O'Casey had bright-red hair and stood six foot seven in his stocking feet,' added Mary O'Dwyer. 'As you can see from the photograph, he was built like a tank.'

Peter swallowed hard before answering. 'Are you saying that he's not my father?'

'You really will both have to excuse me. I cannot tell you any more,' the woman insisted.

'But you are the only link! Was Eamon O'Casey not my real father?' demanded Peter.

'You will have to ask Elizabeth that. I can't help you any more.'

'But she won't tell me a thing!' snapped Peter. 'All my life I've been in the dark. Every time I try and approach the subject, she closes up! She doesn't even know we've come here. I didn't even know you existed until I read your name and address on my birth certificate.'

'You must leave here now. I'm sorry. It's up to Elizabeth to tell you the facts, not me.'

'If he's depending on her telling him, he'll wait for ever!' Catherine interrupted.

'I'm sorry, truly I am. Please leave.' She led them to the front door and held it open. Peter was last to leave. 'Mrs O'Dwyer, if you change your mind we're staying in Dublin at the O'Donnell Arms; it's off O'Connell Street. We have a room there.'

The woman remained silent as they went outside into the chilly evening air. As the door closed behind him, Peter felt as if part of himself had been put into suspended animation.

'What now?' asked Catherine.

'Who knows.' Peter shrugged and put his arm around her as they walked off towards the main road. 'Who knows.'

The lace curtains moved slightly at the bay window of the house. Mary O'Dwyer watched them leave with a feeling of despair. Guilt hung over her like a heavy shadow. Later that night she went down to the basement and moved the old trunk away from the wall. She eased back the stone slab with difficulty, her age and creeping arthritis now making the simplest of tasks difficult for her. The stone finally moved aside and she lifted out the canvas and leather bag Elizabeth had left behind all those years ago. As she began dusting off the years of sediment, the silver-grey embossed German eagle and swastika became visible once again. She knew what must be done.

DUBLIN
Saturday, 26 March 1966

PETER AND Catherine spent the following morning in Dublin, arguing with the assistant registrar over access to all the death certificates relating to the name Eamon O'Casey. They had little to go on. All Elizabeth had ever said was that his father had died in 1945, nothing else. The old registrar was as patient as he could be under the circumstances.

'Look, what you're asking could take me days. I'll see what I can do, but maybe you should check with the Dublin newspapers. They regularly print all the death notices. If your father died here in Dublin, you reckon in the early half of 1945, then his name will show up somewhere in the death notices, but somehow I don't think it will.'

'Whyever not?' asked Catherine.

'After your phone call yesterday, I had one of our clerks do a cursory check through our records. There's only two listings for an Eamon O'Casey dying in 1945.' He read from a scrap of paper. 'Eamon Patrick O'Casey died on 20 April, aged eighty-one, and Ignatius Eamon O'Casey died on 12 November, aged seven years and three months.'

'Then that's it.' Catherine felt utterly dejected.

'Not necessarily,' replied the man.

'What d'you mean?' said Peter excitedly.

'Now, as I said yesterday, it may be that he died somewhere in one of the counties and somebody's slipped up in telling us. Remember, those were awful confusing days, you know.'

'We'll follow it up. Thank you,' said Peter.

'I'll make a few inquiries myself. Give me a call around Tuesday. I might have something for you then.'

'Thank you again.' Peter shook hands with the man before following Catherine out of the fusty office. 'Well?' he asked her.

'Now we try the newspapers.' She endeavoured to sound optimistic.

The rest of the day was spent in Dublin's central library, leafing through the second-page death notices of each yellowed copy. Peter thanked God that someone had been meticulous enough to keep the editions in proper order, each month's papers filed in a separate cardboard box. It was coming close to four o'clock and the offices were closing. Peter was looking forward to a large steak, if nothing else, when Catherine suddenly sat forward in her chair.

'Wasn't Eamon's father called Martin? There's a front page headline here stating how a Martin O'Casey was murdered in Cork. Shot dead at the quayside on 8 June 1945.' She passed over the newspaper.

'Let me see.' Peter pulled the file across the table.

'It has to be him. What'd you think?' She leaned over his shoulder as he started reading the column.

'I've heard Elizabeth speak of her father-in-law many times. She talked more freely about the old man than she did about anything else.' He read on. Martin O'Casey was described as a wanted IRA terrorist, a commandant in the outlawed organization. 'Catherine! He was in the IRA!' He looked up at her. The photograph of Martin O'Casey was blurred and of little help, but the description of him tied in with what he had heard about his supposed grandfather. In the remaining few minutes they searched for any death notices that might have related to the old man, anything that might have pinned him down more clearly – perhaps a lead to another relation – but there was nothing of consequence, just follow-up stories and speculation about what O'Casey had been involved in.

As they walked back to the pub, Peter's head was spinning. Catherine could see that the tension and pressure were starting to tell on him. When they strolled inside, the landlord called Peter over.

'Young man, there's someone over there to see you.' The landlord signalled towards the snug, just off the main bar area. It was Mary O'Dwyer. Peter went on in alone.

'Mrs O'Dwyer?' He was astonished by the woman's reappearance.

'I had to see you before you flew back to America.' She stood up and handed over a brown-paper parcel.

'This arrived with you at my house in 1945.'

'So I wasn't born in the house, then?' He frowned.

'I think you'd better sit down. You can call in your wife there, she should hear this also.'

Peter beckoned over Catherine from just outside the glass doors. Mary O'Dwyer began by explaining Elizabeth's arrival at the house with the baby. She then related as best she could all that she had been told about the U-boat landing at Dingle Bay. Peter and Catherine looked on in amazement, finding each piece of information even more incredible than the last. It took the woman almost fifteen minutes to tell all she knew and by the end Peter's head was about to burst open with tension.

'Then who am I?'

'I wish I could tell you that. Even Elizabeth said she didn't know. The only German she talked about was an SS general called Schiller or something. You came ashore in the arms of a nurse, who was subsequently killed during the fighting. That's how Elizabeth found you. I can tell you, son, that without Elizabeth you would have died there, as presumably the Germans thought you had.'

'And the last time you saw my mother was when she left with Martin O'Casey to board the ship at Cobh?'

'Yes. Then just before Christmas that same year I received a short note from her. She had arrived in America safely but gave no forwarding address, and that was the last I heard from her. I suppose she was too frightened of being traced by the IRA. You see, both my husband and Martin O'Casey were murdered by the IRA. By the way, Elizabeth included a banker's draft, which I've kept to this day, uncashed.' She removed the bank draft from her handbag and showed it to them. Peter recognized Elizabeth's signature immediately. The draft had been for a thousand dollars and was dated Friday, 30 November 1945.

'Thank you.' Peter had almost forgotten about the parcel sitting on his lap.

'I'm afraid it isn't much. I threw out all the baby powders and powdered milk after you left. It was all marked in German anyway.'

She stood up to leave.

'Mrs O'Dwyer, the place in Dingle Bay where you say the Germans came ashore, what was it called again?' asked Catherine.

'Meadowlands Farm . . . yes, I'm sure that was it. Elizabeth mentioned it several times. She could never understand how the place had been called after a meadow since there wasn't one there in the first place. But this is Ireland. That's good enough reason in itself!' She forced a smile.

'Goodbye.' Peter smiled at the woman, but she was already half-way through the glass doors.

'I feel so sorry for her.' Catherine sighed. 'Her life crashed around her all those years ago and much of it was caused by Elizabeth, indirectly or not.'

Peter unwrapped the parcel. The dusty canvas bag smelt fusty and stale.

'Look at the side.' Catherine pointed to the side furthest away from Peter. The German insignia had been wiped clean of the dust and grime. As he unzipped it, part of the cloth gave way. He removed a small blanket. Then he found baby clothes, some of which looked hand-made, and apart from that there seemed to be nothing else.

'It's just a useless bag!' As he tossed it aside, something rattled in the bottom. Catherine heard it and picked up the bag. There was something metal at the bottom of it. She lifted it out.

'What do you make of this?' She showed Peter a solid-gold tie-pin, depicting the German eagle with a swastika surrounded by laurel leaves just underneath – an exact copy of the insignia imprinted on the side of the canvas bag.

'It looks real enough.' Peter examined it in closer detail. The back of the two-inch-wide pin was engraved. 'Catherine, look!' He pointed to the name. R. SCHILLER. 'It's the same name that Mrs O'Dwyer mentioned. Is this Schiller my father? A bloody Nazi!'

LONDON
Tuesday, 29 March 1966

ON CATHERINE'S insistence, they had taken time off from their investigation and spent the weekend touring the west coast. No matter how he tried, Peter found he just could not relax; his mind kept drifting back to the search. Through one of Catherine's contacts they found out that the World Jewish Congress had an office in London, so that Tuesday morning, they flew across the Irish Sea to London.

The office was a veritable mine of information. They had files on all the major war criminals and leading Nazis who were still at large following the Nuremberg Trials. The young office manager, called Franke, was disinclined to impart any information to them initially, but then Catherine's press card swayed in their favour. The file on

Rudolph Schiller had been forwarded by the Documentation Centre in Linz, run by the famous Nazi-hunter Simon Wiesenthal. Amazingly, there was not one clear photograph of the SS general who had been personally responsible for the murder and torture of thousands of Jewish men, women and children.

'Mr Franke, have you ever seen one of these before?' asked Peter, showing the man the tie-pin.

'Yes, I've seen these before, but only in photographs. If I remember correctly, the owner's name should be engraved on the back.' He turned it over and gasped. 'Where did you get this?' He was immediately suspicious again.

'We found it. Somehow it made its way to Ireland, where we've just come from,' Peter replied nervously.

'You must tell me more. This is very significant. Schiller is still believed to be at large and wanted for his part in the Holocaust! Please, come with me. I need to get your details.' He beckoned them to follow him into the next office.

'Please wait here, while I get someone to join us. You really don't know just how important a find this is.' He looked at the tie-pin again before setting it on the table. 'Each senior SS officer and Nazi party official was presented with such a pin in recognition of their outstanding service.' He picked up the telephone receiver and dialled the extension number. It rang continuously.

'More like outstanding butchery!' Catherine interjected.

'Presented by whom?' queried Peter.

'By Hitler. He handed them out at his birthday in 1944. Please, excuse me, I must get this gentleman before he leaves the building.' He set the receiver back and rushed off, leaving the door open. It took him five minutes to locate Ludwig Marx, the director of the London office, himself a survivor of Auschwitz, but by the time both men returned, the room was empty.

'They've gone!'

'You shouldn't have left them alone. Search the building, Franke. They must not get away. Quick, man!'

But it was all too late. By the time Franke had reached the front door of the offices, Peter and Catherine were already aboard a red double-decker bus, heading towards Marble Arch.

HILTON HOTEL
Minutes later . . .

McCLEAN greeted the call with scepticism. He had been given many false leads in the past by Marx and only as a favour to Wiesenthal had he continued to receive the man's phone calls. The issue of wanted war criminals was becoming more and more a matter for Interpol and the free world's police forces.

'All right, Mr Marx, I'll see what I can find out. You say they were both American and the girl showed a press pass in the name of Catherine Beaumont? Now, what about the young man? He was called Peter what?'

'My manager here can't remember. He only remembers the girl calling him Peter several times, that is all. I am sorry. This is the first real evidence we've got on this monster Schiller.'

'All right, I'll see what I can do. Thank you and goodbye.' McClean set the receiver down and turned to the white telephone on the other side of his desk, dialling the London number as he flicked through the information he had before him. The call was quickly answered.

'Coleridge.' The man's public school accent was as familiar to McClean as decent whisky.

'You one-eyed dog!' he snarled down the telephone.

There was a momentary silence before the man answered. 'McClean! Good God, man, are you here in London?' asked Coleridge.

'Checking on how well you're measuring up to my old job.' McClean laughed. He hadn't seen his assistant since the time he'd walked out of the Old Admiralty Building, having punched his section head. 'Ian, we have to meet. It's professional.'

'McClean, I don't know. You're taboo around here. There's a red file running on you.'

'Coleridge, do you remember that little Irish job you attended to during 1945, the case involving the German U-boat on the west coast of Ireland?'

'Dingle Bay actually, why?'

'Someone's been asking questions,' snapped McClean. It was enough to whet the man's appetite.

386

'I can be at the George and Dragon inside twenty minutes,' suggested Coleridge.

'Make it in fifteen and the drinks are on me.' McClean chuckled.

IRELAND
Wednesday, 30 March 1966

PETER AND Catherine flew back to Ireland the next morning. It was more a romantic expedition than a realistic attempt to find out about his past. Peter wanted to see the place where he had been brought ashore before he returned to the States. Catherine reluctantly agreed to the return visit and they headed out in search of Meadow-lands Farm.

Coleridge found their trail easily, although he was more used to being desk-bound these days. A lot of people believed intelligence work to be terribly dashing and exciting – agents jetting into the sunset, beautiful women and a glamorous life-style. In fact, ninety-nine per cent of those working for the SIS were pen-pushers of one sort or another. Very few had any experience in the field, and those who had had almost forgotten how to load a gun, never mind fire one. Coleridge found the chase invigorating. Peter and Catherine had rented a car at Dublin airport and on the form were obliged to state where they would be travelling to and the purpose and duration of their stay. Catherine had simply written 'Short holiday at Dingle Bay, Co. Kerry'. It was like taking candy from a baby. Coleridge rang back to McClean and briefed him before following on.

Peter and Catherine had spent all afternoon combing the country-side and shoreline for the farmhouse. It was a pointless exercise. Eventually Peter had to admit that their visit had been an utter fiasco.

'Let's get the hell out of here,' he suggested.

'That's the best thing you've said all day, Peter.' She kissed him on the lips. The walk back up the cliff was more difficult than either had anticipated. Most of the limestone path had crumbled, weathered away to almost nothing, and even the parts that survived were fairly unsafe and could give under the pressure of a foot. They were both relieved to get to the top. Catherine stopped.

'What's wrong?' asked Peter, panting slightly.

'There's a car coming down the track.'

By the time they reached their own hired car, the other vehicle had already pulled up alongside. The man had alighted and stood in front of their car. As they approached, he took out a gold cigarette case and lit a cigarette. 'Peter O'Casey, I presume? And you're Catherine Beaumont.' He spoke in a clipped English accent. 'My name's Coleridge. I'd like to have a chat with you both.' He drew on his cigarette, before offering the open case to Catherine.

'Who are you?' she asked, declining the offer.

'I work for the British government, investigative work.' He produced an official-looking identity card with his photograph in the top right-hand corner. 'I got a call from the offices of the World Jewish Congress in London. They say that you two ran out on them after whetting their appetite.'

'What's it to you?' snapped Peter.

'Let's say that neither of you is going anywhere until I get some answers.' He smiled, dangling their car keys in his free hand. 'Perhaps we can talk this thing through over dinner this evening. I know a fabulous little place just up the coast from here – the lemon sole is absolutely divine.' He smiled again. 'Then I'll run you both back to Dublin in the morning and get you booked on a flight to New York. You'd be safer on it.'

'Why?' Catherine didn't like being shoved around.

'Because it's quite conceivable that certain gentlemen may want to get their hands on young Peter here.'

Peter and Catherine stared at each other. Suddenly they both felt extremely vulnerable. 'I was planning to save this for a little light reading for you both on the journey back home, but you may as well have it now.' He removed a copy of *Flair* magazine from the front seat of his car and handed it to them. Elizabeth's face was on the front cover. Coleridge flicked open the marked page for them. He had circled Peter's photograph in pencil. 'If by any chance this Schiller person is still alive, he might just put two and two together and come after you.'

'Why?' queried Catherine.

'The Nazis obviously reckoned Peter here was dead, but Schiller might just want him back. After all, he left his calling card, the tie-pin, didn't he?'

'What do you think?' asked Catherine.

'Frankly I don't know, but if Peter's mother is in any way mixed up with these Nazis, she could be facing criminal charges, remember that.'

'She's not mixed up! I'm sure of it,' he insisted.

'We'll see, shall we?' Coleridge suggested.

DUBLIN
Thursday, 31 March 1966

IAN COLERIDGE brought them to the companies' register in Dublin. It didn't take long for them to find the details relating to Oisin Enterprises Ltd. Catherine and Peter scanned the list of directors. There were five names in all, none of which struck him as being familiar, all with addresses in Ireland.

'And you say my mother actually owns this company?' He frowned.

'Yes, apparently she created it to purchase the site where the Germans landed. It also marks the spot of certain unmarked graves, including that of your mother's late first husband, Eamon O'Casey.'

'So what you're saying is that this Oisin Enterprises is nothing more than a holding company?' Catherine spoke up.

'Quite,' replied Coleridge.

Peter scanned the list. It was only on second glance that he faintly recognized one of the names – the company secretary, a solicitor called O'Neill, with a business address in Connaught Street. Then he looked at the fourth name on the list, Fred Rickman, care of the same Connaught Street address. 'Catherine, look at this name. I'm sure this man worked for my mother at one time, but he's American, not Irish. Remember the hullabaloo in the press when he killed himself, here in Dublin?'

She recalled vaguely. 'But the address?'

'Look again. It's the same Dublin address as this other director called O'Neill. It's just a postal holding,' replied Peter.

'Perhaps we should pay this Mr O'Neill a visit,' suggested Coleridge. 'Connaught Street isn't far from here.'

They drove the short distance and then pulled up at the address listed. Catherine got out of the car and went over to the door to examine the brass plate. The name of the second director was on it all right. He was a solicitor and notary public. Peter followed her, while Coleridge waited for them outside.

'What does it mean?' he asked.

'I've seen this before, dozens of times. A company's registered office can be anywhere, but with small companies such as this one obviously they use the company solicitor's or accountant's office as the registered address. It is quite legal for another director to have his registered address at the same premises, provided he uses that address as his business address. Your Mr Rickman obviously did just that. Why don't we ask Mr O'Neill just what Oisin Enterprises is all about?'

The offices were on the first floor. A woman sat at a glass-topped desk in the centre of the white-walled office. All but one wall had grey filing cabinets up to a height of six feet, reducing the narrow confines of the room even further.

'Can I help you?' The woman looked up from her typing.

'We'd like to see Mr O'Neill, please,' answered Peter.

'May I ask what it's in connection with?'

'Oisin Enterprises.'

'You don't have an appointment?' She checked her diary.

'No.'

'Names please?'

'I'm Peter O'Casey from the Goldmann Corporation of New York. This is my PA.'

The woman excused herself and went into the adjoining room after knocking on the door first. Catherine gave Peter a dig in the side.

A middle-aged man came out to greet them. 'Mr O'Casey?' He took in Peter's jeans and floppy sweater. 'Please, step inside.' He beckoned them both into his office, shaking their hands as they went by.

The room was about the same size as the outer office but appeared bigger because of the lack of office furniture. Apart from a small desk and a row of four chairs set aside the facing wall, the room was bare. The man lifted over two of the chairs and set them in front of his desk before sitting down himself.

'Sorry for asking, but would you happen to have a business card?' Peter pretended to fumble in his wallet. 'Sorry, Mr O'Neill, but I'm travelling light. In a hell of a rush to get back to New York.'

'Would you have a driver's licence or anything to identify yourself? Just a formality, you understand.'

'Sure.' Peter pulled out his licence and handed it over to the man. The solicitor recognized the address as being the same as his client's private home address. He examined it carefully before handing it back.

'You wouldn't be any relation to Mrs Goldmann?'

'Her son.' That seemed to do the trick. The man's face lit up. 'I'm sorry, I should have realized. It was the name that threw me.'

'My father's.'

'I see.' The man flushed. 'I've only ever had the pleasure of speaking to your mother on the telephone, a lovely lady indeed.'

'Was that when she set up the company?'

'Well, as a matter of fact, your Mr Rickman had already done all the spadework. Poor man, it was just awful.'

'What was?'

'Why, his death, of course, just after the meeting.'

'Meeting?'

'The meeting between Mr Rickman and myself, to set up Oisin Enterprises.'

'How did you settle on that name?' asked Peter.

'According to Irish legend, Oisin was the son of Finn MacCool, the Irish giant. Apparently it was your mother's idea. She said it reminded her of someone.'

'And to the purpose of my visit, Mr O'Neill.' Peter glanced over at Catherine. 'My mother is thinking of winding up the company.'

'This is very sudden!' The solicitor was shocked.

'She tends to make up her mind on things fairly quickly. She sent me over here to find out the state of play, what the company is up to.'

'Mr O'Casey, I don't understand. Your mother knows perfectly well that the company is not doing anything. At present it's purely a holding matter, having secured the title pertaining to the land in County Kerry.'

'But you pay men to guard the land, don't you?' Peter had to think fast. He didn't want to cause too much suspicion before he got the answers.

'Well, yes, in a way, but that's all taken care of from America. The cash used for maintaining the property is channelled through the Bank of Ireland here in Dublin and I oversee the payment of accounts.'

'How much land is there altogether?'

'Off the top of my head, I'd say around two hundred acres, including part of the shoreline, of course. Mr O'Casey, I can tell you that all this rather puzzles me. Your mother just wanted the land kept as it was. The old family home in Ireland, a sentimental attachment, she said.'

'Well, it seems all that has changed. Only two days ago she told me she wanted to sell or use up the option to mine the property.'

'But there's nothing to mine. Your mother is fully aware of the

391

survey reports that I sent her. She was trying to ascertain if anything was buried on the land. At one time she had almost every inch of turf lifted by mechanical diggers.'

'Really?' Peter cocked his head, looking over at Catherine. 'Well, thank you for your time, Mr O'Neill. It's been a pleasure.' Peter beat a hasty retreat, quickly followed by his wife.

They relayed their findings to Coleridge on the way to the airport. There was nothing left for them to do. It was time to go home. Coleridge saw them both safely into the departure hall and up to the customs line. 'I feel much safer now, knowing that you two are on your way back home.' He shook Peter's hand first, then Catherine's.

'But will we be any safer there?' asked Catherine.

'There's a friend of mine on his way to see Mrs Goldmann. His name's McClean. He knew her during the war. He has the contacts to ensure your safety. I imagine that he'll be waiting to meet you at the other end,' Coleridge reassured them. 'Have a pleasant flight.' He watched as they passed through customs and down the corridor to the boarding gate.

Once the Boeing jet airliner disappeared into the low cloud over Dublin, Coleridge called Whitehall. The number rang for some time before it was answered. 'Sir, this is Coleridge. The turkeys have flown back home.' He listened for a moment, before echoing his superior's opinion. 'My sentiments exactly, sir. Let them keep the mess in their own backyard.' He listened again for several moments. 'McClean's got himself into this, he can get himself out. I quite agree.' A smile spread across his face. 'Thank you, sir. I'll see you when I get back.'

NEW YORK
9 a.m., Friday, 1 April 1966

ELIZABETH had reluctantly left Key West and returned to the city at Hoover's request, meeting him at the Goldmann Corporation offices on 42nd Street. She had no sooner arrived than the call came through to her from Dublin. She listened to O'Neill for several minutes. At least they knew Peter was safe for the present. The solicitor had checked with Aer Lingus and confirmed that Peter and Catherine were both on the scheduled flight back to New York. Elizabeth set the receiver down and stared out across the Manhattan skyline. It had changed over the years since she first arrived on the liner from Ireland. A lot had changed since then, including her relationship with Peter. It seemed the more she tried to communicate with the young man, the worse things became. Then Hoover came into the office suite, clearly in a fluster.

'The switchboard tell me you had a call from Ireland,' he said.

'It's Peter. He was there. Apparently he's on his way back to New York right now. Oliver, that boy is becoming a liability to himself as well as to me.'

'Elizabeth, you have to see him when he gets back. Smooth things over with him. Patch up your differences,' he suggested.

'If only we could.'

'Have you seen this?' He handed her a copy of the *New York Times*. The headline read 'REPORTER MURDERED'.

Elizabeth scanned the subheading and first paragraphs. Ed Morrisey's body had been found on a garbage dump in the Bronx.

'The bastard finally got his just deserts,' commented Hoover. 'The police are blaming his death on some street gang. They've picked up nine or ten hooligans already.'

'It's too convenient,' mused Elizabeth, worriedly.

'Well, at least we don't have to worry about buying *Flair* magazine any more. With Morrisey out of the way, I think that'll be an end to the witch-hunt.'

'I hope you are right.' Elizabeth flicked back her hair and massaged her neck.

'I suppose it could be worse,' said Hoover.

'Could it?' She held out her arms to him. Elizabeth needed him now, not just as a business partner but as her only friend. He held her closely, as she let her usual hard façade crumple into tears.

JFK AIRPORT
10.40 a.m., Friday, 1 April 1966

ELIZABETH had the car meet them at the airport. Peter was heading for the showdown with new hope in his heart and a woman at his side who loved him. Elizabeth waited for them in her penthouse office. Hoover showed Peter and Catherine in just as coffee was being served.

'So, you've finally returned.' She walked across and kissed him on the cheek before turning her attention to Catherine. 'Welcome to our

393

family, Catherine. I want to apologize for the way I treated you.' She hugged the younger woman, kissing her at the same time.

The show of emotion stunned Peter. His aggression abated.

'Mother, I would like some answers,' he said firmly, but politely.

'Of course you would, and I will answer all your questions later. First, though, there are some ground rules to go over,' she insisted, still the dictator. 'I think it would be safer if both of you go down to Florida and remain there at the house for the time being.'

'Wait a minute, Mother,' interrupted Peter. 'I've got some important questions for you. Most importantly, I want to know who I am!' Elizabeth looked at him with a mixture of shock and apprehension. 'Just whose blood is running through my veins?' he demanded.

'What should it matter to you! You've had everything that money could buy – well, nearly everything.' She glared over at Catherine. The smile had vanished. 'You've had everything and given me nothing in return!' she exploded.

'Who am I?' he demanded.

'I don't know!' she fired back at him in frustration.

Peter fell silent for a moment, staring at Elizabeth. 'But I'm German, aren't I?'

'It's possible.' She stepped forward. 'But you're my son, Peter, you always have been, you always will.'

'You've never loved me! You sent me away when I was seven years old and you've been avoiding me ever since . . .'

'Stop it!' She turned away, trying to hide her grief.

'Even before I was sent away, when I was little, someone else looked after me. It was always somebody else!'

'No!' She turned back to him. 'You've got it wrong! I love you, I love you!' She rushed out of the office, almost pushing Catherine into a large rubber plant as she exited. Peter stood in silence.

'I think she means it, she really does love you,' commented Catherine.

'She has a funny way of showing it then,' he replied.

Hoover reappeared at the door. 'What happened? Where's Elizabeth?'

'Gone,' replied Peter coolly.

Hoover pulled Peter by the arm. 'Gone where?' he demanded.

'What the fuck does it matter?' retorted the young man.

Hoover slapped him across the face. 'Don't you ever speak about her in that tone again! Are you too stupid to see that she loves you? She'd do anything for you. You are her only son! The only child she could ever have!'

'What are you saying?' snapped Peter.

'Work it out for yourself, Mr Know-all.' Hoover pushed him aside and left.

Peter sank down in one of the chairs. Catherine remained silent. He would have to work that one out for himself. Later on perhaps they would go down to Key West after all. At least they would be on their own and away from any confrontation with Elizabeth.

KEY WEST, FLORIDA KEYS
11.46 a.m., Saturday, 2 April 1966

ROSETTA was busy working in the kitchen, preparing Peter's favourite – one of her paella dishes – when she noticed the truck pulling out of the side road at the entrance to the property. She imagined it was some delivery man who'd taken a wrong turning. She left the vegetables in the sink, drying her hands on her apron as the truck came up the driveway towards the house, stopping by the service entrance. She waddled outside through the utility room to meet the driver.

'Inter-County deliveries. We've got some carpet and rugs to deliver here.' The young man jumped down from the cab of his truck, smiling at Rosetta as he walked forward with his delivery docket.

'I know nothing about no delivery,' she maintained as he handed her the paperwork.

'A Mrs Goldmann placed the order. That's her name right there.' He pointed to the signature at the bottom of the pink form.

'That is the mistress all right. But she said nothing to me about no delivery.' She was perplexed. The young man shoved his cap back, scratching his forehead.

'Well, lady, I sure as hell ain't takin' this lot back to town. I've already wasted half a day findin' this place.'

She was about to speak when someone grabbed her from behind and covered her face with a cloth. The chloroform worked almost instantly. In less than five seconds she was out cold and in less than the same time they had carried her back into the kitchen. The two men returned to the van, opening up the rear door and pulling out a large rolled rug. The younger man went first, followed by his blond-haired companion. They knew their way through the house and moved straight to the lounge. Both men looked at each other for a

395

second. Then Roth pointed towards the sound of voices coming from the swimming pool at the other side of the house. They quietly tiptoed through the conservatory until they were standing at the french windows. Through the fluttering nylon curtains Roth could see the young couple playing in the pool. Peter was chasing his wife across the shallow end, splashing her as she screamed.

Roth walked out on to the terrace, calling out to Peter. 'Excuse me, but we were told by the maid to bring a delivery into the house. Where do you want it?'

'What delivery?' Peter looked up annoyed at the intrusion.

'A rug.' Roth glanced back at his young partner, propping up the Persian rug as he pretended to examine the pink delivery docket.

'Leave it with the maid. Where is Rosetta anyway?' he asked.

'On the telephone, Mac. Sounds as if she's talking to a girlfriend.' Roth smiled.

'Typical,' groaned Peter, climbing out of the pool. 'Catherine, stay put while I sort this out.'

She waved back to him, climbing out on the opposite side of the pool. Peter walked over to the younger man. 'Just leave it in the lounge, in front of the fireplace.'

The man smiled and carried the rug back inside. As Peter went through the french windows, the door was suddenly closed on his body. Peter groaned at the sudden pain. A powerful hand then gripped his arm, now jammed on the inside. Almost immediately he felt the sting of the injection, He tried to call out to Catherine, to tell her to run away, but she was already racing to his aid. Peter felt his eyes closing, his head felt fuzzy, then nothing.

Grabbing hold of a deck chair, Catherine swung it at Roth, missing the man and smashing it into the glass door. She hurled herself through the debris at the German, but he brushed her aside with a single swipe of his forearm. She had no sooner landed on the floor than the younger man had her pinned down by the arms.

'Let me go, you bastard!' she cried, seeing Peter lying slumped on the floor. Before she could do anything, she was pulled around on to her side, her nimble body pinned against the cold marble surface of the lounge floor. Catherine screamed but there was no one to help. Roth knelt down beside her. He ran a hand through her damp blond hair, his eyes almost signalling compassion.

'This will not hurt, I promise,' he whispered.

The other man already had her left arm held outstretched against the floor. Roth quickly found a vein just below the elbow joint.

'Let me alone!' She struggled with all the strength she could muster. Roth jabbed the needle in and emptied the syringe, holding her head in his hand the whole time.

'I am so sorry. You are so lovely.' He stroked her cheek just as she began to black out.

Catherine was not unconscious, yet she was totally helpless. She was aware of them having let her go. She was lying on her back now. She tried to get up and managed to roll over on to her side, but only just. She watched, unable to speak, as the two men unrolled the rug and set Peter on to it, carefully rolling it up again. Already she was sweating. Her stomach felt as hard as a rock. She was hot and cold simultaneously. What was happening to her? What did the man mean when he said he was sorry?

The blond-haired man was locking the conservatory door. She could just see the almost pained look on his face as he turned and walked away, picking up his end of the rolled carpeting. Catherine grabbed hold of the coffee table but slumped back on to the floor again. Something rolled off the glass-topped table beside her. It was an empty syringe, the one he'd used on her. Then she was suddenly fighting for breath. Her nose seemed blocked and she panted for air. She slumped face-down on to the floor, her mouth still open, her eyes gradually becoming lifeless.

3.01 p.m. – that afternoon . . .

ELIZABETH and Hoover had followed on down to Key West. The scene at the house had divided them completely, but contrary to what her husband was saying, Elizabeth knew she would stand a better chance of getting Peter back by handling things her own way and without any interference from the police. As they stood arguing in the kitchen, the telephone rang. Elizabeth answered it quickly.

'Yes?'

'Shelley's Service Station on the main highway. The call-box in twenty minutes.' The caller had Midwest origins. There was a pause for a moment, then he spoke again. 'Be there or else . . .' His threatening tone was enough for Elizabeth.

'I will,' she said firmly. The caller hung up.

She had no sooner replaced the receiver than Hoover restarted on her.

'So what did they say?'

'I've to go to a call-box.' She snatched the keys of her sports car off the kitchen table.

'You're not going anywhere until we've had a talk,' insisted Hoover.

'Oliver, I've no time for this!'

'I still say we call in the FBI,' insisted Hoover.

'No, Oliver, we could jeopardize Peter's safety if we do that. The message was very clear on that score,' replied Elizabeth.

'Elizabeth, a young woman has been murdered! Rosetta is missing! We can't conceal that from the police.'

'We have to, don't you see?' she said frantically.

'No, I don't!' He tried to grab hold of her but she pushed him away.

'Leave me alone!' she shouted. 'Look, the way the girl was left it looks like a drugs overdose or even suicide.'

'Is that all you think about? Your image?'

'Don't be ridiculous.' Elizabeth tried to control her temper. 'Oliver, we have to meet this thing on their terms.' She tried to reason with him.

'So what are their instructions?'

'That's my business, Oliver! Mine alone!' she insisted, picking up her bag and rushing out to the car before he could stop her.

Hoover watched the red Ferrari get booted through the gears as it disappeared up the winding driveway away from the house. Wiping the perspiration from his forehead, he returned inside and picked up the telephone. As he dialled the number, he stared through the glass doors towards the body now lying covered by a sheet on the conservatory floor. He averted his eyes as the telephone began to ring. ✔

'Yeah?' The man with the Midwest accent answered.

'She's just left,' Hoover said impassively.

'We'll be in touch.' The man hung up.

Elizabeth went to the service station on the highway as directed. She waited outside the telephone booth and checked her wristwatch. It was 3.23. The caller was late. She pulled back the folding door and picked up the receiver just to make sure it was working. It was. The glass booth was fusty and smelt of stale tobacco. She waited outside, shielding her eyes from the glare of the hot sun. Were they watching her? Was it some sort of a trap? Perhaps they wanted her as well? An articulated lorry appeared through the shimmering heat and drew up outside the service station. Two rough-looking men alighted from the cab and started to approach her. Panic seized her. All she could imagine was being taken herself. Elizabeth climbed inside the booth and closed the folding door, putting her back against it, her heart palpitating. To her amazement and relief, the two men simply walked past into the diner, ignoring her completely. As she breathed a sigh of relief the telephone started ringing. Elizabeth jumped at the sound. She let it ring several more times before plucking up the courage to answer it.

'Yes?' she said softly.

'Elizabeth O'Casey, I believe.' She recognized the man's voice but couldn't place it. There was a deep Germanic tone to it. 'Are you well?' the voice continued in English.

'Who is this?' The man had referred to her as Eamon's wife. Why?

'Why, I'm the man who killed Finn MacCool!' The caller laughed.

He had used Eamon O'Casey's codename. Elizabeth's blood turned almost to ice. 'Schiller!' At last, the rat had surfaced.

'You have something belonging to me, Mrs O'Casey. I want it back.'

'And will you return my son unharmed?'

'Your son?' She heard him chuckle. 'That is very good, very funny!'

'Schiller, don't play with me. Is he all right?'

'Of course he is.'

'What about my maid, Rosetta?' she persisted. 'Look, if it's money that you want, you can have it! All that I have.'

'I intend to, dear lady, but first of all I want back what is mine: "The Three Brothers".'

'And then what?'

'We will discuss that when we meet. Meanwhile, you should transfer at least one billion dollars into any one of your four Swiss bank accounts.'

'A billion! Where on earth would I raise that sort of money?'

'Your business empire, I am reliably informed, is worth three times that amount. Borrow it, if you must. You have just one week. Then we will speak again.'

'How? Where? How do I know you have Peter and that he's still alive?'

The line was dead.

Elizabeth knew there was only one man who could possibly help her now. After returning to the house, she placed a telephone call to

Vienna. She was surprised at the ease with which she was able to reach Simon Wiesenthal. Hoover listened at the door of the bedroom as Elizabeth spoke.

'Herr Wiesenthal? Thank God!'

'Mrs Goldmann.' He recognized her voice even over the long-distance cable.

'Something's happened. They've got my son.' She held back the tears.

'Don't say any more,' he cautioned. 'Are you in Florida?'

'Yes . . . but how did you . . .'

She was interrupted before she could finish.

'Stay exactly where you are. Someone will be with you very shortly. Do you understand me?'

'Yes . . . I . . .' She was lost for words.

'Trust me and just wait.' Then he was gone.

Elizabeth hung up and wiped the tears from her eyes. Only then did she realize that Hoover was standing in the doorway. 'Help is coming,' she said.

'What help?' he inquired. Elizabeth shook her head.

'He knew I was here,' she said absently.

It was a little after 5 p.m. when the helicopter soared in from the sea and hovered some three hundred feet above the house. Elizabeth reached the window just in time to see the two-seater Bell helicopter land in the gardens, close to the tennis court. As she walked out on to the terrace a lone figure had already emerged from the aircraft and was walking hurriedly towards her. The visitor was a tall man, grey-haired and seemingly in his fifties, but with an obvious agility, confirmed by the way he ascended the terrace steps three at a time. Elizabeth didn't recognize the man until he removed his sunglasses.

'Mrs Goldmann.' McClean gave her a reassuring smile. 'It's been a long time.'

CAFÉ ROYAL, LONDON
Wednesday, 6 April 1966

IT WAS NOT an easy task. Elizabeth started by asset-stripping what she could, quietly and efficiently. She had several parties interested in various aspects of the business. Inside three days she had secured just over five hundred million dollars, all of which was transferred into a Swiss bank, just as she had been told. Oliver Hoover had spent his time between the money markets in the Middle East, London and New York, borrowing heavily on the remaining corporation assets. It had taken much longer than anticipated. He had to be extremely careful not to create rumours of financial collapse for the entire business empire, and he wasn't all that successful in maintaining secrecy.

In London questions had been asked about the meaning of the borrowing and Oliver Hoover was fast running out of answers. The City's private banks were a tight-fisted bunch at the best of times and were acutely nervous about any fast dealing. They had their own pace; gentlemen didn't need to rush. That put Hoover at an instant disadvantage. Not only was he in a hurry but he was American to boot! He kept his luncheon appointment with Lord Hetherington, the chairman of Stroud and Sefton Merchant Bank, the largest private banking company in London.

The Englishman had chosen the Café Royal for the meeting. Oliver Hoover arrived some minutes late, which did nothing to improve his prospects. He was escorted by a waiter to one of the private dining rooms. The room was long, capable of seating up to forty people, but only a single table had been set. Just one man sat at the far end of the oak-panelled room. Charles Hetherington was reading the *Financial Times*.

'My lord.' The waiter was obviously used to his lordship's patronage. 'Mr Oliver Hoover, my lord.' The waiter looked disdainfully at Hoover before walking away. Charles Hetherington folded his paper but didn't rise. Instead, he extended his hand to his guest. 'Hoover, isn't it?'

'Oliver Hoover.' He offered his card to the Englishman.

'Please, sit down, Mr Hoover,' continued Lord Hetherington. Hoover sat down directly opposite him.

'I knew your old partner, Wendell Caldwell, very well. He was quite a character. His passing must have been a tragic loss to all of you on the New York exchange.'

'It was.'

The menus arrived seconds later, the waiter moving to a position just outside range of hearing yet attentive to every detail.

'I'd recommend the rainbow trout at this time of year – most succulent, the sauce is exquisite.'

Hoover played along, joining in the small talk, when suddenly, towards the end of the main course, the Englishman came straight to the point, somewhat bluntly. 'How much?'

'I beg your pardon?' Hoover set his fork back on the side of his plate, almost choking on a small fishbone.

Lord Hetherington dismissed the waiter. 'How much money are you needing?'

'Overall around half a billion US.'

'And you are looking for all of that from Stroud and Sefton?'

'I've just arrived from Tokyo. I can borrow an equivalent of around two hundred on collateral the corporation owns in the East.'

'So you're looking for another point three billion from us, right?' he mused. Hetherington had already known, of course. His Mid and Far East contacts had already briefed him thoroughly on the issue in advance of this meeting. With the war reaching new heights in Vietnam, the general unrest throughout the region and China's growing political power, some of the Goldmann interests in the Far East looked to be in jeopardy. Lord Hetherington liked to know who he was dealing with, especially their weaknesses. 'Just what's in this for us? What carrot can you offer besides payment of our high interest rates?'

'Carrots?' Hoover shook his head. 'The loan will be short-term, no more than four or six months. The corporation will sell off excess interests if need be to raise the sum for repayment.'

'Why not do that instead? Why all the rush?'

'The corporation has an option to complete by the end of this week. We lose it if we aren't in a position to buy at that time. Selling off our own assets will take time.'

'I heard you've already sold off almost half a billion on Wall Street, just a few days ago. That means you're getting together a billion-dollar package. What are you doing, Hoover, old man, buying Shell Mex and BP?'

'Then it wouldn't be British, would it?' Hoover was annoyed by the man's condescending tone.

'Sorry, old chap. I'll need to know a lot more about your business before I can put something like that to my board.'

Hoover sat forward. 'You know as well as I do, you could authorize three times the amount I'm after without going anywhere near your board of directors!' Hoover clenched the side of the table in frustration.

'Information, Mr Hoover, that's what I need. Then, when I'm satisfied I'm dealing with a solvent company, we'll discuss terms, and I don't mean interest levels. If I'm to give you what you need, we at Stroud and Sefton will want a "piece of the action", as you Americans say.'

'What piece?' inquired Hoover.

'The bank would want a seat on the board of the Elizabeth Goldmann Corporation, with a minimum five per cent share-holding.'

'Go to hell!' snarled Hoover.

'Hoover, think about it before you burn your bridges. Here's my card. You can get me at that private London number this evening.' He set a gold-rimmed card between the prongs of Hoover's fork. Then he stood up. The attentive waiter was over beside him instantly, drawing back his chair for him. 'Don't leave it too late, old boy. Ring me by ten o'clock if you are interested. Enjoy the rest of your meal. It's on me.' Then he strutted out, his military bearing still evident after almost forty years in banking. Oliver Hoover threw his napkin across his plate, he'd just lost his appetite.

MAYFAIR
That night . . .

IAN COLERIDGE had been keeping a close eye on Hoover since his arrival in London. He used his family relationship with Charles Hetherington to get himself access to the American's dealings. He called at his cousin's town house late that night. He knew Hetherington did not approve of his 'seedy profession', as he so often referred to it. The man had offered him several jobs in the City and Ian's flat refusal had only enhanced his older cousin's determination to succeed.

The doorbell rang twice before the elderly butler let Coleridge in. 'Mr Ian, so good to see you again.'

'Crozier, how are you?' He patted the old butler on the arm.

'Well, sir, well. His lordship is in the drawing room, awaiting you. You should go right in.'

'Thank you.' Coleridge headed for the massive Georgian drawing room. Charles Hetherington was sitting in a wing-backed library chair beside a roaring fire, flicking his way though an Ian Fleming novel.

'Ian, dear chap. How wonderful to see you again. Come over here and warm yourself.' He stood up, shaking his cousin's hand. 'You look tired,' he commented.

'The hours.' Coleridge managed a smile.

'The hours don't seem to matter to this fellow – ' he waved the book at him – 'James Bond, now there's a man for you.' He laughed.

'Since when have you taken to reading spy stories?'

'Tell me, Ian, is it really like that?' The clock on the mantelpiece struck ten o'clock. Charles Hetherington sighed. He had misjudged the American after all.

'Of course it is. I'm only in it for the girls and fast cars.'

'I suppose you're still driving that old Riley?'

'You mean Betsie. Actually she's parked outside.'

'Whatever will the neighbours say!' exclaimed Charles.

'I'm adding colour to the neighbourhood,' insisted Coleridge.

Charles Hetherington tossed aside his book. 'Brandy all right?' he asked, going across to the George I bureau and unlocking it.

'Your good health.' He handed a large glass to his cousin.

'Cheers,' replied Coleridge, sipping the Napoleon brandy.

'Tell me, Ian, how is Grace these days? Is she still living with that fellow?'

'I'd rather not talk about that if you don't mind.' Ian Coleridge downed his brandy more out of necessity than enjoyment. He was still smarting from his short but very fast-paced marriage to a young débutante from Oxfordshire. She had left him after just sixteen months, having run off with an out-of-work musician.

'Quite! Drink up and I'll fix us another. You'll stay for a little light supper, won't you?' He pulled the rope at the left side of the Adam fireplace, taking it for granted that he would. 'I had the most frightful luncheon today at the Café Royal.'

'Food bad?'

'No, it was the company! An American.'

The door opened again, 'Ah, Crozier, the Major will be staying for supper. Have Cook throw together some of that smoked salmon she got yesterday, perhaps a salad too.'

'Very good, my lord.'

The telephone rang on the desk beside the curtained window. Charles Hetherington checked his watch against the mantel clock. It was five minutes past the hour. Coleridge went over to the cocktail cabinet and began to pour two more brandies. He swilled one around in his hand as his cousin answered the telephone.

'Speak,' Hetherington snapped, listening to the caller for a moment. 'Yes, Mr Hoover, have you reached a decision?' Another pause. Coleridge noted his cousin's lips curling at the edges. It was clearly news to his advantage. 'Excellent. That's five per cent on the board and a borrowing at the fixed-term rate over three months.' There was another short period of silence before he spoke again. 'Very well, Mr Hoover, I will agree to stretch to six months for an extra per cent on the borrowing. Have the papers drawn up and delivered to my office first thing in the morning. I can sign by the afternoon and instruct the release of funds by closing tomorrow.' He listened again, turning as Coleridge handed him his brandy. 'Thank you and good night to you.' He replaced the ivory-handled receiver back on its stand.

'Oliver Hoover wants money?' commented Coleridge, sitting down on one of the two library chairs beside the fire.

'So that is the reason for your visit.' Charles Hetherington rounded on him immediately. 'What is it? What's he done?'

'Nothing yet,' insisted Coleridge. 'Charles, will you do me a favour? After the transaction, would you be so kind as to furnish me with all the details of this deal? It's a matter of national security, I assure you.'

'Is the bank risking exposure?'

'No. From what I know about the Goldmann Corporation, they have more than enough assets to cover any losses.' He raised his glass to his cousin. 'Cheers.'

THE PLANTATION HOUSE, HAITI
Evening, Wednesday 6 April 1966

THE *Lady Christina* had brought Peter to the quiet peninsular property in the northern region of Haiti. The small plantation was perfect. The only access was by sea, the rest of the four-hundred-acre property being surrounded on all sides by dense swampland. The yacht was moored in the deep water of the quiet bay below the main plantation house. Schiller looked down over the moonlit water as he sat relaxing on the terrace. He was eventually joined by a man in a white coat.

405

'Herr Renan, I think you should know that the young man is coming round now,' said the doctor. 'As we slowly reduce the effects of the drugs, his memory will return. It is entirely dependent on how quickly you wish his memory to be restored.'

Schiller rose without saying a word and followed him back inside. Peter was sitting on a large leather sofa, his head propped to one side, resting on his shoulder. Schiller went over to him, drawing up a chair and sitting opposite, just a couple of feet away.

'How are you feeling?' he asked in a soothing tone.

'Who are you? Where am I?' Peter tried to peer through the blur. His eyes could still not focus properly. His head throbbed with pain. A shadow passed across him and then a voice cut through his jumbled thoughts as someone flashed a bright light into one of his eyes.

'He's OK.' The doctor flicked off his pencil torch again and stepped back.

'Peter?' Schiller stroked his shoulder.

'Where am I?' repeated Peter.

'All will be revealed,' replied Schiller. 'Sleep some more. You will see much more clearly in the morning.'

Peter felt a hand patting him gently on the arm. As he began to drift off again, he heard the same voice, now using a tough, demanding tone and speaking in German. Then Peter drifted away to a softer, more comfortable plain.

The next morning Peter was shown into the same room after showering and shaving with a battery razor – they had denied him any razor blades for some reason. The room was bright and cheery, with the pale sky showing between the fluttering white curtains. He walked to the french windows and out on to a balcony, looking out over lush tropical vegetation and the bluest sea he had ever seen. He stared down into a crystal-clear bay, secluded and without any sign of human life. The large yacht he thought he'd remembered seeing the day before had gone now. Out to sea the morning's mist obliterated everything beyond the three-mile marker. Somewhere in the distance a foghorn burst forth intermittently. Gazing up, he saw he was on a hillside. Above, the mountains were blanked out by a heavy, swirling mist which, like some massive gas cloud, was slowly creeping down to meet the sea.

'Good morning!' The voice startled him. Peter turned. He had been so busy studying his new surroundings that he hadn't heard anyone approach. The man appeared to be in his fifties, with greying stubbly hair. He was tall and muscular with a black leather patch over his left eye. The skin around the left side of his face was wizened and twisted, obviously the result of burns at some time in the past. As the man approached him, Peter noticed that he had a slight limp and he held his left arm in a permanently bent position, his hand gloved.

'Who are you?' asked Peter.

'My name is Schiller.' The man smiled and stepped forward to shake Peter's hand.

Peter ignored the handshake. 'Listen, I don't know who you are or how I got here.' Peter shook his head. He felt very confused. 'I'm not even sure of just who I am.'

'Pieter, my dear boy, don't you remember? You had a most terrible accident. You had severe concussion. That is why you cannot recall.' Schiller patted him on the shoulder. 'Time is a great healer. The doctors say you will make a full recovery.'

Peter rubbed his eyes. 'You haven't answered my question, sir. Where am I?'

'You're in the Republic of Haiti,' replied Schiller.

'Why am I here?' insisted Peter.

'For your own protection, Pieter. There are those who would want to cause you harm.'

'Why?' he demanded to know.

'Do you remember the name Elizabeth Goldmann?' Schiller pushed him a little.

'My . . . my mother.' His memory was hazy. 'She's my mother,' he said anxiously. 'We live in Long Island. No, come to think of it, the house was somewhere else.' He shook his head. What the hell had happened to him? 'Have you kidnapped me?' he demanded.

'No, not kidnapped. Rescued,' Schiller assured him. 'Elizabeth Goldmann is not your real mother.'

'What the hell do you mean?' growled Peter, his blue eyes sparking with fresh energy. For a moment Schiller started to think that the young man was too strong-willed to allow the drugs to suppress his conscious mind.

Schiller faked his shock. 'My, my, did she never tell you? Tell you about your real mother and father?'

'What are you talking about? Did you know my mother and father? Who were they? I want to know about them! I want to understand!' He was becoming excited.

'In due course.' Schiller laughed. 'For the moment accept that Elizabeth Goldmann is not your mother, and nor is any Irishman your father.'

407

Peter stepped back from him slightly. 'Has this anything to do with a tie-pin?' he asked cautiously, not sure why he'd even said it.

'Come. Come inside. We shall get some breakfast.' Schiller went indoors, followed slowly by Peter. 'Now, what's all this about a tie-pin?'

'A gold tie-pin, with a swastika,' Peter replied slowly as he sat down at the breakfast table opposite Schiller. 'It was found in a canvas bag my mother – ' Peter paused upon using the word 'mother' again – 'my mother brought with me to Dublin during 1945!'

'Indeed.' Schiller broke into a knowing smile. 'I wondered where my tie-pin went to all those years ago.' He laughed, putting his hand in his pocket. 'Here, one of my men recovered it from your bedroom.' He produced the gold tie-pin, setting it on the table in front of Peter. 'Have you any idea of the history behind it?'

Peter looked down at the gold pin, the German eagle with the swastika underneath. He vaguely remembered being told something about it. Why could he not recall?

'It was presented to me personally by Adolf Hitler,' Schiller said proudly. 'A great moment for me. It seemed appropriate that I should pin it on you all those years ago.'

'You are my father?' Peter's face contorted.

'No, Pieter. Proud as I would be to have you as my son, alas I am not.' He smiled at him. 'I am going away for a few days. When I return, you will see exactly what I am talking about.'

'And in the meantime I remain a prisoner here?' snapped Peter.

Schiller handed him a bread basket. 'In time you will learn, my boy. Your privilege is much greater than you could ever have imagined, even in your wildest dreams.' Schiller smiled at him. 'Now try some of the sesame toast. I can thoroughly recommend it.'

KEY WEST, FLORIDA KEYS
4.02 p.m., Saturday, 9 April

THE TELEPHONE rang three times before Elizabeth had the courage to answer. The crowded room fell still as she lifted the receiver.

'Yes?' she said tentatively.

'How good it is to hear your sweet voice again.' Elizabeth shivered upon hearing his voice again. Sarcasm was evident in Schiller's tone. Elizabeth looked over at the slow-winding spool of the tape-recorder beside her.

'Is my son all right?' She followed the procedure exactly as McClean had told her.

'Pieter is in good health and amongst friends.'

'Schiller, if he is injured in any way, the deal is void,' she insisted.

'You look even better than I remember,' he said, and her blood turned to ice.

She looked up at McClean. The Scotsman shrugged his shoulders. 'What do you want from me?' Elizabeth forced herself to maintain control.

'You have some nerve, I'll grant you that, my dear,' Schiller said coldly. A dreadful silence followed.

'Are you still there?' She spoke in a very low voice. There was no reply. 'Hello?'

'All right,' continued Schiller. 'If we can keep some restraint in this conversation, the better it will be for you.'

'I was reading about you in *Flair* magazine,' he continued. 'It was very graphic. You clearly have made quite a few enemies in America.'

'And you are no exception,' she added, getting a laugh from him.

'To business. My associates confirm that one billion US dollars have been deposited in your number three Swiss bank account. That is very good. I am pleased to see that you acted wisely in this matter.'

'The money will be transferred to you once Peter is set free.' She was reading from the notes McClean had given her.

'The money must be transferred first,' insisted Schiller.

'Very well.' She looked up at the other faces. 'And what do you suggest?' she added. There was silence again. It was as if someone else was speaking to Schiller. A faint whisper could be heard on the crackling line.

'Here is what you must do. You will instruct your Swiss bankers to purchase gold on the market to the tune of one billion dollars. This must be completed immediately. The gold bullion should then be transported to Key West.'

'I . . . I don't know. It will take some time to organize.'

'Don't try and mess about with me!' Schiller raised his voice menacingly. 'You will do exactly as you are told and get it, down to the very last pfennig's worth. Do you understand me?'

'Yes, I understand.'

'I have two more stipulations,' he went on. 'You will purchase a

409

boat, a large fishing trawler, one of the commercial kind, adequate to carry the gold. The boat will be loaded at Key West, at the old boatyard there.'

'Where?' She played for time.

'Just do it,' he insisted.

'Very well,' she said obediently. 'You said you had two stipulations.'

'So I did.' He chuckled again. 'Can't you guess?' He was playing with her.

'"The Three Brothers"?' She felt crushed.

'Ten out of ten.'

'Agreed.' She swallowed hard.

'You have exactly four days in which to carry out my instructions.'

'Four days! You can't be serious!' Elizabeth protested.

'If you think we are not serious, have a look on your private beach.' The telephone line went dead.

Elizabeth flicked the button several times but it was no use. The Mossad engineer shook his head and switched off the tape-recorder. 'We've lost him.'

Hoover reached over and comforted Elizabeth. 'You did well.'

'Is there any way of telling where that call was made from?' she asked.

The Israeli engineer shook his head for a second time. 'He could have been anywhere, from Tijuana to Argentina.'

Nico Giovanni flew out of the room, followed by McClean. Both men drew their guns as they followed the path through the palm trees towards the private beach. The golden sands lay deserted apart from a small, white cardboard box sitting on top of a large boulder, just beyond the high-tide mark. It was tied with red ribbon, of all things. McClean checked the area first, in case whoever had set it there was still hanging around. The place was deserted. He looked out to sea. There wasn't a vessel in sight, although he knew one could have been hiding amidst the myriad tiny islands scattered around the Keys.

'I was swimming here just an hour ago,' said Nico. 'How the hell did they put it here?' He looked around, through the trees and across the shrubs and low-lying vegetation. Whoever had left it would have had to pass through the immediate grounds of the house if they'd approached from inland.

McClean circled the four-foot-high granite boulder. The ebbing tide had receded, removing any tracks left in the soft sand. But at the bottom edge of the rock a small section of dry sand had remained unaffected. The scuffmarks of a flipper were still evident. 'Here's your answer!' shouted McClean, replacing his 9mm Beretta in the waist-band of his trousers.

'A boat?' Nico ran over to him.

'Scuba-divers,' answered McClean.

Nico raised an eyebrow as he stared out across the glistening sea. 'The bastards could even be watching us right now.'

'Would you care to do the honours?' McClean motioned towards the ribboned box.

Gingerly, Nico approached the boulder. He looked back at McClean, who shrugged. Casting caution aside, he undid the red ribbon. Then, lifting the lid, he quickly stepped back. 'Well, it didn't blow up!' He tried to hide his fear. Stepping forward again, he peered over the rim and looked at the contents. McClean watched as the man turned away, doubling over as he started to retch.

Hoover followed Elizabeth out on to the terrace as they waited for McClean and Nico to return from the beach. 'We'll get Peter back, if it's the last thing we do,' he said softly.

'I don't know any more.' She stared at him. 'Before that call I would have said yes, but now . . .' She shook her head. 'You had better contact Switzerland and start the purchase of the gold.'

'OK. We'll play their game,' agreed Hoover.

Nico appeared at the top of the path. She stared at the cardboard box he was carrying. 'It's a hand,' he said bluntly. Elizabeth's heart raced, imagining Peter's hand inside. 'Oh, dear God! Is it Peter?' she cried.

'It's not Peter's,' Nico Giovanni assured her. 'But maybe you'd have an idea.' He looked at Hoover.

As McClean consoled Elizabeth, Oliver Hoover reluctantly went aside with Nico and examined the box for himself. He recognized the gold ring on the blackened middle finger. It had been a present from Elizabeth. He fought back the terrible urge to be sick as he returned to his wife's side.

'Oliver?' she asked hesitantly.

He squeezed her hands in his. 'It's our maid, Rosetta. They've just returned her right hand.'

Elizabeth cried out before rushing back inside the house, heading directly for the sanctuary of her bedroom. Nico watched how Hoover reacted. He had a guilty look about him as he followed his wife into the house.

Nico drew McClean aside. 'These neo-Nazi bums seem to know our every move.'

'You think there's an inside plant?' suggested McClean.

'I mean Hoover himself.' Nico deliberately kept his voice low. 'I

411

heard it on the street that he was compromised with a hooker in some two-bit sleaze joint in South Queens. These guys took a lot of saucy snapshots.'

'You know who they were?'

'No, but I can guess,' Nico said confidently. 'You only take shots like that when you want something.'

'Like what?' inquired McClean.

'Like everything that we do here.' He handed McClean the box, much to the Scotsman's disgust.

Hoover left for Europe that night. Three days later the gold arrived in Miami, kept under guard at one of the main banks while they awaited further contact with the Nazis. Hoover's job on the Continent was now at an end. He rejoined the others at Key West, more than a little bemused to find a number of Nico's 'family' now guarding the house at Key West.

THE OLD BOATYARD, KEY WEST
2.17 a.m., Wednesday, 13 April 1966

McCLEAN approached Elizabeth on the flood-lit quayside. She was standing at the edge of the old dock, watching the trawler being loaded with provisions. 'Mrs Goldmann, I think we should talk.'

'About the weather?' she replied coyly.

'Please don't play games with me. I know you've been hunting for Schiller for quite a while now.' McClean's eyes widened. 'Why?'

'That is between myself and Schiller.' Elizabeth dismissed the question.

'Not any more. People have already died because of whatever it is between you two.'

'I can't help you, Mr McClean.' Elizabeth went to leave.

McClean reached out and grasped her arm. 'Have you ever heard of "Nemesis"?'

'She's the Greek goddess of retribution, isn't she?' Elizabeth looked surprised.

'And vengeance,' added McClean. 'It's also the name of an ultra-secret neo-Nazi group led by Schiller and some others.'

'Really?'

'I think you've something belonging to "Nemesis". Your first

412

husband, Eamon O'Casey, seemed to be the link. At first I reckoned it was stolen Reichsbank gold bullion. Then there was the issue of the jewels you used to develop the Costello Construction Corporation.' He paused a moment.

'Please go on,' Elizabeth replied, nervously withdrawing her arm from his grasp.

'But it's something much more tangible than that, isn't it?' He searched her face. She was hiding something all right. Elizabeth remained silent and unresponsive. 'You came to the States with your son Peter. He was only a month or so old, isn't that right?'

'Mr McClean, I agreed to help you in the hope that you could help me understand why these madmen are hell-bent on destroying everything I have ever striven for. But now you're speaking in riddles.' She went to leave, but McClean gripped her firmly by the arm this time.

'You're hurting me!' she snapped, raising her voice just enough to draw the attention of some of the workmen.

'Listen to me a second!' pleaded McClean, his eyes ablaze. 'Just supposing these neo-Nazis are serious about doing something other than avoiding a hangman's noose and dying of old age. Just supposing they need some sort of a figurehead, a rallying point for their minions, giving their cause some purpose again. What then?'

'McClean, you make no sense!' Elizabeth pulled back.

'Peter isn't your natural son, is he?'

'Now you are insulting. Leave me alone!' Elizabeth strode off. He followed her. 'I told you, go away!' she shouted again.

'What if Peter is actually Adolf Hitler's son? His flesh and blood! Think about that!' He headed off down the dock.

Elizabeth watched him walk away. Stunned by his frankness and audacity, she was by now trembling. She had always blotted out Peter's origins, accepting him as God's gift in recompense for her great losses. Yes, she knew him to have been undoubtedly German and probably the son of some high-ranking official, but Hitler? The suggestion was preposterous! Or was it?

Two American Express security lorries trundled into the dock, their headlights blazing and hazard warning lights flashing. They were flanked on either side by armed motorcycle escorts and followed closely by a vanload of security guards. The lorries drove slowly up alongside the boat and stopped.

Elizabeth returned to her car and got in, watching the first crates being hoisted aboard the trawler and lowered slowly into the main hold. By now the entire dockside was crawling with security guards and Nico's men. She knew that she was stuck there for the duration of the loading operation. Even if she'd wanted to, she couldn't get out of the place. Her head thumped and her neck felt as stiff as a poker.

McClean had got right through her mental defences. She kept going over and over again in her mind all the mannerisms that Peter had adopted. She thought back to his early stages of development. The first steps he had taken for himself. The first time he had called her name. The day he had cut his knee in the park. The tantrums and moods. Could this child have been the offspring of such a monster? Hitler had been a sick man, she had read that much. Towards the latter part of his life the man had been dependent on a variety of drugs. There had even been the suggestion by several learned sources that he was impotent. One even suggested that he had lost a testicle, the result of his injuries in the trenches during the First World War.

Yes, Peter indeed had dark hair and piercing pale-blue eyes, but so did a thousand children she could pick out in any one state in the Union. Yes, he had his moods, was quick-tempered and had an incredibly high IQ, but so had she. He could easily have picked up his intemperate habits from her own behaviour, and as for his IQ, she rightly or wrongly believed that her own influence in his early development and the proper schooling had much to do with bringing out the best in him. How dare this man McClean suggest such a thing! Who gave him the right? Yet why would he say it? What had he to gain? What if he was right? Elizabeth's heart pounded. She felt as if her chest was about to explode. If he was right, what did it mean? Was Peter in danger or was he going to be hailed as the new saviour of National Socialism? Would her own people even allow him to live? The Israeli government had proved itself unrelenting in pursuit of these Nazis. What if Peter suddenly represented some sort of threat to Israel's existence, what then? She looked up. McClean was leaning against the side of the car.

'I suppose I owe you an apology,' he said.

'Forget that.' She paused. 'Look, we must speak.'

'Shoot.' He got into the car beside her.

'Have you any evidence to support your suggestion about my son?' she asked firmly.

'Not exactly.' McClean eased himself back in the seat. 'I can tell you that a baby was taken out of Berlin just before the Russians seized the city. The child was then transferred to a U-boat in Kiel.'

Elizabeth sighed. 'Peter came from that U-boat.'

'I thought as much.' McClean sat forward. 'That would be the same one you told Herr Wiesenthal about when you saw him in New York originally.'

'Yes.' She rubbed her tired eyes, no longer surprised at his intimate knowledge. 'And Schiller was on board.'

'You spoke to him?'

'Yes.' Elizabeth shook her head, trying to dislodge the memory of their confrontation in the Irish farmhouse.

'Eamon was a brave man,' said McClean comfortingly. 'The best double-agent we had. German Intelligence believed he was working for them, but all the time he kept his allegiance to us. I'll never understand how he managed to get away with it for so long.'

'His real allegiance was to Ireland,' Elizabeth corrected him.

'We knew that. That wasn't a problem for us. It was something I'd have expected from a man of his principles.'

'And how would you have handled it if he had lived?'

'We would probably have been on separate sides, he and I. Our common enemy would have been defeated and in my line of work you've always got to have an enemy of some sort or other.'

'But you're no longer with British Intelligence?' she inquired.

'We didn't see eye to eye. The Israelis made me an offer I just couldn't refuse.' He smiled back.

'And so you've been hunting these war criminals ever since?'

'Yes. The difficulty being that until just recently I didn't have the evidence to prove Schiller and company were in fact still alive.'

'What makes you so certain about Peter?'

'I'm not, but I'm backing a hunch.' He looked at her, praying he was wrong.

KEY WEST, FLORIDA KEYS
2.00 p.m.

TWELVE hours later Elizabeth received a further call at the house.
'Yes,' she answered, trying to remain calm.

'I'm glad to see that you are, what do they say, "playing the game".' Schiller's voice made her tremble.

'What have we to do now?' She no longer wanted to mince words with this creature. He'd won. All she wanted was her child back again.

'Put on your husband. He will understand what I am about to say,' insisted Schiller.

415

'Oliver.' He took the receiver from her. McClean watched as the perspiration began to trickle down Hoover's neck.

'Yes?' Hoover fidgeted nervously with the telephone.

'You have the vessel loaded up?' continued Schiller.

'Yes, everything is ready,' he replied.

'Good. Now listen carefully, as an ex-naval officer you will understand what I am about to tell you. You are to set sail from Miami following a southerly course on the co-ordinates that I am about to give you and you will keep an open radio channel as follows . . .' Hoover started scribbling down the information, not that it was absolutely necessary, with the tape-recorder still running as always.

Nico motioned McClean to step outside. They walked around the pool, considering their options. 'I knew something like this would happen.' The little Italian sounded pleased with himself. 'It could be their biggest mistake.'

'I've received fresh orders from Tel Aviv. They won't sanction a military operation so close to United States territory.'

'So what are ya trying to say, McClean?' Nico glared back at him.

'They won't give me the muscle I need.'

'I've got muscle, plenty. I can put two hundred soldiers on the streets of New York in one hour. Give me the target and we'll take these bastards out for nuthin'!'

'Just for the kicks?' McClean smiled.

'Something like that,' agreed Nico.

'I've got to warn you, these people are professionals. They don't mess about.' McClean was sceptical about Nico's commitment.

A switchblade flicked up in front of his face, barely an inch from his nose. 'We'll carve 'em up like pigs!' Nico grinned back at him.

'You know, I think you've just convinced me.' McClean capitulated.

THE OLD BOATYARD, KEY WEST
10.30 p.m.

THE SEVENTY-FOOT trawler was called the *Dolphin*. The chartered vessel was perfect for what they wanted: slow enough to be easily paced and big enough to take aboard the precious cargo of gold bullion. The trawler had been in dry dock throughout the winter, whilst having a complete overhaul. It came without a crew, which

416

presented a slight problem for Hoover. He didn't relish the idea of heading out to sea into an unknown situation with a bunch of amateurs. To placate him, Nico contacted his Miami 'cousins' and procured four sailors, all with 'family' connections.

The crew list was finally decided late that night. Elizabeth returned to the docks, dressed in a pair of jeans and a sweat-shirt. She came aboard the boat carrying a small holdall, clearly ready to stay a while. McClean braced himself for what he knew would be a confrontational meeting. They all sat at the dining table amidst the cramped confines of the boat's galley to discuss the matter.

Nico Giovanni sat on one side of the table beside David, the Mossad communications expert who had been monitoring the telephone calls. Hoover sat opposite them, with his invited guest, a tubby man in his fifties, on one side and Elizabeth on the other. McClean squeezed in next to Nico as Oliver Hoover opened the discussion by introducing the stranger as his old navy pal, Jimmy Drexel. It raised a few eyebrows, but McClean had to concede that, with his navigation ability, the man was a necessity. With the four sailors from Miami, Drexel and himself, Hoover was quick to announce that there was room for only two more. McClean stated that David would not be joining them, as his contribution was no longer necessary, and the explanation seemed to suffice. Elizabeth could readily see what was coming – with Nico and McClean added to the crew list, she was being deliberately excluded.

'I insist upon coming,' Elizabth said.

'Honey, it's out of the question. We haven't the room,' replied Hoover.

'It's my gold. I have the right,' she insisted.

'The lady's got a point there,' Nico said.

'You keep out of this,' snorted Hoover.

'You gonna make me?' retorted Nico threateningly.

'Maybe I just will at that!' Hoover jumped up and leaned across the table. The blood drained from his head as he felt the glinting point of the stiletto pricking the underside of his chin.

'Careful, or I might just pick you with it,' said Nico in a low tone.

'Stop it! Stop it, both of you!' cried Elizabeth, slamming the table with both hands.

'Put it away,' whispered McClean, before turning his attention to Hoover. 'And you sit down.' Hoover didn't need to be asked twice. 'Before this goes any further, I want to say something,' insisted McClean. There was silence from around the table. He directed himself specifically at Elizabeth as he continued. 'This is going to be no picnic. None of us knows exactly what we're getting into. Now, the crew are essential, and I have to agree that Mr Drexel here falls into that category. As for the rest of us, this isn't a large vessel. There's only limited sleeping and living accommodation. Now, I'm going because I have to, it's my job.'

'An' I'm going to keep him company,' Nico piped up.

'And I'm not?' said Elizabeth.

'Everyone on this boat will have a job to do. You don't.' McClean tried to be as gentle as he could with her. 'Your job is here.'

'You are forgetting one thing. It is my son out there. Furthermore, Schiller wants the jewels. I'm not handing them over to anyone else.' McClean shook his head. 'McClean, I paid for the charter of this vessel, I have the right!'

McClean looked across at Nico. The little Italian nodded reluctantly. 'Very well,' McClean capitulated.

'I object!' interrupted Hoover.

'She's going!' McClean shouted him down as he pointed his finger at Elizabeth. 'But understand one thing, Mrs Goldmann, this is going to be run as a military operation. Out there you take orders, not give 'em.'

'Agreed.' Elizabeth smiled for the first time in days.

'We'll leave just before dawn,' decreed McClean.

12.05 a.m., Thursday, 14 April 1966

THE NIGHT went by slowly for everyone. Nico waited up on deck for the arrival of the four men from Miami. He sat with his back against the wheelhouse, staring up at the stars, when his attention was caught by Hoover emerging from the crew quarters. It wasn't until Hoover was at the gangway that he realized Nico was watching him.

'So there you are.' He tried to sound casual.

'Goin' somewhere?' asked Nico suspiciously.

'The ship's chandlers at the end of the dock,' he said, a little too nervously for the Italian to accept as natural.

'But it's after midnight.'

'I've a new VHF radio to collect. Any objection?' he asked sarcastically. Nico remained silent. Hoover took a step forward, raising his voice. 'What's wrong? Don't you trust me or something?'

'What's wrong here?' McClean came up the gangway past two armed security guards.

'I'm being questioned by this idiot like some common criminal, that's what's wrong!' shouted Hoover.

'Take it easy,' insisted McClean.

'I was just askin' where the guy was goin',' said Nico.

'So where are you going?' asked McClean.

'You too!' Hoover glowered back. 'I'm going to the chandlers' office to pick up a radio, special delivery from the suppliers at Fort Lauderdale. They are staying open specially for that reason and if you don't believe me, come along and see for yourself.'

'OK, OK.' McClean raised his hands in surrender. 'I'm sorry, I guess we're all just a little on edge.'

'You can say that again.' Hoover glared at Nico before disappearing down the gangway.

'Can you two not bury the hatchet?' McClean sat down beside the Italian.

'Oh, I've no problem buryin' it.' Nico grinned, standing up to get a better view of Hoover walking off down the quayside. 'In him.'

'Once he's on the boat he can't be of any more value to them.'

'"Big George" Francetti's taking my place on the *Dolphin*. He's old but he's as strong as an ox. His job will be to look after Elizabeth. You can rely on him. He'll be arriving with the boys from Miami just before you sail.'

'What about the weapons?' asked McClean.

'They're bringing the "hardware" with them.'

'Good.'

'Look, if I don't get a chance again to say it, I wish you luck.' They shook hands.

'We'll need it,' McClean said, and of that he was certain.

'Now, if you'll excuse me, our pal Hoover might get lonely by himself.' Nico hurried down the wooden gangway and off into the darkness after Hoover.

The manager of the chandlers' was delighted to see Hoover arrive. It was well past his bedtime and the merchandise had arrived over an hour previously. Hoover paid cash for the radio, checking inside its box before accepting it. To the manager's further annoyance, he had to wait while his customer used the payphone. Hoover kept his voice low and his back turned to the elderly shop manager as he spoke.

'We're leaving around dawn.' He listened for a few moments. 'She's going too and so is Giovanni.' At the far end of the shop the manager publicized his frustration by deliberately rattling the door as he drew down the roller blind in readiness to close up. Hoover strained to hear the question. 'I've only seen two guns so far. McClean has one and so has Giovanni.' Another pause. 'Wait a minute!' He raised his voice, lowering it again as he continued. 'I don't care about me, but I don't want my wife to come to any harm, is that understood?' Silence this time. 'Do you hear me? Hello?' Somewhere between his last two questions the man had hung up. Hoover stared at the receiver in his hand. For a moment he was tempted to redial, then the manager made up his mind for him.

'Hey, mister, you finished yet?'

'Yes.' Hoover replaced the receiver and started walking towards the door.

'Ain't you forgettin' somethin', mister?'

It was only then that Hoover realized the precious radio was still sitting on the counter. He went back, picked it up and hurried from the premises. Nico emerged from the shadows of the adjacent alleyway. He'd seen everything that had gone on inside the brightly lit chandlers' store.

4.09 a.m.

'BIG GEORGE' Francetti and four other men arrived in a stretched limousine. The security guards were all dispatched by McClean and the Mafia 'soldiers' proceeded to come aboard. Hoover watched in amazement as the guns and ammunition were loaded from the limousine's truck. Apart from a .303 heavy machine-gun he counted at least a dozen French-made Mat49 sub-machine-guns and four cases of ammunition.

Minutes later they cast off, with Drexel taking the wheel. Hoover walked the length of the trawler before realizing Nico was not aboard. After checking below deck, he rushed up into the wheelhouse. Elizabeth was standing next to Drexel as he slowly steered the boat away from the quay.

420

'I can't find Giovanni,' said Hoover, a hint of panic in his voice.

'I heard McClean say he was staying behind,' replied Drexel. He glanced over at his old friend. He'd known him long enough to realize that something was troubling him. 'Say, everything OK?'

Hoover was silent.

'Oliver?' inquired Elizabeth.

'Excuse me, I've got to plot our course,' he said, immediately disappearing below deck again.

'I wonder what's the matter with Oliver?' Elizabeth looked over at Drexel, who shrugged. 'And Nico didn't even say goodbye,' she added.

The words were lost on Jimmy Drexel. He had other things on his mind, the most important of which was to finish a fight he and the other guys on the USS *Cheyenne* had started twenty-one years ago. He wasn't going to miss this for the world!

Elizabeth stared out to the open sea beyond the coastguard station. The die had been cast. There could be no turning back now. The only way was forward, and straight into the mouth of hell.

They headed due east until outside territorial waters. As they cleared the fifty-mile limit, Drexel climbed up on top of the bridge housing and tied the flag to the side of the radar housing. Oliver Hoover looked out of the wheelhouse and eyed the little emblem fluttering furiously in the sea breeze as the boat cut steadily through the waves at twelve knots. Jimmy Drexel had hoisted the USS *Cheyenne*'s personally adapted battle flag, a bear rampant on a background of red, white and blue. It had been one of Abe Charles's ideas to boost morale when things were at a low ebb aboard the *Cheyenne*. He'd got the idea from a story he'd read about Teddy Roosevelt. Little did the old fool know that his moral-boosting exercise was at long last about to have material consequences.

PART SEVEN

'Flesh from my Flesh'

'At last, here is one of my own kind –
Bone taken from my bone, and flesh from my flesh.'

Genesis 2: 23

THE PLANTATION HOUSE, HAITI
7.15 a.m., Thursday, 14 April 1966

PETER AWOKE to find the doctor standing over him again, checking his pulse and respiratory system. As the man moved away from the bed Peter sat up, supporting himself on his left elbow. The sharp pain he felt in his armpit was momentary. When the doctor had left the room, Peter drew back his unbuttoned pyjamas and examined himself. There was a little bruising around the muscle but apart from that he could feel nothing else. He looked again. At first he thought it was a mosquito bite, then he realized he was staring at a needle mark.

After showering in the adjoining bathroom, he declined breakfast, quickly getting dressed into the bush shirt and corduroys that had been left out for him. He passed the man called Roland Kruse as he headed down the road towards the shore. Kruse was standing talking to one of the security guards. The guard walked off as Peter approached, slinging his Armalite rifle across his shoulder.

'Good morning, Pieter. Did you have a pleasant night's sleep?' asked Strassmann.

'Yes, thank you, Herr Kruse,' replied Peter. He had met the man just once before, the day he arrived in the small aircraft, landing by the aid of its floats just inside the calm bay below the plantation house. His recollection was hazy. Peter looked into the man's steely-grey eyes, a little unsure of what he saw. Was it adulation? He dismissed the idea as preposterous.

'You are going to the shore?' Strassmann continued. 'Don't stray too far along. The bay is perfectly safe, but the rocks at the point can be a bit tricky – tides and the occasional high wave. You could get pulled in very easily.'

'Thanks for the advice.' Peter dismissed the man's comment and strode on down the road. As he rounded the bend towards the bottom, he glanced back. The man was still watching him. Strassmann waved. Peter ignored him and walked on. He thought about his position as he walked on to the soft white sand. The man called Schiller hadn't been around for the last day – apparently he had had to go to Port-au-Prince on business. Peter had accepted it without question. He knew he should do nothing to interfere with his position at least for the present. His head still felt fuzzy and his memory was only coming back faintly. He kept seeing the same image in his mind:

Elizabeth's face, angry and then compassionate, and something else. It was a swimming pool. He could see the water reflecting up on to a ceiling or something. A man or someone was standing over him. He could hear a girl's voice faintly, then nothing. He shook his head, treading on to the damp sand as the waves withdrew and scooping some of the salt water up on to his face.

He stopped, staring out at the small powerboat circling the edge of the bay, before walking round the crescent-moon-shaped beach. They were watching him! It took him twenty minutes to walk to the rocks. The granite outcrop jutted into the sea, a mixture of lush flora and stone. A large breaker smashed over the point, showering water thirty feet into the air. He started climbing, curious to see what was on the other side. Just as he started winding his way up between the massive boulders, he was almost thrown back on to the sand. A small two-seater helicopter swooped up from the other side of the point, its black belly barely skimming the rocks. Peter ducked instinctively, crouching between the boulders as the aircraft swung up into the sky, its rotor blades beating a changing pitch as it swooped back down again towards him. The helicopter then banked and headed inland, skipping above the trees before disappearing behind a small ridge. Peter gave a deep sigh of relief. Maybe Herr Kruse was right after all and it was safer on the beach.

ABOARD THE *DOLPHIN*
7.15 a.m., Sunday, 17 April 1966

THE FISHING boat was three days out of Key West and following the coordinates heading on course into the Gulf of Mexico. Elizabeth had spent most of her free time on deck towards the bow of the vessel, thinking and trying to understand her relationship with Peter. It was her fault, she could see that now; all the pushing and shoving to make her mark, to get somewhere, to amount to something. She had been so determined to recover what the bastards had taken from her father and family, she hadn't fully understood what she had done to Peter. Jacob Bronowski had tried to tell her, even dithering Oliver had tried his best, but she hadn't taken one blind bit of notice. To her, there was only one way – her own.

She leaned against the bulwark and stared out at the empty horizon. The good weather that had accompanied them since leaving

426

port had now left them. The sea had started to get gradually choppier; dark thunder clouds were threatening and the winds had picked up. Elizabeth looked at the bow. The rusty hull was getting sprayed with water as the trawler went down into the deep troughs. Hoover was going around the vessel checking all the hatch covers and ensuring that everything was secured and battened down. They didn't speak as he passed by. They had hardly communicated since leaving Miami.

The boat had been travelling a route along the Tropic of Cancer now for almost twenty-four hours, heading in a westerly direction, just as Schiller had instructed. For some reason she had expected the Nazis to have been in contact immediately they were outside territorial waters. After all, no one wanted this thing protracted. The waiting game was becoming tedious. She looked around. How were they going to be contacted? Would it be by another vessel, or possibly a helicopter, or perhaps Schiller had another U-boat somewhere? A clap of thunder came from some miles off the starboard bow. The grey clouds were fast darkening. The storm was going to blow right over them.

Elizabeth headed below to the galley to prepare breakfast for the crew. By the time she emerged up into the wheelhouse with coffee and flapjacks, they were already riding a roller-coaster of deep troughs and white-tipped waves which pounded against the rusty hull relentlessly. The momentum of the waves had started to make Francetti ill, but the sight of the biscuits was too much for him. He rushed outside on to the navigation bridge, emptying his stomach contents over the guardrail. For the next three hours the boat battled against the elements, forced to run with the storm at one stage, because of its ferocity. Elizabeth breathed a sigh of relief when the sea-state began to calm again. The engine-room had reported an excessive intake of water and the bilge pumps were working flat out to rectify the matter. As a result the *Dolphin* was now temporarily reduced to a speed of just four knots and was over sixty miles off course.

Suddenly, there was a flurry of anticipation at the wheelhouse. McClean came rushing towards her, the excitement on his face obvious before he spoke.

'They've made contact!'

'Thank God.' She closed her eyes and said a short prayer. Then she realized something. 'But we're off course!'

'It's all right. Your husband explained to them about the storm. We've to continue on this course, transmitting our co-ordinates on VHF radio every hour,' he continued.

'Why?' She looked at him.

'Probably to plot a rendezvous,' he replied. 'Excuse me, I've got work to do.' He went back, checking on Hoover and Drexel in the wheelhouse, before disappearing below into the cramped crew quarters. Elizabeth watched 'Big George' Francetti and one of his men, who were already setting up the heavy machine-gun on top of the forecastle. One of the other sailors reappeared on the well-deck, a sub-machine-gun now slung over his shoulder. All around the vessel the atmosphere was electric.

'And now for battle!' grinned Drexel, just as McClean slid back the wheelhouse door and came inside.

McClean smiled at the man. He'd taken a liking to him ever since first meeting him. Apart from being a constant wit, he could cook the best southern fried chicken McClean had tasted in his life. He went a long way to make up for Hoover's broodiness. McClean watched him twiddle with the controls on the VHF set as he retuned it. His hand was shaking. Drexel let go of the wheel a moment and produced a large .45 Colt pistol from the waistband of his trousers, pulling back the firing mechanism as he checked the chamber. He looked over at Hoover and winked. He said little, but his eyes spoke for him. He was looking forward to a confrontation.

'One thing, chaps,' McClean cautioned both of them. 'I want a clear battle plan before we go into action. These people are going to be well prepared. I don't want anything to spoil our chances of getting the boy back in one piece.'

'Be realistic, McClean,' snapped Hoover. 'What chance do you really think we have of getting him back? He can finger these people. They'll waste him, just like they did the girl and our maid.'

McClean never answered. He was staring over Hoover's right shoulder. Hoover turned to find Elizabeth standing outside the open window next to him, despondency etched across her face. She had heard every word he'd said.

1.20 p.m.

THE WEATHER had changed considerably, with the squally showers blowing off towards the south-east. They had increased speed to eight knots and had continued to transmit every hour, on the hour, but without further response. Hoover had stayed at the helm most of the time, splitting his rest periods with McClean and

Drexel. It also kept him out of Elizabeth's way. McClean checked the radar monitor. It had a twenty-mile range, but still nothing showed. Then suddenly there was a blip to the south-west.

'What do you make of this?' He called Hoover over to the radar monitor.

'From the way it's moving, I'd say it was an aircraft,' replied Hoover. After watching the image for a few moments, he stepped out of the side door of the wheelhouse and focused his binoculars on the horizon, but he could see nothing. He waited. A couple of minutes later McClean called out to him.

'See anything yet? It should be about twelve miles away!' he called.

Then Hoover saw the tiny speck. It was slowly growing larger. An aircraft, flying towards them at around a thousand feet. 'I see it!' he cried.

'Get everything up on deck. No guns!' ordered MClean.

Elizabeth was first up at the starboard rail alongside Francetti. 'So this is it.' Francetti smacked the rusty guardrail with his head, relieved that something was finally happening after the days of frustration. He then ran forward and covered up the heavy machine-gun with a canvas tarpaulin. As the aircraft came closer, it began to circle the boat. It was then they all realized it was a flying boat.

'I don't understand.' Elizabeth was perplexed. 'They will never be able to transport the gold by air.'

'They'll have another ship somewhere near by. The aircraft is probably just to look us over,' replied Francetti.

The aircraft was a twin-engined Dornier Do-24 flying boat. It had originally been ordered by the Dutch government for work in the West Indies. It was an old aircraft, but reliable and quite a common type around the Caribbean, used mainly by small operators and shipping companies. The boat's crew watched as the red flying boat banked around them, checking the vessel out. It maintained a wide circle for several minutes before flying off in a figure of eight towards the east and circling back again.

'Hello? This is the *Dolphin* calling aircraft circling us. Come in!' Hoover called out on the VHF radio.

McClean moved beside him. 'Nothing?'

'Not yet.' Hoover shook his head. 'What's that bastard playing at?'

'He'll speak to us in his own good time. Just maintain this course,' replied McClean, checking the western horizon. The sun was fast disappearing. Very soon it would be dark. Following a shout from

Elizabeth, McClean went outside in time to see the aircraft land just off their starboard bow. It bounced high before finally settling amidst the slight swell. McClean heard the radio crackling again and peered inside just in time to hear Hoover speaking into the microphone.

'Send. Over,' he answered.

'Hove to and prepare to be boarded. Any weapons you are carrying must be left on the bow deck. Is that understood?' The voice was snappy and confident.

Hoover looked across at the Scotsman. 'Perfectly,' he replied, tossing the microphone back on top of the radio set. 'They're going to take over this ship!'

'We'll see.' McClean went back out on deck and spoke to Francetti. 'They want all the guns on the forward deck. Do it.' As he went to head below, the burly Mafia lieutenant grabbed his arm.

'Are you serious? We came here for a fight.' He bared his teeth.

'Nico says you take orders well, so do it!' insisted McClean, pulling himself free and disappearing down the stairwell.

He slipped forward in through the service hatch and into the main hold. He quickly scaled the metal ladder, locating the small plastic box he'd deposited up on a ledge in the bulkhead before they'd set sail. He switched it on, flicking the red switch twice. The warning light on the top of 'the sandwich box', as David had called it, began to flash. He carefully set it back again, letting it drop down the back of the inner metal-plating skin and making doubly sure that it was still suspended by the wire attached to the bolt on the ledge. Then he hurried back on deck, in time to see a small inflatable dinghy with three men on board pushing away from the flying boat.

He slipped forward to where Francetti and two of his men were setting down the last of the weapons with the rest. 'This don't feel right, McClean,' he protested.

'It will.' McClean removed a small black object, the size of a pillbox, from his trouser pocket, sticking it underneath one of the sub-machine-guns.

'What the hell . . .' Then 'Big George' started to grin.

Inside a couple of minutes they had been boarded. There were two in their early twenties, fit-looking and seemingly European, both carrying Czech-made Scorpion sub-machine-guns on straps around their necks. The third man was clearly the leader. He was older, with blond hair and what seemed to be a permanent grin across his sun-tanned face. Roth walked up to Elizabeth as his men trained the stubby-looking machine-guns on the crew.

'My compliments, Mrs Goldmann.'

'Where is my son? Is he on that aircraft?' she snapped.

'In good time,' he retorted. 'Is this all your crew?'

'There are nine of us altogether,' she replied.

Roth looked them over, starting with Francetti. His eyes scanned along until he saw Hoover, standing just outside the wheelhouse beside Jimmy Drexel, and finally stopped at McClean, standing on the port side of the vessel. His eyes ran back again until they met with Hoover's. The American was cringing. For a second Hoover wanted to go for the man's throat. Jimmy Drexel seemed to sense what he was thinking and rested a hand on his old friend's shoulder.

'Take it easy, Ollie.'

'I presume that all the weapons are on deck?' Roth glanced forward to where one of his men was now standing next to the small arsenal.

'Just as you ordered.' McClean stepped forward, standing on top of the deck cover across the main hold. The German turned partly to face him.

'Major McClean?' Roth asked, grinning.

'I certainly am,' McClean said drily.

'Perhaps, Major, you and I will have a little chat later, soldier to soldier.' Roth turned his attention to the others, waving for them to move. 'Everyone is to move over to the port side.'

McClean glanced down at the walnut butt of the revolver protruding from the clip holster on Roth's right hip. From the bulk of the gun he correctly judged it to be a .357 Magnum. From over Roth's shoulder he could see the dinghy being drawn back to the aircraft by means of a thin nylon line. Reinforcements wouldn't be long in arriving. They were all made to stand in line along the port rail, with Roth's other associate keeping his gun trained on them.

'If everyone remains calm, then no one will get hurt,' continued Roth, standing with his legs apart and arms akimbo. 'The object of this exercise is to transfer, not to get killed.' He reminded Elizabeth of a photograph she'd seen of an SS officer addressing prisoners at one of the camps. 'You, show me the gold.' He pointed to Jimmy Drexel.

'Me?' Drexel prodded his own chest.

'Do as he asks,' insisted McClean.

Jimmy Drexel moved aft. Roth followed, signalling for his men to keep watch on them.

'This sucks. Where's the other ship?' Francetti whispered to McClean.

431

'I think we can conclude that Peter is not on the aircraft,' said Elizabeth. She watched as McClean mumbled something to Francetti.

'And I think we'd better hurry up,' insisted Francetti, looking over at the dinghy now on the way back to the boat, carrying three more men.

Checking that the nearer of the two guards wasn't watching, McClean whispered to Elizabeth, 'Cause a distraction.'

Elizabeth stepped forward, defiantly shouting, 'Where is my son? I demand that you tell me!' Elizabeth addressed her remarks to the young German standing on top of the cargo hold.

'Shut up!' he snapped.

'How dare you!' Elizabeth moved forward slightly, full of indignation, just as McClean depressed the miniaturized radio controller in his left hand.

There was an immediate explosion as the device went off amidst the weapons on the fore deck. The German was caught in the small blast. Stunned and temporarily blinded, he was thrown off his feet, crashing semi-conscious on to the deck. Oliver Hoover pulled Elizabeth to the deck, shielding her with his body as McClean moved forward to take the nearer man still standing on top of the cargo hold. After the momentary distraction of the blast, the young German swung his Scorpion sub-machine-gun around to open up on them. Francetti moved like a cat. He produced a knife from inside his shirt sleeve just as the German's finger went inside the trigger guard. McClean braced himself, expecting the worst; the German had been too quick for him. Suddenly the knife flashed past him, barely missing his arm before embedding itself in the German's throat. The man staggered back, the gun firing harmlessly into the air as he fell backwards on to the deck. McClean snatched the gun from him leaving the young German writhing, his face already purple as he clutched helplessly at the knife embedded in his windpipe.

'Take over! I'm going after the other one!' he shouted to Francetti before charging aft.

Before the second German could recover his senses, Francetti's men had jumped him, kicking him in the face and wrenching the gun from his neck. The men in the dinghy had already stopped rowing upon hearing the small explosion and seeing their comrade disappear from view under the bulwark. They trained their guns up towards the deck of the fishing boat, one opening up with a short burst as one of Francetti's men afforded him a target. The Mafia 'soldier' was hit in the chest and head. The bullets pitched him backwards.

McClean was half-way down the stairwell when he found Roth. The German had his arm around Drexel's bull neck. The muzzle of the .357 Ruger revolver had ruffled the skin under the American's right ear.

'Drop the gun,' said Roth calmly.

Back on deck Francetti's men had armed themselves. Francetti glanced through one of the weep-holes in the bottom of the bulwark's metal plating. The bullets bounced off the plating, sending up a small cloud of dust and salt into his face as he rolled aside. Hoover crawled forward to him. Francetti grabbed one of the fallen Scorpion machine-pistols checking it was undamaged, before sliding it across the deck to Hoover.

'I take it you know how to use it?' he asked sarcastically.

'I'll try.' Hoover took it, his hands shaking.

'I'll stop these bastards from boarding. You just keep your wife safe,' ordered Francetti.

Hoover nodded and started working his way back to Elizabeth. Francetti shook his head. He'd be lucky if Hoover didn't shoot himself in the foot. The burly Italian snapped out some hurried orders to his men. Then, keeping his head low and timing his action, he bounced up, firing instinctively over the side of the boat, just as the leading German started to climb up the rope ladder. His sudden action took the Germans by surprise, one of his bullets hitting the leading man in the shoulder and knocking him into the water beside the dinghy. His comrades opened up. The Mafia 'soldier' closest to Francetti was hit in the face. He smacked forward into the bulwark before pitching over the side into the sea.

Suddenly a grenade was lobbed on to the deck, exploding a split second after it clattered over the deck timbers. The explosion sent a shudder through the vessel, enveloping the main deck in smoke and killing another of Francetti's men outright. The man's pitted and charred body lay spread-eagled across one of the cargo hatches, while his friend, shielded by his body, had escaped with a shrapnel wound to the leg.

'Ammazzati!' screamed Francetti, as he trained his sub-machine-gun at the other two men. But he didn't see a third gunman directing a rifle at him from the observation platform aboard the aircraft. The rifle cracked just once.

McClean emerged into the wheelhouse, followed by Drexel, with Roth's gun still at his ear. The German quickly assessed the situation. He saw the dead lying scattered around the deck. The only movement came from Elizabeth and Hoover, huddled together in the middle of the well-deck, next to a cargo hatch. Hoover was pointing a sub-machine-gun towards the now-swinging gate at the boarding hatch.

'Go out and tell that idiot to throw away his gun,' ordered Roth.

McClean glanced over at him, assessing his chances of getting at the German.

'I think you'd better do as he says,' blurted Drexel, by now sweating profusely.

'And no funny business,' warned Roth. 'If you have any doubts, check out the aircraft observation window.'

McClean stepped outside on to the bridge section. As he stared across to the flying boat, he was looking directly into the sights of a rifle.

'Hoover! Drop the gun! It's all over!' he shouted.

'Do as he says,' urged Elizabeth, seeing Roth appearing with Drexel at the wheelhouse window.

'I . . . I feel so inadequate,' hissed Hoover.

'If it's any comfort to you, so do I.' She removed the gun from his shaking hand and set it on the deck.

Roth pushed Drexel outside and called for his men to board. '*Schnell!*' he shouted.

The first of them appeared at the gangway opening, rushing forward and shoving McClean on to his face on the deck. As he was being roughly searched, McClean looked over towards Francetti. The big man was sitting with his back up against the bulwark, a hole drilled between his still and open eyes. The remaining Mafia 'soldier' was manhandled over beside him after being similarly searched. McClean recognized the pain etched across his face.

'You got hit?' McClean asked.

'My left leg.' The man winced in pain as one of the Germans pulled his arms behind his back and handcuffed him. McClean was next. He braced himself as the handcuffs were tightened, nipping the skin on both wrists.

As Hoover and Elizabeth were being brought over to join them, something happened on the bridge section, next to the wheelhouse.

McClean turned in time to see Drexel wrestling with Roth. He had one hand on Roth's gun and the other on the German's throat. In a single movement Roth brought up his left forearm, breaking Drexel's grip and chopping him on the side of the neck with the edge of his taut hand. The American fell on to his knees. Without hesitation, Roth aimed the gun and fired. The .357 Magnum bullet hit Drexel on the top of the head, exploding the cranium and

434

showering the wheelhouse wall in blood, tissue and bone. Elizabeth shrieked as Jimmy Drexel's body jerked and convulsed before crashing on to the deck.

8.00 p.m.

OVER THE next two hours the decks were cleared of everything; the bodies had all been dumped down in the engine room. McClean and the remaining Mafia 'soldier' were now sitting on the floor of the crew quarters, below the wheelhouse. They were still handcuffed and now had their feet tied with nylon rope. Elizabeth was lying on her back on one of the bunks, handcuffed and tied from behind. Hoover had been taken away from them the moment Roth regained control of the ship and McClean had written him off as being in league with the neo-Nazis. Suddenly, Hoover was shoved down the stairwell by Roth. The sight of Hoover confirmed his innocence of all such charges. One of Roth's men pulled him on to his feet. His hands were cuffed in front of him and he had been badly beaten. His face was purple, his nose clearly broken and his right eye almost closed. Blood was still trickling from his mouth and, from the state of his shirt, he'd been bleeding for some time.

Elizabeth turned around to see her husband. 'My God, Oliver. What have they done to you?' She shuddered at the sight of him.

'I was just explaining to Mr Hoover here that it is better to co-operate than to fight the inevitable.' Roth looked over at Elizabeth. 'Probably why so many of your sort went so quietly to the showers.'

'You scum!' Elizabeth struggled to get up, but she couldn't in the narrow confines of the bunk.

Roth grinned as he unlocked Hoover's handcuffs and made him stand with his back against one of the supports, an encased steel pillar in the centre of the cabin. He quickly relocked the handcuffs, leaving Hoover fixed firmly to the pillar.

'Just tell me, is my son all right?' she demanded. Roth ignored her. 'Please! Is Peter safe? For God's sake, tell me!'

'I am informed that you have a package for Herr Schiller,' said Roth finally.

'Tell me about my son!' she insisted.

'He's fine,' snapped Roth. 'Now, where is the package?'

'I want to see my son.'

435

Roth shook his head, clearly exasperated. Elizabeth squealed as the German grabbed her by the hair and twisted her head up towards her husband. Elizabeth's eyes widened as Roth casually raised the .357 Magnum revolver to the side of Hoover's skull and cocked back the hammer. She remembered how casually he had killed Drexel. He would do it again. She knew he would!

'It's in a holdall, under this bunk,' she assured him.

Roth raised an eyebrow as he let go of her hair. Elizabeth's head thudded on to the bunk as Roth rummaged through the loose clothing and life-jackets to locate the yellow holdall. He dragged it out, emptying the contents over the table. The battered black metal box had been stuffed into the bottom of the bag. The lid was broken and tied up with a piece of string. He broke it, opening the box and checking the contents. 'The Three Brothers' glinted back at him.

Without a word of response, Roth opened the emergency hatch at the side of the stairwell, jamming it ajar. Then he disappeared up the stairwell, carrying the metal box under his arm. McClean watched as Roth closed the upper hatch, leading to the wheelhouse.

'Now, why did he do that?' mused McClean.

'Oliver? Are you OK?' asked Elizabeth, looking over at her husband. His head flopped forward.

'It doesn't matter,' he whispered.

'Oliver, I'm sorry, really I am,' she continued.

He raised his head. 'Don't apologize to me.' A tear trickled down from his uninjured eye. 'I don't rate an apology.'

'You are very brave and I love you,' she reassured him. From the sound of his voice, they'd kicked loose most of his teeth as well. Elizabeth closed her eyes to it all.

'I don't deserve it . . . I got us into this.'

'What?'

'It's all right, Hoover. We got ourselves into this,' McClean butted in, trying to save Elizabeth any further pain.

'It's time she knew!' Hoover glared. 'You suspected it anyhow.'

'Oliver, what are you talking about?' She turned her head to see him.

'I've been tipping them off all along about your movements . . . I'm so sorry.'

'Why?' she asked dazedly.

'Blackmail.' He raised his head and looked directly at her. 'You know how it is, I can't resist a pretty face.'

436

'Oh, Oliver,' she groaned. Then she heard the sound of the engines starting up. 'What's that?'

'It's the sea plane,' answered McClean, looking down at the man handcuffed next to him. He was writhing in agony. The Italian gritted his teeth against the pain in his leg as he spoke up. 'Hoover, what were they doing with you besides kicking you senseless?'

'I had to take them around the vessel . . . They've set time-charges and explosives along the shaft tunnel and in the bottom of each of the watertight bulkheads.'

'What!' cried Elizabeth. 'But that doesn't make sense.'

They all heard the aircraft drawing steadily away from the boat. It was taking off.

'It makes perfect sense,' answered the Italian. 'They plan to sink us.'

'But the gold! That makes no sense!' she protested.

'How deep is the water here?' McClean turned to Hoover.

He had to think for a moment before answering. 'About two hundred feet, I think.' Hoover looked over to the Italian for confirmation; the man nodded.

'There's your answer.' McClean shook his head. 'They sink her and then, at some later time they come along and lift the gold. All neat and quiet and no traces.'

'And Peter?' Elizabeth was in despair.

'Mrs Goldman, let's face it, they never had any intention of releasing him in the first place,' replied McClean.

Moments later the first explosion took place. The entire cabin shook. Then another, followed quickly by two more, almost simultaneously. All along the bottom of the hull the sea water started to flow in. Inside ten minutes the vessel was listing badly to the starboard side. The cabin lights flickered and then went out. They were in total darkness except for a small red emergency light just above Elizabeth's bunk. They waited in silence. It took almost the same time again before the water reached them. The vessel had now tipped forward, bow first, but still pitching to the right.

'Not long now,' commented the Italian, seeing the water flood over the bottom of the emergency door leading up from the main hold. He had no sooner spoken than they heard another sound. It was several more seconds before they realized it was directly over them. 'What the hell is that?' he asked.

McClean thought he knew who it was and he prayed he was right. The water started to cascade in at a greater rate, filling up the tiny cabin very quickly. It had reached his chin by the time the door to the wheelhouse was kicked open. Flashlights scanned the cabin, voices calling out above the noise of the helicopter's engine.

'Thank God!' cried Elizabeth, as the men jumped down into the water.

'Get the woman out first!' insisted McClean.

'He's going under!' shouted Hoover, as he watched the injured man slip beneath the oily surface of the water. One of the rescuers dived in and recovered him. The Italian was helped up to the deck, coughing and spluttering.

'Come on, McClean, you'll catch your death in all this cold water.' McClean looked up upon hearing the familiar voice. David jumped down into the water and helped McClean to his feet, reaching under the water and cutting the bonds around his ankles.

'You took your time.' McClean smiled up at the Israeli.

'Hurry!' David called out to his companions and a further two men scrambled down and carried Elizabeth up towards the main deck.

'Oliver! Get Oliver!' she cried, struggling to see her husband as she was lifted clear of the upper hatchway.

'We'd better hurry. This thing's going to disappear any second,' said David, looking over at one of his men still working to free Hoover. 'Hurry up, Uri.'

'We have a problem here,' said the man, struggling with Hoover's handcuffs. 'We've no cutting equipment with us.'

The vessel lurched violently and gave a deafening groan. The water started pounding in through the emergency hatch. The boat was on its way down.

'Get out! Leave me,' insisted Hoover.

'No!' shouted McClean. 'I'm not leaving without you!'

'Didn't you hear what they said!' screamed Hoover. 'Leave me!'

'He's right, McClean.' David dragged McClean over to the stairwell. With the handcuffs still on him, McClean was in no position to argue. As McClean was lifted up through the hatch, David went back to see if there was anything he could do. The boat gave out a final and deafening groan, like nothing Hoover had ever heard in his life.

'We have to go!' David pulled his assistant back to the stairwell, shoving him up it.

'Tell her I'm sorry,' Hoover called out to the Israeli, over the noise of the rushing water. 'Promise me!'

'I promise.' David saluted the man. Then he disappeared up the stairwell. Hoover twisted his head as far as he could to watch the Israeli reach safety. Then he closed his eyes and started to pray aloud.

'Our Father, who art in heaven . . .'

David had no sooner jumped aboard the hovering helicopter, than the fishing boat began to disappear amidst a frothing white sea. The Mossad agent looked into the back of the helicopter, where Elizabeth had her head buried into McClean's shoulder. As the aircraft banked, David looked out of the side window. From what he could see in the moonlight, the boat had already vanished. Only the escaping air, still bubbling to the surface, now marked the spot. As he looked back at Elizabeth he thought of his promise to the American. It would have to wait.

THE PLANTATION HOUSE, HAITI
10.30 a.m., Wednesday, 20 April 1966

PETER WATCHED as the *Lady Christina* loomed out of the sea mist into the bay. The yacht had been absent for over nine days. He was mulling over in his mind just where it might have been to when Strassmann came on to the veranda beside him.

'Beautiful, isn't she?' he said.

'I suppose,' replied Peter casually.

'Are you looking forward to the dinner party this evening?'

'Should I be, Herr Kruse?' Peter stared back at him.

Strassmann's grey eyes twinkled. 'An auspicious occasion. And you, young man, will be the guest of honour.' Strassmann patted him on the shoulder and went on back inside. 'By the way,' he added, 'we will be dining aboard the *Lady Christina*.'

Peter returned to watching the massive 350-foot long white yacht as it dropped anchor. Already three powerboats were circling the vessel and one of Schiller's helicopters was aloft, positioned just further out to sea. He wondered who might be on board to merit such attention. Whoever they were, they must be extremely important.

8.01 p.m.

SCHILLER had returned with the yacht. Peter had been informed of his presence in the massive plantation house just after five o'clock that evening, but he didn't see him until later, when he came to the bedroom to escort Peter to the yacht. He was shown in by the ever-attentive native servant he had left with Peter just before his departure the previous week. Peter had dressed reluctantly in a white tuxedo. He had just poured a drink of orange juice and started listening to some Mozart on the record player when Schiller interrupted him.

'Good evening, Pieter.'

Peter turned on hearing his voice, the glass dropped from his hand. Schiller clicked his fingers and the servant rushed forward and started picking up the pieces. Peter didn't notice the man at his feet. He was too busy staring at the black uniform that Schiller wore. He recognized it instantly from his historical studies. Schiller was wearing the full dress uniform of an SS Gruppenführer.

'The Schutzstaffel!' Peter was open-mouthed.

'You are not honestly shocked, are you, dear boy?' Schiller limped into the room, clicking his fingers again for the native servant to leave.

'I'm not sure,' replied Peter. 'The war ended in 1945, did it not?'

'Not for us. Come, they await.' Schiller grinned.

'But I . . . am Jewish.' He was frightened, suddenly more terrified than he could ever have imagined.

'I told you before, you only thought you were Jewish. That is what they wanted you to believe. Pieter, you come from pure Aryan stock, the purest there is! Now, come, they are waiting to meet you.'

ABOARD THE *LADY CHRISTINA*
8.26 p.m.

THEY WERE ferried over to the yacht by helicopter, landing on the helipad beside the pool deck, at the stern of the vessel. As Peter walked from the helicopter into the upper section of the ship, he

440

stopped in his tracks. The place was covered in Nazi banners, every one a relic from Germany's past. He looked back. Schiller had halted and was talking to another man, also dressed in SS uniform. 'Why am I here? What has all this to do with me?' he asked impatiently.

Schiller excused himself from the other officer and rejoined Peter. 'All in good time. Very shortly you will know everything.' He guided Peter downstairs. 'By the way, henceforth you will be required to speak only German for the remainder of the evening. I believe your command of the language is quite good.'

'Passable,' said Peter coldly. His head still felt fuzzy. He was certain now that it was the medication the doctor had been giving him. But he had failed to tell them that he was starting to remember more and more about what had happened to him recently. He was aware of the girl called Catherine, but not what had happened to her. He felt he loved her and she him, but apart from that nothing else. At the bottom of the steps the main corridor of the yacht was lined with SS guards, again in full dress uniform, each man wearing the armband of the Leibstandarte SS Adolf Hitler, Hitler's own personal bodyguard! These were all hand-picked SS men, specially chosen above all others, not just because of their purity of body, heart and mind but for their outstanding loyalty to just one man. Peter was starting to convince himself that it was all a masquerade, and in rather poor taste, until the doors opened to the stateroom.

There before him stood a gathering of over forty men, all dressed in the various uniforms of the armed forces of the Third Reich. At the top of the room hung a large Nazi flag with a swastika, draped from one side to the other. In the middle hung a large oil painting of Adolf Hitler. The general chatter slowed almost to a silence. The uniforms parted and a general hush fell over the entire gathering. Peter braced himself as a tubby little man in a brown uniform swaggered forward from the middle of the crowd. Martin Bormann threw his arms around him, hugging him like a long-lost son. For a moment Peter thought that this stranger might well be his father! Then Bormann stepped back from him.

'Pieter, welcome. From the bottom of our hearts we bid you welcome. This is indeed an auspicious moment – to come home on the day you are recognized as a man, this your twenty-first birthday!'

Bormann started to clap and the others followed. Then in traditional manner they began stomping their jackboots on the floor. The entire vessel echoed to the sound of their feet.

Finally, after more than a minute, Martin Bormann waved for

them to cease. He stepped forward again, taking Peter by the arm and guiding him towards the top of the room, seating him beside himself at the top table. Two further tables had been laid out, running down from either end of the top table and forming a U-shape. Bormann then clapped his hands and the gathering took up their respective seats. Martin Bormann gestured for Peter to sit down and then did so himself, the rest following suit. The officers talked amongst themselves, but Peter noticed that it was all a great deal more muted than before. He couldn't get over how they were all staring at him. They seemed to be comparing and assessing him. Peter noticed Strassmann sitting at the end of the top table, next to Schiller. Both men were involved in a deep discussion on some matter. Several times Strassmann pointed down to one of the SS officers seated at the bottom of the right-hand table. Peter stared at the man. For some reason the blond-haired man was familiar. Roth looked back at him, a wide grin on his face. Peter smiled back.

'The doctor says that you are making excellent progress,' commented Bormann.

'No one has yet said what was wrong with me,' retorted Peter.

'Haven't they?' Bormann glanced over at Schiller, who was still in conversation with Strassmann. 'Pieter, you had a fever, quite delirious. If we hadn't located you, God only knows.' He patted him on the arm. 'By the way, I must compliment you on your German. How did you come to learn the language so well?'

'I taught myself.'

'Magnificent!' Bormann was really impressed. 'And so well, but of course to you it must come naturally.' Peter ignored the compliment.

'I'm sorry, but I don't think I caught your name?' Peter said, somewhat sarcastically.

'My name is Bormann. Reichsleiter Martin Bormann.' He sampled the wine, then nodded agreeably to the wine waiter standing behind him. 'Sometimes, however, it is better to call me by the name of Keller, but I would be deeply honoured if you were to call me Martin.'

Peter, shocked to the core, swallowed deeply.

The dinner went on for several hours, each of the courses interspersed with speeches. Throughout the evening a quintet of musicians played chamber music and a rendition of some popular Bavarian folk-songs. As the evening wore on, Peter was still none the wiser. He had looked forward to finding out finally about his true origins, no matter how bad the news might be, but now he was just wanting out of the place. Eventually the musicians ceased playing and filed out, followed by the waiters.

Roth then got up and locked the double doors, whilst two of the other SS officers carried a large cine-screen over and set it in front of the door, extending it out to its full height. As the lights were dimmed, Peter could hear a cine-camera starting to whir away. He glanced back. The massive flag behind him had parted just above the painting. A large camera lens, not unlike ones he'd seen in movie houses, was protruding from a small rectangular window close to the ceiling.

'Now you will see,' whispered Bormann.

Peter looked back at him, just as the music started playing – marching music, similar to what he'd heard on some old German newsreels. He focused on the screen as the film sprang into life. It was footage of Hitler walking about at the Berghof on the Obersalzberg. The gathering immediately started clapping, settling down again after a few moments. Hitler had two Alsatian dogs with him. He was throwing a ball for one to fetch, whilst the other walked obediently by his side.

'He had a way with animals, you know,' whispered Bormann.

Peter looked back at him curiously. Bormann smiled and patted him on the arm again.

The film switched to Hitler walking up the steps of the Berghof, with Eva Braun beside him. The two dogs were not to be seen. Peter supposed this was different footage that had been added to the reel. As they reached the top of the steps, Hitler waved towards the camera, as if embarrassed by the cameraman's presence. Eva Braun stretched up, kissing him on the cheek. Hitler then raised a finger, as if admonishing her. Then she pecked him on the other cheek, much to the enjoyment of the gathering. The film ran on for another ten minutes, whetting the appetites of all those gathered – all, that was, except Peter. Then, as suddenly as it had started, it stopped.

Peter thought this was the end of the little show, but then the camera started whirring again and another image flashed up on to the screen. It was of a large library. The camera carefully zoomed in on the figure sitting in a red leather winged library chair. It was Hitler again, but this time he looked older than before. Peter was shocked. None of the film footage or photographs he'd seen of the Führer had ever depicted him like this. Then Hitler started to speak, his voice a little slurred, but strong and concise.

'*The future will determine whether we were right or wrong.*' Adolf

Hitler's nasal tones echoed around the stunned gathering. *'My conscience tells me that we won a great battle over the hearts and minds of all men. Our thousand-year Reich is not lost, but has merely taken on a new form. The metamorphosis has been a painful one and Germany has suffered. Our young men have spilled their blood for this. That is why we must not and will not fail!'* Hitler raised his fist, shaking it towards the camera. *'My son is destined to take over this challenge! My son is the heir, to help guide us towards our real destiny! For this reason my son . . .'*

The rest of the words were lost on Peter. Through his tired, numbed mind all he could hear were the incessant words *'my son, my son, my son, my son . . .'* It was him. *He* was *the* son. *He* was Hitler's son! Him, Peter O'Casey-Goldmann, a practising Jew!

Peter's mind was numb. He couldn't think. He sat staring at the man's lips moving, his arm shaking, his eyes glaring back at him. Yes, it was in the eyes. He had his father's piercing blue eyes. Of that there could be no doubt whatsoever. The film ran for another half-hour, with Adolf Hitler again and again talking about the furtherance of the Reich and something called 'Nemesis'. The two were indivisible, he said. The time was coming for them to retake the power, the real power, the financial power.

No one, not even Martin Bormann, seemed to notice that their guest of honour was in a state of shock. He hadn't moved a muscle or blinked an eyelid during the entire film. As the lights went up, everyone stood, all except Peter. Bormann was first to give Peter the straight-arm Fascist salute. Peter hardly noticed. He was in another world.

'Sieg Heil! Sieg Heil! Sieg Heil!' shouted Bormann. The rest followed, joining in the chorus.

Peter finally looked up at Bormann. He then slowly stood, too overcome with emotion to say or do anything, although what he was feeling was not in tune with what these men wanted. He took a five-minute standing ovation before Bormann steered him from the room, leaving by a side door.

Schiller and Strassmann followed as Bormann brought Peter into his private suite. The room was panelled in yellow pine, the thick-pile carpeting a pastel blue. All the furnishings were in white leather. In his hallucinating mind, all Peter could see was the blood of millions seeping out from the leather stitching of each of the sofas and chairs set around a low glass table at the centre of the room. Bormann guided him over to one of the seats, whilst Strassmann poured out some brandy for his masters.

'Did you even suspect?' asked Schiller.

'No. I had thought it was you,' replied Peter. Schiller laughed.

'How do you feel about it?' asked Bormann.

'I . . . I am not sure.' He was concerned not to alarm them too much. 'I presume my mother was Eva Braun?'

'Eva Hitler,' corrected Bormann. 'They were married secretly in February 1945. Both Schiller and myself were witnesses.'

'But I always thought they were married in Berlin, just before . . .' Peter was lost for words.

'That is so. A ceremony took place on 29 April 1945. It was done for other reasons.'

'Reasons?' mused Peter.

'You will have plenty of time to adjust, and to understand,' Bormann assured him, avoiding the issue. 'Ah! Refreshments.'

Strassmann brought over a silver tray containing four brandy glasses. Against his will, Peter accepted. He needed it. Bormann looked across at Schiller, signalling his approval with a gentle nod of the head. Peter drank some of the brandy, immediately coughing. They laughed as Bormann went over beside the fireplace and raised his glass to yet another portrait of Hitler, this time of him sitting by the lakes on the Obersalzberg.

'I give you our Führer!' he said.

'The Führer!' echoed Schiller, raising his own glass, as did Strassmann. Peter couldn't bring himself to follow suit. They were all staring at him now. What could he do?

'Pieter? Is something wrong?' asked Bormann, the smile still on his face.

'I . . . I am sorry. I was just thinking.' He raised his glass.

'The Führer,' repeated Bormann. They all drank, all except Peter. Whilst raising the glass to his lips, he feigned sipping the brandy.

'And "Nemesis"!' continued Bormann.

'"Nemesis"!' repeated the two SS officers.

They all drank again, Bormann emptying his glass and licking his lips.

'A memorable evening, Herr Reichsleiter,' Strassmann complimented Bormann.

'And it is not over yet, Strassmann, my dear chap. We have many a toast to drink this night. Is that not so, young Pieter?' He realized the confusion on Peter's face. He was staring at the man he knew as Kruse. 'Ah! You are quite right, Pieter, we have all been required to live under *noms de plume*. I fear SS Sturmbannführer Strassmann is no exception to the rule, but for this one night we have broken our own rules, in honour of your homecoming.'

'But where is my home?' asked Peter absently. His mind flashed back again to the swimming pool. Catherine was running towards him calling out his name. He looked up and saw a man, and for a split second he recalled the man's face. It was the blond-haired SS officer at the end of the table!

'Pieter?' Schiller was beside him.

'It has been a strain for the young man,' said Bormann. 'Perhaps the doctor should be called to give him something.' Strassmann immediately picked up the telephone to speak to the bridge.

'I am perfectly all right, thank you.' Peter tried to steady himself.

'Nevertheless, I think it would be best,' insisted Bormann. 'We only want the very best for you, my boy.'

'What is "Nemesis"?'

The question stumped Bormann a little. He looked over at Schiller first before replacing the receiver. '"Nemesis" is an organization that was established as a direct consequence of your father's wishes. The Führer, in his infinite wisdom, decreed that a small, select band of us be charged with the task of creating "Nemesis". It all started one rather stormy night at a castle at Wewelsburg. Perhaps you've heard of the place?' Peter shook his head. 'The chief object was to maintain power anywhere in the world through exerting financial pressure.'

'Is that not a little naïve?' suggested Peter.

'Naïve!' Bormann roared. 'Did you hear that?' He laughed, poking fun at the comment.

'Pieter, it has worked,' said Schiller, adding, 'it *is* working.'

'So what is my role in all this?' he replied.

'That's more like it, dear chap!' Bormann handed his glass back to Strassmann to get it recharged.

'We envisage you emerging as the new leader in Germany . . . eventually.'

'And what if I do not wish this?' Peter dared to ask.

'Pieter, you are your father's son. You cannot escape that,' Schiller assured him. 'And I think it now appropriate that you should have this.' Schiller removed the heavy gold signet ring from his pocket and handed it to Peter. 'It was given to me by your mother.'

'Eva Braun.' Peter took the ring, examining the swastika emblem.

'Eva Hitler,' corrected Schiller. 'As Reichsleiter Bormann has just said, contrary to public knowledge, the marriage ceremony in the bunker was not the Führer's first. They had been married in secret at the Berghof.' Then he smiled. 'Just two months before you were born.'

'But my date of birth is in May 1945.'

Schiller shook his head. 'Not so. You were born at Obersalzberg on 20 April, a month earlier than you imagined.'

'It is also your father's birthday!' Bormann piped up eagerly.

'I see,' acknowledged Peter, staring down at the ring in his palm. It was embossed with the Nazi swastika, surrounded in laurel leaves.

'Look at the inscription on the inside band,' urged Schiller.

Peter held the ring towards the light of a table lamp and looked at the faded lettering. He could barely make out the engraving. It read: '*Heute Deutschland! Morgen die Welt! – Adolf Hitler, 1938*'.

'Today Germany . . . tomorrow the world,' Peter read from the inscription.

'It was your father's, his personal ring,' said Bormann. 'And now it is yours, Pieter!'

'What happened after I was born?' asked Peter.

'SS Gruppenführer Schiller brought both you and your beautiful mother to Berlin some days after you were born, just before the British bombed the Berghof and attempted to murder you. We got you out of Berlin just before the Ruskies overran the city.'

'So that was how I ended up in Ireland?'

'*Ja.*' Bormann nodded. 'It surprised me a little that you had found out about that. I believe you even found old Schiller's gold tie-pin!' He chuckled.

'My father's death . . .' Peter's mind was racing now. 'The film I just saw, he was much older than I had expected.' He ran his hands through his hair, before trying to rub the tension away from the back of his neck. He looked up at Bormann. The man was smiling! Suddenly the truth dawned on him. 'He didn't die in 1945 after all . . . Did he?'

'Excellent! Magnificent!' Bormann threw his hands in the air. 'Do you see that, gentlemen – the analytical mind, the brilliance of deduction! Truly his father's son.' Then he walked over, leaning down and clutching Peter by both shoulders. 'No, he did not die.'

'Incredible!' Peter sat forward. 'Wait until old Professor Snyder back at Yale hears about this one!' Then he realized the stupidity of what he had said. Snyder and the rest would never know about it, they never could. He was about to apologize for his foolishness when he detected something from Bormann. 'When *did* my father die?'

Martin Bormann looked at Schiller. Neither of them had wanted things to go this far this quickly.

'Herr Bormann, *is* my father dead?' Peter stood up.

'Show him,' commanded Schiller, motioning for Strassmann to lock the door from the stateroom. That done, Bormann went across to the portrait, clicking a small switch on the side of the picture frame. Immediately the fireplace opened back, revealing a metal staircase running parallel with the room.

'Come,' insisted Bormann, leading the way down the staircase. Peter followed, then Schiller and finally Strassmann.

The staircase ended under the lounge. Bormann opened another door, using an electronic combination lock on the wall beside it. The door slid into a slot in the bulkhead and he walked in, flicking on the main lights. Peter shielded his eyes from the glare. A young doctor stood up from his desk over in a corner of the room, switching off his angle poise lamp. Bormann signalled for him to leave. The man exited through another door, leading, from what Peter could see, into a similar room next door.

Peter looked about the place. The room smelt of disinfectant and had the sterile appearance of an operating theatre. The walls, ceiling and floor were all metal, shiny and spotless. At its centre was an operating table and on the other side from where they stood was a large bank of machinery and something that looked like a giant 'iron lung'. The tank was made from steel, well over eight feet in length and sitting almost five feet off the deck. Its top was curved and a series of bolts ran along the hermetically sealed seams at intervals of six inches.

Martin Bormann went over and fiddled at a small control panel. He then beckoned Peter to his side. As he reached him, Bormann pointed down to a glass panel on the 'iron lung'. Peter peered into it, but it was pitch black and there was condensation on the outer face of the glass. He rubbed away the condensation with his hand as Bormann switched on the internal light. Peter jumped back in horror. Strassmann supported him.

'It is perfectly all right, I assure you. Our doctors at the country club have access to the finest medical and research facilities known to man,' said Bormann.

Peter returned to the viewing panel and looked inside. Adolf Hitler peered back at him through a swirling white mist. Hitler's head was covered by a tight silver mask which stretched around his face, leaving a small open oval section stretching from chin to forehead to allow the face to be viewed at all times. From what Peter could see, the rest of his body was also fitted in a similar skin-tight suit, his father's gloved hands crossed over his chest.

'Your father is in suspended animation,' continued Bormann. 'Our cryogeneticists have frozen his body. The Führer could stay there for ever, frozen and perfectly preserved in this support system, the ageing process halted.' He patted the side of the steel tank. 'The white mist that you see is the gas from the freezing process.'

Peter looked again. 'But his eyes are open!'

'And so they should be.' Bormann moved beside him. 'The doctors painted a protective synthetic layer over the eyes to protect them.'

'But why?' Peter still didn't understand.

'Because, dear boy, the Führer will need them again some day.' He pointed down into the tank. 'Don't you see,' he said gleefully, 'your father is alive!'

Peter couldn't believe what he was witnessing. Schiller took up the story. 'We knew from our early freezing experiments at Auschwitz that we could suspend life for a time by freezing the body in a certain fashion. When the Führer discovered that he was suffering from an inoperable heart complaint, he had the wisdom immediately to sanction further cryogenetic investigation, no expense spared. Of course, scientists in the United States were already doing it with laboratory animals. With what our people already knew, all we had to do was develop along the lines of the American experiments. Our own medical people in Argentina designed and built the support system and tank.'

'But why?' demanded Peter.

'Some day soon medical science will perfect the heart transplant, without serious risk to the patient,' replied Bormann. 'Great advances are already being made in South Africa by a Professor Barnard and his team. Our information is that they are making preparation in Cape Town to carry out the first human heart transplant within the next year. Of course, it is experimental and highly dangerous. When the risk factor is adequately reduced, the Führer will be ready to rejoin the world again,' he said with confidence.

'He was put in there alive, but who says he will come out that way!' Peter was aghast.

'He knew all the risks, Pieter. The Führer took the decision himself, based on scientific fact and logic,' insisted Schiller.

'Pieter, your father also knew that within another month, perhaps two, he would have been dead, and in that time other vital body organs could have also been damaged,' added Bormann. 'It was a simple and painless procedure. A body preparation which he helped complete himself, followed by a simple injection. The freezing was extremely rapid. He is neither conscious nor unconscious. His brain functions, but with a minuscule level of activity.'

'But the risks! What if this apparatus breaks down?' continued Peter, more curious than concerned.

'We have a back-up system on board.' Bormann went over to some steel shutters on the adjacent wall. 'Behind there is another tank.'

'My father lies here, yet my mother is dead?' Peter looked at Bormann.

'Your mother chose to die, Pieter,' said Bormann, without hesitation. 'She did it out of pure love and devotion to both you and your father.'

'My mother committed suicide? And with me just born?' Peter felt hurt and abandoned.

'Don't you see? It had to be. There was no other way,' insisted Bormann. Peter looked again at Schiller. The SS general was glowering at Bormann. 'She had to die in the bunker. There was no other way out,' added Bormann.

'*Götterdämmerung*,' said Peter absently, referring to the historical term used to describe the last days of Hitler in his Berlin bunker during late April 1945. 'The twilight of the gods.'

'Excellent, you have studied well,' complimented Bormann, glad to try and change the subject. 'But of course, I am forgetting that modern history is your forte.'

'You said she chose to die.' Peter couldn't let the matter rest there.

'Your mother was a very brave woman. She was also a pragmatist,' continued Bormann. 'She knew the risks of escaping from the bunker along with the Führer. For her to have disappeared also would have ensured a witch-hunt.'

'But how? Their bodies were both supposedly discovered in the chancellery garden.' Peter was perplexed.

'*Ja, bodies* were discovered,' replied Bormann, sounding rather proud of the fact. 'Realizing defeat to be inevitable, the Führer sanctioned a secret operation codenamed "Herron". A volunteer impostor took his place. With a little plastic surgery and the switching of dental and some medical records, the corpse resembled the Führer in every detail. Of course, to ensure complete safety, an attempt was made to burn both bodies in a shallow pit in the gardens above the bunker.'

'An attempt? I don't understand you.'

'It was quite deliberate. Even those witnessing the funeral pyre had no idea, but the physics of such an operation were futile. In reality we knew that the bodies would not burn completely, but just enough to remove such things as fingerprints and any possible evidence of cosmetic surgery.'

'And a pregnancy,' quipped Schiller.

'Quite.' Bormann moved over beside Peter. 'After the bodies were buried, the only remaining problem was to ensure their proper and quick discovery. In due course, once the Russians overran the complex, they found several willing witnesses prepared to show them the grave.'

'If anything went against our plans, it was the Russian attitude towards the affair.' Schiller spoke up again. 'Stalin's refusal to allow the Americans or British to investigate the bunker and suicides themselves stirred up suspicion, but we have been fortunate.' He stroked the 'iron lung'.

'How could any man allow his wife to sacrifice herself for him?' Peter stared down into the viewing panel of the tank.

'Pieter, to answer that, you must first understand just what it was like during those final days.' Bormann took a step closer. 'Berlin was ravaged. There was little chance for any of us to get out alive. The Russians had us surrounded on all sides and were squeezing our city defences. The perimeters were diminishing hourly. For the Führer to attempt to leave, and perhaps be captured in the process, was more manly than to die. I can assure you that he was distraught at the thought of leaving his beloved.'

'In fact, we had to administer an anaesthetic in order to ensure his co-operation,' added Schiller.

Bormann glared back at him for having revealed the fact. 'Your father is a very brave man, Pieter.'

Peter said nothing. He stared down into the swirling mist inside the tank. He could feel his father's eyes staring back at him.

'Come.' Schiller put his arm around Peter's shoulders and guided him back towards the staircase. 'This, of course, is not the Führer's normal residence. We are in the process of transferring him for security reasons, but everything, I can assure you, is perfectly safe for him. We have a team of three doctors on board whose sole job it is to see that your father remains safe.'

'And well . . .' whispered Peter as he walked on up the narrow stairs ahead of Schiller.

THE PLANTATION HOUSE
11.03 p.m.

THE TROOP-CARRYING helicopters swooped in from the east, landing behind the plantation house. David led his five-man team towards the house, while McClean took his four men and the signals specialist down towards the beach path to cut off any retreat, or for that matter reinforcements. The helicopters immediately lifted off as planned. David's men cleared the lawns, weaving through the palm trees and keeping to the shadows until the very last moment. Then, in a sudden dash, the black-clad agents cleared the last yards to the rear veranda of the three-storey plantation house.

They knew the layout of the place down to the position of the furnishings. Each man had his job to do. Silently jumping on to the wide veranda, David gave the signal. Immediately they burst through the house, taking the rear rooms simultaneously. The silenced 9mm Uzi sub-machine-guns popped away as the Mossad agents sanitized the lower reaches of the house. Gradually they worked their way up, finding little resistance. Apart from a couple of guards in a kitchen who got blown away over their bowls of spaghetti and a handful of servants, the place was empty.

David gathered the native servants together in the dining room, asking them some questions in French, but he got little response from them. Then, when he tried a few words of Creole, several of the servants nodded; they understood. After a minute he found what he wanted to know. David cursed to himself as he examined, through his binoculars, the *Lady Christina* at her deep-water anchorage in the bay below.

Their intelligence had been brilliant and their luck had held until now. The Israelis had been keeping a watchful eye on events following the *Dolphin*'s departure from Key West. The tracer McClean had triggered aboard the fishing boat had pinpointed their exact location on the Tropic of Cancer. From two tracking stations David had got a fix on the boat inside minutes. The Israelis had watched on their radar screens as the flying boat had come and gone. Unbeknownst to Roth, he had been tracked right back to Port-au-Prince. From there it had been a straightforward task to locate the Nazi hideout. The Israelis had had their own way until the *Lady Christina* arrived back with Schiller, but now everything was up in the air again. What they had thought would be five minutes on the ground was thus set to become very protracted indeed.

David pulled off his light woollen balaclava as he rushed over to join McClean.

'Well?' asked the Scotsman.

'Clean,' panted David. 'Our intelligence was perfect, right down to the last detail, except for the most important one. The place is empty!' He pointed down at the yacht. 'Party time. That's where they are, including the boy. A party of some kind. Important people, according to what the servants say.'

'How many on board?'

'Forty or fifty at the party and around another thirty guards. They should be easy enough to spot. They're all in SS uniform!' McClean looked back at him in amazement. 'So what now?'

'Plan two. We take Nico Giovanni at his word and see just how good his boys really are.'

'Simon isn't going to like this,' commented David.

'I don't give a shit!' answered McClean, turning to his signals operator. 'Call up the choppers and get me "Mad Dog" on the emergency frequency.'

ABOARD THE *LADY CHRISTINA*
11.09 p.m.

BORMANN and Schiller had resumed their conversation with Peter up in the suite above the medical deck. Strassmann went over to the cocktail cabinet and started replenishing their empty glasses while the two older men continued their conversation with Peter.

'There is something in all of this that I don't understand,' Peter said.

'And what might that be, dear boy?' prompted Bormann.

'My father,' Peter found the word difficult to say. 'In the film he mentions me, his son. Just when did you know about me?'

'Pieter, the Führer never gave up hope, even after you had been lost to us,' responded Bormann.

'Lost?'

'You see, dear boy, we thought that you were dead. The Goldmann woman deliberately tricked us.' Bormann sat down beside him. 'In Ireland, you were brought ashore from a U-boat, by

453

Gruppenführer Schiller here. You were to transfer to an awaiting aircraft. The arrangement was for your father and myself to continue on to our final destination by U-boat, thus the line of succession of our glorious Third Reich was protected. But in Ireland we were betrayed. The Irish scum that we had paid to assist us began to get greedy. They tried to kill you.' Bormann pointed towards Schiller. 'See on Gruppenführer Schiller's face, the terrible injuries inflicted upon him as he tried in vain to protect you.'

'I had you removed to a farmhouse for your safety,' Schiller interjected, glancing over Peter's shoulder in time to see Strassmann slip the small tablet into Peter's wine glass. Seconds later, Peter accepted a further drink from Strassmann. 'Thank you,' he replied, sipping some of the red wine.

'Our enemies deliberately attacked the farmhouse, knowing you were inside. Your bodyguard and nurse gave up their lives for you, Pieter.'

'Meadowlands Farm,' replied Peter, his memories of Ireland faintly stirring.

'You know the place?' Bormann was surprised.

'I've been there. The Goldmann Corporation owns the property.' He took a further mouthful of wine. Almost immediately his vision became impaired.

'Now you see! *Ja?* The lengths these dogs will go to just to decieve you, *ja?*' Bormann replied excitedly. To his delight Peter nodded back. 'Pieter, dear boy, they have deceived you all your life.'

'Now I see,' replied Peter, his mind already floating on another level. 'Now I see.'

Bormann gave a satisfied grin. With the aid of the drugs Peter would be completely won over within a matter of weeks. The scientists at the country club could indeed work miracles.

THE BAY
11.11 p.m.

THE TWO war-surplus MTBs cut around the point from the east. Before the German patrol boats knew what was happening, the deck cannons from the MTBs had blown them out of the water. The guards on the upper decks of the *Lady Christina* sounded the alarm.

Throughout the yacht, horns blasted. Everywhere men rushed to their posts. In the stateroom the party stopped instantly.

'Get to the armoury!' Roth took the initiative. 'Follow me! *Schnell!*' Immediately everyone charged out towards the aft section.

Nico Giovanni was in the leading MTB. He steered the plywood boat towards the yacht as his men fired the deck cannon and heavy and light machine-guns at the yacht. The forward section of the upper deck area exploded just as the other MTB's gunnery crew hit the hull amidships. The Germans fired back with everything they had. Whilst the Nazis possessed only small arms, the MTBs were at a Mexican stand-off. There was absolutely no way they could board the vessel without sustaining serious casualties. Nico kept up the pressure, racing in as close as he dared to the vessel and drawing the Germans' attention away from what was really happening.

The single helicopter dropped like a stone into the rear section of the yacht. David and McClean led the way down the ropes, jumping the final ten feet on to the deck. They were immediately engaged by a handful of black-uniformed SS guards. The Germans opened fire as David tossed a grenade amongst them. Two of them died instantly and the remainder were finished off when McClean sprayed them with his Uzi. As the final Mossad agent dropped on to the deck, McClean gave the signal to move out. The team was on its own until they could find a way of getting Nico's people aboard.

They shot and blasted their way down through the vessel. The Germans had grouped well and were giving as good as they got. Inside minutes the Israelis were down to six. McClean recalled the surveillance photographs of the yacht. There was an engineering door just above the water mark and towards the ship's stern. If he could locate and open it, Nico's men could get aboard. With David and the others still pinned down on the helicopter deck, McClean got one of the men to follow him. They climbed over the side, swinging down under the sun canopy and on to the deck below. Instantly they came under fire from the stairwell opposite. McClean fired back, shooting the man through the head.

'OK?' he shouted to the other agent, who had twisted his ankle badly on landing during the exchange of gunfire.

'Let's go,' the Israeli shouted back.

They headed down into the stairwell, tossing two grenades in ahead of them. Waiting for the explosions, they rushed on. From the bottom of the corridor a couple of SS officers opened up with Armalite rifles. The man with McClean went down, having taken a bullet in the hip. He had been flung backwards into the wall.

'I'm hit!' he cried.

McClean turned back from the head of the next staircase and emptied his gun into the Germans, hitting one in the chest and forcing the other man to take cover. Clipping on a fresh magazine, he rushed back, grabbing the Israeli under the arm and dragging him with him. Just as they reached the next stairwell, the German officer fired again, barely missing them. The Israeli fired instinctively from the hip. His Uzi jumped in his hand as the 9mm bullets sprayed the German, killing him instantly.

'Well, at least it hasn't affected your aim!' said McClean.

'Leave me! Find the door yourself,' replied the man.

'Go to hell!' he rebuked him.

THE MAIN DECK
11.23 p.m.

O N DECK David was finding it very tough. He was considering abandoning ship if matters got any worse. Roth was now leading a band of soldiers up his left flank. If they managed to get to the far end of the swimming pool and over to the helicopter pad, his men would be caught in the cross-fire.

DECK THREE
11.24 p.m.

B ELOW DECKS, Peter had been kept with Bormann and Schiller in the main lounge, while Strassmann had disappeared outside the moment the shooting started. Schiller wasn't frightened, but he was uneasy about the way Bormann was reacting. The fat ex-Reich Leader was waving a silver- and pearl-handled Walther PPK pistol about like some kid with a toy. In the excited state he was in, Schiller imagined he'd be safer in the middle of the gunbattle upstairs.

'Call in the helicopter and get us off this ship!' Bormann demanded.

'We have to stay here,' insisted Schiller, his own pistol already drawn. 'Strassmann will let us know what is happening when he gets back.' He looked over at Peter outstretched on the sofa. He was almost unconscious.

Somewhere above there was another explosion.

'If he comes back!' retorted Bormann.

MAIN ENGINE-ROOM
11.27 p.m.

McCLEAN HAD made it to the engine-room. He shot the two white overalled engineers as they tried to close the pressure door in his face. Helping his comrade along the narrow metal gangway, he reached the engineering cargo door. McClean checked the door catches. They were either frozen with rust or locked. Pulling the bag of grenades from around his neck, he hung them on the centre of the double doors before dragging the badly bleeding Israeli behind one of the boilers.

'Keep down and cover your ears!' he shouted over the noise of the twin generators. Aiming carefully and flicking the Uzi on to single shot, he fired. The exploding grenades blew the sea doors wide apart and himself on to the deck. It didn't take long for the message to get through to Nico. His MTB was alongside and discharging the Mafia 'soldiers' instantly. Nico then joined McClean and the wounded Mossad agent.

'You OK, McClean?' Nico smiled.

'I am, but he isn't.' McClean pointed down to the Israeli. The man had virtually passed out.

'Enzo!' Nico called over to one of the 'soldiers'. 'Get this guy back on to our boat and wait for us. We got some unfinished business upstairs.' He grinned widely as he followed McClean.

ON THE MAIN DECK
11.43 p.m.

THE BATTLE was more even-sided now. Very soon the Germans were being driven back by the superior fire power. Enzo checked the Israeli again. The man was unconscious. He covered him up with

457

a blanket on the deck of the MTB and turned to climb back into the yacht's engine-room again when the bullet hit the Italian in the temple. Strassmann jumped the short distance from the blown doors to the motorboat. After checking to see it was clear, he waved for the others. Peter was first, assisted by Bormann, then Schiller. They cast off and slipped away in the darkness, leaving Roth and the others to stand or die. But some of the neo-Nazis had other ideas. It was a hard struggle, but finally Nico's men beat the Germans back until one of their officers offered to surrender conditionally to them. They were still negotiating when news reached them of the missing MTB.

'Schiller with Peter. It has to be,' said McClean.

'I'll call up the chopper,' replied David.

The helicopter landed a few minutes later, taking off Nico and McClean. They flew directly towards the plantation house. The MTB had already docked at the small jetty. As the helicopter's searchlight drifted towards the house, they caught sight of them. Strassmann opened up with an Armalite rifle as the others reached the veranda and the relative safety of the house. The helicopter pilot flicked open the cap of the red button on top of his joystick and squeezed. The heavy 7.62mm shells cut wads out of the manicured lawn beside Strassmann. The pilot struggled to steady the aircraft as he went to fire again. For a few seconds the searchlight lost Strassmann. When the pilot regained position, the target had vanished into the night.

On McClean's instructions they landed at the rear of the plantation house, where Elizabeth was waiting, having just been brought in by one of the other helicopters. She was very pensive.

'Peter?' She could hardly bear to ask.

'He's in the house.' McClean looked at Nico. 'Let's go.'

They walked to the house, Elizabeth waiting on the rear veranda with Nico whilst McClean went inside. He quickly located the Germans in the library, where Bormann was trying to call in assistance on a high-powered radio set which had been concealed behind one of the bookshelves. Schiller had already collected his personal papers and 'The Three Brothers' from his safe and was standing beside the windows, looking across the bay towards the yacht. Several fires were burning on her main deck. McClean's eyes fell on Peter; he was sitting in one of the chairs beside the fireplace, his face distant and strange.

McClean walked into the room behind Bormann, jabbing his Uzi into the man's rolls of flab. 'One move and you're history,' he whispered. Then he called out loud, 'Schiller, drop the pistol. Then slowly turn about.'

Schiller froze. With some hesitation he let the pistol slip from his

458

hand on to the parquet floor. Then, very slowly, he turned around. 'You must be McClean.' Schiller shook his head. 'And Roth said you were dead, along with the woman.'

'Just shows that you can't trust anyone these days,' answered McClean. 'Good labour's hard to find, General, isn't it?' Schiller looked back at him disdainfully. McClean continued. 'Now the briefcase, General, toss it into the centre of the floor.'

The curtains fluttered in and around Schiller as he continued to stand at the french windows. 'Is there no chance we could strike up some deal?' he said coyly.

'Not a chance in hell. Now get rid of the case,' McClean replied, looking curiously at Bormann, standing next to him. 'You know, even plastic surgery can't enhance a pig at heart.' He smirked.

'What happens now?' demanded Bormann pompously, ignoring the insult.

'You should stand trial, but . . .' McClean shrugged as he flicked the Uzi on to single shot.

'But what?' asked Bormann anxiously. The look on McClean's face told him. Bormann started to back away, moving towards the centre of the floor. 'I don't even know you! For God's sake, you fool! I can pay you well! *Nein! Nein!*' Then a single shot echoed through the house. Bormann fell on to the floor. He grasped his paunch as he drew himself up on to both knees. A dark patch started to form quickly across his brown tunic. He clutched his stomach in vain with both hands, then blood began oozing between his fingers. 'I don't even know you,' he repeated in a groan.

'But you knew a Jewish woman called Anna, didn't you?' McClean fired again, shooting him in the groin. Bormann gave out a sickening scream as he collapsed on to the floor, writhing around, twisting and turning in every direction.

'Kill me!' he cried, howling like an injured dog.

Instead of finishing the job, McClean returned to the side of the room again. He looked over at the SS general still standing beside the french windows.

Schiller shook his head. 'You don't frighten me, Major McClean. You don't frighten me at all.'

Bormann's screaming reached a new height. Finally, McClean held the Uzi single-handedly and fired on automatic. The Reichsleiter's body was lifted off the floor and shunted several feet by the force of the 9mm bullets tearing through his body. The shooting finally stopped. McClean stared down at the still form beyond the smoking muzzle of the machine-gun.

'Does that give you some sort of satisfaction, Major?' Schiller had just finished speaking when Elizabeth entered through the other set of french windows. She was holding a silenced .22 Mauser pistol in her right hand.

'You!' Schiller's mouth dropped open upon recognizing her, but she never even looked at him. Instead she went across to where Peter was sitting, at the far end of the long room. There was a blank expression on his face, a combination of the drugs and trauma. She knelt down next to him, gently stroking his head and caressing him. 'Get away from him, you Jewish trash!' snarled Schiller.

Elizabeth ignored the German as she kissed Peter again, running her hand through his dishevelled hair, before standing. Then she turned towards Schiller, training the Mauser on him as she approached.

'You have the floor,' said McClean, stepping back.

'McClean, what's going on here?' shouted Schiller. 'What does this idiot Jewess think she's doing?'

McClean said nothing and Elizabeth kept slowly coming. 'You killed them all. My father, my brothers, my sisters, my nieces and nephews,' she said in a measured tone.

'McClean? As one soldier to another, a clean death?' he implored. But the Scotsman had already backed into the doorway opposite. It was obvious he wasn't going to intervene.

'You kill because you enjoy it, don't you?' Elizabeth halted just two yards from him. Not waiting for an answer, she added, 'My father, how did he die, Schiller? Did you try and make him beg for mercy?'

'Your father?' Slowly the memory that had so often haunted Schiller throughout all these years came back with a vengeance. As he stared into the woman's eyes, all he could see was Peter Goldmann coming alive in them. His confidence drained from him. '*You* are Goldmann's daughter!' He was aghast. She moved a fraction closer and he backed away, his shoulder brushing against the light switch and dousing the overhead lights. He could still see her clearly in the moonlight streaming through the windows. The wind suddenly picked up and the curtain blew in around him again. Peter Goldmann's dying words came back to him – 'With all my heart and soul, I curse you.' The words stuck in his mind. He tried to move. Suddenly he felt a choking sensation in his throat, immediately imagining the hands of the old man upon him. He raised his right hand to his neck, but it was no use – he was pinned in position by a strong knee digging into his back.

The lights came back on again. Schiller could see McClean standing across the room beside the main lighting panel; the Scotsman was grinning! Schiller's nightmare began to slip away again. He glared at Elizabeth, his eyes challenging her to kill him. It was no longer Peter Goldmann that he saw but his daughter standing before him now. The choking suddenly increased; he wasn't imagining it. It was real, deadly real. The wire cut deeper into his throat, slicing the skin and soaking his white shirt and tunic in blood. Behind him, amidst the fluttering curtains, Nico Giovanni slowly applied the pressure, deliberately avoiding the possibility of snapping Schiller's neck and giving him a hastier end. Schiller tried to show no sign of fear as he looked into the woman's face. Already the wire had cut down to the windpipe.

Elizabeth watched as the last remnant of life was forced from Schiller. The SS general began to turn blue as the garrotte now cut through his windpipe. As Nico let go, Schiller slumped on to his knees, the wire garrotte still stuck half-way through his throat. Schiller's eyes flicked as he rasped for air. He raised his right eye and looked at Elizabeth one last time. Then Nico slid the garrotte from his throat and Schiller keeled over on to his back. He was struggling now, not so much for breath as to avoid showing the woman any anxiety. Just when she thought it was all over, Schiller's right arm shot out and grasped her ankle. Elizabeth was horrified. She wanted to scream but instead she instinctively raised the gun and fired into his face. The silenced Mauser coughed once, the .22 bullet blowing away Schiller's remaining eye. The SS general was suddenly still.

Nico Giovanni came out from behind the flapping curtains, a smile on his face as he rolled up the wire garrotte and shoved it inside his pocket.

'My papa always said there was no point in rushin' a good thing.' He grinned.

'And I think my father would concur exactly.' Elizabeth forced a smile before turning her attentions again to Peter.

The seventeenth-century grandfather clock began to strike midnight as she was half-way across the floor. A second later, she felt the massive explosion. It shook the entire house to its foundations. She knew what it was without turning round to see the massive fireball licking skyward from the stricken yacht. As the clock chimed a twelfth time Peter blinked, just once, as if suddenly released from his trance. As she knelt down in front of him, his face slowly formed into a faint smile.

EPILOGUE

BONN
Early January 1976

THE MAN at the top of the boardroom table looked around at his colleagues. 'Then it is agreed?' he asked in a polished voice.

The other directors tapped the table with their pens, the usual form of approval in such matters. The man pressed one of the switches on the intercom panel beside him. Moments later a voice could be heard around the boardroom.

'Kruse here.'

The chairman spoke into the gadget again. 'Roland, thank you for being so patient with us.'

'My pleasure,' replied the voice.

The chairman continued. 'Roland, I have the honour of inviting you to fill the existing vacancy on the Central Council of the Bundesbank. Would you do us the honour of accepting?'

'The honour would be mine, Herr Kohl. Thank you. I accept,' the voice answered respectfully. Immediately the other directors started tapping the table again.

Back in his office, the recipient switched off his telephone intercom. Karl Strassmann stood up from his desk and walked over to the tall window overlooking the Rhine. He opened the window, breathing in the cold crisp air. 'Nemesis' was one step closer to becoming a reality.

TEL AVIV UNIVERSITY
Spring 1976

PETER WAS standing in front of the blackboard in the well of the auditorium, summing up the essence of the morning's lecture – an analysis of Nazi philosophy and ideology and the views of the working classes in Germany at the time Hitler came to power. The students were spellbound by the university's youngest professor of modern history.

He had taken his mother's family name by deed poll, for it had seemed the only sensible thing to do. It also afforded him an air of anonymity in his newly adopted country.

Professor Goldmann's lectures were renowned for their electricity and depth, especially those he gave on his favourite subject – the Second World War. As he wound up, Peter looked over at the back row and smiled at his mother and the old rabbi. Elizabeth blew him a kiss, embarrassing him slightly. Jacob Bronowski stared proudly down at his protégé.

'As I said earlier, all the major historians who have written about the Hitler phenomenon disagree on many issues relating to the dictator's life, but they all agree with the following conclusions . . .'

As he spoke, a man slipped into the rear balcony, cantilevered above the main lecture floor, remaining in the shadows as he listened to Peter.

'With all his victories and defeats, Adolf Hitler's last will and political testament reveal to us that he learned absolutely nothing from these experiences. He maintained to the bitter end that the Jews were responsible not just for the destruction of the Third Reich but for all mankind's ills. He either would not or could not accept any blame for the millions that had perished during the black years of his regime.' He paused, drawing the lecture to its close.

'Next week's lecture will be on the Spanish Civil War. Suggested reading is listed in your study notes.' Peter gathered up his papers. 'Any questions?'

A young man in the second row raised his hand. 'Professor Goldmann, how certain can we be that Adolf Hitler actually did kill himself on 30 April 1945? The evidence seems perhaps inconclusive, does it not?'

'Yes, I agree, it is inconclusive. Perhaps I can put it another way. I think in all our hearts we know that at the very least a little of Adolf Hitler still remains alive. You cannot stamp out an ideology by the death of one man, or even a million men. Only time can do that. Above all else, the memory of Hitler gives us caution, caution to examine ourselves and consider our future with the utmost care.'

'Professor?' A girl student in the fourth row spoke up. 'Does it not strike you as sinister that National Socialism in Germany disappeared almost without trace, virtually overnight?'

'That is a valid point.' Peter smiled. He was getting through to these first-year students after all. 'Yes, the structure of National Socialism collapsed and there is little evidence to suggest it went underground. The Allied governments would like to propagate that notion, and perhaps with the vast amounts of investment capital they are still pouring into West Germany under the Marshall Plan, they are a little nervous about adverse effects on their speculations.' The class broke out into laughter as the bell rang, signalling the end of the lecture period.

'Ladies and gentlemen, I thank you.' Peter smiled back as the students gathered up their belongings and started filing out.

McClean remained in the shadows. As Peter turned to wipe the blackboard clean, his blue and white yarmulke was visible on the back of his head. From the balcony he watched as Elizabeth helped the old rabbi down the steps towards the front of the lecture theatre.

'Rabbi, will you tell my son that he is to come home with me for Passover next week?' Elizabeth said loudly.

'What is this, Peter? You make your mother worried? You make her beg?' Jacob Bronowski goaded him gently.

'Uncle Jacob.' Peter turned around from the blackboard, a grin across his face. 'I have said nothing about avoiding Pesach. My mother, as usual, makes a mountain out of a molehill! And all because I have been invited to speak to the Knesset.' He bent forward, kissing her on the forehead. 'If it makes you happy, Mother, I will be at the house in Jaffa to help with *bedikat chametz*.'

Elizabeth hugged him. 'My son, the presidential adviser, and he still has a little time for me,' she teased him as she looked back at Jacob Bronowski. The old man smiled back at her and then at Peter, who shrugged his shoulders. The first students for the next class appeared at the rear door of the lecture theatre, and started filing down into the auditorium.

'Come, Jacob, we must let this important young man get on with his work,' Elizabeth said, guiding the old rabbi out of the side door next the podium. 'We will see you later?' she called back to him.

'Around seven o'clock,' Peter answered.

'Oh! I nearly forgot.' Elizabeth turned back to him, removing a small package from her handbag. 'This arrived at the house for you by special delivery. It's from Switzerland.' She handed over the small box-like object to her son.

'My old watch,' replied Peter hastily. 'I sent it off for repair.'

'I didn't know it was broken.' Elizabeth frowned.

'It wasn't, until I dropped it at the pool-side last month!' Peter made a joke out of her suspicion. Elizabeth laughed. 'I'll see you later.' He started packing up his books and notes.

'We'll expect you at seven. Don't be late,' she called back to him as she reached the door.

'I won't.' He waved back at her. As the door swung shut behind them, Peter opened the package, revealing a small blue leather presentation box. He opened the hinged lid and stared at the signet ring with the Star of David now as its centrepiece before examining the inscription around the inside band: *'Heute Deutschland! Morgen die Welt! – Adolf Hitler, 1938'*.

Peter placed the ring on his right index finger – just as his father had always worn it!

McClean watched the smile on Peter's face. Simon was wrong after all. There was nothing to worry about. The newly appointed Israeli adviser on war crimes investigations was as sound as Simon was. He slipped out again, careful not to alert anyone below. From the corner of his eye, Peter glanced up at the swinging door at the rear of the balcony. The smile had developed into a sardonic chuckle. He had fooled them. He had fooled them all.

A NEW BEGINNING...